FREE CITIZENS

FREE CITIZENS

BOOK THREE OF THE DERIVATES RISING TRILOGY

LIV EVANS

Free Citizens
First published by Liv Evans in 2024
ISBN 9780648812296

For any enquiries please visit www.livevans.com.au

Cover designed by Piece d'Arterie (Instagram @piere_d_arterie)

Editing: Nicole Zoltack

For my children.
You are the light of hope in a world full of shadows.
Never let anyone tame your spark.
Xx

1
____

SCRAPS

TIME PASSED STRANGELY when one was locked in a small, white cell with bright lights on at every hour of the day.

There were no clocks, of course, so Scraps measured the passing of time by how many meals they had brought him. It was quite the challenge, as the Government did not provide the standard lunch or dinner fare Citizens consumed. Instead, Scraps was given bland meal replacement bars. They reminded him of his years in the Derivate Training Facility and made it impossible to figure out just how long he had been in the room.

Following the first two meals, Scraps tried to sleep. It was difficult when the lighting was so bright. He did not dare ask for it to be lowered, though. Whilst he was certain the wheels of the Government were working in full force outside his cell, he was not inclined to draw attention to himself.

Not that Scraps was really waiting for anything. From what Sway and Hawkeye had said, the Underground was going into lockdown. Scraps had given up his opportunity to return to that bastion of safety, and he would do so a hundred times over if it gave Flit a chance to get away.

He was stuck in this cell. Hopefully, she was safely tucked away in the Underground.

After finishing the fourth nap and thirteenth meal since he had arrived, Scraps set the plain foil wrapper on the crisp, white sheet beneath him. He removed his shoes and set them off to the side of the bed, the base of which flowed out of the floor and into the wall in a single seamless slab, opposite the only door in the room. There was a toilet with a sink in the cistern in the corner of the room. Everything was the same radiant white that made his eyes ache. Apart from the bed and the toilet, there was nothing else—no sounds of the city in the distance, no window to peer out of, no interesting smells wafting in through the single narrow vent lining the wall above the door.

Nothing but the stark room and an immeasurable stretch of time.

As Scraps got off the bed and stepped towards the middle of the room, he realised that wasn't entirely true. He was also in the room, and while he still had control of his own mind and body, he would use them. He had eaten enough meal replacement bars to feel like he had some energy to burn, and he was tired of trying to sleep only to wake and not know whether a minute or five hours had passed. One thing he could always count on to help him pass time was a good workout, and he didn't need anything fancy to do that.

Scraps wasn't foolish enough to think keeping fit would help him escape. He knew that was not going to happen, not while he was a captive of the Government. What he hoped it would do was keep his mind off the near-constant replay of Flit's face when she had realised he was surrendering. The memory was nearly enough to have him try to fight his way out of that building single-handedly. That would do nothing but get him killed faster. If he wanted to see the woman he loved ever again, he needed to be smart about it.

Just as Scraps started his warm-up with a deep lunge, the door to his cell opened, and two armed Registereds walked in with a woman dressed in a Government uniform between them. Her smooth, honey blonde hair sat at the nape of her neck in a neat twist, and her light blue eyes surveyed Scraps with a mixture of apathy and suspicion.

"Mr. Parkes, my name is Agent Greene. Follow me."

Without waiting to see if he would comply, Agent Greene turned on her polished heel and walked out. The two Registereds who accompanied her gestured for Scraps to move.

As he walked past, he took in the designations stitched to their uniforms. The man on the right was much older than him but was a high-powered telecoercionist, CC-9832. The woman, TB-219, was only six years older than Scraps and was a mind-reader capped at level B, making her the most powerful mind-reader Scraps had ever met outside of—

Scraps stopped that train of thought and focused instead on counting the number of windows he passed on the way. He counted the corners and turns, even though any attempt at escape would be futile. He was determined to keep his mind busy. Distracted.

The sterile, gloss-white-panel-covered corridors of the level seemed to follow the layout that most Government buildings close to Centre One did. Of course, each of these doors had to be opened by Agent Greene, but as they left the corridor that held his cell, they moved into a more open space surrounded by interrogation rooms. Some of them were occupied, judging by the opaque glass, and Scraps wondered how many other Free—

Once more, he stopped thinking. That was a dangerous past time in current company.

Greene led them across the space and opened the door to an interrogation room with a full wall window that had a view of the Hub. Scraps was unexpectedly grateful to notice the sun rising slowly above the horizon, casting the entire city outside in shining rays of powder blue and orange.

Sunrise.

Like the rest of the floor, this room was stark and utilitarian, but it was tinged peach with the strains of dawn. There was a sleek steel table in the middle of the room, with one chair on the window side and two chairs on the door side. A man with slicked-back black hair and dark brown eyes already occupied one of those chairs. He glanced at Scraps with clear contempt before he nodded at the woman who had brought him in.

"Sit." Greene pointed to the single seat on the window side of the table.

Scraps turned his back on the beautiful view and did as commanded. There was no point antagonising the agents. Flit would have been fighting like a wildcat, but he would remain calm.

It was one of the reasons he had surrendered himself before she had a chance to.

"Mr. Parkes, I am Agent Hector. I suspect you already know why we have brought you in?" Hector leaned back in his seat, narrowing his eyes at Scraps.

Scraps' heart beat faster. He nodded mutely. Citizens were entitled to legal representation in situations like these. However, he was unsure of how many Citizens would actually know that, which made him feel as though he needed more information before deciding how to play the situation.

"The fact you tried to run makes this far more cut and dry than you could imagine," Agent Hector informed him. "Do you know where your wife is at this very moment?"

Scraps shifted in his seat, acutely aware of the telepath standing by the door. He looked down at his hands, noting the wedding ring still on his finger. It was a solid reminder of the reason he was in this room. "No."

It wasn't a lie.

Hector turned to the telepath, who pressed her lips together but nodded. Scraps could only hope that the question and reaction meant that they did not know where she was, either. He closed his left hand into a fist, and covered it with his right, blocking the ring from his view and theirs.

Good.

"At nine o'clock in the morning three days ago, a group of terrorists ignited several blasts that killed over fifty Citizens and wounded countless more," Hector continued. "Those blasts disabled the maglev system. They then illegally accessed the Government's media servers and broadcast lies to the population of the Hub."

"Now, given the recent attack on the Department of Advanced Human Research's new facility, we have a few hints about who may be part of this rebel group." Greene leaned forward, steepling her hands on the table. "There are only a few places the Free Citizens could have gotten the information they needed to achieve both."

There was more silence, as if they were hoping Scraps would ask what they were talking about, or claim he knew nothing about it, or maybe confess to something.

He let them sit with the silence, allowing himself to appear to be too stunned to speak.

"Now, Mr. Parkes, the Government is not unreasonable. We understand that simpler folk have trouble knowing why it is important to follow rules and what 'for the good of all' really means," Hector said.

The sheer lies and condescension in his words set Scraps on edge. It wasn't something that normally bothered him, but between the sensory deprivation of the cell and not knowing if Flit was safe, he was burning on a shorter wick. He took a breath and stamped down the unhelpful emotions.

"We know who gave the Free Citizens the information. We also know that you and your wife got home at five-thirty in the evening the night before the attack and did not leave until you fled," Greene explained, her eyes not leaving Scraps. "So, you did not commit these acts yourselves."

Scraps looked between the two agents, not sure where they were taking this discussion. If they thought he and Flit were the ones that shared the information, why was he not already imprisoned? Why hadn't they already turned him into one of those unthinking, unfeeling living dead in their research facilities?

Hector leaned forward, resting his hands on the table. "Given the information we have, the Government would like to offer you an opportunity—"

"A lifeline, if you will," Greene added.

Scraps blinked.

What were they playing at? The reason the Government had been in power so long was because they followed their procedures and made no exceptions. If they were offering Scraps a "lifeline" they must be desperate.

The Registered mind-reader shifted on her feet, her eyes darting to Scraps before she looked away. Scraps ran his thumb along the underside of the table and focused on the cold smoothness of the metal against his skin.

The agents put a set of datapads on the table, displaying an array of documentation. Scraps didn't need to look closer to recognise them. He forced his eyebrows into a confused furrow and shrugged, as if he was not sure what he was seeing.

"We do not believe that you and Ava knew what you were getting into, Mr. Parkes. You both have exemplary employment and behaviour records." Hector rubbed the stubble on his chin. "Here is what happened. You moved to the Hub, met some of the wrong sort of people, and got caught up in something larger than yourselves."

Greene leaned forward and swiped the screens of the datapads. Instead of Government documents, they were now showing images of him and Flit before and after their work reviews. They must have pulled those from so many different cameras.

"So, we are here to give you a choice." Greene lowered her voice so Scraps had no choice but to lean in closer to hear her. "You can accept the punishment for the treason that you have committed, or you can work with us to stop this nonsense. Nip it off at the bud. You do not need to get any more blood on your hands."

If they could find those documents and images, what else could they find?

Scraps sat back and rested his palms on his thighs. The agents had enough evidence that he knew it would be foolish to deny it. All he could do was try to protect the last few secrets they didn't seem to be aware of.

He met Greene's expectant gaze. "Nobody was supposed to die. That was not part of the plan," Scraps said, letting his genuine frustration creep into his tone.

Once more, TB-219 confirmed this with a nod.

"Good. Now, to prevent that happening again, you need to help us." The sharp edge to Greene's tone dulled somewhat.

"And what would that entail?" Scraps asked, certain it was something he would not like.

Hector crossed his arms over his barrel chest. "You know the Free Citizens, and we need an inside man."

Scraps' fingertips dug into his own thighs. "You want me to spy on them for you?"

"Organisations like the Free Citizens are just like weeds, with roots that spread wide. We may pluck out those who committed this atrocity, but there is little point in doing so if there are others waiting in the wings," Hector explained. "Who are they? What resources do they have? What are their long-term goals?"

The idea of turning on the Free Citizens made Scraps ill.

"They concealed much of that information from me," Scraps said slowly, looking between the agents.

Hector shrugged. "If you want don't want us to lay charges against you, you will need to go back in there and do a bit of research. I heard you're good at that."

"May I have time to consider your proposal?" Scraps asked. He needed time to think.

Alone.

Greene frowned and pushed back a few strands of honey hair that had fallen across her freckled cheek. "You have until this afternoon to make your decision. Otherwise, we will begin the paperwork for your official arrest. Once that has started, there is no going back." She got to her feet, her chair dragging against the floor with a grating screech. "Before you return to your cell, we need to know if you have met the leader or any of the other Free Citizens."

Adam's face flashed through Scraps' mind before he could stop it. He was tempted to lie, but with a telepath in the same room, that would be a very unwise decision. "Yes, I have."

Both agents turned to the mind-reader, who nodded grimly. Satisfaction glinted in Hector's eyes as he stood beside his colleague. They exchanged a meaningful look.

Greene gestured for the Registereds to open the door. "Think carefully about your decision, Mr. Parkes. We will get the information we need from you. How we get it is entirely up to you."

The Registereds peeled away from the wall and walked over to stand on either side of Scraps. He got off his chair and turned to make for the door. Greene and Hector walked off in a different direction once they hit the hallway, but Scraps did not try anything stupid. Any attempt at escape would fail within moments. The grim set of the telepath's lips told him as much.

Scraps didn't even dare think of anything other than the offer until the Registereds shut and locked the door of his cell behind him. Letting out a deep breath, Scraps felt far more relieved than he had any right to, but the idea of giving the Government intelligence on the Free Citizens made him sick to his stomach.

As he walked over to the bed in his room and picked up the discarded silver meal bar wrapper, he tried to imagine what Flit would do in this situation. A faint smile tugged at his lips at the string of profanities she would throw at the agents. While he was relieved she wasn't there to dig them deeper into trouble, he missed her fire.

Whilst trying to figure out how to handle his undesirable predicament, Scraps replayed the conversations with the agents over in his mind. His attention snagged on a detail he hadn't processed while the conversation was happening.

Mr. Parkes.

They had called him by his alias. They thought he was a Citizen, and they wanted him to work for them. If they knew the truth of who he was, of *what* he was, then they would have no mercy. The Underground had warned he and Flit that their covers would not hold up to greater scrutiny, but whatever they had done had gotten him through to this point. He could not take that opportunity for granted.

If he wanted to survive this, he would need to keep his cover intact.

He would need to play by their rules.

2
———

FLIT

HAWKEYE WAS the first person Flit saw when she woke up in the Underground.

He was also the first person she punched when she woke up in the Underground.

Flit, not noticing that she still had the bracelet inhibitor around her wrist, had then tried to teleport across the medical bay to make Sway the second person she would punch. Instead of the satisfying feeling of flickering across the distance, her entire body sizzled with purple sparks of agony. The distraction gave Sway enough time to react, and with a single word, he sent her back into a state of deep sleep.

The second time Flit woke, she was cuffed to the bed at her ankles and her wrists. As she tugged at the restraints, head still groggy from the telecoercion-induced sleep, she heard a familiar voice.

"It's only to make sure you don't go punching your friends again, Flit." Physie stepped into Flit's line of sight.

Flit narrowed her eyes at the matronly woman as Hawkeye, the skin surrounding his left eye a deep, satisfying purple, stepped up beside her.

"He can't go around with that kind of asymmetry on his face," Flit snapped, jutting her chin in the direction of Hawkeye's black eye. "Come closer. Let me give you a matching pair, arsehole."

To his credit, her best friend did nothing more than roll his eyes. "Flit, we had to—"

"Where's Scraps?" Flit's demand cut off whatever insufficient excuse he attempted to make.

She tried to sit up, but the restraints were tight enough that she snapped back against the mattress with a grunt.

"We've got our micros looking for him as we speak." Hawkeye came a little closer.

A mix of panic, rage, and utter betrayal surged through Flit. It was so deep, so visceral, that the edges of her vision blurred as her eyes burned with tears. "Let me out of here!" She thrashed against her bonds. "I have to find him. I have to—"

"Flit, stop!" Hawkeye leaned forward, grasping her shoulders and pinning her down.

Physie's bustled over and fixed her with a warning glare. "Stop! You're going to hurt yourself."

"Let me go, now!" Flit tried to teleport again, and those familiar purple sparks seized her.

Pain sizzled in every cell of her body. She pushed passed it, willing herself to teleport with every ounce of force she could muster.

Scraps was out there somewhere... and he loved her. She could not leave him in the custody of the Government. She would die before she let them keep him.

She had to get out of the Underground, now. With a cry of frustration, Flit turned and bit the hand Hawkeye was using to hold her down.

"Fuck!" Hawkeye yelped and jumped back.

Physie's eyebrows shot into her receding hairline, and she slammed her shoulders against Flit's hips to hold her down. The older woman pushed Flit deep into the bed, even as she thrashed with renewed vigour. "Patch, sedative! Stat!"

Out of the corner of her eye, Flit saw Patch running over with a syringe in his hand.

"Don't you dare!" Flit screamed, voice growing hoarse. "Don't you fucking dare!"

There was a flicker of genuine regret in Patch's eyes as he

plunged the syringe into the side of her neck and mouthed, "I'm sorry."

The fight left Flit's body with a frustrated groan, and her eyes grew heavy.

WHEN THE EFFECTS of the sedative wore off, Flit's eyes were even grittier and harder to open than before. From what she could tell, they had moved her to a private room. It was one of the smaller medical bays used for patients requiring more privacy. Barely bigger than her old room in the Residence, it was as cold and clinical as places got in the Underground.

Flit tried to move, and the warm metal of the inhibitor cuff shifted against her wrist. She was still restrained. She let out a low growl just as the door to the room opened.

"Flit, remain calm." Harmony's gentle tone was laced with a subtle coercion as she, Divvy, and Acumen entered the room.

Flit glared at the leaders of the Underground even as her rage subsided. Her heart, which had been pounding against her chest, slowed, and her breaths became longer, smoother. She hated Harmony for using telecoercion on her like that, but thanks to the white-haired woman's intervention, Flit couldn't get angry about it even if she tried.

Most likely sensing her thoughts, Acumen looked at both leaders and nodded subtly, as if confirming her docility. On another day, she might have called him a traitor for his complicity, but she couldn't summon the outrage to do so. His lips twitched into a frown.

"Where's Scraps?" Flit asked, the fire and passion gone from her words. It sounded more like she was inquiring about the weather than the man she loved.

Divvy ran a hand through her deep red hair and looked down at Flit's wrist, the one with the inhibitor on. "We traced him to the holding facility in North One. Beyond his location, we couldn't find anything else."

Being in holding was better than being sent to a research or internment facility, but the lack of further information was alarming. Tracking meant that the Government was giving itself some sense of accountability. Slipping off the radar often implied darker intent.

"What's the plan for his extraction?" Flit asked.

Reaching across to pat Flit's hand, Divvy said, "We can't extract someone without enough intel and certainly not from a Government stronghold. You know that."

Flit shifted her hand as far away from Divvy's as the cuffs would allow. The inhibitor on her wrist shifted as she moved. "Are you two here to take this off?" She nodded towards the device.

"That depends," Harmony said slowly. "If I take that off, are you going to disappear on us? Are you going to head back to the Hub to get Scraps?"

"No."

Harmony looked at Acumen who shook his head, exposing Flit's lie.

Harmony sighed. "It's staying on."

"It's for the best, Flit," Acumen said. "The surface is a mess. I know you want to get him back, but you're more likely to get captured than to rescue him."

Fine, Flit thought petulantly at Acumen, *be a dick.*

If she was unable to show her anger and frustration with her tone, thanks to Harmony's coercion, she would use her words to get her disgust across.

"What about the cuffs, then?" Flit asked. "I look like some Government experiment, being strapped to the bed like this."

Divvy grimaced. "Those can come off when you promise not to attack anyone else down here."

"Let me get one punch in on Sway, and I'll give you my word."

Harmony sighed and shook her head.

Silence fell in the sterile room while Flit waited to see if one of the leaders would give in. Her silence was the only power she held, so she clung to it for as long as she could before conceding.

"Whatever. I promise I'll behave."

"Finally a truth," Acumen said, nodding towards the leaders.

"Good." Harmony's serious expression settled into something a little more sympathetic, a little gentler. "I'll get one of the medics to check you out. You can go into quarantine with the others, but we'll be watching."

Flit was just about to ask why she would be in quarantine, but then her Intelligence training came back to mind. Given how cut off the Underground was from the surface, they needed to quarantine agents to reduce the risks of the transmission of viruses that would hurt the community. Usually, this process was only set in place for agents who worked in cities other than the Hub or if there were any new viral breakouts. There were enough half-halfers living between the Underground and the Government's capital that most threats from the Hub were mild enough. The decision of whether to implement a quarantine was an important one though, as they had to balance the impracticality of having inactive members waiting around against the slight possibility of contagions being introduced. There were stories of how the population of the Underground had been devastated by such things in the early days, and Flit was glad she was not the one who had to make those decisions.

While she was lost in thought, Harmony, Divvy, and Acumen made their way for the door.

"Wait," Flit called after them. "If you hear anything about—"

"We'll let you know," Acumen promised her.

Divvy tapped at the screen by the door and scanned her handprint. The cuffs on Flit's wrists and ankles unlocked and retracted into a panel in the bed frame. "Anything else?"

Resisting the urge to ask how long the order to remain calm would hang around, Flit shook her head. "No, all good. Thanks."

She sat up straighter on the bed and stretched her arms and legs to get the muscles used to moving again as Harmony, Divvy, and Acumen walked out.

The moment that the door slid shut behind the two leaders, Flit groaned and slumped onto the bed. Much to her own dismay, she realised the telecoercion was probably for the best. If it were up to her, she would have throat-punched her way out of the Underground. Unless she happened upon some flame grenades.

Flit tilted her head to the side. That didn't sound like such a bad plan.

Her amusement was short lived.

Given how even the best laid plans had gone awry in the past few weeks, she needed to stop, take a breath, and get her head around things before she came out fighting.

Desperately needing to move around, Flit hopped off the bed. She winced when her feet hit the floor. Every part of her protested. Her muscles and joints were all locked up in the worst way possible. She didn't even bother walking straight away. Instead, she used the bed to help her balance and started with some basic stretches.

It was another couple of minutes before the door opened again. Flit looked up to see Patch smiling warily.

He edged his way into the room. "Harmony and Divvy promised you wouldn't hit me."

"That was nice of them." Flit straightened up and rolled her shoulders. Her knees felt stiff as she tried to walk over to him. "How long have I been out for?"

Patch took her arm, guiding her back to the bed. "Three days."

Flit stumbled over her own feet. "Three days?"

"Well, it took you a while to wake after you first came in, because Yavin had to do her thing—"

Leg pain all but forgotten, Flit stumbled over to the wall of the medbay. She opened the door to the small ensuite and stepped inside to look at herself in the mirror. Sure enough, she saw her own hazel eyes and chocolate hair instead of Ava's honey brown hair and brown eyes.

Flit's stomach lurched.

They had conducted the phenotype manipulation on her when she was asleep. Without her consent. On top of that, they had kept her sedated for three whole days without medical justification. It was an utter violation of her autonomy and her rights and something she thought only the Government was capable of.

The sparks of outrage flared in Flit's gut, but the residual telecoercion still in her system saw them fizzle into something different, something more disappointed and melancholic. She wanted to get to the Hub to retrieve Scraps, but she couldn't do it looking like herself. Her facial features were attached to the file she had used when she lived with her parents, a profile that was supposed to be deceased.

Patch leaned against the doorframe. "If it helps, they reverted the pheno work on all of the agents."

Hearing a note of guilt, Flit peered at Patch more closely. He was clearly trying to remain professional, but she got a hint from the expression on his face that he was not too fond of the reversals either.

"With everything going on," he continued, "they've recalled all agents and half-halfers indefinitely. It's going to be pretty crowded, but I haven't seen Control or Intelligence this flustered since... well, ever."

Flit vaguely remembered Hawkeye referring to something dangerous happening in the Underground before he had betrayed her and had Sway knock her out.

"What happened?" she asked.

Patch jutted his chin at the bed. "Why don't you sit down? I can take your obs while I explain. The sooner I get the medical stuff sorted, the sooner you can get back to the others and glare at Hawkeye and Sway."

Even if Flit wanted to demand information right away, she did not feel like arguing with Patch. He had always been good to her, and seeing him again made her feel a sense of comfort she didn't realise she had been missing on the surface.

"Okay."

Patch's smile brightened at her acquiescence, and he escorted her back to the bed. When Flit had settled against the crisp sheets, Patch gently pressed one palm against her forehead and wrapped his other hand around her wrist. He closed his eyes, concentrating on using his abilities as she had seen her mother do countless times. It was a good minute before his eyes fluttered open.

"Everything's looking good." He let go of her and sank down onto the bed at her side with a heavy sigh. "I know you've got a lot on your mind, but everyone is fragile now. We had a series of big explosions in a range of tunnels. They were around the same time as the explosions in the Hub. Rumours are that it's connected—"

"That's impossible," Flit blurted.

The Free Citizens didn't know about the Underground. They couldn't have attacked them too. It had to be some kind of coincidence.

Raising his hands in supplication, Patch said, "I'm just telling you what I've heard, okay?" He waited for Flit to nod before he continued, "The explosions caused cave-ins in our critical exit and supply tunnels. We lost twelve people, which is surprising given the scope of the damage. Control classified it as a targeted attack and said we had to withdraw to the mid- and deep-level tunnels for safety. They apparently recalled all agents for their own safety and so we could muster our forces."

"Scraps and I weren't on the recall list," Flit recalled.

He nodded. It didn't seem like news to him. "Sway and Hawkeye got thrashed for going up there after you. I've never seen Shadow or Acumen so angry before."

Flit's heart seized. She could understand Shadow being pissed she was back. He was a cold prick, but Acumen? That cut deep. She thought of him as a friend. So did Scraps.

"Between the refugees Hawk brought back the other week and the explosions, Control have been really distracted." Patch shrugged a little helplessly. "I think it was a blessing for Hawk and Sway, really. Everyone is too busy to do anything about it. Harmony and Divvy grilled them for hours, but apart from that, they seem to have gotten away with it."

As furious as Flit was at Hawkeye and Sway for leaving Scraps behind, she was touched they had taken the risk to retrieve them. She didn't want to think about it for too long, lest she go soft when she saw them. Instead, she focused on getting more information, so she knew what she was walking into.

"Refugees? What refugees?" she asked, knowing full well who they were but knowing she needed to pretend otherwise.

Patch looked around surreptitiously and leaned in. "The general population don't know about them yet, but you'll be in quarantine with them so I suppose it can't hurt to tell you." He shrugged as if there was no point hiding anything "Around two weeks ago, Hawkeye disappeared and then came back with a dozen people including—" He stopped, his eyes wide.

"Who?" Flit leaned closer.

She hoped everybody had made it down safely. She didn't know what she would do if something bad had happened to Fortune.

Pressing his lips together, Patch seemed to withdraw. "Actually, I'm not the one who should be telling you this. Why don't we go to the common room? You can find out for yourself." He slid off the bed and offered Flit a hand, helping her to her feet. "Come on, I'll take you to the others."

Flit accepted Patch's hand and got off the bed, wondering just what sort of story Hawkeye and Fortune had spun about how they had met and whether she and Scraps had been implicated in the process.

3

———

SCRAPS

IF THE CONSTANT presence of the bright sterile lighting wasn't enough to stop Scraps from sleeping, he had the added worry of the agent's offer to keep him up. The hours dragged as he weighed up his options.

The first and most obvious was that he could stand on principle and refuse the offer. Getting freedom for Derivates and Citizens was important. Like Flit, he wanted to see a world where future generations did not need to hide themselves out of fear if imprisonment and torture.

However, refusing to work with the Government only had one outcome. He would end up in a place like the Department of Advanced Human Research. If he was put into a permanent coma and experimented on, it would reveal the truth of his biology, and his principles would not matter at all.

If he kept his chin held high, the Government would bring him to his knees.

He couldn't fight on his knees.

Scraps' second option was to just do what the Government wanted. For some reason, Adam had taken a shining to him and Flit. He was confident could return to the ranks of the Free Citizens without complication. After the way Adam had consistently twisted their goals and missions, Scraps wondered if it was better to turn him in. The only problem was that the other members of the group did not deserve the fate awaiting them if he did so.

Chris' and Liana's friendly faces came to mind when Scraps considered taking the Government's offer. They were two wonderful friends who had shown him and Flit such kindness. Of course, Flit and Scraps had deceived them by not telling them what code 6B meant, but he could not imagine they would resent them for it if they ever found out the truth. They might even understand.

Scraps was formulating a third option when the door to his cell opened. The same two Registereds from earlier that day stepped in. His thoughts ground to a half, and he focused instead on his concern about seeing the agents again.

"You must come with us," the female telepath commanded.

Scraps rose from where he was sitting on the edge of his bed and followed the pair through the halls. This time, it was easier to remember the path they took through the corridors, and he was not surprised when they stopped at the same interrogation room. The view outside the window startled him. It was mid-afternoon judging by how the city outside was flooded with light. He took in the reflection of the building he was in from the windows of the one on the opposite side of his street and tried to calculate where he was.

The telepath gestured towards the window. Agent Hector tapped the datapad he had on the table in front of him the glass turned opaque, obscuring Scraps' view of the world outside.

"Mr. Parkes, take a seat." Hector gestured to the chair Scraps had vacated earlier. He spun the datapad around and showed Scraps the screen. On it was a standard-looking Government form. "Do you know what this is, Mr. Parkes?"

Scraps perched on the edge of the seat. He frowned as he read the entry field titles. "No, this is entirely unfamiliar to me."

"I imagine it would be." Greene reached past her colleague and scrolled the screen up to the title of the document. "You have never been incarcerated before. This is what we need to fill out if you don't accept our offer."

Scraps sat back in his chair. "I have already made my decision. You do not need that form."

Hector's brow twitched at the comment.

Greene nodded. "A wise choice." She tapped the screen to turn it off. "Why don't you start by telling us what you already know."

Scraps took a deep breath. His stomach churned with guilt and wondered if he could ever forgive himself for what he was about to say. "The leader is a man named Adam. I don't know much more about him, to be honest, but... he is dangerous."

Hector and Greene turned to the Registered telepath. She nodded. The two agents exchanged smug glances.

"By all means, Mr. Parkes," Hector said with a wide, sweeping gesture. "Please continue."

TWO HOURS LATER, Scraps emerged from the front doors of the building containing the holding cells. The facility was in North One, which was only a few blocks away from his apartment in West Two.

He brought up an arm to shield his face against the glare of the late afternoon light. Upon first glance, the streets around him appeared busier than he anticipated. As he was wondering why, he noticed that the extra foot traffic in the area did not consist of Citizens. Instead, Registereds and Government Agents were posted at close regular intervals, watching the pedestrians and hurrying along anyone who stopped to chat or gawk around. Derivate presence was normal on the streets, but Scraps assumed this new level security was a reaction to the maglev attacks.

After spending an hour telling the agents what he knew without giving away the names of anyone other than Adam, they had taken their turn to tell him their expectations. In return for his *freedom*, they wanted him to ingratiate himself with Adam once more, so he could report the Free Citizen's plans to them.

Now that he was away from any telepath, he could freely admit that it wasn't going to happen. The third option, the one he had settled on was only reporting dangerous missions that would cause too much collateral damage or loss of life, like the dangerous ones Adam had surprised them with. With any luck, he could persuade the Free Citizens to consider more sensible things and then take a step back to stay out of their business.

The challenge, the agents had said, would be explaining his "wife's" absence. Normally, Flit and Scraps were inseparable. After disappearing off their friends'—and indeed, the Free Citizen's—radar for three days, it would be a hard sell. In the end, the agents had promised to forge some travel documentation to make it look like *Ava* had gone to visit her sick mother in Eastbay. They also promised Scraps they would do their best to find her.

Scraps sincerely hoped they didn't.

With any luck, Flit was just where she needed to be.

In the Underground.

Safe.

Walking down the busy streets, Scraps was certain the Government was still watching him. He couldn't afford to put a foot out of line unless he had an escape plan set up.

When he reached their apartment, Scraps was startled by how empty it was. The Government had come in to fix the glass and give the place a clean sweep. His and Flit's datapads had been returned to their beside tables to charge, and he shuddered at the thought of a group of Government workers combing through their place. Still, the agents had shown no sign that they knew the truth of Scraps' biology, so the Underground must have done a good enough job keeping the place free of any suspicious elements.

Before he settled in, he inspected every possible inch of the apartment for bugs and came up empty. Everything appeared to be where it was supposed to be. Odd.

Deciding it was safe to settle in, Scraps sat on the edge of his bed and picked up his datapad. He avoided looking at the side of the bed that Flit slept on. It took all his restraint to stop himself from running out the door. He knew how to get back to the Underground, but if he left, the Government would follow him right back down there.

Nothing, not even his own safety, was worth leading the Government to that last bastion of safety for Derivates or to the woman he loved.

Instead, he focused on the notification flashing on the datapad screen, telling him he had over three dozen new messages.

The messages were from Adam, Chris and Liana, and Jane, all asking where he had been and what was going on. Scraps walked back into the living room and sunk onto the couch as he started to answer the messages with profuse apologies. Ava's mother, he explained, had taken very ill. He hadn't even been thinking beyond supporting her to have the common decency to message them back. Chris and Liana immediately requested a dinner catch-up. Adam said that he would meet Scraps at Nightmix that weekend to debrief, and Jane let him know that she expected to see him in the morning.

Once he had sorted out his inbox by putting the messages in the folders for their respective recipients, Scraps sat back and looked around. He had just been about to call out to Flit to see what she wanted for dinner, but then he remembered she wasn't there.

The look in her eyes when he had told her to go still stung. There had been betrayal there. Fear too. Not for herself, but for him.

He hadn't even been thinking at the time. All he had known was that the Government was closing in on them and he had to buy some time for the others to get away. When he had seen the agents pointing their weapons at Flit, he had been overcome by a desperate desire to protect her. If anything happened to her, it would ruin him. He couldn't imagine his life without her in it anymore.

Yet there he was, sitting alone in their apartment, unsure if he would ever see her again.

Still, he would much rather be alone than have Flit in Government custody. There was no way she would have gotten through three days in a cell without losing her temper.

Despite the sense of loneliness that crept over his skin like a cold chill, he was pleased things had turned out the way they had. He just needed to figure out how to get back to Flit and the Underground as safely as possible.

With a new sense of resolution, Scraps pushed himself off the couch and went over to the kitchen to make dinner. If he was going to put a plan together, he would need to take care of himself. As minimal as his appetite was, he refused to let his mind or body go weak.

$$4$$

FLIT

"IF YOU'RE HERE to punch me again, you can turn around and walk your arse right back out," Hawkeye muttered as he looked up from the game he and Sway were playing on the narrow camp bed they were sitting on.

Flit stood in the doorway of the packed shelter with Patch by her side. Dozens of people stared back at them. Some were undercover operatives who she recognised from her youth. They acknowledged her presence with blank stares or slight waves and returned to what they were doing. The others, scattered around the room, were from the facility she and Scraps had raided. There wasn't even a single flicker of recognition in their eyes as they blinked back at her. No sense that she was the same person who had saved them.

Good.

"Harmony made me promise to behave," Flit said, returning her attention to Hawkeye. She walked past a few of the refugees to reach him. Patch followed along, giving the seated pair a bit of a wave. "She also, rather persuasively, convinced me that I was not mad at you."

That new, ice-cold rage Flit had discovered over the past few weeks was notably absent, even with her new frustrations. Logically, she knew she was mad at him, but she couldn't summon the emotions or the drive to act on them.

Hawkeye screwed up his face at her confession.

"Calmness is a surprisingly good look on you," Sway said with a shrug.

Flit twitched. "Don't get used to it."

"Right." Hawkeye stood and smoothed his black fatigue pants down over his thighs. "I know you're upset with me, and I am genuinely sorry about how things turned out, but it's good to see you. Is it too much to ask for a hug?"

His words cracked with such vulnerability that Flit let out a soft puff of breath, her eyes stinging as she nodded.

"Good."

The tension in Hawkeye's request melted when he stepped closer and wrapped his arms around her. Everything about him was so familiar—his warmth, his strength, his smell. Flit bit her lip as she rested her head against his shoulder. She couldn't recall how many times he had been there to hold her when she had been struggling. Even though part of her hated him for what he had done, she still loved him.

"I wish we had another choice," Hawkeye whispered, warm breath rustling the hair laying over her ears. "But he saw we were trapped. He bought us time to get back to safety. If he hadn't—"

"Stop," Flit blurted, her shoulders shaking. "I can't do this right now."

Hawkeye's chest deflated as he dropped the topic and hugged her tighter.

Sway groaned. "Shit. Either get a room or sit down." He threw the datapad in his hands onto the bed. "I know reunions are good, and it's nice to see you alive and kicking, Flit, but you got some explaining to do."

Flit pulled away from Hawkeye.

Patch, who had moved around to stand beside Sway whilst Flit and Hawkeye were embracing, cleared his throat. "Actually, I brought Flit here with the promise that you two would give her an update." He waved his hand in the direction of the rest of the room, to the refugees and returned agents. "She's missed a lot."

Hawkeye's eyes widened. "Oh, shit. I should have told you right away. I'm sorry." He put both hands on her shoulder. "It's probably a good thing Harmony worked some coercion on you because what I have to tell you next is big."

Flit rolled her eyes, her foot tapping on the ground. "Just spill, already."

"We rescued some of the people in this room from a Government facility just outside of the Hub. While we were there, we found someone we were not expecting," Hawkeye begun.

It was hard, but Flit did her best to pretend to be surprised. "Oh?" It sounded impatient, but that was better than coming off as knowing.

Sway got to his feet. "I need you to listen to everything I say before you react, okay?" he said, keeping his town low and calming. "Hawkeye found Fortune."

Flit blinked, her breath catching in her throat. She knew that already, of course, but Fortune had told her she would wipe their memories of meeting Flit, so she had to pretend otherwise. She let her mouth drop open and her eyes widen. "W-What?"

Resting a hand on her shoulder, Hawkeye said, "Rook and Fortune were in the facility these people came from. Rook was in poor health, and he was unable to return, but Fortune did."

"Rook was alive?" Flit blurted, bringing her hands up to cover her mouth. All she needed to do was think back to the look on his face before he had kissed her. Before he had died. That was enough to have tears brimming in her eyes.

Hawkeye nodded. "He *was*," he said, getting choked up himself. "He tried so hard to stay alive, but they did things to him—"

"He died, but it sounds as though he was in pain," Sway cut in. "I know that's hard, but we have Fortune. I know how much you loved her. At least she survived."

Scrubbing her eyes, Flit straightened up and looked around. She didn't see Fortune in her earlier scan of the room, but she could really do with one of her motherly hugs right about now.

"She's speaking to Shadow in another room at the moment," Patch informed her. "I saw them going into bay three earlier."

Flit made a show of sinking onto the bed beside Sway and resting her head in her hands. She took several deep, shaking breaths before looking back up at the three guys. "I want to see her."

"We can't interrupt them," Patch warned.

Hawkeye looked between Flit and the door, as if she was a flight risk. It was a fair assumption. If it really was news to her that Fortune was alive, nothing would stop her from storming that room.

She jumped to her feet, to make it look like she was going to go anyway. Hawkeye slid between her and the door and grasped her hands.

"Flit..." He inclined his head in the direction of the other people in the room. "I know you're keen to see Fortune, but there is a lot more to the story. Let me introduce you to some of the others."

So, he was going with the distraction technique. Clever.

Without giving Flit a chance to argue or tug out of his grasp, Hawkeye linked his arm with hers and dragged her across to the other side of the room, towards a familiar head of red hair.

"Layla! I have someone to introduce you to," Hawkeye announced as they approached.

The attractive, feisty woman turned to face Flit, and while she eyed her warily, she had a warm smile for Hawkeye. Flit called upon every ounce of restraint she had to stop from smirking at the memory of Layla giving Hawkeye a solid fist to his face. Clearly, that animosity between them was gone now.

Interesting.

"Hi, I'm Layla. I take it you're another returned agent?" Layla stretched out her hand for Flit to shake.

Flit noted that she was out of that horrid Government jumpsuit. The bandage on her left forearm was gone, revealing a peppering of small circular scars on the inside of her arm.

"Kind of," Flit said noncommittally, not wanting to accidentally jog her memory and undo whatever Fortune had done to her memory. "Sorry, but I don't recognise you."

Sway glanced around before leaning in and whispering conspiratorially, "That's because she's never been here before."

Flit forced a frown onto her lips and made her eyebrows furrow as she looked Layla up and down. She would be lying if she said she wasn't enjoying this at least a little bit. "Well, you're not from Longbeach... and you don't have red eyes and a tattoo, so you're not Registered."

"That's because she isn't!" Sway blurted, unable to contain his excitement.

Flit threw up her hands, enjoying the chance to be a bit dramatic. "Are you a Citizen, then?" she snapped, feigning impatient confusion.

"No, I'm a microkinetic." Layla's voice dropped to a whisper. She glanced at Hawkeye who nodded, encouraging her to continue. "I was born in the Hub to Citizen parents."

Just as Flit opened her mouth to speak, Patch squeezed her hand. "I promise we'll explain, but we've already drawn too much attention. Why don't we sit down for a while and chat over a game of Fifty-Two Pick-Up?"

Pressing her lips together and pretending to be annoyed, Flit turned and led the way back to the bed Hawkeye and Sway had been sitting on when she arrived. The others followed her, and for the first time in weeks, she felt a genuine sense of amusement as she wondered what story they would tell her.

⁓⁓⁓ 🔥 ⁓⁓⁓

IT JUST SO HAPPENED THAT Fortune had fabricated an excellent story. Hawkeye explained that he had been on a standard surveillance shift in Intelligence when he had noticed some odd movement in the Old City readouts. He said he had done his absolute best to get through to someone in charge, but his calls hadn't been answered, so he'd decided to investigate by himself. Ever since his injury, he had been resentful of having to take a back seat, and this had been a regrettable attempt on his part to feel useful again.

Fortune had done such a thorough job of convincing Hawkeye that the story was the truth that Flit could see the frustration and embarrassment on Hawkeye's face as he explained what had happened. She felt a smidgen of guilt for letting him wallow in those emotions, but she had no other choice. If the truth of what had happened in that facility got out, she and Scraps would get into serious trouble, and it could expose the Free Citizens to scrutiny they didn't need.

When Hawkeye finished his side of the story, Layla jumped in. "Since we got down here, the leaders—"

"Harmony and Divvy," Sway provided.

"Yes, Harmony and Divvy have asked us to keep quiet about where we came from. They are concerned that, with the recent tunnel collapses, it may cause undue panic." The redhead looked around, as if checking to see if someone was eavesdropping. No one in the shelter seemed to care much for them, though, as they were too busy doing their own thing.

"But they know that you weren't Registered or from the Underground. What was their reaction like?" Flit asked.

Hawkeye leaned closer. "As non-reactionary as ever. They didn't even bat their eyelashes."

"They had Acumen question me and some of the others yesterday, but it was more of a casual conversation than anything else," Layla supplied.

Flit let out a low whistle and leaned back as she took in the fact that Harmony and Divvy wanted to keep such important news to themselves. Everyone in the Underground deserved to know the Government had been lying and that there were more people like them living on the surface than they anticipated. Still, there were other things to worry about.

"Tell me about these tunnel collapses," she said.

"There's not much to tell." Patch shrugged and scratched his chin. "We lost around twenty percent of our network and all but one of our concealed emergency escapes. People died. Others were injured, and we think some may still be trapped. They haven't said who or what caused it, but..." He gestured around them with an open palm. "...this kinda speaks for itself. They haven't done such an extensive recall since Longbeach."

The implications in his words were clear. Longbeach had been the Underground's last satellite site. Now, the facility they were in, the one just below the Hub, was the last bastion of resistance. They were all that was left.

"So, since the collapses, everyone's just been sitting here?" Flit raised her eyebrows.

Hawkeye rolled his eyes. "Well, that we know of, but I am sure a lot is happening outside of these walls."

"I got a message from Link today. Apparently, all the Security patrols have been—" Just as Sway was about to dish the dirt, the door to the shelter opened, and a familiar woman stepped in.

"Fortune!" Flit was so relieved to see the woman's tanned skin and grey-peppered brown hair that she forgot about the inhibitor she was wearing. She tried to teleport over to hug her and cried out as the purple sizzle zapped through her and lit her nerves on fire. She fell back against the cot she was sitting on.

"Flit!" Fortune's voice was full of such concern. She crossed the shelter in seconds and pulled Flit into a tight hug. "Oh, thank goodness you're here. You're safe."

Fortune's hug was firm, and familiar, and almost enough to undo Flit.

The older woman pulled back and held her at arm's length, looking her up and down. Her eyes lingered on Flit's hazel ones and her chocolate brown hair, most likely noticing that her features had been reverted to their natural state.

Fortune's lips curled into a mournful frown. "Rook—"

"I know. Hawk told me," Flit spluttered.

Fortune merely nodded and pulled her into a tight hug. "That friend of yours, Scraps... he isn't here." Her voice was barely loud enough for Flit to hear above the murmur of conversation in the shelter.

Flit shook her head against Fortune's shoulder, static pulling strands of hair from her plait. "Don't worry. We'll figure something out. We need to talk but not here. Just hold tight for a little longer until we get out of quarantine."

With a heavy sigh, Fortune pulled away from Flit again and cupped her cheek with a warm, smooth palm. "Well," she said, voice loud enough for the people with them to hear, "I never thought this moment would come, but I am so, so happy to see you again, my darling girl."

Flit sniffed and blinked away the genuine stinging in her eyes. "You too, Fortune, you too." Flit held tight onto Fortune's hand as Layla slid over on the cot to make room for them.

"Any word on when we're getting out of here?" Sway asked, looking impatient. Flit could only imagine that he was aching to see Link again.

"Shadow said tomorrow morning. We've got to do some medical checks and a debriefing first." Fortune sat straighter as she pulled Flit against her side. "Until then, we can just hang tight here. I was given the impression that there is a lot of work to do around the place thanks to the collapses, so we might as well enjoy the downtime while we have it."

Even though the idea of helping the Underground recover from the latest tragedies was enticing, Flit had other plans—namely, getting back to the Hub and finding Scraps so she could kiss his annoying face, tell him that he was stupid for giving himself up like that, and then telling him she loved him too.

5
____

SCRAPS

AFTER THE LAST FEW DAYS, Scraps had come to think a knock on his door was a bad thing.

As he sat alone in his apartment, eating his pre-packaged dispenser dinner, the knocking was the last thing he expected to hear, but it was there—assertive, persistent, and unaccompanied by any disclosure of identity.

He looked between his half-finished meal and the door. If he didn't answer it soon, the neighbours might hear it and get suspicious.

Non-residents usually didn't have access to the building unless someone buzzed them in, so the visitor either lived there, somehow had gotten granted access, or had broken in. Scraps did not find any of those options particularly desirable, but he wouldn't be able to solve the mystery by sitting at the dining room table.

Scraps got up, brushing his hands off as he walked over to the door. He took a deep breath before he held his hand up, ready to hit the access panel. "Who is it?"

There was a pause and the shuffle of shoes. "Your friend."

Scraps blinked. He knew that voice. He resisted the urge to frown and opened the door. "To what do I owe the pleasure of this visit?"

Adam gave him a large, fake smile that didn't reach his eyes. "I was in the neighbourhood. May I?" He gestured to the living room behind Scraps.

If he hadn't been given a mission by the agents, Scraps would have told Adam to leave. He had thought he would have to seek Adam out, so he tried to be grateful for the fact he would not have to do the legwork. Also, if it meant he could avoid going to Nightmix on the weekend, then perhaps it wasn't a bad thing.

"Of course. I was not expecting you, but it is good of you to drop by." Scraps stepped back and gestured for Adam to come in.

Scraps shut the door behind them and led the way to the lounge room where he invited Adam to take a seat.

The older man looked around, taking his time to drink in his surroundings before finally sitting. "Where is Ava tonight? Out with Liana?"

"Her mother is unwell. Ava is in Eastbay with her," Scraps said. As much as he hated the lie, he would rather not let Adam know where Flit really was.

"Ah, hopefully her mother gets well soon." Adam didn't sound entirely genuine about it, and Scraps' scepticism was confirmed as the man continued on, unperturbed, "I know things didn't go quite as you planned the other day, but I hope that hasn't tainted your enthusiasm for the cause."

Scraps had to make a conscious effort to unclench his jaw so he could reply. "Not at all."

"Good. I just stopped by because I wanted to discuss that added responsibility we talked about before our attack on the maglev system."

"Oh?" Scraps hummed.

Normally, he would ask for information, but he avoided it this time. If Adam volunteered the intel, at least he could say he didn't lure him out. It was a hair-splitting distinction, but it eased Scraps' moral concerns enough to stop him from giving up.

"It's probably a good thing that I caught you alone," Adam started. "I can tell that Ava is not fond of my approach to things. She has some good insights, but she is a little too fiery. That kind of resistance has the potential to sow disorder into a group."

Scraps pressed his lips together. Flit wouldn't have resisted if

Adam's plans were sound and sensible, and if he wasn't trying to turn his own freedom fighters into suicide-bombing extremists.

When Scraps didn't respond, Adam continued, "You, though, you think things through. You have a quiet logic about you, and that is what I really need. What the Free Citizens need. I know I made some changes to our mission last week, but they needed to happen, and Ava would have made it too difficult."

It took a great deal of effort for Scraps to contain the anger building inside of him. He wanted to tell Adam that he was right, that Ava would never have approved that strategy because it was terrible. Scraps didn't condone it, either. He wanted to explain that Adam clearly knew very little about what the Free Citizens truly needed because Scraps was certain suicide bombing was not on that list. But he didn't say any of that. He couldn't. The Government needed him to get information from the Free Citizens, and the Free Citizens needed him to protect them from Adam's madness.

"I didn't enjoy concealing the plan from you. It isn't what the Free Citizens stand for, but that mission needed to have a real impact. EMPs would have been too easily fixed." Adam shook his head as his jaw was set with determination. "Not only did we fully destroy several important transport mainframes, but we spread the kind of awareness that will lead to more joining our cause. I spoke to those who gave their lives for our cause before the mission, and they did so gladly."

Despite how earnestly Scraps disagreed with Adam, he smiled and nodded even as his gut twisted and throat constricted. The effort it took for him to stay silent was painful, and he finally understood what Flit had to battle with daily.

"What do I have to with all of this?" he asked.

"Everything, Brian." Adam patted Scraps on the shoulder. "I need you to step up to the plate. The Free Citizens responded well to your calm, considered leadership. It compliments my vision for the group. I don't need the wonderful wildfire that is your wife." Adam smiled when he said that last bit, but it was only to dull the backhanded insult of it. "We need your steely logic. Sure, when Ava gets back, I am more than happy for her to manage things by your side, but if we are going to succeed, your voice needs to be louder than hers, if you get what I mean?"

"I do." Scraps' cheeks started to ache from the neutral expression he forced onto his face. "I am not sure when Ava will get back, but I promise I will heed your words." Scraps gave Adam a small salute. "For the good of all."

The moment the words slipped his lips, Scraps knew he shouldn't have said them. Even though he attempted to deliver them with a tone of sarcasm, he was never good at conveying such social complexities. As much as he wanted to point out that Adam was acting just like the organisation he hated, Scraps needed to be more tactful about it. The last few days had been stressful, and he was missing Flit, but it was no excuse for slipping up.

"That is not our motto." Adam rolled his shoulders as he narrowed his eyes at Scraps.

Scraps scraped for the first excuse that came to his mind. "Maybe it should be. Maybe we should reclaim it and live up to its true meaning."

Adam stared at him for almost a full minute. Scraps refused to look away or back down.

In the end, Adam pressed his lips together and got to his feet. "In a couple of nights, I will send you a message and let you know where we can meet instead of going to Nightmix. Don't tell anyone else about the location. Not even Chris and Liana. Is that understood?"

"Of course. I will see you there." Scraps rose and led Adam to the door.

When Adam was gone, Scraps reheated his dinner and sat down to eat. He'd eaten four spoonfuls before the doorbell rang again. He looked back over at the living room to see if Adam had left anything behind.

He hadn't.

With a heavy sigh and a longing glance at his cooling meal, Scraps got up and made his way to the door again with light, cautious footsteps. When he reached the door, he leaned against it. "Who is it?"

"Chris and Liana. And we have food." Liana sounded far too

excited, and there was a rustling as Scraps imagined her holding up whatever bag she carried to emphasise the point.

Scraps opened the door. Despite the visit he just had from Adam and the way his neglected stomach rumbled at yet another interruption to his bland but nutritious dinner, he smiled.

"To what do I owe the pleasure of this visit?" Scraps stepped back and gestured for the couple to come in.

"Outta my way, this is hot!" Liana rushed past and set the bag on the table, flapping her hands to cool them down.

"Jane told us that Ava had to go back to Eastbay on family business." Chris took his time shaking Scraps' hand. "Someone's gotta make sure you're taking care of yourself while she's away."

With a groan of disgust, Liana held up the half-eaten processed, prepackaged dispenser meal. "Ugh, see? Told you he would do this." She threw it straight into the trash compactor.

Scraps' mouth dropped open. "I was eating that."

Chris patted Scraps on the shoulder. "Don't worry, buddy. We've got your back."

Without needing to ask where things were in the kitchen, Chris and Liana had dinner set up on the table for him within moments. He watched in silence, swallowing a ball of appreciation. After growing up the way he had, it still amazed him that people performed these kinds of thoughtful acts for others and even more so that they thought him worthy of them.

"Please tell me you're hungry," Liana said, adjusting the last fork on the table.

Scraps' mouth watered as he walked over to the table. "I certainly am."

Liana beamed. "Fantastic because I'm starving. Let's eat before it gets cold."

The three of them settled in around the dining table.

"So, about the other day—" Chris begun.

"Not now, please," Scraps blurted. He had just picked up the fork. All he wanted was to eat his dinner.

Chris blinked, clearly shocked by the sudden shut-down.

Scraps might have been happy for Adam to incriminate himself, but he did not want his deal with the Government to ensnare Chris and Liana as well.

"Sorry, I did not mean to be abrupt," Scraps said. "I just... It's been a very long few days, I miss Ava, and I just want to enjoy a quiet night with my friends."

Chris' expression softened.

Liana reached across the table to pat his hand gently. "Then let's just have a quiet night, hmm?"

Scraps was grateful his friends did not argue. Instead, as they ate, they fell into a comfortable, casual conversation. For a short while, Scraps was able to forget his own worries. Of course he missed Flit, but there was something healing about the thoughtful kindness of his friends.

After dinner, Chris took care of the dishes while Liana and Scraps set up a movie for them all to watch. Liana gave him free rein of the selection, so he picked a movie that Flit was adamant would be terrible. As they watched, Chris made every effort to make fun of the bad parts. It was a good distraction that kept them up far too late.

When Chris and Liana finally left, Scraps was utterly exhausted. Far too much had happened within such a short span of time, and he was grateful for the warm, restorative shower he had before tumbling into bed.

Still, no amount of fatigue or good company was enough to camouflage the fact that the bed was cold and empty beside him. Scraps wasn't sure how he had gotten so used to sleeping next to someone else in such a short time, but with Flit gone, he couldn't settle in properly. The night felt far longer than it should have, but he did not regret his decision.

6

———

FLIT

THERE WERE SO many people in the emergency shelter that the nighttime snores, rustle of sheets, and mutters of sleep talking were almost as loud as the buzz of daytime conversation. It made it near impossible for Flit to sleep. Even though the coercion had made her mind foggy around the edges and her extremities weak, her hands and feet bounced in time with her racing thoughts. She spent so much time spinning and fussing with the wedding ring still on her finger that her skin hurt. The more time that passed, the more desperate Flit became to get up and *move*.

Flit wasn't sure what time it was when she crept to the door and tapped the panel beside it. A red light flared, indicating it was locked from the outside. She swore under her breath. She glanced over her shoulder to make sure no one was watching and then tried the door again.

Still locked.

Flit slammed her hand against the panel and turned around. She was just about to walk the perimeter to find another exit when the door hissed open behind her. Flit spun, ready to bolt out, but Shadow stood in the threshold.

"Trying to escape, I presume?" Shadow's voice was flat, without a hint of amusement.

Flit shrugged, resisting the urge to look past his shoulder. It wasn't like she could teleport out anyway.

"This room is being monitored. There's no point acting coy." Shadow stepped back into the hall and gestured for her to join him with a wide sweep of his arm. "Luckily for you, we have some new intel to share. Come with me."

If that wasn't good timing, Flit didn't know what was.

She stepped into the tunnel, caught between wariness that this was a trap and an undeniable sense of curiosity at Shadow's offer. She waited until they were a few metres down the hall to ask, "So, what is this about?"

Shadow held up a hand to silence her.

"But—"

"No."

Flit gritted her teeth. "Shadow."

"Confidential information isn't shared in hallways, Flit," Shadow snapped. "You should know better."

"Then walk faster so we can get to a secure room quicker."

Judging by the twitch on Shadow's face, he was barely restraining the urge to throttle her. He went to say something but shook his head and increased his speed. Flit nearly had to run to keep up. They didn't have far to go, though. They turned out of the corridor the shelter was in and back towards the rear part of the Intelligence area, passing through the network of tunnels between them and the rest of the Underground.

Shadow pressed his palm against the panel by the door, and it slid open. The room beyond was small with a plain metal table and two chairs, one of which was occupied by Harmony.

The older woman's face softened into a gentle smile. "Flit, thank you for coming. I hope you're not mad at me for waking you?"

With a dismissive wave, Flit said, "Nah, you're fine. I was having trouble sleeping anyway."

"Harmony, do you want me to wait out here?" Shadow stepped aside to let Flit into the room.

"No, I'll walk Flit back to the shelter afterwards. Thank you, Shadow. Go and get some rest." Harmony took a datapad off her lap.

Flit walked into the room and sank into the spare seat. The

metal was cold through the simple pants she had been given to wear to bed in the shelter.

When the door closed, Harmony put the datapad on the table between them and set her hands either side of it. Flit watched her warily, still annoyed about being compelled to remain calm earlier. The command had worn off, but the indignation hadn't.

"Earlier, Divvy and I said we would let you know if we had any news about Scraps," Harmony explained.

Any wariness Flit felt dissipated at those words. She leaned in. "And?"

Harmony pressed her lips together. She tapped the screen, and a video started. It looked like run-of-the-mill surveillance footage from a standard Government office space. "This is footage from the lobby of the interrogation rooms in North One. That's the—"

"The holding facility you tracked Scraps to," Flit interrupted.

She stared at the screen, transfixed as people seemed to go about their business, as if it were just any other office in any other building. She wasn't sure if she wanted to see what Harmony had to show her, but she couldn't have torn her eyes away if she tried.

After a few more seconds of the uneventful feed, one of the doors opened, and two agents stepped out with Scraps between them. A whimper escaped Flit's lips as she saw him. He looked pale, tired, and drawn, but he wasn't wearing an inhibitor or even handcuffs.

"He's alive," Flit whispered, reaching towards the screen but stopping just short of running her fingers over it. She was going to ask when the footage was taken or if they knew where he was now, but something she saw stalled her questions.

A shiver rippled down her spine as Scraps' face set in a grim smile, and he shook both of the officers' hands. Flit's breath caught in her throat at the casual motion, goosebumps rising on her arms.

"Based on this evidence and further surveillance, we believe that—"

"No!"

Harmony gave Flit a sympathetic smile that was edged with pity. Instead of speaking again, Harmony changed the footage to show the street outside of their apartment. Scraps was walking along the pavement, free and unharried, and then turned and entered their building as though it was any other day. "This was taken earlier today. He went straight home following release from the holding cells. We were unable to gain footage of the apartment itself, but he is free, and he is home."

Flit wasn't stupid. She could see the evidence. She could even understand why they might deduce that Scraps was working with the Government, but she knew Scraps. She knew him better than she knew herself. He was on their side.

"We're also concerned he may have been connected to the recent tunnel collapses," Harmony explained.

As much as Flit wanted to rage, as much as she wanted to argue, Harmony's accusation hit her like a punch to the guts. She could barely breathe, let alone speak. She shook her head as she tried to catch her breath. "Harmony, you know that's not—"

Harmony reached across the space between them and took Flit's shoulders gently in her soft, warm hands. "Flit, sweetheart, we know you would never do that. I have no doubt you were completely unaware of any of this."

"Scraps didn't have anything to do with it either!" Flit met Harmony's gaze and held it with all of her conviction. "Besides, we were never apart. He wouldn't have had the time."

With a slight tilt of her head, Harmony asked, "What about the times when he went for a run? Those were at least an hour, once a day. And... you did sleep while you were in the Hub, didn't you?"

Flit blinked at the insinuation. Preposterous! Harmony and Divvy had been so complimentary of Scraps before they had left, and he had more than proven himself to everyone in this blasted place.

"Harmony, I'm sorry," Flit begun, pulling back and shaking her head. "You're wrong. Scraps had nothing to do with any of that, and he is not working for the Government. This is bullshit. If you give me a chance, I'll go back up and get him. I'm sure he has a perfectly logical explanation for what you saw with the agents." As Flit was speaking, she got to her feet and stepped back. She did not like where this was going.

She had to get out of there. She had to clear Scraps' name.

"Flit, sit down," Harmony said firmly.

Flit plonked back down into the chair. Her mind railed at the command.

"Harmony, let me stand up," Flit demanded.

Harmony's gaze caught Flit's, so Flit squeezed her eyes shut.

"There were times when you and KC-847 were apart in the Hub," Harmony said. Even without eye contact, there was such influence behind her words.

The worst part was that it was true. Flit couldn't deny that even if she tried.

"He went for runs frequently."

Another undeniable truth.

"Sometimes, you'd wake up in the middle of the night to use the restroom, and he wasn't there beside you," Harmony continued, her voice slithering into Flit's mind, the oily tendrils coiling around her memories and taking a vise-like grip on them. "Whenever you would ask about it, he would say he'd just gone for a walk to clear his head."

Lies.

But... why did it feel like the truth?

"You started to suspect there was something going on but just dismissed it as him having trouble adjusting to being back on the surface."

"I started to suspect there was something going on..." Flit's voice was so weak as she repeated Harmony's horrible words. Despite how much they wavered, they wormed their way into her mind. They sounded like the truth.

She jammed her hands against her ears and shook her head. "No, no, no!" The hard metal of the wedding ring she wore as part of her cover story pressed against her skin and she struggled to keep her resolve.

Harmony only spoke louder. "But now you have seen the videos. You know the truth. KC-847 betrayed the Underground. He plotted to destroy us."

Tears sprung to Flit's tightly closed eyes. The pressure of them was so immense that they started to ooze from the corner of her eyelids. Even muffled by her hands, Harmony's words took root in her mind and spilled out of her mouth. "KC-847 betrayed the Underground. He plotted to destroy us."

A soft hand squeezed Flit's shoulder. "I'm so, so sorry, Flit." The sympathy in Harmony's voice was sickly sweet and full of poison. "It's not your fault that KC-847 was able to infiltrate the Underground. This is clearly a plan that went beyond all of us. It was so very brave of you to share your concerns with me. Thank you so much for being honest with me. Thank you for telling me that KC-847 had to be behind this. I hope this helps you move on from him. You do not need to go after him. He will just betray you again."

"I do not need to g-go after KC-847. He will just b-betray me again." A violent sob wracked Flit, making her entire body shake. The world tilted around her, and the edges of her heart felt razor sharp and ice cold.

"Oh, shh..." Harmony wrapped an arm around Flit's waist and helped her to her feet. "I know it's hard, love, but we're here for you. The whole Underground is here for you." The older woman walked Flit to the door. "Don't worry, sweetheart. I'm going to take you back to the shelter, and you can get some sleep. We will talk again in the morning."

The rest of the trip back to the shelter passed in a blur of tears and shadows. Flit felt like a complete idiot. She thought of the people who had been killed and injured in the collapse, of the people who were possibly still trapped. Her people. The Underground's people... and she had led KC-847 right to them.

7

SCRAPS

EVEN THOUGH SCRAPS had trouble getting to sleep, it was a restful night once he finally succumbed. He woke feeling better rested than he had in days. He was strongly tempted to ignore his alarm and sleep a little longer, but he decided against it. He had woken in a good mood and had to take advantage of it, so he got up, went for his first morning run in almost a week, and came back to get ready for work.

When Scraps got to the office, he settled into his pod and logged into his console. He opened the prep work for his next job, the Derivate Training Facility, and tried to read. For some reason, he had trouble getting through it. He hadn't realised just how quiet his day would be without Flit. Even when they were both working hard, Flit made some kind of noise, whether she was muttering at her work, or her clothes were swishing against the desk as she swivelled from side to side on her chair, or she exhaled a frustrated groan when her system wasn't working fast enough... It was all an ambience he was accustomed to, and it was hard to work without it.

Then, it dawned on him that he hadn't spoken a single word since he had woken up.

He shut the files and rested his elbows on his desk then put his head in his hands.

It was too much.

Judging by the policy review information Scraps read, he

wouldn't be able to do the Derivate Training Facility on his own. It was a lot of work, and he didn't want to push his luck by spending more time than necessary in the facility. He was skating on thin ice with the Government as it was. The last thing he could afford to do was annoy someone and have them uncover the truth about him.

He had a feeling Flit would be disappointed in him. She had been so hopeful that the facility would reveal some useful information they could report to the Underground, but Flit wasn't there. She was gone, and Scraps was not quite as good at noticing that kind of thing as she was, so the whole review would just get him into more trouble than it was worth.

Scraps opened his messaging application and put Jane's address into the *To* field when he looked over his shoulder to see that Jane was sitting in her office, scrolling through something on her screen, looking calm. He got to his feet and decided to talk to her in person. Even though he had warned Flit against doing the same thing before, he figured it would be good to keep up the rapport Flit had built with her.

When Scraps knocked on Jane's office door, she looked up, and her eyes widened a little with surprise. She gestured for him to come in. "Brian, how can I help you?" she asked, swiping her screen to sleep and steepling her hands on the table.

"I've been looking over the material for the Derivate Training Facility, but I do not think I can do it without Ava. It's a large project with a short time frame."

Jane frowned. "You don't think Ava will be back by next week?"

Scraps shook his head. "I don't know when she will be back."

Although what he really meant was that he didn't know *if* she would be back.

With a sigh, Jane rubbed her eyes. "I can probably pull Gary off the hydroponics job and send him with you."

That, Scraps thought, was the most repulsive idea. He disliked Gary intensely and did not want someone who was clearly so anti-Derivate put on the job.

"Liana should be free soon," Scraps suggested, thinking back to a conversation the previous night. Or was it that morning? "She's almost done with her current review."

Jane shook her head. "Her clearance level is different."

Scraps furrowed his brows as he tried to think up a way around it. "Can she have temporary access?"

Jane peered towards office where Liana sat, working away in her pod. "Let me think about it, okay? I'll let you know who your partner is before the end of the day. Just keep going with your prep."

"Copy that," Scraps said, turning and heading back to his pod.

He hoped Liana wouldn't be angry at him for volunteering her. She might have been almost done with her current review, but she had spent a good part of the previous night complaining about how many other jobs she had on her plate. Perhaps, Scraps thought, he could sweeten the deal by offering to help her with some of her work if she helped him with his.

Scraps hoped Liana would agree. He and Flit had discovered that their Citizen friends were polite to Derivates and believed they should have rights. Seeing Liana's reaction to the facility would really help Scraps figure out whether or not he should tell her and her husband the truth behind Code 6B. It was a secret that neither he nor Flit enjoyed hiding, and it would be good to know he had some allies if his or Flit's true identities were revealed.

Scraps was too deep in his work that afternoon to immediately check the partner assignment Jane sent through. In the end, he didn't need to go to his mail app to get the news. Instead, a soft knock made him look up from his computer. Liana stood outside the pod, smiling at him.

"Come in," Scraps called, spinning around in his chair.

Liana opened the door and stepped in. "What is all this about the Derivate Training Facility?" she asked, plonking down in Flit's seat.

"Ava was supposed to do the job with me, and I'd rather not have Gary replace her." Scraps shrugged. "Out of everyone in the office, I thought you've got the right point of view to approach it fairly."

For a moment, Liana seemed to consider it as she kicked back in Flit's seat and looked down at her hands. "I don't know if it is the right assignment for me. I don't think I'll like what I see there."

The frown on her face made him think he was right about her, that she wasn't as comfortable with the use of Derivates as everyone else around them seemed to be.

"I don't think you will either, but that doesn't make it any less important to see." Scraps reached across the booth and gently patted her hand. "The only way to fix an uncomfortable truth is by facing it head on. We can't run from it."

Scraps' voice was low, but he wondered whether there was much point trying to be quiet. He had no doubt that Agent Greene and Agent Hector were listening in on his every word. They were also expecting him to do things to get more information about the Free Citizens, so it would not come as a shock to them if he went to investigate another facility.

He needed to be seen to be continuing with his life to fool both the Government Agents and the Free Citizens. People wouldn't get suspicious unless they had reason to be, and until Scraps could find a way to get back to Flit safely, he would ensure his behaviour was beyond reproach.

After time to think and a heavy sigh, Liana conceded. "I'll do it. At the very least, I'm looking forward to working with you. You and Ava are so efficient. It'll be good to get the opportunity to learn all your tricks."

"It is nice to have a chance to work with you, too," Scraps said, truth ringing from his words. "Before I prepare your information package to get you up to speed, what do you already know about Derivate training?"

"Er... I mean... they train them, right? To use their abilities. So, there must be some sort of policies around that." Liana scratched the back of her neck as she gave a small shrug.

Scraps frowned. Clearly, the Citizens were not given as much information on the lives of Derivates as Derivates were given about Citizens.

"Yes, they train them. There are relevant policies and procedures. The children are born and raised in the facilities, so you will need to prepare yourself for seeing that. Also, there will be a range of powers on display. It will be important for you to trust the process and to not panic if you see something you wouldn't see on the street."

"Oh, I'll get to see them using powers openly?" Liana sounded more enthused.

"Well, it is a training facility..."

"Right, of course." Liana cleared her throat and nodded. "But when you say born and raised in the facilities—"

"That is not a euphemism. You will need to brush up on your knowledge of the development trajectories for Derivates. The facility houses every age from newborn through to senior years. I can send you some information, if you would like?"

"That would be very helpful. Thank you." Liana sighed. "I should get back to my desk. I've got a lot of reading to do." She stretched as she stood then smiled at Scraps before leaving him to his work.

Scraps immediately began going through his files and putting a package together for Liana containing the policies and procedures she needed to brush up on. He added in some important papers related to the rearing and treatment of Derivates, too, to give his friend some context for what she would see. He had always understood that the Citizens gave very little time considering how Derivates lived, but for one as empathetic and caring as Liana to have no real idea was a surprise.

The deep dive into the Government's database was as infuriating as it was enlightening. Since learning the truth of what happened in the Department of Advanced Human Research, Scraps had not had a chance to truly sit down and look for more information and evidence about the origins of Derivacy. Between their work and extracurricular troublemaking, he and Flit did not have time for such things.

As he sifted through document after document, he wished Flit was there. This was probably the only material she would be interested in reading, and there was a lot there to digest that he wanted to discuss with someone else who would understand.

There were a lot of familiar documents that Scraps gathered to copy to Liana—in-depth information about each Derivate ability, the classification system, and the designation conventions. All ones he had grown up reading and reciting. In fact, he could have recited them to Liana if she was still in his office. In addition to the foundation documents, he shared the rules and regulations every Derivate student was expected to follow. As he read through them, a knot formed in his chest, writhing with resentment and frustration. The familiar words blurred his vision, and he couldn't believe that he used to live his life by them. Things like the prevention of social bonding, reinforcing their function as a service in society rather than individuals...

Scraps had assumed other Derivates felt the way he did. From the outside, they were all very good at following orders. The punishments were too dehumanising for anything else. What Scraps hadn't realised, that he now knew from meeting Fortune and the escapees she had with her, was that were plenty of Registereds who had been able to see through the lies. Even Bookworm, Patch and Link's mother, said she made a purposeful break.

Even if he was late to the party, in terms of discovering his own mind, Scraps was determined to do his best to prevent others from suffering the extent of brainwashing that he had felt. They had to know that there was a chance for a meaningful, self-directed life out there.

Scraps was just finishing up his folder for Liana when a new message appeared in his inbox. It did not have a listed sender or subject title, but he opened it to find a short, straight-to-the-point directive there waiting for him.

To: Brian Parkes
From: H & G
Subject: Meeting Scheduled
Compulsory rendezvous tonight at five. Floor three of East Two-North One: Government History Museum. Come alone. Do not tell anyone about the contents of this message.

It hadn't been all that long since he had last seen the agents, so Scraps couldn't help but wonder what they expected from him. Surely anyone who worked in this kind of field knew that information would take time to acquire. However, the fact Adam had come to visit him at his apartment the previous night might have something to do with it. He didn't really have much to tell them. He hoped they would be okay with that.

Scraps was about to reply to the message when it disappeared from his screen. He tried looking through the junk and trash files, but it wasn't there. Judging by how it left behind no trace, Scraps assumed there was some clever coding or micro-work going on. The fact the agents wanted to hide their message was interesting in and of itself. Were they concerned about their own internal people finding out? It also showed Scraps that it was possible they were accessing his profile in all sorts of ways he might not be aware of.

Instead of dwelling on the possibilities and implications, Scraps concentrated on his work. Reading through the policies and procedures that used to rule his life, albeit from a different angle, was more difficult than he had anticipated. The sense of underlying resentment he felt for the Government since learning the truth swelled in his chest, turning a tidy, patient urge into something with sharper edges and more insistence. It gave him the drive he needed to push through his discomfort in the hopes he would be able to use what he learned to benefit others like him. Thankfully, this assignment Flit had stolen was the perfect way to do that.

8

———

FLIT

"SHE STILL HASN'T WOKEN UP?"

Hawkeye's voice broke through Flit's misery.

A finger gently poked her shoulder.

"She is still alive, right?" Sway whispered back.

Hawkeye groaned. "Obviously, idiot."

"Don't get pissed at me. I don't know what her sleep schedule is like."

"Oh, what, and I do?"

"I figured you'd have some idea. You were crushing on her for most of your life."

The weight of the pause between them held the implication of a nasty glare. Flit could even imagine the death stare Hawkeye would be giving Sway for bringing that dirty laundry back out into the open.

"She's a heavy sleeper," Hawkeye finally conceded, "especially when she's upset, but I would have thought she'd be awake the moment the lights went on, given the situation."

"I'll go get some cold water. That'll do the trick."

Finally, Flit rolled onto her side and peeled one eye open to peer at the dunderheaded duo. "You know I can hear you two arse-holes, right?" Her voice was raspy as it clawed its way out of her throat. A night of crying had that effect on a person.

"Good morning Flit. How nice of you to finally join us!" Sway clapped his hands together in mock delight. "Harmony and Divvy said that we're all going to be getting out of quarantine this afternoon. If you slept any longer, we might have left you behind."

"I'm good with that," Flit huffed and shifted back to her stomach, burying her head into her pillow and wishing everyone and everything around her would just disappear.

There was a much more discretely whispered buzz of conversation above her and then footsteps slapped against the concrete shelter floor. A few minutes later, whoever had left returned with an extra set of shoes clacking along with them. The edge of the collapsible cot Flit was on sagged, and a warm, gentle hand settled on her shoulder.

"Flit, sweetheart, what's going on?"

Fortune's motherly voice broke Flit all over again. A pathetic sob burst from her lips.

"Oh, hey, it's okay. Come here." Without asking, Fortune leaned down and wrapped her arms around Flit before pulling her closer for a tight embrace. Flit sank into it. "I know it's hard, but we'll find him."

Flit choked on her own tears. Twenty-four hours ago, Fortune's words would have been the perfect reassurance. Now? Flit wished she had never met KC-847. So much death and destruction could have been avoided if she'd just followed protocol.

It was several minutes before Flit worked through enough tears and gasps to be able to speak. She didn't want to tell the others the truth, that KC-847 had been the one behind the tunnel explosions, but she could trust Fortune. She was just about to say something when Fortune's body stiffened around her, and a new voice echoed over from the other side of the shelter, near the exit.

"Attention, everyone," Divvy called, causing the returned agents and the facility refugees in quarantine to fall silent. "Thank you for your patience. Our medical teams have been working diligently around the clock to ensure you are all free of any harmful surface contaminants, and you have now been cleared to join the general population."

A buzz of excitement sizzled through the room, and it was

enough to have Flit peel away from Fortune. She looked around, her swollen eyes and bleary gaze focusing on Harmony.

"As you know, a lot has happened in the past few days" Harmony said, addressing the crowd, "so before we let you go, we are gathering the members of the Underground for a meeting. You will join us, and we will explain to everyone there, at the same time, where you have come from. After that, you will be assigned guides to help you settle in. We will leave in five minutes. Please gather up any belongings and use the facilities before we depart."

The energy in the room changed as soon as Harmony finished her announcement. Everyone got up and started to move around, gathering the meagre belongings they had brought with them or acquired whilst in quarantine.

Hawkeye and Sway looked between Flit and the chaos.

Fortune just waved them away. "Go and prepare, okay? If you see Layla, tell her that I'm with Flit. We'll join her and the others at the door before we leave, so we can all go together."

With a new task to take care of, her friends busied themselves.

Fortune gently pulled herself away from Flit and raised a hand to brush away her tears. Flit met her questioning deep brown eyes and sniffed.

"What's going on, Flit?" Fortune whispered.

Flit's throat was suddenly too tight. It was hard to breathe, let alone speak. Fortune was patient. though, but just when Flit finally found the words, a hand settled on her shoulder.

"Ah, Flit... here you are."

Wincing, Flit turned to see Divvy behind her. The pity on her face only made Flit feel more miserable.

"Sorry if I'm interrupting. Harmony and I would like you to walk with us. I am sure Fortune will be fine with her own people." Divvy's smile was warm, even though Fortune fixed her with a sharp look.

"My own people?" Fortune asked, not letting go of Flit.

Divvy waved a hand dismissively. "My apologies. I didn't mean it like that. We are your people, of course. All I meant is that Layla and the others from the facility look up to you. They will benefit from your familiarity as we head into the Underground proper."

A tight frown twisted Fortune's lips as she looked between Flit and the group Sway, Hawkeye, and Layla were gathering on the far side of the shelter.

"It's okay. You go. I'll be fine," Flit promised, telling herself that she really was fine with it, that her encouragement had nothing to do with the fact she was delaying the inevitable.

Fortune did not appear entirely convinced judging by the prominent appearance of her crow's feet, but she didn't argue. "I'll check in with you after."

After a final tight embrace, Fortune slipped off the cot and went to join the others.

Divvy leaned in closer and offered Flit a hand to help her up. "I know this is a tough time for you, but we're so grateful for your honesty," Divvy whispered, taking her hand back when Flit ignored it and stood under her own volition. "It was brave of you to tell Harmony the truth. Your loyalty to the Underground is admirable. We'll be sure to let everyone know."

Right now, Flit didn't feel particularly loyal to the Underground. Not with how much chaos her relationship with KC-847 had caused. She didn't want to argue, though. There were too many people around them, and she didn't know if she had the energy for it after a sleepless night. The best she could do was dry her eyes and press the back of her cold, shaking hands against her puffy cheeks as she followed Divvy over to wait beside Harmony.

After five minutes, everyone was standing by the door, waiting for the two leaders of the Underground to show them out of the room they'd been stuck in for days. Flit fell in directly behind Harmony and Divvy when they led the way out. The halls passed in a blur as they walked through the familiar passages. Flit knew she should have been excited to be back in the Underground, at the prospect of seeing her parents and her friends again, but she was genuinely concerned about what they would think of her once they found out the truth. She wasn't the only one that had fallen under KC-847's spell. They would never have met him if it weren't for her. She had rescued him. She had been his steadfast champion from his earliest days with them, and she had gone out of her way to show them he could be one of them.

Oh, how wrong she was.

Eventually, the group stepped out of the tunnels and into the large, yawning cavern that held the hydroponic gardens and the Residence building. It was a welcome, familiar sight. The gardens were still perfectly tended, the rows of lush greenery filling the earthy-scented space with a tang of fresh life. The building they surrounded was just like the apartment buildings in Old City, but instead of towering into the sky above, this one disappeared into the roof of the cavern. It was an odd sight, almost like the structure was a giant pillar supporting the jagged ceiling, but it felt like *home*.

The gardens around the Residence were unusually quiet, but when they got into the building itself and moved to one of the large meeting spaces on the ground floor, it was evident why. It was impossible to gauge exact numbers, but judging by the swell of the crowd, they had to have everyone not on active or critical roles gathered.

The crowd rippled as the newcomers approached, shivering almost like a single living thing. Heads turned in their direction, and whispers fluttered through the room.

Divvy gestured for those who had been in quarantine to wait at the back of the group. She turned and edged around the crowd, towards the small stage set up at the front.

"Come with me." Harmony took Flit by the elbow and led her towards the stage.

Voices followed them as they moved, and Flit stared at the speckled concrete beneath her feet to avoid the familiar faces she knew would be looking at her for answers.

"Wait here." Harmony positioned her right by the stage.

Flit wanted to teleport the hell out of there, but the inhibitor was still on her wrist. She pulled down the sleeve of her jacket to make sure it was covered.

The Derivates gathered fell into an anticipatory hush as Harmony and Divvy strode to the middle of the platform.

"Thank you to everyone for making your way here and waiting patiently for us to arrive," Divvy began, addressing the crowd with a deep, serious tone. "It is unfortunate that whole-population meetings have come to be associated with tragedies, but such is the nature of life at the moment. Before we provide you all with eagerly anticipated updates, I want to thank each and every one of you for your hard work and sense of community during this difficult time."

"The residents of the Underground never cease to amaze and inspire me," Harmony added. Her tone sounded so loving, so motherly.

Flit looked up to see her gracing the crowd with a warm smile that they lapped up. Everyone leaned closer as she spoke, the praise falling on desperate, thirsty ears.

"As you are all aware, we have called off the work teams who were sent to perform rescues in the collapsed tunnels. The window for viable life has passed, and we need to preserve the health and wellbeing of those who are still left with us."

Several audible sobs broke the silence, and Flit winced, wondering if those people were waiting, hoping to hear loved ones had been rescued.

"Our administration will approach the nearest and dearest of those who we have lost to organise farewell ceremonies," Divvy explained. "This will begin immediately after we dismiss this gathering."

Whispers bounced around the space as people took in this news. For the first time, Flit glanced at the crowd. The panoramic view of the familiar sea of faces, worn pale and strained by the stress of recent days, felt like a gut punch to her. She tried to pick out her own nearest and dearest in the crowd, but she was too close to everyone and too short to see over the first couple of rows of heads.

"Now, as some of you may have noticed," Harmony said, raising her voice to signal it was time to listen again, "there is a group of mostly unfamiliar faces at the back of our crowd. Given recent events in the Underground and the terrorist actions occurring above ground, we made the difficult but necessary decision to recall our Intelligence operatives. We were lucky enough to be able to retrieve all but one."

The tension in the crowd returned as people doubtlessly wondered if someone they knew was now stranded in Government territory. Flit felt as if a cold bucket of water had been dumped over her head. The only person who hadn't returned was KC-847, and it was going to remain that way.

"In addition to reuniting with the brave souls who risked their lives on the surface, we are also welcoming some new refugees," Harmony continued, "people who, with the assistance of some Underground members, were able to break free of the Government's torture facilities and make their way to safety."

The buzz of surprised conversations filled the room.

Harmony had to raise her hand and call out, "Everyone! Please, stop talking!"

The people in the front few rows heard her and passed the message back through the crowd like a wave rolling away from the shore.

When silence fell once more, Harmony turned to Divvy and nodded.

"Thank you. I promise we only have a couple more announcements to make." Divvy tucked a loose strand of her red hair behind her ear. "The first is that the newcomers and returned agents will be assigned buddies to help them reintegrate into the Underground. We will announce the list of people selected to act in that capacity at the end of the meeting. If you hear your name, please stay behind."

As far as news went, that last tidbit was met without much concern. Flit had to imagine that more than a few people were eager for the meeting to be over, so they could see if any of their old friends or family members were amongst those returned.

"Finally, we wish to share with you the conclusion of our investigation into the recent tunnel explosions," Harmony announced, her words greeted by a mixed outpouring of curiosity, celebration, and concern.

Flit's entire body tensed, and her face flushed with dread. Once more, her throat became tight, and it was difficult to breathe. She stared straight ahead, not focusing on any one person in front of her, hoping that she could avoid attention by pretending she didn't exist.

"After interviewing the recently returned agents from the surface, it came to our attention that one of their number had been acting suspiciously." Harmony gazed at the crowd, her usually friendly face stern and set hard. "Following further investigation, we found evidence that the ex-Registered, KC-847, who had come to be known to us by the name of Scraps, was responsible for setting and detonating the charges."

The uproar was so loud that it drowned out Flit's thoughts. The sonorous howl of voices echoed in that new emptiness inside of her and fed the seeds of guilt that had taken root. Her vision blurred, but the feeling of a soft, warm hand on her shoulder brought her back. She blinked the distortion away to see Harmony beside her, holding her, supporting her to remain tall.

Divvy gestured to a Control worker at the side of the room, and the man pressed a button on a wall panel. A long, piercing beep sounded through the space and stopped all conversations in their tracks. Divvy nodded, and the beeping stopped.

"We will provide more information in time, but we want to apologise to you all. We allowed and encouraged KC-847 to become an active member in our community, and Harmony and I personally feel responsible for his actions," Divvy said, her stoic expression cracking as her voice warbled, as she admitted her own oversight. "However, we were not the only one fooled. KC-847 proved that anyone is capable of hideous deception. We wish to thank Flit for coming forward and sharing her concerns."

Blood roared in Flit's ears. The air in the room shifted as more people than she could count turned to her. It took a great deal of restraint to remain standing, to keep her chin up, even though her eyes were burning with tears of shame and her heart was lying in jagged shards at her feet.

Harmony wrapped an arm around her shoulder and squeezed her gently. "To anyone in the Blue Team or who came to call the traitor friend, please do not blame yourselves. You were embodying the very ethos of the Underground. You were making space for a person who you thought needed refuge. Please retain your sense of kindness, of acceptance. That is what makes us different from those living above."

The crowd responded to this with mixed levels of agreement, but they didn't return to the loud outbursts from before. Everything after that was a blur as Divvy took a small datapad from her trouser pocket and read the list of names for the buddies. She finally dismissed the crowd, and people started to filter out of the room.

"Flit!"

Shocked by the ferocity with which her name was called, Flit glanced up, stunned.

"Flit!"

Both of Flit's parents pushed against the tide of the crowd, barging their way through until they tumbled to a stop in front of her. They both looked battered, bruised, and exhausted, but the relief in their eyes was palpable.

"Oh, thank goodness!" Without another word, Tinker wrapped Flit in a strangling embrace.

Her father joined in, and the air between them was filled with grateful mutters and profuse words of love.

The familiar scent of her parents, and their unconditional affection, was enough to make Flit crumble. She fell into their arms and let the rest of the world around them disappear.

Eventually, her father pulled back, straightening up and smiling through his own tears. "Sorry to break the mood, but my back just isn't what it used to be," he said, making both Flit and Tinker laugh.

"You still look just as good, though."

Flit's parents turned at the voice of the newcomer, and gasps fell from their lips.

"Fortune?" Tinker covered her mouth with her hands.

Fortune smiled and nodded.

"Rook? Vector?" Flit's father asked, hope dancing in the words.

"Unfortunately, it is just me," Fortune confessed, her own eyes shuttering with pain.

Tinker shook her head and pulled the other woman into a gentle embrace. "I'm so sorry," she whispered.

Fortune patted her back and gave Stride a grim smile over his wife's shoulder. "I have made my peace with it."

Just as she extricated herself from Tinker's embrace, a streak of blonde barrelled into her.

"Fortune!" Swipe wrapped herself around the older woman. "I can't believe you're alive!"

As Rook's childhood best friend, Swipe had grown up around

him and his parents. Fortune had always treated Swipe like a daughter, especially after she lost her parents in the attack on Longbeach.

What followed was a cascade of reunions and embraces. The rest of the Blue Team and Flit's other closest friends all came over to welcome her and Fortune back. The excitement of the occasion was overshadowed by the fact that each and every one of them steadfastly avoided all mentions of KC-847. Still, being back with her friends and family was a balm to Flit's aching soul.

"I hate to cut this reunion short," Swipe said, interrupting a conversation about what the Blue Team was up to now the Underground was on lockdown, "but I need to show Fortune to her new room. I have a shift tonight." She linked her arm through the crook of the other woman's elbow.

"Will you be able to join us in the Mess for dinner? I think this reunion calls for a celebration," Clarity said with a warm smile at Flit and Fortune.

"No," Swipe said, frowning. "But if you give me an hour to get Fortune settled, I would like to see the Blue Team in my room for an emergency meeting."

"Sure thing, Captain." Tweak gave her a mock salute.

"Captain?" The word spilled from Flit's lips.

Swipe smirked. "You and Hawkeye left us. Luckily, I was there to pick up the slack. If you want to rejoin the team, you're gonna have to get used to calling me boss. See you in my room in an hour." Swipe winked at her before patting Fortune's hand and leading the woman away, leaving Flit slack-jawed in her wake.

9

<hr>

SCRAPS

SCRAPS STOOD outside East Two-North One, staring up at the glass and steel monolith with a frown. He had been permitted inside the Government Museum on precisely one occasion: the mandatory excursion all ten-year-old Registereds attended as part of their history and social studies classes. Being allowed out of the training facility always caused quite the buzz, and Scraps vividly remembered the sense of wonder he had felt at being in the city he would one day be charged to protect.

Although when Scraps and the other children from the '07 birth cohort had left the training facility, it had been under the cover of darkness when the rest of the city was asleep. They had been fitted with circlet inhibitors, shuffled onto one of ten heavily armoured shuttles, and driven from the training facility and straight into the basement parking of East Two-North One.

From the parking lot, the children had been taken straight up to the museum in the service elevators, only to find it had closed more than two hours earlier. Apart from their chaperones, museum security, and their teachers, there were no other people in the space. No chance to see any Citizens up close. No opportunity to get a better idea of what made them so precious that these children should lay down their freedom to protect them.

The view Scraps had now was the one he had hoped for at the

tender age of ten, but now that he had it? He wanted nothing to do with it.

Despite the revulsion churning in his gut, Scraps squared his shoulders and walked through the front door of the building. The agents were inside, and he refused to risk everything he was working for because of some bad memories.

Getting through security was a breeze, as the building was nowhere near as heavily guarded as the other Government buildings in the Hub. He crossed the lobby with ease, passing tourists and students alike on his way to the elevator, and joined the short line for the cart designated for the sole use of museum visitors. When it was his turn, Scraps hopped into the elevator with a woman and her son, the young boy chatting excitedly about one of the exhibitions he was hoping to see. The elevator rose higher and higher, and when the arrival tone rang and the door opened, the boy disembarked with the same level of energy and excitement that Seeker in the Underground seemed to possess. It made Scraps smile, but he couldn't get past the knowledge that neither he nor Seeker had been born with the same privileges the young Citizen had. Scraps couldn't even imagine what it was like to have a mother.

Scraps found it a little harder to breathe as he stepped into the lobby. Immediately, the pre-recorded strains of a computer-generated greeting loop chimed through the room.

"Welcome to the Government Museum, the best place to learn about our great history and how the Government takes care of all of its Citizens..."

Scraps pressed his lips together as he observed the area. People milled about the large, open-plan lobby. The floor was the standard gleaming white, with shining chrome displays holding holographic screens acting in the place of walls. Each one had information about the exhibition which covered everything from the war that started it all to modern politics and agriculture. Apart from the Government's publicly accessible intranet, the museum was the best place to find anything and everything about the ruling body's history. Not only was there information, but there were artefacts gathered from all points in their history that gave very tangible evidence of the Government's achievements.

Unsure of where he was supposed to be meeting the agents and aware he was five minutes early, Scraps figured he should move along. Standing by the elevator and waiting for the Agents would make him look suspicious. He recalled Flit's strategy for sneaking around and decided that looking like he was there with a purpose was the best idea. Therefore, he turned, picking the closest exhibition space to venture into, pleased the educational video cycle inside was just about to refresh so he would have some entertainment while he waited.

The first room was large and kept purposefully dark. The walls were made of screens featuring monochrome images of Old City before it had fallen into disrepair. A mishmash of varied architectural aesthetics and building materials, the city couldn't have looked more different to the gleaming Hub.

"The world before the Government's stewardship was disorderly and dangerous," the automated voice said in a smooth, matter-of-fact tone.

As Scraps walked in deeper, holographic projections danced around him. Old-fashioned cars screeched through the streets, and projected people yelled and shook fists at one another.

"People struggled to survive. Necessities such as clean water, food, shelter, and work were hard to come by. The people of Old City, and other metropolises beyond, were forced to resort to violence and crime to fulfil their needs."

Scraps kept walking, memories of his visit as a child flooded back to him. All those years ago, he had lapped up the stories. He absorbed every single word as a fact, as undeniable proof that the Government was right. That what they were doing was for the 'good of all'.

As the projected people continued their scavenging lives, the lighting in the room took on an ominous red tinge, and a group of faceless, featureless people started to fill the end of every street on every block of the dilapidated city. The others stopped, turning to face the new threat. Low sounds of fire crackling, and sirens faded in as the faceless army advanced. Small gestures of the arms were used to bring down chunks of buildings, to fling cars into walls, and to trap people in terrifying deaths.

"Just when the previous administrations truly lost control, a new breed of chaos was brought about, thanks to the unethical experimentation of a misguided research centre."

The logo of a double-helix, with the word *Helix Corp* danced in the sky over the buildings as they slowly crumbled. Scraps watched, transfixed despite his repulsion, as the lies the Government told about their history unfolded around him.

"The brilliant minds at Helix Corp were twisted and bent into creating a new breed of humans. These beings looked just like ordinary people but had terrifying abilities which they used to gain control of the vulnerable city."

Concussive blasts and screams were added to the audio track, and a subtle bass timed like a thudding heart rate made everything more visceral. Scents of smoke and wet concrete wafted across the room, and hot air blasted from the vents in the ceiling. Even though Scraps had seen it all before, his muscles tensed and eyes widened as he was sucked into the atmosphere.

"These new beings, Derivates, wrought havoc upon the cities of old in their quest for control. Just as hope was almost lost—"

The crumbling of the city reached a feverish pace, with people forced to flee the amassing faceless army. It looked like the Derivates were going to win, but then, a new logo flashed across the projection—the familiar hands cupping an oval around joined links of a chain.

Scraps' attention snagged on the logo, and he tilted his head to the side. His stomach lurched as he realised that the chains in the Government's logo looked suspiciously like the double helix in Helix Corps'. It had to be a coincidence, of course. There was no way they were linked... was there?

"The Government was formed. Determined to save humanity and restore order, peace, and prosperity, they reclaimed the situation. Led by eight outstanding citizens from each of the critical city portfolios, these Oligarchs made the decision for the newly formed Government. Their anonymity was the key to ensuring they were not swayed or bribed by the corruption of corporations like Helix Corp. Together, the Oligarchy orchestrated the righteous attempt to save their civilisation. They stemmed the Derivate tide and offered safety to the human

*refugees. The Government set down the foundations for a new way
life."*

Dozens of armoured vehicles and aerial assault vehicles
swooped into Old City, chasing the Derivates away while the
fleeing citizens stopped and cheered, the jubilation ringing through
the room as the panicked bass heartbeat morphed into a triumphant
thumping.

Any thought Scraps had previously about the link between the
Government and Helix Corp was forgotten as he watched the
defeat of his ancestors, as he was forced to listen to all of the lies
painting them as rabid, monstrous aggressors.

*"The last vestiges of rogue Derivates poisoned water sources and
exposed entire cities to nuclear radiation. The Government, determined to create a safe world once more, tracked the Derivates down
and the Oligarchy oversaw the creation of new megacities that would
have enough resources and opportunities for all Citizens."*

Scraps jumped back as a projection of The Hub rose from the
floor where he stood. Centre One towered over him. He blinked up
at it, bewildered as the image shone with lights, just like the glass of
the real city did when the sun beat down upon it. In contrast to the
decimation all around, it was a glowing hive of hope and wonder.

*"After years of starvation, violence, and terror, the Government
created a new world. Everything we did then, and we do now, is 'for
the good of all'."*

The peripheral projections of Old City faded, their light seemingly sucked into the Hub as it glowed brighter and brighter.

Scraps' younger self had been transfixed by this display.
Inspired by it.

He now recognised the exhibition for what it was.

Lies.

The Underground's records of the war were few and far
between. Scraps had read them, but his research had not revealed
any new insights. However, his time with the Underground had
taught him everything he needed to know. The Government had
twisted history to fit their own narrative. The clever tableaux, and
the consistent messages they pushed for generations, sold the lies.
They gave Citizens and Derivates alike comfort. With a story like

this burned into the impressionable minds of children, how could they ever doubt that Derivates were inherently dangerous and that the Government deserved their allegiance?

Left standing in the glowing core of the projected Centre One, anger and confusion welled inside of Scraps. The Government had kept its promises, for the most part. Homelessness was almost completely eradicated. Starvation was unheard of. Any people who were capable of working had jobs available for them. There was economic disparity, of course, but opportunities for advancement were boundless, though it all came at a cost.

Freedom.

Two years ago, Scraps would have scoffed at the concept, but now? It plagued almost every waking moment. He had finally gotten a taste of muted freedom in the Underground. He had learned to laugh, love, and live.

Flit was right.

It was nothing more than a tiny sample of what they *should* have. Since returning to the surface, Scraps had learned that the Citizens felt the same about their own lives. Even their choices were controlled, albeit in more subtle ways. The sheer amount of people flocking to the Free Citizens' cause proved one thing.

Everyone craved freedom.

"Ah, nothing like a solid history lesson to remind you of what is really important." A heavy hand clapped Scraps' shoulder.

Whirling around, hands raised defensively, Scraps froze when Agent Hector took a step back and arched an eyebrow at him.

Agent Greene rolled her eyes. "Please excuse my colleague. He can be a bit abrupt at times."

Scraps looked between the two agents as his hands fell to his side and nodded to them both in turn. Then, movement near the door drew his attention. The same telepath who had been present at the interrogations in North One stepped into the room. The darkness in the room made it impossible to catch a hint of her expression beneath the reflective glass.

Tearing his attention away from the Registered, Scraps said, "Agent Greene, Agent Hector, I assumed you summoned me here for a reason?"

Hector raised a stubby finger. "One moment..."

The projection of the Hub disappeared, leaving them standing in utter darkness. After a second, the outer projections of Old City rebuilt around the room, and the automated voice began its tale again.

Hector stepped closer once there was enough noise to cover their conversation. "What do you have for us?"

Scraps' eyebrows furrowed. "What do you mean?"

"Need I warn you that playing dumb will put a swift end to our agreement, Mr. Parkes?" Hector grumbled. "We saw the flickers on the security feeds outside your apartment before your friends visited you for the night. There was almost half an hour of inter-ference."

Scraps blinked, impressed. He had no idea Adam had gained access to that level of security. It reminded him of just how little he knew about the man.

"Ah, that. I was not aware he had access to the systems," Scraps conceded with a frown.

"He?" Agent Greene stepped closer, her eyes wide with antic-ipation.

As much as it grated Scraps to be in his current predicament, he had little choice. His loyalties had changed so much over the past two years. What difference would one new shift make?

"Adam." Scraps steeled himself as he betrayed the man who had become as much a blessing as a curse. "The leader of the Free Citi-zens. He came to see if I was willing to accept more responsibility within the group."

The agents hung on his words.

"And?" Greene urged.

"And I said yes." Scraps' voice was clipped as he shifted on the spot. "I figured that would help me get the information you require."

"That is perfect, just the position we need you in." Greene smiled. "The leader, Adam as you call him, is slippery. We need all the information you can get on him without exposing yourself."

"I do not have anything else on him," Scraps admitted, trying not to let the voice-over of the exhibition affect him as the screams and heartbeat intensified.

"Will you be seeing him again soon?" Hector crossed his arms over his chest, and Scraps got the feeling that they were hoping for more.

Scraps nodded.

"Where will you meet him?" Hector pushed.

"I'm not sure yet. He said he would let me know beforehand."

The agents turned to the Registered, who nodded subtly beneath the projections of the crumbling, war-ravaged city.

Hector and Greene fell silent, but as they turned back to Scraps, something passed between them.

"I trust you will keep us up to date?" Hector eyed him.

Scraps resigned himself to the path. "How am I supposed to contact you?"

"You don't. We'll contact you." Greene stepped closer and leaned in. She was close enough that her minty-fresh breath fluttered in the space between them. "You're doing the right thing. I can understand the lure of the Free Citizens, but they aren't helping anyone. They're just killing people and creating chaos. Your self-loathing will be worse if you let any more people get sacrificed in some ill-advised stoush for anarchy."

That was easy for Greene to say when the Government's idea of freedom worked in her favour. Still, Scraps forced a grim smile onto his face. "You are right. I do not want anyone else to die because of Adam's bad decisions."

The bright, towering projection of Centre One shot up between Scraps and the agents as the tableaux neared the end.

Scraps watched the agents through the bright lights of the holographic building. "Will that be all?"

He was exhausted. He just wanted to go home.

"Yes. We'll speak again soon." Hector nodded in farewell before turning and gesturing for Greene and the Registered to follow him.

Eager to escape the room before he had to listen to the voice-over again, Scraps gave the agents a few minutes to get a head start before he made for the elevator. Despite being alone for the trip down, Scraps didn't relax. He knew the Government watched him closely. He could not afford even the smallest slip-up.

Already, his mind was racing, trying to find ways that he could lessen the impact of his betrayal. Not too long ago, telling the Government about traitors would have made him proud. Now? Well, it made him feel like the second-rate human the Government had raised him to believe he was.

10

FLIT

ONE WEEK AGO, the last thing Flit thought she would be doing was moving back in with her parents. If anyone had suggested it to her, she would have happily told them where to shove that idea. It wasn't because she didn't love her parents, she really did, but she preferred living with KC-847. Or she did before she heard the truth. Now, her heart was sore, and the guilt threatened to drown her, and she just wanted to live alone to escape the tension that came with her parents trying to resist the urge to ask what had gone wrong.

The tunnel explosions had happened while Flit's parents had been working in the Underground. They had been expecting to return to their apartment in the outskirts of the Hub that night, but they had instead been assigned a small, two-bedroom apartment in the Residence. Given the fact they had no warning to pack their things, they were living on the trademark mishmash of hand-me-downs and scavenged items the Underground reserved for people in need. Flit, luckily, had stashed some of her own things in storage, which had been given to her parents while she had been in quarantine.

It didn't take long for her parents to show Flit around the modest apartment. When they finished, the three stood in the living room, no one quite willing or ready to break the awkward silence that fell between them. The tension grew until it was an unreach-able itch on the back of Flit's neck.

"I'm going to take a shower and change before I head to Swipe's," she told her parents, still flabbergasted that she was grateful she had to see Swipe again.

Tinker pulled Flit into a tight hug, probably for the hundredth since their reunion. "Let me know if you need anything, okay? It's not good to shut yourself off. Your father and I are here if you need us."

"I'm fine, Mum," she lied, kissing her mother on the cheek and peeling herself out of the embrace.

Flit gave her father a lacklustre smile before disappearing into her new room. She found her clothes in the wardrobe and made her way to the bathroom.

The scalding temperature of the water and the rhythmic patter of the spray on her back was a much-needed balm for her woes, but it was temporary. The relative silence gave her thoughts room to be noisy in her head. In the past, Flit had preferred to drown in her own thoughts than be around others and pretend things were okay. It was why Hawkeye had gone to such lengths to pull her back into social events after Rook's disappearance. This time, though, Flit's head was a horrible place to be. She kept conjuring up her memo-ries of Scraps—the kindness, loyalty, and affection. She remembered the shared smiles and stolen kisses, the promises that it was them against the world... his dramatic confession of love.

With a growl, Flit slammed her hand against the shower control panel and stopped the water.

"It's KC-847, not Scraps," she whispered, correcting herself out loud. Thinking of him as Scraps just made it harder to stay angry at him.

Flit dried off a little more roughly than she should have with the overly scratchy towel and dressed quickly. She stomped out of the bathroom, pulling her sopping hair out of the neck of her tank top, not caring that it saturated a thick patch of fabric right down the middle of her back.

"Wowsers!" Her father whistled as she stepped out of the bathroom. The steam from the shower billowed out in a cloud behind her. "Were you trying to create a sauna or something?"

Flit frowned at him.

Tinker groaned. "Stride!"

Her father shrugged innocently. "What?"

Tinker just shook her head. "You go catch up with the team, sweetheart. We'll be here when you get back. Do you want us to organise to have dinner here, or would you like to go to the Mess?"

The thought of walking into the Mess given the current circumstances made Flit's stomach churn. "Here is good. Thank you. See you both soon."

Flit stalked through the halls, tugging on a jacket to cover up the bracelet inhibitor and gritting her teeth. With all the reunions, she had forgotten to ask for it to be removed. She added it to her list of things to be done if she could be bothered showing her face around the tunnels.

The path to Swipe's room from her parent's apartment wasn't that different to the one from her old room. She was pleased she didn't run into anyone along the way and hoped she could continue to avoid people this easily for a while. When she knocked on the door, it opened right away to reveal the entirety of the original Blue Team. The conversation they were having stuttered to a halt as Flit stepped into the room.

"Don't let me stop you." Flit shut the door behind herself. She looked around for somewhere to sit, but Sway, Link, and Clarity were already sitting on the bed, Swipe was perched on the edge of her desk, and Hawkeye and Tweak occupied the only two chairs. Flit leaned against the wall and crossed her arms over her chest.

"So, what's the deal?" Swipe asked.

"What do you mean?"

Everyone watched her with anticipation.

"Sway and Hawkeye said that, last night, you were punching and fighting your way around quarantine to get back to Scraps." Swipe hopped off the edge of the desk and crossed over to stand in front of Flit. "Then, this morning, you were curled into a pathetic ball and agreeing with Harmony and Divvy when they said Scraps was behind the collapses. So… what's the plan, and how can we help get him back?"

"There is no plan." Flit could not hold Swipe's piercing blue stare. "KC-847 did it. He fucked us over. End of story."

"KC-847?" Swipe spluttered, horrified.

"Yes. He was never Scraps, he was just KC-847 pretending to be one of us," Flit snapped back. "It was all just a lie to make us trust him."

"Bullshit!" Swipe snapped, stepping close enough that Flit could feel the huff of her hot breath. "It's bullshit, and we all know it. He wouldn't do that, and you do not have to try and get him back alone."

Flit balled her hands into fists and shoved them into the pockets of her cargo pants to avoid slamming them against Swipe. "Get out of my face."

"I will when you tell the truth," Swipe spat, tilting her head to the side and using her height to stand over Flit.

"You want the truth?" Flit threw her hands up in the air. "I'll give you the fucking truth. He'd go for really long runs. Sometimes, he'd leave the apartment in the middle of the night. I thought he was just trying to clear his head, that he was having trouble read-justing to the surface." She slipped out from between Swipe and the wall, and walked over, pressing her palms against the door and leaning over, shaking her head. "I wish he was having trouble read-justing. That would have been better than him coming down here to hurt everyone. To destroy more of the Underground…"

Silence fell behind her until footsteps broke through and she felt a warm arm around her shoulder. "Flit, that can't be true. Scraps was our friend too. We know there is no way he would ever—"

"Well, he did!" Flit turning on Hawkeye. "He did, okay? Intelli-gence have footage of him consorting with Government Agents who just let him walk away after capture! How the hell would he get away with that if he wasn't in their pocket, huh?"

Flit scanned the faces of her other friends and saw that they all looked as torn as Hawkeye and Swipe seemed to be.

"This doesn't feel right," Link muttered, getting to her feet and taking Flit's hand. "I know you believe what you're saying, but—"

"Get out of my head." Flit snatched her hand back and struggled to fill her mind with blackness.

"The videos don't mean shit. Without context, we can't know for certain what happened," Swipe insisted. "If you were the only one who trusted him, I'd be on your side... but you weren't. He won over everyone in the Underground. Even Acumen!"

"It's not that hard to fool Acumen," Tweak said in a low voice.

"Bro!" Sway threw Swipe's pillow at Tweak's head. "Shut the fuck up."

Swipe rolled her eyes and planted her hands on her hips before she rounded on Flit again. "Here's the deal. I don't believe you, and we're going to get him back with or without your help."

"Swipe..." Clarity shook her head. "I don't think that's wise. We can't bring him back here without proof he's innocent. Who knows what people will do to him?"

"Then find the proof!" Swipe spun to face the remaining members of the Blue Team, staring at them as if it were obvious.

"I suppose I can try and track down the videos Flit was talking about," Tweak offered with a shrug.

Swipe nodded. "That's a good start."

"I can do some poking around in Intelligence and Control," Hawkeye offered. "See if there are other explanations for the collapses."

"Now we're onto something." Swipe's disparaging grimace curled into a satisfied smirk.

"Flit, what are you going to do to help?" Sway asked. From the encouraging look on his face, Flit figured that he was trying to rope her into their doomed investigation.

"Me? I'm going to stay out of your way." Flit slapped her hand against the panel by the door to open it. "If you arseholes won't listen to me, then I have nothing left to say you."

Feeling utterly betrayed by their lack of empathy and support, Flit turned her back on her friends and walked away.

11

___

SCRAPS

THE REST of the work week went by quietly for Scraps. He spent his office hours preparing for the investigation of the Derivate Training Facility the following week. His nights were for catching up on shows that Flit didn't like watching and adding extra time into his workouts. With each day that passed, he had to work harder to fill the Flit-sized hole in his life.

He didn't realise how dull life was before he had met her.

Still, as he shut down his console for the weekend and made his way home, he couldn't help but wonder if Adam had forgotten about him. He had yet to hear anything about how to get to the Free Citizens meeting that night, and that worried him. He was counting on his connection with the Free Citizens to keep the Government away from his other, more dangerous secrets.

Walking into the empty apartment, Scraps went straight to the fridge to sort out dinner. Even without knowing if or when Adam would summon him, he had to eat.

Cooking turned out to be the only thing Scraps found easier without his girlfriend around. Flit was even more chaotic in the kitchen than she was elsewhere in her life, and that was saying something. The meals Scraps cooked were always delicious and nutritious when he was able to follow the recipes he found. If Flit was around when he cooked, she would throw in a little bit of this, or add a little bit of that, or change up some instructions. Sometimes, the flair worked.

Mostly, it didn't.

At least Scraps didn't have to worry about cleaning up after some of the Flit-inspired kitchen disasters.

Still, he would happily scrub charred marinade off every frying pan and implement in the kitchen each night if it meant having Flit back.

Scraps was just putting the finishing touches on his simple salad and chicken meal when the doorbell chimed. He wiped his hands on a tea towel and slung it over his shoulder as he went to open the door.

"Oh… hello." Scraps' eyebrows furrowed as he saw the young woman dressed in a courier's uniform, chewing on some gum and holding up a bag of delicious-smelling takeaway containers. "You have the wrong house. I didn't order anything."

"Brain Parkes, right?" The woman swapped her gum from one side of her mouth to the other.

"Ay, yes. That's me." Scraps peered up and down the hallway, suspicion rising.

The woman shoved the bag against his chest then blew a pink gum bubble that popped obnoxiously close to his face. "Then this is yours. Have a nice night."

Before he could protest, she turned and walked away.

"Odd." Scraps shut the door and took the food to the kitchen. He pulled the containers out and started to look at the array of noodle and meat dishes that all appeared perfectly palatable. Just as he lifted the second last container out, a soggy piece of paper hung off the bottom. He peeled it off and flipped it over.

South Twelve-West Fourteen. Floor Three. Seven PM.

It took a moment of staring at the obscure address for Scraps to see the message for what it was. The meeting point for tonight. He closed his fist around the paper and glanced at the clock in the corner of the display on the kitchen wall.

"Oh, crap."

Scraps needed to leave right away if he wanted to get to the meeting on time. It was so far away that he would have to change maglev tracks several times to reach it.

With an energised sense of haste, Scraps covered the plate of chicken salad and shoved it into the refrigerator, along with the takeaway containers. Figuring it would be best if he looked like he had a reason to be out on the streets, he shed his clothes as he walked towards the bedroom. He changed into his running gear, and pulled his jogging shoes on, tying them clumsily with telekinesis before dashing for the door.

SCRAPS HAD NOT TRAVELLED at night since the attack, and he found that the Government had increased the amount of Derivates and Law Enforcement Officers on the streets and at the maglev stations even more so for the evening hours. There were still several detours in place due to the damage done by the Free Citizens' attacks, and it meant that Scraps had to catch five trains instead of the standard three he had been anticipating.

The billboards and screens that normally held advertising content or various businesses were now split down the middle, half paid advertisements and half warning from the Government.

Citizens are reminded that loitering is not permitted at maglev stations.

If you see something concerning, report it to your nearest Law Enforcement Officer.

The Government acts for the good of all. You should too.

Even if he wanted to ignore the signs, they had included the message into the maglev station announcements as well. By the time Scraps got off the train and onto street level, he was just about ready to compromise his cover and use telekinesis to blow up the speakers, just to avoid hearing 'for the good of all' one more time.

Once Scraps was on the street, he had something else to focus on. South Twelve-West Fourteen was in a rather undesirable part of the Hub. It wasn't horrible, there were no parts of the city that were particularly sordid, but it was known for its manufacturing facilities and housed workers who tended towards trades. They were important jobs, but the social structure in the Hub didn't hold their positions in high esteem. Therefore, they were farther away from the buzzing hive of the central city, and the area was not quite as well provisioned.

The building itself was only ten stories tall, and from the signs outside, it looked to hold the workshops of several prominent textile companies. Floor three, as Scraps learned when he entered the building and checked the listing of companies, was a uniform business.

During the short elevator ride, Scraps was struck by the vast difference between meeting in a nightclub and a textile workshop. He was initially curious as to why Adam would chose such a venue for a rendezvous, but the moment the elevator doors opened, Scraps had his answer.

Beyond a low reception desk, the floor was filled with row after row of machines. Some of them were automated, but judging by the amounts of seats, there were some parts of the fashion manufacturing process that could not be completed by machinery alone. All the desks were empty, but the production line responsible for laser cutting segments of fabric was churning away loudly along one side of the building.

Even with just those few machines running, the noise was deafening. Scraps did not want to imagine what it would be like in the middle of the day, with all the machines joining the chorus. He covered his ears with his hands as he looked around, feeling relieved when he spotted Adam waving at him from halfway down one of the rows of desks, a few columns away from the cutting machines. There were half a dozen people dressed in various casual outfits gathered around Adam, none of whom were familiar to Scraps.

He didn't bother calling out a greeting in return. They wouldn't hear it anyway. Instead, he approached them, taking in his surroundings and calculating his best escape routes, just in case.

"Thank you for joining us," Adam called above the din as Scraps approached. He gestured to the people gathered. "I know I normally do introductions, but the Government has been sniffing around so I'd rather people to retain their privacy."

"Good call," Scraps said out loud, somewhat relieved that he would not have any names to try and hide from the telepath assigned to follow Hector and Greene. Still, Scraps gave the three women and two men nearby a polite nod in greeting.

"It's hard to talk above the noise, so I'll keep it brief. This factory specialises in the production of uniforms for several high-end corporate organisations." He gestured towards the machines cutting outlines in crisp fabrics. "I managed to get hold of patterns and fabrics used in Government uniforms, so we're going to go about producing some for future missions." Adam turned to Scraps with a grin. "I know it isn't what you're used to, but I want you to make sure this goes smoothly. We can use this factory every third night, at this time, for two hours at a time. Everyone gathered here knows how to construct the uniforms. We just need you to keep an eye out, make sure they stay safe. Can you do that?"

It wasn't the most exciting plan, but Scraps was glad for it. He secretly wondered if Adam had an ulterior motive. Perhaps he was going to use the uniforms to get people into better places to blow up ... but he would handle that if it happened. For now, creating counterfeit Government uniforms was simple. Scraps could also gather information about the types of uniforms and the quantities created, which might string the agents along for a while.

"Yes, I'll take care of them while they work," Scraps said with a casual salute to highlight his acceptance.

Adam grinned and clapped him on the shoulder. "Excellent. This will keep you busy for two weeks. I'll check in with you when you get closer to finishing this project. If you have any problems, leave your lounge room light on while you're at work for the day, and I'll get in touch with you."

Scraps nodded. "Copy that."

Adam patted his shoulder a final time before stepping aside to speak to the people gathered. After a minute, they all split up and went to a few different machines to begin their work. Adam waved at Scraps and walked to the elevator, and Scraps wondered exactly how Adam would be aware that he left the light in the lounge room on.

As alarming as it was to think that Adam was monitoring him, Scraps was not entirely surprised, so he chose not to linger on the fact. Instead, he focused on the task at hand. He walked up and down the aisles of machines that the others had chosen to sit at and observed their work. He stopped at the end of one row, where a woman was unwrapping bolts of fabric and sliding it onto the feed hooks of a cutting machine.

Scraps never paid much attention to fashion, but he knew the different Government uniforms well. The deep grey, cross-woven material they were using was favoured by the Law Enforcement Department. The other bolts of fabric were still wrapped in opaque black plastic, so he kept moving and resolved to come back later when they were unwrapped.

After getting an idea of the fabrics and pattern shapes being used, Scraps was certain the uniforms would be ones just like the Citizen Officers wore. They were tightly controlled by the Government, each one having a chip sewn into it to identify its owner to any environmental scanners, with replacements being unobtainable unless a rationed uniform was returned in a swap. It was much the same deal for Derivate uniforms, which he had found mildly interesting when he would overhear the Citizens he worked with in the Law Enforcement Department complaining about it during quiet times.

Satisfied that he had a good idea of what was going on, Scraps spent the rest of the evening walking the perimeter and checking the exits and windows. This part of the city was relatively quiet at night, with only workers who were in plants that operated twenty-four hours moving along the well-lit streets.

After two hours, the woman who had been feeding the fabric into the cutting machines approached Scraps. With the noise, he barely heard her in time to turn around before she reached him.

"We're done for the night. We've stored everything where Adam told us to, so it's time we get out of here. If everyone gets into the elevator together, I can reset the alarm," she explained.

"Let's do that." Scraps peered around to see the others pushing the edges of some wall panels back into place. They had cleaned up the evidence of their work well.

They all went to the elevator together. When they were in the tight carriage, no one spoke. The woman who had been setting the fabric leaned over the control panel in the elevator to set the alarm and then straightened as they descended.

"It's probably best if we stagger our exits," Scraps said, "and make sure we go in different directions. Is there anyone who needs to leave together?"

"We do," two men said, stepping closer to one another. No one else spoke up.

"Then you two leave first. I'll count the rest of us out, okay?"

Everyone nodded, and Scraps was relieved that this lot of people seemed far more compliant than the hotshots at the research facility a few weeks earlier.

Scraps did exactly as he said, stepping out of the elevator with the others and then encouraging the two men to go first. He approached the door with the rest of them and then staggered their exits, letting one go next then allowing the final two women to leave at intermittent intervals before finally exiting for himself.

On the trip home, Scraps tried his best to think up a story to tell the agents that would downplay what the Free Citizens were brewing. When he got home, he saw a message from Chris and Liana blinking on his comm screen, asking why he was not at Nightmix. He felt terrible as he typed up a false reply, citing a headache and the desire to get an early night. Scraps had grown fond of his two friends, so he wanted to keep the thoughts of them as separate from his thoughts of the Free Citizens as he could. He would happily turn Adam over to the Government, but the others? They didn't deserve that fate.

12

FLIT

THE DAYS that followed the meeting in Swipe's room passed in a blur. Flit didn't leave her family's apartment. Even walking beyond the confines of her room was undesirable, as the look of concern on her parents' faces made her stomach swirl with a mix of frustration and betrayal.

To his credit, Hawkeye visited several times a day. On the first few occasions, he had attempted to reason with her. He would ask her why she thought KC-847 was guilty and then argue with her every time she provided a rational reason. As if he was there with them on the surface and had evidence contrary to hers.

After the third such argument, Flit had told him he could either piss off or shut up. He had chosen the latter. Instead of talking, they'd picked up the controllers of some of their old favourite console games and lost themselves in the digital world.

With the distraction of the games and Hawkeye's consistent presence, Flit started to second-guess her own conviction. When she entered into a flow-state of playing, her mind wandered back to those nights in her apartment in the Hub with KC-847. Even though she *knew* he had left her while she was sleeping, she could not recall a single time she had woken to find his side of the bed empty. She also remembered times where KC-847 showed off the stats and tracking after returning from his daily runs, where he would walk around with that cute, smug grin when he could show that he was getting faster and faster each week.

As the gaming sessions wrapped up, Hawkeye would inevitably fill her in on progress outside of her room, with the reassignments to provide better security and news from above about how the Government had added extra security in the strictest crackdowns since the early days of their regime a century ago. It was a much-needed reminder of the things she and KC-847 had done to help the Free Citizens and to get information for the Underground. If KC-847 really was working against them, wouldn't he have tried to sabotage her at every turn? Instead of ruining their attempts, he had gone along with them and even led the charge in some ways.

It turned out that, given space, it was much easier for Flit to question her own mind than when people were doing it for her. Her thought spirals were counterproductive for her scores in game, but Hawkeye hadn't even teased her about it. It meant the visits, which had initially been somewhat frustrating, turned into an opportunity for her to really think about things. If she was on her own, her emotions would get the better of her, but having Hawkeye around helped Flit keep herself together, even for a short time.

It was towards the end of one such visit that a loud knocking interrupted the final point scoring round of Flit and Hawkeye's game. Flit's eyebrows furrowed.

Hawkeye paused the round as he rubbed the back of his neck and looked between Flit and the door. "Are you gonna get that?" he asked, voice cracking.

Flit narrowed her eyes. She'd heard that tone enough times to know he was up to something. "Hawk... what have you done?"

Her sandy-haired friend just shrugged and threw his controller down on the end of her bed. "So, I'd better get going. I'll get the door if you won't." He hopped to his feet and walked over to it.

Just as Flit was about to call Hawkeye something unsavoury, he opened the door to reveal a familiar face that took her breath away.

"Hello, Flit," Fortune said with a warm smile. "Hawkeye."

"Ah, Fortune. Fancy seeing you here." Hawkeye's voice was stilted as he gave Flit a *please-don't-punch-me* smile.

"Hawk, you're an arsehole," Flit snapped. She would have teleported to her feet if the inhibitor around her wrist hadn't given her a painful jolt as she attempted it. Instead, she groaned and stumbled off the bed instead. "But it's always nice to see you, Fortune."

No matter what the situation was, Flit could never be mad at Fortune.

"See you tomorrow!" Hawkeye left the room and shut the door behind himself but not so quickly that Flit missed the satisfied smirk on his face.

Fortune peered around the room. "This is a lot neater than I'm used to from you," she teased in a light tone.

"Yeah, I gave away most of my stuff before moving to the Hub. Kinda makes it hard to cover the floor with clothes when you barely have enough to cover your own body," Flit conceded. She waved to invite Fortune to sit on the end of the bed.

"Sorry I didn't come by earlier. I heard you weren't doing well, and I figured a bit of space might help. I've also been busy trying to get my head around how things have changed here since I left," Fortune said as she took Hawkeye's vacated seat on the wrinkled blankets.

Flit sank back onto the bed too. "Surely it hasn't changed that much?" She massaged her arm around where the inhibitor cuff sat. After each discharge of power-blocking energy, she felt like she'd just sprained her muscles.

Fortune shrugged. "You were here for over a year after I was taken, and you haven't really been out and about since returning. It's not so much a physical or visual thing... it just *feels* different."

"Ah, that... Yeah, there was a lot of tension after all of the collapses before I left." Flit glanced at the older woman, taken aback once more by just how much her time away had aged her.

Flit understood what it was like to lose a lover, but she couldn't imagine the pain of losing a child. On top of that, she didn't even know the extent of what Fortune and Rook had gone through before their rescue from that blasted facility. With everything Flit and KC-847 had found at the other branches of the Department of Advanced Human Research, she couldn't even imagine.

"It's not quite that," Fortune conceded, frowning as she looked around the room. She opened her mouth to say more but shook her head ever so slightly. "But forget it. That's not why I'm here. How are you?"

A helpless laugh spluttered from Flit's lips. "Miserable? Frustrated? Confused?" Flit groaned and threw herself back on the bed. "Fuck, I don't even know any more."

The covers crinkled as Fortune shifted closer and took Flit's hand in her own warm, soft one. "What don't you know any more?"

"What I think, and what I feel. What's right, and who to trust. It's such a bloody mess, Fortune." Flit held her hand a little tighter and closed her eyes. "My emotions are all over the place. Sometimes, in the quiet moments, all I can think about is how I fucked everything up. I rescued a Registered who came down here and set explosions off that killed some of us." Flit rubbed her face with her free hand. "Then, when I start moving around, waking my brain up, and doing things, I think that it's impossible. I mean, Harmony and Divvy showed me the footage of KC-847 being released from the Government's holding facility. How did he get out? They had to have known that we were involved with the Free—"

Flit bit back the rest of the comment on instinct. She'd been so careful since returning to the Underground to avoid even thinking about the Free Citizens, let alone talking about them. She had no doubt the leaders of the Underground would be far less forgiving if they knew just how far her involvement with that maglev attack had gone. It had been such a brash risk to take when she had so many links to the Underground. If she had been captured, she would have dragged them down with her.

KC-847 could have too.

But he didn't.

Or at least, he hadn't. Not yet. Enough time had passed that the Government would have advanced on the Underground and exterminated them if they knew.

"What did you see on the footage, exactly?" Fortune asked, breaking Flit out of her revelations.

Flit opened her eyes as she thought back to that night. It was all such a tangle of sleeplessness and emotion. It was so hard to remember exactly.

"He was in the lobby with an agent. They exchanged some words I couldn't hear. Then they let him walk out."

"So, what do we really know, then?"

Flit sat up, released Fortune's hand, and combed her fingers through her tangled hair. "He had to have been captured. There was no way he could have escaped."

Fortune nodded. "And?"

"Well, judging by the time stamp on the footage, he was either with them for several days, or he just returned for a meeting," Flit continued. "If they knew he was Registered, then they would have put him back into service. If they thought he was one of us, there's no way they would have let him go, right?" There was hope in her tone as some of the fog in her brain started to lift.

"They don't show mercy to our kind."

"Does that mean we assume they don't know he is a Derivate?"

The corners of Fortune's eyes crinkled. "Did any of you use your abilities during the escape?"

Flit shook her head. "I couldn't because there were too many of us. Hawk's aren't visible. KC-847 was running with the rest of us, and... Sway did, but that was just to knock me out when the Government were distracted."

Fortune's crow's feet smoothed as she smiled. "Then I'd say that probably saved him."

Flit let out a breath of relief.

"So, if they don't know that he is a Derivate, but they are aware you had something to do with the maglev attacks..." Fortune trailed off after her summary.

"Then there's probably a good reason they let him go, and whatever it is, it doesn't mean he is necessarily the one who caused the tunnel collapses?"

Fortune got to her feet and brushed down her trousers. "That is what I'm hoping." She cupped Flit's cheek. "You're a superb judge of character, Flit. Scraps seemed like a good person when I met him, and with the way he looked at you..." Fortune's voice cracked, but she swallowed her emotions and continued, "There's no way he was betraying you when he looked at you like that."

I love you, Flit.

Those four words echoed in Flit's mind and seared away some more of that mental fog. There was still a horrid itch in her thoughts, a doubt that refused to let go... but it wasn't as powerful anymore.

Using the hold on Flit's cheek to pull her closer, Fortune placed a gentle kiss on Flit's forehead. "From the dark circles under your eyes, I can tell you're having trouble sleeping. Please, get a good sleep, and then come to the Mess tomorrow. Everyone would love to see you, and I have a feeling the Blue Team would like to hear about our discussion today."

Reluctantly, Flit agreed with Fortune. She glanced down at the wedding ring she still wore on her finger. For some reason, she had not been able to bring herself to take it off. She smiled as she remembered the conversation they'd had about relationships before she reluctantly put it on. That was before he had said he loved her. Before he had sacrificed himself to save her from the Government. Looking back, she wasn't sure how she'd let herself become so swept up in the notion of Scraps' guilt. She'd never been one to take someone else's word for something, and she was furious that a misinterpreted six second video had clouded her judgement.

"I'll see you tomorrow," Flit promised.

"WELL, FUCK ME. SHE HAS EMERGED!" Sway called out above the din of conversation as Flit arrived in the Mess.

The way everyone within a four-meter radius stopped eating to turn and look at her made Flit want to turn back and walk out. Instead, she rolled her eyes. "Is it any wonder I haven't left my room when there are arseholes like you waiting out here for me?" Her teasing tone had the gawkers chuckling and shaking their heads before they returned their attention to their own business.

"Naw." Sway elbowed Hawkeye. "And you said she'd lost all sense of humour."

Instead of adding fuel to Sway's fire, Hawkeye slid over on the bench to make room for Flit between Sway and himself.

The Mess was busier than Flit had seen it in the longest time. With all Underground members on local duties only, the covert agents from the surface returned, and the added numbers of the refugees, every single seat and bench was taken.

Even the table the Blue Team favoured was far more crowded than usual. There were three extra faces beyond the usual team of Hawkeye, Swipe, Tweak, Sway, Clarity, and Link. Layla was seated between Hawkeye and Fortune, and Patch had joined them too. Flit was pleased that the table didn't feel empty, but the last memory she had of sitting on the metal bench was with Scraps' thigh pressed alongside hers as they had eaten together.

"Flit? Did you hear me?"

Jumping slightly, Flit realised Clarity had asked her something. When she looked up, everyone at the table was staring at her. Swipe, in particular, had daggers in her gaze.

"Uh... no. Sorry," Flit admitted, pulling her mind out of the memory and focusing on the present.

"I was wondering if Posthoc had spoken to you about rejoining the team? Or will you be with Intelligence now?" Clarity asked. She reached into the middle of the table and retrieved one of the crystal geodes that Link had put there as decorations. She turned it over in her fingertips as she waited for a response.

"If another team member defects to Intelligence, I'll lose my shit," Tweak muttered, stabbing at the sole remaining potato on his plate with a vengeance.

"I don't really think they're trusting me to do anything at the moment." Flit raised her hand and let the sleeve of her oxblood leather jacket slip down around her forearm to reveal the inhibitor.

A low whistle escaped from Sway's lips. "They still don't trust you to stick around?"

"Would you?" Tweak asked.

For the first time in the past few days, Flit wasn't sure of that answer. Up until her discussion with Fortune, she had been sitting firmly in the camp of staying in the Underground. However, her recent revelations and the recession of some of that doubt had her thinking about a trip to the Hub again. Not that she would let anyone else know that. She had to look like she was behaving herself. Which, for once in her life, she was.

Mostly.

"I'm sure they'll sort something out soon." Hawkeye waved his hand dismissively. "We've got too much going on to tolerate idle hands. Layla and the others are even being offered job assignments."

The way Hawkeye smiled at the red-headed woman beside him made Flit sit a little straighter.

"Oh? Where are they putting you guys?" Patch asked, leaning in. "We could always use some extra helpers in the Medbay."

"I've been assigned to the kitchens." Layla pressed her lips together in a failed attempt to hide her discontent.

Fortune chuckled. "Yes. They're being very careful with us. I'm stuck in Supply."

"You used to be in Control!" Flit blurted, unable to believe that someone who had been as valued as Fortune had been being thrown into mediocrity.

"It's just plain insulting," Swipe said, finally taking a break from the death-stares she was levelling at Flit to speak.

"After what happened with Scraps, they're bound to be extra careful with new people." Link gave Fortune and Layla an apologetic smile before she turned her attention to Flit.

Flit had a feeling that the telepath was watching, probably listening, for her reaction. It was the first time someone had mentioned Scraps since Flit had arrived at the table. Given the way their last interaction had gone, they had to be wondering.

It seems like a stupid, arrogant idea to keep the people who were held by the Government away from the planning. They probably have important information we could use to deal with whatever bullshit reason they have for blocking us in here, Flit thought as she maintained eye contact with Link.

Link nodded ever so slightly before her expression changed. "Oh! Do you know Swipe is now the team leader?"

Flit eyed the other woman and let out a sigh. "Yes, she mentioned it the other day. Better than Tweak or Sway, I suppose. You'd be fucked if you had them in charge."

Tweak picked up the much-maligned potato on his plate and threw it at Flit, who caught it with ease, squished it in her hand, and threw it back at him. He let out a squeak of surprise and batted it away from his preciously coiffed dark locks. Laughter rounded the table, and Flit sank deeper into her seat at the warm familiarity of it all.

The conversation turned into a recount of the patrols the remaining Security team members had been on that day. As Link and Sway were telling a story about a new patch of giant mutant roaches they had found around some of the heating vents, Swipe leaned across the table.

"So, have you changed your mind about what we discussed the other night?"

Flit looked around to make sure no one was listening, and her eyes fell on Fortune. She was so glad to have the caring, clever woman back in her life. "I think there could be many reasons Scraps was seen leaving that building. I want to find them."

Swipe's crimson lips curved into a wicked smile. "Well, it's about bloody time."

The daggers that the blonde had been staring at Flit were gone, replaced instead by a smug visage of victory.

Flit let her have the win. It was as close as she would come to letting Swipe know she was probably right.

Eventually, Flit was drawn into main discussion to provide some truth to an extremely exaggerated story Hawkeye was telling Layla about his prowess against a rogue roost of mutant bats. The embellishments served to widen the redhead's eyes and have her lean in closer for the details. It was only when Flit saw it was an embarrassing attempt at flirting, rather than a genuine belief that he had actually achieved anything in that fight, that Flit let Hawkeye have his fun. It had been years since she'd seen her best friend flirting with someone, and the lengths he was going to make himself look good amused her.

The rest of the night went on, and for a short time, Flit was thrown back into the past, to a time before tunnel explosions, sinister Government facilities, and the death of so many wonderful people. She let herself savour the moment.

WHEN FLIT RETURNED to the apartment she shared with her parents, she immediately sensed something off. The first sign was the fact both of her parents were standing there with broad, fake smiles plastered over their faces.

"Flit! How was dinner?" her mother asked, walking over and draping an arm around Flit's shoulder, guiding her away from the door and through the living room area.

"Um... not bad?"

Flit's words were punctuated by her father's uneven footsteps as he gave her a wide-eyed look of... *Concern? Worry?*

When they rounded the small wall that separated the living space from the dining room, Flit understood what her father was trying to convey.

Warning.

Sitting serenely at the small, square table was Harmony.

Flit had to stop herself from instinctively stepping back. She felt as though a cold bucket of sludge had been dumped over her head.

"Flit, it's lovely to see you. I thought I'd come in and check on you, see how you're going?" Harmony said, her smile as bright as her blue eyes.

Remaining on her feet, with her parents standing behind her, Flit put her hands in her pockets. "I'm okay."

The room fell into silence as Harmony frowned, watching Flit, apparently waiting for her to say more.

"Harmony, can I get you a drink or something?" Tinker stepped out from behind Flit.

Harmony shook her head. "I won't be staying long. I appreciate the offer together. Although, I would like privacy to speak to Flit."

Flit looked back at her parents over her shoulder and frowned. Was Harmony expecting them to leave their own apartment? The leader was certainly making no moves to get out of her seat.

"We can go to my room," Flit offered, leading the way before Harmony had an opportunity to argue. She held the door open and let the other woman go first before she followed her in and closed the door behind them.

"I'm sorry I requested privacy. I just wasn't sure if you felt comfortable talking to me about how things are in front of your parents. Family relationships can be complicated sometimes." Harmony walked over and perched on the edge of the empty desk in Flit's room.

Waving a hand dismissively, Flit sat on the corner of her bed.

"It was really hard seeing how upset you were when you first learned of KC-847's' betrayal," Harmony said gently, her natural charisma making Flit look up.

The instant their eyes locked, Flit got caught in Harmony's intense gaze.

"How are you feeling about that now?"

"It still hurts," Flit confessed. It wasn't a lie. Even though she had started to doubt the situation, it was still an uncomfortable one.

"It probably will for a while. You clearly loved him dearly," Harmony said, once more in a kind, empathetic tone.

Love, not loved, Flit thought to herself. *It isn't a past tense thing.*

Instead of answering and risking a lie, she just nodded.

"Hopefully soon, you'll be ready to get back to work. I heard you've just been locking yourself up in your room. I understand that you're hurting, but people need to see you out and about. So many of them look up to you," Harmony explained as she rested both hands against the edge of the desk and leaned back. "Where would you like to work? Technically, you're part of the Intelligence team. Would you like to continue that? Or would you prefer to go back to the Blue Team?"

"I haven't given it much thought," Flit said when what she really meant was *I need to figure out what I plan to do before I decide where to work.*

"That's fair. Think about it. Then come and see me and let me know what you'd prefer. I can get that inhibitor removed when you do."

Instinctively brushing her fingers over the bump in her sleeve caused by the inhibitor, Flit frowned. *Why not do it right now?* It almost felt like an ultimatum. She was tempted to ask Harmony that exact question, but she had a feeling she wouldn't get a straight answer anyway.

"I will. Thank you."

For a few moments, Flit and Harmony just stared at each other. Then, rather suddenly, Harmony rose from her perch on the desk and walked over to Flit, clapping a hand on her shoulder. "Thanks for speaking to me, Flit. Please don't ever hesitate to come and see me if you need anything, okay? Even if you just want to talk."

"Thank you."

Flit looked at the older woman, surprised by the personal offer of assistance. Even though they weren't like the Government, there was a structure in the Underground that meant Harmony and Divvy were often too busy for ongoing, casual discussions like that with people who weren't the head of a department or in some other position of authority. The offer, as lovely as Flit might have once thought it was, now made her suspicious. Did Harmony really want to help her, or was there some ulterior motive?

"Good." Harmony did not let go of Flit's shoulder. She just returned her gaze for a moment before resolve set behind her eyes. Something churned in Flit's stomach, but she was unable to look away before Harmony added, "Now, please do not forget how heartbroken you are, how KC-847's obvious betrayal is eating away at your heart. You will push through the pain and come to me tomorrow morning to tell me you decided to rejoin the Blue Team. You will be too upset by the situation to discuss your motives properly with anyone in the meantime. If anyone asks about KC-847, you will tell them that he betrayed you and betrayed the Underground."

The coercion in Harmony's voice was so strong that Flit's mind went blank for everything other than what the leader had told her. The sense of betrayal and frustration returned stronger, and Flit staggered back, her eyes wide and heart thundering in her chest. "My heart is breaking... He betrayed me. Us."

"That's a good girl." Harmony turned and walked towards the door, but just before she held her hand out to open it, she paused and caught Flit's stunned gaze over her shoulder. "And you're not going to remember I told you to do any of this, either. The concerns about the betrayal, the decision to rejoin Security... they are all your decisions. The only thing I did here tonight was check in on you and offer you a non-judgmental ear."

And then, Harmony left.

By the time Flit's parents walked into the room, she was sitting on her bed in tears, once again wishing she had never met KC-847.

13

———

SCRAPS

THE MORNING of the Derivate Training Facility audit arrived faster than Scraps anticipated. He was fully prepared, of course, at least when it came to the work itself. However, the strange churning in his gut as he woke for his run told him that maybe, emotionally, he was not as ready as he had thought.

It had been well over a year since he had been Registered, and several years since he had left that facility. Coming back to the Hub had shown him that he was able to keep his new, rebellious resolve without issue. The real concern was that the Facility had been such a big part of his life before he had moved to the Underground. He had grown up there, and it was where his brainwashing and servitude had been cemented.

Seeing Agent Greene and Agent Hector at the museum had dredged up memories, and he'd only visited it one time as a child. He wondered what it would be like to go back to the place where it all started. Would it add fuel to his desire to usher in an end to the Government's regime? Or would it drag his mind back to that mindset he had worked so hard to reverse?

Scraps' concerns were there the moment he woke up from a rather restless sleep, and they followed him right up until his feet hit the pavement and he started to run. Flit had always found his dedication to his exercise routine, any routine in general, amusing. She was a far more chaotic kind of person than he was. He knew she chafed at the idea of any routine and particularly at purposeful exercise, but he found a sense of comfort and predictability in it all. It helped him keep focused.

The streets were still quiet at the time Scraps went for his run, but even without many Citizens moving about, there was still an increased Registered presence. Every block corner had an officer wearing a dark Government uniform and blacked-out visor. Some of the Government buildings he ran past had an entire team standing at their entrance. He made sure his mind was clear as he ran past them, but between the posted guards, he was pleased by how things had changed since the attack on the maglev systems. The Government felt rattled enough to continue to expend their resources, and if the uniforms being counterfeited by the Free Citizens were any indicator, the tension the surveillance was causing would only drive their insurrection to greater heights.

When Scraps returned to his apartment, he went for a quick shower, dressed in his work clothes, and got breakfast sorted. A notification tone rang through the apartment, and he called out, getting the screens integrated into the living room windows to switch on and display the incoming message.

To: Brian
From: Liana
Subject: How are you?
Brian! I hope you had a good weekend. Just checking in to let you know that I woke up late and will have to meet you outside the facility. See you there.

Scraps wouldn't need to leave quite as early as he thought if Liana planned to meet him at the facility, so he spent some extra time sitting on the couch and scrolling through the policies he had transferred to his datapad. He wished he could have sent some of them to Flit and Shadow. Even if it wasn't something they were looking for, it would help them understand what he and the other Registereds grew up with and, he hoped, remind them that they still had a fight on the surface.

Eventually, Scraps had to turn his datapad off and get ready to leave. The trip to the Derivate Training Facility passed in a blur as he went over the audit schedule in his mind. The people from the Facility had, at least thus far, been somewhat more cooperative than the people he and Flit had dealt with in the Department of Advanced Human Research. He figured that Citizens and Government workers alike were far more used to the perverse treatment of Derivates and, therefore, those carrying out the procedures did not feel as much of a need to defend themselves and conceal the truth.

The streets around South One had changed since he had left the facility. He had not gone back into the vicinity since returning to the Hub, so it was quite a surprise to see the way that the buildings on either side of the facility had been coopted by the Government and turned into additional training and housing spaces. He had read about it in the briefing, of course, but seeing it was different. The need for extra room escaped him, though, as the birth rate of Registereds was closely monitored, as was the assignment of their living quarters to different barracks and departments around the city.

Scraps wasn't able to think on it for long, as Liana arrived just on time. She was always punctual and polite. He appreciated that about her. Another thing he was pleased about was that Liana was less likely to veer off on a side mission while they were in the building. He loved Flit, but it would be a much simpler job with Liana, even if it meant he would probably be unable to steal any information.

"Brian! Lovely to see you." Liana pulled him into a hug by way of greeting. When she stepped back, her smile faltered. "I've been wanting to work with you for ages. From what Ava said, all of the planning and organisation is all on you. So many people in the office could do with a kick up the butt to help them improve the admin side of things. I'm looking forward to gaining some insight from you."

Despite his anxiety around the situation, Scraps laughed. "Well, it isn't that difficult. I'm not sure if you'll see anything special here today in terms of my performance. Ava was right. I'm all about the admin and planning. She was the one who made the real connections and discoveries… but I hope it is a useful endeavour for you all the same."

Her shoulders and jaw set, Liana turned to look at the building. "This is the second most hated review after the Department of Advanced Human Research." She rubbed her forearm as she took in the extra guards around the building. "After we do this, I think Jane is going to owe you and Ava one heck of a thanks for taking them both on. I know Gary was keen to do this one again, but we've all been sceptical about how well he's done the reviews in the past. It's no secret he hates Derivates, but no one else wanted to go in there."

Scraps blinked and had to restrain his annoyance at Liana's comment or at least at the truth behind it. It wasn't her fault. She was just pointing out the obvious.

"Why is that?" he asked.

She shrugged. "I think people are just intimidated by all the powers and stuff." She raised her palms to show that she did not agree with that line of thinking. "But they all have control chips and stuff, right? It's not like they could do anything."

"I highly doubt they would want to, either. They aren't wild animals who can't control themselves. Besides, the consequences are quite severe if they act out of line," Scraps said, wanting her to know that there was more than the control chips stopping the Registereds from hurting Citizens.

Including all the brainwashing.

And the lack of autonomy.

And, of course, basic humanity.

If Flit was here, she might have just launched into the first argument with her best surface-side friend. Scraps almost wouldn't blame her, especially knowing about Code 6B and the likelihood of Chris and Liana bringing a Derivate child into the world. Unlike his girlfriend, Scraps knew he had a job to do and held that as highest priority.

In order to put a stop to any further conversation, he gestured towards the front door of the building. "Shall we?" He turned and started to walk while Liana fell into step beside him.

GETTING through the security screening process was about the same at the Derivate Training Facility as it was at Centre One. However, that was an increase from what Scraps remembered growing up. The security at the facility tended to focus more on keeping Derivates in than keeping Citizens out. After all, very few Citizens would be either daring or caring enough to bother trying. Not that there was anything interesting for them to gain by breaking in.

The main foyer itself was just as Scraps remembered it—cavernous, modern, and decorated in that white-stone and sleek-silver-metal style the Government preferred. It was about as welcoming as any corporate office building in the city. After seeing the different apartment buildings in the Hub and the homes in the Underground, it was apparent to Scraps that this was not a place anyone would call homely. The large reception desk in front of the elevator bank was always staffed but seldom used, as the building rarely got visitors.

Or at least, in the past the reception desk was rarely used. As Scraps and Liana made their way over, there were ten neat lines of uniformed Registereds waiting patiently across the span of the counter.

"This place is busier than I expected," Liana noted as she joined on the queue that seemed to be moving the fastest.

Scraps frowned as he looked around. Every single person lined up was a Derivate. The patches on their uniforms indicated a wide range of ages, abilities, and power levels, and the uniforms covered all assignments, from city maintenance to special operations. At the very front of each line, the person speaking to a receptionist would spend a few minutes discussing whatever matter they had brought before being directed to the elevator bank that was reserved for the accommodation levels.

"It certainly is," Scraps muttered under his breath as they shuffled forward.

Liana turned back to face him. "Do you think—"

"Sir! Ma'am!" A female security officer approached them. The patch on her shoulder indicated that she was a high-level telecoercionist.

Scraps had to work to keep his mind clear. Not because she could read it. More because he was worried someone else in the room would.

"Yes?" Scraps turned to face the woman, taking in her salt and pepper hairline and deep red eyes.

"There is no need for you to wait in line here. Please, come with me."

Scraps and Liana followed the woman around the crowd of waiting Derivates, right to the administration desk, where the receptionist had just sent a young woman off to the elevator bank. Predictably, the Derivates in the line behind them didn't utter any complaint, but Scraps had to hide his frown at his preferential treatment.

"Oh, thank you." Liana glanced between the security officer and the receptionist. "My name is Liana Perez, and this is Brian Parkes. We're here from the Research and Development Department to conduct the annual policy and procedure review. We are expected on level thirty-five," she explained confidently.

The receptionist nodded and tapped at her screen. There was a slight pause, most likely while the security readers built into the room locked onto their chips, and then, she nodded. "Very well, Ms. Perez and Mr. Parkes, you're cleared to head straight to level thirty-five. Have a nice day."

When Scraps and Liana stepped aside, they were rejoined by the telecoercionist who said in a quiet, flat tone, "I will ensure you have private and priority access to the next elevator."

It was no surprise when they turned the corner that each of the ten elevators in the lobby also had a long line. They weren't quite as crowded as the ones for reception, but if they had to wait to speak to a receptionist and to catch the elevator, Scraps and Liana could have been easily forty-five minutes late for their supposed start time.

Just like she did at the line for reception, the telecoercionist walked them around the side and then stood between them and the queued Derivates. When the elevator arrived, she held the door for them with one hand as she raised her other to stop anyone else boarding. She then pressed the screen icon for level thirty-five before letting go of the door. "Have a good day, Sir, Ma'am," the telecoercionist said before stepping back and letting the door shut between them.

When they were in the elevator, Scraps finally frowned. Telecoercionists and mind readers of that level were usually only employed within the ranks of Derivate security for one reason: to keep an eye on their own kind. Scraps hadn't been in the presence of a security officer like that for a long time. In the past, he had respected the difficulty of their position. Just like his role of returning runaways, he had believed it was a worthwhile pursuit. Now, though? He understood that he and people like the security officer were some of the more sinister players in keeping Derivates complicit. If they couldn't even trust their own kind, then where could they possibly go for help?

"What do you think the Derivates in the lobby were doing there? They had uniforms from all different departments," Liana muttered as the elevator carried them up higher into the facility.

The question broke Scraps out of his musings and tore his attention away from that uncomfortable stirring of guilt in the pit of his stomach. "It sounded like they were being assigned new accommodation within this building, which is odd, as they would have other lodging closer to their postings. This facility was designed for people until they receive their first postings at the age of eighteen or for those older ones retraining."

Liana frowned. "There's a lot of weird stuff going on in this city at the moment."

Scraps knew better than to respond. Both he and Liana were involved in the exact events that had caused the Government to take extra precautions. As the elevator stopped and the doors hissed opened, Scraps wondered whether the reallocation of Derivate housing had something to do with that too.

A Citizen employee stood behind the reception desk across the sleek foyer. "Good morning. How may I help you?"

"Hello," Liana said brightly as she and Scraps approached the counter.

She introduced Scraps and herself just like she did downstairs, and the woman politely asked them to wait whilst she retrieved another worker who showed them into an open-plan office space beyond the foyer. The spacious room reminded Scraps of the office he and Liana worked at in Centre One, with soundproof pods that made the large space oddly quiet given the amount of people sitting at the desks.

The worker who showed them around explained that they had been assigned a pod to conduct their review in. A Security Officer would be available to escort them around the premises if they needed to assess anything in person. Scraps thanked the worker and stepped into the pod with Liana.

"Well, I guess this will be our office for the next several days," Scraps said as he sat down at one of the desks and swiped the screen to bring the system to life. He logged in with his credentials as Liana sat down behind him at the other desk.

"Several days?" She tapped her own screen. "You don't think that we'll wrap this up by tomorrow afternoon?"

Scraps shook his head. "I do not think so. Given the amount of accommodation reassignments, we will need to dive into the policies of several different departments to ensure that the requirements are met for the staff members that are now staying here."

"What do you mean?" Liana spun on her chair as she watched him.

"Well, different roles have different rest and nutrition requirements. This facility was set up to handle the needs of people from birth through to eighteen based on a set schedule of study and exercise. The workers will have vastly different ages and requirements," Scraps explained, still working his way through the computer system to retrieve the policies and procedures they required. "So, in order to ensure the needs of each worker are met, we have to learn how they are accommodating, feeding, and provisioning for adequate rest environments."

Silence filled the pod. It was a good few seconds before he'd finished opening all the documents he required and turned to find Liana staring at him, open-mouthed.

"Do you know all of the departments this well?" Her voice was voice tinged with awe. "Geez, no wonder you and Ava were always able to get out of the office on time. Do you have a photographic memory or something?"

Scraps laughed and shook his head. "I just study a lot and retain information well."

"Right." Liana didn't sound entirely convinced. Still, she clapped her hands together. "Where do we start?"

14

———

FLIT

THE NEXT MORNING Flit woke early, feeling more tired than she was when she had gone to sleep. Her emotions had been on such a wild ride for so long that she didn't know which way was up anymore, and it was taking a toll on her body. Still, she reluctantly rolled out of bed and dragged her feet to the bathroom in hopes a shower would help her wake up.

Her hopes had been somewhat met as she emerged in a puff of soap-scented steam and dressed for the day. Even though she was still feeling miserable and betrayed, Harmony had been right the previous night. It was about time she got out of her funk and back to work. The one positive from her terrible sleep was that she had woken with more clarity around what she wanted to do for work. Anything other than rejoining the Blue Team just felt *wrong*. She couldn't quite put her finger on the reason, but she was used to following her gut, so she didn't question it.

Flit decided to make her way to the Mess for breakfast before going to Control to speak to Harmony about her job assignment. She wasn't sure if she would be given immediate duties, so it would be better to have a full stomach just in case.

The Residence was a hive of activity. One of the problems, she guessed, with having so many people in the Underground. She had no idea what was going on beyond the few tunnels she had ventured down recently and found that a kernel of curiosity was growing in her.

Flit hoped her reassignment to Security might help her gain insight into how the Underground was planning to handle this lockdown in the long term. They had always relied on supply runs for the medicines and other necessities they were unable to produce in their caverns and tunnels, so they couldn't hide away forever. Before her trip to the Hub, Flit had found that most of the residents of the Underground had grown resigned to their life in the darkness. These new restrictions only served to further highlight how powerless they were, especially after more explosions and more deaths. She had been so caught in her own drama that Flit hadn't been able to gauge the temperature of the rebels.

Luckily, when Flit walked into the Mess, there were a few familiar faces sitting at the Blue Team's usual table. Flit retrieved a simple breakfast of toast and fruit and then turned to survey the room. She was just about to walk towards her table when a hand settled on her shoulder.

"Hey, stranger. It's nice to see you out and about," Acumen said with a wide smile.

Flit frowned at his hand and then at him. She shrugged him off. "You mean, after you tattled to Harmony and Divvy and made me keep my stupid inhibitor on longer?" She pulled the sleeve of her jacket down her wrist self-consciously and imagined birds. All kinds of big, pointy-beaked, flappy-winged birds.

Acumen winced. "Look, I'm just doing my job," he said, shaking his head. "I know you're pissed at me for it, but I want to make sure everyone down here, including you, is safe."

"Then congrats," Flit snapped. "You and the rest of Control are doing miserably."

Pinching the bridge of his nose, Acumen sighed. "I forgot how long you hold grudges for." He let his hand fall and stood straighter. "For what it's worth, I'm pissed at myself for not sensing Scraps' betrayal too. I'm the one who gave the final tick for his trustworthiness. I'm annoyed that the Underground got caught up in that, but also, I'm sorry you got your heart broken. If I could go back and change it, I would."

Birds, birds, and more birds. That was all Flit wanted to think about. Not her own doubts... and certainly not her conversation with Hawkeye and Fortune. Just a whole flock of birds swarming around her mind.

"All right, all right. I get it. I know when I'm not wanted," Acumen said, raising his hands and stepping back. "But if you change your mind, come find me, and we can chat."

"Not likely," Flit said in a false, cheery tone as she stepped around him.

She clung to her tray of food instead of throwing it at Acumen like she really wanted to. She pictured throwing her apple at the back of his head, and Acumen instinctively reached up to rub the spot she had imagined throwing it.

With an immature sense of satisfaction at her petty win over Acumen, she turned around and walked to the Blue Team's Table. As she approached, Fortune, Layla, Tweak, and Link broke out of their discussion to greet her. Fortune's greeting was particularly welcome as the older woman rose out of her seat and pulled Flit into a tight embrace. When Fortune finally let go, she shifted to the side so Flit could sit between her and Layla.

"I wasn't expecting to see you out here," Link said with a warm smile.

Flit shrugged as nonchalantly as possible. "I've moped around enough," she said, even though her eyes still felt gritty from crying herself to sleep the night before, "and I've decided I want to rejoin the Blue Team. I figured I should get up early to go and see if I can speak to Harmony or Divvy about a possible assignment before the day ramps up and they get too busy."

Tweak raised an eyebrow at her between spoonfuls of cereal. "You want to rejoin security?"

"Why wouldn't I? Or have you lost faith in my judgement?" Flit frowned as she glanced at him. "Or is it because I invited a traitor to the Underground and was stupid enough to fall in love with him? Go on, Tweak. Say what you really mean."

Tension rose between them, where a moment ago there had only been easy familiarity.

Tweak's eyebrows furrowed, and he went to say something.

But Fortune beat him to it. "That's not how you felt last night."

"Well, things have changed. He's a traitor. That's all there is to it."

"Flit, I think—"

"I don't want to talk about it," Flit snapped, a sudden urge to end that line of conversation bursting out of her.

Fortune and Link shared a look, and Fortune sighed and sat back in her seat. There was silence at the table, with the hum of distant conversation and the scraping of utensils against plates acting as a backing track.

The Blue Team and Co were never good at sitting in silence, so it was barely a minute before Tweak spoke up. "I, for one, never had any faith in your judgements to begin with, so there was nothing to lose." Tweak winked, making Link laugh awkwardly, and Flit couldn't help but smile at his familiar teasing tone. "But, really, you were in Intelligence! Why the hell would you come back to clearing roaches and getting covered in bat shit when you could sit at a desk and do nothing but tap a screen all day long?"

With a roll of her eyes, Flit replied, "Yeah, because I'm the type of person to voluntarily sit on my arse all day." She was about to say more, but her mind flicked back to the dreary monotony of working in Centre One with KC-847. She shook off those memories. "I just want to be useful again. I was good in Security, and I know these tunnels better than I know myself."

"Well, we'll be happy to have you back," Link said.

"*We* might be," Tweak muttered, "but I have a feeling Swipe won't be. She's down a patrol partner, and I think she'd rather gouge her own eyes out with rusty nails than work with you."

For the first time that morning, Flit questioned whether rejoining Security was a good idea.

Fortune sighed. "Oh, for goodness sake. It's not that bad. You're both grown women, and it's about time you learned to get along."

Poor Fortune had been dealing with Flit and Swipe's rivalry since Flit had started dating her son years ago. Fortune had made a point of making sure Flit and Swipe knew that she loved them both in equal measure. She always seemed to deal with them the same way that Flit had seen parents with more than one child in the

Underground manage any sibling conflicts—with a roll of the eyes and a heavy dose of exasperation.

"I'll play nice if she does," Flit said in a tone that was one part playful and two parts serious. She felt a little guilty when the statement earned her one of Fortune's disparaging but fond grimaces. It was an expression she'd missed sorely while the woman had been gone.

Then, just like she used to, Fortune changed topic instead of feeding Flit's amusement. "I'm going to the Catacombs this morning. I haven't been down there since getting back. Would you be willing to come with me?"

Flit blinked. The expression of love and resignation on Rook's face moments before his true death flashed through her mind. She thought of his handsome face. Of the taste of his lips. Of the way it felt to hear him say that he loved her one last time. Suddenly, her eyes were stinging again, and she had to dig her fingernails into her palms, using the crescent-shaped bursts of sharpness to draw her out of the painful memories.

"Sure. I'll come with you after I speak to Harmony or Divvy."

"Great. I'll go with you to Control, and then we can head down together after that."

"Sounds good," Flit said when what she really meant to say was *that sounds like more than I can deal with right now.*

Fortune turned to the redheaded woman. "Layla, will you be all right to hang around for a bit while Flit and I are gone? You can always head back to your room and catch up on reading if you like?"

"Oh, I might hang around here for a bit longer before heading back." The apples of her freckled cheeks turned slightly pink.

Link smiled to herself and looked down at her breakfast.

Tweak snorted. "You mean, you'll keep pushing that breakfast around on your plate until Hawkeye arrives, so you can eat it with him instead of us?"

Layla's hand froze on her spoon, and she stared up at Tweak. "Um, no. I'm just not hungry yet. Besides, Hawkeye and I were going to catch up and figure out what training modules he would run me through later today."

Flit hid her own smile behind her toast. She certainly understood what Tweak was implying, and she couldn't help but think that he was onto something. Flit had seen the interest on Hawkeye's face right after he had first met Layla, even though she had just punched him in the face. Flit couldn't help but think that her best friend was finally over her, and Layla seemed like a lovely woman for him.

Conversation turned from teasing Layla about the changes to the shift rotations and the implications for mealtimes. Flit couldn't have given less of a crap about that topic, which meant she had a good excuse to eat her toast before it got much colder. When she was finished, she caught Fortune's attention, and the two excused themselves from the table. They took their dishes to the collection area and then left the Mess.

The tunnels just outside the Mess were still busy. Fortune explained that everyone with a job had been given rostered eating times to ensure appropriate availability of seating. It was odd seeing meal times formalised like that. In the past, people just tended to show up as they desired. Flit understood the need for more order now, to ensure there was enough food to go around, but it just felt *off*.

It was almost like she had left for her mission and returned to a different place altogether.

It wasn't until they were transitioning from the grey utility tunnels to the white ones that led to Control and the other various departments that it was clear enough for Flit to break the silence.

"So, they've put you in Supply? You must be bored out of your brain."

Fortune shrugged. "Given how many of us are down here and how unexpected the lockdown was, Supply is surprisingly busy. It's monotonous work, but I'm just pleased I have something to do besides stare at a wall all day. Especially because Harmony and Divvy seem to be suspicious of myself and the other escapees."

Flit let out a soft hum. She supposed that was true. Almost anything must have been an improvement compared to that hideous place the Government had the nerve to call a research facility. Still, it was hard for her to shake the memories of how things were before Fortune had left. She had been one of the key leaders of the resistance at Longbeach before that sanctuary had been lost, and ever since arriving in the Underground proper, her sharp intelligence and keen decision-making skills had been put to good use.

"It just doesn't make sense to me," Flit said as they walked. "They've got you back now. You've got insider knowledge of the Government's most cutting-edge facility, and they assign you to distributing sacks of grain or scrubbing service tunnels."

Fortune chuckled morbidly. "It makes perfect sense to me."

Before Flit could ask what she meant, they turned a corner into the wide corridor that ended in the thick, reinforced blast door that led to Control. Still, she turned to face Fortune and went to speak.

The older woman merely shook her head and mouthed the word, "Later."

Even though the puzzle of what Fortune was trying to imply by her comment bugged Flit, she didn't argue. She trusted Fortune enough to know she would keep her word.

They walked along together until they reached the blast door, and Flit pressed her hand against the access panel. Instead of opening, as it would for someone assigned to a shift in Control, the screen lit up with the words *Please Wait*.

After almost a full minute, the face of a Control operative appeared on the screen. "How can I help you today?" the older man asked.

Flit remembered seeing him around the tunnels, but she couldn't quite recall his name.

"I'm here to speak to Harmony or Div—"

"Do you have an appointment?"

"No, but I only need a minute of their time." Flit frowned.

"If you don't have an appointment, then you can't see them."

"Maybe if you take a minute, call them, and let them know it's me, they might be able to make a tiny bit of time," Flit suggested, her annoyance growing at the stone wall the man was throwing up between her and her goal.

The man looked directly at the camera, his face a mix of disdain and annoyance. He was about to say something when Fortune stepped into his range of view, right behind Flit's shoulder.

"Hex, it's been a long time. How are you?" she asked smoothly.

Hex's eyes widened in surprise as he saw Fortune. "Well, I'll be damned." He shook his head. "I heard rumours you were back with us. It's nice to see you again. What can I do for you?"

"I'm just here to accompany Flit to see Harmony and Divvy. I know they're probably busy, but it's rather important," Fortune said with a warm smile.

"Oh, of course. Come on in." Hex's face disappeared as the screen went black.

"You've got to be kidding me."

Fortune let out a soft laugh and leaned closer. "You catch more flies with honey."

The door beeped, and with a metallic hiss, it opened slowly. Beyond the door, Control was in full swing. Every console had a worker at it, with the screens showing everything from security footage of the Mess to glitchy Government news feeds.

Hex walked away from a security station beside the door and stood in front of them. He reached out and shook Fortune's hand. "Okay. They can see you. They said that they just finished up their current meeting. Come on in, and head to meeting room ten."

Hex gestured down the corridor to the right of the main space. It led them to a suite of meeting rooms, many of which Flit had been in before for reasons varying from job assignments, to debriefing, to reprimands. Mostly the latter.

They got halfway down the white corridor when a door opened and Acumen stepped out. He seemed preoccupied, but he smiled as he spotted Flit and Fortune approaching. "Thanks for interrupting that meeting. It was getting a bit boring."

"We're not here to bail you out." Flit crossed her arms.

"Either way, I'm hungry. I forgot to grab a snack in the Mess earlier. Might go get myself a crunchy apple." Acumen winked at Flit as he stepped aside to let her and Fortune into the room.

Flit wished she really had thrown one at his head earlier.

Acumen snorted a laugh as she walked past, and she just glared at him.

The room beyond contained a large oval table with an illuminated touch screen surface and a dozen chairs spread around it. At the far side of the room, Harmony and Divvy sat nursing stainless steel thermoses, most likely containing coffee or tea to get them through a long day of leading a besieged group of rebels.

"Flit, Fortune, lovely to see you both. Take a seat." Divvy smiled and then pressed a button on the table to shut the door once they were inside.

"So, what can we do for you?" Harmony asked in a kind voice, sitting forward and smiling at them both.

"I'd like to rejoin the Blue Team," Flit said, figuring there was no point adding any fluff or prelude to her request.

Divvy looked surprised, and Harmony's face twisted into an expression of delight.

"Oh, fantastic," Harmony said. "I'm sure the team will be pleased to have you. It's about time you start getting back into the swing of things. I know you're heartbroken about KC-847, but it's important not to dwell on that."

Flit shifted in her seat, thinking about her earlier conversation with Tweak and Fortune and how uncomfortable it had all felt. Fortune was right. The night before, Flit had been convinced that Scraps was innocent, and she had been ready to launch into investigation mode. Then, after talking to Harmony, she'd fallen headfirst back into that spiral, into that unyielding certainty that KC-847 had tricked them, tricked her.

Running her fingers over the top of the touch-responsive table and leaving a trail of blue light in their wake, Flit sighed. "Is there any way I can take a look at that footage again?" She didn't dare to look at Harmony and Divvy. "I know I've already seen it, but something just feels *off*."

"There's nothing to be gained by torturing yourself further, Flit," Divvy said gently, reaching across the table and taking Flit's hand.

Flit looked up into her reassuring face and bit her lip.

"Besides, you won't find anything new on it," Harmony added in an unexpectedly sharp tone that had Flit looking over at her immediately. "We've had our best micros and Intelligence operatives look over that and other evidence, and he is guilty beyond doubt."

The words hit Flit like a punch, knocking the breath out of her chest.

"Flit, I know this is hard for you to accept, but KC-847 lied to you. He betrayed you. He tricked you into falling in love with him so he could use you to get information and ingratiate himself with the Underground."

Tears filled her eyes. She wanted to deny it, but there was such a sense of gravity to Harmony's claims that she knew they had to be true.

With a rustle of clothing, Fortune draped a comforting arm around Flit's shoulder.

Suddenly, that foreboding sense of Scraps' guilt lifted. The weight of Harmony's accusations, the steely truth in her words, dissolved.

"But—"

"There is no but," Harmony said firmly. "He is guilty, and that is the truth. You know it, and there will be no more denying it."

Growing up in the Underground, Flit had been around plenty of telecoercionists as they used their powers against others. It was an interesting thing to witness, the way their tones shifted and the sharpness of their command asserted itself against another. When it wasn't aimed against her, Flit could still tell what they were doing, the more amateur ones at least. It was an uncomfortable sensation Flit remembered well... and right now, she felt it again. That familiar gnawing pit opened in her stomach, only this time, she knew *she* was the one who the command had been intended for.

Flit glanced at Fortune, wondering if she could sense what was going on. As a telecoercionist herself, she would be more likely to sense it than Flit. Then again, Harmony was one of the most powerful telecoercionists the Underground had ever seen. Maybe Fortune didn't know.

Just as Flit had begun to think Fortune was oblivious to it, the other woman raised a hand to Flit's cheek and tilted her face down to press a soft kiss against her forehead.

"I know it's hard to hear, love," Fortune whispered, "but maybe it's time to let go." Then, pulling Flit to her chest in an embrace,

Fortune looked over her head. "If you'll excuse us, I think Flit needs some time to process this."

"Oh, of course," Divvy said gently, also apparently oblivious to how twisted the situation had become. "We'll get her reassignment sorted, and she can start tomorrow. She can take the rest of the day to compose herself."

"Come on. Let's go." Fortune gripped Flit's arm firmly enough that she couldn't pull away and guided her to stand. She looped her arm through Flit's elbow and led her out.

Flit wanted to turn around and ask Harmony what the fuck was going on, but she let Fortune lead her out of the room. The second they were in the corridor, the meeting room door shut between them and the two leaders, Flit hissed, "Did you sense that?"

"Shh, not here." Fortune tugged her arm to make her walk faster.

Flit pressed her lips together and nodded. For once, she was more than happy to keep her mouth shut.

15

SCRAPS

SCRAPS AND LIANA spent time going through the various policies he had pulled up earlier. After two hours of constant scrolling and reading, Liana got to her feet and stretched, rolling her neck and shoulders as Scraps closed the document they had just completed.

"Ok, I'll let the Security Officer know that we're good to go."

"Wait!" Scraps' stomach dropped, and his hand froze over the screen. His heart beat a little faster. He had learned enough about emotions over the past year or so to identify what he was feeling.

Anxiety.

"What is it?" Liana's tone held a flutter of exasperation.

"I think we missed a couple of child and adolescent education policies," Scraps blurted.

Liana rubbed her forehead. "I don't think we need to pre-read those, Brian. Perhaps we can go for a wander, get started in the areas we've already read up on, and then come back to the extra policies when we need to." She pointed to the computer. "I'm not quite as good at remembering these things as you are. There's no point in me reading them now."

Glancing between the screen and his friend, Scraps' shoulders fell. She was right. They should have stopped reading over an hour ago, but he kept pulling up policy after policy, feeling like he needed to know more. At least, that was what he told himself. Now that he thought back, they didn't need to read even eighty percent of what they did.

"You're right." Scraps stood up, swiping the screen to locked mode without looking at it. "It's time to get started. I propose starting at either end of the life span and then going chronologically rather than jumping around. Which age group should we handle first?"

"It, uh... it's been a rough news week for Chris and I on the children front." Liana pulled her neat black braid over her shoulder, fretting with the slight curl at the end, below her hair tie. She seemed to disappear into her own mind for a minute before she said, "I think I'd rather start with the seniors." She tapped the screen of her datapad to call their escort.

"Okay, sounds good!" Scraps sat back. He wanted to say something, to find some kind of platitude to let her know that she and Chris wouldn't have their life dictated by the Government forever, but a busy office space in the Derivate Training Facility was hardly the place.

Then, Scraps froze. Would the Derivate Training Facility have any policies referring to the code Chris and Liana had been given as justification for their inability to have children?

Before the Government had raided their apartment, Flit and Scraps had stumbled across the policies surrounding 6B, which contained the criteria classifying Derivate status, particularly of those born to non-Derivate parents. He and Flit had long discussions about whether to tell their friends and ultimately decided they would, but it was not the right time.

What would happen if he and Liana stumbled across that code here?

The thoughts were cast from Scraps' mind as he and Liana were joined by a neatly dressed Registered with a designation of KD-1325. The designation indicated that the man was a telekinetic who was one category lower than Scraps had been when he was capped and that he was the twenty-fifth born Derivate in the year one-hundred and thirteen, making him five years younger than Scraps.

Scraps watched the man as he introduced himself in a crisp, robotic tone and gestured for Scraps and Liana to follow him to the elevator bank. He couldn't help but stare as he tried to figure out if he had ever seen this particular macrokinetic in the training room. Of course, it was impossible for him to know every other Derivate who might have been in the facility at the same time as he had been, but sometimes, they crossed cohorts to help with training, and Scraps might have been paired up with him at some point.

As the trio walked towards the elevator, Scraps found his memories of training spilling over the high walls he had built around them after moving to the Underground. All the early morning wake-ups, the meals of bland, tasteless nutrition bars, hours upon hours spent in drills from the age of five all the way through to his graduation at the age of eighteen.

"Sir?"

KD-1325's voice broke though Scraps' memories, and he realised they reached the elevator and both the Derivate and Liana were waiting for him to join them inside.

"Oh, s-sorry," Scraps stammered, hustling into the carriage and watching the doors close.

Liana requested the level they needed to visit the adult education floors, and Scraps glanced at KD-1325. He had a neatly shaven face, as per Government regulations, but his dark hair was just a hint longer than the maximum length. His eyes were such a dark crimson that, in the right lighting, it would probably be easy to miss that he was a Derivate. Well, if it weren't for the white-outlined black tattoo of the Government's logo on the deep brown skin of his neck.

For an outlandish, illogical moment, Scraps wondered what the man might have been named if their world were different. He wondered what *he* would have been named. Scraps was merely a product of the Underground's naming conventions and Flit's sassiness. Would things have been different if his people were never forced to flee the main cities? If they weren't forced to identify themselves around the trait that was both a source of power and a cause for oppression?

When the doors to the elevator opened, Scraps felt as though the breath had been sucked out of him. Despite the sudden sense of déjà vu that spread throughout his body, he felt Liana watching him. He schooled his features into a neutral expression and followed her out.

Following his graduation, Scraps had moved out of this particular building and into one that held quarters for people working in his part of the city. He had returned once or twice for training reasons. Now that he thought of it, this floor had been the one he had spent the most time on the last time he had visited for some advanced law-enforcement training.

As KD-1325 led them over to the reception area, Scraps couldn't help but notice how *busy* the floor was. Usually reserved for training sessions that the local department sites were too small to handle, this level should have been a relative ghost town. Instead, the halls beyond reception were buzzing with people in their active-duty wear marching purposefully from place to place. The walls, lined with floor-to-ceiling windows designed to give an easy view of what was going on inside the spacious training spaces, were now opaque, with the wide double doors to each room shut for as far as Scraps could see down each corridor.

"Good morning. How can I help you?" the receptionist asked as they approached.

"We're here from the Research and Development Department to conduct the annual policy review," Scraps said. "We have clearance and would like our guide to be able to show us through the various rooms so we can ensure appropriate policies and procedures are being followed."

The receptionist looked down at her monitor and swiped through a few screens before nodding. "Access granted. You can ask KD-1325 for help with navigating our system."

"Thank you very much," Liana said with one of her usual warm smiles.

With that, KD-1325 turned to Scraps and Liana, awaiting their orders.

"Let's start with the room closest on the left. Each one needs to have the rest and training regulations required on a panel in the room, so we should check that," Scraps said, pleased they weren't put with a telepath.

The truth was, there were so many ways they could check that the rooms were compliant with that rule. Most required little more than a two second systems check on any network panel. Liana would have known this too. However, she didn't seem to want to argue. When her eyes met Scraps', there was a flicker of understanding in them. They were both on the same side, after all, and she had to be as curious as he was about what was going on. He wasn't sure what they would find, but any information to help the Underground, and possibly the Free Citizens, was welcome.

Their guide, apparently none-the-wiser to their needs or their deception, led them over to the room as directed. He automatically moved towards the communication panel and requested entry. It took a few minutes, but the door slid open, and he gestured for them to head in.

Thankfully, the training room was oriented so that the door was at the rear of the space, allowing any late arrivals or early leavers to come and go with minimum disruption. It also meant that very few of the uniformed Derivates sitting at training consoles knew to look up when Scraps, Liana, and KD-1325 entered.

The trainer at the front of the room, a middle-aged man with a horseshoe of hair around an incredibly smooth and shiny scalp, grazed his attention over them as he spoke.

"As you are aware, timely first aid is the key factor contributing the survival of a patient. If CPR or an appropriate wound dressing is provided whilst waiting for medical evacs or medics to arrive, then it means the professionals will better be able to do their job." The man raised his hand, the gesture triggering the blank screen behind him to a video with the basic steps of first aid. "Statistically, and thanks to the Government's excellent health programs, most calls the emergency services deal with are in relation to lifestyle diseases. However, you will learn skills beyond those required to tend to such maladies. The Government has mandated that all incoming field agents are aware of crisis-level medical intervention."

Scraps blinked. If he had to guess, there were probably around thirty trainees in the room. All were wearing uniforms from different and decidedly non-combat departments. He wondered what had gone so wrong with the job allocations that they needed to reassign this many people to this kind of thing.

"Ma'am? Sir? The panel is this way."

KD-1325's quiet, deep voice broke through Scraps' musings, and his shoulders tensed as he realised he was staring.

"Thank you." Scraps gently tapped Liana's forearm, as she seemed to be as transfixed as he was, and then led her to the panel they came for.

The two made a show of taking their time to inspect every part of the menu they could get away with while eavesdropping on the training behind them. Just as Scraps thought initially, the trainer went on to explain that the kind of injuries they would learn to treat —lacerations, piercings, crushes, internal haemorrhaging, and burns. Despite his earlier confusion, Scraps realised that this was just another sign of how the Government was changing operations due to the actions of the Free Citizens. He was surprised that they were trusting Derivates, other than microkinetics, to handle these kinds of matters. Then again, Derivates of all sorts were posted on every street corner and in every building with any level of importance, so if the Government were suspecting another strike, it made sense to have them prepared.

Which meant that the Government was concerned.

"I think we're ready to move to the next room," Liana whispered, stepping between Scraps and the presentation at the front of the room.

KD-1325 led them out of the room. The automatic response was enough to tell Scraps that the man was doing his job. He was listening in on them carefully enough to know when to move on without being asked.

The three left the room as quietly as they had come and then went into the next and the next and the next.

There were no less than three hundred Derivates assigned to duties like administration, traffic control, distribution, and city maintenance who were being trained in treating traumatic injuries. With only ninety-ninety Derivates being birthed every cohort and the expectation that individuals worked in some capacity between the ages of eighteen and seventy-five, the quantity of Derivates in training on one side of this floor alone amounted to around five percent of the entire Derivate work force. Pulling that many people from their duties was never done on this scale... and this was just one day.

Following what they found in the adult level, Scraps and Liana decided to inspect the adolescent level next. After checking out with the receptionist, Scraps and Liana made their way to the elevator under the guidance of KD-1325. They didn't need to wait long before they stepped in. Instead of letting himself dwell on the fact that they would be visiting a level of the building that Scraps was intimately familiar with, he thought about how interested Flit would be in what he had just seen. He didn't know how he was going to do it, but he had to find a safe way to get her a message, to get the Underground a message. Even though he wasn't exactly sure what was going on, he had a gut feeling this information was critical.

The receptionist on the next level was a tired, white-haired man who seemed like he just wanted a good nap. "Identification and purpose?" the man drawled, not even looking up.

"Brian Parkes and Liana Perez from the Research and Development. We've come to do our—"

A soft beep interrupted Liana as she spoke, and the receptionist said, "Access granted."

Liana blinked. "We just need to—"

"Access *granted*," the man repeated with an impatient and dismissive flick of his hand.

Liana looked between him and KD-1325.

"This way," KD-1325 said with the slightest shrug of his shoulder as he walked through the security gates beside the desk. "Where would you like to start?"

Scraps walked through and came up to stride alongside the Derivate. "In the simulator training rooms first. Those have the most stringent usage protocol," Scraps explained, instinctively walking off in the right direction and leaving his guide to follow *him*.

If KD-1325 thought his knowledge of the building was odd, he didn't say so. However, the look Liana gave Scraps was enough for him to slow his steps. It was hard to pretend he didn't know the building as well as he did. He could probably navigate his way through with his eyes closed. As it stood, he had to remember his cover. Brian Parkes had no reason to know the intimate layout of a building that Citizens were rarely ever granted permission to enter.

The simulator training rooms in this facility were like the ones in the Underground but ten times larger and far more technologically advanced. They were usually used to train Derivates in basic hand-to-hand combat. They were also used to generate fitness and obstacle courses, as the Government didn't really want their Derivates learning to fight too well.

All of Scraps' memories of the training regimen were wiped clear as they arrived at one of the largest simulator rooms and looked in through the viewing window. Inside, at the far end of the room, stood twenty adolescents in full assault combat fatigues. They were arranged in four rows, staggered formation. The rest of the room was filled with projections of city corners and dishevelled Citizens with improvised weapons. As Scraps and Liana watched, a young woman in the middle of the back row yelled a command, and the macrokinetics in the front row raised their arms to send a wave of force at the projected Citizens. As they stumbled, the second row raised their hands, and the walls of a building burst apart, water spraying out and splattering against their foes. The final row, made up of teleporters and most likely remote viewers, paired off. Each teleporter transported their partner directly into combat range before retreating again.

Scraps turned to KD-1325. "Regulations state that group tactics are restricted to numbers of no more than five, and the projections are never allowed to represent Citizens."

KD-1325 stared at Scraps for several long moments, his head tilted slightly to the side. "The rules have changed."

"When they changed the rules, did they also change the policies?" Scraps asked, figuring that was a much safer way to gauge how quickly the changes were put into place and how well thought through they were.

KD-1325 bowed his head apologetically. "I do not know. I can show you to the nearest consoles that will have the information, though."

"That sounds helpful."

It warmed Scraps to see that she was just as polite with the Derivate as she was with her Citizen colleagues.

Once more, Scraps and Liana followed KD-1325 into a training room. This one was far more chaotic as the sounds of simulated battle rang through the space, and holographic projections shifted all around them. Liana walked far closer to Scraps in this space, watching the training adolescents with a mixture of awe and wariness. The console at the rear of the room was easy to navigate, but there were no new policies or procedures to be found.

Liana leaned closer to their guide. "How long ago did the new training regimes start?"

"It is fairly recent. Perhaps three or four days ago," KD-1325 replied, voice halting.

"Did they make any announcements about changes?" Scraps asked, figuring it wasn't too off topic.

KD-1325 shook his head. "No. The timetables just changed. The security team was given a briefing the morning of the first training sessions, but that was only so we knew to expect a significant increase in traffic. There were a lot of changes after the attacks on the maglev system that were pushed through with little explanation."

Scraps listened on with growing interest as the Registered gave more information than he would have dared to in the same position.

The man seemed to cotton on to Scraps' interest and cleared his throat. "However, it is not my role as a Derivate to expect such. I just follow my orders."

Knowing better than to push, Scraps just nodded. "We can handle any issues that arise from upstairs. I think it might be worthwhile making notes of the conditions while we are here, and I also think it would be helpful to speak to someone in charge on this floor so we can get a better idea of hours and expectations." Scraps pulled a datapad out of his pocket and glanced at Liana with a grim sense of determination. "Let's get down to business."

16

———

FLIT

FLIT WAS quiet the entire trip to the Catacombs. She held onto Fortune's arm and let the older woman guide her along as her own mind skidded to alarming conclusions. However, it wasn't until they stepped into the cavernous burial site that Fortune finally stopped and looked at her.

"Where is Rook's stone?"

The mention of her beautiful, wonderful ex-lover was enough to shake Flit back to reality. She bit her lip. She'd been so caught up in her own distractions that she hadn't considered what this moment meant for Fortune.

"This way."

It was Flit's turn to do the directing. She wove along the familiar path through the headstones and dodged the damp stalagmites as necessary. Every few steps, there was an eerie whooshing sound from a nearby, underground river, or they could catch the rhythmic dripping of water from the large, rocky ceiling. The whole area was just as damp and musty as Flit remembered, and it was such a stark contrast to the crisp, fresh scent of the memorial forest just outside of the Hub.

When Flit took the final turn towards Rook's memorial site, she froze. A familiar figure with a perfect blonde braid stood by the stone.

"Ah, I was just about to leave. I thought I might have missed you," Swipe said, glancing between Fortune and Flit.

A sizeable, immature part of Flit wanted to ask Fortune if they could come back another time.

"We were just delayed a little. Control was busy," Fortune said, clearly having expected the telekinetic to be waiting for them. She and Flit walked closer to Swipe. "It turns out we were right. Not that I wanted to be, of course, but yes, Harmony was using telecoercion on Flit."

"Wait, what?" Flit stopped in her tracks and narrowed her eyes as she looked between the other two women. She had come to that conclusion herself as she'd made her way to the Catacombs, but she'd thought it would have been just as surprising to Fortune.

Apparently not.

"Oh, come off it. As if Scraps would ever turn on you." Swipe rolled her eyes. "And, even worse, as if you would ever believe he was capable of it."

Flit had a natural instinct to argue with Swipe, but she couldn't. At least, not about this.

"We suspected something was going on from the way your moods were ebbing and flowing," Fortune explained, her voice soft despite them apparently being alone in the cavernous space.

"Yeah, we just had to figure out who was fucking with you," Swipe added. The sense of victory that had twisted her lips into a smug grin faded, and she looked at Fortune. "I mean, I was hoping it wasn't Harmony. That... that just makes this even messier, right?"

Flit felt like she was several steps behind in the conversation. It was a distinctly uncomfortable vulnerability that had her gut churning.

"Yes, it does make matters more difficult," Fortune conceded. "However, we're not without—"

"Wait!" The word spluttered from Flit before she could stop it. "If she was using telecoercion on me, why didn't it work this time? Why did it work all the other times but not just then? Today was the first time I felt like I could argue with her. I would have if you weren't there."

Fortune shifted her weight from one foot to another, and Swipe tilted her head with interest.

"You mean, she tried it on you, and it failed?" Swipe's confusion reassured Flit that she wasn't quite as far behind as she'd thought.

Flit nodded, but it was Fortune who spoke first. "That's actually the other reason I wanted to go with you, Flit, and why I wanted to speak to you both here." Fortune gestured around them. Here was one of the spaces in the Underground that wasn't currently overcrowded or reduced to a busy thoroughfare.

"There's more?" Swipe let out a tired sigh.

"There's more." Fortune ran a hand through her grey-dusted brown hair. "And I want to tell you both, but I need you to promise you won't share this information with anyone. Also, you'll need to keep a tight rein of it in your thoughts."

Despite her frustration at Harmony's use of telecoercion and the confusion about what was going on, Flit was intrigued. "You can trust me."

"And me," Swipe added.

"Good." Fortune straightened up and took a deep breath. "The facility that Rook, myself, and the others were at was an experimental one. There were a lot of things they were testing, but the one they seemed most dedicated to was the development of a new psionic talent."

Flit's eyebrows rose. "But that's not possible. The psionic abilities have remained the same forever."

Fortune shrugged. "They were convinced that enough exposure to a newly discovered type of radiation would help turn certain powers into a new type, one that would cancel out others. They tried using it on so many of us, and it usually ended up turning on the host and killing them." She turned to Flit. "That's what happened to Rook, why he was on those life support machines. He survived a lot longer than most, but because he was..." She smiled fondly to herself. "...well, wilful... they went over the top with the exposure. For me, though, they got the balance right."

"Hold up." Swipe leaned closer. "You're saying *you* have this new ability?"

"Yes." Fortune straightened her shoulders. Some of her hair fell out of the low ponytail it was in and brushed against her olive skin. "In addition to telecoercion, which I'm having a little trouble accessing at the same level as I used to, I have the ability to block other powers. I need to be touching someone to be able to do it, but it's why Harmony's telecoercion didn't work today."

In a rare and surprising turn of events, Flit was speechless.

She thought back to when she and Fortune had been in that Control meeting room and distinctly remembered the comforting weight of Fortune's arm around her shoulder.

"Well, shit." Swipe let out a low whistle. "I'm guessing all this secrecy means that not many other people know?"

"Only Layla," Fortune conceded. "At least, down here, that is. The Government is fully aware it was successful. From the gossip I overheard when the experimenters thought I was sleeping, I'm the only success thus far."

"Wait!" Flit remembered the conversation she and Scraps had with Fortune in the shelter on the outskirts of Old City. "You mentioned at one point that the Government were experimenting on you with the same radiation they used to make the gun. Is that what caused your power to mutate?"

"Yes." Fortune frowned. "They must have done something to change the operational impacts of it, but I believe it's the same thing."

"Does your negation work on every ability?" Swipe asked.

"I've tested it against fellow telecoercionists and telepaths. The next phase was supposed to be the movement-based classes." Fortune looked between Swipe and Flit, a hint of encouragement in her eyes.

"Well, I'm wearing an inhibitor, so my powers won't work anyway." Flit smirked at Swipe. "Go on. I know you're aching to hit me with your best shot."

"My pleasure." With a laugh, Swipe raised her hands.

Draping an arm around Flit's shoulder, Fortune sighed. "Please start with something small. If we have to explain what happened in the infirmary, we may draw suspicion."

Flit didn't bother asking why her safety wasn't the main reason Fortune encouraged caution. It would be the least likely thing to change Swipe's intentions. The idea of getting caught was much more effective.

Swipe squared her shoulders and took a deep breath. "A slight push on the left shoulder."

Then, a breeze rushed past Flit's body, but it didn't even rustle her clothes. It was more like the *sense* or *intention* of a breeze.

"I'm sure Fortune didn't mean to go *that* easy on me," Flit muttered.

Swipe drooped her hands. "I didn't!"

"It was probably the equivalent of a good shoulder slam." Fortune tutted, shaking her head. "Not quite what I meant by starting small."

"Oh, come on. I have faith in you," Swipe said without a hint of remorse.

Flit laughed. For once, she didn't care that Swipe's comment was filled with the clear animosity that was a hallmark of their relationship.

It worked.

It really worked!

Flit turned to Fortune, the action making the other woman's arm drop from around her shoulder. "This is crazy! It has so many possibilities!"

Fortune raised both of her hands as she laughed softly. "One step at a time," she said gently. "I need to keep it quiet because I don't want to get discovered, and I can't help but think that there is way more to Harmony's use of telecoercion than just wanting a scapegoat."

The enthusiastic amusement that had taken over the conversation slipped into the background at the mention of a scapegoat.

"If Control had to blame someone, why pick on Scraps? Why not blame the Government?" Swipe put her hands on her hips as her neat brows furrowed in confusion.

"That would make people want to get back at them," Flit said slowly. "One of the reasons things returned to normal so quickly after Heft's betrayal was because people thought it was one of our own turning on us. Once Heft was dealt with, it was problem solved."

"Yeah, but they didn't read the extra stuff we found in Old City." Swipe kicked at some of the gritty ground beside her.

"I have a theory about that." Fortune cleared her throat. "Remember what Scraps told me about Heft?"

"Wait, you met Scraps? How?" Swipe crossed her arms over her chest.

Flit winced at the slip on Fortune's part. No one was supposed to know she'd seen Flit and Scraps in the Hub.

"The less you know about that for now, the better. I'll tell you when the time is right, and I can be certain we don't have any nosey mind readers poking around," Fortune promised, "but the real issue is that I was following a concerning trail of information before the Government found me and the fact I've picked up almost where I left off means I'm on to something."

Flit remembered the start of that conversation. She, Scraps, and Fortune had been interrupted by Hawkeye's arrival and hadn't been able to finish it. Still, the implication that there was a traitor in the Underground was clear.

Swipe's lips parted, and her eyes widened. "You think there's something dodgy going on down here?"

"It goes back to when we were in Longbeach." Fortune glanced at Swipe, a wariness drawing her crow's feet tight. "If I tell you this, you need to promise not to say or do anything. I'm handling it."

"Okay. I promise," Swipe said far too quickly.

Fortune hesitated, but then she sighed and started speaking. "A month or so before Longbeach was destroyed, we got a message from Control in the Underground telling us to move to this facility. They said it would be safer to have everyone under the same roof, so to speak, you know, to make it easier to protect everyone. I thought they got scared after we lost the camp at Hartford, but... we didn't want that. We were all comfortable where we were, and we saw no reason to move."

"Why would we?" Swipe's eyebrows furrowed. "At least we had access to sunlight and trees there. At least we had fresh air."

"Exactly." Fortune looked away, her eyebrows creasing. "We

told them we weren't going to move. Then, a month later, there's some sort of leak that led the Government right to us. Everyone assumed one of our agents had screwed up. After we settled in here, I decided to investigate. I had a feeling there was more at play than general Government Intelligence. All my leads pointed to something internal. My family was 'found by the Government' just as I was making headway. I think that means I was on the right track."

"I... I assumed it was the marriage application." Swipe glanced at Flit, pressing her lips together, guilt flushing her cheeks. "But you're saying you were betrayed?"

"I believe so. Our capture wasn't Flit's fault or Rook's. It was mine. I should have been more careful," Fortune said as she took both of their hands.

Swipe would never apologise, but as her eyes narrowed, that discomfort turned from shame to fury. "It was just perfect timing. Sick bastards must've figured it was a perfect cover."

"Agreed." Fortune gave Flit a reassuring squeeze before letting both of them go. "I must have trusted the wrong people to help me. I won't make that mistake again."

"*We* won't make that mistake." Swipe held her chin high as she stepped closer, every part of her stance letting Flit and Fortune know she was in.

Flit had spent her entire life believing the Underground was better than the Government, that they stood for freedom, and choice, and respect, but everything that had happened since Hawkeye and Sway had come up to retrieve her flew in the face of that. The fact they weren't on the recall list. The way her physical appearance had been tampered with without her consent. How the leader was using telecoercion to turn her against the man she loved to cover for something he didn't do. The lies they were telling everyone to keep them quiet and under control...

"What are we going to do about this?" Flit asked, throwing herself into the ring as well. There was no way she was going to let the leadership of the Underground get away with this. Not when so many people trusted them with so much.

Fortune's expression turned from one of concern to a determined grimace. "We're going to find out what's really going on here."

AN HOUR LATER, Flit, Fortune, and Swipe emerged from the Catacombs with a new sense of shared resolve and a plan. Given it was still early days since Fortune's return, they had to play it careful. The first thing they needed to do was decide who they could trust. Then, they needed to figure out how to get more information.

For Flit and Swipe, the question of who to trust was easy. They both agreed, without reservation, that the members of the Blue Team would have their back. There might have been squabbles and teasing within the group, but they were more family than colleagues. They were also, as Swipe was keen to point out, very doubtful of the lies Harmony and Divvy had been spreading about Scraps. They, like Swipe, had been trying to figure out how to go about getting him back, but they weren't willing to act without Flit being on their side.

As much as Flit wanted to get back to the surface to bring Scraps back down, they had to be clever about it. With most of the population invested in his guilt, it could potentially be a death sentence for him. They would need to clear his name, at least with some people who could help hide him, before they went out for retrieval. She wished that she could volunteer for the role, but it would be far too obvious it if was her.

One challenge Fortune predicted was that Harmony would continue to use her telecoercion on Flit. Despite Flit's desire to confront the woman, it would be useless. It was decided between Flit, Fortune, and Swipe that it would be best for Flit to continue playing along with the lies, at least for now. If Harmony and Divvy thought she was still under their control, they would have no reason to up their game. The only real concern was that Harmony would corner Flit when she was alone. It would cause too much suspicion if Fortune went everywhere with Flit. No amount of discussion between the three had been able to come up with a viable solution so, for the moment, Flit had resolved to roll with it. Now that Swipe and Fortune knew what was going on, they would help her remember the truth if she was caught out.

The retrieval of Scraps was only one of their concerns. They also had to consider that Harmony and Divvy had thrown the entire Underground into a lockdown with no end in sight. Thanks to that, they knew nothing about what was happening above ground. Fortune and Swipe both said that things at Longbeach had started off with small security breaches and "protective" and "proactive" withdrawal of agents. It hadn't been too much later that the site had been destroyed. Fortune's family and Swipe were among the very few survivors.

The thought that the Underground could go the same way as Longbeach terrified Flit. Right now, with so many of their exits cut off, they were sitting ducks. If there were genuine concerns that the Government had found them, they needed to make efforts to prepare, to run evacuation drills and find somewhere safe for people to run to, and to train people to fight.

Despite Flit's utter desire for an uprising, they weren't ready. If they faced the Government, they had to be sure they gave it their best shot. Swipe and Fortune agreed with her, and they had all decided that, if their leaders wouldn't prepare their people, they would have to do it themselves.

"So," Fortune said, glancing between Swipe and Flit as they stood in the tunnel outside of the Catacombs, "what are our priorities?"

Swipe rolled her shoulders back and held her chin held high. "We need to figure out what is going on above ground and why we're in a lockdown."

Fortune nodded.

"We need to figure out where they are keeping Scraps and what we need to do to get him back," Flit added, standing a little straighter. "Then, we need to prepare the others for a fight."

"We can do this." Fortune put one hand on each of their shoulders. "Now, let's get back to the main tunnels and go about our business."

Swipe looked at Flit. "You're on patrol with me this afternoon."

For the first time, the thought of a patrol with Swipe didn't make Flit want to groan. Maybe it had more to do with the fact she would be on patrol than who she would be going with, but Flit wasn't going to question it.

"I'd better go the Medbay to get this taken off, then. I don't want to be useless on patrol," Flit said, holding up her wrist with the bracelet inhibitor.

Swipe snorted. "Your lack of powers isn't what makes you useless."

There was little malice in the comment. It felt more like playful teasing.

Flit just rolled her eyes and started walking down the tunnel with Fortune, leaving Swipe scrambling to catch up.

THE MEDBAY WAS SURPRISINGLY quiet given the expanded population of the Underground. As Flit walked in, there were a few patients scattered on the beds with simple-looking ailments requiring basic first aid. Beyond that, though, it was a calm environment for Patch and Physie. Patch seemed to be going through some admin on one of the monitoring stations, and Physie was at the far side of the room restocking supplies.

"Flit!" Patch waved at her as he stood up from one of the monitoring consoles and walked over. "How have things been? Are you injured? You haven't started working yet, have you?"

The rapid-fire questions made Fit smile. It seemed her teammate's brother was pleased to see her. "I'm okay, thank you. Just here to see if I can get this..." She raised her hand in the air so that the metal inhibitor bracelet caught the light. "...taken off."

"Oh." With a frown, Patch gestured for her to follow him over to the monitoring station. "I haven't seen any orders come through for that, but let me just put a request in, and hopefully we can get it off as soon as possible." After tapping at the screen for half a minute, Patch glanced around. "Let's go to one of the private rooms while we wait for a reply." He stood up. "Physie, Flit and I are going to examination room three."

Flit wasn't sure exactly why they needed an examination room, but she wasn't about to argue. She could do with a quiet place to relax for a while where most people wouldn't think to find her. She'd grown tired of the looks of pity or betrayal she had been getting lately.

She followed Patch. She was about to ask how he was going, but the moment he shut the door behind them, he turned on her.

"What's going on with Scraps?"

Flit blinked. "What do you mean?" she asked, deliberately vague.

"He didn't do what they say he did," Patch said, leaning back against the wall beside the door. "I shouldn't bust confidentiality, but I had some great conversations with him before you guys went to the Hub. There was no way he was lying that whole time."

"Well, Harmony and Divvy have a video showing him in a Government building, so..." Flit trailed off, trying not to sound too unconvinced.

Patch raised a single eyebrow. "Right, because that's solid evidence he bombed the Underground." He shook his head and held up his hand. "Look, you can say what you need to say for whatever reason, but I know he wouldn't betray us. Do you want to know the only thing I'm more certain of?"

Flit should have cut the conversation off, but her curiosity got the better of her. "What?"

"He wouldn't betray *you*."

All of the breath was knocked out of Flit. The memory of Scraps miming *"I love you"* before being swarmed by Government Agents flickered through her mind. She looked up at Patch. The fact he said they'd had some good conversations made her wonder what they were about, but she knew better than to ask. All she knew was that, as she looked at Patch, his entire body was tense with the strength of his conviction.

"Thank you," Flit whispered. She swallowed and looked away from him. "I..." She stopped. She wanted to tell him more, she did, but she still knew too little. Maybe later, maybe after she, Fortune, and Swipe had some more concrete evidence and could make a—

"Don't feel like you have to say more than that," Patch said, as if picking up on Flit's indecision. He wasn't a telepath, but he was quite emotionally intelligent. "It's clear there's more going on here than meets the eye. You've got a habit of getting twisted up in all sorts of plots. I just want you to know that, if you need help, I'm here for you. And Scraps."

Flit looked into his eyes then. She really looked at him. He had the same smooth dark brown skin as his sister, Link, but his eyes were a softer shade of brown that stood out beneath his raven black hair. The smile that curved his lips was genuine and kind.

"I'll remember," Flit promised.

That seemed to be enough for Patch. He straightened and walked over to the console on the wall in the examination room. He tapped at the screen and grinned. "Ah, looks like we got the all-good. Why don't you take a seat on the bed, and I'll get that inhibitor off you."

Flit willingly did as she was told. She walked over to the bed and sat on the edge of it. Her feet didn't touch the floor, so she crossed her legs at the ankles to make sure she wouldn't squirm around too much. Patch tugged a loop off his belt which had a series of RFID tags hanging over it. He held it against the screen of the console and waited for half a minute for it to beep. Then, he walked over to Flit. She held her wrist out to Patch, who gently took her arm with one hand.

"I know it will be tempting to teleport off this bed and probably not stop after that, but... please don't. You haven't teleported for almost a week, and it's likely to sap your energy faster than usual. You need to take time to warm back up to your usual range, okay? Don't go burning yourself out."

"I won't," Flit answered, perhaps a little *too* quickly.

Patch just sighed as he held the RFID tag against her wrist until the bracelet unlatched. He caught it before it fell to her lap.

"You can probably just burn that little bitch of a thing," Flit said, taking her wrist back and rubbing her other hand against the skin that had been in contact with the metal.

With a snort, Patch shook his head. "Oh, if only I could. I hate that they're using these now. This isn't what we do down here."

Flit's mood sobered almost instantly at Patch's comment.

"There's been a lot of that going around lately," she said, reaching up and raking her fingers through her hair.

The hair they changed back to chocolate brown without consulting her.

She let out a sigh and then looked at Patch, determination shining in her eyes. "But I plan to change that very soon."

17

SCRAPS

"WELL, you two look like you've been hit by a hover truck," Chris stated as Scraps and Liana entered the apartment.

At the end of their workday, Liana had insisted that Scraps went home with her so they could have dinner together. She still seemed fixated on the idea that the microwave meals he was eating were not good enough. He had given up trying to tell her otherwise after the fifth round of rebuttals from her. Either way, he figured it would be good to discuss what they had seen at the facility in private.

"We've just spent the day at the Derivate Training Facility." Liana set her bag on a hook near the door.

Chris, still standing in the kitchen of the open-plan living area, leaned against the bench. "And they've taken to hitting all people from Research and Development with hover trucks now?"

Liana sighed. "I... I don't know what to say. I've can't process what we just saw."

"War," Scraps said.

The statement made both Chris and Liana gawk at him, open-mouthed.

"It looks as though they are preparing for war."

"Surely it's not that bad," Liana said in a tone that told Scraps she didn't even believe her own protest. Oh, he had no doubt she wanted to, but it was hard to rationalise what they had discovered at the facility.

"They've never allowed Citizen-like projections in training before. They're bringing in hundreds of Derivates from different, non-defensive departments to learn combat skills, and they are providing field medic training to every Derivate on staff." Scraps stiffened and pressed his lips together. "I do not know what else they could be doing."

Still staring, open-mouthed, Chris blinked. "They *what*?"

"It's true." Liana ran her fingers through her raven hair. "We've only looked at the adolescents and adults, but Brian is right. There are provisions for those two age groups to all go through combat and medic training over the next two weeks."

"That doesn't sound normal. Or right." This time, Chris looked to Scraps in hopes of an answer.

"It's definitely not either. They haven't even written the processes and procedures for it."

A spark of mischief flashed behind Chris' blue eyes. "Does that mean you can pull them up for it? Put a pause on their preparations."

That, Scraps thought, was a question he had been asking himself since he had realised what was going on.

His mind drifted to the two agents who were watching him and to the fact the Government knew he was part of the Free Citizens and was expecting information. Scraps wanted to do what he could to shut the war training down, but the risk was too great.

"I do not think that is a good idea," Scraps admitted, the words feeling like grit as they scraped up his throat and worked their way out of his mouth. "If we interfere, we will be brought under close scrutiny that I do not believe we can afford."

"But... we can get more information, right?" Liana sounded hopeful. "All of this will be very useful to Adam."

Scraps did not want to encourage this discussion. He wanted to maintain plausible deniability in case he was subjected to inspection by a telepath.

"Oh, Adam would want to hear about this for sure," Chris agreed. "We clearly scared the shit out of them if they are preparing like this. It also means we should probably be prepared for these lockdowns and curfews to be tightened."

"The Free Citizens won't like that," Liana muttered, face paling somewhat.

"No, which means that *we'll* need to start preparing for a fight too." Chris turned to Scraps, looking far too excited about the prospect of a battle.

Scraps knew he was right, but he wanted to protect his friends. He couldn't have this conversation with them. With Adam, yes. He didn't mind implicating Adam. He was dangerous, and the Free Citizens needed a better, less unhinged leader.

So, even though Scraps knew Chris was waiting for confirmation or some kind of plan, he just cleared his throat. "What's for dinner?" he asked.

Chris and Liana both stared at him for a moment before bursting into laughter.

Liana clapped a hand on his shoulder and led him to the kitchen. "Ah, Brian. You're hilarious."

Scraps did not mean to defuse the tension, merely change the topic. Still, he wasn't about to complain. He had achieved his goal, even if it wasn't quite the way he'd hoped.

He and Liana moved into the kitchen to help Chris sort out the plates, cutlery, and drinks so they could enjoy their meal.

That night, when Scraps got home, he was still shocked by the reality he had seen. Not only was the Government clearly readying themselves to fight the Free Citizens, but the knowledge that, if he were still Registered, he would be in that building with the others, preparing to kill Citizens who were doing nothing more than trying to fight for their freedom sickened him to the core. Despite his distaste of having to act as a double agent, he was keen to see what Adam would do with this new information. Did the Free Citizens have the numbers to fight back against the Government? Against the Derivates? Would they?

Pushing his thoughts into a neat little box in his mind, Scraps readied himself for bed. In addition to spending the next few days at the Derivate Training Facility, he would also need to return to the clothing factory to continue his part in Adam's plan. Whatever that was.

Despite his initial concern about reliving his past when he ventured back into the familiar facility halls, his childhood brainwashing was the last thing from Scraps' mind as he slipped into bed. He let out a heavy sigh as he turned his head to the left and ran his hand over the cold sheets beside him. More than anything, he wished Flit was there to discuss this with. He closed his eyes and told himself that he would just have to figure this out on his own.

THE NEXT DAY, it became painfully evident that Scraps' assumption was right. The rigorous training schedule continued for the adolescents and adults, and he and Liana spent most of their time looking at the conditions and scrambling to determine if there were any policy violations. Of course, there were vaguely worded clauses in every policy that referred to it being possible to alter approved training schedules in times of 'need'. It made their work a little more complex, but in the end, there was nothing they could do. Every concern they raised could be shot down due to it being a 'time of crisis'.

It was just before lunch on the third day of their investigation when Liana flopped back in her chair and groaned. "There's nothing we can do." Frustration seeped from every syllable.

"I believe that is quite on purpose," Scraps agreed in a low voice, glancing at the review she was typing on her screen and noting that was almost done, "but that is something we can discuss later. If you're finished it, we can begin work on reviewing the child, toddler, and infant levels."

Liana bit her lip.

Scraps had known her long enough now to comprehend the flicker of pain that passed over her face as he mentioned children. Scraps felt a squirming of guilt in his gut at the fact he and Flit had discovered the reason the Government had denied her and Chris procreation rights and had not told them.

At least, he thought, the next part of their investigation should be simpler policy wise. He'd gone through the care and education requirements for Derivate children, and they were fairly straightforward.

"KD-1325?" Scraps called out, causing the man standing just outside their cubicle to turn around to face them. He had been assigned to guide them again. "We're ready to visit the child education levels now."

"Very well. Please follow me."

Seeming almost entirely unenthusiastic, Liana slid out of her chair. She retrieved her datapad off her desk and shook out her limbs. "Lead the way."

Scraps gave her what he hoped was a reassuring smile before following her and the Registered out of the office space and towards the elevators. Once more, Scraps felt as though he was going back in time when they stepped into the reception area of the education levels. Of course, as a child growing up here, he and the other Derivates had been made to use the stairs at the rear of the building to access these levels as part of their daily movement requirements, but he had still seen enough of the reception area when he had been chosen to run errands that it brought back all kinds of memories.

After being ushered past the reception area, Liana commented that this level did not look all that different to the adolescent education levels. She was, Scraps decided, right. The layout was similar, and there was no décor or concession that the space was for children beyond slightly smaller chairs. It lacked the bright colours and teaching displays of Citizen schools and the chaotic art and paintings scrawled across educational areas in the Underground. The rooms were just as sleek and clinical as any other space in the building.

"Oh, now that's cute."

Scraps turned to see Liana looking into one room set up like a lecture theatre. A large screen at the front played some sort of geographical introduction to the layout of the city and what was probably the entire birth cohort of ninety-nine eight-year-olds were sitting at their desks, tapping at datapad screens and taking notes.

Brows furrowed, Scraps stepped closer and pressed his hand against the window. He thought back to the children he'd met in the

Underground, the lively Seeker, Kindling, and their friends. There was no way they would have sat down as calmly as this group of children.

"Cute but not natural," Scraps said with a deep frown. "The control chips are likely set up to enhance docility and focus. Those children look around eight."

Liana winced. "How long are their lessons?"

"Ninety minutes," Scraps and KD-1325 said at the same time.

KD-1325 looked at Scraps, his features neutral, but curiosity flickered behind his eyes.

"They usually have a schedule of five ninety-minute lessons per day. All breaks are ten minutes, with the exception of the break between the third and fourth session, which is forty-five minutes," Scraps rattled off, knowing the schedule by heart.

KD-1325 was still watching, but Scraps was beyond caring.

"Are... are all the lessons like this?" Liana turned away from the window this time and directly addressed KD-1325, her forehead creased with concern.

"No," the Registered conceded. "The first lesson in the morning or last lesson in the afternoon, depending on the age group, is for ability training. Those usually require more active participation."

As Liana asked more questions, Scraps turned his attention to the room full of children. There was an armed Citizen supervisor at the front of the room, but apart from that, there were no teaching staff in the space. That many children should have been split up into at least four groups, each with their own tutor.

"I am guessing the lack of staff here is due to the extra training going on for adults," Scraps surmised, not realising he was interrupting the discussion that had continued without his input.

"That is correct."

Scraps was about to ask to see another room when his eyes were drawn to the screen at the front of the lecture theatre. The grid map of the city zoomed out to show how neatly organized the towering buildings were from a bird's-eye view. Scraps had seen the layout like that a hundred times over, but this one was different. Instead of just highlighting the main buildings, like Centre One and the

Derivate Training Facility, this had green areas pinpointed on dozens upon dozens of buildings across the map.

"What is that?" Scraps asked.

Then, without asking for permission or waiting for it to be granted, he walked past KD-1325 and Liana into the room. The armed Citizen glanced over, but when KD-1325 appeared at Scraps' shoulder, he looked away, disinterested.

The even-toned voice-over that was used for automated educational modules sounded through the room. "Please use your datapad to record the safe houses across the city. You will be tested on these at the end of the module. They will be important in cases of civil unrest as you must know where to regroup."

Scraps' stomach churned as rage surged in him.

The green lights on the map changed, stretching out into square outlines. Each encapsulated four blocks of the city before stopping, the perimeters throbbing as they formed a grid over the city.

"Each of these cells constitutes a group you will be assigned to. Just in case reassignments are required during a situation, you will need to be aware of the limits. Please take time to shade these in on your datapad maps."

"Brian?" Liana's voice was soft with concern.

Scraps looked at the map, trying to memorise the boundaries of each group and the location of each safe house. He wished he could take a screen recording of it all, but that would get him into a lot of trouble.

"Yes?" he asked, without looking away from the screen at the front of the room.

"I-I... um..." The uncertainty was thick in Liana's stammering.

Scraps didn't have the mental capacity to respond to her concern. He knew they would only get a few minutes to copy down things like this on their personal datapads, and he didn't want to waste a second. In allowing them in during this lesson, the Government had unwittingly exposed he and Liana to a map of where their people might be in case of an *incident*, and he had to take advantage of that.

"Sir, Ma'am, is there anything I can help you with?" The Citizen officer stepped between Scraps and the screen.

Barely managing to stop himself from gritting his teeth, Scraps fixed the Citizen with a forced smile. "We're here to review the policies and procedures surrounding the education and housing of these children. It appears their new study schedule is beyond said policies. Can you please direct us to an appropriate overriding policy or a senior member of staff to discuss this matter with?"

The man blinked at Scraps. "Uh, I can tell you who the manager is," he offered, glancing at KD-1325, as if that really should be his job.

"No need. We'll just be moving on. Thank you." Liana wrapped her hand around Scraps' forearm and led him from the room. When the door slid shut behind them, she looked up at him. "What happened in there?"

Scraps could not answer that honestly given their location. Instead, he gestured to the next room. "Nothing," he lied, "but we should continue our investigation. Have you recorded the breaches of the policy in the new schedule?"

Liana held up her datapad. "I have. Would you like to see them?"

"No, I trust you," Scraps said without a second thought or hint of irony. "We should continue, though. I have a feeling there are more breaches we have yet to uncover."

With a nod of agreement, Liana turned and led the way to the next room.

Scraps used the silence of the walk to go over those safe house locations again. The pattern was simple to recall if he was able to remember the four closest surrounding Centre One. He just hoped whatever else they found on this level did not wipe that memory from his mind.

18

FLIT

BEING BACK on patrol *should* have felt like coming home.

Flit might have even relished it if things had not changed so much.

Having Swipe as her patrol partner was only one of the problems. Granted, she and the other woman had reached a silent agreement that they would not verbally snipe at each other en route, but that just meant they were both working in awkward silence.

The patrol routes were significantly different too. Flit could understand why as they made their way through the tunnels. It was impossible to ignore just how much destruction had been caused by the last round of collapses. With only one exit route left, almost all their patrols focused on monitoring the mid-level tunnels surrounding their main habitation levels.

Each tunnel was surveyed and checked at least three times a day. Before she had started her first patrol a few days prior, Flit had been given a rundown of their new priorities. They were to check the pipe pressures as usual, but they were also required to look for any odd items or new plumbing or electrical connections. The Intelligence team's experts were still excavating and analysing the destroyed tunnels, but the consensus was that bombs had been planted on key pipeline junctures that lead to critical failures in surrounding areas.

Flit and Swipe slowed their pace as Flit ran one of the sensor devices over a service pipe. All of the changes to prevent future explosions seemed especially redundant if Scraps really had been the one to cause them as he was now unable to return. Still, she supposed Harmony and Divvy were creating a smokescreen to cover up the fact they probably had no idea who it really was. At least it was keeping people in the Underground calm enough.

"This all looks good," Swipe said as the sensor beeped and flashed a green light at them.

Flit tucked the device back in her pocket. "Then let's head back to base."

Even though it annoyed Swipe to no end, Flit did her usual leap-frog teleporting as they made their way back to the main tunnels. The short hops were a good way for Flit to flex her powers again after wearing the inhibitor for days. Swipe just sighed and rolled her eyes but didn't bother commenting on it. It also had the bonus of distracting Flit from the awkward lack of conversation.

Their route meant they had to return to the armoury via the tunnels that led them past the Intelligence rooms. Rounding the corner to the main entry, Flit and Swipe paused. Two people were leaning against the wall. A man and a woman were standing very close, the man's hand resting against the woman's hip.

"Hawk? Layla?" Flit called out, smirking when they sprung apart as if they were oppositely charged magnets. "Nice to see you both."

"Coming to visit Hawkeye for his break, Layla?" Swipe asked, also apparently unable to resist the urge to jump in on the light-hearted teasing.

"O-Oh, uh—"

"No, actually, we were waiting for you two," Hawkeye said, glaring at them both as Layla tried to stutter out a reply. "You're late."

Flit nodded slowly. "Oh, right. Yeah. That's totally what it looked like."

Hawkeye's face started turning red. "Or you could just piss off, and I'll get back to work."

"Oh, Hawkeye, you're so cute when you're flustered." Swipe winked at Layla. "Don't you agree?"

It was Layla's turn to blush.

Hawkeye's glare only hardened. "We need to chat. We'll go to the armoury with you. It should be empty."

Instead of giving into the banter any further, Hawkeye turned and led Layla, Flit, and Swipe through the tunnels and towards the place where the Security teams stored their gear. Sure enough, when they arrived, the space was empty, and the long shiny steel table in the middle was clear and clean. Thanks to the patrols being tightened around the living zones, it was rare that anyone returned covered in roach guts or bat shit anymore.

Flit removed her daggers from her hip holsters and set them down. "What was so important that it couldn't wait until dinner?" she asked as she carefully detached the flame grenade bandolier from her belt.

"I've got an offer from Shadow for you," he said, looking between Flit and Swipe.

"The same Shadow who was more than happy for Scraps and me to be left off the recall list?"

Hawkeye sighed. "There's only one Shadow."

"Then you can tell *Shadow* to fuck off."

Beside Flit, Swipe paused. Her hands hovered over her utility belt as her neatly shaped brows creased. "But... you're like obsessed with Shadow. You've been licking his boots for as long as I've known you."

While Hawkeye snorted a laugh at Swipe's comment, Flit cast Swipe an annoyed glare. "Did you not just hear me say that he was happy for Scraps and me to get stuck in the Hub?"

"He doesn't make decisions unilaterally, you know. He's part of a team. Like all of us are down here," Swipe muttered as she returned to disarming herself.

"The offer extends to both of you," Hawkeye said, pushing past the tension as he put his hands on the bench and jumped up to sit on the edge. "All of us, actually."

"Me too?" Layla's eyes brightened. She tilted her head to the side in curiosity, a few strands of her red hair falling from her neat braid.

"Yeah, of course. Why else did you think I made you wait in the tunnel with me?" Hawkeye asked.

Layla's shoulders fell, and she shrugged.

"Oh, it's not that," he said. "I just wouldn't waste your time if—"

Swipe let out a low whistle. "Hawk, stop. You're just digging yourself a deeper hole."

Hawkeye scratched the back of his neck.

Flit felt a little sorry for him. She shook her head. "Please, just tell us whatever it is you wanted to tell us."

That perked him back up. "He's got some... extracurricular ability training he would like to offer us all."

Whatever Flit was expecting, it wasn't that.

"Why extracurricular?" Swipe asked, sounding interested. "Why not a reassignment?"

"Because reassignments are all very official, and Shadow wants this low-key. Besides, if you get reassigned, we lose more Security operatives, and we can't afford that right now," Hawkeye explained in such a smooth, easy tone that it all sounded quite logical.

"And why didn't Shadow bring this offer to us himself?" Flit asked.

Hawkeye raised an eyebrow at her. "You really need to ask after that reaction?"

"And what, he was thinking you'd be able to smooth it over?"

"Can't I?" Hawkeye challenged.

As much as Flit wanted to roll her eyes at her friend, she couldn't. The prospect of something extracurricular from Shadow, despite how much of an arsehole he'd been a few months ago, was alluring, and if he was desperate enough to send Hawkeye as a messenger, it must be important to him. Flit couldn't help but feel a surge of power in this situation.

"Okay, I'll bite. Tell us more, please," Flit conceded. She set her bandolier in her locker and then leaned against it, crossing her arms over her chest as she waited for Hawkeye to fill them in.

"Well, Shadow wants to gather more information than his current team and role restrictions will allow." Hawkeye's voice dipped low as he gestured for everyone to step in closer. "He has a lot of operatives, but none with the kind of…" He glanced at Flit. "…spark and motivation that we have here."

"I tried to give him plenty of information over the past few months, and he didn't want a fucking bar of it."

"Well, I guess he's changed his mind." Hawkeye shrugged. "Either way, we'll all benefit from training and information. Layla, Shadow also wants to learn a lot more about the network of Citizen-born Derivates you were in touch with. He'll help you work on your micro skills too. From what he's heard, you've got a lot of raw power, but he wants to help you harness it."

"I've never had any formal training. I'm up for it. The people who helped me out in the Hub could really use some allies too."

"Do you think they'll want to join us?" Flit asked, looking at the redhead.

"I can't speak for all of them, but they certainly don't want to join the Government," Layla said with a shake of her head. "It'll be hard to get hold of them, though. They stay hidden for a reason."

"I'm sure we'll figure something out," Hawkeye said with a reassuring smile. He reached out and squeezed Layla's hand before turning to Swipe. "As for you, he thinks you're our best shot for training up a macro who can work without overt gestures. Your control is excellent. Your yield is high. If he can help you get those gestures under wraps or help you move to mental control only, you'll be invaluable."

"I'm already invaluable." Swipe bristled for a moment, clearly wanting Hawkeye to know that she wasn't keen on his choice of words, before she let her posture relax. "But… if he thinks I can get to gesture-free, then I'm down for it."

"And what about me, then?" Flit asked, seeing as the other two were in.

"One word," Hawkeye said with a wicked grin. "Translocation."

"Ah, fuck."

Flit could have resisted any sort of temptation other than that. She hung her head, defeated. She would probably have to kiss Shadow's arse the whole time, but the ability to teleport to all sorts of locations—seen or unseen—was too good to pass up, especially when she needed to rescue Scraps.

"So, I take it you're in?" Hawkeye was more than a little smug, and Flit nodded. "Great. Shadow's wants us to meet up with him tonight. He's booked out a VR Suite in the Residence, and he's going to write it off as some sort of simulation training. I don't quite know how they'll keep it private, but I saw him talking to Cogs earlier, so she'll probably work her micro-magic."

A thrill of excitement ran through Flit despite her reservations. She wasn't sure what Shadow would be asking for in return, but he knew what she was like. Most people in the Underground did. She figured Shadow wouldn't have wanted her in on his plans if he didn't think she would be good for it. The best thing, Flit thought, was that this was clearly off the record. Off the record plans were the best kind.

"I'll see you there," Flit said with a determined nod.

"Great." Hawkeye stepped back and smiled at Flit. Then, he turned his attention to Layla. "Want me to walk you back to the Residence? The tunnels between here and there can be a little confusing."

Flit shook her head as she turned back to her locker and took off her jacket. She hung it up.

Swipe walked over, opening the locker just to Flit's right. "Think he's gonna take her via forty-two on the way back?"

Flit snorted with laughter.

19

SCRAPS

IF THERE WAS one thing Scraps was certain of by the end of the day, it was that the Government were preparing for war.

It has been a theory before, when he and Liana had reviewed the adult and adolescent units, but the real confirmation came from the child floors. In addition to teaching them where the safe houses were in the city, their regular classes covering literacy, numeracy, and civics were all replaced by extra power training and the euphemistically named "team-work tactics class".

It took Scraps and Liana the remainder of the day to work their way through the policies. It truly horrified Scraps that children as young as five were being prepared for battle. He would have thought they would keep the children somewhere safe, somewhere central. Instead, they were planning to send them onto the streets.

A twisted, dark part of Scraps thought it was a rather clever strategy. Even the most Derivate-hating Free Citizens would have trouble fighting back against children.

Scraps shook his head to rid himself of that thought as he rode up the elevator of Liana's apartment building with her. Once again, she had invited him over for dinner after work. He didn't even really think about his answer. He had been too caught up with his own thoughts as he followed her home.

When the elevator stopped, Liana led the way to her apartment, and the moment they were inside, she walked over to the couch and collapsed onto it.

"That was worse than I could have imagined," she said, sounding so, so tired.

"Liana, babe? You home?" Chris walked down the hallway and smiled as he saw Scraps. "Hey Brian. I take it you had another long day?"

Scraps just nodded in reply.

"They are training kids to fight, Chris," Liana said, lifting her head off the couch and looking at him.

"Isn't that what you said yesterday?"

"No," Scraps said before Liana could speak. "Yesterday, we were talking about children thirteen and up. Today, we saw them training kids from the age of five."

The usual, happy-go-lucky smile Chris wore faltered. He ran his hands over the casual pants he was wearing. "Surely not? That... I-I..." he stammered to a stop, speechless.

"We can't fight kids." Liana sat up straighter. "I know we want to bring the Government down, but I cannot fight against someone who isn't even old enough to drink." The conflict in her voice was evident, and her face was pale.

"Derivates are never allowed to drink."

Liana looked at Scraps, her dark brows furrowing deeper. He wasn't sure what he was hoping to achieve with his comment, but it wasn't intended to further confuse her.

Chris walked over to sit beside his wife and gestured for Scraps to join them in the living room. "I guess it was too much to ask that the Government keep it between the adults, huh?"

"I am not surprised." Scraps walked over and sank onto an armchair. He looked at the full-length window wall of Chris and Liana's living room and out at the city beyond. "They want to maintain control. They will do anything within their power to do so. They've been brainwashing and enslaving children for a century. Why wouldn't they use them in a battle?"

Scratching his head, Chris' frown deepened. "Well, when you put it like that..."

"I wish we could invite them to join us," Liana said, looking down at her lap.

"What?" Scraps tilted his head to the side.

Liana shrugged. "I don't know. I just think… Here we are, ready to fight for our freedom, but we have nothing to complain about compared to the Derivates."

Scraps watched his friend closely. He already knew that Chris and Liana did not waste time belittling Derivates, but what Liana was now saying was something else entirely.

"I wonder if they hate the Government as much as we do?" Chris leaned closer to his fiancé.

Scraps pressed his lips together and kept his thoughts to himself on that particular matter.

"I don't know." Liana gave a light, helpless shrug. "The one who has been showing us around, KD-1425—"

"1325," Scraps corrected, tightly-pressed-together-lips be damned. Both Chris and Liana glanced at him.

"Ah, sorry. KD-1325 did slip us little bits of information I doubt his supervisors would approve of," Liana continued, a slight blush on her porcelain cheeks. "I don't know if that equates to him hating the Government, but…"

"I've noticed a few Derivates not being quite as honest as they should be, too," Scraps conceded.

Chris leaned back in the couch, crossed one arm over his chest, and rubbed his chin with the other. "I wonder if that's something we should look into? How would we even go about it?"

"We need to consider what Adam would think about that. From what I've seen, he would see this as a Citizen movement," Scraps suggested. There was something about Adam's zealotry that made him feel as though anyone who did not fit into his narrow view of the world would be seen as opposition.

"We'll have to think about it," Liana agreed. Then, her shoulders fell. "But I'm worried about tomorrow. Surely there isn't anything the babies and infants can be trained to do."

Scraps chewed over her comment. He didn't remember being that age himself, but he did recall the few times he had gone to that level to run errands throughout his childhood and adolescence. He hadn't thought anything of the bland walls and strict, unaffectionate caregivers at the time. Now, he had seen the way Citizen and Underground children grew up, and he knew that what the Derivates had was a poor comparison.

"They may not be training them for war, but have you seen how Derivate infants are raised before?" Scraps shifted in his seat. He considered, once more, the fact that any child Chris and Liana had might be a Derivate.

"Not really. Why?" Liana asked.

"It's not what you would be used to seeing for Citizen babies. It's... efficient."

Chris frowned, lines creasing in the corner of his eyes. "Efficient?"

Scraps smoothed his palms over the legs of his pants as they grew unexpectedly clammy. "They aren't really raising children. They are raising permanently indentured workers. Things like affection, emotional nourishment, and leisure are not a priority."

"But they're children," Liana protested, looking genuinely dismayed. Chris took her hand in his own.

"Not in the eyes of the Government. They are future workers, nothing more." Scraps' muscles tensed. He hated the words, but they were the truth. "Did you learn much about Derivate life when you went to school?"

He and the other Derivates had spent years learning about the Citizens and their rights, and their privileges, and how they were a higher calibre of human beings. He had always wondered what the Citizen children learned about Derivates.

Liana frowned, but Chris shook his head. "Ah, no. Not really. We learned that their powers are dangerous and that they aren't human like the rest of us. That's why the Government has to be so careful with them. That's it." He turned to Liana, who gave a kind of helpless shrug, as if that was the same for her.

The tension in Scraps' jaw radiated to his head and made it ache. That was all? Derivates spent every moment of their lives dedicating themselves to Citizens, and those Citizens knew nothing about them.

"Why? Did you learn something different in Eastbay?" Liana's voice was gentle. Coaxing, almost.

That was when Scraps realised he had made a mistake. His hands clenched at his thighs as he stuttered, "Uh, no. N-Not really. I just did my own research. I was curious, I guess."

"Ah, okay." Liana nodded. "Do you mean before you were assigned the facility review?"

"Yes," Scraps admitted, partially because he had already lied enough, but he was also curious about their reaction. "I thought the way they were treated seemed unfair, but I wanted to have all the information before making that decision."

"And?" Chris urged.

"I was right."

The words came out sounding so very simple. So matter-of-fact.

They didn't surprise Chris and Liana, either. He looked at his friends, at the two Citizens he had come to trust above all other non-Derivates, and the lack of judgement in their eyes was reassuring. Liana, in particular, he had found to be so empathetic and understanding. She was a kind-hearted, gentle person. He thought of her reaction to the facilities thus far and imagined her heart breaking even further tomorrow. Then, he wondered if there would be anything about code 6B in the facility, and guilt gnawed at him.

"Liana, what we see tomorrow will likely be emotionally challenging," Scraps started slowly.

Liana's grip on Chris' hand tightened. "It was bad enough seeing adults being treated like that, and then the children today..." She looked away, her eyes welling with tears.

"If you want to call in sick, I can finish the review alone," Scraps offered. It wouldn't be easy for him, but at least there would be no surprises.

Chris shifted so that he was looking at Liana more directly. "There's no shame in taking a step back when you need to. No one outside of this room has to know," he said in a low voice.

Biting her lip, Liana shook her head. "I can't do that. My life has been comfortable because of the protection provided by Derivates. It would be so disrespectful to step back now. If this is the life I live and the privilege I have, I owe it to them to learn about what it has cost."

The words hit Scraps and knocked the air from his lungs. Never before had he heard such a thing from a Citizen. Never before had he heard such respectful sentiments.

He swallowed and took a deep breath, committing to his next statement before he could change his mind. "There's something else."

Both of his friends looked over at him, a little surprised by the interruption, as though the intimate conversation made them forget there was someone else in the room.

"There's more?" Chris asked. There was enough strain in his tone to indicate that another piece of news might just be too much, but Scraps had committed, and it would seem odd to fall silent now.

"There was not a good time to tell you this until now. Ava and I wanted to, but things kept happening with the Free Citizens, and..." He paused, knowing he was about to cross a line.

Chris and Liana both leaned in, hanging on his words.

"And?" Liana urged.

"It is highly classified, but there is evidence that Derivacy is a spontaneous genetic mutation, not merely an inherited trait." Scraps paused and watched his friends for their reaction. They just blinked at him, so he added, "Ava and I think it is the reason the Government insists on genetic matching before procreation. They need to avoid the chance that a Derivate child will be born to Citizen parents. It ruins their entire narrative."

Chris and Liana paled.

"You mean they won't let us have children because they may be Derivates?" Chris asked.

"That is what Code 6B refers to."

Liana's mouth opened and closed several times.

"We're not the only people who got coded. We've been speaking to others who have dealt with the same thing." Chris' voice grew short and hot. "This is... I—" He stopped, turning to his to his fiancé. Any further protest died as he saw the look in her eyes.

"I don't care," she whispered fiercely. "I don't care if they'll be

Derivates. I'll love them all the same. I just want a child with you." Tears sprung to her eyes and spilled down her cheeks.

Suddenly, Scraps felt like an imposter. He cleared his throat. "I, uh... I think it is time for me to go home. I will see you tomorrow, Liana."

Scraps gave them an awkward nod as he skirted around them.

20

FLIT

"WHERE ARE YOU OFF TO?"

Flit paused, frozen next to the front door of the apartment she was sharing with her parents. It had been a very, very long time since her parents had questioned her comings and goings in the Underground, and her mind reeled back almost ten years. The natural defensiveness she felt when people questioned her reared up, and her shoulders instinctively tensed.

When Flit turned around, she saw the excited and curious expression on her mother's face, and her posture softened. She wondered if her defensiveness had less to do with being questioned and more about the fact she was doing something she really shouldn't be doing. Even if Shadow was high up in the chain of command, he was clearly convening these meetings outside the usual channels.

"Just catching up with some friends in the VR suite," Flit lied.

Flit's father perked up. "It's good to know you're getting out of your room more. We were starting to worry about you for a minute there."

"I may fall hard, but I bounce high," Flit said with a grin and a wink that made her parents' smiles widen.

"Well, enjoy your night. We'll probably be asleep by the time you get back," her mother informed her.

"Is that code for 'don't make a lot of noise when you return'?"

Tinker laughed. "Yes, pretty much. Good night, Flit."

"Good night, Mum. You too, Dad."

Flit turned and opened the door, a warmth blooming in her chest as she made her way down the halls of the Residence. As much as she and her parents could get on one another's nerves, leaving them behind in the Underground to go undercover in the Hub had been one of the most difficult things she had done in her life. She had been too busy in her time up there to think much about it, but since returning, the truth of what she had been missing was so clear. She had no doubt she would have uncovered that if she spent more time in the Hub.

Instead, Flit thought about the other gaping chasm in her chest as she made her way through the graffiti and art-laden halls of the Residence to get to the VR Suite. It felt wrong trying to live life like normal in the Underground while Scraps was stranded and possibly in danger in the Hub.

His face flashed in her mind, his lips moving as he admitted that he loved her, and her hands shook. She balled them into fists and shoved them in her pockets. It wasn't like she was being idle. She, Fortune, and Swipe had a plan, and she was going to start working on translocation. She was going to rescue him. Soon. She would accept no other outcome.

"Hey, you're early!" Hawkeye's cheeks flushed as Flit walked into the suite, and he jumped up from the bench he was sitting on, elbow to elbow with—

"Hi, Flit." Layla leaned back against the wall and tried to look casual.

The room was large enough to host a party of eight VR players. As such, there was plenty of seating available. There was no need for Hawkeye and Layla to sit quite so closely. Unless, of course, they wanted to.

The itch to make a teasing comment was so visceral that Flit twitched with the effort it took to stop herself. "Hey, guys. All good?"

"Yeah, we were just discussing a few things that have come up on the news recently." Hawkeye walked to the opposite side of the room to make a show of fiddling with some of the VR controls.

Settling into the spot Hawkeye had just vacated, albeit with a bit more space between herself and Layla, Flit raised an eyebrow. "Oh? Anything interesting?"

"They've tightened their security significantly. The attacks of that rogue band, the Free Citizens, must have really rattled them," Layla supplied.

Flit noted her enthusiasm. "I bet. Any more news on that group?"

"They've been quiet. Nothing new." Hawkeye watched Flit warily. "I doubt the Government would really report anything anyway."

"True." Flit's fingers drummed against her knee.

Having Hawkeye still in Intelligence was helpful. The rest of the Underground had been cut off from accessing any live news from above, so he was in a privileged position.

"Anything suspicious in the news that sounds like it could have been a cover-up for Free Citizen activity?" she asked.

"Not real—"

Hawkeye was interrupted as the door opened, and Swipe walked in with Shadow following behind her.

"Ah, look what the cat dragged in." Flit narrowed her eyes at Shadow as he walked straight over to the control panel where Hawkeye was.

"I happen to think cats are rather enchanting creatures," Swipe said, leaning against the wall opposite where Flit and Layla were.

"Flit's ire is directed at me," Shadow drawled. He tapped the controls, and the glass on the walls turned opaque.

Flit didn't bother denying it. "I may be willing to forgive you if you pull through on this whole translocation thing."

"Ah, I see you had to pull out the incentive," Shadow muttered to Hawkeye.

Hawkeye raised his hand defensively. "Even being her best friend doesn't get me a free pass."

"I do intend to uphold my offer to train you. Whether you can achieve it or not, well, that's up to you," Shadow said. If he had paused, Flit would've swore at him, but he continued, "However, I want to thank you all for being here. As I asked Hawkeye to mention, I want you to keep this training confidential. There are a lot of moving pieces in the Underground, but I am relying on you all to exercise your discretion."

"What's in it for you, though?" Swipe crossed her arms over her chest and watched him warily.

"The knowledge that we'll have appropriately trained operatives ready to act when we need them."

Well he certainly isn't mincing his words.

"Ready to act?" Layla's voice was wary as she sank back.

"As much as I would love to give you more detail, I can't," Shadow said, voice firm. "All I can say is that I need to know there are people in the Underground who are ready to fight. I understand that, apart from Hawkeye, you're all cut off from what is happening on the surface. That can lead to a false sense of security."

"Then why aren't we preparing everyone?" Flit teleported to her feet so that she was leaning against the wall beside Hawkeye.

A simple raised eyebrow from Shadow was enough to tell Flit all she needed to know. No one wanted the rest of the Underground to think they were preparing for a fight. Flit thought this was a terrible idea, but arguing would only make Shadow rethink his offer.

"Okay, so how is this going to work?" Flit pushed herself off the wall and bounced from foot to foot, eager to get started already.

"I'll be training you myself with Hawkeye's assistance," Shadow said, glancing at Flit. "After Hawkeye's done helping us, I'm going to ask Scope to help him work on his range and acuity." Then, he turned his attention to Layla. "I've enlisted Cogs to help you. She's probably the best micro we've got, and she knows how to keep a secret."

"And me?" Swipe asked.

Shadow gestured between Swipe, Hawkeye, and the control module. "Hawkeye helped tweak the training program to develop mental control for macros. You'll be able to run it easily enough."

If Flit wasn't mistaken, there was an air of disappointment around Swipe as she nodded. Swipe had been in the Underground for long enough to get a good idea of who the more powerful macro-kinetics were, and Flit was certain she would have been as eager to have one of them teach her as Flit was to have Shadow teach her translocation. Or, at least, as eager as Flit from two years ago would have been. Current Flit, not so much.

Layla seemed more confident after Shadow's comment. She perked up and got to her feet as well. "When do we begin?"

"Tonight. I can translocate you to where Cogs is, and then Flit, Hawkeye, and I will head to another training room. We'll train every night at this time unless I tell you otherwise." Shadow walked towards the middle of the room.

A look of concern tugged at Swipe's features. "What about the Security roster? Flit and I may get nights."

"We'll deal with that if it happens," Shadows said so dismissively that Flit narrowed her eyes at him, wondering what he meant by *if*. She didn't bother asking, as he continued speaking to Layla, "Now, I assume you haven't translocated before. It may cause strong nausea. It's best if you don't hold your breath and if you give yourself time to recover. Cogs knows what it is like, so she'll go easy on you."

A green tinge came over Hawkeye's face at the mention of translocation, and Flit chuckled. She playfully nudged him, and he rolled his eyes.

"If you're ready, come over here. I'll need to make physical contact with you to bring you along." Shadow held out his hands for Layla to take.

"It's great. You'll love it." Hawkeye's voice was tense and his face stiff.

It was such a blatant lie that both Flit and Swipe chuckled.

"It's not the worst," Swipe promised, apparently trying to make up for the fact she had just been laughing.

"Geez, talk about shittiest pep talk ever," Flit muttered. She walked to Layla's side. "Some people find it disorienting or nauseating, but they are in the minority. Translocation will take a little more out of you than regular teleportation, but there are never any lasting side effects. You'll be fine. I promise."

With a surprising amount of eagerness, Layla strode over. "I've never teleported before. I've always wondered what it would be like. A bit of nausea won't deter me." She slapped her hands against Shadow's.

"Excellent." Shadow stepped closer as his fingers curled closed over hers. "Now, don't forget to breathe."

Then, they were gone.

"I hope she doesn't get sick," Hawkeye muttered, frowning as his brows furrowed.

Playfully bumping her hip against his, Swipe said, "If she does, you'll be able to comfort her. It's not all bad."

"Bloody hell. Every time there's a new person in this place, people rush to pair them up. It's juvenile." Hawkeye's comment radiated indignance as he turned his nose up at Swipe.

"I wouldn't be saying it if you two weren't staring longingly at each other every time you thought the other wasn't watching," Swipe muttered.

Hawkye glanced at Flit for support.

She raised her hands defensively. "You know I don't like agreeing with Swipe. Please don't make me do it."

"You're insuff—"

Shadow reappeared in the room and looked at Flit and Hawkeye. "You two ready to go?"

Shoulders sagging, Hawkeye nodded. Flit did too.

Shadow told Swipe the password she would need to access the training program before he stepped closer and took one of each of Flit and Hawkeye's hands, and the world shifted around them.

Blinking quickly, Flit took in her new surroundings. A grin spread across her face at the sheer awesomeness of getting to experience translocation again. Despite her annoyance at Shadow, she found herself getting excited about the prospect of finally learning how to do it for herself.

The room they were in looked like a standard observation suite, with a console and a trio of large blank screens on one wall. The standby image disappeared as Shadow approached it and worked the controls. The image on the screen changed, and they were then looking at a plain, almost cell-like, concrete room.

"So... how do we do this thing?" Flit asked, too impatient to wait for Shadow to speak of his own accord.

"First, you wait here, and don't touch anything." Shadow

stepped towards Hawkeye and took his hand. "You're coming with me. Ready?"

Pale skin turning green, Hawkeye gulped. He pressed his lips together, as if that would help him reduce the nausea. Flit didn't get a chance to remind him to breathe before they both disappeared and then reappeared in the room on the middle monitor. A split second later, Shadow faded out of that room, leaving Hawkeye alone and reappearing beside Flit.

At the sudden disappearance of the senior member, Hawkeye's frown deepened, and he started rocking back and forward on his feet.

Shadow reached over to the console and pressed an icon for a microphone. "Hawkeye, can you hear me?"

The remote viewer jolted to attention, turning this way and that until he found the camera in the room. He waved at it. "I take it that the flashing red light means that we're connected by video and audio?"

"Copy that, Hawkeye. Flit and I are going to begin. I suggest that you remain perfectly still. We'll be starting small, but even that could end poorly," Shadow warned matter-of-factly, leaving Hawkeye looking even more concerned than he was nauseated.

Shadow reached into his pocket, pulling out a tiny microchip with a flashing red bulb on it. It was no larger than a grain of rice.

"This is what we'll be using to start with. I know you can already relocate objects within line of sight, so this is the next natural step. Your task is to get this chip into that room without going along with it. If I were you, I'd aim to set it at least a metre in front of Hakeye's feet. It's biodegradable, so it should do minimal damage if you teleport it somewhere inside him."

Flit's stomach dropped, her confidence sinking like a lead balloon as she looked past Shadow, taking in Hawkeye's unsuspecting face on the screen. "Why don't we just start with an empty room?"

The look Shadow gave her was disparaging. "If we had endless time to work with, we would. Why? Are you not capable of this?"

"Of course I can!" Flit snatched the microchip from his palm.

Shadow's face remained stoic, but she caught a flicker of amusement behind his eyes.

Bastard. He enjoyed torturing her.

"Then pull yourself together and get to it." He gestured for her to step closer to the console. When Flit complied, he continued, "The reason that Hawkeye is in that room is because he is familiar to you. You care about him. I could have just shown you the video feed of the room, but we need to increase your chances of success. The element of risk will make you think about things a bit more before you jump in."

Poor Hawekeye stood in the other room, perfectly still and entirely innocent. The only giveaway that it was a live feed was the occasional blink and the steady rise and fall of his chest under his black training singlet. Flit wondered if he knew that he was being used as bait. Surely, Shadow would have warned him?

Tapping at the console again, Shadow brought up two additional views from different cameras in the room, giving Flit a good idea of the dimensions and nature of the space beyond the single image.

"Look at the room on the screens. Use the view to build a three-dimensional reference in your mind." Shadow's voice had lost its usual cool efficiency and turned into something calmer, almost meditative.

"Can't we just use a three-dimensional holographic representation?" Flit asked, her brows furrowing.

"You won't always have that option. If you are going to need a visual reference, you'll be lucky to get even a live feed. Most of it will be from memory, so you're just going to have to get good at this aspect. Now, concentrate."

Flit nodded. Straight out of the frying pan and into the fire, it seemed.

"Picture the room in your mind like I told you... When you've got that, bring Hawkeye into that space, standing just like he is in the feed. Don't take your eyes off the screens," Shadow continued.

Flit tried to empty her mind of everything else. She let go of Harmony and Divvy's betrayal, of the oddness of her new alliance with Swipe, and the gnawing pain of Scraps' absence in her gut.

With each breath, she zeroed in on Hawkeye and the room around him.

Shadow continued, "Remember what it is like to be standing next to him. Can you hear the steady cadence of his breathing? Can you smell the sharp spices of his aftershave?"

Hawkeye was almost as familiar to Flit as she was to herself. She knew the smell of him instinctively, she knew exactly how his laughter reverberated in her ear canal. She had teleported with him enough to have an ingrained understanding of his density and distribution and the comforting heat that always radiated off him.

"When you're ready, send that microchip into the room. Aim for a metre in front of where he is standing..." As he trailed off, Flit thought Shadow would be silent, but he added, "Take your time, Flit. Go for precision over speed."

Flit measured her breathing and allowed herself to sink into the moment. She didn't want to mess up and hurt her friend. She had already done that once, and that was enough for her. So, for the first time in her life, she truly *focused*. She was fully aware of how the air conditioning made the hair by Hawkeye's ear flutter. She imagined what it would be like to be a metre away from that, where the cool swell of that filtered air would be slightly different. How it would caress the side of the grain in her hand as it fell to the floor.

Taking another deep breath, Flit sent a surge of power into the grain and—

It was gone.

There was an awful cracking sound, and the monitor she had been so fixated on bloomed with weblike fractures. The veins raced out from where the microchip had embedded in the screen. The image flickered, the screen groaned and shattered, and glass shards fell like rain all over the console.

"Ooops..."

Flit's heart hammered in her chest as she waited for Shadow to rip into her.

"If that had gone into the room, it would have been in the perfect position," Shadow said. His footsteps crunched as he stepped onto the glass shards. He used the console to change the view so the front-on angle that had been on the now destroyed screen moved to the left side instead. He bent over to retrieve the blinking microchip. He held it out for Flit. "Try again."

Bolstered by the unexpected praise, Flit took the chip.

"This time, really get your mindset into that room. It's a real room, not just an image on a screen," he advised. Then, with an amused glint in his eyes, he added, "And don't worry. Hawkeye's not made of glass. He won't shatter if you accidentally get that chip stuck in a muscle."

Flit gulped, certainly hoping Shadow was right.

21

SCRAPS

IN RECENT WEEKS, Scraps had difficulty finding things to be grateful for. However, as he caught the maglev from the Derivate Training Facility to his apartment, he was grateful that the atrocities he and Liana had uncovered for the children, adolescents, and adults were not repeated for the infants. Their investigation into the living conditions of the youngest and most vulnerable Derivates had revealed that, whilst the nursery was running on skeleton staff, the babies were still being cared for as they were supposed to be.

Despite his own relief, Scraps had sensed Liana's lingering horror as they had worked. Her reaction had driven home the reality that she and other Citizens really had no frame of reference for the perfunctory way Derivates were raised. The babies were kept in their separate cribs and were brought out for routine movement and mealtimes, as well as socialisation sessions. However, there was no affection in it. No warmth. There were several occasions where Scraps had seen Liana watching the little ones, her hand instinctively brushing over her own stomach. It only made him wish he could have shut the place down. He couldn't help but think that, if Flit were here, she would have done it anyway, risks be damned, but he wasn't as good as thinking on his feet as she was, and it just made him miss her presence more.

When Scraps arrived home, he made himself a quick dinner and got changed into his casual gear. He had politely declined the offer of dinner at Chris and Liana's. As much as he wished he could have the night to sit and clear his own head, he had to go to the factory. He wasn't sure when Agent Greene and Agent Hector would call on him again, but he had to find something, no matter how small, to feed to them so he could retain his freedom. Scraps also hoped he could gather something worthwhile enough to feed back to the Underground, too.

The trip to the textiles factory took longer than Scraps remembered. When he got there, the noise was enough to have him wishing for the night to be over. As he paced up and down the aisles, he stole glances at the garments that were being made. They were starting to come together as the Free Citizens had moved from cutting to sewing. In addition to Officer uniforms, he thought it was possible there were also some in there for maintenance or hospitality workers. He wasn't quite sure which at this point.

After what felt like a long day and an even longer night, Scraps helped the Free Citizens leave the factory safely and made his way home. In the office the next day, he spent time with Liana on the report for the Derivate Training Facility. The sheer number of urgent changes to the Derivate's lives meant that the pair had their work cut out for them. Scraps fell into the pattern of working, sleeping, and repeating, with visits to the textiles factory peppered in every third night.

IT WASN'T until a week and a half later that something happened to break the routine Scraps had fallen into.

"Adam?" Scraps paused in his patrol of the textile factory floor as he saw the man step in through the main door.

Although there was no way Adam had heard Scraps' surprise over the noise, he must have seen it in his expression. He looked around, frowning at the machines that caused a constant, loud hum to fill the space. Without even trying to speak, Adam gestured to Scraps and then to the office in the corner of the factory floor.

With a nod of understanding, Scraps walked past the woman who was putting the finishing touches on some Government maintenance uniforms. Adam paused along the way, leaning in to speak to the woman because the machines were so loud.

Adam arrived in the office shortly after Scraps and shut the door. He pressed a button on the wall, and there was a soft hum in the room before some noise cancellation technology kicked in. The office itself was small, the desk layered with fabric offcuts and every corner littered with thread and dust. It took Scraps a moment for his mind to recalibrate after the noise and in the chaotic new visual environment.

"I thought I would drop by and check on progress," Adam said by way of introduction.

"We're almost done," Scraps informed him, although Adam could probably see from his walk through the space. "The Maintenance uniforms are just getting their final touches and the other ones should be done the next time we come by."

"That's good to hear. They will be right on time too."

A short, heavy silence followed Adam's statement, almost as though he was waiting for Scraps to ask what they would be on time for. The older man watched Scraps carefully, but he didn't flinch or balk. As much as he wanted to know what the plan was, he also wanted Adam to believe that the trust between them was complete, that he would do exactly as asked.

When it was clear Scraps wasn't going to pry or question, the thin-pressed lines of Adam's lips softened into a half-smile.

"We'll be getting some new supplies sent through. There will be other uniforms manufactured after these. The crew will know what to do with them, but I want to change up our security plans." Adam walked over, leaning back against the desk.

"Are there problems with the way I am handling it?" Scraps asked, figuring this was safe. It was good to try to ensure he was doing his best work.

"Oh no, not at all," Adam said smoothly. "If anything, it's the opposite. You're too good at other things to be stuck here babysitting the textiles production."

Scraps knew he *should* be pleased about this news. He *should* be keen to get back into a better position to acquire information and help the Free Citizens, but the last time he helped plan something, it had gotten terribly out of hand. He didn't want to be part of more destruction.

"What else would you like me involved in?" Scraps tried to keep the wariness out of his tone.

"We'll discuss it at Nightmix on the weekend. Same day and time as usual." Adam's tone was dismissive enough that Scraps knew there was no purpose pushing him for more information. There wasn't really time anyway, as Adam quickly followed up by asking, "So, how's Ava? Is she due back anytime soon?"

Even though Scraps wasn't the best at interpreting social nuances, he knew that was a loaded question coming from Adam. "No. She's still with her mother. She wants to spend as much time as possible with her while she can."

The lie came surprisingly easy after having told it so many times. He figured it was because it wasn't entirely untrue. If he worked off the assumption that Flit had reached the Underground safely, he had no doubt she was enjoying her time with her parents. She and Tinker argued a lot, but the familial love was undeniable.

"Do you need anything from me in the meantime?" Scraps was eager to change the subject.

"There will be two couriers coming when you're here next. They should arrive at the end of your allocation to pick up all the uniforms. Please make sure the boxes are ready to go." Adam gestured towards the factory where the tailors were still working away.

"How will I know that they are the right people?"

Scraps' caution made Adam's face shine with approval. "They'll have our logo painted on their forearms. If they don't show you them as they approach, assume the situation has been compromised and distract them so the others can get out safely. I'm sure you're able to handle yourself."

There was no hesitation as Scraps nodded. The Citizens he was working with, while lovely enough, were just civilians. He would be far better placed to hold any enemies up whilst they escaped, and he felt as though it was the right thing to do.

"Very well." Scraps resisted the urge to salute like he used to when he was given similar order.

Old habits, it seemed, died hard.

Apparently satisfied with the conversation, Adam left the room and wandered around the factory before saying his farewells and exiting the premises.

Scraps finished up the rest of the night in much the same way he had the previous ones. Even though he was well used to dealing with routine and monotony in the name of duty, he was somewhat pleased to know he would soon be doing something different on his evenings. Besides, the more information he gathered, the more likely it was he would have something to take back with him when he left the city and returned to the Underground. Even though he hadn't been recalled, it was something he was considering more and more the longer he was away from Flit. He just wanted to make sure he had enough intelligence to take back with him, to make sure he didn't disappoint her, to make sure the time they spent apart was worth it.

Scraps was pleased when he got home that night. After a long day of report writing, the constant hum of the sewing machines, and the strain of being alert for so many hours, he was keen for the rest. He stifled a yawn as he made his way to his apartment. When the door shut behind him, he removed his shoes, leaving them neatly beside the entrance. Then, he turned straight for the kitchen. As much as he wanted sleep, he knew he needed to eat first.

Scraps had only taken a couple of steps before the sound of knocking made him jump. He pressed his lips together as he spun around and stared at the door. Part of him wanted to groan at the interruption to what was supposed to be his rest time, but after a second knock, his survival instincts kicked in. He took a slow, steadying breath as he walked over and opened the door to reveal Agent Hector and Agent Greene.

Scraps forced a smile onto his lips. "Ah, hello." Given their timing, Scraps thought they must have been watching him.

"May we come in?" Greene asked as she started to step in the door. She might have lilted the end of the sentence to make it sound like a question, but she wasn't really asking for permission.

Stepping back and sweeping his arm towards the living area, Scraps did not protest. It would only make him seem defiant, and he could not afford to do that right now. He shut the door and followed Greene and Hector to where they were standing in the middle of his living room.

"To what do I owe the pleasure of this visit?"

"We would like an update on the movement of the Free Citizens. We've noticed that you've been spending some nights outside of your apartment quite regularly." Hector's voice was matter-of-fact.

Scraps' years of training and work allowed him to read Hector's intention immediately. By mentioning that they already knew he had spent time outside of his apartment, they were telling him not to dance around the truth.

"Correct. I was asked to work on a project with the Free Citizens. They were manufacturing uniforms," Scraps confessed but quickly changed topic. "However, Adam has asked me to return to the Free Citizens meetings this coming week. It is the first time he has invited me back to the main group since the maglev attack, so I believe that is a good sign I am earning his trust again."

The glance that Greene and Hector shared at Scraps' confession made him think he had said the right thing. Letting them know that there was something possibly interesting coming in the future had torn their attention away from the more informative truth about the uniforms.

Hector crossed his arms over his chest. "Did he explain why he had a change of heart?"

"He said I was too good to be wasted on manufacturing, and he wanted me involved in *other things*. He did not elaborate, but I should learn more this weekend," Scraps explained plainly.

Given it was all true, the words came easily. Scraps was pleased they didn't bring the telepath with them when they visited. For some reason, they must have thought he was not going to try and lie to them.

"And I trust you will inform us of whatever these plans are when you become aware of them?" Greene asked slowly, watching Scraps through narrowed eyes.

"Of course," Scraps replied. "What if they ask me for information in their planning process? How would you like me to handle that?"

"Tell them you need to research it. Then run it by us first." Hector spoke with enough ease that it was evident he had accounted for this already. "We need to ensure you're valuable enough to them to keep you in on their plans but that you're also not giving them anything we can't afford to lose."

"We need you in place for as long as possible," Greene added. "They will plan regardless of whether you are there or not, so we may need to give a little to get a little. We just want to avoid further casualties."

"Agreed." Genuine guilt twisted in Scraps' gut. "I am appalled at how the maglev mission ended. That was not why I became involved with the group. They have become a danger to themselves and others."

Even though Greene and Hector devoured Scraps' words with avid approval, Scraps didn't really tell them the full truth. Yes, he thought the Free Citizens had become a danger to themselves and others, but he still believed them to be less of a danger than the Government.

In hopes of encouraging the agents to leave his apartment sooner rather than later, Scraps changed the direction of the conversation back to the promise they had made him when they first captured him. "Have you made any progress finding my wife?"

Greene shifted uncomfortably. "No," she admitted, that single syllable low and twisted with discontent. "We will continue working on that, though, so long as you keep your end of the bargain."

"I will." No progress finding Flit was good progress, as far as he was concerned. "Is that all?"

Bristling at the clear dismissal, Hector narrowed his eyes at Scraps. "I should ask you that. Did you leave anything out of your report?"

"I'm not sure what else you would want to know." Scraps didn't shy away from the disdainful expression on Hector's face.

"What do the Free Citizens uniforms look like?" Greene asked.

Scraps blinked. *Free Citizens* uniforms? Did the officers really have such a lack of understanding about their targets that they thought they would create their own uniforms? The whole point of the organisation was to step away from that kind of branding.

"I don't know." It wasn't really a lie, but playing dumb would only get him so far. "It's hard to tell what the pieces will look like when they are finished. I believe there is a lot of dark fabric, though. Beyond that? It's not really within my realm of knowledge."

"Get us pictures," Hector demanded. "When you have that evidence, as well as news of what Adam wants from you, use this to contact us." He held out a small, acorn sized device with a single button on it. "It will send us an alert that you wish to speak to us."

"Copy that." Scraps took the device and walked to the door. He opened it for them. "I will speak to you both soon. Good night."

The agents hesitated at the second dismissal of the night before resigning to the fact it was time to go, and they walked out.

Scraps happily shut the door behind them. He let out a heavy sigh and threw the paging device onto the couch across the room before heading for the bathroom. He was well and truly done with the day and was looking forward to crawling into bed and finally letting his mind switch off for a while.

DURING THE TEMPORARY reprieve from visiting Nightmix, Scraps had forgotten just how loud the venue was. He walked right past the bouncer and into the dark, throbbing club beyond. The coloured strobes and holographic flecks of fireworks that burst into the darkness revealed a sea of tightly packed, writhing bodies.

Even though Scraps was not much of a fan of the nightclub, his mind wandered back to when he had been here with Flit in that sensual, revealing silver dress of hers. His body started to respond to the memory, and he squashed it down. There was no sense getting caught up in things he could not have. He still had a mission to complete.

Flit had a much better ability to find their friends in the crowd than Scraps did. With the vast array of outfits and body types on display, it was difficult for him to tell everyone apart. He spent the better part of half an hour wandering around the club before someone found him.

"Brian!" Andy stepped in front of him and put a hand on his shoulder. He barely heard her say his name, but he could read her lips well enough.

Scraps smiled, despite himself. As much chaos as the Free Citizens had caused in his life, he had met some good people amongst them. Andy was one of those. She had helped Flit without a second thought when that rogue microkinetic had been murdering innocent civilians. Thanks to a good knock on the head, she didn't remember much after they had dropped her off home, but Scraps still knew the truth.

Leaning closer so she could hear him over the music, Scraps said, "Hi, Andy! Sorry it took me a while to find you. Where is everyone?"

Andy waved away his apology. "They're down there already. Meeting started an hour ago. I'm just up here catching the stragglers. Head on down."

Not bothered to yell again, Scraps just smiled and nodded at her. She let her hand drop from his shoulder. He skirted the undulating tide of bodies on the dancefloor, darted around the long lines of people waiting to order drinks, and finally made his way to the back of the club. The fact he was now spying on these people did not sit well with him, but he could not put it off any longer.

It was easy enough for Scraps to find his way to the office and to open the passage that led to the bunker beneath the building. As Scraps walked down the narrow concrete tunnel, the thumping of the club faded behind him and was replaced by a new buzz of conversation from ahead.

The bunker held more people than he had ever seen in there before. Scraps guessed that there were easily thirty people squeezed into the space. Adam was at the rear of the space, standing on a new desk that must have been brought in recently. He gestured towards a box on the ground beside him, finished that statement, and looked across the crowd at Scraps.

"The fake ID chips, paired with the uniforms we have manufactured, should be more than enough to get our stealth team into the target buildings to retrieve the information we require," Adam said. "I take it the pick-up went well?"

Scraps straightened at the question. He had overseen that exchange the night before. "Yes, it was smooth. Everything was ready on time, and the collection went ahead."

What Scraps didn't mention was that the Government Agents wanted pictures of the uniforms. Thanks to some quick thinking, Scraps had searched a quiet part of the production floor for some of the uniforms being made during the day by the company. They were just standard uniforms for some food factory. Instead of taking a photo of the security uniforms the Free Citizens were manufacturing, he had taken a photo of those. He figured that it would give the agents something to think about and throw them far off the scent of what the Free Citizens were actually doing.

"Excellent." Adam clapped his hands in delight. "Everything is in place. I'll assign members to the strike team later tonight. If you want to be part of it, or if you don't, please come and see me. We need to get numbers solidified before tomorrow, so we can adequately plan for the incursion."

With that, Adam jumped off the desk and started speaking to a couple of people nearby. Scraps was about to weave his way closer when Chris and Liana stepped up beside him. He smiled at them in greeting.

Liana leaned in closer, resting her hand on his forearm. "You're not going to be part of that, right?" she asked, sounding wary but speaking low enough to avoid being overheard by those around them.

Scraps gave her what he hoped was a reassuring smile. "I don't plan on going on any of the missions."

That seemed to be enough for Liana as she stepped back.

"What are you doing?" Chris asked.

"Just going to check in with Adam. He said he had some ideas for how he would like me to help out."

Chris nodded. "Want us to come with you?"

For a moment, Scraps considered it. He did not like Adam, and he did not trust him, but he also did not wish to drag Chris and Liana into more of the drama the Free Citizens were most likely planning, drama that he was certainly going to be dragged into. "No, I will be okay. Thank you for the offer, though."

With that, Scraps turned and started to make his way to the front of the room. There were so many new faces around him, but he did his best not to pay them any mind or attention. The more people he could identify, the greater the chance the freedom-seeking Citizens could get captured because of him. He had no intention to make the Government's persecution of its people any easier.

When Scraps got to the front of the room, Adam stopped the conversation he was in and opened his arms wide in greeting. The grin that pulled at his lips almost split his face in two. "Ah, Brian! It's good to see you. Are you ready to help me plan a riot?"

22

———

FLIT

TIME PASSED at an odd pace that had every part of Flit screaming with frustration. On one hand, her translocation training was coming along well. She had always considered herself naturally skilled at all things teleportation related. After just a fortnight of lessons, Shadow had to begrudgingly agree. But despite her good progress with translocation, the fact that Scraps was still in the Hub somewhere got less and less palatable. The knowledge made Flit feel like she was a pot of water on a stove, slowly working towards an unstoppable boil.

"So, you managed to move a barrel from one room into another in one piece?" Swipe asked over her meal, sounding utterly unimpressed.

"Yes," Flit replied, not letting Swipe's scepticism get to her. She kept her voice low, given they were seated in their regular corner of the Mess. "Tomorrow, I'll be trying to go myself."

Swipe ran a hand through her smooth blonde hair in frustration as she looked at Fortune. "Are we seriously pinning all of our hope on the fact that Flit can translocate without getting herself half stuck in a wall?"

Fortune, who had been ignoring the sniping up until now, fixed Swipe with a look of disapproval. "I wouldn't put it that way, but yes."

"Then I hope for Scraps' sake she can hurry up and get her shit together," Swipe muttered, shaking her head.

"You just worry about keeping on top of the patrol schedule, okay? We will need the longer and farther routes over the next week. You'll also need to make sure you can swap people around without suspicion," Fortune warned her.

"Don't worry. I've got my part in this sorted."

"Hey, guys!" The conversation was interrupted by Hawkeye as he and Layla approached the table.

Apparently, they had been making good progress with their own training, too, with Layla learning more about technological manipulation from Cogs, and Hawkeye's range increasing steadily thanks to his lessons from Scope.

"Ready to head to the sim?" he asked.

Flit quickly picked up her cup and downed the last of her drink. She and the others had organised a private meeting in the simulator for the night. Hawkeye had some important updates for them regarding their plan to get back to the surface and retrieve Scraps. Flit had been impatiently anticipating the meeting for three days.

"Ready as we'll ever be." Flit got out of her seat and smiled as she looked over at Hawkeye and Layla.

The pair had been spending significant amounts of time together over the past few weeks. When she had asked Hawkeye about it, he said that it was nothing more than information sharing. Given the chemistry she'd seen between them on multiple occasions, she didn't believe it. Still, she stopped pestering him about it. He'd tell her what was going on when he was ready.

Fortune and Swipe got up, and they all dumped their trays in the cleaning area before leaving the Mess. The walk to the Residence was quiet, but there were plenty of people milling about the lobby and social areas when they got there. Way more than usual, given the increase in their population. After everything the Derivates had gone through over the past century, it broke her heart that there were more people living in the Underground now than ever before. If anything, they should have been up on the surface and free decades ago.

When they reached the simulator, there was already someone in there. Flit watched Hawkeye to see if he was expecting this.

"Hey, Cogs." Hawkeye gave the woman a small salute.

She gestured for everyone to sit down on the stools that were spaced around the room. "Good to see you all. I don't have long, so we'd best get this started ASAP," she told them.

The group didn't need telling twice. Everyone sat down on a stool.

"Thanks for coming along. I know it's not easy for you to sneak around," Hawkeye acknowledged.

"We all need to do our part." Cogs dismissed the concern in his tone with a shrug. "Have you explained the plan already?"

"Not yet. I wanted to wait for you in case they had any questions. Do you have the data?"

Instead of answering, Cogs waved her hand at the screen at the rear of the room, and it flared to life. Several time and location stamped images came up on the screen. Flit had just sat down, but she teleported to her feet when she saw the photographs of Scraps. She walked closer, taking in the details on the images, noting the various Hub buildings in the background. Then, she noted the date, and her head snapped towards Cogs.

"Were these really just last night?" Flit asked, not sure how to feel about it.

On one hand, seeing Scraps out and walking about, apparently completely without issue, was good. The last thing she wanted was for him be in Government custody and being tortured or exploited like other Derivates had been. However, the hairline cracks of doubt that Harmony had installed still plagued the foundation of her trust in Scraps. She knew he wasn't working with them, but... why would they let him go free? That wasn't like the Government. There had to be something else going on.

"Yes. I managed to hack in the Government's server last night. They left a backdoor open when they reset for some maintenance. It's lucky I did, too, as the new firewalls they have up are... Well, they are using some crazy code to protect themselves now. It seems they are arming their tech just as well as they are arming their streets." Cogs reached up, taking turns to point to each of the images.

Returning her attention to the screen, Flit noted the people in the background. She let out a low whistle as she counted more than two dozen Derivate and Law Enforcement uniforms in the background of just three images.

"Any word on that rogue group of Citizens? Are they the reason for all the extra security?" Flit asked, trying to be as vague as possible even though there were no telepaths in the room.

"There wasn't anything on the news archives I could access while I was skimming through last night," Cogs admitted.

"The Government don't like looking as though they are concerned," Layla interjected. "It must be pretty serious for them to go to this level."

Flit had to admit there was a special sort of satisfaction that came along with the knowledge the Government was scrambling to protect their arses. Even though the maglev attack had gone so poorly, the Free Citizens had achieved something important. They had shaken the Government.

With that knowledge, Flit returned to her seat and leaned back against the wall. She inspected the pictures from a distance, hoping more clues about what Scraps was up to would come through.

"I didn't have much time to go through the footage, but I was able to ascertain that Scraps is still going freely between his apartment and his office building in Centre One." Cogs waved her fingers again, and a video sequence jumped from camera to camera, showing the familiar route between the apartment and the office. "Every now and again, he diverts his path in the evenings. The locations I could find were in... North One-West Three, and North Four-East Three."

A smile tugged at Flit's lips at the mention of the first building. That was where Chris and Liana lived. The fact that Scraps was still spending time with them filled her with a sense of relief. They were good people, and the last thing she wanted was for Scraps to be isolated. Even if he wouldn't have minded, he deserved to be around people who cared about him.

"What's in those buildings?" Swipe leaned closer, as if trying to put together pieces of a puzzle.

"What isn't?" Layla grumbled, shaking her head. "Each block in the Hub is like a miniature city in and of itself. There's apartments in almost every building, and then there are a lot of service and commercial properties too. He could be visiting anything from a hair salon to a nut factory."

Flit had the answers, but she kept her mouth shut just in case anyone took issue with the fact Scraps was friends with some Citizens. She also didn't want to give away the location of Nightmix just yet.

"What's important is that we know he is moving around freely," Fortune said, watching the footage as it replayed. "And that he is back in the apartment around the same time every night."

Swipe nodded. "So, if I can fix the security routes and timetable just right..."

"We will have the opportunity to get up there, grab Scraps, and bring him back," Hawkeye finished the thought.

Flit's heart skipped a beat. "What's our window of time for this?"

If it was soon, she would have to hustle on the translocation training. Sure, she was starting with moving herself that night, but getting to a building in the Hub and returning safely with Scraps was another matter entirely.

"Well, we need to do more than just get Scraps," Layla said, shifting uncomfortably.

Hawkeye rested a hand on her forearm. "Go on. You can trust them."

"I have some contacts back in the city," Layla confessed. "I want to see if they are still around."

"What will these contacts be able to do?" Flit asked.

Layla shrugged. "They're not equipped like you guys are. They are a bunch of Citizen Derivates and regular Citizens who are in hiding for some reason or another. It's a bit of a mayday style network. We work on getting people out of bad situations and then offer them shelter. We didn't have a chance to do much more than that, but they could do with a purpose."

That certainly piqued Flit's and Swipe's interest. The others seemed to already be aware of this information, and Flit realised this meant she and Swipe were the ones who Layla wasn't sure if she could trust. She let it slide. Harmony had wiped the woman's memory of who it was who had actually saved them from the facility. So, apart from being her crush's bestie and the woman who was sleeping with the potential traitor, Layla had no real reason to trust her with anything. Still, Flit was grateful for that amount of information at least. It sounded as though they could be potential allies.

"We think it could be useful to have some contacts above ground. Maybe if things start moving up there, and the leadership down here see an opportunity to strike, we may be able to finally do something about our living situation," Hawkeye said. His eyes met Flit's, and he gave her a warm smile. "It was bad enough before, but now we're not even allowed to leave the main tunnels. I worry we're going to die in a trap of our own making."

"Finally, someone bloody gets it," Flit cheered.

"So, how are you planning to get up there?" Fortune asked, ignoring Flit's comment and looking between Hawkeye and Layla. "Swipe rearranging the rosters can get you a couple of hours at most. Anything more than that will be too suspicious."

"That's where Flit comes in," Hawkeye admitted with a sheepish smile.

"Flit's only just starting to translocate herself tonight," Swipe protested.

For once, Flit agreed with Swipe's lack of faith in her abilities. Not so much because she didn't think she could translocate, but because there was a big difference between individual teleportation and teleporting others.

Hawkeye shrugged. "Then she's going to have to get her shit together. Fast."

"It's the only way we can get to them up there," Cogs interjected before Swipe could say something more forceful. "You can't be gone for longer than the time of a patrol, and you can't be seen on any of the cameras that have been installed to monitor the only entrance and exit tunnels left for us to use. I can work a little bit of magic on them, but I need to save that for emergencies."

"And we don't want to put Cogs at risk by getting her to do too much, too soon," Hawkeye added.

They both had good points, Flit thought. It was still early days, far too early for them to show their hands. It was better to try and do what they could with what they had, even if it meant Flit had to hurry up and learn a skill in a matter of weeks that usually took people months or years to master. She wasn't intimidated, though. She knew she could do it. She had to.

Scraps was depending on her.

23

SCRAPS

"YOU'VE CERTAINLY GATHERED a lot of new weapons over the past few weeks," Scraps said, straightening up and turning to Adam, who was waiting by the exit of a storage room at the back of a small convenience store a few blocks away from Nightmix.

According to Adam, this convenience store was not the only place he had supplies. He made an allusion to having other strongholds, but when Scraps had asked them about it, he had changed the topic and opened more crates. There were more than Scraps could count in a quick glance, all full of a variety of weapons and other important items. It was a good haul but also a little concerning that Adam and the Free Citizens had managed to amass so many supplies.

Adam leaned against the door frame, his eyes twinkling with amusement. "The tip you and Ava gave us a while back has proven immensely useful. I thought that, after the maglev attack, the Government would have cleaned up after itself a little better. Apparently not."

Scraps tugged the lid off a nearby crate and to reveal a batch of easily concealable pistols stacked neatly inside. "Do the Free Citizens know how to use these weapons?"

"How hard can it be?" Adam scoffed. "You flick the safety off, point, and shoot."

Years of taking orders from uninformed or lazy senior officers as a Registered had trained Scraps to hide his responses to such stupid comments.

"It is not quite that simple. If they do not know the right hows and whens of using these kinds of weapons, they are just as much a liability to us as they are to the Government."

The leader of the Free Citizens dismissed Scraps' concerns with a wave of his hand. "The chances they are going to use the weapons are minimal. They are just for show."

"Are they loaded? Functional?"

"Yes, and yes."

"Then they will get used." Scraps slammed the lid shut and turned to Adam. "If you want me to plan this with you, then you also need to factor in time for me to give our people basic training."

"We don't have time—"

"That is not negotiable."

The vehemence in Scraps' interruption made Adam press his lips together.

Scraps had even surprised himself.

Shaking his head, Adam chuckled. "You're sounding more and more like Ava every time I speak to you."

"I married her," Scraps said, the expression on his face hardening as he thought of how determined Flit would be to make sure this was done properly. "I would clearly choose to take that as a compliment. Please do not presume to use it as anything other than that."

"Wow, you're tightly wound. Is everything okay?" Adam stepped closer and let the door slide shut behind him, blocking off the view of the small, closed convenience store beyond.

Somehow, the question only made Scraps angrier. There was something in the way Adam looked at him that made him wonder if that was on purpose... if the other man was trying to throw him off his game.

"It will be when I can provide weapons training to anyone coming into contact with these," Scraps said, getting back to the issue at hand.

"Fine. Whatever. So long as the timetable isn't impacted, I don't care if you teach them how to ice-skate naked on top of a chessboard." Adam retrieved a small, handheld device from his pocket. "Are you going to be available over the next couple of nights to finalise the plans with me?"

Scraps shifted on his feet and gave the simple answer of, "Yes."

However, as he stood there, he knew it was far more complex than that. He had received a message that morning from the Agents demanding information about his meeting with Adam. He had agreed to meet in a few days. Of course, he was planning to give them minimal answers and as many red herrings as possible, but the reality was that if he was sneaking out every night, it was likely they would get even more suspicious.

"Great. Nightmix will be the best place if we're doing weapons training. Conscripting Trey and Petra to the cause was the best thing I ever did. Their club makes an excellent cover for all sorts of things." Adam grinned, probably thinking himself very clever, and then looked at Scraps. "So, I'll see you at the club tomorrow, then?"

"Copy that," Scraps said with a nod as he walked towards the door.

Adam put a hand on Scraps' shoulder. "We're relying on you, Brian. You're not going to let us down, are you?"

Scraps resisted the urge to shrug his hand off. "No. I will do my best to keep as many of us alive as possible."

"Good. We're close to having all the pieces in place for this mission. I'm hoping we can really start to fight back soon."

"Is there anything else you need from me before then? Aside from helping the recruits?" Scraps asked, wanting Adam to tell him more.

"There are a few things we need. My next priority is securing some identity chips we can use for other missions, but I've already got plans to handle that." Adam let his hand drop. "For now, just get our people up to scratch with their weapons. I'll handle the rest."

Scraps hesitated at the smug look in Adam's eyes when he mentioned *the rest*. He was tempted to push, but he also had to avoid appearing suspicious. In the end, he just decided to nod in agreement and to keep his worries under wraps for another time.

As he made his way out of the storage room, he walked through the aisles of food and sundries and wondered if the Government had any idea of just how much was hiding in the heart of their own city.

THE NEXT WEEK left Scraps feeling utterly exhausted. His worries about Adam's plans faded to the back of his mind as he spent his days working and trying to keep his cover together and then the dark hours at Nightmix, training a bunch of inexperienced Citizens how to not shoot themselves in the foot while putting their pistols in their holsters.

It was far more difficult than it should have been.

Even though Scraps had spent many years training and studying, he found that trying to keep up a cover was exceptionally tiring. With Flit around, he had a constant reminder of what they were working towards. Now, the only thing he could think of was that he had to find a way to help the Free Citizens rile up the Government while keeping them out of danger. In addition to that, he had no idea how any of his actions would impact his own kind, and after the investigation at the Derivate Training Facility, he felt the yearning to return to the Underground grow. It was so hard to ignore. The only thing that stopped him from giving in was his concern that running there now would bring the Government with him. No matter how badly he wanted to be amongst his own kind, that was a price he was not willing to pay.

All the concerns were running through Scraps' mind as he left for work in the morning after only a couple of hours sleep thanks to his time with the Free Citizens. He got into the office right on time, as usual, sat down in his stall and started his system. Once it was ready, he opened a report he was working on for a policy within his own department. It was not long before Scraps lost himself in the words, letting the rules, regulations, and the process of report writing ease his worries.

Just as Scraps settled into a good flow, a knock on the door to his pod pulled him from his thoughts. He turned around, expecting to see Liana or even his manager, Jane. Instead, he frowned as he saw a pair of Registered Derivates standing there. It took a moment for his mind to connect positions with the faces, but when it did, he put a mental wall up around his thoughts.

Scraps got to his feet and opened the door of his pod. "TB-219, CC-9832, to what do I owed the pleasure of this visit?" he asked politely, his mind flashing back to the first time he had met this pair.

When he was being held by the Government. Just before he met Hector and Greene.

"We have been asked to escort you to level twenty-three to discuss a highly classified... policy review," TB-219 informed him, her voice stilted as another employee walked past, peering at them curiously.

"Ah, right. Yes, that review," Scraps said. "Let me just retrieve my datapad, and we can be on our way."

"You do not require—" CC-9832 began.

TB-219 held up a hand to stop him. "Please gather your equipment. We have time," she said.

CC-9832 pressed his lips shut, and TB-219 turned her back on the pod and clasped her hands in front of her as she waited. Her partner followed suit, seemingly a little more reluctant.

Scraps was grateful for the understanding from the telepath. Keeping his cover in this office would help with his ability to continue to blend in. If any of his colleagues thought he was involved in anything untoward, it would make his job, and his role as an informant for the Government, that much more difficult.

After tucking the datapad under his arm, Scraps turned his console onto standby and stepped outside into the main office. He tried to look as nonplussed as possible as he followed the Registereds—the *Derivates*, he mentally corrected himself—towards the elevator.

The ride down to level twenty-three was silent, and Scraps took great interest in noticing just how tightly fastened his left shoe was compared to the right. He wiggled his toes. It really was quite tight. How had he not noticed that before? He figured he must have been distracted that morning when he had tightened them. Most likely because he knew he had to figure out what to have for dinner that night before he left for work. He had eaten out far too much lately, and he was craving the simplicity of a home-cooked meal. He hadn't really bothered cooking since Ava wasn't around, and that meant he would need to do an order for shopping as well. He ran a mental catalogue of the ingredients he knew he had in his—

"Uh, Sir? This is our level," TB-2199 said, cutting into his purposefully absorbing and distracting train of thought.

"Ah, thank you very much," Scraps said with what he hoped was a winning smile. It just made the telepath furrow her brows at him as he disembarked from the elevator.

The two walked Scraps through a series of security checks. For all intents and purposes, this looked like a regular office level in what Scraps was guessing was a finance department. There were projections of budgets and pay rates all around as they walked through a maze of corridors to a meeting room at the back of the space that had a floor-to-ceiling window with a view of the building opposite Centre One. There was a round table in the middle of the room, where both Hector and Greene were seated.

"Mr. Parkes. Thank you for joining us. Please, sit," Greene said, gesturing to the only other chair at the table, opposite of them and in front of the large window.

Scraps turned his back on the view of the building across them and took the offered seat. The Derivates came to stand on either side of him, and he resisted the urge to look at them. He had no doubt they were here to provide security and assurance that he was telling the truth.

"You've been a busy man, Brian," Hector said, crossing his arms over his chest and leaning back in his seat. "I hope you are ready to share what you've been doing with the Free Citizens over the past few weeks."

"They are planning an attack on the facilities they made uniforms for," Scraps said without hesitation. "I've been with them participating in self-defence training so that they don't go in and hurt themselves."

"So that *they* don't go in?" Green raised her eyebrow. "You're not planning to go with them?"

"No. I have no desire to do that," Scraps admitted.

Greene looked over her shoulder to where TB-2199 was

standing for a moment before asking, "What is the point of the attack?"

"They want to make their presence known. Ruffle some feathers, so to speak. They hope that it will be the first in many to let the other Citizens know that there is another option," Scraps said, quoting Adam almost word for word.

"And what are they attacking?" Hector urged.

Scraps shrugged. "The uniforms were from the hospitality department, so something related to that? There may be chemicals or something they want to get from there."

"Are they planning to kill anyone this time?" Hector asked, derision clear in his tone.

"No," Scraps said, lips fell into a wry frown. "But that was not their intention last time either, and they did."

Greene signed and glanced at her partner, who was too busy trying to stare Scraps down to return the look.

"We need you in on that attack," Hector told him. "If we can track your movements and record what you're experiencing, we can better understand where they are and prevent damage."

Scraps shifted, his gut clenching uncomfortably at Hector's comment. "If I do that, and they get caught, then I might blow my cover working for you."

"If you get caught, we'll handle it," Hector said dismissively. "However, our main priority will be letting them get as far as they can without doing damage, so we can learn about their tactics. We want to give them as much rope as they need to hang as many of themselves as possible. We need you on the inside for that."

Hector's word choice made Scraps shift uncomfortably. He might not approve of the methods the Free Citizens were using, but so many of them were just good people who were trying to find a way to live their lives. The idea of giving them more rope to hang themselves with sat wrong with him. However, he thought, it was better than letting Adam convert them into suicide attackers. Better alive and restricted than free and dead.

"So, you want me to go to capture that evidence?" Scraps asked, wanting to confirm this point.

"Correct." Greene leaned forward, resting her elbows on the

table. "We also need to see how far Adam has woven himself into the wider community. This may be a good way to sniff them out. Have you heard of other cells or met any new people?"

"I have seen more people at the meetings," Scraps confessed. "Apart from the uniforms and the meetings I attend, I do not know if there are more groups involved."

Hector frowned but nodded. "Well, that is something else you need to do for us. If you can tell us where these other cells are, we may just be convinced enough by your loyalty to put extra resources into finding where they are keeping your wife."

The mention of *Ava* made Scraps' body tense. He turned, staring at Hector. He wanted to argue that he was already doing what they had asked, but then again, he wasn't sure that he wanted them to find—

"I will let Adam know I am available for the raids. I am sure he will appreciate knowing I want to join him again," Scraps said quickly, not wanting to let his thoughts about what happened to Ava settle between them.

"Excellent." Hector clapped his hands together as he rose from the table. "I'll be waiting for your full report. If you hear anything urgent, use the device we gave you to let us know you need to speak with us."

Greene shifted on her seat cushion. She opened her mouth then paused as she looked between Scraps and Hector. Then, she sank back a little and asked slowly, "Does that sound acceptable, Brian?"

"Yes," Scraps said, even though he felt he had little choice in the matter.

"Then you're free to get back to work," Hector gestured towards the door.

Scraps made his way back to his own office. CC-9832 and TB-219 escorted him right up until the elevator doors opened on his level. He was pleased they remained in the carriage when he stepped out. Not only because it would look suspicious, but because it was becoming increasingly difficult to ignore the sense of satisfaction he felt at the success of his lies.

He only hoped he could keep the charade long enough to keep everyone safe.

WHEN SCRAPS WAS on his way home that night, the rare sound of sirens wailed in the distance. The Derivate and Citizen officers lining the streets were taut with tension, and they all seemed to hold their weapons or hands at the ready rather than standing watchfully at ease. Scraps frowned and told himself it was none of his business.

He was lost in the task of distract himself by figuring out which café he would visit for dinner before heading to Nightmix when the datapad in the bag against his hip started to buzz. A thick blanket of foreboding settled over him as he retrieved the device.

To: Brian
From: Andy
Subject: Dinner
We're opening Nightmix early. Come join us for dinner ASAP!
Xx Petra, Trey, Andy

All plans Scraps had for cooking were wiped from his mind. It took a fair amount of restraint to resist the urge and run to the nearest maglev station. Instead, he turned in the opposite direction of home and walked in a brisk yet orderly fashion.

24

FLIT

"AND THAT, my friends, is how you translocate!" Flit pumped her fist into the air and let out a jubilant hoot.

Instead of being in the viewing room with Shadow, she was standing in the target room all on her own.

At her age, she had teleported tens of thousands of times. It always felt *right*, like she was using some skill that was inherently hers. Translocating, though? Flit had never felt such a rush of exhilaration and success.

"Yes, yes, that is all well and good," Shadow drawled through the comms, "unless you happen to need your left boot."

Flit paused mid-sway of her happy-dancing hips and looked down at her feet.

"Ah, fuck."

Just as her shoulders sagged, her boot appeared beside her. "Thanks," she muttered as she shoved her foot into the still-warm footwear. The last thing she wanted was for Shadow to have to send her a damn shoe on a mission.

"Don't worry. That was, if I have to admit, a rather successful first attempt. At least you kept all of your important clothes," Shadow informed her as he appeared beside her. "Are you willing to try again?" He narrowed his eyes as he looked her up and down. Then, he looked at the watch on his wrist and noted Flit's heart rate, which was being sent to him from the small sensor on her chest.

Flit didn't need to see the numbers to know she was still within safe limits.

"Hell yeah." She stepped aside and concentrated, but he put his hand on her shoulder and shook his head.

"Not unseen, not yet," he said. He teleported them back into the observation room. "I still want you to use the visuals. Now that you've got it, it will get easier, but don't move too far too fast."

"I need to get this down—"

"I appreciate your tenacity, but there is no use *getting this down* if you burn yourself out or lose half a limb—or worse—in the process," Shadow warned.

Resigned, Flit sighed. "Yeah. Gotcha."

She had to stop herself just short of mentioning the fact that she had people relying on her. She wasn't sure how much information Hawkeye had shared with Shadow about their plan to retrieve Scraps and to find some new allies, so she wasn't going to blow the secret.

Instead of worrying about the fact she had to learn faster and more efficiently, Flit squared her shoulders and looked at the screen at the exact spot she had translocated to just moments ago. She sucked in a deep breath, wiggled her toes in her boots, and focused of the feel on her clothes. She set her intentions and then jumped—

"Fuck yeah!" Flit cried out as she appeared in the exact same spot. She then paused, looking down at her shoes, and then noticed she had brought both along this time. "Double fuck yeah!"

"I don't know whether it is the teleporting or the excitement that has your heart rate spiking right now," Shadow called through the comms. "Either way, I think that is enough for today. Tomorrow, we'll pick it up again. Same place, same time. See you then."

Flit had been training with Shadow enough to know that was his way of saying good night. She didn't even bother walking back into the observation room, knowing he wouldn't be there if she did anyway. Instead, she turned and let herself out of the room before making a more than a dozen short-range, rapid-fire teleports to get back to the Residence. For the first time in a long while, she felt her body dragging and putting up some resistance.

Translocation was definitely more draining than regular tele-portation.

Just as Flit appeared at the front door of the tall, underground apartment building, a loud alert tone sounded through the cavern. The plants growing down the front of the building shook against the graffiti-covered walls. She froze on the spot as the klaxons blared. The few people who were strolling through or tending to the hydroponic gardens paused and looked up at the speakers lodged high in the cavern walls.

Finally, a voice broke through the unnerving wails. *"Attention. A population-wide meeting has been scheduled for ten minutes' time in the Residence Meeting Room. This is compulsory for all residents unless an explicit order is given to you by your manager or residential leader."*

The klaxons resumed for another mind-clobbering minute before the same message was repeated. The announcement was on its third and final round when Flit walked through the doors. The entry level of the Residence building was a hive of wary whispers. She assumed that the people there had previously been just enjoying their afternoon.

Peering around, Flit hoped to see someone she knew in the space, but her friends and her parents were nowhere to be seen. She debated sticking around, but she remembered the last time there was a full-scale meeting called and how people had been urgently reassigned. If that happened to her, she wanted to at least be refreshed.

After a hurried shower, Flit emerged from her room dressed in a casual pair of tights, a plain tank, and a soft, warm black jacket. She munched on an energy bar she had grabbed from the kitchen and mused that her parents must have been on shift. She hadn't checked in with them that morning to figure out what their plans were for the day. Concern jolted through her as she realised that this could be bad news. It was possible that something had happened, and one of her parents were injured.

Normally, Flit had a rule to not eat while teleporting as it had resulted in a few concerning choking incidences in her younger years. This time, however, Flit broke her own rule without thinking.

Despite the fact she had a mouthful of chocolate energy bar in her mouth, she teleported the rest of the way down the corridor and impatiently tapped at the elevator control screen. When the doors opened, she noted that the carriage was full of people travelling down from the higher levels, and she groaned. She didn't linger, though. She folded the silver wrap back over her snack and shoved it in her pocket then made her way to the emergency stairwell.

When the Residence had been built, it had been designed knowing full well what type of people would be residing in it. As such, the stairs had a void running straight from top to bottom. It made it an easy way for teleporters to move around in a time crunch.

Leaning over the railing, she looking up and down the void and yelled, "Teleporter moving to ground floor. Anyone else around?" Her voice echoed through the concrete structure, and when she did not hear any protests, she peered over the edge and picked her destination.

A heartbeat later, Flit's feet landed on the ground floor concrete, and she strode towards the door that led to the main lobby. When she arrived, she had to stop. Even with the people lost in the recent collapses, the population of the Underground was at its highest point in a long while. Between the rescues from the facility and those recalled from missions and hybrid living, the main space was packed.

If it was anyone else, they would have given up on the hope they would find their friends in the crowd. It was simply too packed to move. Flit wasn't daunted, though.

"Sorry, just passing by on your left—" she said before, "Oops! My bad. Just gonna squeeze—"

With a few more platitudes and apologies, Flit made it to an area where she could climb on a ledge surrounding a structural pylon to get a good view of the space. She was looking around when Harmony and Divvy entered from a door at the back of the meeting room. They were flanked by Acumen, Shadow, Posthoc, and a few other leaders. A few storage trunks had been moved in front of the crowd for them to stand on. After they were both settled, a hush fell over the space, and tension crept into the quiet gaps in conversation.

"Thank you to everyone for your prompt assembly," Divvy began, her tone as serious as ever as she scanned the crowd. "Before we begin, I want you to know that everyone in the Underground is safe, and we are not facing any direct threats."

The tension that had been gnawing at the room lessened slightly as there was a collective exhale.

Flit considered using the moment to slip off her perch and make her way over to where she saw her parents by the door. However, Divvy quickly resumed speaking, and Flit decided she would have a far better view of the crowd's reaction to whatever the news was from where she was.

"We have received word that there has been an incident in the Hub. Tonight, at approximately five PM, a group calling themselves the 'Free Citizens' attacked a production facility in the city. The Government is being vague about which facility they attacked, but three casualties were recorded, and it is clear from the response that further casualties are expected," Harmony explained.

Divvy, who had been standing stoically beside her fellow leader, cleared her throat before adding, "Given the escalation in combat on the surface, we are planning to bolster our defences. We do not have any concerns for our immediate safety, but we cannot ignore the growing unease above. If we were to get caught in the crossfire, it could end up in the decimation of our population."

Chatter rippled through the crowd in a rolling wave. Flit over-heard a variety of sentiments being shared. Who were these mystery attackers? What were they trying to achieve? Did they know about the Underground? What was the point in increasing defences when it had nothing to do with them?

Flit pressed her lips together to resist the urge to speak lest she blurt out what she knew, which was far more than anyone around her did.

Although, all Flit really wanted to know was where Scraps was. As much as she detested how Adam had turned the maglev plot into a suicide attack, she still wanted the Free Citizens to succeed. She wondered if they had cottoned on to the fact she and Scraps were missing.

Harmony called for silence. "To ensure we can appropriately

protect our population, we will be tightening our current movement restrictions. The general population must not travel beyond the painted tunnels. Only authorised personnel will be allowed beyond these boundaries."

Gasps of surprise sounded around Flit. There were three over-arching classifications of tunnels in the Underground, each referring to the use and origin as well as relative elevation of each. The Surface-level tunnels were the retired subway, highway, storage, and service tunnels from Old City and much too close to the surface to be safe for the Underground residents. The deep-level tunnels were all the natural ones that most people avoided, save for the Catacombs, Sapphire Beach, and a few others recreational locations. Most people spent their days in the mid-level tunnels, which were the ones that were furnished and fitted out by the early residents of the Underground. Out of these, only the ones connecting the Residence to other critical locations such as the Mess, Medbay, Control, Training, and so on were actually painted. The other mid-level tunnels were just concrete-lined and not as frequently used. It was a rarely used distinction, but it was clear Harmony and Divvy were using it now.

Pulling their boundaries tight enough that only "painted" tunnels were accessible meant that any location that was not a living or working space or a thoroughfare between such was out of bounds. In terms of absolute area, it was like restricting the entire population of the Underground to one of the multi-function outer level towers in the Hub. It wasn't much room for anyone wanting to stretch their legs... or to escape the close supervision of their leaders.

"If you have to wonder who will be authorised, you can safely assume you are not one of them," Divvy clarified. "I know this may seem extreme, but I know the Government will increase their scans of the city and its surroundings to locate these terrorists. I've *seen* it." She gently touched her temple, confirming her use of precognition.

Flit almost choked on her next breath. *Terrorists?* Of all the things she would call the Free Citizens, terrorists was not one of them. Did Control not know anything about the group?

Or did they know, and was there a reason they were making them out to be extremists?

Even though Flit was never one to believe in the whole "enemy of my enemy is my friend" approach, she certainly believed the Underground should be looking into possible allies.

"Alterations will be sent to anyone who is currently performing duties requiring them to go beyond the painted tunnels. This includes, but is not limited to, members of Security, Intelligence, and Supply. If you have scheduled shifts, please ensure you speak to your direct supervisor before embarking on these, as they have likely changed."

At Divvy's latest revelation, Flit glanced around. Finally, she was able to locate Swipe, who was standing with Layla, Clarity, and Link. All four were wearing gym gear, so Flit imagined they had been interrupted mid-evening exercise session. The women were muttering to each other. Their plans to get Flit, Hawkeye, and Layla out away from the direct supervision of their superiors would be severely reduced by these changes.

The announcement had continued as Flit's mind reeled. She shook herself back to focus and returned her attention to the two leaders at the front.

"We do not have all the information we would like to have right now, but we have our teams working on it. However, we would like to open the floor to questions. If we do not have answers right away, we will endeavour to find them as soon as possible," Harmony promised.

She had barely finished speaking when Tally, the cranky old man who had found Flit and Scraps when they had been investigating a storage hold, spoke up. "What will we do for things we aren't growing down here? We will need supplies!"

There was a murmur of agreement from the crowd.

"As always, the people in charge of calculating our need versus supply ratio have been doing an admirable job of keeping things up to date," Divvy assured him in a low, patient tone. Her blue eyes shone, and the light softened her features. "I've had a look at several outcomes for what we have and what we anticipate, and they are all favourable. However, we will continue to monitor these closely."

Harmony nodded along, and added, "If this restriction persists, we will ensure we can make up for any shortfall in supply. That, however, is a discussion for another time."

A wave of calm reassurance rippled over the group at Harmony's last line. It was a subtle hint of indirect coercion that was so cleverly done that even Tally crossed his arms over his chest but stayed quiet. However, people towards the back of the room didn't seem quite as effected by it.

"Will we still have the right security and maintenance around our oxygen supply?" a woman standing by the rear door asked.

"Of course," Harmony said, sounding as if it were obvious. "Our pipelines and filters remain in optimum shape. Restricting resident movement has no impact on that. Critical operations will continue as required."

Even though Harmony had a point about the pipes not being impacted by human restrictions, Flit could understand the mindset of the questioner. She had always felt that living in the Underground was like being buried alive in some ways. Now, the walls of the coffin were just squeezing in tighter and tighter around them. The thought alone was enough to have Flit questioning the air quality and wondering if it was getting a little harder to breathe.

"How long will this be for? Surely it isn't sustainable," Tally called out again, earning him disapproving, narrow-eyed stares from both Harmony and Divvy.

"Thank you again for your concern, Tally, but Divvy and I are trying to brief everyone and would prefer you save any specific questions for later," Harmony said. Her tone was even, but there was a coercive kick to it that had Tally shrinking back. "As for how long the lockdown will last, at this stage, we're not sure. I can confidently confirm that it will be for just as long as we need to ensure our survival, and not a minute longer."

Bullshit, Flit thought. She would have said it too, if she hadn't witnessed Harmony using her telecoercion throughout this meeting. She was already on the leader's radar, and she couldn't afford to draw any more attention to the fact that she was not under her coercive suggestion any longer.

"Why aren't we using this opportunity to formulate a way to get out of here instead of retreating?" someone from the back called out. Flit wasn't sure who, but she appreciated the question.

"That is a fair question," Harmony said, her voice far too patient and gentle to be genuine. It set Flit instantly on edge. "The truth is, we don't have enough information about these Citizen terrorists to know what would happen if we reached out to them. Even if we did, they appear to be rabble-rousers rather than a genuine threat at this point."

Flit frowned. The "rabble-rouser" comment wasn't far from the truth, but at least the Free Citizens had the guts to stand up for themselves.

"If we decide to make a move on the surface, it must be with the absolute certainty of a win. We may be restricted down here, but we lead good lives," Divvy added, her eyes moving over the crowd as she adjusted her tone to something more caring. "Your lives are worth more than a whim and a fantasy."

A whim?

A fantasy?

Flit was struck by the painful temptation to teleport over to the leaders and to give them an idea of what her current whims and fantasies were. Instead, she balled her hands into fists and shoved them into the pockets of her jacket. From the way the crowd was taking in the news, they believed Harmony and Divvy's crap. After all, why would they argue? All they had known, for generations, was the desire to hide away, to scrape, to survive. All they had ever done was accept the darkness because they had been told the light was too dangerous for them.

Even though there was danger on the surface, there was the possibility of freedom too. The possibility of thriving rather than just surviving. The others might have been content with their lot, but Flit yearned for more, not only for her, but for all the Derivates being dominated by the Government.

There were a few more questions about rosters and the like, but Flit ignored them. She was too busy trying to sort through her own anger at the situation. Even though the concerns about being stuck were taking up the most space in her mind, there was also a good chunk of it that snagged on the fact this whole thing messed with her plans to get Scraps back.

Given how events had unfolded in the Underground after the maglev attack, Flit knew that bringing Scraps back to the Underground proper right away would be foolish. It wasn't enough to just retrieve him. They had to find proof that he wasn't involved in the tunnel collapses. They had to find a way to protect him from manipulation, as well. Harmony's use of telecoercion on Flit had been a gut-punch. Flit wanted to give the woman the benefit of the doubt and believe that it was because it was easy to blame Scraps and ease the worries of the others. However, she wasn't confident enough in that to expose Scraps to the woman. If she convinced him to confess, then he would be walking into a death sentence.

A zing of pain sizzled through Flit's arms as her nails dug sharply into her palms. The tension in her limbs was growing, and she just wanted to leave. She wanted to speak to the others, to find somewhere she could bring Scraps. Considering that their plan was for her to translocate, they could probably just find somewhere else to start their journey. The starting point for translocation mattered far less than it would have for sequential teleportation. Perhaps they could hide Scraps in someone's room and just sneak food back to him.

As much as Flit loved her parents, she wasn't sure they would keep the secret safe if she brought Scraps back to her own apartment. She had no reason to request an apartment of her own either, especially when there were so many new people in the space filling every spare room already. A lot of the others in her team only had single rooms, but she was sure one of them would be willing to share if needed.

A heavy sigh broke Flit from her train of thought.

"We should cancel our plans to meet tonight," Hawkeye said as he approached her with some of the other Blue Team members. "Everyone's on high alert. I'll do a bit of research in the meantime, and we'll get together tomorrow night instead."

"Shall we head to dinner, then?" Layla asked.

There was a general murmur of agreement.

As the group turned and started walking in the direction of the

Mess, following the flow of foot traffic, Flit said to the others, "I managed to translocate tonight. I still need to work on non-live image locations, but... I did it."

From the way her friends grinned at her, Flit could tell they were containing cheers of excitement. It would have been far too suspicious in the current climate. Still, the way their eyes shone with the acknowledgement of her achievement added a little swagger to her stride.

25

SCRAPS

THE CITY WAS WARY.

That was what it felt like as Scraps made his way to the club. All of the streets had extra guards posted, Citizen and Derivate alike. They kept people moving along. Anyone stopping to take a break or peer around was questioned. Scraps avoided the maglev stations after he heard some people on the street whispering about the fact that they were utterly packed with patrolling officers. Scraps was concerned there might be some telepaths down there. On the streets, it would be fine because he could keep walking. Trapped on a station platform, though? He would have to control his thoughts so tightly he did not want to risk it.

Even Nightmix felt off as Scraps approached. For once, there was no line out the front of the building. The long walk to the club meant that it was somewhat late by the time Scraps arrived. Normally, the line would have snaked out of the club by now, with people eagerly waiting to get in early and immerse themselves in the strobing lights and thumping music.

Thanks to his personal connection with the owners of the club, Scraps never really had to wait for entry. He could just skip the line, and the bouncers would let him in without a second thought. His VIP access had little effect when there was no line.

Inside, the club was a poor shadow of its usual self. The music and the lights were still in full swing, but the crowd of partiers was thin enough that Scraps could make his way to the back of the room with ease. He tried to be inconspicuous about it, acting as though he was scoping for a table or a good spot to hang around.

The Free Citizens meeting wasn't scheduled until later in the night, but Scraps didn't care that he was early. He needed to speak to Adam one-on-one. He needed information about what had gone down and why he had been kept so completely out of the loop.

Scraps thought back to his discussion with Greene and Hector, and he hoped they would believe him when he said he had nothing to do with the attack. Scraps was walking a very fine line with the Government. If they had any reason to investigate him further, they would learn about his connection to the Underground. If he left now, he had no doubt they would track him. His only hope to keep Flit and his friends safe was to play his new role perfectly.

When Scraps finally sidled up to the office door, he knocked on it a few times. It took a minute, but the door was eventually opened. He was greeted by Andy's teal hair and a bright smile that was at odds with the mood of the rest of the city.

"Hey! You're early." Andy stepped back to let Scraps in without needing an answer.

"Yeah, I heard about what happened tonight. I need to speak to Adam," Scraps said. As much as he thought Andy seemed to be a nice person, he was keen to get to the bottom of the situation.

"He's downstairs with Petra and Trey now. What's it like outside?"

The question made Scraps frown and his forehead crease. "Tense. Disconcerting."

"Are there any announcements on the big screens?" Andy walked over, sitting on the edge of the office desk and leaning back to rest on her hand as she watched him.

"What kind of announcement would you be expecting?"

It was then Andy's turn to frown. She glanced between Scraps and the entrance to the tunnel that led to the bunker and raked a hand through her hair. "I think you should go speak to Adam." There was a hint of apology in her tone.

Scraps nodded, walked to the back of the room, but paused before the large screen that covered the hidden panel door. "Did you know about whatever it was before it happened?" He looked back over his shoulder to watch the woman.

Andy's shoulders sagged. "He asked me to do a bit of digital magic for him, but I didn't realise what it was for. Petra and Trey didn't know what was going on until he showed up early with a couple of people just after we opened."

Letting out a huff of frustration, Scraps shook his head. "Thanks," he said, genuinely grateful Andy was willing to share that with him. "I'd better get down there and see what this is all about, then."

The rough concrete passageway was as familiar to Scraps as his own apartment. He had traversed the path so many times over the past few weeks. With how busy the Free Citizens had become, there was almost always a low hum of conversation emanating from the bunker at the end. Like everything else tonight, though, it was different.

"How are we supposed to tell her family?" Trey's raised, almost frantic voice echoed down the tunnel. Scraps heard him before he saw him.

"We aren't supposed to," came Adam's smooth reply.

Some might have considered his tone to be calming, but there was an undercurrent of dismissal in it that had Scraps set immediately on edge. He picked up his pace.

"Of course, we tell them!" Petra argued just as Scraps entered the bunker. She looked as though she might say more, but she froze, peering over Adam's shoulder at him.

Slowly, Adam turned. His lips stretched from a disgruntled grimace into a wide smile. "Ah, Brian! I'm glad you got our message." Turning his back on Trey and Petra, Adam strode across the concrete floor.

"What is going on?" Scraps demanded, not giving Adam time for further meaningless pleasantries.

"We managed to acquire the identity chips we spoke about the other night. They are secure with one of our members as we speak. We'll be able to move forward with our plans sooner than we thought." Adam clapped Scraps on the shoulder and then kept his hand there, leading him over to the desk they used for strategising.

"We cannot move the plan forward. The group are not well trained enough." Scraps dismissed the idea immediately. "And whilst I appreciate you telling me what was acquired, you did not actually tell me what happened."

"We lost two people," Trey blurted, earning him a look of reprimand from Adam.

Scraps felt as though a bucket of ice water had been dumped over his head.

"We did not *lose* two people," Adam said smoothly, returning his gaze to Scraps. "Two people bravely gave their lives fighting for our cause. Their sacrifice will help us bring down the Government."

"Sacrifice? It was friendly fire. Jill died because—"

"Enough!" Adam barked sharply, raising his hand to cut Petra off. She flinched away, and Trey stepped between her and Adam. "Leave us. I need to speak to Brian privately."

It was a show of how much Adam had taken over the space that Petra and Trey left their own bunker immediately.

Scraps waited until the sounds of their footsteps had receded before speaking. "What happened?"

In the seconds that had elapsed since his rather brutal dismissal, Adam regained his composure. He stood in front of Scraps and leaned back against the desk as casually as he would if they were discussing the weather.

"I understand that people will be hurt by the death of two members, but if we don't move on from this quickly, their loss would have been in vain," Adam said. "What I am interested in now is seeing how we can best respect their legacy. I've been thinking about this plan we have, and I want—"

Scraps' jaw tightened. "I do not want to hear it," he said, not caring that he was being rude and cutting Adam off. "You told me that you would include me in plans. You didn't, and now two people are dead, and the entire city is more heavily guarded."

Adam's gaze sharpened as Scraps spoke, his eyes narrowing ever so slightly. It was a look Scraps had seen on many people before, and he knew that this moment could make or break his place in the Free Citizens and potentially ruin the only reason the Government were letting him walk free.

"So, you need to make a decision," Scraps said, squaring up to Adam and deciding he needed to use strength to fight strength. "Either you tell me everything from now on, or I turn around and walk out and forget all about you and the Free Citizens."

Scraps held Adam's intense stare. He kept his chin high and his face set with determination. He thought back to the night they attacked the human research facility and the way Flit had stared the man down. Adam was all about the power games, and right now, he needed Scraps more than Scraps needed him. In his time training the other Free Citizens to shoot and fight, Scraps had earned their respect and camaraderie. If he left, especially after two people died, Adam would have trouble keeping everyone calm and in line.

From the way Adam's gaze started out calm and collected and slowly morphed into something hard and piercing, Scraps knew Adam was aware of the nature of the situation too.

"Fine," Adam conceded. He pointed at Scraps. "But you need to understand something, Brian. This isn't a game. This isn't child's play. If you want to be involved, you need to acknowledge that we have started something that will either end with us winning or us dying."

Shoulders tensing with annoyance at the condescension in Adam's tone, Scraps watched the man carefully. He was tempted to tell Adam that he knew much more about the need for change than Adam ever would. Adam might have chafed at the way his freedom had been curbed, but Scraps had been born into slavery.

"I assure you, Adam, that I am very well aware of the stakes," Scraps said, voice low and even, supremely calm despite the rage boiling in his gut.

Something in Adam's eyes flickered with surprise and approval at Scraps' words. "Then you'll stop fucking around and finally work with us to implement the training you've been insisting on?"

"Yes." Scraps knew it was now or never. "But only if you agree to follow my advice and stop lying to me."

Adam stared at Scraps for several long moments as the two men stood there. Then, the tension in Adam's posture trickled away, and a wide, victorious grin stretched his pale lips thin. He reached over and patted Scraps on the shoulder. "Good. I knew I could count on you," he said, all bluster and confidence where there had been defensive wariness a moment ago. "Now, I need you to help me figure out how to best deliver the news of Jill's and Michael's sacrifice. If we leverage the situation just right, I think we can really light a flame under our more reluctant members."

Scraps knew who he wanted to light a flame—no, a giant bonfire —under, and it certainly wasn't anyone other than Adam. Still, he had to play along. As much as the thought of twisting the needless death of two good people to serve a cause weighed uncomfortably on his shoulders, he was *in*. Adam had taken the bait, and now Scraps was going to see what the Free Citizens were really capable of.

26

FLIT

MORNING CAME with a strong sense of clarity and determination for Flit. After waking up with her first alarm, Flit dressed and freshened up for the day, had a quick breakfast with her parents, and teleported her way to Hawkeye's bedroom door.

"We need to move things along faster," Flit said firmly. "If this lockdown bullshit is going to continue, we need to act before we run out of time or surveillance increases."

Rubbing his eyes and stifling a yawn, Hawkeye muttered, "What?"

"We need to hurry up and rescue—"

All sense of Hawkeye's tiredness disappeared as he grasped Flit's forearm and hauled her into his room. "Shhh! Are you crazy?" He shut the door behind her. "We can't just go talking about those plans in the halls!"

Flit rolled her eyes. "I was out there waiting for you to get your arse out of bed and open the door. There was no one there."

"You can never be too careful." Hawkeye shook his head and sighed. "Regardless, I have something to show you. I found it yesterday and thought you'd want to see it."

Instead of launching into her tirade about why they needed to reschedule that cancelled meeting from last night ASAP, Flit pressed her lips together. "You're just trying to distract me."

"Maybe." Hawkeye shrugged. "But I need to hit the restroom

and take a shower before we talk business. At least you'll have something to keep you occupied."

Despite her best intentions to cut off any more foolishness, Flit was curious, and Flit was never good at resisting her curiosity.

Hawkeye didn't even bother waiting for an answer as he walked over to the screen in his small studio apartment. He went through a complicated maze of folders that he tapped on so fast Flit could barely follow. "Do you remember when you recorded a message before you left for your undercover mission?"

Flit's eyebrows furrowed. "Yes."

"Well, do you remember Scraps recording one too?"

Flit snorted. "Yeah. Shocked the heck out of Shadow. Why?"

"Sit." Hawkeye pointed to the end of his bed.

Flit frowned. "Why?"

"Just. Fucking. Sit."

There was enough impatience in Hawkeye's tone that Flit teleported over to the end of his bed and planted herself down on the tousled blankets.

When Flit was settled, Hawkeye tapped the screen a final time, and Scraps' face filled the window. Flit gasped as she saw him there with his red eyes, blond hair, and Government tattoo. Over the space of their time in the Hub, she had come to think of him as the tawny haired, blue-eyed man she was living with. Seeing him again like that, like he was when she fell for him, opened an aching chasm in her chest.

"What... How..."

Hawkeye gave her a gentle smile. "I figured he was the kind of guy to take up the offer of a recording. Thankfully, Cogs was able to work her way into the system and steal a copy of this for us."

"Do you know what the message is?"

Hawkeye shrugged. "It felt wrong to watch it beyond the bit where he mentioned it was for you. It's been a while, so you should take some time to watch it. It might help."

Flit's eyes prickled with emotion, and she nodded.

With a gentle squeeze of her shoulder, Hawkeye said, "I'll be in the shower. Let me know when you're done. I won't come out before then, okay?"

"Thank you," she said before he left her alone with the recording.

Flit tapped the remote-control panel beside Hawkeye's bed. She kept her gaze on Scraps as he came to life before her.

"If you are listening to this message, then something must have happened to me," he began in that serious, stoic tone she remembered so fondly.

Scraps paused a moment as if in thought. He swallowed hard and took a deep breath.

"Flit." A small smile formed on his lips at her name, and the tears that had been welling in Flit's eyes slid down her cheeks. "I'll never forget the way we met. I was surrounded by flesh-eating rats with no way out. You could have left me to die, a Government Derivate, trained by and representing everything you hated."

He looked away from the camera, his eyebrows furrowing with the emotions of the memories. When he looked back at the camera several heartbeats later, Scraps' expression transformed into something confident and determined.

"But you didn't. You couldn't. You saved me and even after I had the arrogance to try and arrest you." He chuckled at the memory as he spoke, and Flit laughed along too.

Oh, how she loved hearing that laugh of his again.

It was always hard to earn a chuckle from Scraps, so Flit treasured each and every one. She enjoyed his stilted sense of humour and the way he found amusement in the odd, chaotic moments they had shared.

"It was our first spar too. I think it went well, considering the circumstances." He shook his head. "You know, I spent the first week in the Underground trying to gather information for the Government and planning how I was going to escape."

Guilt had Scraps' posture sagging, and Flit held her breath. She couldn't believe she had ever been taken in by Harmony's lies.

"But you showed me what I could have, how I could be more than I was. The others helped a little too, but it was mostly you. Without you Flit, I would just be another mindless drone, enforcing a corrupt regime without a conscience. You gave me something worth fighting for. *Someone* worth fighting for." He smiled again, wider.

Flit felt a smile tugging at her own lips too, and her heart felt as if it grew three sizes in her chest. She wished she could reach out and run her fingers of his familiar jawline. She wished she could tell him she loved him. And, oh, how she wished she could hear him say it back. Not under life or death circumstances, but in the calm intimacy of a quiet moment just like this.

Then, Scraps cleared his throat, pulling Flit from her daydream. His expression hardened, and his tone was serious again as he spoke. "Back to the issue at hand. The mission. I want you to know that no matter what happened, I chose this." He looked down at the floor for a moment as if remembering something.

Flit shifted on the edge of Hawkeye's bed, her breath caught in her throat as she waited to hear whatever it was that had Scraps so pensive.

"Seeing how you were with Hawkeye after the last mission, you are probably going to blame yourself for whatever happened—maybe not fighting hard enough or not doing enough to stop it—but that isn't true. You always give it everything and you never give up." He moved his face closer to the camera, staring right into the lens.

Heart fluttering in her chest as if he was looking right at her, Flit instinctively leaned forward.

"So, no matter what..." He paused then swallowed hard, a steely sense of resolve overcoming him. "Keep fighting. Don't give up. You will free the Underground. Though I might not be there see it, I want you to know that I..." He paused again as if he couldn't find the words before surging forward with a wide smile curled in the corner with regret. "I'm betting on you. I have been all along."

A sob spilled from Flit's lips, and she pressed a hand against her hammering heart. Even though she had missed him so deeply over the past few weeks, she had never wanted to feel his arms around her as badly as she did in that moment. The tears that spilled were short-lived, though. The sense of faith and trust he had in her fed the glowing coals of resistance in her gut, making her desire to help her people fare with a new sense of purpose and passion.

The sound of the shower running had stopped at some point

during the message, so Flit teleported over to the door and knocked on it. When it opened, Hawkeye's hair was still wet, and he was standing with a towel wrapped around and concern etched on his face. "Is everything—"

"We're going to get him, and when we bring him back, we're going to raise hell down here," Flit said.

Hawkeye's grimace turned into a grin, and he pulled her into a tight bear hug. "You bet your arse we are!"

"I DON'T KNOW what has come over you, and I'm not sure if I should be pleased or concerned," Shadow said as Flit teleported back into the observation room and took a long swig of water from her bottle.

After half a dozen successful translocations to the other room using only mental visualisation as reference, Flit was exhausted physically but emotionally exhilarated. "Why would you be concerned?"

Shadow raised his eyebrows at her. "You've never been good at hiding your motives. You wear your emotions in the sparkle in your eyes. I've seen that look on your face before. You're up to something, and I think it is better if I don't ask what it is."

It would have been entirely plausible for Flit to try to dismiss his concerns, to tell him he was just imagining things, but she respected him too much to treat him like a fool.

"I think it's better you don't ask, either."

Rubbing his brow and shaking his head, Shadow shut down the observation screens with his free hand. "I know the warning is likely redundant, but be careful. We've got a lot of parts moving behind the scenes to make sure everyone in the Underground is safe. Experience has told me that telling you 'no' only makes you more determined, so all I will say is stop for a moment. Think about whether what you're doing is really as important as you think it is. And... don't risk anyone else in your shenanigans."

Flit crossed her arms, her bottle tucked against her chest, and leaned back against the wall. "You're not going to try to stop me?"

"No."

Shadow's short answer was intriguing. He didn't qualify it with anything. He didn't roll his eyes or change his posture in challenge. He just watched her seriously. There was something in his gaze that made her think that this wasn't some kind of trap. He genuinely meant to keep out of her business.

"Is there anything else you need to practice before you attempt whatever it is you're planning?"

"Are you... Are you serious?" Flit asked, eyes wide.

"If you're going to take risks, I'd rather you be as prepared as possible."

Given the fact Shadow was already working on upskilling her for some purpose he wasn't sharing yet, Flit figured they both had something to hide. If she asked for more, she had a feeling he wasn't likely to snitch on her. After all, if anyone read her mind, he would automatically fall into the category of suspicious.

"Translocation with a passenger." Flit jutted her chin out, holding his gaze and wondering if that would change his mind about not prying.

Shadow stepped forward. "Once you've got translocation down, taking someone else along isn't really much harder. You're already skilled at knowing how to keep your passenger safe for line-of-sight. It's the same deal." He reached a hand out to her to make the physical contact required for such a task. "Although translocation is more disorienting for the person you're taking along than line-of-sight. Prepare to jump back or take a spare pair of shoes with you. The chance you're going to get vomited on is infinitely higher."

Flit snorted a laugh at the last piece of advice and stepped closer, taking his offered hand. "Shall we start with a visual reference?"

"No, that would be taking a step back." Shadow straightened his stance. "I don't think failure is on the agenda for you this evening."

"It never has been." Flit grinned at him.

She closed her eyes, took in a slow breath through her nose, and pictured the room adjacent to the one they were in.

Then, Flit proved Shadow right.

SCRAPS

TWO NIGHTS AFTER SCRAPS' heated conversation with Adam at Nightmix, the leader of the Free Citizens knocked on the door to the Scraps' apartment. They had agreed to wait before speaking privately again because they did not want to risk getting together too soon and drawing the attention of the Government. Well, Adam didn't want to. Scraps knew that he was already well and truly on their radar and had warned the agents that he would be having this precise meeting. They were expecting a full report some time over the next couple of days.

"Adam, come in." Scraps held the door open.

Wearing a plain pair of black pants and a dark grey jacket, Adam stepped past Scraps and walked in. "I didn't say anything last time, Brian, but being here reminds me of just how lucrative it can be to work for the Government. Your job has given you some nice luxuries," he said as he walked across the entry area and over to the lounge room with the wide, low couch and the floor-to-ceiling windows. Beyond the glass, the sky was dark, but the city was awash with a spectrum of lights and colour.

"The job has also allowed me to gain some important information to help our cause," Scraps noted. He wasn't the best at picking up on social slights, but Adam's tone and the reference to the benefits Scraps got from working for their enemy didn't sit right with him.

"For which I have been very, very grateful." Adam wheeled around to face Scraps. He peered towards the hall that led to the bathroom and bedroom. "No word about Ava's return, yet?"

Scraps shook his head. "She wants to spend as much time with her family as she can."

"Pity. I thought she was dedicated to our cause and understood the sacrifice necessary if we are to prevail."

Shifting on his feet and trying to keep his face neutral, Scraps said, "Oh, she does, but right now, she is where she needs to be. I am more than competent to help you." Then, to try and get Adam's mind off the fact Flit might not be dedicated, he said, "Besides, there is far less arguing when you and Ava are not in the same room. Enjoy the quiet while you can. When she gets back, she will be far less accommodating than I am."

That earned a genuine laugh from Adam. "True, Brian. Very true." Adam walked over to the dining table and helped himself to a seat. He slipped a hand inside his jacket and pulled a datapad out of a pocket in there. "Join me."

As Scraps waked over, he was unsurprised by the audacity Adam had to invite Scraps to sit at his own dining table.

"You know, this place reminds me of somewhere I used to live."

"Oh, so you have had the privilege of a well-paid job before too?" Scraps asked, reflecting Adam's own implication from earlier.

Adam tapped the screen of the datapad to turn it on and started working through some password-protected files to open an array of schematics and documents. "Yes. More so than you could imagine."

"Did you work for the Government?" Scraps probed, wanting to know more about the mysterious man across from him.

"I was part of the Oligarchy," Adam said as casually as if he was speaking about the weather.

Scraps' eyes bulged, and his mouth dropped open.

Looking up from his datapad, Adam raised an eyebrow and smirked. "Surprised, Brian?"

Realising he must look ridiculous, Scraps snapped his mouth shut and blinked away the dryness in his previously wide eyes. "Yes, I must admit I am. I assumed you had connections in high places, but I did not think you were in that high a place."

As much as Scraps hated himself for it, a sense of awe rose within him. The Oligarchy were the small, select group of people chosen to oversee the Government and its holdings. Their identities were kept secret to avoid them being hunted or bribed, but it was well known that they could be working for any Government department at any level. The idea that your own office-buddy could be secretly sitting in on the meetings and making ruling decisions in the Government was enough to keep most workers on their best behaviour.

"Are... are you still part of the Oligarchy?" Scraps asked, suddenly wary.

What if he wasn't the only double agent? What if this was all some Government plot to root out dissenters and deal with them before a full-scale uprising could develop?

"No." Adam pushed the datapad along the smooth frosted glass surface of the dining table and gave Scraps his full attention. "I escaped before they could come after me. Let's just say that my apartment..." He gestured around at the sleek trappings of Scraps' abode. "...and everything else I used to own is now in their possession."

"Where do you live, then?" Scraps asked. He had never really given much thought to the matter. Adam always just appeared in the places he was needed. That was all Scraps previously needed to know.

"That's a good question," Adam said, sitting back in his chair, "but we're not here to talk about me. We've got a lot of planning to get through." He pulled up a map of the city on his datapad.

It was no easy task for Scraps to squash his curiosity. Was Adam on the run? He had assumed he was just hiding in plain sight, much like Scraps and the other Free Citizens were, but if he had tried to escape the Oligarchy, he must be well and truly on the run. Scraps imagined it must have been quite difficult to evade Government surveillance whilst remaining in the heart of their main city, so he could only guess that Adam still had a lot of important contacts in high places.

"Brian?"

Adam's voice snapped Scraps from the internal whirlwind of

questions rushing through his mind. "Sorry. Please, go on."

With a shake of his head, Adam pointed to the map of the Hub with its perfect grid layout. He traced a finger around the outer bounds of the city. "I want to gain control of the entire outer rim. If we get enough of a cordon going, we can implement a siege."

Leaning forward, Scraps knitted his eyebrows together. That was not at all what he was expecting. They were so far away from having the resources they needed for that kind of thing. There was far too much to consider before even thinking about it.

"Sieges are an outdated military tactic," Scraps said, frowning. He had studied a wide range of subjects for leisure when he had lived in the Derivate Training Facility. He was familiar with ancient warfare approaches. "They rely on the fact that resources cannot be easily transferred between sites. If we start a siege, the other cities would have reinforcements here within hours."

"Oh, Brian." Adam sighed, shaking his head. "Do you really think that the Free Citizens you've seen here are the only ones I have under my wing?"

Well, yes. That was exactly what Scraps thought with the exception of a drabble of people here and there who he had heard of but never met.

The silence from Scraps was enough of a confirmation for Adam.

"The outfit we have here is wider than you can imagine. You know that I have other cells in the city. I also have mirrored groups in every city and major living centre." Adam zoomed out beyond the bounds of the Hub until the satellite cities appeared on the map. Scraps noted the glowing dot where Eastbay was, just one of the glimmering stars in a constellation of the population.

"The other teams must be quiet, then. I haven't heard anything about them—" Scraps pressed his lips together before he could finish that rather stupid comment.

Amusement glimmered in Adam's eyes when Scraps made the connections in his mind. Of course, they hadn't heard anything about cells in other cities. The Government were barely broadcasting anything about the local Free Citizen attacks. Why would they report on the happenings in other locations?

"It's always telling, you know, watching someone's expression as they finally start connecting the dots." Adam leaned back in his seat, cockiness written all over his relaxed posture. "I'm pleased to know that I still have some tricks up my sleeve, even for you."

Scraps tilted his head forward, hoping it came across as a respectful nod. "I must say I am impressed." He reached over, zooming back into the Hub and trying not to let the throbbing dot of Eastbay make him think of Flit. "Tell me more about this siege you want to pull off."

Adam grinned. He seemed content enough to tell Scraps all about his plans.

True to his word, he explained that he had acquired many resources from the outer cities, including inroads into the broadcasting networks that controlled not only the media, but the entire flow of internal information. He explained that the uniforms that Scraps' small group had made and the computer chips the fatal incursion had gathered were enough for a small team of insurgents to infiltrate the Hub's Network Hive and plant bugs that would allow them to have control of the communications networks.

"Once we have control of the flow of information and communication, we can isolate the cities whilst projecting an impression that it's business as usual in each one," Adam explained, pride shining on his cheeks, which had become increasingly ruddy with his fervour as the conversation deepened. "Meanwhile, we will be slowly tightening the boundaries of the siege and gaining more control."

"Control is all well and good," Scraps said slowly, "but it won't be long before the Government realises something is wrong and starts fighting back."

There were simply too many people in the Hub, too many sources of information, that no charade could be held for too long.

"I'm counting on that," Adam said simply. "Like we did with the broadcast after the maglev mission, I plan to let the populace know of our cause when the time is right. I think we'll have an influx of numbers then."

Scraps sat back, looking at the map. "What are our number like now? We have a lot of ground to cover and hold."

Adam watched him for several long, tense moments. Scraps felt as though Adam were truly trying to gauge just how much Scraps could be trusted with. Then, he opened a spreadsheet on the datapad with a list of cities and numbers beneath each.

Scraps let out a low hum of surprise as he saw far more people signed to their cause than he anticipated.

"Better than you thought?" Adam asked with a chuckle.

"That is far more workable than I had imagined."

Adam closed the spreadsheet and reclined in his chair. "We just need to figure out our timeline, and then we can say that this uprising is well and truly under way." He swiped to a notetaking app and glanced up at Scraps. "Before we do, though... I need to ask you a few questions."

"Of course." Scraps was wary, but given the amount of information Adam had just given him, he had a feeling that the man already deemed him worthy of trust.

"Will having Ava in another city distract you from our cause?"

Scraps blinked as he considered it, surprised that they were jumping back to the topic of Flit. Well, not Flit. *Ava.*

"No, I do not think so."

"I would prefer something more certain," Adam said. "You either tell me, one hundred percent, that you can dedicate yourself to the uprising in the Hub, or I can swap you and the leader in Eastbay. It would mean you are fully responsible for that cell and their mission, but I know you are capable. The current leader has the same kind of tactical mind as you, so I will happily have either of you as my wingman here."

The question stirred up so many thoughts in Scraps' mind. Adam and the others were constantly asking after Ava. If he were with a different group of people, who had never met her, it would be far easier to dismiss their questions. However, Eastbay was the city they were transferred from, so he was unsure if his current identity would hold out there, but would it even matter? Even though all Government cities were well guarded, Eastbay was very different to the Hub. It might be easier to slip out of Greene and Hector's noose there and return to the Underground.

"I can see I've given you something to think about." Adam took the datapad off the table and tucked it into his jacket pocket. "A lot of things, really. I'll give you a couple of days. Come and see me at Nightmix at the usual time and let me know what you want to do." Rising from his seat, Adam smoothed the creases out of his pants. "Either way, you have potential to do great things for the movement. We don't have much time to waste, so I will be waiting on your decision and expecting you to hit the ground running."

The commanding octave of Adam's voice had Scraps almost saluting as he rose to his feet. The man sounded every bit the Government official when he spoke like that. Luckily, the Underground had thoroughly drilled any saluting or "for the good of all" out of him.

"Very well. I'll have an answer for you then."

Scraps was grateful for the opportunity to think it over. He had been given so much information to process. Then, he wondered how would he hide it from the telepath that always with the agents.

"See you then." Adam was over at the door, about to leave before Scraps realised the man had said farewell.

"Wait!"

Adam raised his eyebrows.

"Why did you leave the Oligarchy? You were at the highest level of power."

"The Government is too far gone." The casual set of Adam's shoulders tensed, and he looked past Scraps out of the window and at the city beyond. "When I was first called into service, I was optimistic. Idealistic. Foolish." The sound of Adam's self-derisive snort filled the air. "I soon learned that the only way to deal with the continued crimes against our freedom was to raze the Government and start anew. Anything else would only be like trying to build a utopia on shit-stained and mould-ridden foundations."

Despite the concerning flicker of fervour in Adam's eyes, Scraps could not disagree with him, so he nodded and watched as the leader of the Free Citizens left his apartment.

Scraps stood rooted to the spot for the longest while as his mind spun with all the information he had learned in such a short span of time. At least, Scraps thought, he understood why the Government Agents were keen to keep track of Adam. They probably figured that they needed to get a better idea of the reach of his network before bringing him in. He was clearly a very powerful enemy. Scraps couldn't even imagine the kind of information the Oligarchs had access to, cloistered in the top level of Centre One as they made their rulings for the city.

With all the revelations, Scraps hadn't had time to really think about how to handle them. The knowledge that the agents would be waiting to speak to him in the morning loomed over his head. Whilst he had gone into the arrangement happy to share bits and pieces, the thought of them knowing the true extent of the Free Citizen's reach did not sit well with him. From the numbers Adam had shared and the plans they had in place, the Free Citizens stood a real chance of making a difference. Scraps still wasn't entirely certain they would win, but the Government would take a damn good hit in the process. Surely that would be enough to make them finally sit up and listen to the true needs of their people?

Then, Scraps mind drifted to his own kind. He should have asked Adam what his plans were for handing the Derivates. He, Chris, and Liana had yet to share the full extent of the enhanced training and tactics that the Government was drilling into the Registereds. If the Government deployed their new forces against the rebels, it could mean casualties in the thousands.

The thought of so many enslaved Derivates dying at the hands of the Free Citizens made Scraps' stomach churn. He could not allow that. He would have to find a way to protect them.

Or, Scraps realised, to let the Underground know what was going on so they could come up and help. Maybe, just maybe, if the Underground came to the surface to help, they could actually win.

All those concerns and more were racing through Scraps' mind at lightning speed as he readied himself for bed. Even a scalding shower and a fresh set of sheets on the bed were not enough to distract him. Scraps had never really had trouble sleeping. He was very good at compartmentalising his thoughts and picking them up again in the morning, but as Scraps tossed and turned in bed, with the new information plaguing his mind, he wished Flit was there with him.

She would know what to do.

28

FLIT

THE MESS WAS LOUDER than usual as Flit walked in.

With the new restrictions on movement, people were getting restless and bored. The recreation areas in the Residence were packed, but there was no real food there. The Mess was where the real keen people wanted to be. Extra tables had been wedged between the existing rows when the refugees arrived, but even then, there were not enough for how many people were squeezed into the space.

Luckily, the importance of the Blue Team's role in protecting the boundaries of their living space meant that they, like the other Security teams, managed to keep hold of their preferred tables without much fuss.

There had been a few instances over the past few days where people had chosen the table in the back corner decorated with an assortment of natural stones and other ephemera to dine at. However, all it took was a member of the Blue Team looking in that direction for them to clear off.

The table itself became more difficult to sit at, just because so many more people had chosen to join them. As Flit approached, squeezing past small groups standing and mingling as they ate from plates held in their hands, she noted that she would either have to sit on someone's lap or steal a chair from somewhere else.

"Flit!" Tweak called out, voice muffled by a mouthful of mash potato. He hip-bumped Sway, who was sitting to his left at the edge of the bench, and almost knocked the blond telecoercionist off his seat. "Sit here!"

Tweak glared expectantly at Hawkeye, who was sitting on his right.

Hawkeye cleared his throat and looked at Layla who was beside him. "Sorry... It's going to be a tight fit," he said, moving closer as his cheeks reddened.

Layla, who was midway through chewing a slab of meat-replacement, smiled back at him shyly and nodded. The shift had their sides pressed against one another, and Flit could imagine their thighs were touching beneath the table.

Flit rolled her eyes. Those two really were getting sickeningly cute together.

"Come. Sit." Fortune waved Flit over from where she was sitting across from Hawkeye.

Instead of walking, Flit teleported to the other side of the bench and looked down at the small space of metal. Hawkeye was right. It was going to be a tight squeeze. She was also worried about the structural integrity of the furniture. She'd only ever really seen four people on them before. Across the table, Swipe, Clarity, Link, Fortune, and Patch were squeezed onto one bench.

Flit shrugged. If the other bench could hold five, surely this one could too. She sank down between Hawkeye and Tweak. When she was settled, they moved in a bit closer either side of her to give their fellow bench mates back some space. It wasn't really the most comfortable arrangement, but Flit didn't care. She wasn't really feeling hungry, so she didn't need the elbow room, and she was too excited about her progress that day to resent the lack of personal space.

"You look smug."

Swipe's comment ensured that the attention of the group remained squarely on Flit.

"You could have gone with pleased. Or triumphant. Or highly skilled and successful," Flit said, more sass in her voice than annoyance.

"Cocky would have worked also," Sway muttered.

Flit snorted in amusement. "Like you can talk." Then, she glanced around surreptitiously. "Besides, you'd probably be cocky too if you had reached full AAA status of teleportation."

The Derivates in the Underground rarely ever spoke about the Government's ability classification levels. They learned them as children, but without the control chips, they were wildly inaccurate at capturing the intricacies of what the rebels could achieve. However, it was pretty common knowledge that the only time a teleporter could reach AAA was if they had translocated. Everyone else, no matter how good their line-of-sight, could only ever reach AA.

It took a good few seconds for understanding to dawn in Sway's eyes, an understanding which rippled around the table. Flit couldn't stop the wide, gloating grin from taking over her face.

"Well... I'm impressed. Not surprised, but impressed all the same," Link said, the first to break the silence in a low voice.

They all knew they needed to be careful about discussing elements of their plan in public places. However, the amount of people and noise in the Mess and the use of certain substitute words, like AAA instead of translocation, meant that they were reasonably safe to speak.

"Thank you," Flit said, figuring she needed to be gracious. Still, every part of her was buzzing with pride at the achievement.

Growing up, Flit had always dreamed about reaching the peak level of her abilities. Of course, it was only ever a pipe dream for most teleporters. That level of translocation was highly unnecessary for life in the Underground, so most teleporters didn't push themselves. It wasn't worth the risk of burnout. The speed of her progress towards her goal over the past few weeks had surprised even her, especially when Shadow's proclamation that she would find translocating with someone else easy turned out to be true.

"That means we can move forward with things," Fortune said quietly, looking around at the group her son used to lead.

"Our next rotation for outer-area patrols isn't for another week," Swipe muttered before shoving a spoonful of potato in her mouth.

The potato was another reason Flit wasn't keen to eat. She would much prefer to raid her parent's stash of dehydrated meals.

With an indefinite restriction on their movement, the residents of the Underground were now forced to return to staple foods that could easily be grown in their restrictive environment. Anything with the ability to provide filling meals for a vast amount of people was favoured, and the meals had started to taste like bland muck.

"We'll find another way around it," Clarity said with absolute certainty.

Everyone at the table turned to face her, and she gave an innocent shrug. As the team's resident precog, they knew that tone well. She wasn't just giving them polite assurances. She had seen a future where they manage to come up with another plan.

Noticing the eyes on her, Clarity shook her head ever so slightly and set the geode she had been fiddling with back down on the table. "Not here."

Clarity's dismissal deflated the burgeoning sense of anticipation at the table, and the team returned to their meals.

Hawkeye leaned in closer, his shoulder brushing Flit's. "Congrats. I knew you could do it. I bet Scraps'll be so impressed."

The first part of Hawkeye's compliment was enough to warm Flit's heart, but it was the second part that really made her day. She was so focused on the fact they were doing all of this to save Scraps that she hadn't given much thought to what he would say when he saw her or what he would do.

Regardless, Flit couldn't focus on that. She couldn't afford to have her mind drifting to all sorts of soft and unnecessary things. Not when the health and safety of the people she was translocating with depended on her having a clear head.

Flit was about to reply to Hawkeye when her stomach let loose a loud, angry grumble. She had indulged in a hearty lunch to ensure she had enough energy to teleport, but her body had consumed far too much energy during her teleports, and she was famished. She had patrol later that night, too, so instead of sticking around, she stood.

"I'd better get home to have dinner with my folks. I'll check in with you guys after my patrol, yeah?" she asked, knowing she and Swipe would need something interesting to offset the drudgery of walking the supply tunnels.

"See you then! I hope you're ready for me to whip your arse in Hoversoft," Hawkeye said, naming a random game to lend more support to their cover story of using the VR Suite for games.

"Ha. Keep dreaming."

Just as Flit was about to move away from the table, Acumen slipped between two people standing nearby. "Hey, you lot," he said, walking over. He rested an elbow on Hawkeye's shoulder as he leaned closer.

The previous laughter died down, and everyone turned towards the newcomer.

Acumen groaned. "Come on, really?" he asked, looking around at all of them. "You should all know there is nothing more suspicious than stupefied silence and mental *la, la, la* when a telepath approaches. I expected better." He pointed at Link. "Especially from you."

"Would you rather we think about birds?" Flit asked pointedly, figuring there was no use denying it.

"Why would anyone want to think about those flying, razor-beaked, disease-carrying vermin?" Acumen shuddered, making those gathered around the table laugh as some of the tension eased. "I'm just over here, hoping for a seat with a group of people who aren't so boring that the best thing they can talk about is training rats to race so they can to bet on them."

"I dunno. That sounds an awful lot more interesting than patrol schedules," Fortune said with a smile and a shrug.

Acumen smiled at her, but it was a stretched, unconvincing thing. "Perhaps I should sit elsewhere, then. I was hoping for something more exciting."

"You can take my seat," Flit said. "I'm sure Hawkeye and Tweak won't mind you squishing your arse between them. I have to spend some time with my folks."

"Flit, wait." Fortune stood. There was almost a collective sigh of relief as those sitting with her on that side of the table shifted aside to get a bit more space between them. "I'll walk with you."

It wasn't a request, and Flit could see concern in Fortune's gaze. Even if there were no worries there, Flit would have been fine with it.

Instead of answering or wondering too much if it had anything to do with Acumen's arrival, she walked around the table and looped her arm through the crook of Fortune's elbow. "Let's go. My parents will be pleased to see you."

However, Flit wasn't being entirely honest. Despite the fact that Fortune and her family had been relatively close to Flit's own before she disappeared, there was an odd tension between the parents now. Tinker and Stride hadn't said anything, but there were no invitations to dinner issued and no offers of hospitality. Like the other members of the Underground, Flit's own parents still seemed to be wary of the refugees.

Talking wasn't really possible as the two women wove their way through the throng of people eating and chatting. When they got into the grey corridors outside of the Mess, the silence between them remained. It wasn't until they reached the quieter junctions between the higher traffic tunnels that Fortune leaned in.

"You don't need to bother you parents by inviting me in. I just wanted to make sure you got home safely. Layla and I have been working on increasing my reach with my powers. I no longer need to touch someone to inhibit them, but I can't risk using them flippantly. I'm not convinced Acumen was just looking for some light conversation. I don't want him telling Harmony you're not under her coercion. We can't afford another round of that, not when we have so much to do," Fortune whispered. "I also wanted to make sure Acumen couldn't read your mind and figure out that you weren't convinced anymore. He's been working much closer with Control than he ever did before, and it worries me."

Flit turned to smile at Fortune as she walked, her shoulder sagging with appreciation. It was nice to know that Fortune had her back and was just as concerned about Harmony and Acumen as she had become. "Thank you. I'm sick of the emotional rollercoaster. I can pretend to be all convinced if I need to be, but I'd much rather have you there with me to ensure it doesn't sink in again."

"Then feel free to call me any time you need to. I'll be sure to check in more often too."

Flit squeezed Fortune's arm with gratitude.

They fell back into silence as they made their way back to the apartment Flit shared with her parents. When she arrived, Fortune stayed for long enough to say hello to her family and to ascertain that Harmony wasn't waiting inside. She gave Flit a warm embrace before she excused herself.

"How's was your day, Flit?" Stride asked when the door shut behind Fortune. He set down the datapad he was doing some kind of puzzle on and smiled at her.

A furtive glance in her mother's direction let Flit know that Tinker was in the living room, thoroughly engrossed in an episode of some silly comedy she enjoyed watching in her down time.

Flit teleported to her father's side at the dining room table. "I translocated today. Safely took Shadow along with me," she whispered, not wanting her mother to overhear.

"You translocated?" Stride's voice was loud enough to make Tinker jump.

Tinker turned, concern flashing in her eyes. "What? Is everything okay?"

"Yes!" Flit blurted then had to follow it up with a calm, casual wave of her hand. "Hawkeye just found something in one of the supply tunnels that Dad has been looking for for a while."

"Oh, that's good." Tinker turned back to her show.

Leaning closer, Stride muttered, "You do know we tell each other everything, right?"

Flit raised an eyebrow at him. "Oh, I can think of some exceptions to that. Did you want me to tell her about the chocolate you—"

"Hey!" Stride poked her shoulder with his bionic hand. "Don't you dare."

The legs of a dining chair scraped as Flit pulled it away from the table and sank into it. "Look, if you tell her, she'll just freak out. I'm really excited about it, and I knew you'd understand."

Stride sighed, but there was a spark of pride in his eyes. "You've officially surpassed your old man. I'm pleased for you, darling. Well..." He paused, frowning. "I would be if I knew it wasn't going to lead to you getting yourself into trouble."

"I'm not going to—"

Flit stopped when her father stared at her with *that* look, the one he always got on his face when he knew she was up to something.

"Fine. Just know that it will be worth it. I promise."

Instead of getting caught in further discussion, she leaned over, kissed his cheek, and then teleported over to her closed bedroom door. She looked over her shoulder and noted that her mother's attention was still fixated on the screen, her back to Flit. With a slow breath, Flit closed her eyes and visualized her room as she had left it that morning, unmade bed, clothes on the floor, and all. With a surge of intention, she teleported into that space. She felt her body shift. There was no sense of pain or immobilisation, which was the first good sign. It meant she felt confident to peel one eye open and then the other.

"Fuck yeah!" Flit whooped as she jumped, fist pumping in the air.

She'd gotten so used to teleporting to the few safe spaces Shadow had set up for her that it was nice to expand her range to something important and familiar. Sure, she could have just opened the door and walked through, but then she wouldn't have tried something new.

Hope and excitement grew within Flit's gut at the thought of her success and what it meant. Her mind reeled back to the last time she had seen Scraps, disappearing beneath a squad of officers after telling her he loved her.

As Flit changed for her patrol, she felt as though she could breathe for the first time in a long while.

Finally, after so many weeks, they were going to get Scraps back.

THE NEXT DAY, it was late afternoon by the time Flit woke. Doing a night patrol meant she hadn't crawled into bed until well past six in the morning. Without an alarm, it seemed her body was keen to get as much rest as it could. When she finally did rouse, it was to the obnoxious pinging sound that alerted her to an urgent message on her comms unit.

Emergency Blue Team training session. Simulator Seven.

The message was attached to a meeting room booking. Flit opened it and realised she only had ten minutes to get dressed to the venue. She wasn't sure what the session was about, but it had been a while since the Blue Team had done a full group session.

She rushed around the room, pulling on whatever training clothes she could find on her floor that weren't too gross. She made a mental note to do a load of washing later and utilised the bathroom before rushing out of the apartment.

Thankfully, Flit's gift of teleportation meant it was hard to be late for almost anything. She made it to the designated room in record time. She was quite familiar with Simulator Seven and wished she was able to directly translocate there, but there were just too many factors involved making it unsafe. Still, as she arrived, she found that almost everyone was there, except for Hawkeye.

There was also someone extra lingering around.

"Layla, you joining the team?" Flit asked by way of greeting as she walked over to where the others were standing.

Layla bit her lip and looked at Swipe, who said, "We'll explain in a minute when—"

The door opened, to reveal Hawkeye toting a heavy-looking duffel bag over his shoulder.

"Well, we can explain now," Swipe finished as the door shut behind Hawkeye, and he dumped the bag on the ground and unzipped it. "We don't have long, so we gotta make this look convincing. Tweak, get into the system and liaise with Cogs. She needs to know we're ready to go."

Flit frowned, watching the team launch into action around her. Her head was still spinning. "What's going on?"

"We're going to the Hub now. Me, you, and Layla," Hawkeye explained as he pulled a jar of interference paint from the bag. He opened it, running two fingers through the silvery goop and smearing it over his cheeks before throwing the jar to Flit.

Knowing exactly what to do with the paint, Flit scooped some of its contents out before handing it to Layla. "Have you used this before?"

Tipping the jar this way and that and letting the light shimmer over the surface of the viscous substance, Layla shook her head. "No, but I know I've seen it before, although I can't remember where."

It was a restricted substance, so specialized that the Underground had only given her and Scraps one jar between them when they had gone on their mission. They had used it when they'd rescued Layla and the others from that medical facility.

That line of thinking had Flit quickly saying, "It's a kind of face paint. The silver shimmer is part of an advanced concoction that helps to confuse any visual surveillance tech. Sometimes they pretend to use it in spy movies. Maybe that's where you saw it." She hoped the information was enough for Layla to not think too much deeper about it. It would be bad if she started recalling that night.

Layla shrugged and smeared the paint across her cheeks, copying the lines as Flit applied her own.

Flit turned to Swipe. "Why now?"

"It's the only time I could get a training room booking for a while. Given that it'll be dinner in a couple of hours, no one will mind having the extra space in the Mess. They won't miss us. Cogs also happens to be at her station for an evening shift, which is a quiet time for Control. I know it isn't much warning, but since you're a teleporting pro now, there is no time like the present."

Normally, Flit was the one in control of her plans. It felt weird knowing Swipe had taken the initiative and gotten everything in line while Flit did her patrol and slept. The timing would work out well too. Scraps should be getting home from work in an hour or so, which meant she could be there to greet him.

Much to Flit's surprise, she found she didn't actually mind this teamwork thing so much after all.

"Here. Catch." Hawkeye threw Flit a tactical belt and a leg holster, already loaded with several flame grenades, a pistol, and her two favourite combat knives.

She raised an eyebrow at him. "We're going in prepared, huh?"

"There's no other way to do it," Hawkeye replied matter-of-factly. He took another belt and thigh holster from the bag and approached Layla. He held the items out to her, and she tilted her head to the side and stared at them as if they were alien artefacts.

"I've never used any of that before," she admitted, reaching out and taking the end of the belt, lifting it higher and frowning.

"I know, but it would be better if you have them just in case than to not have them and need them. You probably won't have to use any of it, but... take it. Please."

For a moment, Layla just stared at it. Then, she bit her lip. "I don't know how to put it on, though."

"Oh." Hawkeye glanced between Layla and the items in his hand and cleared his throat. Flit was about to offer to help when he found his voice again. "All good. I can help you get into it. That's easy."

Flit smiled to herself as she got her own thigh holster situated. The awkward tension between Hawkeye and Layla was just the cutest. She was happy for her friend. It was clear the two were very into each other. She just wished they would hurry up and admit it. Life was too short to not be honest about stuff like that.

While the trio sorted out their weapons and gear, Hawkeye pulled a trench coat out of the bag for each of them. The other team members worked on initiating the simulator protocol. Flit was adjusting the long, fitted black fabric and buttoning it up at her front as she overheard Swipe and Tweak muttering about adjusting the interface and monitoring. It sounded as though Tweak was chatting to Cogs as well. It was hard to know for sure, but Flit had heard of tech-oriented Micros using networks to communicate in code rather than written or verbally.

When Flit, Hawkeye, and Layla were all fully dressed and standing together, Swipe left Tweak's side and joined them. She looked them up and down. Flit in her black trench, Hawkeye in a dark grey one, and Layla wearing something that looked more like a deep navy women's dress coat. Swipe reached into her pocket and held out a wristlet communicator for each of them.

"These are apparently on a private network," she explained. "You'll only be able to communicate with one another. The Government won't—"

"Shouldn't!" Tweak called out from where he was standing across the room. "Cogs and I make no promises. The Government *shouldn't* be able to track or hack them, but there are always exceptions."

"Fine." Swipe rolled her eyes. "The Government *shouldn't* be able to interfere with them. You've got around four hours to get your shit sorted and get back here. I've got a crate being delivered by Fortune just before dinner for our precious cargo. It'll take him down to a hospitable storage room while we find a better place for him to hide out."

Flit's heart soared. She looked at Swipe, suddenly overcome with gratefulness. If Flit hadn't been so susceptible to Harmony's brainwashing, if she hadn't been so consumed with her own short-sightedness, she would have been able to contribute more. "Swipe, thank you."

Swipe held up a hand to stall any further comments. "Don't thank me. Just bring that hunk back with you safely, just like you were supposed to the first time."

On another day, the comment might have held some bite but not this time

Swipe gave her a smile as she stepped back. "Also, don't teleport my friends into a wall and fuck shit up. Got it?"

Even though the genuine possibility of that happening was enough that it shouldn't have been funny, Flit laughed. "Don't worry. I've got this," she promised as she stepped over to Layla and Hawkeye. "Ready?" she asked, holding her arms out for them to step closer so they could translocate together.

"Yes!" Layla said, sounding keen.

Hawkeye was greener than Flit had ever seen him.

With a sigh, Flit said, "I'll take your stoic silence as a yes."

She wrapped her arms around them, closed her eyes, and hoped for the best.

29

SCRAPS

"BRIAN, the feedback from the Derivate Training Facility review is in."

Scraps looked up from the report he was working on as Liana stepped into his pod. Her usually cheery expression was marred by worry as she mentioned the reason for her visit.

He couldn't blame her.

After the information he had given to Chris and Liana not that long ago about the fact any child they had could be a Derivate, he wasn't sure what the memory of that particular report would hold for her. He glanced at the time and frowned at how late it was. He wanted a good chunk of time to go through the feedback, but there was only an hour of work left.

"That's great," Scraps said, spinning his chair so he could face his friend. "Do we need to go through it tonight, or can we wait until tomorrow so we have more time?"

Liana's shoulders sagged, and she looked at the datapad she was carrying in her right hand. "We *could* wait, I suppose..."

The way she trailed off told Scraps that they could not, in fact, wait. Several months ago, he would have just taken her words at face value. However, he knew better now. The way she wouldn't meet his eyes and the slow tone told her all he needed to know.

Forcing a smile on his face for her sake, he pointed to her datapad. "Do you want to go through it in my pod or your office?"

Regaining her pep, Liana looked at the desk that had been empty since the Underground had retrieved Flit. Her lips twisted into a frown. Scraps wouldn't have minded if she sat in Flit's seat again, but Liana shook her head. "Let's go into my office." She stepped back and waited in the doorway of the pod to keep it open while he got to his feet.

Scraps said hello to a few of his colleagues as he walked through the office space. He had become popular enough on the floor due to the extra effort he consistently put into his work. He had a sense that a few people were also somewhat envious of him. Still, everyone was all smiles as he passed. He had to walk by Jane's office on his way to Liana's as well. Through the glass walls, he noticed she was preoccupied by a conference call. Even though she was busy, Jane still managed to smile at him as he walked by. He gave her a small wave and then stepped into Liana's glass-walled office.

"Take a seat. I'll just sign into my account. It should already be up on the screen." Liana moved to the chair on the opposite side of the desk as Scraps took the one closest to the door. Liana slid around the oval table, so she was sitting beside Scraps, and she tapped the glossy surface to bring up the tabletop screen.

"So, is the feedback positive?"

"I didn't want to go through it without you. It felt wrong," Liana said, focusing on the screen as she opened the document they had submitted. There were highlights all throughout the body of it, linked to comments left by their superiors and the staff at the Derivate Training Facility. "I was genuinely surprised and impressed by your depth of knowledge when we did our investigation. I shouldn't have been, given how much you know about almost everything."

Scraps preened at the compliment. "I just like being thorough."

Liana chuckled. "Brian, I think thorough is an understatement for your work. Honestly, you were a lifesaver in that place for so many reasons." This time, when she caught his eye, he knew she was talking about more than just the review itself. She looked as if she wanted to say more, but instead, she shook her head and started on the first comment.

Half an hour later, a knock at the door broke Scraps and Liana from their work.

"Who's that?" Liana sounded just as confused as Scraps was wary.

Once more, Scraps was met by the now-familiar faces of TB-2199 and CC-9832, Hector and Greene's Derivate pair.

He stood up. "I, uh… I'll see what they want," he offered before Liana could stand. He walked over and opened the door. "Um, good evening, officers. What can I do for you?" he asked, trying to keep it casual.

"We are here for you, Mr. Parkes. Some of the financial planners who are overlooking your latest investment statement just want to ensure you have all the information you require," TB-2199 said in a rehearsed cover story.

Scraps glanced at Liana over his shoulder.

"It's almost the end of the day. You might as well sort that out and head home. I'll catch up with you in the morning," Liana said, looking between Scraps and the Registereds with interest. She squashed it down as she closed the document they were working on. "Take care, Brian."

With a nod of acknowledgement to his friend, Scraps turned to the Registereds. "Very well. Lead the way please."

The Registereds led Scraps through his level, drawing a few looks of interest from his workmates. He ignored the curiosity. Given the wide range of departments they often worked with, it was not unusual for Registereds to escort people to and from meetings on unfamiliar levels.

This time, Scraps was led all the way down to the second level which housed an entire complex of meeting rooms for casual use. Even though each room was made of clear or frosted glass walls and they were all well-lit, it was a little like walking through a maze to get where they needed to go. The walls of the room they stopped in front of were fully opaque, and Scraps had guessed the agents probably switched on the privacy function the moment they got in there.

"Good evening, Brian," Greene said as Scraps walked in. She gestured to one of the many empty chairs at the generous round table.

Scraps took a seat and waited until he heard the door slide shut behind him to say, "I spoke with Adam."

Greene tilted her head to the side curiously, and Hector leaned in, elbows on the table.

"I know they were behind another attack recently," Scraps said, working hard to keep his mind uncluttered. "They are working on other plans. Adam has given me some details, but he is waiting to tell me what is really going on. He's quite cautious."

"All clever fugitives are," Hector noted with a wry smile. "What are they working on next?"

This was the part that Scraps had difficulty sharing. "It seems as though they destroyed some servers on their latest incursion. They reset some identification files so they could get their people into places they aren't supposed to be in."

Green and Hector looked to TB-2199, who was behind Scraps' right shoulder. Whatever they saw made them both settle into their seats a little more.

"Does this have anything to do with the uniforms they manufactured?" Hector asked.

Scraps nodded. "They are going to use them to sneak into the hospitality facilities they want to access."

A memory of seeing the officer uniforms on the Free Citizens' sewing machined flashed through his mind as did the one of him taking pictures of the hospitality uniforms on the production line.

The sound of a foot scuffing the floor behind Scraps made his grasp tighten on his knees. His mouth went dry, and he realised his mind had slipped. He paused, waiting for the Registered behind him to say something, to tell the agents, to ruin everything he was working towards.

Hector's head tilted to the side as his dark eyes flicked over Scraps' shoulder. He raised an eyebrow at the telepath.

Scraps' breath caught in his throat.

Then... nothing.

Scraps had to resist the urge to turn around and gawk at the Registered. Why wasn't she telling Hector what she saw? There was no way she would have missed that. It was her job.

"So, some sort of hospitality facility?" Green asked, leaning forward and taking the attention away from Hector and the odd exchange.

"Adam didn't say anything about that," Scraps said honestly. He was careful with his words but truthful all the same.

Green and Hector exchanged a look. "Then keep going until you can get us the right information. We need more," Green told Scraps.

"Okay. I will do that." He felt as though the agent's words were a dismissal, but he didn't dare stand without permission.

"Mr. Parkes, please follow us. We will escort you back to the elevator," TB-2199 said stiffly.

There was no way Scraps was going to think twice about that. He got to his feet, nodded in farewell to the agents, and turned to let the Registereds lead him back through the maze. He remained alert to ensure they were leading him in the right direction. Thankfully, he had a lot of experience with tunnels, and it was easy to tell that they were doing just as they said they would.

The Registereds stopped at the elevator bank and remained with him while he waited for the car to arrive. When it was a couple of floors away, TB-2199 caught CC-9832's attention. "I will escort Mr. Parkes to the ground level. You can finish for the day if you like. I think you have an afternoon shift back at the facility," she informed him.

CC-9832 didn't argue. He just gave her a salute and turned to walk back into the maze, most likely to the elevators designated for Derivates.

Then, TB-2199 turned to Scraps. "You're playing a dangerous game," she whispered, her lips barely moving.

The blood in Scraps' body ran cold. He remained silent.

"Only a select group of people think of us as *Registereds*," she stated, bringing her hand up to adjust her collar, covering her mouth in the process. "If you get another telepath at some point, be careful. You are far looser with your thoughts than you think."

Before Scraps could say anything, the elevator arrived.

TB-2199 leaned in closer. "They are getting suspicious. They cannot breach the security network in your apartment to spy on you." She reached out, holding the door open for him.

Scraps nodded, too shocked to say anything. Instead, he stepped into the elevator and thought loudly, *Thank you.*

He wasn't quite sure what he was thanking her for yet, but he felt as though it was far more than he imagined.

TB-2199's covert concession and warning haunted Scraps for his entire walk home. It was already getting dark in the city, and he normally used the trip to take in the way the view transitioned from bright sunshine and blue glass to the multi-coloured reflections of the encroaching dusk sky. He liked how the electric lights flared to life and peppered the buildings with constellations of multicoloured stars.

It was hard to enjoy his usual routine after that meeting. The intensified presence of law enforcement following the most recent Free Citizen attack had yet to show signs of abating. If anything, Scraps almost felt as if there were more dark-uniformed officers on the streets.

As he walked past one corner, he saw the designation of one of the Derivates. He couldn't see their face through their dark visor, but he made out the *TD-2413*. The 24 of the birth year indicated that the Derivate was not even eighteen years old. Scraps had to stop himself from staring as he realised a minor was guarding a street corner.

Spotting the adolescent made Scraps think of the review he and Liana worked on. As he walked home, he held up his wrist and tapped out a message to her.

To: Liana
From: Brian
Subject: My Apologies
Sorry I had to leave early this afternoon. I am looking forward to discussing the feedback from the facility with you in the morning.

Scraps had barely taken five steps before his he received a reply.

To: Brian
From: Liana

Subject: RE: My Apologies

We have so much to discuss. Also, Chris and I would love it if you joined us for dinner tomorrow night.

Despite the situation, Scraps smiled and typed out an *'That sounds good, thanks.'* in reply.

With that sorted, he returned his attention to his walk. Five minutes later, he was walking into the lobby of the apartment building. He rode up in a car that was just as full as usual, given the fact a lot of office workers seemed to finish work around the same time. When he got to his floor, the promise of being in his own space became even more alluring. There was something about getting into the privacy of the apartment that made him feel as if he could relax a little.

It was one of the rare nights that Scraps didn't have any plans. As he reached the front door, he tried to figure out what he was going to do with his time. He figured it would probably be good to cook a nutritious dinner to start with, something with some flavour that he couldn't get from the microwave meals he had been heating up in his rush to get to Nightmix. Perhaps then he could sit down and play a game while he tried to figure out how to get the information he had recently gathered to—

"Flit?"

Scraps froze by the front door as it shut behind him. He heard the lock automatically click, but he couldn't think about that or the fact that he shouldn't have said her name. All he could focus on was Flit.

Flit, who was standing in the living room, wearing a matte-black trench coat that clung to her chest and flared around her shapely hips. There were smears of silver interference goop across her cheeks, but that did not detract from the knowledge that it was *his Flit* standing before him.

Flit, whose eyes had returned to the beautiful hazel shade he still dreamed about, whose hair was once more that sleek, chocolate brown.

"Hey, you." Flit smiled, her chest rising and falling a little faster as she watched him. "It's been a while, huh?"

Even though his throat had constricted, Scraps managed to splutter, "Far too long."

That was all it took.

One moment, Flit was standing by the expansive lounge room window, and the next, she was in his arms.

Her lips found his, and she melted against him. He wrapped his arms around her. Holding her felt even better than he remembered.

30

FLIT

AFTER THE WEEKS of longing and the horrific mental manipulation, being in Scraps' arms again made all the pain disappear. It was as if the past month hadn't happened at all, as if Flit had never left.

Scraps still tasted the same. His body was just as solid and warm against hers. His arms fell around her, his hands settling in just the right place to make her let out a sigh of relief into their passionate kiss.

Flit never wanted it to end, but the sound of a throat clearing from the living room made Scraps pull her behind him and hold his hand up. That pose told Flit he was one second away from throwing some shit around to protect them.

"It's okay." Flit put her hand on his shoulder.

Hawkeye and Layla peeled away from the window they were leaning against, and Hawkeye scratched the back of his neck. "Sorry to interrupt. I know this is an emotional reunion. It's just that we don't have much time to waste."

As much as Flit wanted to throttle Hawkeye for ruining the moment, he was right.

"What do you mean?" Scraps turned to face her.

Flit looked up into his familiar eyes of his and felt as though she would melt. "We're here to take you home. We've got something else to do before we leave, but we wanted to give you some warning so you can pack up here, and then we'll be back to get you."

The curiosity on Scraps' face turned to concern as his eyebrows furrowed. He dipped his head and lowered his voice. "What do you need to do? I should come with you."

"It's too much of a risk," came Layla's voice. Scraps frowned as he turned to face her, and Flit kept her hand on his arm. "If our location is compromised and we have to run, you could draw the attention of the Government. Flit's facial features will take time for the system to decode now that her eye colour has been restored. Yours is still too fresh on the system."

Scraps cupped Flit's cheek and ran a thumb over her jawline. She instinctively leaned into the intimate touch as she met his gaze. He seemed to register the changes in her, and he nodded reluctantly. "Do you need any weapons or anything? I still have the stockpile the Underground gave us when we came up here."

Flit pulled her trench coat open and showed him the belt gear she had underneath. "We're good. It's probably best for you to get yourself armed up. Just in case."

"Why? What do I need to be—" Scraps began then stopped and frowned again. "Wait. How did you get in here? I'm being heavily monitored."

It was impossible for Flit to resist the urge to grin. "Translocation."

Scraps' eyes widened. "Flit, that is incredible!" He pulled her in for a tight embrace. Much to Flit's dismay, the moment ended with Scraps pulling back and holding her at arm's length. "Where do you need to go next? Do you have a safe way to gauge that location? What if there are people there? What if they have changed the furniture layout?"

The concern in his voice made Flit's cheeks warm with affection.

"Ah, we've got that covered. Believe me, Layla and I have no intention of getting half stuck in some desk." Hawkeye pulled the sleeve of his jacket back and looked at the wrist device he was wearing. He tapped the screen several times. "Flit, come over here and tell me if this will work."

Flit clung to Scraps and bit her lip. She didn't want to step away. However, time was of the essence, so she slid her hand down his arm and laced their fingers together before leading him over to where Hawkeye was holding out his wrist.

The screen of Hawkeye's device showed a scene of what looked like an ordinary living room with a worse-for-wear couch and a drooping potted palm. Flit was about to ask how long ago the image was taken when there was a flicker of movement that made the palm fronds move, showing it was a live feed.

"I wouldn't stake my life on it. Can you give me the address? Show me the location on a map? Help me visualise the scene a bit better with a different view? Maybe a bigger one," she added as she stopped squinting. She did not have nearly enough detail to make a safe jump to that location.

"You can connect it to that." Scraps gestured to the large screen on the nearby wall.

Hawkeye shook his head. "Who knows who has access to your network. It's not worth the risk."

Flit was getting a sinking feeling about the mission prospects. If they couldn't get a clear image, they wouldn't be able to contact Layla's people. It wasn't a deal breaker, but given the odd things happening in the Underground, they needed all the allies they could get.

"Actually," Scraps started slowly, a smile forming on his lips, "I found out just this evening that the Government have been unable to breach the security network in this apartment."

Those words brought back the accusations Harmony and Divvy had made, and Flit hated the way a shiver of worry ran down her spine.

"How do you know?" Hawkeye asked. Flit gave him a grateful nod, relieved he had asked the question that would have made her feel like a traitor to voice.

"It's a long story," Scraps said. When Hawkeye just kept staring at him, he squared his shoulders. "After you came to get Flit, I was captured by the Government. They don't know I'm a Derivate, but they do know I am connected to the Free Citizens. In return for my freedom, they asked me to be a double agent for them. I have been feeding them half-truths ever since whilst keeping an eye on Adam and his people. I heard from one of the Registereds working from the agents today that they are starting to grow suspicious because they cannot breach the network in this apartment to spy on me whilst I am home."

Flit blinked. There was a lot to digest in Scraps' words, but the overwhelming feeling she got was one of relief. The videos Harmony and Divvy showed her made sense now, and as she watched her boyfriend speak, she knew that he had always been truthful with her. Perhaps too truthful at times.

"Right." Hawkeye cleared his throat at the frank confession. "Well, in that case, let's give it a go."

Scraps gently squeezed Flit's hand before he untangled his fingers from hers. He walked over to help Hawkeye get the network set up. Flit took the time to spin in a slow circle and look around at the apartment that she and Scraps had called home. As much as she longed for that feeling of relief she got from walking through the front door after so many difficult days and nights... it just didn't feel the same anymore. Too much had happened.

That was when Flit realised nowhere felt like home anymore.

When she had been living here with Scraps, it had felt like the apartment was just a holding location, a place for them to retreat whilst they tried to complete their mission. When Flit had been dragged back to the Underground, she had found it had changed. It wasn't the place she had left, and it certainly was no longer a place that she felt safe.

Then, it dawned on her.

Home was no longer a place.

It was a *person*.

"How is that?" Scraps turned around and smiled at her.

Flit's heart skipped a beat. She wanted to teleport over to him, to take him in her arms and disappear for a while, to revel in each other's presence, to revel in being *home*.

Instead, she let out a slow breath and nodded, pushing back the emotions. She still had a job to do.

She turned her attention to the large screen on the wall and took in the improved image. The size and resolution allowed a far greater, more detailed view. "I can work with that."

"And you wanted a location?" Layla asked, finally stepping away from the window. She held out her wrist and showed Flit a simple map with a ping on it. The location in question was on the opposite side of the city, more towards the outer edge.

The location was in the lower rent part of town, where people tended to work in the service and sanitation industries. As a child, she had gone there with her parents to explore the different types of cuisine it offered. The produce was fresher and the recipes more authentic than other regions of the Hub had. Her parents had always favoured good flavour over speed and convenience. Memories poured back through Flit, and she smiled to herself as the location became tangible in her mind.

"All right, I've got this," she announced. Hawkeye grinned at what she thought must have been the confidence in her tone. Then, she turned to Scraps. "We shouldn't be too long. We just need to touch base with some of Layla's contacts."

Scraps stepped towards her. Panic tightened his features, maybe because their time had drawn to a close.

She held up a hand and swallowed her own emotion. "Don't say goodbye. Don't wish me luck," Flit said quickly. "I will be right back. I promise."

"Did you... When you left, I said—"

"I heard you," Flit promised, her vision wavering with brewing tears. "And I want to hear you it again when I get back. If you say it now, I won't want to leave, okay?" She balled her hands into fists at her side to stop herself for reaching out for him.

The worry creasing his brows softened, and the corners of his lips curled. "Okay," he replied, locking his gaze with hers. A zap of electric energy passed between them.

"Hawk, Layla, let's go," Flit said, gesturing for them to come closer. They obeyed, walking to her side and stepping into a huddle. She had just enough room between their bodies to return her attention to the screen on the wall as she wrapped her arms around them. "See you soon, Scraps," she said with a warm smile before willing them to move.

THE APARTMENT LOOKED JUST like it did in the image Flit had been shown. The breeze that had fluttered the house plant proved to come from a broken windowpane just off to the side. It certainly gave off the rundown, mayday group kind of vibe Layla had described when she had first explained what they did. With a sense of relief, Flit stepped back and rolled her shoulders.

"The trust you two are showing in me is highly impressive," she muttered as Hawkeye and Layla peeled apart. She slid her hand beneath her trench coat to rest on the hilt of the dagger tucked into her tactical belt.

Hawkeye gulped back his nausea. "Teleporting is just about the only thing I trust you with." Judging by how green his face was, his teleportation-sickness was in full swing.

Layla tucked a strand of red hair behind her ear and peered around, biting her lip. She looked fine but wary. "It's quieter here than I expected. This place used to have so many people camping out."

"How do we know that the Government haven't cottoned on to the existence of this place?" Hawkeye asked.

"We don't, but this was the safest way to try and—"

Just as Layla was about to explain, the door to the living room slid open. Flit drew her dagger and held it out in front of her as two people burst into the room, guns in hand.

"Who brings knives to a gun fight?" the dark-haired young woman at the front snapped, her pistol pointing directly at Flit. She tilted her head, the tight headphones on her head blaring music so loud even Flit could hear it. Flit was just about to make a witty comeback when the woman yelled, "Layla?"

"Iris!"

Iris leapt at Layla. Hawkeye moved in to intervene but skidded short just as Layla opened her arms and the two embraced. Instead, Hawkeye glanced between Flit and the other person who had come along with Iris. A person with pink hair, a decidedly wary look on their face, and a gun in their hands that was lowered but not holstered.

Flit just shrugged helplessly at the show of enthusiasm. She had hoped Layla would introduce them all, but she didn't seem to be in a hurry to do so. Flit was just about to open her mouth, when Iris turned around, her face contorted with excitement. "Mitch, you're not going to believe this! We were right. The Government did get Layla. She was stuck with them for the whole year, up until an underground group called—" She paused, frowning, and looked back over at Layla. "Wait... literally called the Underground?" She shook her head. "Wow. Original, but whatever. They rescued her! And there are a bunch of them down there, all surviving outside of the Government's gaze."

The verbal torrent made Flit blink. Then, she sighed. The music, the wordless transfer of information...

"Yep, I'm a telepath." Iris winked at Flit.

"Clearly the music isn't terribly effective at blocking out all the noise, huh?" Flit chuckled to herself.

Iris shrugged, her shiny black leather-look jacket creaking. "It's more for the background buzz than anything in the immediate vicinity."

"As lovely as this conversation is," Mitch said, looking around suspiciously, "how did you get in here? This place is our last safe house."

"Trans—" Hawkeye started.

"Location?" Iris cooed with surprise. She glanced at Flit. "Damn... I thought that was an urban legend."

"*Urban Legend* just happens to be my middle name," Flit said, grinning wickedly. That earned a groan from Hawkeye and a spluttered laugh from Iris.

"We're not here to bolster your ego, Flit," Hawkeye hissed, rolling his eyes.

Flit teleported to his side and nudged him in the ribs. "Bolstering my ego is the prime directive of any mission."

"The Underground chose to send these two with you?" Mitch snapped, looking between Flit and Hawkeye sceptically. "We're all fucked."

"Well, the Underground don't really know we're here," Layla admitted, lowering her voice. "They have kind of cloistered themselves in lately. Shutting off all ties to the surface and what not. But... there are a few of them..." She paused and smiled at Hawkeye. "...well, a few of *us* who want to put an end to the oppression."

Iris held up a hand. *"Us?"* Her eyes flicked between Hawkeye and Layla. "Oh, damn. Well, you look cute together."

Layla blushed furiously. "How are you guys going? Have you got many people at the moment?" she spluttered, clearly eager to change the topic.

"We lost a whole lot in raids around the time you got captured," Mitch informed them, still clinging to their weapon, finger on the trigger. Clearly, they were far more suspicious than Iris, who reminded Flit of an over-eager puppy. "We thought that might be the end of it, but we did our best. We've had a massive reprieve over the past few months. There's this random bunch of Citizens who think their lives are shit. They've been spray painting logos and attacking locations. It's a good diversion for us. We managed to regroup."

A chain of emotions played over Layla's face throughout the explanation. Regret, concern, pride... determination. Flit smiled to herself at the mention of the Free Citizens but kept her thoughts reined in. Iris tilted her head and raised an eyebrow at Flit, but Flit kept her mouth shut and her mind on track.

"Will you be ready to mobilise?" Layla asked.

"Mobilise?" Mitch asked, frowning. "For what?"

"I wanted to see if you would join us. We are working on a plan to convince the Underground to make a stand. It would help to know we have friends up here that are ready to join us," Layla said, laying it on the line. "Flit's translocation is just a drop in the pond of the level of skill and training the Underground have. Imagine it, guys! A whole civilisation of people who were able to enhance and refine their powers without fear or limitation. We have a real chance here, and we all want the same thing."

"We never said we wanted to fight," Mitch said, even though the firearm in their hands painted a different picture. "What would we be fighting for, anyway? Who else would run the show? Certainly none of our lot would want to. It's a hot mess, but at least we know where we stand. We just want to stay out of the way. Mind our own business."

"And how long do you think the Government will let you do that for?" Flit asked, tilting her head to the side. "You said that you've already had a few raids. Imagine living in a world where you won't have to worry about *any* raids."

"That sounds dangerous," was all Mitch had to say in response.

The room was silent save for the rumble of music from Iris's headphones as she and Mitch locked eyes. Flit had no doubt Mitch was pleading their case with Iris telepathically. It wasn't possible for Iris to reply unless Mitch was also telepathic, but Flit had spent enough time with Derivates with that power to know it was possible to hold a decent one-sided conversation with someone you knew well enough.

Then, almost as suddenly as the silence had fallen, it was broken by Iris. "We have recently acquired some Drone contacts. Even that lot are getting uneasy."

It was a slight change of topic, but the volunteering of information felt like a tentative agreement in Flit's mind.

"Drones?" Hawkeye's eyebrows rose in question.

"Oh, that's what we called the Registereds," Layla said, wringing her hands as she looked at Flit apologetically.

"You know they didn't have a choice in the matter, right?" Flit snapped, all of the time she spent defending Scraps coming back to the forefront. "They didn't ask to be born into that shithole of a system."

"Yeah, but they do have a choice to keep hunting us down," Mitch argued.

Heat rose under Flit's her skin. "They put control chips in their heads. They brainwash them from birth!"

"Okay, okay!" Iris stepped between Flit and Mitch and raised her hands. "So, this is going to get heated if we let it continue. Let's just go with the knowledge that there are some of the Drones—" She paused, glancing at Flit as Flit sent a few choice swear-word laden thoughts her way "Sorry, Registereds... A few of the Registereds have broken free of the brainwashing and are willing to talk. How about we get in touch with our people and see what we can dig up? Between us and them, we might just be able to bolster your numbers. What do you say?"

Despite the tension in the room, Layla's face lit up with excitement. "That would be perfect. Thank you!"

Hawkeye nudged Flit and wiggled his eyebrows at her. She was unable to resist the urge to smile. They weren't sure what to expect, but this was something.

"How do we contact you?" Mitch asked.

"We'll come back here when we can. We just need to get the right opening." Hawkeye reached into his pocket and withdrew a bracelet that had a charm on it, just like the one he had given to Flit before she left for the Hub. "I don't give these out lightly, but Layla promised that you guys could be trusted, so... if you run into an emergency or you have something urgent to share with us, crack this and we'll do our best to get to the location ASAP."

The suspicion on Mitch's face splintered, and they looked at Iris before finally tucking their gun away. With a flick of their fingers, the bracelet zoomed into their hand. "You're just taking Layla's word for this?"

"If we won't take a risk to help you, what reason do you have to trust us?" Hawkeye asked in a tone that told them that it was just that simple for him.

Mitch put the bracelet on their wrist and nodded. "I hope we don't need to use it."

"Me too," Hawkeye agreed.

The group fell into an awkward silence for a few moments before Iris bounced on the balls of her feet and spluttered, "Are you guys gonna go now? I'd love to watch you translocate!"

Flit laughed to herself. "I mean, sure. Who am I to squash your dreams?" She reached out for Hawkeye and Layla, who cuddled closer, but then Flit looked over at Iris. *I'm looking forward to working with you and your people. It's time for the Government to fall.*

Iris returned Flit's thought with a lackadaisical salute.

Flit closed her eyes and then willed them back to the apartment.

Back to Scraps.

31

———

SCRAPS

THE INSTANT FLIT LEFT, Scraps felt the weight of the situation dawn on him.

Immediately, he regretted letting her go without him. He should have fought against it. He should have demanded she not leave unless he was by her side.

Seeing her again, so unexpectedly, had made him feel as if he had been hit by a hover truck. The encounter still whirred in his mind, and there were so many things he wished he had said and done. He shook his head, wondering at the fact that he had ever managed to function around her to begin with. He'd forgotten how magnetic her presence was, how distracting it was to be in her proximity.

Scraps shook himself out of his stupor. Flit had told him to pack. She was planning to take him back to the Underground.

Without further deliberation, Scraps raced into the bedroom. He tore through the wardrobe to find the plain duffel that he and Flit had used in the past and then got to his knees, pulling the loose panel off the floor and taking out the gear that the Underground had given them.

As his hand closed around half-empty tub of interference paint, he paused.

"We just need to figure out our timeline, and then we can say that this uprising is well and truly under way."

Adam's words came back to haunt Scraps, and his breathing hitched.

"You have potential to do great things for the movement. We don't have much time to waste, so I will be waiting on your decision and expecting you to hit the ground running."

Slowly, Scraps lowered the tub of interference goop back into the crevice. Then, he reached in and pulled out the guns he had just put into the duffel. He kept unpacking until the duffel was empty and replaced the floor panel over the cache as his heart split in two.

He couldn't go with Flit.

Instead of packing like Flit asked him to, Scraps went to the living room and sat on the arm of the couch. His knee bounced up and down, heel tapping as he waited for her to return. He tried to find the right words to express why he was going to turn down the one thing he had been yearning for since she had been torn away from him.

Scraps lost track of time as he sat in that room. The city outside darkened completely, and the familiar lights of the building across from his twinkled almost like stars. Then, just as he was starting to worry, Flit, Layla, and Hawkeye reappeared in the living room.

"That went well!" Flit's voice bubbled over with excitement as she stepped back from her companions. She turned, smile growing wider as she saw him. "Come on. Let's get—" She stopped speaking. Her eyebrows knitted together as she looked at Scraps, and then at his feet, and then around the room as if searching for something. "Scraps? Where's your bag? We have to go."

The expression on Flit's face made it hard for Scraps to speak at first. He swallowed his last regrets in a silent gulp and said, "I cannot come with you, Flit."

Flit blinked. "What do you mean you can't come with me?" Her voice verged on the edge of panic.

Scraps stood up and walked over, taking her hands. "I'm making significant progress with the Free Citizens. Adam told me about a plan he has to take down the Government, and it sounds promising. If I come with you, then we will no longer have anyone on the inside."

Realisation dawned in Flit's pretty hazel eyes, along with a flare of hurt.

"We managed to get in contact with Layla's people. A whole group of Citizen-born Derivates who may be able to help us. We don't need the Free Citizens." Hawkeye stepped closer.

Layla nodded, putting her hand on Hawkeye's shoulder. "They even have Registered contacts. They are going to see if they can mobilise them too."

It wasn't enough.

Scraps knew the Derivates alone would not be enough. The Government had so many resources and so many people...

"Scraps, can I speak to you privately, please?" Flit asked, voice stiffer than Scraps had ever heard it.

"Of course."

He took her hand and walked out of the living room and down the hall with her, leaving Layla and Hawkeye whispering to each other in their wake. They made it to the bedroom, and he slid the door shut behind them. Then, without warning, Flit tugged him back to face her and leapt into his arm.

Her kiss was fierce, passionate, and so full of emotion that Scraps stumbled. Then, his back hit the door, and he wrapped his arms around her. He wasn't sure what was going on, but there was no way he was about to question it. Not when he needed it so badly.

As much as Scraps wanted to live in the moment, Flit was the one to end it. She was panting slightly, and her cheeks were flushed the most alluring shade of pink. When she looked into his eyes, the desire he saw there made him clear his throat.

"I want to come with you, I really do, but I can't. If—"

Flit cupped the back of his head and drew him close until their foreheads were touching. "I know," she whispered. "Fuck... I hate it, but I know."

Scraps froze. That wasn't what he was expecting.

"You... you are not going to try and convince me to come with you?"

A strangled groan escaped from Flit. "I want to. I can't tell you how much I've missed you. It... It's been fucking hard down there,

Scraps, but if you think you're onto something up here that may turn the tide of this war, then... you have to stay."

A surprising wave of relief washed over him. It was difficult enough for him to commit to his decision. He was grateful Flit wouldn't make it any more challenging by fighting him on it.

"I want to be with you. I really do. I just know that we cannot live like we were living in the Underground forever. I think this is it, Flit. The Free Citizens are rising. The Derivates are rising. This is the best chance we've had to fight for freedom in a hundred years."

Flit wrapped her arms around him, pressing their bodies together. "What did you discover?"

There were so many things Scraps would rather say to her, but he knew that they were working with a limited time frame.

"Adam used to be an Oligarch."

Flit muttered a particularly colourful swear word that Scraps had read on graffitied walls but had never heard spoken out loud.

"He has been orchestrating similar attacks to the ones here in all the major living centres. Of course, the Government hasn't publicised them because it wants to maintain a front of control," Scraps continued, trying to be as concise as possible "He intends to gain power around the perimeter of the city and to essentially lay siege to the Hub. He'll have people ready to take down communication networks to throw them off."

"And while that's down, it might be our chance to help out," Flit said slowly. She pulled her forehead away from his and met his gaze. "Do you think he'll let the Underground join the fight?"

That question made Scraps press his lips together with concern. "I am not sure," he conceded. "He is such a consummate liar it is hard for me to get a read on him."

"Damn... I wish I could help. What did you tell them about me? Did they ask where I went?"

"Your mother is sick in Eastbay," Scraps said, letting her know with his tone that this was not a concern. "It is best it stays that way. If you come back up here, it would be dangerous. I've got the Government monitoring me constantly, and we cannot risk rousing suspicion and turning their attention towards the Underground."

A small flicker of hope that had settled in Flit's hazel eyes fizzled out, and she let out a huff of agreement. "So, you stay up here, keep an eye on the Free Citizens, and figure out if we can throw our lot in with them."

Scraps nodded.

"And I'll go back to the Underground and try to get them ready to mobilise," Flit continued.

Scraps nodded again, and the sigh Flit let out after was a heavy, regretful thing. He cupped her cheek and ran his thumb over her soft, flushed skin. "How will I let you know when I have more information?" he asked.

The more they planned now, the higher their chance of success. The higher the chance of success, the sooner they could be together without worrying about the Government.

"I'll try to translocate back when I can," she said. "They've locked the Underground down. We're restricted to painted tunnels only. It's getting hard to do anything without being seen, but I'll make it work." Flit glanced over her shoulder, as if she could see through the door before adding, "And I'll see if I can get one of those emergency beacons off Hawkeye for you. Just in case."

"Thank you."

Flit leaned against him again, her embrace so tight that he knew they were both delaying the inevitable. He wished there was more he could say, but if he started, there would be too much. They didn't have the time for a full report of everything that had happened since they had been torn apart.

There was the sound of vibrations against skin, and Flit tilted her head to look at her wrist. A frown pulled at her already down-cast features.

"What is it?" Scraps asked, brushing his thumb over her cheek.

"Just Hawkeye checking in and reminding me that we need to get back ASAP," Flit muttered. She looked up at his eyes, and he knew what had to happen next.

Scraps was just about to tell Flit it was okay, that he understood she had to leave, when her lips found his and caught him in a passionate kiss.

After so long without her touch, the intensity of this kiss made him groan into her mouth. She clutched at him, and he turned around, pressing her back against the door and leaning down to deepen the kiss.

Before Scraps knew it, Flit's fingers were tearing his fly down, and he was returning the favour.

"You should go," Scraps managed to blurt between bouts of fervent kisses.

"I should." Flit let go of his pants to push her own down around her ankles. She was wearing high, lace up boots that would take an eternity to remove and then replace. "But this is more important."

Her words were the most arousing thing he had heard in the longest while, and he was not about to deny her. He stepped into the circle created by her pants and then reached down, grabbing her thighs and lifting her up so she could wrap her legs around him.

As much as Scraps dreamed about taking his time, time was a luxury they did not have. So they did the best with what they had, and the precious minutes they were able to steal were enough to remind Scraps of the pure bliss he could achieve with Flit.

When they were done, he held her in his arms as he gently lowered her to her feet. He pressed a kiss against the part in her chocolate brown hair and breathed her in. "I love you, Flit," he whispered, unable to hold the words back any longer.

Flit tilted her head back, and she trapped him in her gaze. Her cheeks were still flushed from their coupling, strands of hair that had been dislodged from her ponytail framing her face. "I love you too, Scraps," she replied. Then, she took a deep breath and closed her eyes. "If I don't leave now, I never will."

Despite the urge Scraps felt to test that comment, he knew that they would have no hope of a peaceful, free future unless he stepped back now. He gingerly stepped outside the tangle of her pants. He buckled up his own and then helped her get dressed.

Once he and Flit were presentable, they walked back out to the living room. Flit clung to him as they went, and before Hawkeye could make a comment, she raised her free hand. "I'm coming with you. Scraps is staying here. I'll fill you in when we get back, but it's the best decision for the cause."

Hawkeye looked devastated as he glanced between Scraps and Flit. "Are you sure?"

"It is not an easy decision, but it is the right one." Scraps guided Flit over to her best friend and transferred her hand to his. "Hopefully it won't be for long." He stepped back as Layla moved in closer to Flit and Hawkeye. "I'll see you all again soon."

Flit nodded, wrapping her arms around her friends before pausing. "Hawk, did you have another one of those bracelets?"

"Unfortunately not, but I'll sneak another one out of Control. You can bring it up to Scraps over the next couple of days. How does that sound?"

There was a flicker of relief inside of Scraps at Hawkeye's offer, at the opportunity offered to him and Flit. The small smile on Flit's otherwise stony features was a gift in itself.

"Excellent. Thank you," Scraps answered on behalf of them both. Then, he focused on his girlfriend. "Please, stay safe. I'll see you soon, okay?"

"Okay," Flit said with a firm not as she wrapped Hawkeye and Layla in a functional embrace. "I love you, Scraps. See you soon."

"I love you too," Scraps said, enjoying being able to reciprocate the emotion.

Then, with one last heavy sigh, Flit was gone.

32

FLIT

"WELCOME BACK, guys. Right on time too." Clarity's voice came through the intercom the moment Flit, Hawkeye, and Layla reappeared in training room seven. "The others were starting to worry, but I knew it would be fine."

Then, a second voice came through the comms. "Hawk, Layla, join the rest of us in training room six. Flit, retrieve Scraps and get him into the crate at the back of the room."

Flit's already gritted teeth crunched a little at Swipe's comment.

"Just come with us. I can explain for you," Hawkeye whispered, wrapping an arm around Flit's shoulder and ushering her to the door.

"Guys, what are you doing? We don't have time to fuck around," Swipe repeated over the comms.

Hawkeye squeezed Flit's shoulders tighter and let her out of the room they were in. At this time of night, most people who hung around in the Residence were over at the Mess eating dinner, meaning the coast was clear for them to slip out of their current simulator room and into the next one.

For the first time, Flit wanted to do what Swipe said so, so very badly. She wished she could just turn around and translocate back to the apartment. Bring Scraps back with her. Forget about this whole mess with the Free Citizens and the Government.

But it wouldn't be right. She and Scraps were making the best decisions they could, and she loathed that it meant they could not be together.

At least he was still alive and free. That was more than she had dared hope for, and she was so incredibly grateful for it. The little bits of information he had given her about the Free Citizens were fascinating too. When Flit and Scraps had first thrown their lot in with the ragtag bunch, she'd hoped they would be able to form an alliance. It seemed that Scraps had really earned Adam's trust, and as much of an erratic sociopath as Adam was, he was bent on bringing the Government down. If the Underground could mobilise, they could ride that energy. They stood a real chance.

Upon entering training room six, Flit couldn't help but feel the attention of all of the Blue Team members on her. Her jaw ached as Hawkeye stepped up beside her, bringing Layla along with him.

"So, the good news is that we managed to get in touch with Layla's contacts. They are wary of us, which is understandable, but they have agreed to reach out to their people," Hawkeye explained, the excitement in his tone evident despite the tension in the situation.

The others muttered to themselves, pleased by this revelation.

Swipe crossed her arms. "And the bad news?" She narrowed her eyes at Flit.

Flit took a deep breath and swallowed her instinctive anger at Swipe's attitude. "Scraps needs to stay in the Hub," she said, speaking slowly so she wouldn't have to repeat herself. "He has made significant inroads with the Free Citizens. They're planning an uprising. Scraps is going to keep an eye on them to see if we can't time something that will work for all three groups."

The indignation in Swipe's features softened into something akin to resignation. "So... now what?"

"Do we just wait around or whatever?" Sway grumbled.

"Obviously not." Flit rolled her eyes. "Waiting for more information from others doesn't mean we sit on our arses and twiddle our thumbs. We need to get our own people ready to fight."

"How do we do that?" Clarity asked, a frown tugging at her delicate lips. "We could barely even get these training rooms to help you sneak out for a while."

"Harmony and Divvy have this place locked down tight," Link agreed.

"Fuck Harmony and Divvy," Flit snapped, her frustration getting the better of her. Her hands balled into fists. "If we let them keep running the show, then we'll be entombed down here forever. They have no intention to do anything other fuck around. We've been doing that for a century now and expecting different results, but nothing has gotten better."

"You're talking mutiny here, Flit." Clarity's voice was barely above a whisper.

Flit threw her hands up in the air. "It's our only option."

Clarity shook her head. "We could try talking to them. You know, properly? Lay out everything that we've done and the contacts you've made outside this room. Maybe they'll change their minds if they know there's more out there."

"Oh, that's a brilliant idea," Swipe said, leaning back against the wall. "Clarity, why don't you use your ability and have a look at how well that'll go?"

With a frown, Clarity said, "You know I can't—"

"You don't need to be a precog to see how poorly that will go down." Flit softened her tone to ease the hurt look on Clarity's face. "I know you want to believe the best of them, Clarity, but they have spent the last month brainwashing me and scapegoating Scraps. They've made decisions to lock us all in here. They have access to all the information and intelligence the Underground has ever acquired. If that isn't enough to convince them, we've got no hope."

There was a general reluctant murmur of agreement, and Clarity sagged.

"If you're not comfortable with it, we understand if you need to step back." Hawkeye squeezed Clarity's shoulder.

"Some of us might just need more time to process this than others." Link stepped up to Clarity's side. "It was one thing when we thought we might be contacting other Derivates to bring back down here, but it is another matter entirely to join those Derivates and a bunch of Citizens and try to overthrow a Government that seems to know little to nothing about us."

"I'm not so sure about that," Hawkeye conceded, shifting on his feet and scratching the back of his neck.

Link glanced at him, and her head tilted to the side. Her mouth popped open slightly, and Flit leaned in, wondering what she'd read from Hawkeye.

"Okay, someone spill. I don't deal with tension well," Tweak blurted.

"Hawkeye has a theory about the most recent tunnel collapses," Link said slowly. She paused and gestured to Hawkeye expectantly.

The sandy-haired remote viewer's shoulders sagged. "We all know it wasn't Scraps," Hawkeye begun. "They know it too, which means they are trying awfully hard to pin the fault on someone. The only reason they'd do that is to cover for something else."

"So, what are they covering for?" Swipe flicked her braid over her shoulder and tried not to appear as interested as the glimmer in her eyes made her appear.

Flit thought about it. Hawkeye was onto something there. Why were they trying so hard to create a false narrative about the collapses?

The first thought Flit had was that they didn't know the cause. Not every incident had a simple explanation. However, they had admitted ignorance before. In the past, they had never shied away from saying they did not yet have enough information to reach a conclusion. So, they had to know what was behind it, and whatever the cause was had to be worse than the idea of being betrayed.

The next thought Flit had was that maybe the Government already knew about the Underground. Having a single rogue actor behind the attacks would make for a much less threatening excuse than the whole Government aware of their existence. The information the Blue Team had found when investigating the gang Heft was running with had been destroyed, or, at least, they did their best to destroy it. However, as that idea grew in Flit's mind, she mentally swatted it away. The Government had never shown any signs of hesitation when it came to snatching up Derivates. If they knew there was a whole colony under Old City, there was nothing to stop them from sending some strike teams down and ending the rebellion. After all, they were pretty much trapped in the tunnels.

It couldn't be the Government.

Then, Flit remembered what Fortune had told her about Long-beach, about the way Control had tried to recall them under the guise of keeping everyone safe, only for the settlement to be raided shortly after.

"They're isolating us on purpose," Flit said. "Think about it. Those collapses were too much of a coincidence to be mere malfunctions. If the Government knew about us, we'd already be dead. So, why are we down here? The only logical reason I can think of is that Control *wants* us to be isolated."

There was a buzz of conversation as the others either protested Flit's suggestion or spoke about how they were getting that feeling too.

"The question is, why?" Hawkeye interrupted the chatter. "It's something I've been trying to figure out, but I haven't had any luck."

"They could just be trying to keep us safe, like they say," Clarity said, ever the voice of reason.

Tweak rolled his eyes. "Then they are doing a shit job of it. We've got one viable exit route left. All it will take is one more emergency, and we'll be sealed down here forever."

"I don't think this is something we will be able to figure out right now," Hawkeye interjected, shaking his head. "The point is that I don't think they'd look kindly on us for wanting to take the fight to the surface."

The group fell to a hush.

Almost a minute passed before the silence was broken by Sway. "We just need a good cover, a reason to make our activities look legitimate while we get things started right under their noses." His usual tongue-in-cheek tone was gone, replaced by something more serious. "The best covers are often those close to the truth. I think it's one of the reasons you were able to break out of your telecoercion, Flit. The idea that Scraps would betray us was so, so far from any possible truth."

"So, what you're saying is we need something that will let people prepare to fight without Harmony and Divvy thinking we're preparing them to fight?" Layla asked slowly, her eyebrows furrowing.

"That's not going to be easy to hide, mate." Tweak shook his head.

"I don't know." Swipe's eyes lit up with the glow of a new idea. "I've seen a lot of things that look like training that weren't."

A gasp from Link made Swipe's lips stretch into a wide grin. "That's brilliant! Tell them. It's perfect!"

The Blue Team perked up at the barely concealed spoiler.

"Seeing as we're all stuck down here, languishing away in the tunnels with nowhere to go and nothing to do, I feel like we should propose a new exercise scheme. You know, get people up and moving. Take their minds off the fact we're basically all trapped down here," Swipe said.

"Exercise?" Flit scoffed. Still, she kept her tone light as it was a good idea. "Should've known that would have been your go-to excuse."

"Don't mock it." Swipe pointed a finger at her. "That hunk of yours would be sad he's missing out."

"That's a good plan." Tweak perked. "I mean... not that any part of me wants to engage in mandatory exercise, but it's a solid cover."

"How do we make it happen?" Layla asked, glancing at Hawkeye.

The tension that had been filling the empty space in the room was now electric with excitement.

Hawkeye drummed his fingers on his thigh as he considered it. "I can speak to Posthoc. I'm sure he'd love the idea. Might even be able to help us get it all together. He's been pretty bored lately with the restrictions reducing how much he has to coordinate."

"Well, that sounds like the start of a good plan," Flit said. "If there's anything you need from me to help, let me know."

There was a reassuring chorus of similar offers from the others.

"For now, our priority is keeping the truth behind this on the down low," Flit said. "If they really are trying to keep us penned in down here, I'm willing to bet they've got their telepaths on the job. Guard your minds."

Once more, the team agreed with her. Even Clarity, who had appeared reluctant a few minutes ago, was standing with her shoulders back and chin high.

"Damn it, Flit. I'm the team leader. I'm the one supposed to be giving those kinds of orders," Swipe said in faux exasperation.

Swipe walked over to a narrow bench that lined the far wall and retrieved a bag she had left there. The rustle of food packets sounded from within, and Flit was pleased she had considered snack for the crew. The thought made her stomach rumble, letting her know that it was past dinner time.

"I'll make the call to get the crate moved," Hawkeye offered as he walked over to Flit. He gestured to where she had her weapons belt and gun settled under her trench coat. "I can take those back to the armoury for you."

"Are you sure? I kinda like them where they are," Flit said, even as she reluctantly started to unbuckle the belt.

Hawkeye ignored her comment, and she eventually got the gear off and handed it over to him. Swipe handed out some energy bars and then used her abilities to float over a duffel for Hawkeye. Once it was packed with their mission supplies, they all shucked off their coats. Hawkeye draped them over the bag and then hugged the bundle close to his chest.

"Okay, let's blow this joint," Tweak said as he led the way to the door. "Flit, I'm on your protection detail. I'll get you back to your folks' apartment safely."

Flit stumbled over her step but easily caught herself before she fell. "On my what?"

"Protection detail," Swipe said, walking up behind Flit and patting her on the shoulder with a wicked grin. She then reached into her pocket and handed Flit a damp, disposable wipe to remove the interference goop from her cheeks. "We all talked and decided you need one of us with you at all times. If you get brainwashed again, we're thoroughly fucked, so we're not going to give Harmony the chance to get you alone."

The satisfaction on Swipe's face was enough to let Flit know that this was highly amusing to her. She wanted to argue back so badly, but she knew she'd just be feeding right into Swipe's hand, so Flit let it go. One thing that she had discovered over the past year or so was that snapping back was fun, but being smart about it turned her sassiness from a form of smack-talk into a weapon.

When the Blue Team left the training room, they split into three groups. Hawkeye and Layla turned for the Armoury. Swipe, Link, Clarity, and Sway announced that they were heading to the Mess, and Flit and Tweak continued up higher in the levels of the Residence.

Flit did not need nor want a babysitter, but she was grateful for the company. Even though she had told herself to be cautious with her hope when she had set out earlier that evening, there was still some part of her that had believed she would be bringing Scraps home. Knowing he was back on the surface, still in the heart of the Hub, and under the surveillance of Government Agents was terrifying. She was relieved he was alive and safe, but she wasn't foolish enough to think that was a permanent arrangement. He was balancing on a knife's edge up there, and she was about to start doing the same thing in the Underground.

As they approached the door to her parents' apartment, Tweak patted Flit's shoulder. She turned to face him, and he gave her a rather sad, sympathetic smile.

"I'm sorry tonight didn't go right," he said quietly, glancing up and down the empty hall with caution. "I know it must be tough, but I'm so glad to hear he's okay. He's a good guy, that man of yours. You'll see him soon enough. We'll all make sure of that."

The emotions Flit had been trying to keep locked up tight in her chest pushed at her inner boundaries, and she choked on her words. Instead of spluttering through a response, she just nodded and accepted the firm, warm embrace Tweak offered.

He gave her a tight squeeze before releasing her. "I'll see you around, yeah? And please, for the love of everything good in these tunnels, don't go getting any ideas and try to escape. We need you."

"Thank you," Flit said. She wasn't sure whether it was for the reassurance, the compliment, or the faith he showed in her. Perhaps it was all three.

Either way, Tweak just nodded and waited for her to walk into her apartment before he left.

When Flit got inside, her parents were eating some dinner they had brought back from the Mess. They'd gotten a plate for her, but she told them she wasn't feeling well.

Flit went straight to her ensuite and was about to step into the shower but paused on the threshold and frowned. Memories flashed through her mind of where Scraps had touched her. Where he had joined with her. How it had felt to have his hands all over her as her back was pressed to that bedroom door. With a heavy sigh, she shut the water off, telling herself she would shower in the morning. She wanted to keep those sensory memories with her for the night. Then, when she woke, she would scrub away all the doubts and focus on steeling herself for what was coming.

33

————

SCRAPS

THE MOMENT FLIT LEFT, Scraps wished he had gone with her. Not for any logical, sensible reason. Purely because he already missed the way her warm hands felt on his skin. The scent of that incredible spot on her neck. How she had tasted when he kissed her.

He had tossed and turned in his sleep that night. There was a part of him that knew he had made the right decision. Staying was his only real option given how deep he was in the scenario. Seeing Flit again had also confirmed that he was on the right path. He was in a perfect position to make a difference.

With a new sense of conviction, Scraps made his way to Nightmix a few days later, just as Adam had suggested. Knowing that Flit would be rousing the Underground and that there was a hidden pocket of allies positioned in the city, Scraps was more confident in Adam's plans than he had been when he had first heard them.

Adam was deep in a conversation with a couple of people from the garment production line Scraps had been assigned to earlier when Scraps walked into the bunker. Adam immediately dismissed the men and rose from his desk as Scraps approached.

"You've got new swagger in your step this afternoon, Brian," Adam said with a wide, almost predatory smile.

Scraps chose to take that as a compliment.

"I'm in," he said, not bothering with any preamble. "Your plan has real merit. We'll need to train more of our people up, though. What timeline are we working with?"

"We'll be initiating our siege in a fortnight, provided my contacts in the communication departments can do their thing," Adam said.

"Two weeks?" Scraps blinked. Proper training would take months.

Adam crossed his arms over his chest, and his eyebrows raised almost to his salt and pepper hairline. "Is that going to be a problem?"

"No, but I do have a question for you."

"Oh? I do like questions." Adam pulled out a chair from under the front of the desk on the same side as his own chair. He leaned on the table with one arm and swept the other towards Scraps. "Well, go on. No time like the present."

There were far too many people packed into the bunker for Scraps to feel comfortable having any sort of real conversation there, however he reminded himself they were all Citizens. With the general hum of conversation, combined with the steady thrum of the bass from the club above, he figured it would have to do.

Just to be cautious, he leaned closer to Adam. "Have you considered how the Derivates factor into this plan?" he asked, keeping his tone neutral.

Scraps had debated how to ask this question over the past few days. He had come to the realisation that he couldn't lead with any ideas. As open as Adam pretended to be to suggestion, Scraps knew better. If the leader didn't think the plan was his own, it was bound to be twisted and warped beyond the initial proposal. Instead, it would be far easier to gauge his receptivity to any alliances by how he responded to the neutral request.

The leader's eyebrows rose. "What do you mean?"

Clever, Scraps thought. The man would give nothing away for free.

"I am curious. It is inevitable that the Government will mobilise them to protect the city, but they aren't our enemy."

"I don't care who it is. If they stand with the Government, they're our enemies."

As firm as Adam's tone was, Scraps had to point out a flaw in his logic. "They do not have a choice. They were born into their jobs and brainwashed to stay there."

"They're tools." Adam shrugged. "They wouldn't know what to do with a choice even if they had one."

Scraps stared at him probably for a second longer than was reasonable. For all the things Adam had to have known as an Oligarch, he still believed Derivates were just tools? Scraps had never wanted to lecture someone so badly before, but he resisted the urge.

"But... what if they do have a choice, and what if some *chose* not to follow orders and wanted to join the fight?"

The snort Adam let out was enough to tell Scraps what he thought of *that* particular idea.

"Then they could fight with us to appease the Derivate sympathisers, I suppose," Adam conceded, sounding as though the very thought of it was ludicrous. "But they will never be like us. I've seen what happens when a group of Derivates try to break free. It's dangerous and chaotic. I'd rather let the Government deal with them. They cannot be trusted. This movement is called the *Free Citizens*."

The edges of Scraps' vision blurred red.

"Now, is that all with the questions, Brian?" Adam asked briskly, moving the conversation right along. "We have an uprising to plan."

Scraps plastered a fake, satisfied smile on his face. "Of course."

IT WAS LATE that night or, rather, early the next morning when Scraps was walking out of Nightmix with Chris and Liana. The extra patrols and Derivates stationed around the city had increased. They could barely get half a block without counting at least three officers on watch. It was a concerning development. If the Government continued to enhance their security, it could only mean they were anticipating further action from the Free Citizens, or maybe there was already further activity that Adam just wasn't telling Scraps about.

After the eye-opening conversation with the leader of the Free Citizens, the rest of Scraps' night had gone smoothly. Adam had explained that they had various safe houses around the outer perimeter of the city, all stocked with food and arms and ready to go. At this stage, they had gathered enough to provision the first ten rows from either side of the edge of the city. As Nightmix was in the eleventh row of blocks from the North and twelfth from the East, they just had a little bit more work to get the club within the boundaries of their siege. That would account for more than half of the city area-wise, but the outer blocks had minimal value to the Government.

The other thing the Free Citizens needed was people trained and able to fight. That was where Scraps came in. The conversation Scraps had with Adam about Derivates was a reminder of the kind of people he could be dealing with and the reality that the Free Citizens would be fighting Registereds, so he resolved to teach them self-defence and to focus on the Citizens giving the orders rather than the Derivates themselves.

In addition to training people in combat skills, Scraps would meet with a group of Citizens Adam had deemed "trustworthy". Together, they would organise a condensed training program that those people could then share with their own cells. Scraps would then continue to train his current group at Nightmix, which Adam had taken to calling headquarters, all whilst working with a selection of already skilled fighters to form an elite strike team.

It was all a sign that things were heating up, and Scraps wished he had a way to contact Flit. He had to be patient, though. She would visit when she got a chance. The knowledge that she and the others were essentially trapped in the Underground was more of a shock to him than Adam's derision towards Derivates. This brought Scraps back to the present moment as he walked silently alongside his two closest friends on the surface.

"It has been a while since we have had a proper chance to talk. Would you both like to come back to my apartment tonight?" Scraps asked, trying to sound casual as they approached the corner where they would normally have to split to walk to their own homes.

"Our place is closer. You're welcome to come to ours instead," Chris offered.

Scraps shook his head. That would not do. There was every chance the Government were listening in at their apartment.

"I have some really tasty cheese and wine at my place that will go to waste if we do not eat it tonight," Scraps lied, hoping their previous preference towards the refreshments would encourage them to agree.

"Well, we can't be complicit in wasting cheese," Chris lamented. "To your place we go!"

Silence draped back over the trio as they completed the journey to Scraps' apartment. It continued as they rode up in the elevator, and it wasn't until they were all inside and Scraps pulled the door shut behind them that he finally spoke.

"I apologise for my subterfuge, but I do not have any cheese in my fridge," Scraps said, feeling somewhat guilty about the necessity of the lie.

Liana chuckled and waved a hand. "I'm fairly certain we both knew that was just an excuse."

Chris nodded in agreement.

"I can order some if you would like? It will not take long to arrive," Scraps offered, walking over to the wall screen in the kitchen.

"Honestly, Brian, it's fine," Chris promised, helping himself to a stool that was tucked under the kitchen bench. "So, what's on your mind? We noticed you were heads-down with Adam for the entire night. He really seems to be confiding in you lately."

As far as segues went, Chris had provided the perfect one for him.

"Adam is very selective in what he confides and in whom." Scraps walked around to the opposite side of the bench and leaned over, resting his elbows on it as he spoke. "He has opened up to me lately, but I think there is a lot more he is concealing."

Liana leaned her hip against Chris' side. "He's not planning something stupid again, is he?"

"Depends on your definition of stupid," Scraps conceded, earning a laugh from Chris. He wasn't quite sure what was funny, but he forged on anyway. "It seems that the plans to rise up against the Government are closer than I imagined."

Any mirth in the room vanished immediately.

Leaning closer, Chris asked, "How close?"

"Two weeks."

"What the—" Liana covered her mouth and muffled a swear word that was one of Flit's favourites. She shook her head. "That's crazy!"

"He's got a plan," Scraps said. Then, he hesitated. He would trust Chris and Liana with his life, but he knew they had no training against the mental incursion of telepaths. Even he was struggling in that department, apparently. Everything he told them had a chance of incriminating them. "I want to share more information with you but not if it will put you both at risk. Suffice to say that if you do not wish to continue with the Free Citizens, now would be a good time to step back. Even though the plan has a chance of success, there are no guarantees that any of us will make it out of the uprising alive."

After being in a relationship with Flit, Scraps had learned that there was a silent communication style that all couples developed even if they weren't telepathic. As he watched Chris and Liana, he could see that happening in real time. So many emotions he could not read seemed to coalesce between them.

"I don't want to lose you," Chris whispered.

Scraps looked away, wanting to give them some privacy for what was clearly an intimate moment, but what Liana said next broke his heart.

"If we don't fight now, you will anyway."

Straightening up, Scraps swallowed an unexpected clog of emotion that lodged in his throat. His mind flashed to the night before, when he had been holding Flit. He knew exactly what it felt like to be in the same position as Chris and Liana. It was only a matter of time before the Government made them confirm an unthinkable decision.

"You know I would have the procedure and pick you over anything else, don't you, Li?" Chris' voice dropped to a whisper.

"I know. I would pick you, too... but that isn't a future either of us want. It will be a burr between us for the rest of our lives. How long can we live, wondering what our lives would have been like if things were just a little bit different?"

"Li..."

"I know somewhere you can go," Scraps blurted, immediately regretting it as Chris and Liana turned to him. He let out a long breath and decided that he had to commit to it now that he had said it. "I... I cannot give you details now, but I may be able to get you to safety. You could hide until this is over."

Immediately and with great relief, Scraps noted the way Chris and Liana's shoulder stiffened.

"I appreciate that, Brian. I really do," Liana said, giving him a warm, gentle smile, "but I couldn't live with myself if I let everyone else fight for the future I want."

"Me either," Chris said, but the way he glanced at Liana told Scraps that maybe, just maybe, he wished she would seek refuge instead.

"Then we need as much information as we can get to ensure we all make it out of this alive," Scraps said, his lips setting into a firm line. He turned and walked over to cupboard to retrieve some glasses so he could get water for them all.

"Actually, I do have something that might be interesting. Or not. I'm not quite sure what to make of it," Liana said slowly.

Hands pausing by the filtered water tap, Scraps looked over at Liana. "It is hard to know what is useful or not without hearing it."

"Well, you've been busy in meetings with Jane and the others about the upcoming sewer system review that I decided to just go through and make the changes to the Derivate Training Facility report myself," Liana said.

Scraps froze. He vividly remembered that being a priority in his mind the night that Flit had visited. The next morning, he had been so lost in his own thoughts that he had just let it go.

"I am so sorry. It slipped my mind. That was not collegial of me."

Liana shook her head and raised a hand to stall any further apologies. "Don't worry about it. I was happy to finish it up. You carried the investigation itself. It was the least I could to. That's not why I'm bringing it up, though."

"Did we miss something in the report?" Scraps asked, wracking his brain. They made a point of being so thorough with their reporting as well as their critique of just how many policies and procedures had been broken and discarded recently.

"No... but I made the changes and then submitted the final copy. It was accepted, and I realised I made a few errors in the policy numbers." Liana leaned in closer. "I went back in to change it... and they had replaced our text, almost word for word, with the report from last year saying it was all good."

"But their compliance was completely different last year. All it would take is for someone to walk into the facility to know that the report was a lie," Scraps protested.

He filled the cups for them, slid two across the bench to Chris and Liana, and then took a sip from his own as he thought the situation through.

"Maybe they don't really care about the review?" Chris suggested with a frown.

Liana sighed and then swirled the water in her glass around. "Then why bother changing it? If they don't care and they don't plan to address it, who are they trying to impress by lying about it?"

"They're not trying to impress anyone. They are trying to conceal the truth." Scraps felt that had to be the only logical conclusion.

"To what end?" Liana asked.

There were bound to be so many possible answers to that. Scraps couldn't be sure what fit best, but he did know the Government was all about spreading the illusion of control. They had a very specific narrative that they were trying to push. If they were seen to be training children and pulling Derivates off all other jobs, that would admit that they were either losing control or trying to gain more. Either one threatened the idea that everything was fine and that they were untouchable.

Scraps couldn't help but laugh. The Government's narrative had to be awfully fragile if it could be threatened by a ten-page report.

When Scraps looked up, he noticed Chris and Liana were watching him warily.

"Sorry." He set his glass down but kept his fingers around the cool surface. "If they changed it, it means they are worried. People would be terrified if they thought the excess show of force was necessary. And then..." Scraps thought of Layla and the Citizen Derivates Flit had gone to recruit. "If there are any Citizens concerned about the Government's treatment of Derivates, that would likely have a huge impact on them."

Chris' eyes widened.

Liana rolled her shoulders back and sat a little taller. "You're right," she said. "I know we're few and far between, but I would be furious and looking to protest if I heard about it. Right now, I'm just spinning my wheels and trying to figure out what we can do to shut it down."

"We can't shut it down." Scraps hated himself for saying so, however information was power, power that needed to be used at the right time to have maximum impact. "But I know how we can make use of it."

That seemed to perk Liana up as she raised an eyebrow at him in question. "Oh?"

"Do you think there is a way to sneak the draft of our report off the Government's network without it being flagged?"

A thoughtful look clouded Chris and Liana's gazes, but Liana shook her head.

"I'm not sure. Information technology is not my area of expertise," she told him apologetically.

"I'm good at planning calendars, booking meeting rooms, and signing people in and out," Chris added with a chuckle that made Liana roll her eyes.

"We will need to look into it," Scraps said, too busy trying to come up with a working plan to indulge Chris' sense of humour. "Adam intends to broadcast more messages city-wide, like he did with the maglev mission. If we can figure out who is putting that together and get hold of that report, we may be able to convince them to add some extra information to it."

"Ah, that's easy! I'll have a word with Andy." Then, Liana

paused and bit her lip. Her cheeks flushed. "I... I probably shouldn't have shared that."

Scraps her hand. "You did the right thing. If we're going to succeed, then we'll need to share important information with each other. Do you think Andy will be open to it?"

Even as he asked the question, Scraps knew the answer. He thought back to a few months ago, when Andy had helped Flit disappear on the surveillance system at that madman's apartment.

"Absolutely," Liana said without hesitation. "Andy's a good person."

"Will she tell Adam?"

"A lot of people love Adam, but I don't think Andy is one of them," Liana said slowly. "She seems pretty pissed off with Adam lately. At first, he was being respectful of the space under Nightmix, but Petra, Trey, and Andy have raised their concerns about the increasing number of people coming in and shipments going out. They're worried about being discovered, but Adam isn't taking their concerns seriously."

That information, while new to Scraps, did not really surprise him. He didn't bother questioning how Chris and Liana knew about it. He was always the last to learn about the gossip and interpersonal drama in any group of people.

"Good," he said, "because I do not think Adam will appreciate us diluting his message."

Liana tilted her head to the side. "What do you mean?"

"I asked him about his plan for Derivates and suffice to say that he does not consider them a part of this movement," Scraps said, trying to be as diplomatic and respectful about the matter as possible.

"Well, that's a load of bullshit." Chris jumped to his feet, his hands gripping the edge of the smooth bench. Liana put a hand on his shoulder. "It doesn't make sense. They've got it even worse than we have."

Scraps took a sip from his glass to cover the smile of relief that crept onto his lips. He took his time to drink then set the glass down again. "I agree... and it is something we need to change. I do not think we can win this thing without them."

A low whistle danced from Liana's lips. "How can we involve them, though?"

"Do you trust me enough to leave that to me?" Scraps asked, looking between them.

"Of course," Liana replied right away. "If you handle that side of things, I'll speak to Andy about the broadcast. She may be able to tell me how to get the information safely off the network. She's good at that kind of thing."

She certainly is, Scraps mused.

"It sounds like a plan," Chris said with a wide grin. "So, was it just the cheese you were lying about or the wine as well?"

Scraps couldn't help but chuckle. He was sure they had more to talk about, but the way Chris changed the subject told him that now was not the time.

"Let me check. I am sure Ava left something behind in the pantry."

As Scraps pulled the cupboard door open, he didn't have to bother trying to hide his smile. He and Flit had made a good decision all those months ago when they'd decided to make friends with Chris and Liana. He only hoped he would be able to retain their friendship when they learned the true depth of just what he and Flit were hiding from them.

"*YOU* WANT A FITNESS PROGRAM?" Posthoc looked up from the files open on his desk, his face the perfect picture of incredulity as he cocked an eyebrow at Flit.

"The whole team thinks it is a good idea," Hawkeye cut in, trying to draw the attention back to himself.

Hawkeye had asked Flit to accompany him to see the leader of Security. Flit thought that it was bound to be counterproductive, but Hawkeye swore Posthoc had a soft spot for her. He'd even thrown in the fact he might feel sorry for her so he'd be more receptive too. Flit wanted to slap Hawkeye across the back of the head for that last comment, but he was right. Beneath all the grumbling and threats, Posthoc was a softie. If Flit had to force a few tears and blubber a bit, it would be well worth it.

"Not you, her." Posthoc waved a hand at Hawkeye dismissively. "Flit, you hate exercise. All you've ever bloody done is complain about it."

Flit shrugged. There was no point denying it. "I hate being bored more."

Scratching his chin, Posthoc asked, "Does this mean that you'll finally get your arse to the gym without constantly whining about it and trying to make up excuses?"

Not a fucking chance, Flit wanted to say. Instead, she looked down at her nails and feigned nonchalance. "Hawkeye said I can be a group facilitator, rather than participant."

Posthoc's snort was loud enough to make Hawkeye jump. "The proposal is to train them, not turn them into sassy smart-arses."

Hawkeye shifted beside Flit and shot her a glare that had the potential to burn through her skull.

"Well, I learned a lot about fitness from Scraps while we were up in the Hub," Flit said, letting her voice crack on his name. "I was hoping I could at least make something good of that whole mess."

Flit had Posthoc right where she wanted him. He shifted uncomfortably in the seat behind his desk and cleared his throat.

"Fine." He tapped the surface of his desk and opened a new window. His on-screen keyboard appeared, and he started typing. "You two get back to work. I'll handle the proposal. I'll have to run it by the other leaders."

"Posthoc?" Flit asked, leaning in closer.

He didn't bother looking up. "Mmm?"

"It might be best if you leave mine and Hawkeye's names off the paperwork... I think a lot of people are mad about us because of what happened with the... well, you know."

"Do you think I'm stupid? There's no way I'm putting your name on it." He shook his head. "Get out of here before I change my mind."

No further dismissal was required. Flit and Hawkeye knew better than to push their luck, so they walked towards the door before they messed things up.

Just as they reached the threshold, Posthoc cleared his throat. "Flit... Hawk?" He looked up at them, bushy grey eyebrows furrowed over his blue eyes. "This is a good plan. I think people will benefit from the distraction. Thank you."

The odds of receiving a compliment from Posthoc were so low Flit was momentarily speechless. Instead of answering, she just gave him a crisp salute and a smile. Then, she slipped her arm through the crook of Hawkeye's elbow and led him out to the hallway.

"Well, looks like you were right," Flit muttered under her breath when they turned into a different tunnel.

Hawkeye stopped walking and stared at her, eyes wide. "First a compliment from Posthoc, then you admit I'm right?" He pretended to slap his own cheek. "I must be dreaming."

Flit playfully bumped him with her hip. "I'm happy to admit you're right as long as this plan works."

"Well, it was a stroke of genius to ask him to keep our names off it."

"I know." Flit's face split into a brief but cocky grin. "So... what are you up to tonight? Any chance we could hit up the sim for a game?"

Now that Flit's training with Shadow had stopped, she was back to the drudgery of twiddling her thumbs in her parent's apartment and short-range patrols.

Hawkeye's cheeks turned pink, and he started walking again. "I'm, um, I'm actually busy."

"Let me guess... a special dinner with a certain someone?"

"That's ridiculously vague," Hawkeye said.

When he didn't follow up beyond that, Flit urged, "So, you and Layla are getting closer, huh?"

There was more silence.

"Bloody hell, don't get all closed-lip on me. I'm so happy for you. She's lovely... and fierce." Flit wasn't sure why Hawkeye was being so secretive about it, but she knew how to make him bite. "I like her. Kinda reminds me of someone I know." She playfully buffed her nails on her shirt in a self-aggrandising gesture.

"Hardly," Hawkeye scoffed. "I wouldn't call you lovely."

Flit let out a belly laugh that felt so good after the drama of the past few weeks. "That's fine. I'll make do with fierce."

She tugged on Hawkeye's arm to draw him closer and rested her head on his shoulder as they walked. They went for the rest of their stroll in companionable silence, and when they arrived at the Residence, Flit stopped in front of the elevator bank.

"I think I'll pop by and see if any of the others are free," Flit said, feeling that quality time with her other friends was well overdue. "See you later, yeah?"

Hawkeye pressed his lips together and eyed her warily. "Where are you going?"

"Probably just to see Clarity." To say she was exasperated

would have been an understatement. "Don't worry. I know I'm under that stupid protection detail. I'll get one of them to walk me back to my parents' level. I think I'll be fine on the lift between here and Clarity's. No one would be expecting me to go there."

"But—"

"Chop, chop!" Flit interrupted, nudging him away. "Don't want to be late for your date with lover-girl!"

Instead of protesting, Hawkeye let out a string of curses that only made Flit more amused as he turned and walked away.

Flit returned her attention to trying to find someone to spend some time with and pressed the button on the elevator. While she waited, she decided that a night with Clarity, the quiet, calm precog, would be good. She made her way to her friend's apartment and knocked on the door. She bounced on the balls of her feet as she waited for it to open.

"Babe, what took you so—" Clarity paused, mouth dropping open and face going white when she saw Flit standing there. She tugged at the hem of the oversized T-shirt she was wearing, probably to make it look like it wasn't the only thing she had on.

"Babe?" Flit waggled her eyebrows. "Not what you usually call me, but I'm down for—"

It was Flit's turn to gawk when she looked past Clarity, who, as far as Flit knew, was still single, to the bed behind her. Complete with rumpled sheets, a bare-chested Sway was leaning back on his arms, wearing nothing but a shit-eating grin.

"Oh, shit," Clarity blurted.

Sway chuckled. "You can't say 'Oh, shit' when you're the one that opened the door. How did you not see that coming?"

"I didn't think to check who it would be! I'm not a twenty-four-seven precog machine, Sway!"

The last thing Flit wanted was to walk in on this kind of drama. She had come here seeking a nice, relaxed night, not to uncover the fact that one of her friends was cheating on another. Sway and Link had been together for so long that even Flit felt the gut-punch at the evidence that he had just slept with Clarity.

"This isn't what it looks like," Clarity said in a quiet, urgent whisper. Clarity reached out for Flit's hand, but Flit snatched it away and stepped back. "Link will be back in a moment. Please, just stick around so we can explain. It'll make sense. I promise."

"Look, you do you." Flit raised both of her hands. "Just be aware that I can't stop Link from reading my mind. I won't say anything because I'm not going to go out of my way to break her heart, but you should consider it. This is not okay."

"So, I couldn't find the moonshine, but I did find—"

Flit jumped with fright and spun around to come face to face with Link as she slipped out of the apartment opposite, the one she shared with Sway. She was wrapped in a worn but still fluffy dressing gown and holding up a full bar of good, Hub-grade chocolate.

"Oh... Oh, dear. I see." Link sighed heavily and looked up and down the corridor. She then grabbed Flit by the upper arm and dragged her into Clarity's room, knocking the precog back as they bustled through.

Clarity quickly shut the door behind them. "Just let us explain," she said, still pleading.

The combination of Sway's overly smug smirk and the lack of clothing on both Link and Clarity was enough of a hint for Flit to calculate what was going on.

"Well, shit. I don't think anyone had bets on this." Flit whistled with appreciation and tipped an imaginary hat at Sway.

"No bets, just hopes," Sway schmoozed with a nonchalant wave of his hand.

Link shot him a look so sharp that he hung his head and pulled the blankets up to cover his chest. "This isn't something anyone else knows about," Link admitted as she finally stopped glaring daggers at her boyfriend.

"Yet," Clarity added, blushing. "We are going to tell people, just not now because... well, you know. There's so much going on down here. We don't want to throw a hand grenade into our lives when we're all stuck in such close quarters."

Relief flooded through Flit. "I'm just glad you two aren't fucking behind her back." She waggled her finger between Sway and Clarity.

"It was Link's idea," Sway said, smug once more.

Link threw the chocolate bar at him. "Stop!"

"Don't worry, guys. Your secret is safe with me."

"You're not going to tell anyone?" Clarity's features lit up with hope.

"No," Flit confirmed. "This is your business and your business alone. If this is what you all want, I'm happy for you." She shoved her hands in the pockets of the cargo pants she was wearing and sighed. "Although it does mean I'll have to find another way to entertain myself tonight."

"You can join us, if you like," Sway offered.

The tone of his voice and the way Link and Clarity's voices rose in a combined, "Sway!" let Flit know that he wasn't entirely joking.

Sway just smiled innocently. "Can't blame a guy for asking."

"You're the worst." Clarity shook her head, but there was a fondness to the supposed insult.

"As fun as that sounds, especially with chocolate involved, I'm going to have to decline." Flit hung her head, pretending to be disappointed. "But I'll speak to Scraps when this is all over. See what we can do, huh?" She winked at them and turned to walk towards the door.

"No!" Link dashed over and grabbed Flit's shoulder.

"I was joking," Flit promised, turning to face her.

"Not that." Link rolled her eyes. "I mean you can't leave."

"Why the fuck not? I certainly can't stay here. You guys aren't even fully dressed!"

With a frown, Link looked down at the robe she was wearing. "Just... give me a second. I'll walk you back to your place. You shouldn't be wandering around alone."

"Wait... who was supposed to be with you?" Sway sat up enough that the sheet fell down to reveal his chest again.

Flit groaned and turned away. "Hawkeye, but he had an urgent matter to attend to. I only rode up in the elevators, guys. Don't lose your shit." She slapped her hand against the access panel, and the door slid open. "Don't worry, Link. I'll wait just outside the door for you to make yourself decent."

Before anyone else could argue, Flit stepped outside and shut the door behind herself. She flopped back against the wall. She considered going to see if Tweak was free, but then she dismissed that idea. Even if he was a micro and he couldn't read her thoughts, he would know she was hiding something right away. Given that he and Sway were best friends, it would be dangerous to risk it. She hadn't spent time with Patch in a while either, but given that he was Link's brother, that would likely end up even worse.

The only other person on the team was Swipe, and there was no way Flit was voluntarily going to seek her out, tenuous armistice or not. And Fortune? As much as she craved to speak to the woman who was like a mother to her, seeking her out would look suspicious right now. She couldn't draw any attention to the fact they were working together.

Flit resigned herself to another night stuck in her family's apartment and was mulling over the benefits of getting to bed early when Link stepped out of Clarity's room, pulling a ponytail full of tightly coiled black locks out of the neckline of her T-shirt. Upon closer inspection, it was the T-shirt Clarity had just been wearing that probably belonged to Sway anyway.

It took an admirable amount of restraint for Flit to stop herself from commenting on the shirt as she started walking, and Link fell into step with her.

"I read that thought anyway, you know," Link muttered, resigned.

"That's your own fault for being in my head."

"You practically screamed it." Link put her hands in the pockets of the pants she was wearing, the same ones she had worn on her patrol earlier that day. "Some days, you manage to keep a solid, tight hold on your thoughts. Other days, you blurt out things like it's going out of fashion."

Flit laughed. "Well, then, my thoughts are a good match for the rest of me."

Link laughed softly. They kept going until they reached Flit's apartment a few levels up. When they walked in, the living room was empty, and Flit let out a sigh, figuring her parents were working.

Instead of leaving right away, Link leaned against the wall

beside the door. "How are you going? It's been a rough couple of weeks."

Pausing on the spot, Flit said, "I'm fi—"

"Please, don't," Link interrupted, pushing off the wall and walking over to take Flit's hand. "You don't have to pretend. You don't have to lie to me or yourself. At least, not right now."

Flit's breath caught in her throat at the sudden request for vulnerability. "Link, I..." She stopped, not knowing what to say or where to start.

Link just pulled her into a warm, surprisingly strong embrace.

Sudden tears burned in Flit's eyes, and she squeezed them shut tightly in hopes to stem the tide. She had been so focused on the next move, on planning the next step, on trying to make things happen that she hadn't stopped to just breathe.

"It's tough going now, but we'll get through this. You'll be okay. Scraps will be okay, too," Link whispered.

If Flit didn't know the telepath better, she might have accused her of pulling the thoughts straight from her mind, but it was unlikely Link would go so far. Not in a moment like this.

When Flit pulled back out of the hug, she dashed away the errant tears that managed to escape and roll down her cheeks. She sniffed and tried to look a little more composed. "Thank you, Link," she said, already feeling better for being able to break down, even for a moment.

"I know you came to seek Clarity out tonight and..." The telepath cleared her throat. "Well, it didn't go too well, but we're all here for you. Not only to kick arse, but for the hard stuff too. If you need to talk or think things at me... or even just sit in silence, I'm your girl, okay?"

Flit nodded, taking Link's hand and squeezing it gently. "You'd better get back, or Sway might think we're having fun up here without him."

Link rolled her eyes. "Heck, I wish I could say that was unlikely, but you're probably right. Take care, okay? And reach out if you need to. There's no point burning yourself out before things come to a head. We need you. This rebellion won't happen without you."

With that, Link stepped back and gave Flit one final smile before leaving the room.

IT WAS early morning two days later when Flit checked her e-mails before getting out of bed and saw a message from Hawkeye.

To: Flit
From: Hawkeye
Subject: You're not gonna believe this!
Flit!
Come to training room seven as soon as you wake up. I heard from Posthoc a few moments ago, and we have approval to implement our program. Everyone (including you) will now be expected to attend mandatory exercise groups at least once a day but with the option to attend multiple times. We need to get together and create a schedule for him before lunch. They plan on announcing it this afternoon so we can get started as soon as possible.

On any normal day, Flit would groan and swear at the idea of having to get up. She would even mutter unkind and inappropriate things about Hawkeye and his insufferable morning energy. This morning was different, though. She had just about given up hope in the proposal getting anywhere and was starting to muse about different ways to covertly training people to fight.

Instead of pulling the covers back over her head, Flit teleported out of bed and started getting ready for the day. She got a second message from Hawkeye telling her that he had contacted the others, and they were going to meet in training room seven.

When Flit left her room, her parents were sitting at the table enjoying some cereal for breakfast. Her mother almost choked on her meal when she saw Flit up and ready.

"Is there some kind of emergency?" Tinker asked, only half teasing.

"Nope! Just got shit to do. See you guys later."

Flit opened the front door and dashed outside, only to slam right into—

"Tweak?" Flit bounced back, rubbing her cheek where it had collided with his shoulder.

The microkinetic groaned. "Don't you watch where you're walking anymore?"

"And you just have a habit of standing outside people's door in silence? Creep," Flit snapped back.

"Not my fault you need a bloody babysitter." Tweak shook his head. "Come on, let's continue this bickering on our way to seven. I don't want to deal with Swipe carrying on if we're late."

That was something Flit could get behind, so she shut her mouth and started to walk beside Tweak. When they reached the elevator, he initiated light conversation about new graffiti he had seen popping up in some of the tunnels on his afternoon patrol the day before. Generally, people kept their creative spraying in the residential tunnels, but Tweak informed her with much amusement that tags and murals were starting to bleed into other areas as well.

The training room was empty when they arrived. The Blue Team all rocked up eventually, and Hawkeye informed her that Layla and Fortune would be joining them. Flit was pleased at the thought of seeing Fortune again, as she had no idea what she had been up to over the past while. She hadn't even really seen Fortune at mealtimes. It was something Flit wanted to rectify and was considering gently convincing her parents to invite Fortune over for dinner, even if it would be a little bit awkward on both sides.

While they were waiting for Layla and Fortune, Hawkeye walked over to Flit and took her elbow, gently pulling her aside. He looked around then slipped his hand into his pocket. He withdrew a tiny, foil wrapped packet and put it in her palm before closing her fingers around it.

"Cogs is going to tear me a new one if I ask for any more of these, but... she gave it to me. I was supposed to be hanging out..." He paused then smiled. "No, I was going to have a date with Layla this evening, but we've shifted it to tomorrow night so I can spend the night at yours instead. We can lock the door in your room and pretend we're playing Virtuball or whatever. Then, you can take it to *him* while I cover for you."

Flit looked down at her closed fist, and her heart skipped a beat. She was overcome with gratitude for the gesture from Hawkeye. From securing an item that was clearly hard to get, to giving up his night with Layla to cover for her, he was proving once again what a good person he was.

"Thank you, Hawk," Flit whispered, uncharacteristically solemn and serious.

Hawkeye squeezed her hands. "Don't thank me. I'm just doing it to stop you moping around so much, okay?"

Then, Hawkeye ruffled Flit's hair, and any soft feelings were long gone. She playfully shoved him away as she tucked the device into her pocket.

The door to the training room opened, and Fortune and Layla walked in.

"Sorry we're late," Fortune said, letting the door slide shut behind them. "Control still haven't assigned any new duties to the Citizen Derivates. It's starting to get a little claustrophobic down there."

Flit winced. She'd been so caught up in her own plotting that she hadn't found the time to go down and visit the people Fortune was clearly working diligently to support. She tried to file it with high priority on the mental list of things she had to do, but it was difficult to think beyond the fact that she would be seeing Scraps again in less than twelve hours.

"Well, this new *exercise* regime will be out by this afternoon if we can get a roster put together," Swipe offered, gesturing for the other two women to join them.

That was enough for everyone to put any other worries aside and start planning what they wanted their secret training schedule to look like. Unfortunately, Flit much preferred training Derivate abilities to exercise, and they had no scope for that with their current proposal. Still, it was a step closer to getting their own people prepared, so she let those with the know-how do what they needed to do to get a good physical program set up. While they worked on that, Flit, Tweak, and Fortune collaborated to group the residents of the Underground and the refugees together.

To ensure everyone was included, Control had made the rare concession to grant them a full list of the names and ages of the people in the Underground. Even though Flit knew there were a lot of them running around in the tunnels, she had never thought to count them. It was reassuring to see the numbers presented before them so clearly. There were nowhere near as many of them as there were Registereds, or Citizen Officers, but combined with the Free Citizens and the Citizen Derivates, maybe they stood a real chance.

The planning session went smoothly and swiftly. Flit and her group finished up the list of people shortly before the other group completed their routine plans for each age group and estimated fitness/ability level.

While they were exchanging information, Fortune leaned in close to Flit and whispered, "How are you going, love?"

Flit took a moment to consider her answer. She smiled and then confidently replied, "For the first time in a while, I'm feeling really good about things."

35

SCRAPS

"I HOPE our summons did not come as a surprise to you."

Scraps looked between Greene and Hector as he settled in the seat opposite the agents. TB-2199 and CC-9832 had found him on his lunch break and told him that his presence was required. As soon as he saw TB-2199, he slammed a mental wall down around his thoughts so hard and fast she blinked at him in surprise before giving him the slightest nod of approval.

"It did not. It has been a while since we last spoke. I knew you were bound to reach out sooner rather than later," Scraps admitted, feeling much calmer in the presence of the two agents than usual. He hoped that did not indicate that he was becoming complacent. "I have some important information for you, so it is good timing."

Greene and Hector were now the ones to look surprised.

Hector leaned in. "What is it?"

"Adam has taken me properly under his wing," Scraps informed him. "He wants to train his people in self-defence. He thinks I can help him do that."

Hector's face contorted in a mixture of discontent. "What he is planning next?"

"He has not given me much information yet. He is intent on building his numbers, though."

"Is that all? It's been over a month, and this is the best you've got? I am not sure if this deal is worthwhile for the Government."

Scraps pressed his lips together and took a slow, deep breath to settle the sudden annoyance at Hector's comment. "I still work full-time hours five out of seven days a week. Beyond that, I often stay back to get extra work completed, like any good Government employee." He put his palms flat on the table and eyed the agent. "Then, the only time I can dedicate to infiltrating the Free Citizens is on Adam's schedule. Which, for the most part, I cannot do because I am too busy working. I must also remind you, as a human, that I also need time to eat, sleep, and use the restroom."

To Hector's left, Greene rubbed her face to hide a slight smile as amusement danced in her eyes.

"Are you saying you want a holiday so you can get more time with the Free Citizens?" Hector snapped, crossing his arms over his barrel chest.

"No, I was merely pointing out the fact that it is quite difficult to get more information when I do not have adequate time to do so," Scraps replied, keeping his voice calm and respectful. "Although, if you are suggesting I use my annual leave to get time off work to facilitate that, I think you have come up with a rather good idea."

Greene's hidden smile turned into a coughed laugh. Hector glared at her, and she cleared her throat. "Do you have annual leave accrued?" she asked.

"Greene!" Hector's chair screeched against the smooth marble floor as he got to his feet. He gestured for his partner to follow him before he stalked outside.

Greene let out an almost imperceptible sigh and rose from her seat to join him in the hall. The door slid shut between the room and the corridor, and Scraps could not hear what was being said. He did not dare look over his shoulder, either. It was not his place to snoop. They would tell him what they wanted him to know.

As he waited in the room, the Derivates at either of his shoulders shifted on their feet and adjusted their stances. Scraps remembered using similar breaks without supervision to do the same thing when he had been working for the Government. It seemed absurd now. They should be able to do something as simple as adjust position without fear, but he remembered being reprimanded for an overly noticeable rise and fall of his chest whilst breathing on guard duty.

The door opened with an electronic hiss, and the agents returned to reclaim their seats. Greene looked calm again, but Hector looked as though he had eaten a lemon crumbed in chilli seeds.

"We need information faster than you are currently giving it to us. If you feel it would assist you to gain Adam's trust and get him to speak to you faster, apply for leave. We can forge a professional development course you can pretend to undertake from home if anyone asks what you need the time for," Hector explained.

Scraps blinked. He couldn't quite believe what he was hearing. "When would you like me to do this?"

"As soon as you return to your desk. We will get someone in our department to interface with your supervisor. We'll explain that it is done under a Government grant of sorts, and she will not be able to refuse," Greene explained in a more relaxed tone than Hector had used.

"Don't think this is an excuse to laze about." Hector sat up straighter and leaned forward in what Scraps assumed was intended to be a gesture of intimidation.

To make the agent feel better about his evident loss of pride, Scraps reclined in his seat, drawing away from the man and allowing him to live out his alpha male fantasies for a moment.

"We will expect more in-depth information. We need locations. Time frames. Specific plans. Get us enough to justify your continued freedom to our superiors. Right now, we're having a hard time doing that."

"Well, I truly appreciate the effort. Thank you," Scraps said.

Hector narrowed his eyes at Scraps, as if trying to see if there was some sort of hidden message in his words. Eventually, his frown deepened, and he rose from his seat. "We will see you shortly. We look forward to the intel you will bring us."

"Please escort Mr. Parkes back to his floor," Greene directed the two Derivates behind Scraps.

Without being asked, Scraps rose and followed the pair out. As he was walking behind them, he kept his attention on the telepath.

"TB-2199 can you hear me?" he asked, hoping he could project his thoughts in her direction or that she was listening in. He didn't care which, so long as she heard him.

Just as Scraps was about to give up hope, the woman nodded ever so slightly as she wound her way through the corridors, past closed meeting room doors.

"Thank you for warning me last time. I am curious about why you did it, but I know I cannot get any complex answers from you. If I ask questions, can you twitch the fingers on your right hand to indicate yes and your left to indicate no?" Scraps thought, keeping the words slow and clear in his mind.

TB-2199's ring finger on her right hand twitched, and Scraps suppressed a smile.

"That is perfect. Thank you. Did you warn me to be careful the other day for a reason?"

A right-hand twitch followed.

All the questions Scraps could think of started with *what* or *why*. They were questions that required more information. They were a luxury he did not have. He tried to figure out how to ask what he was really wanting to know, but they didn't have nearly enough time.

"Am I the first person you have helped like that?"

As they rounded a corner, TB-2199 flexed her left hand in an assertive indication of *no*.

Scraps was fascinated, but they only had a few more turns before they would reach the foyer. Once they were in the elevator, the confined space would make it far too difficult to stare at her hands without being noticed.

"Are you doing it because you don't agree with the reasons they are being held?"

This time, TB-2199 twisted back to look at him and then tapped the silver Government logo on her shirt before returning her attention to the corridor ahead.

"You don't agree with the Government?"

She turned sideways to skirt around some people who clearly didn't think it was worth taking one step towards the wall to allow others to pass easily. As she did, she slipped her right hand behind her back and flexed her fingers before closing her hands into a fist.

Scraps frowned as he dodged the workers who refused to move, and even though they ignored him, he was fully aware that being able to express his discontent on his face was a privilege in a place like this. *"Are there others like you?"* he asked just before they turned into the foyer.

There was another right hand shift before she let her arm fall back to her side.

A thrill ran through Scraps at the thought of that. *"Do you want to do more about it?"*

CC-9832 slipped back into place beside his colleague as they walked across the marble floor towards the elevator. He reached out and hit the call button for the elevator.

TB-2199 turned her back to the elevator wall, looking every part the attentive guard as she fixed her focus on Scraps and brushed some stray hair off the side of her face with her right hand in a slow, purposeful manner.

The floor indicator above the elevator ticked closer and closer to their level far too quickly.

"Do you have any contacts outside of the Derivates within the Government?"

The corner of TB-2199's lips turned down in a dissatisfied frown, and her head shook in what could have been confused for a slight tic.

"Then let me see what I can do." Deciding that he was already in so deep that one more question couldn't possibly do any more damage, Scraps thought, *"Would you be willing to fight against the Government?"*

A soft ding sounded, and the elevator arrived. TB-2199 stepped closer to the wall and slid her right arm across the door recess to hold it open for Scraps. "Please," she said, bowing ever so slightly but maintaining eye contact.

Scraps knew she was doing more than asking him to enter the lift. He returned her confirmation with a nod, and she and CC-9832 followed him in. The people already in the elevator frowned and shuffled out of the way, and TB-2199 remained close to the control panel, whilst CC-9832 stood behind Scraps.

"If I can get you out, will you be able to find a way to leave your barracks?"

The way that the telepath brought her right hand up to rest on the handle of her stun baton told Scraps everything he needed to know. She would be willing to try to leave if she had a way out. He would just need to find one for her.

LATER THAT NIGHT, Scraps wiped a sheen of sweat off his forehead with the back of his arm. He looked at the people assembled in front of him, a hodgepodge of Citizens from all different parts of the city dressed in an array of clothing that was just the right kind of neon or shiny for the club above but terrible for combat training. In addition to the friends he had made within the Free Citizens, there were a couple of people he recognised from the raid on the Advanced Human Research Facility. There were also several others he had never seen before. All of them sucked greedily on water bottles as they slumped against the cool concrete walls of the bunker below Nightmix. There was a general disagreement between the groups as to what they disliked the most—Scraps' lectures about tactics during warm-up or the physical exertion of the training itself.

"It does get easier, right?" Petra asked, frowning over her bottle.

Scraps nodded. "Yes. The more consistently you work out, the easier it gets. Well, unless you increase the difficulty. By that stage, you may enjoy the burn, so it becomes less of a chore."

"Enjoy the burn?" a man at the rear of the group asked. "Are people really that masochistic?"

"I am." Scraps shrugged.

The exhausted expressions on the Citizen's faces neutralised as footsteps echoed on the concrete behind him. The huffing and puffing that had filled the room quietened.

Adam's voice echoed through the space, a low pitch that

matched the muffled music thumping above their heads. "You will have to get used to it if you want to be part of the uprising."

Apparently reenergised by the leader's comment, Scraps' students stood at attention.

Adam waved a hand at them dismissively. "Don't worry. I'm going to make you do more. From what I've seen, you're all making sound progress as it is. I'm just here to speak with Brian. Please collect your things and make your way out in staggered formation. We will see you again soon."

A general hum of quiet conversation sounded as people did just as they were asked. Liana and Chris, who had been near the rear of the group, winked at Scraps and pointed at Andy before they walked past. Scraps hoped they would get the information they needed from the teal-haired hacker.

"Please do not forget to wear more practical clothing next time!" Scraps called after the exiting group before he turned his back on them and faced Adam. "So, you are pleased with the progress? I wasn't aware you were watching."

"I'm always watching," Adam said in a casual tone that was more alarming than threatening.

Scraps shifted on his feet and let the comment wash over him. "Good. As you said, they are making sound progress."

Adam led the way towards the desk at the other side of the bunker. "Trey said you had something you wanted to tell me before I introduce you to the Elite Strike Squad."

"He was correct." Scraps glanced around to see that the bunker was empty except for two of the Citizens he hadn't met before. They were waiting by the exit, adding some cans of spray paint to the Free Citizen's stash from the pockets of the jackets they had folded over their arms.

"What can I do for you?"

Lowering his voice so he could not be overheard, Scraps said, "I have applied for a *learn from home* style course and some annual leave to do it. I have no work commitments for the next two weeks."

The end of the comment hung in the air. They both knew that work would not be a priority in the weeks after that whilst the city was under siege.

Adam's blue eyes flashed with approval. "Clever." He patted Scraps on the shoulder. "Clever and timely. I assume you are telling me this so that you can do more for the cause?"

"Yes." Scraps stood at attention, shoulders squared and chin high. "Helping train the Citizens and the strike team is good, but I want to do more."

"I knew you were a good choice to be my right-hand man." Adam stepped around the desk and leaned over, activating the screen on its smooth surface. "We are just about ready to go for our infiltration of the Network Hive. How would you like to join them?"

Not at all, Scraps thought, but he said, "I can do that."

"Good." Adam opened an application on his screen and typed out a message to someone named *Harry*, telling them there would be a *+1* for tomorrow's meeting. "If you get here at eight-thirty in the morning, you can inspect the new shipment of weapons we secured."

"Perfect. I will be here promptly at eight-thirty," Scraps promised with false enthusiasm.

The conversation ended when voices echoed down from the tunnel leading into the bunker.

Scraps was relieved to see that the people wandering down were dressed far more practically than the last bunch of Citizens had been. Even though what their clothes were suitable for the nightclub as far as colour or accessories went, they had favoured far more stretchy outfits with better coverage. It was a clear indication that they knew what they were in for, but they also had the sense to try to blend in. Scraps hoped it was also a sign they would be far better to work with than the previous strike group.

"Hello everyone, thank you all for coming!" Adam called out, sounding every bit like a gracious host welcoming people to a formal dinner party. He stepped out from behind the desk and strode over to the group of four Citizens.

Scraps wondered if this was the full strike team. It certainly was small. Then again, he wouldn't put it past Adam to have other people hidden around the city. He wasn't the kind of person to expose all of his plans in one go.

"Thank you for coming. I know you are already all very well versed in the kind of skills you need to fulfil your missions, but I figured it couldn't hurt to get in some more time together as a team," Adam said as he waved Scraps over to join them. "Before we begin, I believe a round of introductions is in order. Stick to first names only and general skills and experience."

Three of the Citizens shifted on their feet, eyeing a woman dressed in a black catsuit with neon green stitches and several strategic slashes in the fabric pulled tightly across her modest breasts. She gave Scraps a rather stiff smile, and some choppy chunks of honey-coloured hair fluttered out of her tight, short ponytail. "I'll start, then. I'm Elise. I've had a career in combat specialty for ten years and a self-protection gym side-business for three."

Combat specialty? Scraps tried to keep his curiosity off his face. The title *combat Specialist* was only used in two Government departments: policing and special operations. Scraps was impressed Adam had managed to find someone with skills that rivalled his own. Not that he would tell Adam that, of course.

"I'm Leo," a surprisingly young man next to Elise said. He had long, choppy hair too, but unlike Elise who stood tall and proud, Leo seemed to shrink back into himself. Even his clothes were a kind of black that swallowed the light around him. "Let's just say I have a lot of practice disappearing and helping—or convincing— others to do the same."

Convincing? The way Leo phrased that rung an alarm bell in Scraps' mind, but he made an effort to maintain a neutral expression.

A stocky but relatively short man at Leo's side gave a small, somewhat awkward wave. "Nick," he said, voice gruff and uncertain, as if he did not enjoy doing this kind of thing. He scratched an old, healed scar beside a misshapen nose, and the biceps under his tight navy t-shirt almost burst the seams of the sleeve. "Years of boxing. I'm not fast, but I pack a mean punch."

Scraps made a mental note not to be on the receiving end of that man's fist.

The tank of a man, Nick, reached over, resting his hand rather protectively on the shoulder of the final person. "And this is Tai. They are our weapons technician."

The final person's eye flicked up from their wrist device, which they had been scrolling on for the whole conversation so far. Beneath closely cut, shock-white hair, they smiled in a way that made their eyes glint wildly. "I'm good at making things go *boom*."

Ah, Scraps thought to himself, *I'm sure you and Flit will get along very well.*

Everyone watched Scraps expectantly, and then he realised it was his turn. "Oh, I am Brian. I have a good knowledge of policies and procedures."

Even though the music from the club above was pounding a heartbeat-like bass throughout the bunker, Scraps could have sworn he would be able to hear a pin drop in the silence that followed his introduction.

Then, Adam laughed.

The sound was so out of place, so sudden, that Scraps jumped. The others, however, all joined in.

Scraps cleared his throat and shifted uncomfortably on the spot.

Adam just laughed louder and thumped him on the back. "Oh, you are too funny Brian," he said, catching his breath. He looked at the others. "Brian is also a talented tactician, quite skilled with combat and weapons, and a fantastic leader."

Some of the awkwardness Scraps felt slipped away at the compliments. It wasn't that he particularly wanted Adam to say nice things about him. He was still wary of the man, but it was nice to hear that Adam valued him for the things he had been trying to provide.

"All of those skills happen to be the reason I have decided to appoint him as my second-in-command and make him the leader of this strike team."

Scraps tensed. He knew he was going to be the second-in-charge, but Adam had not said he would be the leader of the strike team, just part of it. His promotion was apparently a surprise to the others as well, particularly Elise, whose brows sharpened into an acute "V" as she swung to face Adam.

"I have been taking point on missions," she said flatly. Scraps couldn't imagine her face could appear any more unimpressed.

"Yes, and you know how much I appreciate that, Elise," Adam said, almost as if he was an exasperated parent speaking to a toddler about to throw a temper tantrum, "but relinquishing the burden of leadership means you will be able to focus more clearly on combat."

"I like the burden."

Adam walked through the middle of the group and patted her shoulder as he passed her. "I like your enthusiasm, but this is not negotiable." His voice was so low Scraps had to strain to hear it.

There was a hint of warning in Adam's words that made the hair on the back of Scraps' neck rise.

"Now, let's get started. Tonight, I want you to focus on training. We will talk about the upcoming mission tomorrow night." Adam walked over to a crate and cracked it open. He reached in, retrieving fully loaded tactical belts and throwing one to each of them.

Accepting the tactical belt, Scraps pressed his lips together. Whilst he was grateful Adam was forewarning them of *changes*, he couldn't help but wonder how many ways the infiltration of the communication server farm could go wrong. He wished he had more time to prepare, but he had a feeling Adam would never allow it, not when they were hurtling towards their proposed siege start date.

Adam did not participate in the combat training, but he always stuck around for the first part where they discussed tactics and techniques. As Scraps was finishing the warmup, he realised he had never seen Adam join any of the physical sessions. From the way his clothes sat on him, it looked as though he partook physically active lifestyle, but could he hold his own in a fight? Would he be a threat? It was something Scraps filed away in the back of his mind for... Well, he wasn't sure when for, and he hoped he would not need to find out.

After stretching their bodies, the group split into a pair and a trio. They worked through some drills that Elise called out, and Scraps finally felt as though he was amongst peers. They didn't have powers, of course, but compared to everyone else he had worked with in the Free Citizens, he could see this group having a chance at success for an infiltration.

Despite a full day of work and two hours of training the general Free Citizen folks, Scraps relished the chance to really push himself to the limits. Whilst Tai wasn't the strongest and Leo was only good for stealth strikes, Nick could take a lot of hits and dish out some bruisers. And Elise? Scraps wanted to pit her against Hawkeye. He had a feeling the remote viewer was the only person he knew who would stand a chance against the clearly skilled operative.

Eventually, the training session drew to a close. Adam stated that people needed to make a move before Nightmix emptied out. He also told Scraps not to forget to be there bright and early the next day or, rather, because the clock had tipped past midnight, that day. Scraps agreed and said his farewells to the others. He took the opportunity while they were discussing something about a previous mission to slip out of the bunker and make his way back to the apartment.

On the trip home, Scraps couldn't help but feel grateful that the agents had approved his plan to take leave. He was starting to feel the impact of being out of the house for close to sixteen hours every day and was looking forward to a good hot shower and crawling into his bed to get some much-needed rest.

36

FLIT

FLIT YAWNED LOUDLY as she slumped back against the couch in the apartment. It wasn't really *their* apartment anymore, but she could not get used to calling it *Scraps'* apartment. It felt too much like a tasteless reinforcement of just how separate their lives had become. She had to let out a bitter laugh as she realised this would have been their reality anyway if she had come to the Hub alone in the first place, just with the roles reversed.

Letting her head loll the side, Flit took in the time that was illuminated in the top corner of the large living room window. She wondered if she should be worried. Scraps was probably visiting Nightmix, but it was close to two o'clock in the morning, and he still hadn't returned.

Speaking of returning, Flit was supremely conscious of the fact she had to make her way back to the Underground in a mere five hours. She and Hawkeye had agreed that they would need to keep to her normal wake time to avoid suspicion if he walked out of her room alone.

It had probably been foolish to hope for a full night with Scraps, for an opportunity to catch up with him and learn how he had been over the past months. They hadn't had the chance to do so when they had seen each other, but she was pleased they had time to reconnect physically at least. Even that heated, rushed encounter was a balm to her soul.

With a groan, Flit looked at the clock again. Her impatience reared its head as she noted only a couple of minutes had passed. Her foot jiggled of its own accord, and it took a fair amount of concentration for her to stop herself from teleporting to a standing position and pacing the floor. She had already worn tracks on the smooth surface earlier that evening. She didn't need to do it again.

Just as Flit was about to give up, the door opened. She ducked for cover behind the couch and watched as Scraps stepped in, covering his mouth and stifling a yawn. He was wearing casual black pants and a tight t-shirt that clung to his sculped chest and arms like a second skin. Flit gulped, and the sound made Scraps tense. His knees bent, and he raised his hands.

Slowly, Flit sat up, keeping her hands where he could see then. "It's just me," she said quietly. She hadn't wanted to risk turning the apartment lights on just in case anyone was watching. As she rose, she knew it would be hard for him to see her features. She was silhouetted by the bright city lights through the window at her back.

Immediately, Scraps' shoulders sagged with relief, and he pressed his hand against the control panel. Flit waited until the door had closed completely to teleport over to him. She looked up into his eyes, and he blinked.

"You are really here?" he asked, voice husky with an exhaustion unlike any she had heard in him before.

Flit reached up and cupped his cheek. His stubble felt so good against her palm. He let out a soft groan and leaned into her touch. She pulled him closer and brushed her lips over his.

"What do you think?" she asked.

Scraps chuckled quietly. "I think you are here. If you aren't and this is a dream, I do not think I want to wake up."

Resting her forehead against his, Flit let out a soft laugh of her own. "Since when did you become such a sweet talker, huh?"

"I am just telling the truth." He leaned in and stole a kiss.

Every part of Flit flared to life with need. She deepened the kiss, and he snaked his arms around her waist, pulling her body against his. Just as she was about to beg him to take her to bed right away, but warning bells rang in her head.

"We can't—" she panted, pulling away from him. Her hands balled into fists, catching the fabric of his shirt in her grasp.

The sense of relief that had been on Scraps' face twisted into concern as his eyebrows furrowed. "What is it? Is everything okay?"

"Yes." Flit paused then shook her head. "No. Not really. We need to catch up. We didn't get a chance to exchange information properly last time, and we really need to get on the same page. I'd much rather make love to you, but we must talk."

Scraps stepped back, letting his hands fall to his side. He looked between her eyes, then her lips, and then nodded. "That makes sense," he said, but he licked his lips as his attention drifted down her body, sliding over the fitted tank and tights she was wearing. "But I need to have a shower. It has been a long day. Would you like to join me?"

Need made Flit's stomach tighten and breath quicken. She forced a friendly smile onto her face and took his hand. "Of course." She led him through the living room, down the hall, through the bedroom, and into the en suite. "Is this apartment still secure?"

"I believe so." Scraps slid his hands around her waist and his thumbs under the hem of her tank, and she whimpered at the feel of his skin against hers. "I saw the Government Agents recently, and they seem to be getting frustrated at the lack of information I can give them. I convinced them to let me take time off to spend with the Free Citizens, but I do not know how much longer I will be able to get away with not giving them what they want."

The plain, matter-of-fact way he spoke about something so dangerous made Flit swallow. "How long have you got?"

"I told them a couple of weeks. If the Free Citizens' plans go the way Adam said they would, I should not have to return to work at all."

It was not something that should make Flit feel relieved, yet she let out a soft breath all the same. Knowing what would happen when the Free Citizens attacked was not something to celebrate, but it was so very necessary.

"What is Adam planning?" Flit asked, trying to ignore the flutter of her heart as he slid her tank top up. She helped get her arms out as he pulled it over her head and cast it aside.

"A siege, as I mentioned. He's just waiting to get the final command stations armed and ready to go. He's asked me to lead a strike team to attack a communication network hub. I do not have much choice, but the team is good. It should be straight forward."

They both knew that no mission was ever straight forward, especially when Adam was involved.

Flit paused, covering his hand as it settled over her bra strap. She could tell he wanted to slide it down, but she caught his gaze. "You need to stay safe, Scraps."

Scraps' expression faltered for the briefest of moments, and he nodded. "I will to the best of my ability."

"Good." There was little more he could promise than that, so Flit let go of his hand. She reached behind herself to unhook her bra, tugged it off, and dropped it onto her tank top. "Is there anything I—the Underground—can do to help?

Just as she asked her question, Scraps leaned down. His lips found her neck as his hands cupped her breasts. She wanted nothing more than to completely surrender to his touch, but... she couldn't. The moment she let go, she had no plans of thinking about anything other than the joining of their bodies.

"One of the Registereds that has been escorting me back and forth between the Agent meetings want to join the cause. We will need to help her find a way out when the time comes," Scraps murmured against her skin.

Head spinning, Flit nodded. Registereds. Escape plan.

Got it.

"I'll get Layla to speak to her Citizen Derivates. I bet they have done that kind of thing before," she said, reaching up to rake her hand through his hair to hold him to her. It had grown in the time they had been apart, and it felt softer as it slipped between her fingers.

"Is there anything I need to know?" Scraps' lips travelled lower down Flit's neck and traversed the ridges and valleys of her collarbones.

I need to feel you inside me, was all Flit could think, but she shook her head and that idea away. *Not yet.* Still, that didn't stop her from pulling at his T-shirt and slowly work it up and off.

"I'm worried that the leaders in the Underground are isolating us on purpose," Flit said, her thoughts coming slowly with the way he was distracting her. Thankfully, she gained more clarity the longer she spoke. "We are trying to figure out what is going on, but we have to be careful. I'm not sure how safe we'll be if they know we're getting curious."

Scraps' lips left her collarbone and travelled lower, towards the peak of her breast. Her hand tightened in his hair.

"Maybe you also need to stay safe, then," he murmured. There was so much tenderness, so much concern in his voice that her heart melted.

"We're implementing exercise classes to cover for combat training," she informed him, even though combat was the last thing from her mind. "Whenever we figure out what is going on, we'll be ready."

"Good." Scraps slid his hands down her body. He hooked his thumbs under the waistband of her tights and panties and pushed them lower. "Is there anything else?"

In a fleeting moment of lucidity, Flit said, "Yes!"

She reached into the pocket in her tights that were now down around her thighs and drew out the emergency beacon Hawkeye had given her. Scraps straightened, the warmth radiating of him withdrawing and leaving Flit wishing she hadn't interrupted. Still, she held the charm out to him. He accepted it in his open hand.

"Thank you," Scraps said. He went to tuck it into the pockets of his trousers, but Flit shook her head.

"Not there." Flit shook out the long chain it was on, a necklace long enough that he would be able to hide it beneath his shirts. She draped the chain around his neck and then pressed her hand against the tiny glass charm, holding it against his chest as his heart thundered beneath her touch. "Promise you won't take it off," she whispered.

Scraps leaned in and kissed her with so much passion that it stole the breath from her. "I promise, Flit," he whispered against her lips. "I love you."

And just like that, any thought of exchanging information fled from Flit's mind. She wrapped her arms around him as he tugged her tights off then lifted her against him. She wrapped her legs around his hips as he stepped into the shower and got the warm water running. She let the feel of his body moving against and inside of hers wash away the fears of the past months and replenish the hope she needed to feel for the future.

Eventually, they had to move from the shower to the bedroom. They spent the wee hours of the morning with each other, relearning the lines of their bodies and all the ways they could join. When they finally fell asleep, Flit was filled with a warm, relieved sense of *rightness*. For just a few hours, she was where she really belonged.

She was home.

"ARE YOU GOING?"

The sheets rustled as Scraps sat up, rubbing his eyes. His voice was thick with sleep, and Flit winced. She hadn't wanted to wake him. After they finished making love, he had explained how busy he had been. The last thing she intended was to steal more sleep from him, not when it was already in such arrears.

"I have to get back before breakfast," Flit whispered back, tugging her tights up over her hips and turning to face the bed. She could just make out his silhouette in the dim room.

A heavy sigh came from Scraps, and it made Flit's limbs suddenly heavy. She teleported over to the bed and sank down onto the edge of it.

He reached out, taking her hand. "I will see you again soon, though?" he asked. "I will need to update you. The Free Citizens are going to act soon. We need to coordinate."

Flit nodded. "I'll come up as often as I can," she promised, even though they both had to know those opportunities would be few and far between. She leaned closer, kissing him, and rested her hand on his bare chest, pressing the small tracking charm between their skin. "And if there is an emergency..."

"I will use the beacon if I can." Scraps' voice was solemn. She knew that he would only do so if it wouldn't put others at risk, but there was no point arguing about it.

Flit closed her eyes against the emotions brewing behind them. The pain of saying goodbye for now was the other reason she had hoped to slip out while Scraps was asleep. They had left their time on such a sweet note, falling asleep in each others' arms. She hadn't wanted to ruin that with the sorrow of parting.

"I'll see you soon. I love you." Flit pulled back out of the kiss and slipped off the bed. She retrieved her tank top and pulled it on.

Scraps laid back down in the bed, resting his head on one hand as he watched her in a way that made her heart skip a beat. "See you soon, Flit. I love you too."

Then, Flit translocated from the room before emotions overwhelmed her.

37

―――――

SCRAPS

AT EIGHT-THIRTY THE NEXT MORNING, Scraps arrived outside of Nightmix. The neon sign that usually indicated that the club was operating was off, the glass tubes nothing but empty, slightly coloured husks of what they usually were. Scraps felt a bit like the sign, still bleary and not quite functioning after a tiring night that he wished had never ended.

It was hard to get Flit—and the way it felt to be with her—off his mind as he looked around the club entrance to find out how to get in. Every time he had come before, the doors had been open with bouncers and a line of patrons out the front. Now, they were shut, and he was stuck trying to figure out if he had forgotten any instructions that Adam had given him about how to enter. He looked around to see if there was a communication panel anywhere, and just as he was about to give up, the door opened.

Petra stood in the doorway, her eyes bright and smile light despite the early hours. Scraps pushed his fatigue aside and returned her smile with a somewhat forced one of his own.

"Ah, Brian. We were expecting you. Come in, come in." She stepped back into the club, and Scraps followed.

Scraps did a double-take as he entered Nightmix. He was so used to the foggy, alcohol-scented interior and the psychedelic, flashing strobes that the well-lit, black painted room around him seemed rather dull.

"Everything okay?" Petra asked as she led her way across the scuff-marked floor towards the back of the space and the office she shared with Trey.

"Oh, sorry." Scraps shook his head. "Just tired. A lot of training and all."

Petra nodded knowingly. "Well, hopefully you will be able to catch some rest soon. We've all seen how hard you're working. It can't be easy. Thank you."

The genuine gratefulness in Petra's tone plucked at Scraps' pride in just the right way to refocus him.

He shrugged, trying to appear nonchalant. "I am doing what I can, just like everyone else."

When the pair entered the office, Trey looked up from the series of spreadsheet files displayed on the surface of his desk. He smiled at Scraps in greeting and gave him a somewhat playful salute. "Nice to see you, Brian. I believe Adam's waiting for you downstairs." He gestured to the panel at the back of the office, which was already slightly ajar.

Downstairs, Adam and a few other Free Citizens Scraps had seen but never really talked to were standing around a stack of crates that stood around two metres wide and came up to Scraps' shoulder height.

Adam looked up upon hearing him enter and gestured for him to join them, with a wide grin on his face. "Perfect timing, Brian. Harry and the others just delivered this shipment. I have a feeling you will be impressed."

The man, who Scraps assumed was Harry, preened. "I even managed to smuggle out a few surprises."

Harry stepped back and entered a code onto the digital lock screen. It released with an electronic hiss, and Scraps and the others stepped back as Harry opened the lid. The inside of the crates were lined with a protective foam and filled with all sorts of weapons, weapons that even Scraps didn't have access to when he was working for the Government. He listened with a mix of awe and wariness as Harry pulled out item after item, waxing on about the benefits of each and just how lucky they were to have them.

Scraps was stunned to silence until he saw a familiar firearm that made him blurt, "How did you get that?"

Everyone had been so enthralled by the macabre show-and-tell that they were all wide-eyed as they looked at him.

Harry tilted his head to the side as he held out the matte black pistol with a large, clear canister at the back surrounding a glowing purple power core. Being so close to it made Scraps queasy, but he worked to keep any signs of that off his face as Harry asked, "You know what this is?"

At that moment, Scraps wished kicking himself wouldn't have made him seem guiltier. He knew it was too late to pretend he hadn't said anything. "Uh, yes," he confessed. "I was assigned to a review of the factory that manufactured part of them. I thought they were still proprietary tech."

"Oh, they are," Harry said in perhaps the smuggest tone Scraps had ever heard. "These were taken right from under the nose of the Government."

A frown tugged at Scraps' lips, and his eyebrows furrowed. The security at the advanced weaponry facilities was second only to that of the upper levels of Centre One. "How did you get them out?"

"I worked for those bastards for too long. I quit, and this morning was the morning I handed in my security passes. Figured I'd use them before I lost the chance. Even if they do figure out it's all missing—and that it was me—I'm off the grid now."

"And we are so grateful for your resourcefulness." Adam patted the other man on the back and looked around the group gathered. "More and more of us are making our final plays and getting off the grid. It's a sign that the uprising is coming. With any luck, the next time we all walk into a Government office, we will be claiming it as our own."

There was a cheer of agreement that Scraps joined in on, perhaps a little too late. No one else seemed to notice.

"Now we have these, we can see about setting our boundaries properly. We have one more mission to handle before we can move forward. Brian here is the leader of our strike team." Adam turned to Scraps and waved an open hand over the crate of weapons.

"What do you think? Will this be enough to help you with your infiltration?"

Scraps had absolutely no intention to attempt that incursion by going in with all guns blazing, particularly not with that cursed purple aberration. Still, he nodded. "That should be sufficient."

There was something particularly sinister about the inhibiting gun. All other weapons would harm Citizens and Derivates equally. It was not a fact to celebrate, but it was a world away from the inhibitor that would only ever harm Derivates. It was a way to rob them of their powers and bring them to their knees, even though their powers were the reason the Government was persecuting them. It made Scraps feel less human than ever before.

"Are all of these weapons in general production?" Scraps had to know what they would be facing when it came time to fight.

"Yep." Harry patted the box as affectionately as one might a child on the back. "Production at the factories is in overdrive. I think they know what's coming. I have some more crates out the back, so we won't be completely outgunned. Not with these babies." He picked up the inhibitor pistol and turned it this way and that so everyone could ogle it. "Don't even have to worry about friendly fire with this one. The discharge only impacts the Appliances." He dropped it back into the crate that made Scraps wince at such casual, careless handling... and at being called an Appliance. "But don't worry, Brian. We have enough for your team and then some."

"Good." Scraps stepped back from the crate and acted as though he was pleased with what he saw. "Now, Adam, I believe we have a mission to plan?"

When Scraps turned and walked away, Adam followed along with him. He didn't initiate a conversation with the leader until they reached the planning desk. Adam seemed happy to perch there and survey his kingdom every night Scraps had attended the headquarters.

"I have plenty of intel gathered for you," Adam informed him as he sat down and Scraps pulled over a chair. "All you need to decide is how best to approach it. Remember, we cannot afford to alert the Government to our plan. Whilst I would happily suggest going in guns blazing, we need to save that for the final act."

I guess that's why you need me. Adam had a penchant for making missions far more complicated and deadly than they needed to be, and Scraps sensed that his own restraint was the true reason Adam had asked for his assistance.

Adam and Scraps sat at the table and looked through the information together. Scraps had to admit that the team had done an excellent job with the reconnaissance. He had everything from security patrol schedules to the food the employees ate in the cafeteria and where it was manufactured. He got a sense that the wide range of information from Adam was almost a test. Would he use the catering information to drug workers? Was the information about the fire-safety sprinklers included so he could use that as a distraction?

There was a lot of to work with. Luckily, Scraps was good at sifting through information.

BY THE TIME Scraps left the club late that afternoon, he and Adam had locked in a plan for his infiltration of the communication server farm. It was built around stealth more than anything else, and even though it wouldn't be easy, Scraps had faith it would work. The only time they would need to use force, at least in theory, would be at the start. Everything after that would go easily provided everyone behaved.

The strike team itself was Scraps' main concern. As much as he understood the importance of having a team for such endeavours, he also knew that an ununited crew could spell disaster. Even the Blue Team, one of the most effective teams he had ever been a part of, had its quirks.

Thinking of the Blue Team made Scraps feel a kind of longing that was new to him over the past few months. The sign of his emotional attachment to the group was something that filled him with a sense of purpose. Even if he wasn't with them, he intended to work with them again. They had given him his first taste of kindness, forgiveness, and friendship. As volatile and ragtag as they could be individually, there was no unit he would put his trust in as much as he would the Blue Team.

Arriving home, Scraps peeled the clothes he was wearing off and went straight for a shower. He wasn't sweaty or tired, but he wanted a chance to wash off and collect himself before returning to Nightmix later for more training. When he reached the crisply tiled room, he got flashes of his interlude with Flit and couldn't help but wonder if he had imagined it all. He had been very tired the previous night, but as he caught sight of the chain she had draped around his neck in the mirror he saw proof it was real. In some ways, he hoped he didn't have to use it. However, using it would mean he might see her again, and a guilty part of him was sorely tempted.

A long, cool shower was enough to bring Scraps back to reality and convince him that patience was the best approach. He needed to help get the Free Citizens ready for their incursion. Flit and the Underground would need their help to rise against the Government. He only hoped he would be able to find a way to forge an alliance between them. The opinion of Adam and words of people like Harry were concerning, but it was nothing he hadn't confronted before.

THE NEXT THREE days passed in a blur of increasing Citizen training sessions and strike team meet-ups. Nightmix was open during the daylight hours under the guise of a "renovation". Really, it was just a good excuse for Adam to bring in an ever-changing array of new people for Scraps to instruct.

It was alarming just how untrained they all were, but the more people Scraps met, the more real it all felt. He tried his best to impart as much wisdom as possible on the Citizens, but the truth was there would be little they could do to ward themselves against the Government, especially since their opposition would include Registereds. Scraps *should* have trained the Citizens to more effectively deal with Derivate abilities, but if he did, it would have not only given away his intricate expertise on the matter but been directly training people to harm his own. He might have been working as a double agent and dancing between the Government and the Free Citizens, but there was no question that his loyalty would always be Flit and the Underground.

Scraps arrived home late from another round of training. Every time he walked into the empty apartment, he felt a pang of disappointment that it would be another night he would go without seeing Flit. Before their first reunion, he had become used to not having her around, not that he had enjoyed it, but he had made a certain level of peace with their distance. It seemed that getting a taste of having her back in his life was enough to remind him of how difficult he found things without her. She was a part of him that he never knew he would miss.

The door to the apartment slid shut, and Scraps went into the kitchen to warm something up for a late dinner. He found the extra training required extra fuel, and even though he did not enjoy eating so late at night, it was the best option he had as he was so busy during his waking moments.

Before Scraps could do more than put the food in the microwave, the doorbell rang. The sound made him jump, and there was a flicker of hope that it would be Flit. However, he immediately dismissed that notion as foolish, given the fact she would just appear within the apartment itself.

Scraps sighed as he walked towards the door. It was either Adam or Agents Greene and Hector. His guess was on the latter as he had said goodbye to Adam less than an hour ago.

Luckily, Scraps had enough time to formulate a viable lie to feed the Agents.

Rehearsing the plan in his head, Scraps opened the door and then froze as he saw the Agents with both CC-9832 and TB-219 at their shoulders this time. He looked past them at the empty corridor beyond and quickly stepped back to let them all in.

The group of four entered his apartment without hesitation. Scraps stood in the main entryway, not wanting to invite them to sit down. He was immediately concerned that they might plant surveillance equipment in his apartment.

As he went to greet them, TB-219 gave him a subtle nod.

"*Should I do a sweep for bugs after they leave?*" he thought to her. She gave him another nod as she stood behind the agents, and he said out loud, "Good evening, Agent Greene, Agent Hector. I am glad you came by. I have some intel for you."

Greene gave him a smile that almost looked genuine.

Hector's face remained unimpressed as he ran a hand over his five o'clock shadow. "I would hope so," the perpetually disgruntled man replied. "You've had a fair bit of time off and evading our surveillance."

"Evading your surveillance?" Scraps frowned.

Hector rolled his eyes.

Greene nodded. "Where have you been spending your time?"

"With Adam, as I said I would be," Scraps replied, genuinely confused. Why would they bother asking something they had to know?

"And where have you been doing that? Security around North Four-East Three is being scrambled. Where do you go when you enter that building?" Hector's voice had a hard edge, similar to ones Scraps had heard several times in his careers.

It was a warning, and Scraps received it loud and clear.

However, he could not afford to give away the truth. Instead, he had to think quickly and hope the telepath in his apartment was truly on his side.

"There is a restaurant on the second floor," Scraps said. He hadn't initially intended to give the restaurant's name as the Free Citizen's base, but he was planning to use it in the rest of his cover, so he figured it was the best option. "It's called Char. They use the noise and foot traffic from the club below to hide their operations. I did not know security there was scrambled. That is concerning."

Hector immediately turned to look at TB-219 over his shoulder. The Registered nodded without hesitation, and the tense set of Hector's frame softened ever so slightly.

Clearing her throat, Greene asked, "What information do you have for us?"

It was obvious she was trying to change topics, and Scraps was grateful for it.

"The catering uniforms they manufactured... they intend to use them to infiltrate some Government event coming up. Apparently, another restaurant has the contract for the catering, and Adam plans to take them down before they can fulfil it and replace them with the staff at Char." The words tumbled from Scraps far too easily. He did not like how accustomed he had become to lying, but he supposed it was an important skill for him to maintain.

"And then what?" Greene leaned in closer, hanging on the anticipation of an answer.

"I assume they will use that to weaken the leaders," Scraps said. "Adam stopped short of telling me the full plan, but it is concerning to think they are attempting to harm people in such a manner. It is underhanded and petty."

Hector, for once, seemed to agree with Scraps. "Petty is one word for it." He crossed his arm over his barrel chest. "Do you know when this is supposed to be happening?"

"In a week and a half," Scraps said, giving a time beyond what Adam's plan actually was. "I assume they want to use the chaos any poisoning will cause to make some sort of move."

"Can you find out what events they intend to target?" Greene asked, sharing a concerned glance with Hector.

Scraps knew from experience that the Government workers loved any excuse for a good meal. He had to act as a security officer at many of them. Nothing too high profile, but there were more elite events that his colleagues had attended in their training.

"I will do my best," Scraps said. That, however, wasn't entirely a lie. He could try his hardest, and no matter what happened, if the information wasn't there to find it would just be too bad.

TB-219's lips quirked in an almost-smile before her face flickered back to neutral.

"I have reached out to some contacts. They will work with their people to find a way to get you out. Help is coming. Please, just hold on," Scraps thought to the woman.

She blinked slowly enough that Scraps could tell it was not just an instinctive action.

"Well, I guess that will have to do. Is there anything else?" Greene asked.

Scraps shook his head.

The two agents shared a meaningful look before saying their farewells. They turned and walked out of his apartment, taking the Registereds with him.

As the door shut behind them, Scraps looked over at his kitchen bench and realised he hadn't started the microwave. He let out a heavy, annoyed sigh. His appetite was gone, so instead of eating, he walked over and put the food away for another day. Then, he took his time to observe the areas where the agents had been standing and walking. Sure enough, right by his front door, there was the tiniest speck of a device, an off-white matte spot on an otherwise flawless door frame. He frowned and considered leaving it, but if it picked up on Flit teleporting into the apartment, it could ruin everything. Scraps reached out, pinching the device and plucking it off the wall. With an extra bit of telekinetic oomph, he crushed it between his fingertips.

It wasn't as if the agents would admit leaving it behind because then they would give away that the security for his apartment was just as scrambled as that around Nightmix seemed to be. It was a weakness they were reluctant to acknowledge.

A weakness he was more than happy to continue exploiting.

38

———

FLIT

THE NEXT MORNING, Flit groaned as she stretched her aching limbs. The people she, Hawkeye, and Swipe had been training filtered out of the room. It had been a busy few days in the Underground with the new exercise regime taking place, not only because there was so much more movement, but so many injuries came out of it. At nights, she would check in with her mother only to hear that more people had aches or sprains from the sudden increase in activity. However, there were other more concerning injuries and concerns in the Medbay—poor mental health due to the lockdown, relationship issues due to confinement, and an increase in ability burnout due to difficulties regulating emotions. It was an ugly combination, but the Blue Team kept working, and Flit only hoped it would help.

"Not enjoying the rigorous exercise schedule, huh?" Swipe asked as she leaned over, reaching both of her toes with ease and showing off her gloriously toned body.

"Not particularly. There's nothing fun about torture."

Hawkeye sighed. "It's hardly torture." He set down the datapad he was holding on a nearby bench. "That group seems to be going well. I think we will start adding in more advanced manoeuvres soon. Flit, are you okay to handle the kids in the next session on your own? I have some things to handle in Control."

"Sure." Flit saluted lazily.

Whilst she enjoyed spending time with the kids, it wasn't like they were actually training beyond basic self-defence. There was no intention to allow the children anywhere near the fighting. Her sessions with them were more to maintain the pretence of a fully-fledged exercise program and to keep them active and distracted.

Despite how incessantly curious the kids were, Flit had become fond of her time with them over the past few days. It was a good circuit breaker between what was proving to be a series of rather intense workouts and the disheartening updates at night. The frequency and duration of the sessions were well beyond what Flit would ever willingly commit to, but they had quickly moved from basic exercises and into boxing techniques. As much as she hated group exercise, she had to admit that they were making progress. It was good to finally hope that they might be prepared for the cluster-fuck that would be their near future.

Flit heard the children before she saw them. Their excited chatter was just enough warning for her to turn around and steel herself for the barrage of enthusiastic hugs that came when they surged into the room. Hawkeye and Swipe laughed on their way out.

The children's minder, Scry, sighed and shook his head. "I'm sorry. I've asked them not to be so... aggressive with their affection."

"But we don't listen!" Seeker cooed as he hugged Flit tight enough to cut off her oxygen supply.

"It's cool," Flit choked. "I don't mind the enthusiasm."

She smiled down at the boy who had shown so much acceptance of Scraps when he'd joined the Underground. Seeker hadn't asked about what happened to Scraps, although Flit could sense the question trying to burst free of him every time he saw her.

Kindling, Seeker's steady friend, grinned back at their teacher. "You always say we're terrible at listening. We just like making you right!"

"Okay!" Flit clapped her hands together loudly. "Let's get this training started before Scry loses it. Everyone, get into a circle. We'll start with warm-ups."

Flit was under no illusion that there was anything special about her that made the children listen. She was a novelty to them, nothing more. She had no doubt that if she continued to teach them, they would become just as sassy with her. Which, if she was honest, she would probably enjoy too much. There was a good reason she didn't trust herself to take responsibility for the younger generation. She would definitely be a bad influence on them.

The children allowed Flit to lead them through a simple round of stretches as a warm-up before they moved into a big circle and threw a weighted ball to each other. As usual, the macrokinetics in the group added a bit of extra oomph into their throws, but Flit let it go.

Just as the game was finishing up, Kindling threw the ball to another child. The little girl was a precog and had been ready to catch the ball every time no matter how many feints the other children employed in hopes of tricking her. This time, she let out a loud squeak, covered her ears, and dodged the ball, letting it thump to the ground.

Just as Flit was about to ask what was wrong, there was a loud banging on the door.

"No!" the little girl cried out, shaking her head. "No, no, no! Tell him go away, please! Please—"

Flit frowned, not sure what was happening.

Scry leaned closer. "I can't see past the door." His voice was quiet as he spoke.

Flit wished there was some sort of opening in the room he could bounce his remote viewing off so they could figure out who was outside.

The pounding on the door resumed, along with some shouting.

"You stay here with the kids, Scry. I'll see who it is," Flit said warily. Her hands naturally reached for where her dagger would be, but she wasn't wearing her belt. Instead, she curled her hands into fists.

After one teleport over to the door, she hit the control on the window to see outside of the room. As she did, she noted a man in the corridor.

When he realised the window was transparent, he slammed his body against it and pounded it with his fists. "Let me see my daughter!"

"Daddy, no!"

The distress in the girl's voice made Flit return the window to an opaque state. "Scry, keep the kids in that corner with you."

With the memory of what the corridor outside looked like emblazoned into her mind, Flit teleported out. The man was back to banging on the door. The smell of alcohol was so strong on him that it made Flit nauseous.

"Buddy, you're scaring the kids," Flit said, making sure she was beyond arm's reach.

Flit had no idea who the guy was. Sure, she had seen him around the place over the years, but she never really paid him much attention. She had a feeling he was either in maintenance or catering or something, but she just couldn't be certain. Without knowing him, she had no real way to figure out what his power was. She had to be careful.

"Let me see her!" The man's demand was hoarse, which Flit guessed was due to way too much yelling. "They won't let me see her. I need to see my daughter!"

Glancing back at the training room, Flit had a feeling that letting him see his daughter would be a terrible idea. She didn't know the family, but she had no intention of letting him anywhere near the little girl, who was already terrified.

"I don't know what's going on, but right now, your daughter is very scared. Why don't we find somewhere quiet to chat, where you can calm down, and—"

"I don't need to calm down!" the man roared, interrupting Flit's attempt at negotiation. "I need to see my baby!"

The man let out a pained groan and reached up, grasping the hair at either side of his head and twitching as if there was some sort of itch he couldn't quite scratch.

Given the lack of command in his voice, Flit figured he was not a telecoercionist. She took note of their surroundings, and there was nothing shifting or bowing the way it would if a macrokinetic was losing control. He could have been a precog like his daughter, but surely if he was, he would see that this path was useless.

Or... was it?

"Okay. Okay," Flit said, keeping her palms up and letting her posture soften, hoping the de-escalation in her own body language might earn a similar one from him. "I can tell you miss her. I don't blame you. She's a sweet kid. Why don't we head into the room next door? I'll go in and calm her down then bring her to you."

Flit had no intention of doing so. However, she needed to get this guy somewhere safe, somewhere she could contain him.

He didn't seem to react to her thoughts or plan, so Flit gathered he wasn't a telepath either.

"No! They say that all the time, and they are always lying. I won't leave until I see her." He turned around and launched himself at the door again.

"Flit? What the hell is going on?" Swipe asked, leaning of the training room next door.

Never before had Flit felt so relieved to see the snappy blonde. "Code zero-one-zero," Flit blurted.

Swipe tensed but not before the man stopped banging at the door. His limbs shook with barely restrained tension as he turned on Flit. Something in his previously drunken gaze sharpened with a clarity that made Flit's blood run cold.

"Go!" Flit yelled at Swipe before she teleported out of the way as the man charged towards her.

There was a loud crash and a yelped curse as the man hit the wall and then reared around to face Flit without pausing. "Flit!" The way he spat her name made it sound like an accusation. "You're the mule fucker."

Flit winced at the term as rage surged within her. She bent her knees and sank into a ready stance as she prepared to dodge him again.

A klaxon sounded down the corridor, and the bright, clinical white lighting dimmed, casting the tunnel in shadows. Red lights spun near the wall speakers, bathing Flit intermittently in crimson and turning the atmosphere into something more alarming.

The man let out a yowl of pain at the sonorous alarms and brought his beefy hands up to cover his ears. "You're the reason my wife is dead!" he yelled through the noise. Spittle sprayed all around the corridor as the man ranted and raved. "If you hadn't brought that bastard down here, he wouldn't have killed her!"

Flit didn't have time to contemplate what he was saying as he launched at her again.

The man might have been drunk and rambling, but he had a stocky build and a hell of a lot of force behind his charges. Luckily, Flit was faster than most people at the best of times. She wasn't worried about having to get out of his way. She was just marvelling at how much damage he would do if he landed a shoulder in her chest the way he was trying to.

"Stop. This isn't the way to get your daughter back." Flit reappeared behind him. She wished she knew his name, wished she had some way to calm him down, but all she could do was try to keep him occupied whilst she waited for reinforcements to arrive and those damn alarms to stop. "Please, calm down, and I will see what I can do to help."

This time, the man's face had gotten so red Flit was concerned about his health. He reached his hands out, and alarm bells rung *inside* Flit's head this time.

"It's too late!" His fists clenched, and the complete and indisputable fact he was a microkinetic became obvious as Flit's body felt like it was being squeezed from the inside out.

In an instant, Flit teleported farther down the corridor. The pain faded instantly, but it was enough of a shock to her system that her head spun. "Attacking me isn't going to fix things!"

The man's entire body shook as though it was going into shock, and Flit teleported behind him before he could launch another attack. However, he was prepared. Whatever adrenaline his body was pumping through had cleared away some of the drunken fog, and he had turned as she teleported, ready with another microkinetic attack.

Flit dodged it with half a dozen short hops that made him scream with frustration. Worry flared in her as she saw crooked hairline fractures of burst blood vessels creeping across his scleras.

"We really need to calm down now, please," Flit called out across the distance between them. "Please, I know you want to see your daughter. You're going to burn yourself—"

A group of people turned the corner and raced towards them. A cry of horror spilled from her as they raised a gun and fired at the man. The sudden bang made him jump. For a heartbeat, time slowed to a crawl. A look of abject realisation dawned in his blood-shot eyes as more blood vessels burst beneath his skin. The red lines snaked all over his exposed arms and neck, just as purple light blazed behind him.

Flit would know that horrid flare of light anywhere.

However, the rays didn't hit the man. Instead, his entire body tore apart as if someone had planted explosives inside his chest.

Time skidded back into motion, and Flit barely covered her eyes with her arms before hot, wet, thick gore splattered all over her.

A ringing that was more obnoxious and intense than the lock-down klaxons whistled through her as she fell to her knees. Her arms dropped to her side as she gaped at the space where the man used to be. Now, just a patch of blood and flesh in the middle of a corridor. In the distance, the person who had raised the gun lowered it, their own face taut with dismay.

They intended to shoot the man, to contain his powers... Instead, his own powers had killed him.

The stress and alcohol, combined with the unexpected noise, had pushed him over an edge he would never be able to climb back over.

Flit's throat became thick with the urge to vomit, and her mouth watered. She swallowed it back as she held up her hands, worried the reinforcements might think she was part of whatever the man was doing.

"Flit?"

The sound of her mother's voice made Flit blink and move closer at the group.

"Oh my goodness, Flit!"

Tinker pushed the gun-wielder aside. Her footsteps sounded sticky as she ran right across the gore. She fell to her knees in front of Flit and cupped her cheeks. "Are you okay? Talk to me, Flit. Are you hurt?"

Flit shook her head, the rapid-fire questions shaking her out of her stupor. She looked down at herself and swallowed back another surge of nausea. "I'm fine," she whispered.

That seemed to be enough to satisfy Tinker. She looked over her shoulder. "Get a clean-up crew up here ASAP."

Two of the team members walked back to a comms panel outside of a training room and tapped away on it. The sirens stopped, and the lights flared back to full power. Flit jerked back, blinking at the sudden brightness. When her gaze cleared, the red splattering the walls seemed more... vibrant.

"What happened?"

Flit looked up, startled that Acumen seemed to have appeared right in front of her. Thankfully, that meant she didn't need to speak. She let her shoulders sag and forced herself to visualise the events, from the little girl screaming right up until the very moment he asked what had happened.

Acumen sighed. "I need to report to Control immediately." He rubbed the back of his neck as he looked at Tinker. "Can you get Flit home? Give her a debrief. You know the situation with Bolt better than I do."

Sliding her hands under Flit's arm, Tinker helped her daughter up. Once Flit was able to stand on her own two feet, her mother wrapped an arm around her shoulders.

"Clean-up crew ETA five minutes," someone reported in the background.

Flit didn't bother looking over to see who it was. It didn't matter.

"Good. Keep this corridor locked down until it's clear. Then get them to Assembly Point A in the Residence. I have a feeling Harmony and Divvy will want to address this immediately," Acumen said before he gave Flit a final look and turned to jog down the corridor.

It occurred to Flit too late that she could have offered Acumen a lift to Control to get there faster. However, she saw the way that the people who had come as back-up looked at her and stepped back as she walked past. She could feel the previously hot blood and entrails slowly cooling on her arms and on the fabric clinging to her torso. She would have to get close to Acumen to teleport him to Control, and she had a feeling no one would want to touch her right now.

One small grace, Flit thought, was that the trip back to the Residence was quiet. It was a well-known procedure that people were to shelter in place until an end-of-lockdown announcement was made. They were never to assume a situation was over just because the alarms stopped. That meant Flit and Tinker had a clear path and a quick journey back to the Residence and up to their apartment.

It did occur to Flit to be grateful that her mother did not need to fill the space between them with unnecessary chatter. The quiet time gave Flit's mind a moment to catch up to reality even though the view of the man exploding, the flare of purple behind him, was burned onto her retinas.

39

SCRAPS

A STRANGE SENSE of purposeful calm settled over Scraps as he tightened his leg holster over his black cargo pants. The other members of the strike team were also gearing up, and it made him think back to preparing for a patrol with the Underground. It had been a while since he had been on a mission, and this one was probably the most important of his life so far.

After almost a week of training, the strike team were finally ready to hit the server farms. They had gone over their roles and the plan countless times, and Scraps was pleased that they all seemed to know what they were doing.

Footsteps echoed down the passage that led into the bunker below Nightmix. Scraps had learned that it was easier to hear people coming during the day, thanks the fact the club was closed. As Scraps looked up, he watched Adam and Petra approach where the strike team were gearing up.

Adam clapped his hands together contentedly as he looked over at them. "Ok team, the van has arrived."

"Have you got the maintenance overalls?" Scraps straightened up and rested his hands on his weapon belt. As stealthily dressed and well-armed as he was, the hardest part of the plan would be getting into the building. The van was how they would get into the loading dock, and the maintenance overalls were the disguise that would hopefully let them slip through the corridors without too much notice.

Petra nodded and smiled at him, but her expression came across as more nervous than encouraging. "Everything you need is in the back of the van, I believe."

Tai looked up from their wrist device, and their eyes widened. "Even the C4 I requested?"

"I told you we are doing this without explosives." Scraps turned to face Tai, a frown on his face.

Tai shrugged. "Eh, it's just in case, you know? There's no point going in there unarmed."

Scraps was about to gesture to the guns and combat knives everyone had strapped to them, but he knew people like Tai. There was no point arguing. It would have been like trying to convince Flit to leave her flame grenades behind.

"Brian is right. The server farm is critical to our mission. We need to ensure it doesn't get damaged," Adam said with a stern look at Tai.

Tai seemed to bristle at the admonishment on Adam's tone, but Nick settled a beefy hand on their shoulder, and they pressed their lips together instead of arguing.

"Right. Well, we all know the plan. Better get into the van," Scraps said, not wanting to waste any more time arguing.

The earlier they got to the building, the easier it would be to infiltrate it. They knew what the rosters looked like, and there was a security shift handover in exactly half an hour. That would be the best window for getting in unchecked.

There as a murmur of agreement from the small team, and they started filing out. Adam was in the lead, explaining something or other about how Andy had hacked the navigation and identification system in the van so Government sensors would pick it up as one of their own fleet. It wasn't, of course, but with the paintjob the Free Citizens had done on the generic hover-van and the way that the tech had been altered, it would be good enough for a short-term ruse.

Just as Scraps was about to walk after the group, he felt a tug on the sleeve of his shirt. He paused, eyebrows furrowing as he glanced at Petra.

"Andy told me to give you this." She reached down through the neckline of her blouse to retrieve a microchip that looked exactly like the one Adam had given him earlier that morning, the one they had to insert into a server so they could get easier hacking access.

Scraps took the chip and tucked it into his left pocket, so he wouldn't confuse it with the one Adam had given him and he had stowed in his right pocket. "What is it?"

"Andy called it... a highlights reel?" Petra screwed up her nose, clearly not understanding what Andy had told her about it. "She said that, even if she lost control of the first chip, no one would be able to alter that one."

A highlights reel and an insurance policy. Scraps appreciated that. He assumed the chip meant that Liana and Chris had spoken to Andy, and she had agreed to help them get extra information into the broadcast Adam would have them make. It was clever thinking to get the information in a different way as well because he had no doubt Adam would attempt to stop anything that was not part of his own agenda.

"Tell her I said thank you," Scraps whispered with a firm nod.

"I will." The nervous expression on Petra's face softened and she smiled at him. "And good luck out there today. If anyone can make this thing work, it's you."

The vote of confidence made Scraps surprisingly grateful. He hadn't spent all that much time with Petra, so it was flattering to think she had faith in him for such an important mission. After growing up as a Registered Derivate, he had been taught to believe that the only reason he would achieve anything was under the guidance of the Citizen Officers. The Underground had done a lot to help him grow his own sense of efficacy, but he had always been part of a team down there.

"Thank you. I will see you tonight at combat training," he promised before he turned to follow the others out.

There was a set of standard, Government-issued maintenance overalls left in the back of the van for each of the group of five.

Whoever Adam had gotten to find or manufacture them had even gone to the trouble of getting them the right sizes.

When Scraps entered the van, he found that Elise was already dressed and buckling herself into the driver's seat. The others were still doing up the buttons. The clothing was just loose enough to hide the bulk of their weapons underneath. It also inhibited access to them, but given the fact that they were supposed to be getting in and out without any violence, it wasn't such a bad thing that it was hard to get hold of their gear. Scraps, at least, had another natural weapon he could use in an emergency. He would be able to keep them all safe.

"Good luck, and make sure you complete your mission objective," Adam said as he slid the van door shut and slapped the side panel twice.

Scraps pulled on his own overalls and then sat on one of the benches that ran along the inside passenger side of the cargo area. He fastened it as Elise pulled the van out of the club's loading dock.

The van glided out of the alley behind Nightmix. It was still early enough in the morning that the streets were quiet. Well, when it came to vehicles, at least. Scraps had grown used to the way Derivates were spaced out on the sidewalks every ten metres or so on the main roads. Despite the increased surveillance, Elise managed to weave her way throughout the grid network of the city with ease.

Scraps had never had a chance to drive in the Hub. That was reserved for Citizens only. He had always been curious about operating a vehicle, but without access to one, he chose to spend his energy on more achievable pursuits.

As the city whizzed by outside the van window, Scraps turned to the others. "Does everyone remember the plan?" He sat up straight and looked at the other three members of the strike team.

"First, we get into the loading dock," Leo provided, hunched over in his seat. With the way his long hair hung over his face and cast shadows over his eyes, Scraps wasn't sure if he was trying to make eye contact or not.

Tai cleared their throat. "Then, we head up to level fifty in the service elevator."

"Provided the security passes in these suits don't trip any alarms," Elise muttered under her breath as she turned a corner.

"While we are up there, we pretend we are running routine maintenance on one of the water coolers, which is right next to a vent outlet," Nick said, voice low. "Then, you and Tai will shimmy through the vent, into the server farm room, and plant the chip."

Chips, Scraps mentally corrected. He nodded. "And what do we not do?"

There was a heavy sigh from Tai. "Not blow things up."

"Or pick any fights," Nick added.

"But we do defend ourselves with lethal force if need be," Elise called over her shoulder.

Scraps' brows furrowed. "Our first order in that scenario is retreat."

"Sure. Right. You do you." Elise's voice was nonchalant enough that Scraps wished they had a formal ranking system in the Free Citizens so he could issue her with a written warning.

Despite the sass and the concern Elise's comment roused, Scraps let all that go as they turned onto the street of their target building. He spent more time looking out the window, half expecting to be stopped by some Government forces. Even though he had done his best to protect the plans and location of the Free Citizens, it was entirely possible that Greene and Hector knew more than they were letting on.

Elise steered the vehicle towards the entrance of the loading dock at the foot of the building. She slowed right down to a crawl to edge closer and closer to the closed gate. Just as Scraps was about to give up hope, the door buzzed and started to roll open.

Leo, Nick, and Tai all gave subdued cheers as the van travelled down the ramp.

"Don't get too excited yet. We've still got a lot to do." Scraps patted his leg and his belt again, satisfying himself that he had his weapons tucked away just right.

One of the others called him something unfavourable, but he just ignored them. He'd been called much worse in his life.

"Okay, looks like we've got a good spot free right near the

service lift," Elise said as she pulled the van into a parking area was marked *For Government Service Vehicles Only*.

The instant the engine stopped, Scraps rose from his seat on the bench and slid open the side door of the van. He gestured for silence and waved Leo, Nick, and Tai out of the vehicle. On the way out, Nick grabbed hold of a heavy-looking steel toolbox that would not only act as a good prop for their disguises, but it also contained all the items they would need to get into the vent and make it appear as though they were servicing a water cooler.

Elise joined the rest of their team as they walked over to the staff elevator. Loitering and gawking around the place would only make them seem more suspicious. Scraps didn't hesitate as he reached forward to press the call button. He knew that there would be a chip reader in the vicinity, scanning to ensure someone requesting access had the right security clearance. Thankfully, the call button lit up green, indicating that the security system had accepted whatever false information the chips had fed it. Scraps would have to speak to Adam about where he got that information later, as it had a lot of potential to be useful in their future rebellion.

They were alone in the elevator for the first four levels before the car stopped and the doors opened. A man and a woman in the same overalls the team wore stepped in. They looked at the occupants, the expressions on their faces making it clear they did not recognise anyone, but the presence of unfamiliar faces did not appear to worry them as they started chatting, apparently picking up a conversation that they had started before they had stepped onboard. They got off around ten floors before the strike team was due to, and those last few levels filled Scraps with a sense of apprehension. What if the pair decided to report them? What if they told someone and there would be a security team waiting on the other side of the doors when they reached fifty?

"We all need to be on high alert," Scraps muttered, his hand instinctively settling on the holster of his gun even though it was hidden beneath his overalls.

The others didn't reply with words, but their postures changed, and anticipation rippling through the elevator car. Without needing to be asked, Nick stepped forward to stand beside Scraps. His shoulders and chest were broad enough that it wouldn't be possible for anyone to barrel in through the doors.

When the elevator doors opened the corridor beyond was clear. The lighting was still on the night-time reserve setting, which made it hard to tell the difference between the glass-walled server rooms and the corridors. The whole level was quiet, but a somewhat eerie low buzz of the powerful electronics vibrated through the air. The whole place felt almost as if it was sleeping, and walking through the corridors was an intrusion on that tentative calmness.

Scraps had spent a lot of time analysing the floor plans they had acquired and was able to lead the others through the space without difficulty. Even though the level was mostly dedicated to the server farms, there were plenty of other meeting and maintenance rooms dotted between the storage spaces.

As they wound their way deeper into the labyrinth of Government technology, Scraps slowed his steps and paid more attention to the numbers on the server room doors. According to Andy, they couldn't just find any server to plug into. The Government were bound to have fail-safes in the network, and she had been very precise about what he was to look for.

The strike team had to go deeper. Scraps was grateful for his time in the Underground, developing his sense of direction and learning how to navigate narrow, almost identical corridors. As they took what had to be their fifteenth turn, he heard Tai muttering something behind him about feeling as though they were rats in a maze.

"We're almost there," Scraps promised, voice hushed.

True to his word, another two turns later, the glass walls gave way to a more solid-looking, frosted surfaces. The lack of reflection helped the team navigate the space, but the lack of light and darker shadows made it feel as if the walls were closing in on them. The heat of the electronics made the walls radiate a cloistering warmth.

Finally, Scraps held up his hand as he passed a meeting room with a water dispenser built into the wall outside of it. He glanced back over his shoulder at Elise, who tapped her wrist device and looked at the screen. After a few seconds, she nodded.

Nick set the bag down on the ground and started running his

hands over the identical frosted panels around the cooler. The seams in the wall were so thin that it was near impossible for Scraps to figure out which was a vent and which was actual wall, but Nick managed it with a minute of silence and some gentle taps. He retrieved a flat-bladed tool from his kit and carefully wedged it into the seam.

"Want some C_4 instead?" Tai offered, reaching into their pocket.

Elise and Scraps gave Tai matching, warning glances. Nick just chuckled and shook his head as he popped the panel off.

The crawl space was tight, tight enough that Scraps couldn't help but wonder if going in himself was a bad idea. Tai didn't seem to have the same reservation as they got down on their hands and knees and started the crawl.

Scraps patted the pocket where he was keeping the chips and then gritted his teeth. He had to make sure those chips were going in just where he needed them to. He couldn't rely on Tai to do his job for him, so Scraps sank to his hands and knees and followed Tai into the darkness of the vent.

Luckily for Scraps and Tai, they only had to crawl about a metre before they reached a vertical shaft. Scraps found it far easier to shimmy up the inside of the shaft than he had found it to squeeze through one on his hands and knees, but the relief was short-lived. The narrow shaft joined a slightly wider horizontal one that they had to bend their bodies into. They kept moving forward, passing over solid sheets of metal interrupted by the occasional slatted vent that let just enough striped light in for Scraps to remember there was more to this building than the darkness they were currently experiencing. Just as Scraps was about to ask Tai if they knew where they were going, Scraps put a hand down on Tai's foot a little too hard, drawing a sharp intake of breath from his fellow strike team member.

"Just opening the panel now," Tai whispered.

Pulling his hand back and waiting for Tai to do their bit, Scraps took a deep breath and resisted the urge to use his power to get the panel off. He didn't like the enclosed space of the vent and hoped that they weren't wasting too much time. It wouldn't be much longer before the security shift handover finished, and the chance of them getting caught would increase exponentially.

"Got it—"

Just as Tai announced their success, there was a loud clattering as the metal vent cover tumbled to the floor in the server room. Scraps froze, blood running cold, certain that someone had to have heard that cacophony.

Up ahead, Tai wiggled closer to the now-open hole. They gripped the sides of the shaft and lowered the top half of their body down. To provide extra stability, Scraps reached forward and held their legs down, not wanting them to fall face first out of the shaft.

After a minute, Tai pulled themself back up into the vent. "Looks like it's all clear," they announced quietly yet confidently before dropping themselves feet first into the room below.

Hoping that Tai's observation skills were sound, Scraps followed along.

The first thing Scraps noticed was the heat. It was worse than a steamy summer day in the wide room. His mind was thrown back to the Blue Team training session so long ago when they had simulated a server room. The thought of Flit's approach to that made him smile to himself despite the nature of the situation.

"Do we put the chip in any one of these?" Tai asked, unzipping the front of their overalls and revealing the black fatigues beneath. They plunged their hands into a leg pocket and pulled out what looked like—

"We're planting chips into the servers, not plastic explosives," Scraps said, suddenly wary.

Tai shook their head. "No. *You're* planting chips. Adam asked me to put a little bit of spice around the room for him. Getting our word out through their network is one thing, but there is no way Adam will let them have the airwaves back." Tai reached into another pocket and pulled out a small, clear case full of remote detonator receivers. "So, if they figure out how to kick us out, we'll evict their farm from this building."

Scraps wanted to argue. The idea of this was beyond unnecessary. There were also other levels of offices that would be impacted by explosions in this one. However, he had to be smart about it. He couldn't afford to fight Tai over this, not when there were three other members of the strike team, who were much closer to the explosives specialist, waiting for them at the other side of the vent. Also planting the explosives would keep Tai busy, so they probably wouldn't notice Scraps slipping an extra drive into the server.

"Very well. You have your orders. I have mine," Scraps conceded with a firm nod.

He pressed his lips together as Tai started pinching bits of the explosive compound off the block and rolling it between their fingertips to make it warm and pliable.

Turning his back on his comrade, Scraps looked for the serial numbers on the server towers around him. Thankfully, they were all organised in a neat grid fashion that made Scraps think of the layout of the Hub itself. Sure enough, as he found the centre of the room, from which all the numbering radiated, he came face to face with a server tower with far more flashing lights than any other in the space. He pulled the chips out of his pocket and looked at the numbers Andy had inscribed on them. Each one had to be plugged into a specific port to ensure optimal access.

Trying to find the right port in the tower was like searching for a needle in a haystack. There were more choices than Scraps cared to count, and even though they were numbered, there were half-numbers and different fonts and so many signs that this tower had been updated and morphed to be so different from its original state.

After locating the first port for the chip Adam knew about, Scraps pressed his finger to the metal beside it while he located the second. Andy had warned that the longer a port was empty, the higher the chance of a breach being noticed, so Scraps decided to prepare so that he could exchange the chips as quickly as possible.

"Almost set?" Scraps called back over his shoulder as Tai's footsteps echoed around the room.

"You can change the chip in about... twenty seconds."

Scraps slowed his breathing and counted down. Given that his body was on high alert, he took his time to ensure he wasn't counting too fast, and when he hit zero, he pulled the first chip out of his pocket, lined it up so he could get it in fast, and then yanked the first out. It was easy enough to slip the replacement in. He was just about to retrieve the second chip when the overhead lights in the room flared on. The bright white of it all was a shock to Scraps' system after the dim lighting of the vents, and he fumbled with the second chip.

"Shit, we gotta move!" Tai called across the distance.

Deciding speed was the most important factor, Scraps used his telekinesis to remove the second chip and put the new one in manually. He completed the swap and collected the two now defunct connective chips before turning and running back towards the vent.

As Scraps reached the vent to find Tai waiting for him, an electronic hiss signalled that a door at the far side of the room had been opened.

40

FLIT

WHEN THE PAIR reached the apartment, Tinker led Flit straight to the bathroom. She left her standing by the door while she started the shower. "Those clothes are sticky. Let me help you out of them."

Flit didn't argue. She held her breath, and let her mother peel her tank up past her face without allowing the fabric to brush against her skin. Flit unbuckled her belt and fly and then held onto one of Tinker's strong and steady arms as she stepped out of her cargo pants.

"You hop in the shower and scrub off. I'll get you a change of clothes," Tinker promised softly. "I'll be right back."

Sure enough, Tinker was gone for barely a minute. Flit had stepped into the shower in the meantime and kept her eyes straight ahead to avoid seeing the way the water had to be turning red and sludgy as it washed the blood off her skin.

When Flit was done, Tinker handed her a fresh towel, and then stepped out while she dressed. At some point, she had removed the soiled clothes without Flit noticing.

Flit hoped she threw them out. She didn't think she would be able to wear them again without seeing that man tearing apart at the seams in front of her.

After she was dressed, Tinker led Flit to the living room where she sat them both down on a couch.

"Who was he?" Flit asked, voicing the question she'd had since she'd seen him outside of the training room.

"Bolt," Tinker started with a heavy sigh. "He works in the maintenance team. His wife was killed in the last tunnel explosion, the ones that happened on the same day you were brought back down here."

Bolt.

Flit burned that name into her memory. Another victim of this stupid, faceless, senseless fight against the Government and all the horrors resulting from their persecution of the Derivates.

"He wasn't coping well with her death and turned to alcohol, medication... anything he could get his hands on," Tinker continued, voice quiet and somewhat jaded. "He was mourning, but his actions were making it unsafe for him to be around his daughter. From what I know, Control made the call to keep them apart, so he's been holed up in his apartment for weeks now."

Turning to her mother, Flit asked, "Then what changed? Why did he suddenly come out now?"

"I'm not sure," Tinker confessed. "I visited him a few times to check on his health, but we were told we were not allowed to say anything to him about his daughter. I... I wonder if he saw the publication of the exercise timetables and thought he could go and get her back? You were teaching the kids class, right?"

Shaking her head, Flit wished she hadn't heard that, that her mother hadn't made that connection. The lure of the classes she and the Blue Team had put together were the reason the man was dead. She knew it without a shred of doubt.

"Don't do that." Tinker reached over, gently holding Flit's chin and making her look up. "Don't blame yourself. He was angry, grieving, and probably high or drunk. He made his own decisions, and he lost control. That's not on you, Flit. You did the best you could. You kept him away from his little girl. Sage didn't need to witness that. She's gone through enough."

It sounds like they both have. Flit shook her head. "How did it get so bad? Why didn't someone try to—"

An announcement sounded through the apartment.

"Attention all members of the Underground," came Harmony's

soothing, deep tone. *"An emergency meeting for every member has been called. Everyone to assemble at meeting point A in the Residence. I repeat, everyone is to immediately make their way to meeting point A in the Residence for a mandatory emergency meeting."*

Flit groaned. "I suppose *everyone* means us too, huh?" She rubbed her face, her hands still warm from the shower that was probably hotter than it should have been. Her skin still felt tight and icky in places, as if the ghost of the blood was still stretching it as it dried. She resisted the urge to scrub at her skin, knowing it was just her imagination.

"Unfortunately." Tinker got to her feet. She leaned over and kissed Flit's forehead before holding her hand out in a silent offer.

Flit accepted it and stood with a heavy sigh. Before her mother could turn around and walk away, Flit leaned in and hugged her tight. Tinker's body relaxed against her, and Flit took a moment to relish her the embrace. They didn't always see eye to eye, but they were there for each other when it counted.

Tinker and Flit stepped out of the apartment to find that the corridors were busy. As usual, Flit decided to avoid the long and slow-moving queue and use the emergency stairs. "I'll get us there faster." Flit said before she teleported herself and her mother down the void and joined the throng of spilling out into the communal atrium of the Residence.

Flit couldn't help but feel these meetings were becoming more commonplace, and the tension increased with each one. Even though people were becoming desensitised to bad news, there was a sense of wariness in the group. She felt as though people were looking at her, as if they knew what had happened, but logically, that was foolish. There was no way for them to know yet. Maybe they were just *assuming* she had something to do with it. In all fairness, she almost always did.

It only took ten more minutes for everyone assemble. Flit figured that the restriction to habitable tunnels at least meant people were nearby. Still, as Harmony and Divvy were translocated into the room by Shadow, they did not waste any time.

"Hello, everyone, thank you for assembling so quickly and so calmly," Harmony called out.

The conversations that had been taking place ended immediately as the denizens of the Underground waited to hear what the meeting was all about.

"Whilst we have been hoping that we will call one of these meetings to share good news, it is my regret to inform you that today is not one of those days," Divvy say, her blue eyes surveying those gathered. "Instead, we come to you with tragic news."

"We lost one of our own today," Harmony announced with a grimace. "It is the latest in an increasing spate of power-related exertion injuries. A fatal instance, in this case."

A ripple of horrified whispers whipped through the room, and Flit's hands started shaking. She was about to shove them into her pockets when her mother took one and gave it a gentle squeeze.

"It was an unfortunate and tragic accident, and our preliminary investigation has shown that there is no fault to assign here," Divvy continued.

Flit frowned. From what her mother had told her, there was a lot of responsibility to go around. She kept her mouth shut, though. Now was not the time to draw attention to herself.

"There is, however, something to be said for a solid prevention strategy." Harmony straightened her shoulders, and her expression turned serious. "We cannot deny that being in close quarters with limited range for movement has meant that we've seen an escalation in interpersonal and domestic conflicts. The instance today was a reminder that, when we as Derivates are under pressure, our abilities are similarly tested."

Perking up, Flit bit her lip at the direction this was going. They had been under restriction orders for so long now that it was getting ridiculous. Cancelling them would be the best thing to do for the people who lived in the Underground. It would also make it easier for the Blue Team to organise their mutiny.

"Considering the fact we do not want another person dying because of this strain, we have decided to implement a new rule," Divvy said. She gestured off to the side, and a couple of Control workers walked in, carting a gunmetal grey crate between them. "In order to prevent further accidents, we are asking that everyone in the Underground wear one of these."

One of the Control workers held the lid of the crate open whilst the other reached in and retrieved a handful of thin metal bangles.

Most of the people in the room were clueless as to the purpose of the items, but Flit blurted out, "Inhibitors?"

Keeping quiet be damned, there was no way Flit was about to let that go without comment.

Dozens of voices rose in horrified protest.

Divvy raised her hands in the air to signal for silence, but it took a good few minutes for the voices to completely die down. "Please understand that we did not make this decision lightly."

"Divvy is right. This was a long time coming, and today was the final straw," Harmony said, backing up her colleague. "It is not a solution we want in the long-term, but until we can ensure your safety, this is the best option to reduce the impact of people burning out or harming others."

"That's what the Government would do!" someone called out from the middle of the crowd.

Flit couldn't have agreed more.

"I understand the concern." Divvy had to yell to be heard above the growing rumble of dissent. "But this is a temporary measure to protect you, and—"

"Hey, have you seen Posthoc around?" Flit whispered to her mother, leaning in closer as an idea formed in her mind.

Tinker's brow furrowed, but she gestured to the back of the room, where Posthoc, Acumen, and a couple of other senior Underground members were leaning against the wall and watching the chaos unfold with matching looks of wariness.

Flit teleported over to an empty space at the back of the room. "Pardon me... Coming through... 'Scuse me," she muttered as she wove through the people gathered until she reached Posthoc.

He glanced over at her, bushy brows furrowing, and raised his hand before she could speak. "Now isn't the time."

"Don't tell me you agree with this." Flit crossed her arms over her chest.

"With everyone wearing inhibitors?" Posthoc shook his head. "Of course I don't, but it isn't up to me."

Flit pressed her lips together as she tried to remember exactly what it was Posthoc used to say when they would complain about another round of training.

"If you don't learn how to control your powers, they will control you." Acumen pushed himself off the wall, a smile tugging at his lips.

Posthoc cocked an eyebrow at him.

For once, Flit didn't mind the fact that Acumen had raided her thoughts. He chuckled and tipped an imaginary hat at her.

"Why don't we put ability training into our exercise classes?" Flit had to raise her voice above the growing protests from the group behind her. It seemed that they were becoming more and more restless as Harmony and Divvy's people started pulling inhibitors out of the crates. "If we give people that outlet to use their abilities and to learn to control them even with everything going on, we won't need inhibitors."

Standing straighter, Posthoc frowned as he surveyed the room. "I'll raise it at our next meeting."

"Next meeting?" Flit blurted, her hands balling into fists.

The leader of Security's shoulders tensed as he turned on Flit. "Is nothing ever good enough for you?"

Flit snorted.

For a moment, Flit thought Posthoc was going to walk away, but Acumen put a hand on his shoulder. "Her delivery is off, as always, but she's right," he muttered. "If you ask in a meeting, they'll say no. You need to bring it up here in front of everyone. They won't want people to turn on them for ignoring a valid alternative."

With a sigh of resignation, Posthoc shook Acumen's hand off. He slipped away from Flit and Acumen as he pushed his way through the crowd. People shifted around him, their frustration at Harmony and Divvy slowly being overtaken by curiosity as Posthoc made his way to the front of the room.

"Thanks for having my back for once," Flit said.

"We're on the same side, Flit." Acumen shook his head. "I just can't afford to be reckless. If it looks like I'm stabbing you in the back, please know there's a good reason for it."

Flit was distracted from replying when she saw Posthoc step up beside Harmony and Divvy. He spoke to them, and from the way the people at the front of the room were leaning in, they could overhear every word. A ripple of conversation passed back through the crowd as word spread of what they were discussing. When Harmony and Divvy tried to argue with him, a pulse of shock went through the group.

"Let us train!" a woman at the front called out.

A series of cheers joined in as the Control workers holding the inhibitors paused and glanced over at their leaders, clearly not sure what to do.

Harmony raised her hand and shook her head. "We understand that our plan is not ideal, but organising the appropriate training is too much of an undertaking and would draw our resources away from the critical task of protecting you all," she said, having the gall to look regretful about her own decision.

"Then let the Blue Team organise it!"

Flit blinked. She wasn't sure who had yelled that from the crowd, but she loved them for it.

Divvy went to protest, but Swipe called out, "We're already running the exercise groups. It won't be that hard to adjust our rosters!"

The crowd showed their support by raising their voices in assent.

"Order!" Harmony barked, making the people who were still cheering for Swipe's suggestion to settle. "This is not a simple matter. We would not be making this decision if there was a better—"

Vicious *boos* rang through the room, drowning out Harmony's explanation.

"We have a better way!"

Posthoc leaned back in and engaged Harmony and Divvy in a terse back and forward conversation. The crowd only grew louder as they waited for the final verdict. When Harmony raised her hands again, an anticipatory silence fell over the room.

"Posthoc has just informed us that he believes it is possible to add ability training into the exercise sessions," Divvy said through what had to be painfully gritted teeth. "Harmony and I have decided to allow it. Thank you to Posthoc for the idea and the Blue Team for taking on the monumental responsibility of ensuring everyone remains safe and uninjured."

The last line was a clear delegation of blame. If something went wrong with this idea, it would land squarely on Posthoc and the Blue Team. It was a concerning thought, and as the leaders of the Underground dismissed the meeting, Flit felt like she and Swipe had just lit the fuse of a bomb they did not know the location or yield of.

41

SCRAPS

"WHICH TOWER HAD THE GLITCH, AGAIN?" came an annoyed, feminine voice.

Scraps pressed his lips together, his heart thundering in his chest as the Government workers entered the room he and Tai were very much not supposed to be in. It was difficult to see where they were, given the sheer number of network towers packed into the space, but he could hear them.

There was a grunt, followed by. "Bloody Centre One. I keep tellin' them to replace the whole server, but oh, no. Can't have the city down for the two minutes it would take."

Tai attempted to jump to grab the edges of the vent. They were too short, however, and panic flickered behind their eyes. Without a word, Scraps tucked the defunct chips in his pocket, leaned over, and clasped his hands together so Tai could use them for a boost. Even though Tai was light, jumping for height was not their strong point, so Scraps put the tiniest bit of telekinesis into his own hands to boost them up.

"They need to redo the air conditioning system in here too. Is it just me, or is this place better than a sauna?" the woman asked. "This is the fifth time the network has glitched just this week. Jodie wants to blame the manufacturer, but nothing was designed to function in this kind of heat or for this long."

Scraps was grateful for the workers' chatter as it let him know they were still at the other end of the room. He used the opportunity to jump and catch the edges of the grate. He pulled himself up, careful to avoid making too much noise. Once he was enveloped in the relative darkness of the shaft, he noted the light streaming in from the opening they had used. He bit back a groan of frustration and quickly shimmied back, looking down into the hole that was left and spotting the vent on the floor of the server room.

From his position, Scraps was able to see the workers' heads as they stood at the tower in the distance. He bit his lip as he weighed up the risk of jumping back down to retrieve the panel or using his powers. In the end, the speed and efficiency of telekinesis won out, and he slipped his hand out of the shaft and summoned the cover to him. He gingerly set it back in position and clipped it in place before rejoining Tai.

As they crawled back through the shafts, Scraps couldn't help but wonder if they had taken too much time. Getting the chips in place was a win, but it wouldn't matter if their team got caught by the Government. Even those most resistant to torture would not be able to fool a talented telepath, especially the Citizens. Scraps wasn't even certain his own meagre attempts would do much, not if his conversations with TB-219 were an indication.

Despite the sense of urgency, Scraps' relief rippled through him as he slid down the vertical shaft after Tai and then waited while Tai crawled forward.

"Were you counting? Is this the right one?" Tai hissed back. Their whisper would have been quiet, but every sound was amplified in the shaft.

"This should be right," Scraps replied. He had been paying attention but had to admit his own count of the vents might have been off as he had foolishly been trusting Tai to lead the way. "Why?"

There was a soft grunt. "The panel's on tight. We can't get out." Tai knocked against it twice, as if testing to see if someone was on the other side.

Scraps was just about to suggest that they swap places when muffled voices from the corridor drifted into the vent.

"What was that?" The tone was low, almost robotic and entirely unfamiliar.

Someone banged on the panel three times, and the sound echoed painfully along the shaft.

"Told ya' already. Water filter's busted. Knocks like that sometimes when the water can't get through." Scraps identified the second voice, even if Elise was putting a bit of a rough accent on. There was another bang that made Scraps jump. "Oh, when it sounds like that, the pipe's getting' close to bursting. Please let us work before I gotta tell your bosses why this level flooded."

There was a general rumbling of voices and then silence. Scraps counted almost a minute before there was a metallic whine, and light flooded into the shaft around his legs.

"Hurry up!" Elise hissed.

Scraps and Tai did not need to be told twice. They slipped out of the vent, and Nick was already replacing it as they straightened up. The team didn't even bother to try and exchange details of their successes. Their only task now was to get back to Nightmix alive and undetected.

All of the lights in the server level were on full, and it felt almost as if they were travelling through a different building. With the added brightness, the reflections of the glass-walled rooms were stronger and more disorienting.

At one point, the team caught sight of some security officers farther down a corridor. The pair, Registered Derivates by the look of their uniforms and their visors, stopped and started to follow the small group.

When Scraps and the others reached the elevator lobby, the Registereds were gaining on them. Scraps tried to keep his thoughts clear as Leo tapped the call button repeatedly.

Scraps was tempted to tell the younger man that the tapping wouldn't make the elevator come any faster, but he had seen enough nervous ticks like that to know it wasn't worth arguing about. Flit had taught him that much at least.

There was a pleasant chime, and the elevator reached their level. Scraps ushered the others in just as the Registereds down the hall started walking faster.

"Halt! Please present your security passes," one called out.

"Oh, sorry!" Elise pressed the "Basement" level and then jabbed the close-door button nonchalantly. "It's closing. I don't know how to stop it!"

The lie was evident as there was a button specifically designed to hold the doors.

Glancing at the Derivates, Scraps held up the fake pass attached to his overalls. The doors weren't shutting fast enough as the security officers gained speed.

"Shit, shit, shit," Tai muttered.

Dropping his security pass, Scraps leaned forward and put his hands on the doors. He made a great show of pretending to try to hold them open, when actually he used a tiny dash of telekinesis to help them shut completely.

There were yells from the other side of the thick metal doors, but they disappeared as the elevator started gliding down the shaft.

Scraps turned to Leo. "Get the security cameras offline, now."

Scraps wasn't sure if that was something Leo was capable off, but given stealth was his thing, he was the safest bet. Leo glanced around the space, his focus narrowing on the control panel. He leaned in, and even Scraps caught the glint of a miniscule lens as Leo's shadow fell over it. The glint wasn't there for long, though. Leo reached into the neck of his overalls and then pulled out what looked like a... crowbar?

"Copy that." The next instant, Leo smashed the bar into the panel screen, and it rained shards of crystalline glass over the floor of the elevator.

With the security sorted, Scraps looked at the ceiling of the elevator. He knew there would be security waiting for them at the basement now, but they wouldn't be expecting them to come out somewhere else...

Crouching low, Scraps prepared himself to jump so he could dislodge a panel on the ceiling of the elevator. He didn't really need to hit it hard as he could put his power into it.

Seemingly sensing what he was about to do, the other team members stepped aside to give him room.

It only took a single attempt for Scraps to jump up and push the roof grid aside. The instant the ceiling was compromised, security alerts blared through the tall, empty shaft.

"Come on. We need to get on top of the car," Scraps announced.

He got to his knees so he could provide the others with a leg up. Even as the elevator car descended, they managed to get on top of it. When Scraps pulled himself up, he hung over the edge. With a subtle swipe of his hands, he used his powers to tug at either side of the sliding doors. There was an awful creek as the force yanked them off their rails and jammed them shut.

That should keep them busy. Scraps sat up and replaced the ceiling panel.

Head swimming at the way the walls whizzed by, Scraps called upon that sense of balance he needed when he was teleporting with Flit. After a deep breath, he looked at the others, everyone's eyes glinting in the darkness.

"When the elevator stops, I'll force open the door for the level above. We'll get out that way. We'll need to hurry, and we'll have to get onto the street as soon as possible."

"Here. You'll need this." Leo held the crowbar out to Scraps.

Even though he did not, in fact, need it, Scraps took the crowbar with a nod of thanks. "Get out of your suits, too," he added. "They'll be looking for a maintenance crew."

The others scrambled as they only had seconds to comply. Scraps turned his own suit inside out and tied it around his waist, so the plain grey inner lining looked like a jacket hanging over his hips. It helped hide his weapons belt.

As he stepped out of the legs of his own suit, Nick asked, "What about the van?" He let out a yelp as his foot got caught on the suit, and he stumbled. Tai reached out with lightning fast reflexes and caught him by the scruff of his shirt.

"We don't need it anymore," Scraps said dismissively. "We get outside, ride the maglev from South Two to North Seven, and we walk to Nightmix. We may need to split up, but if we do, the club is our regroup zone. Understood?"

The others nodded as the elevator slowed to a stop.

There was no time to waste. Scraps jumped up and started to

climb a ladder on the side of the shaft. The ceilings in the building were high, so it wasn't as easy as just reaching for the next level. However, the fact the ladder forced them into single file meant no one could see the way Scraps simply waved to get and hold the doors open to the "Lower Ground" floor.

Glancing out tentatively, Scraps was pleased that there was no one around what looked like a storage and maintenance level. He hopped out and then leaned over to give everyone else a hand up.

"Do not run. It will be suspicious. Stay calm, measured, and they will think you belong," he advised.

As they reached the stairwell that led the to the ground floor and their escape, the thundering of tactical boots on concrete rang through the door like a desperate drumbeat. Gingerly, Scraps wedged the crowbar between the ground and the edge of the door so it could not be opened, and they all waited with bated breath as the officers bypassed their door and kept running down.

After the footsteps faded, the team burst into the stairwell and made their way up. The lobby was not yet in lockdown, and as they walked out of the building unassailed, Scraps could only hope that the locked elevator door would keep the security team busy until his own team was well clear of the area.

On the way back to Nightmix, they seemed to draw the eyes of some of the Derivates assigned to guard the streets. To avoid suspicion, the group split into two. Nick and Tai peeled off to take the train from the first mag-lev station, while Scraps, Elise, and Leo kept to the streets and walked to a station a few stops down the line.

The concern they were being watched followed Scraps every step of the journey. He resisted the urge to check over his shoulder more than would be normal and was able to make it the rest of the way to the club without being caught.

When they got back to the bunker, they found that Nick and Tai had beaten them there. There were not many other people in the space, but Adam was at his desk, on an audio call with Andy.

"They know that someone was messing with something?" Adam asked, frowning and gesturing for Scraps and the others to join him by the desk.

"Yes, but Brian did a good job of swapping the chips over

quickly. I was able to get into their system pretty fast, and I have been spending the last hour creating some little booby traps and false leads in their networks that should keep them occupied for a while," Andy's voice filtered up from the tabletop screen Adam was leaning over.

A sense of disappointment filled Scraps. Sure, they had gotten in and out safely, but if the Government figured out what they had done, the whole thing would have just been a waste of time and energy.

"When you say a while..." Adam trailed off. He looked up at Scraps, as if the answer would determine just how annoyed he would be at him.

Andy sighed, the breathy sound backed by a frequent pitter-patter. Scraps could have sworn that no rain had been forecast for the day. He had checked that morning when he woke, wanting to know the conditions for the mission. Then, he realised it was prob-ably the rapid beat of Andy tapping at a keyboard. They were working so fast that Scraps was impressed.

"If we can get a couple more hackers in on this, I may be able to hold them off for another day or two. Just depends, though," she said, sounding distracted.

"On what?" Adam straightened, crossing his arms over his chest.

"On how good their micros are."

Scraps frowned. He knew for a fact that the Government filtered every technologically skilled microkinetic into their computer systems from the moment they left the training facility. He could only hope that tactic had changed now they were preparing for an uprising. Perhaps, he mused, they would have pulled some of the micros away from defence to put them into offence.

Suddenly, a thought that had initially been reassuring filled him with dread. If the Government were to turn their full team of micro-kinetics against the Free Citizens, they would be in trouble.

Then again, they still hadn't broken through the protection the Underground had put on his and Flit's Hub apartment. Not that the apartment was guarded by the Free Citizens, but it was at least a good sign that there were some micros out there more powerful than the ones the Government had trained.

A heavy thump broke Scraps from his thoughts as Adam slammed his fist against the desk. "I'll reroute our hacking resources to you. They're under your command. Please don't leave as much of a mess as my strike team did."

Before Andy could reply, Adam glared up at the strike team, who had fanned out around his desk in a loose semi-circle. They were all tight-lipped and stony faced as Adam stood there, the silence between them simmering with disdain.

"Given the parameters, there was no way to complete that mission without triggering some sort of alarm," Scraps said, keeping his head high and refusing to let Adam unleash his disappointment on Scraps' team.

"Good leaders don't blame the mission parameters for their own failure," Adam snapped, crossing his arms over his chest.

The instinct to apologise to Adam and accept responsibility was strong. The only thing that stopped Scraps was the anger radiating off his fellow strike team members. Scraps thought back to his time in the Underground and what he had witnessed there when it came to leadership and teamwork.

"Good leaders back their teams." Scraps let the words fall over his companions like a thick blanket of reassurance, smothering the simmering tension and letting them know he would not allow them to burn. "We did the best we could. We all got out alive, and we succeeded with the mission objectives. If we had more time to plan or gradually infiltrate, we could have done this more stealthily. You gave us a couple of days, so you got the best that a couple of days could buy you."

Jaw twisting and clenching, Adam glared at Scraps. "You'd better hope the Government don't detect those chips before we're ready."

In that moment, all Scraps could do was stare at the selfish, pathetic man before him and feel sorry for him. He had invested so much of his pride in his ability to control the success of the Free Citizens that he had lost sight of what it was truly about.

Scraps wouldn't make that same mistake.

42

FLIT

THE BLUE TEAM didn't waste any time.

Following the dismissal of the gathering where Harmony and Divvy had tried to convince everyone that wearing inhibitors would be in their best interest, Flit and Swipe called for an immediate meeting. There were no arguments with the request, even when everyone including Fortune and Layla squeezed into Swipe's modest studio apartment.

At first, no one spoke. The silence was thick with a heady mix of disbelief, betrayal, and outrage. It was one thing to use inhibitors on people accused of crimes or needing immediate protection, but suggesting that the entire population wear them?

"They... They were planning this," Flit blurted, shaking her head.

All eyes turned to her.

"Surely not," Hawkeye said, although his tone told Flit he didn't *want* to believe it, not that he *couldn't*.

With a wild gesture towards the door that made Tweak jump back, Flit snapped, "They had crates of inhibitors ready, didn't you see? They were just gonna hand those fucking things out like they were rations or something."

"Flit's right," Swipe said, keeping her chin high. The direness of the situation was such that not a single snide comment was made about the fact that Flit and Swipe never agreed on anything. "Why would they need crates of inhibitors if they didn't intend to use them?"

Flit nodded. "I bet they were just waiting for something like this to happen."

"I mean, it is pretty suspicious." Tweak ran a hand through his hair and shrugged. "They weren't the old inhibitors, either. Like, I would give them a bit more benefit of the doubt if they pulled together all the past models, but no... those were that weird new tech they used on Flit."

"The same tech developed from a weapon the Government are using to subdue Derivate abilities."

Everyone in the room was quiet as Flit brought that connection to light.

Flit looked around, not surprised to see how some of her more reserved friends appeared to withdraw into themselves. Every single one of the Underground Derivates in the room loved their home. They had spent their whole life believing that the system they lived in protected them from the oppressive one above ground. They were convinced that their life in the dark tunnels was worthwhile because the heat of existing under the Government's scrutiny would burn them to a crisp, but what were they to do now that their beloved home had become suffocating?

"We need to organise a training schedule," Fortune announced. She stepped forward from where she was leaning against a wall. "We need to do it quickly. If we don't move fast, we may lose momentum and opportunity."

"What's to stop them changing their minds?" Sway frowned.

There was a general murmur of agreement.

"Absolutely nothing," Fortune conceded, "which is why we need to take advantage of every moment we have. The last time I caught whiff that things down here weren't quite right, my family were betrayed. Now, my son and husband are dead. I will not..." she faltered, her voice cracking. She sniffed and took a deep breath. "I refuse to allow that to happen again."

Link gasped, her eyes wide. "You think the Underground told the Government about you, Rook, and Vector."

The way Fortune straightened her shoulders and stood taller

spoke of a stoic strength that Flit had seen in the woman on so many occasions. Given everything that had happened over the past few years, Flit couldn't help but wonder how many other secrets her second mother-figure was carrying.

For the benefit of those gathered who had not heard it before, Fortune launched into the story of her suspicions about the leadership of the Underground. Judging by the parted lips and slumped shoulders, the rest of the team were just as alarmed about the revelations as Flit had been when she'd first heard them.

"So, what do we do now?" Clarity asked. "At the very least, they can't hand any of us over to the Government now they've got us trapped down here."

A small, irreverent laugh spluttered from Flit. A couple of the others gave her concerned looks. However, Flit didn't care. The situation had gotten beyond ridiculous.

"You're not trapped so long as you are willing to fight," Layla said.

It was rare that she ever spoke when they got together as a group. She seemed uncomfortable when everyone turned to face her. Flit had seen Layla with her own people, where she was confident and smooth. For the first time, Flit wondered what it was like for her to discover that a whole different society existed right beneath her feet all along, a society where she wouldn't have had to pretend to be someone else her whole life.

Fortune reached over and gently patted the redhead on the back. "Layla's right. Even when we were imprisoned in that facility, we managed to fight in our own way. Heck, Rook went down fighting."

Where there could have been pain and grief, Fortune's voice rung with pride.

Flit blinked back the unexpected stinging in her eyes at her last exchange with the man she one thought she would marry. Those whispered, heated words... The way he wanted to go on his own terms and take an entire Government facility down with him.

"She's right," Flit said, a new resolve filling her. "We have a perfect opportunity to start preparing people. We said we would do this ability training, so we do it. We schedule as much as we can for as long as we can."

Tweak cleared his throat. "Yeah, but what about Harmony and Divvy? Am I the only one who noticed how pissed they were when Flit and Swipe spoke up?"

"They'll find a way to undermine us." The words that Fortune spoke came with such a lack of emotion that everyone knew it was a simple fact. "Until then, we do what we can for our people. And... when they inevitably find some way to shut it down—"

"We fight," Flit said.

Fortune nodded. "Then, we fight."

LATER THAT EVENING, the Blue Team had their training plan completed. They sent it through to Posthoc, who approved it immediately. They were scheduled to start first thing the following morning and had reorganised their exercise allocations into power-based assignments. As a well-oiled security unit, they knew that mixed teams were stronger teams, however they needed to determine where everyone was at with their own abilities before they made decisions about efficient team assignments.

One thing Flit was pleased about was that, as a teleporter, training her fellow teleporters meant they needed bigger spaces to work with compared to the others. Posthoc had approved a rare exemption to the movement restrictions to allow them to go down to the storage tunnels once they moved past their initial assessments. In reality, it was a small concession but one Flit was excited about. She wasn't the kind of person to enjoy being penned in. The restrictions felt like a constant itch she was unable to scratch.

"I thought for sure that Harmony was going to flip her lid when you spoke up," Stride muttered, looking at Flit over the forkful of mashed potato he had been avoiding eating for the past five minutes.

It seemed the blandness of the potatoes had an inverse correlation to the amount of freedom in the Underground. For the sake of her tastebuds, Flit sincerely hoped the restrictions would not get worse.

"I don't think you went about that the right way," Tinker said, eating her own meal without complaint or hesitation, "but I do agree with your sentiments."

It was the first time during the meal that Flit's parents had actually spoken. Flit knew that they were both wary, given what she had witnessed earlier that day. It still haunted her, of course, but she figured it was something she would be able to process when they were safe and free. Right now, she needed to forge on. She couldn't afford to get distracted.

"If you want help training the teleporters, I wouldn't mind doing something other than counting the dwindling stock. Again," her father offered.

Perking up, Flit leaned her elbows against the table, her meal all but forgotten. "Really?"

Stride nodded and grinned bashfully. "Yeah, well, I know I'm rusty but this old dog still has some good tricks."

"What time will you be free?" Flit smiled. She hadn't spent much time with either of her parents since... Well, she couldn't quite remember when, but it was well overdue.

"I've got a morning shift each day, so I'll be free after lunch."

"Don't forget you need to help with the restocks in the medbay every second afternoon," Tinker reminded him.

A dismissive wave from her father told Flit exactly what he thought about that particular duty.

"And please don't do anything foolish. It's been a while since you've pushed yourself, and I don't want you getting hurt," Tinker added, her tone low as she eyed her husband.

Flit avoided the urge to chuckle to herself. Clearly, she had gotten her own impulsiveness from her father.

"Ah, I'll be fine. Don't you worry about me." Stride patted her hand. "Besides, getting back up to scratch is what this whole training thing is about, right, Flit?"

Before Flit could answer, there was a knock on the door to the apartment.

Flit froze as she looked at her parents, and the worry mirrored in their wide eyes told her that they probably had the same concern she did. They sat in stunned silence until a second, more insistent knock sounded.

"I... I suppose I should get that. Flit, love, why don't you go to the bathroom?" Tinker set her fork down as she got to her feet.

As much as Flit didn't want to run if Harmony had tracked her down, she also knew there was wisdom in retreating at certain times. Without arguing, she teleported off her chair to a spot down the hall right in front of the bathroom. She opened the door, stepped in, and locked it behind herself just as Tinker reached the front door.

Leaning against the door, Flit tried to make out the muffled words from the other side of the apartment. It wasn't an easy task, but after a minute, there were extra sets of footsteps, and then her mother called, "Flit? Come out. It's Hawkeye and Layla."

Relieved, Flit was about to translocate out of the bathroom and into the hall when she remembered she hadn't yet told her mother about her new ability. She had told her father, of course, but if she started using the movement style haphazardly, it would be sure to arouse suspicion from her mother. She walked out normally instead and was confused to see her friends holding gaming console controllers.

"Did you forget we were playing tonight?" Hawkeye asked, tilting his head to the side ever so slightly.

"Forget what?" Flit paused at the way he narrowed his eyes at her. "Oh, uh..." She ran a hand through her hair. "My brain's a bit fried after today."

"You don't have to play if you don't want to, Flit. It's perfectly okay to be exhausted," Tinker said in a tone that had fooled many of Flit's friends into thinking she was a far gentler mother than she really was.

"It's probably exactly what I need." Flit shoved her hands into her pockets and shrugged. "My brain won't switch off properly anyway, so I think I need to kick Hawk and Layla's arses in Virtuball before I can actually sleep."

Hawkeye snorted. "Not bloody likely."

"Do we have to play Virtuball? You two always gang up on me," Layla huffed.

They'd never played before, but her acting skills came across well for selling whatever ruse she and Hawkeye were concocting.

"Yep, we do. I'm the one in need of distraction, so it's my pick. Sorry!" Flit walked over, giving her father and mother each a kiss on the cheek. "Good night, guys. This is gonna be a competitive night, so there's little chance I'll be coming out. See you both in the morning."

Both Tinker and Stride appeared pleased that Flit had found something to distract herself, and she was fairly certain she heard her mother whisper "thanks" to Hawkeye before they disappeared into her room.

When the door was shut behind them, Flit leaned back against the door and crossed her arms over her chest. "So, what's going on?"

Layla perked up. "We thought it was time we paid my contacts a visit," she said, glancing between Flit and Hawkeye. "It's been a while, and given how things down here are unfolding, we need to touch base before it gets more difficult to move around unnoticed."

"I wouldn't put it past my parents to check in later tonight," Flit warned, focusing her attention on Hawkeye.

The remote-viewer gestured to the bed. "I'm sure some strategically placed pillows and clothes under the blankets will convince them that we all fell asleep in here."

Flit shrugged. "Wouldn't be the first time."

"I'll stay back to make sure everything's okay. I'm sure you and Layla can handle this," Hawkeye said, putting the console controllers down and turning the screen in Flit's room on. "If you're not back in a couple of hours, I'll be worried. You shouldn't need longer than that."

"Are you good with this?" Flit asked Layla.

"If Hawk trusts you, so do I."

"Naw, now that's just cute."

Flit pushed herself off the door and walked around Layla and Hawkeye to go to her wardrobe. She retrieved a dark leather jacket. She shrugged it on over her black tank and then got to her knees, pulling an old, shoe-box sized metal crate out from the back of the cupboard. Flit opened it to reveal some flame grenades and interference goop she had managed to stash down there.

"Where did you—" Hawkeye paused, shaking his head. "Actually, I don't want to know. I shouldn't be surprised you're stashing heat. You're probably squirrelling it away at every opportunity you can get."

Flit got back to her feet and kicked the now empty box to the back of her wardrobe and tucked the flame grenades into her pockets. She opened the jar of goop and smeared some across her cheeks then passed the jar over to an alarmed-looking Layla. "I like being prepared. I'm sure we won't need any of it."

Layla took the jar and smeared her cheeks with the goop as well.

"You better not need it." Hawkeye's voice holding a hint of warning that Flit felt went deeper than just safety concerns. He stepped closer, resting his hand on the small of Layla's back. "All you need to do is check in with the Citizen Derivates. That's it."

"And Scraps," Flit said.

Hawkeye frowned. "You're not going to disappear into the bedroom again and leave Layla waiting, are you?"

Ignoring Hawkeye's jibe, Flit reached her arms out for Layla.

Layla stepped closer without hesitation but did look back over her shoulder. "I'll see you later. Don't worry about us. I trust the others with my life."

Hawkeye did not seem as confident and grimaced. "Do you need a picture of the safe house again?"

Flit shook her head. "Nope. It's all up here." She tapped the side of her head and winked before wrapping her arms around Layla. "Ready?"

Layla nodded, and after a deep breath and purposeful moment of concentration from Flit, the pair disappeared from Flit's bedroom and appeared in the deserted living room of the safe house. They stood side by side, facing the door the others had entered through last time. Flit could only hope their presence would trigger the same alarms as it had previously.

"I'll never get over how cool that is," Layla said with a low whistle.

"Yeah, it's pretty fun." Flit figured there was no point in

humility when it was genuinely cool. "How are you going with your powers, by the way? I know you never really got a chance to train them properly."

The smile on Layla's face brightened. "Pretty well. Cogs is… She's a genius. I'm lucky to be working with her. The only thing I could really do was mess around with physical cells and stuff. Heating, cooling, breaking, that kind of thing. Tech was never really my thing, but I'm becoming more interested—and more competent—with it now."

"That's good. And how are you settling into the Underground in general?"

"It was a lot at first," she said with a sheepish shrug. "Harmony and Divvy put some restrictions on what we could and couldn't share. It made it really hard to settle in because when I was around others, I had to watch every single thought."

That piqued Flit's interest. "What sort of stuff did they prohibit?"

"All of the stuff about Citizen—" She paused, almost as if choking. Then, her lips pressed tight, and she shook her head.

The look of utter resignation on her face made Flit furious. "That coercion must be bloody strong."

"They renew it every couple of days," Layla confessed. "It's why we're all in the temporary rooms and not the Residence. It's easier to contain us."

"Why doesn't Fortune stop it?" Flit couldn't imagine she would be happy about the arrangement.

"She's been working on expanding her reach to a radius rather than touch, but we can't risk it working and someone spilling the beans," Layla admitted. "Besides, the information won't have much impact on anything really. It's more just historical stuff. Interesting, sure, but not critical. I don't know why they want to hide it to be honest."

Flit lowered her voice to a whisper. "Is it the stuff about spontaneous Derivacy?"

The way Layla's eyes widened meant Flit could tell she had hit the jackpot. "How did you find out?"

"I have my ways." Flit shrugged. She decided it was probably better to steer the conversation away from her *ways*. "I guess Hawkeye knowing too meant it was easier to relax around him, hey? I'm glad to see you've moved past threatening to turn his brains to mush."

Layla's entire body tensed, and it took Flit several seconds too long to realise she had fucked up.

Flit had a fond and vivid memory of the first time Hawkeye and Layla had met. The look on his face when she had pinned him to the ground and threatened him like that had been part fear and part admiration. It was rare that Hawkeye met anyone who could get a good punch in on him, but Layla had managed it. However, following that meeting, Fortune had agreed to use her telecoercion to encourage her people to forget they ever saw Flit and Scraps. There was no doubt the Underground would use their telepaths and postcogs to figure out where the newcomers had found out about them, and Flit and Scraps couldn't afford that suspicion. Whilst Flit had fond memories of witnessing that highly amusing interaction firsthand, Layla would have been convinced that she didn't meet Flit until after she had been recalled.

"I-I, uh..." Flit stammered, looking away and trying to think of a good excused.

"Hawk told you about that?" Layla blushed and pressed her lips together.

Relief flooded through Flit, and she put a hand on Layla's shoulder. "Oh, don't worry! He didn't tell me much more than that." Then, she stopped and frowned. "Actually, he's told me very little since I got back. He's always been pretty private about relationships."

"Except for when he liked you..."

Flit could have choked on her own tongue at that comment. She had no idea what to say beyond, "I, uh, I actually didn't know about that. I think I was the last person to find out."

"That's what he told me," Layla confessed. "So, you're really not into him, huh?"

"Eww. Fuck no." Flit's reaction to that was visceral enough that a laugh spluttered from Layla. "He's my best friend, of course, and an infuriatingly good guy. But kissing him? Nuh-uh. Definitely not something I'll do ever again."

"Sorry. I know it's none of my business..." Layla trailed off, a pretty pink blush dusting the apples of her cheeks. "He just talks about you a lot. Worries about you."

"We've been through a lot together. That's just what he does," Flit promised, "and really, why wouldn't he talk about me a lot? I'm fucking awesome."

The cocky comment had the impact Flit was hoping for as Layla laughed again. The tension in her shoulders eased, and she turned to smile at Flit. Flit bumped her with her hip and grinned.

"I don't have to go all BFF on your arse and warn you not to hurt him, do I?" Flit asked, adding a threat of playful toughness to her tone.

Layla shook her head. "Nope. No intention of doing that. Even if things don't work out between us, I'll always appreciate how much he has help me settle and process things."

That response, while not a surprise, still warmed Flit's heart. Even though she was not attracted to Hawkeye, she really believed he deserved someone to cherish him for the wonderful person he was. It was one of the reasons they had been friends for almost as long as they could talk. Flit had brought out a bit of bravery and fire in the shy boy, and he had taught her restraint. Well, he had at least *tried* to teach her.

"Please don't tell me the most interesting thing you two have to talk about is some guy. That's disappointing for two bad-arses like you."

Flit didn't need to look to know who it was. The mumble of muffled music through headphones was a dead giveaway.

"Iris!"

Once again, Layla leapt at Iris and nearly tackled the woman with an enthusiastic embrace. It was a lovely sight, even given the dilapidated surroundings. It was odd, though, as Iris appeared to be alone. As much as Flit was pleased there wasn't a cranky, gun-toting pink-haired person aiming a rifle at her, she worried for Iris.

"Mitch is on the way. Don't worry," Iris said, plucking the concern straight from Flit's head.

"Have you tried heavy metal instead? Surely the more enthusiastic drumming would be doing a better job of keeping you out of my head than that electro-synth shit."

Iris's laugh was full and high. "Oh, I should have known you'd be a metal kinda girl with that coat."

Just like Hawkeye didn't flinch when Flit teleported erratically around him, Layla didn't even question the odd conversation Iris seemed to be in the middle of. Flit smiled to herself. Friendships were wonderful yet undoubtedly odd things.

"So, as much as I'm pleased to see you, to what do I owe the pleasure? I assume you didn't come all this way for a hug?" Iris kept an arm around Layla as she looked between Flit and her friend.

The comment was enough to dull Layla's shine and have her let out a heavy sigh. "The leaders in the Underground are imposing more restrictions. Hawkeye wanted me to check in because we don't know when the next chance will be."

"If the leaders are getting like that, then how do you propose any real alliance will work?" came Mitch's voice as they stepped up behind Iris.

"If they keep going the way they are, they won't be the leaders for much longer," Flit said matter-of-factly, expressing something the Blue Team had danced around but not acknowledged in their meeting earlier.

To Layla's credit, she didn't even flinch at the comment.

Mitch did not seem pleased, though. "And how do you expect us to trust a splinter cell who are planning to overthrow their leaders? What's to say you won't stab us in the back the moment you get the chance."

The question made tension radiate through Flit's jaw as she gritted her teeth.

"They're not doing this lightly," Layla said in a tone that was meant to placate Mitch, but it only annoyed Flit even more.

"We've been stuck down there for a century, and every round of leadership has progressively forgotten the fact that humans weren't meant to live in the dark." Flit crossed her arms over her chest.

Mitch appeared to cling to their gun a little more tightly, but Flit ignored the gesture for the intimidation tactic it was.

"We can't do it anymore, especially given what's happening up here. There has never been a better time to fight back, and if we don't take it, we might as well seal ourselves in the tomb we've made down there." Flit kept her arms crossed and her chin high. There was not a single doubt in her mind about this pathway, and she wasn't about to let concerns from someone who had no idea what the Underground was like change that.

"And you still want us to be a part of that?" Mitch kept their hands on their weapon, but their shoulders sank, and some of the tension in the room eased.

Layla stepped forward, pulling away from the shelter of Iris' body and putting herself more in Mitch's line of sight. "We *need* you to be part of that," Layla said earnestly. "Did you have any luck with your Drone contacts?"

A ripple of anger ran down Flit's spine and made her flinch. Flit was about to correct the language when Iris caught her gaze and subtly shook her head. She pressed her lips together to stop herself from spitting out her protest.

"Actually, we did." Mitch lowered the weapon completely as they turned to face Layla.

At least you trust her, Flit thought to herself spitefully.

The corner of Iris's lip quirked up.

"The numbers of possible defectors they gave us were higher than I expected," Mitch continued, apparently oblivious to Flit's annoyance. "We'll need help to get them out, but we should be able to shelter them."

The urge to say *"I told you so"* was strong enough that Flit had to bite her tongue to stop herself. Instead, she took a steadying breath and asked, "What kind of help do you need?"

"Anything we can get," Iris blurted, earning her an annoyed look from Mitch.

Flit couldn't help but wonder if Mitch ever had a light or friendly thing to say.

Iris snorted. "Nope. Never."

Both Mitch and Layla frowned, but Mitch ploughed on, "We have plenty of room for them to hide, but that's the extent of it. We can't risk anymore of our own people. Our numbers are too low."

"Then give me their details. I have a contact who may be able to help with the extraction," Flit said, knowing Scraps would make it a priority. "He doesn't have shelter for them, though, so this sounds like a good arrangement."

Mitch scratched their pink hair and frowned. "You want me to just give you the details? Just like—"

"Do it," Iris said, her tone more decisive and serious than Flit had heard from her so far. "She's not here to fuck around, Mitch. I don't know who her guy is, but she's convinced this will work."

Flit wasn't sure whether to be annoyed at the intrusion or grateful for the support.

"I'd go with grateful," Iris suggested.

With a heavy sigh, Mitch said, "You'd better not fuck this up."

"Oh, don't worry," Flit said with a confident grin. "I won't."

43

———

SCRAPS

SCRAPS SAT on a stool at the kitchen bench in his apartment eating a microwaved meal. He had left Nightmix half an hour earlier after a full day of training Citizens. It had been a long, exhausting day, and Adam's annoyance had lasted the entire time. The leader had spent his time in constant communication with Andy and her team of hackers as they worked their technological magic to stay ahead of the Government tracing.

The meal tasted bland to Scraps, but he supposed it was because he was also tired and not really paying attention to what he was eating. He was too busy thinking about having a shower and heading straight to bed when sudden movement in the lounge room made him jump. The container his meal was in clattered to the floor, splattering the smooth surface with pasta and sauce.

"Woah, it's okay. It's just us." Flit held up her hands, and her leather jacket creaked. She was dressed casually, with a black tank and well-loved cargo pants. She stepped away from Layla and smiled. "Sorry to surprise you."

There was not a single surprise that Scraps would have welcomed more in that moment. He carefully stepped over the spilled food and walked over to pull Flit into a tight embrace.

He nodded at Layla in greeting before dipping his head and pressing a kiss against Flit's hair. "You do not need to be sorry. I'm happy to see you."

Flit let out a soft sigh and rested her head on his chest. The tender moment was short lived, though.

Flit took a deep breath and looked up at him, forcing him to pull back slightly so he could look at her properly. "We need to talk."

Her features shifted into that determined expression he knew all too well. Given Layla's presence, he guessed that she was there on business.

Gesturing to the couch, Scraps suggested, "Then why don't we sit down?"

The trio moved over to the main lounge room area and sank down onto the comfortable couch. After the day he had, Scraps wished he could just take Flit's hand and disappear into the bedroom with her. He would have been ecstatic to just be able to hold her through the night.

"So, Layla and I just spent some time with her Citizen Derivates," Flit explained, diving right in. "They have some Registered contacts who they say want out."

That interested Scraps. Given that he already knew a Registered who wanted to escape the Government, it was not a surprise to find there were more. It did make him curious, though, as to how many of his previous comrades had broken free of the brainwashing on their own. He wondered why he had been so indoctrinated. The Underground had to put a great deal of effort into reversing the Government's impact on him.

"How can I help?" he asked.

Flit smiled at him. "They're able to house them, but they do not have the resources or ability to break them out."

"They've always been more focused on being a refuge than activists," Layla explained, shifting to the edge of her seat. "They're not well trained, either. It was safer for us to just mind our own business and focus on staying alive rather than trying to learn about the traits that had us on a wanted list."

"That makes sense." Scraps was not going to judge her people for trying to survive. "I will see what I can do to help. I have my own Registered contact who I want to break out. I wonder if they know each other."

"These ones work in the sanitation department," Flit explained.

"They've been given a lot of extra duties now, due to the Government's preparations. However, they are still picking up the garbage on the route in the early mornings. They have just cut the evening shift, is all."

One of the reasons the Hub always looked so clean was because the Government had a meticulous sanitation schedule. Garbage routes were worked twice a day, with Derivate staff assigned to switching on the incinerators below each city building on each visit. Initially, it had been a job that was given to Citizens, but following some unsavoury incidences and criminal uses of the incinerators, the positions were reassigned. Scraps supposed it was also far cheaper to get the Derivates to do it anyway, so the Government could spend the money they would have used on wages elsewhere.

"So, I should be able to make contact with them during their shifts?" Scraps asked, pleased that they were working those jobs. They would probably be far easier to contact than people who worked under close observation of Government officials.

"In theory, yes." Flit straightened up. "However, they are all assigned to different security details with these new changed the Government has made. It means that their disappearance is going to make quite a splash."

That was going to be a problem. Scraps leaned forward as his mind ran through the resources at his disposal. "How many people are we talking?"

"Twenty-four that we know of." Layla rested her hands on her lap, but her fingers were pressed hard enough against the fabric of her cargo pants that the tips of them were turning white.

"It's a good start," Flit said, smiling at her. "Hopefully we can get more out later."

Twenty-four was a lot to get in one go. However, he supposed it was probably better that way. The Government would be on guard the instant they realised their assets were missing. As much as he would prefer to take a couple at a time, it wasn't practical.

"What are we going to do about the chips? There's no point getting them out if their kill-switch activates." As Scraps spoke, his hand instinctively drifted to the back of his neck and over the skin where he used to have a scar from the removal of his own chip. It had been removed when his physical appearance was changed for his undercover identity, but there were days where he swore he could still feel it.

The look on Flit's face told him that she hadn't considered this. "If Layla's people can't do anything about them, let me know. I'll bring you someone who can."

"Understood." Scraps looked out the floor-to-ceiling window at the city beyond. He was home earlier than usual tonight, and the lights of the city were still slowly blinking to life beyond his walls. It was a reminder of how vast the Government's capital was. "How will I know I've got the right people?"

"The team you're looking for start at building South Eight-East Nine at four in the morning and work their way west," Flit explained. "Layla's group are only in South Six-East Eleven. I'll give you the coordinates, but you won't have far to get them."

Scraps' mind drifted to his mission earlier that morning and just how problematic Government surveillance had been to the outcome of that. "How do we avoid detection on the cameras?"

"The team have a few micros," Layla said, perking up. "Nowhere near as skilled as Cogs and the others from the Underground, but they've practice messing with Government tech."

"That is good," Scraps said, "but I would need to contact them prior to the mission to ensure I do not inadvertently put them at risk during the handover."

"Oh!" Flit reached beneath the collar of the dark jacket she was wearing and gingerly pulled a long silver chain up and over her head, careful not to smudge the interference goop on her cheeks.

Flit held it out to Scraps, and he noticed a simple pressed metal circle on the end. He took it from her and inspected it closer, and his eyes widened in surprise as he saw a coin like the ones he used to read about as a child, a form of currency used well before the Government formed. There were so many of the coins around that they were abundant in museums and private collections, but seeing one dangling off the end of a chain had to be rare.

Gesturing to the necklace, Flit said, "This belongs to their leader. If you show them this, they'll know it's you. I've given them a physical description too."

"Don't worry. They won't shoot you on sight," Layla promised.

Until Layla mentioned shooting, it hadn't been a concern of Scraps. Truth be told, he was more worried about it now that she brought it up than he would have been if she had said nothing at all. He supposed she was trying to be helpful, though, and thanked her anyway.

"They also have one of the emergency beacon charms. They can use that if they have trouble with the chips or anything." Flit looked down at Scraps' chest.

Sensing what she was looking for, he reached down his shirt and retrieved the emergency charm she had given him previously. Then, he draped the necklace with the coin over his head and tucked both pieces into his shirt.

Scraps was just about to ask how things were going in the Underground when there was a knock on his door. He, Flit, and Layla all froze.

"Who would that be?" Flit whispered, her body tensing as if she was prepared to fight.

"Probably a couple of Free Citizens," Scraps lied as he got to his feet. He didn't actually know who it was, but it didn't matter. He couldn't let anyone know Flit was there.

Even though Flit pressed her lips together and peered past him, she nodded. "I should go then, I suppose."

The look on her face told him that she didn't want to, but they both knew their time was up.

Scraps cupped her cheek, brushing his thumb over her soft skin as he leaned down to kiss her. "Stay safe," he told her, even though he was fairly certain she wasn't the one in possible imminent danger.

"Always," she whispered nonchalantly. "I love you." She stole another kiss but teleported away before it could reach a point that would have been considered lingering.

Flit reappeared beside Layla, who stood and smoothed her pants down. Flit gave Scraps a lazy farewell salute and wrapped her arms around Layla. The two disappeared, and Scraps took a moment to suck in a deep steadying breath before he walked over to the door and opened it.

One moment, Scraps was opening his mouth to greet Greene and Hector, and the next, CC-9832 and TB-219 stepped out behind the agents, holding guns and pointing them at him.

"I strongly suggest you let us in," Hector grunted, keeping his voice low.

Blood running cold with adrenaline, Scraps stepped back and tried to calculate his best option. He considered using his ability to shove the intruders out of the way, but without knowing what they wanted, it might be premature.

"Of course." Scraps stepped to the side and turned, keeping his back to the wall. If they walked in far enough, he could slip out past them if need be.

"Get where we can see you in the middle of the room." Hector's tone indicated that there would be no negotiating.

Scraps did as he was told and raised his hands, keeping his palms forward so they could see he was not carrying anything.

When the agents and the Registereds entered his apartment, CC-9832 shut the front door.

"What's going on?" Scraps asked, looking between the agents.

"Don't play dumb with us," Hector snapped. "We know the Free Citizens were involved in that incursion at the server farm. We need to know what they did there and why you didn't inform us of it. Don't bother trying to lie about it, either. We have proof."

Scraps was just about to open his mouth when CC-9832 spoke. "Agent Hector, remain exactly in that position. Do not speak or vocalise in any way."

The command in his voice was strong, but being classified as a level C, Scraps knew the telecoercion would likely only last a short while. Both Derivates turned their weapon on Hector. Scraps' eyes widened, but he kept his attention on Greene.

"Listen closely, Parkes. I will say this once and once only," Green muttered under her breath, her striking blue eyes catching his and freezing him in place. "I used to believe in the Government, but lately, they've been getting it all wrong. It isn't about 'for the good of all' anymore. It is just mindless control. The Free Citizens are right. Something needs to change. For that to happen, you need to leave. You need to remain hidden. I don't trust Adam, but TB-

219 trusts you. Go back to the Free Citizens and make sure Adam doesn't ruin things."

Shock kept Scraps silent. He dared not move out of concern that this was some sort of trick.

"You don't have long, *Brian*," TB-219 hissed, emphasizing his cover name. "Pack a bag and go. The Government has decided that they no longer want you as an informant if they cannot trust you."

The concern that had been haunting Scraps over the past weeks reared at the telepath's comment. *"Do they know I'm a Derivate?"*

TB-219 shook her head almost imperceptibly.

That gave Scraps a small measure of relief.

"I am working on a plan to get you and some other Registereds out," Scraps thought as he backed slowly towards the hallway. *"If I send a message and some instructions to your private inbox, will you be able to respond?"*

TB-219 seemed to think it over for a moment before nodding. Scraps wasn't sure how she would make it work, but that was something she would need to figure out. He just had to trust her.

"Parkes, we don't have time to stuff around. Move it!" Greene barked, sounding more impatient than Scraps had heard her before. He gathered it had to do with the fact she was clearly doing something her partner would not agree with.

Scraps did not need to be told twice. He raced into the bedroom and pulled the hidden panel off the floor in the closet to retrieve an empty black duffel. After filling it with his modest stash of weapons and supplies, he ran to his dresser and grabbed a couple of basic items of clothing. He was about to walk out when he saw Flit's old datapad on top of the dresser. Snatching it up, he switched off the connectivity before shoving it into his bag. Nestled on top of his clothes and weapons, it was the only thing he had on him that contained photos and messages the pair had shared. Running to the Free Citizens now mean that he would not be able to tell her how to contact him, so it would be a while before he could see her again. He wished he could leave her a message, but he had no doubt the Government would raid this place and run through it with a fine-toothed comb.

When Scraps returned to the lounge room, the intruders were still in exactly the same position.

Greene looked up at him. "We can give you a five minute head start," she warmed him, glancing at CC-9832 for confirmation. The telecoercionist nodded. "After that, I won't be able to protect you. Get yourself to the Free Citizens. Please, for the love of freedom, make sure Adam doesn't turn this into something we will all regret."

Even though his mind was still whirring with this new turn of events, Scraps nodded. He was not about to let his shock or confusion get in the way of his survival. He gave the agent a crisp, respectful salute before he walked briskly towards the door.

"Thank you, TB-219. I will reach out to you soon. I hope you and CC-9832 stay safe," Scraps thought before he left his apartment for what might be the last time.

44

———

FLIT

UPON RETURNING TO THE UNDERGROUND, Flit could not shake off the discomfort of how she and Layla had to leave Scraps behind. Even though he had guessed it was the Free Citizens, the way that his posture had stiffened indicated that they were not necessarily welcome guests.

"Hey, are you okay?" Layla asked, breaking from her whispered debrief with Hawkeye to look at her.

Shaking herself free of her own thoughts, Flit nodded. "Yeah, I just wish we had time to figure out what the Free Citizens were up to."

A grim expression settled on Hawkeye's face. "Maybe we can have another game night tomorrow, and you can go up and check?"

Tomorrow felt like forever away with the worry churning in Flit's gut, but it would have to do. She had no idea how long the Free Citizens would be with Scraps tonight, so it was the safest option. "Sounds like a plan."

Hawkeye and Layla stayed with Flit, and the trio connected some of the gaming controllers to play for a while. Flit found it difficult to get her head into it. It was hard to concentrate on fun and games when there was so much going to shit in the world around her. However, when she realised Hawkeye was going soft on Layla and inadvertently giving her an advantage in the game, Flit's competitive nature reared its sleepy head.

It was almost early morning by the time Layla and Hawkeye left. Flit made her way to have a shower, tired and yawning but feeling far lighter for the company. She collapsed into bed feeling as though she had lived several weeks in the space of a day. When her eyes closed, her mind threatened to veer back to the image of Bolt imploding right in front of her. She took several long, deep breaths and imagined instead what it would like to be able to curl up against Scraps' side and to drag his arm around her. The vivid memory of feeling of his embrace, of how the rest of the world couldn't touch her in his arms, washed over her. It was a fading recollection, but it was still enough to chase away the darker thoughts for now.

Perhaps, Flit thought, she would see if she could spend more time with him the following night. The hope in that idea was enough to help lull her into a deep, exhausted slumber.

THE NEXT DAY came with a flurry of activity as the Blue Team began their power training sessions with their fellow Underground Derivates.

At first, the change of schedule had everyone mixed up. Some people showed up for the wrong sessions as they hadn't check the new rosters that were sent out. Flit and Hawkeye had to seek out Posthoc to ask him to send the updates again as an urgent, Underground-wide alert.

Once everyone knew where they were supposed to be, the mammoth task of skills assessment began. The Government, as Scraps had told Flit, had a very rigorous and structured process for this, but measuring and recording abilities was not something the Underground did as a rule. They far preferred to let the person train however they were able to, and this resulted in a very difficult system of classification.

Separating everyone by ability made it easier to work through the base-level skills, but Flit was struggling to find ways to record things methodically until her father joined her after lunch. The change in recording meant she had to go back and reclassify everyone she had tested that morning, but it was worth it. They needed to get a move on and enact the great idea Hawkeye had. They would pair them up with Derivates of other ability types, so they could test their own powers and learn more about others. Flit was also grateful for her father's help because it meant he was in charge of keeping the young kids in her post-lunch group in line.

Despite attempts of various people to try and maintain the fact that certain powers had little reflection on a wielder's personality, there were some stereotypes that Flit just found held true, particularly for teleporters. As she sat and attempted to reorganise names into the columns her father had suggested, she had to work hard to ignore the way her father frequently had to call out particular children and ask them to relax.

A lot of the other groups would be facing their own issues by having so many of the same power type in one room. Flit could only imagine that the deafening silence in the telepathy room would be pierced by arguments when less favourable thoughts were snatched from minds. She also pictured Swipe having her hands full, trying to keep the younger macrokinetics from throwing each other around too much.

The teleporters, though? With so many kids in one space, all trying to dart around the room, it became a genuine, life-threatening hazard. All it would take is for two kids to decide to teleport to the same apparently empty spot, and—

"Shimmer!" Stride called out, voice firm. The tone made Flit think back to all the times he had told her off as a child. "For the last time, stay put! You almost clipped into the window last time. Do you want me to have to explain to your parents why we returned you with only one arm?" For emphasis, he held up his own prosthetic arm and waved it about.

Stride's prosthetic was a pretty good stand-in, but even Shimmer's little brown eyes widened as she noticed the way the limb didn't quite move as normal. She grabbed her right arm with her left and shook her head. She seemed resolved to stay put after that, but the warning didn't deter any of the other cheeky kids.

Eventually, Flit worked her way through the recording side of things and was able to join her father. Together, they started doing the skills check with the kids. As expected, there was a ride range of competency.

Before beginning training that morning, Flit had been dreading the initial drudgery of the testing and admin. However, as they wrapped up, she found herself surprisingly exhilarated by the process. Some of the other Derivates seemed to think of their powers as just another part of them, as something as simple as their vocal tone or visual acuity. Flit was fascinated by it, though. The small differences between what one person was able to do but another struggled with was a point of interest for her.

Assessing her fellow teleporters gave Flit a chance to see just how nuanced and individual each person's ability really was. It made the idea of a simple, Government-like classification system seem even more foolish. There were some who could move items around easier than themselves and others who had incredible long-range skills but struggled to do short hops. The variance in the abilities was puzzling. Flit found she was keen to work with her comrades to try and enhance their abilities, and for a moment, she could almost forget why they were doing it.

When they finished their assessments, Flit sent the files through to Hawkeye, and then she and her father started packing up. As they did, a question came to Flit's mind that she had never considered before. She looked over at her father as he stacked some of the seats the kids had sat on whilst waiting for their turn.

"Hey, Dad." Flit put her datapad onto standby, tucked it under her arm, and teleported to a standing position.

Stride paused, eyebrows furrowing. "What's up? Did we forget something?"

"No, we're all good." Flit leaned back against the wall and crossed her arms over her chest. "I was just wondering what you would be doing if we didn't have to deal with all this."

"Probably helping your mother sort out some medical supplies."

A laugh spluttered from Flit. "No, I meant 'all of this' in general. Like, say we didn't have to worry about the Government or the Underground. If we were just free to be us... what would you be?"

The question clearly stumped Stride. Flit could relate. When the thought had occurred to her earlier, she'd realised it was never something she had considered. She wondered if anyone in the Underground had. For so long, they had been focused on survival, on putting one foot in front of the other, on protecting themselves, that the idea they could do anything else felt abstract.

Flit had spent a lot of time preaching about how the Underground needed to work for their freedom, but she had never really thought about what she would do with it if she actually got it.

"I've never really thought about it." Stride frowned as he rested his elbow on the stack of chairs beside himself and drummed his fingers on the seat of the top one. "Being in Supply is really just a way to pass my time. I haven't given much thought to what else I could do." He seemed to shake himself out of the melancholy the thought was luring him towards and smiled. "Why? Do you know what you'd like to do?"

"Not really," Flit confessed, alarmed by how little she had been able to dream beyond the mere basics of not being persecuted for the simple act of existing. "But today was quite fun, and I'm looking forward to working with people to get the best out of their powers. Maybe something like that?"

Stride gazed at her as he rubbed his salt-and-pepper, stubble-coated jaw. After a minute, he nodded. "I could see that. You've worked so hard to get where you are. You would have some really valuable insight to share with others."

The way he said it made Flit grin.

"Maybe you can speak to Posthoc about a change of assignments? A lot of the training has fallen onto Shadow lately. I'm sure he'd like someone else to help."

Cold hard reality slapped Flit across the face. She stood there, just blinking. That was not what she had been asking. She wanted to know what he would do if they were free. She was tempted to correct her father, to tell him that she had no intention to do that, but she decided to keep her mouth shut. As much as she loved him, she didn't know if he would approve of the scheme the Blue Team was brewing, and she didn't want him to get caught up in it.

AFTER DINNER, there was a knock on the apartment door. Flit was the first to answer it. As she was expecting, Layla and Hawkeye were on the other side wearing matching smiles and holding game controllers. Tinker and Stride welcomed them in with great enthusiasm, and Flit knew her parents were pleased that she seemed to be getting back to "normal". She felt guilty for lying to her parents, but it was necessary.

Flit, Layla, and Hawkeye made their way to her room and shut the door as they had the night before. Hawkeye walked over to connect the controllers. Flit pulled off the dressing gown she had donned after showering earlier to reveal a comfortable pair of tights and a tank. It was her usual, go-to outfit, but she knew Scraps wouldn't be expecting her to dress up for him. He was never overly bothered about that kind of thing.

"We can stay here for the night if you like. We'll blanket-and-pillow-pile your bed, but your parents seem to leave us alone once we're in here," Hawkeye said, moving to sit at the end of the bed beside Layla.

"You sure I can trust you two alone in here?" Flit asked as she combed her fingers through her hair and eyed her best friend.

Hawkeye leaned back on his hands and cocked an eyebrow at Flit. "I don't know. Can you?"

All Flit could do was laugh as Hawkeye's face grew smug. She had plenty of comebacks, but she decided to let him have this one. She liked Layla, and she enjoyed the way her company brought back some of the lightness in Hawkeye's personality.

"Right. Well, I'll see you two later. Don't wait up." Flit winked at them before she translocated.

In the blink of an eye, Flit found herself in the apartment in the Hub.

Except... it was nothing like how she left it.

The first thing she noticed was how the wall panels had been torn off to expose the pipes and wires behind. Shattered crockery lined the cupboards and peppered parts of the floor. Every single door except for the front was wide open, and anything that could be disassembled was lying in parts of the floor.

Flit froze, her heart stalling in her chest. Her mind slammed her into the past, to the last time she had arrived in the Hub with such anticipation, only to find her lover's home trashed.

"Scraps?"

His name tumbled from her lips in a startled cry.

She launched into action, teleporting down the hall. She looked into the bedroom to find the place in complete disarray. Her eyes darted around the room as fast as her brain could process, and all she could see was chaos.

"Scraps?" She teleported across the bedroom and into the bathroom. "Shit, Scraps?"

Flit could hear the increasing desperation in her own voice. She ran back into the bedroom and fell to her knees on the pile of clothes at the foot of the wardrobe. She pulled at the floor panel, only to find that their secret hiding place had been completely emptied of contents.

The sound of the front door opening echoed through the space, and Flit translocated back into the lounge room.

"Scraps, thank—" she started, her frazzled mind naively hoping for the best.

Instead, she came face to face with the laser-sights of half a dozen Government-issued rifles.

Several red spots settled on her chest.

"Oh, fuck."

Before the agents could squeeze their triggers, Flit was gone.

The instant her feet reappeared on the floor of her bedroom, she fell to her knees, panting.

Layla and Hawkeye, who were sitting on the end of her bed and kissing enthusiastically, sprung apart.

Hawkeye was at her side in an instant. "Flit? Oh, shit. What happened?"

Flit looked into the familiar green eyes of her oldest friend, and she could sense herself spiralling back to a dark place she couldn't afford to go. It felt too easy to do when she was around him.

She shook her head as she jumped to her feet. "I... I can't... I'm sorry," she muttered before turning and bolting from her room.

Even as Flit fled the apartment, Hawkeye, Layla, and her parents calling after her, she had no idea where she was going. It wasn't until a few minutes later, when she had burst into the corridor of holding cells that had been repurposed into bedrooms for the facility refugees that she realised where her feet had taken her.

"Fortune?"

The voice that cried out from Flit sounded strangled even to herself.

A door farther down the corridor opened, and Flit sobbed. She teleported to where Fortune stood and collapsed into her waiting arms.

"H-He's gone, Fortune," Flit blurted. "Scraps is g-gone."

Flit was barely cognisant as Fortune gently guided her into one of the small, cell-like rooms and sat her on a lumpy bed with scratchy, overly-starched sheets.

Fortune put a hand under Flit's chin and tilted it up. She looked directly into her eyes. "Tell me everything," she whispered with such compassion that Flit broke.

45

———

SCRAPS

THE NEXT MORNING, Scraps woke to his early alarm with a blaring headache. He sat up, keeping the blankets close against his chest as he rubbed his eyes. The radio static and chatter that had become the constant soundtrack to his new living quarters were just as loud as they had been all night. It was hard to get away from the noise, and the crates of guns that he had stacked around the corner he was sleeping in did little to create a buffer.

As much as Scraps wanted to go back to bed, he had set his alarm for a reason. He got out of bed and stretched his arms and legs. With the amount of people coming and going from the bunker, he'd decided it would be better to sleep in his clothes rather than pyjamas. He wanted to be ready for anything or anyone.

When Scraps walked out of his makeshift corner shelter, he noted that Andy and the small team of hackers Adam had relocated to the basement were hard at work. Even with the growing pile of energy supplement wrappers building up on the desks, Scraps still marvelled at the stamina of the group. It was three AM in the morning, and they were still up. They had been working nonstop on their devices, dialled into the chip Scraps had put in the Government server. At first, their priority had been deleting or altering security footage to remove evidence of the identity of the strike team members, but that had quickly given way to using the uplink to lay false leads for the Government to work through as well as divert the attention of the micros who were trying to find the location of the network breach.

Scraps was about to bypass the group and head for the walkway that led to the club and the restrooms, when a growl from Adam made him stop in his tracks.

"What do you mean, only twelve hours?"

Adam walked over to stand behind Andy. Or, Scraps thought, stand *over* her.

"We're doing everything we can, Adam. They're throwing more micros at us than we can handle." The teal-haired hacker barely glanced at him. "Unless you can get us another team, then we'll be lucky to last half a day."

Even standing a few metres away, Scraps heard Adam's breath rattle through his tense frame at that revelation. "I'll get you back-up," he snapped before turning and stalking over to his desk. He didn't even look up as Scraps walked past.

After sorting himself out in the restroom, Scraps returned to the little corner he had claimed as his own. So far, he was the only member of the strike team who had needed to seek refuge. Adam had questioned this initially. If the Government had gotten through Andy's camera patches, why hadn't they found the others? Scraps had palmed it off to the fact that he had such a high clearance level. Luckily, there were no telepaths around to know he was lying and expose his liaisons with Greene and Hector.

The fact Greene had allowed Scraps to go still stunned him. He had known that TB-219 was doing her best to keep his secrets hidden, but finding out that CC-9832 and Agent Greene were complicit was a revelation, to be sure. Just over a year ago, Scraps had been utterly brainwashed by the Government. The only dissenters he had known were the ones he had dragged back to the Hub and thrown in cells. Why would they speak up against the organisation promising order and stability?

Scraps knew better now, of course, but there was a web of shame wrapping itself around his organs that grew every time he learned how many people had broken free of the lies without needing so much intervention. What was wrong with him that he had been so utterly susceptible?

Returning to his little refuge, Scraps retrieved the datapad he had packed from his apartment in his rush to escape. He tapped the screen to bring it to life and looked down at the message that was waiting for him.

To: Brian Parkes
From: Government Transport Allocation Service
Subject: Bus Schedule
Dear Mr. Parkes,
Thank you for your inquiry. As requested, the shuttle bus you have booked will be at South Eight-East Nine at 4:30 AM. Your driver will be on a strict schedule, so please note that delays or last-minute route alterations will not be allowed.
Kind regards,
Tania Bates
Booking Agent 219

An odd mix of relief and concern made Scraps sit straighter. He had spent the previous day covertly concocting a rescue plan for the Citizen Derivate's contacts between training the Free Citizens in combat. It wasn't easy, as Adam seemed to want to consult with him in every spare moment. Whilst the leader was talking about the different bases they had secured and how they were trying to organise a final delivery of weapons and armour, Scraps was too busy trying to figure out how to get his ex-colleagues away from the grip of the Government.

In the end, Scraps realised that the best way to get the Registereds out was trying to use the Government's own resources. With the amount of officers lining the streets to provide extra security these days, anything else would be too suspicious.

Scraps' entire plan relied heavily on assistance. It had been a risk, reaching out to TB-219, but the creative message she had sent him had been entirely worth it.

Provided the plan went off without a hitch.

There was just one more thing Scraps needed to do.

He set the datapad aside and got dressed in a dark grey sweat pants and a black hooded jumper. He put on some running shoes and made his way over to the makeshift tech station.

Thankfully, Adam's tantrum minutes ago meant that he was busy over by his own desk, which gave Scraps free passage to walk over to Andy. He rested his hand on the back of her chair and squatted down beside her.

"Andy, I apologise for the intrusion... but I have a favour to ask of you that is of an urgent nature," Scraps whispered.

For a moment, Scraps thought she had ignored him. Just as he was about to ask her again, she tapped her projected keyboard assertively even though there was no tactile reason to and then got to her feet.

"I'm due for a bio break. Walk with me," she said. She didn't wait for him as she turned and strode towards the exit.

Scraps waited until they were out of view and, hopefully, earshot of the bunker to say, "I know you are very busy, but I have a secret mission I need to go on. It would help very much if I had digital eyes and a talented hacker helping to doctor security footage."

Andy held up a hand in a motion requesting silence. Scraps nodded and pressed his lips together. They reached the bathroom, and she grabbed the sleeve of his hoodie, yanking him into the stall with her and shutting the door.

"When you say secret..."

"Adam doesn't know. Nor do I want him to."

Andy rubbed the back of her neck. "I'm pretty strapped for resources out there... but I may be able to help. How long do you need overwatch?"

"Around an hour, hopefully no more," Scraps said, the timing of his plan like clockwork in his head. "Starting in half an hour's time."

She sighed heavily. "If I do this, we will lose some of our lead on the server farm case. Is it worth it?"

"It is a matter of at least twenty-four lives and potential future allies," Scraps informed her. Given the fact she would be watching him over the various networks she would access, there was no use hiding the truth from her.

"Then I'll do it."

The unquestioning conviction in Andy's tone warmed Scraps through.

He explained the plan to her, and she didn't even flinch when he told her that he was saving Registereds. She did ask where he was planning on taking them. He was unable to give her too much in the way of details, and she did not seem bothered by the lack of information.

"Are you okay with keeping this from Adam? I know I am asking a lot of you," Scraps asked when they finished talking about the details of the plan.

Andy frowned and nodded. "I've heard him talking about Derivates before. I don't think he would take this well. Also... he's pissing me off at the moment, so he can get fucked."

A smile came unbidden to Scraps' lips at the sass in her tone. It reminded him of Flit, and he could see why the two had started getting along so well before she had been taken back to the Underground.

"Very well," Scraps said. "I'd best be going, then. Thank you."

The pair left the bathroom, and Andy returned to her station immediately. Scraps did not have much time to waste, so he went straight over to Adam, who appeared to be sending messages.

Scraps approached the leader. "I am heading out for a run. I'll be back in a bit."

Adam didn't look up from his screen, but he did frown. "I don't think that's wise. There's too much heat on you."

"It's still early morning. It will be fine," Scraps said nonchalantly. "Besides, I want to see what security is like out there for myself and see if I can work out any more emergency escape plans. You know, just in case."

"Whatever." Adam huffed with annoyance and waved a hand in Scraps' direction. "Just get back here ASAP. I have things I need you to handle."

"Copy that," Scraps said.

He jogged out of the room before Adam could rethink his decision.

HALF AN HOUR LATER, Scraps was on his second lap of South Eight-East Nine. Whilst the Derivates on guard duty along the street paid him little mind on his first lap, they seemed to notice him on the second pass. He looked at his watch as he ran, figuring it would be easy to pretend he was checking his pace, even though he was really looking at the time.

Just as the hour ticked over to four AM, he saw a bus stop in the driveway of building South Eight-East Nine. The door hissed open, and a line of Derivates filed out. They split into pairs and followed invisible paths smoothly as they dispersed between the buildings on the block. Without giving himself time to overthink it, Scraps jogged towards the garage entrance of the nearest building. He followed behind the duo heading straight for it but waited until they had opened the maintenance door beside the vehicle ramp to quicken his pace.

The Derivates stepped into the building when Scraps was about two metres away. Knowing that he had little option, Scraps held his hand up in a stop motion to telekinetically hold the door open. He figured it probably had an alarm, so he just kept his pace as he ran through. He let it shut behind him, but the Derivates spun to face him as the echoes of his footfalls must have startled them. It was hard to tell much about them with their uniforms and reflective visors, and the lighting was dim enough that he couldn't quite read their designations.

"Halt. This is a restricted entrance," the Derivate on the left warned, holding their hands up in a ready position.

The posture alone was enough to tell Scraps that this was a fellow macrokinetic. They were all trained to stand in the same way. After so much training in the Underground, Scraps saw how it restricted individual achievement and expression.

Scraps reached into the collar of his hoodie and pulled the coin on the chain out. He wasn't sure if either of other wary folk would recognise it, but he had to try. "I am here on behalf of Mitch and Iris," he said, figuring it was more truthful than saying they had asked him to be there. "We don't have long, but I am going to get you and the others to safety."

The macrokinetic flicked her visor up and stepped back, her expression was wary. The person behind her previously had their hand on the radio switch by their ear, but they lowered it.

"I know that you must be concerned right now, but I used to be like you. My designation was KC-847," Scraps said, voice low. To prove his point, he used telekinesis to rustle some wastepaper that was discarded in a corner nearby. "I worked in the Department of Law Enforcement. I managed to get free, and now I want to help you and the others do the same. We do not have much time, so we need to go. Now."

The duo remained silent throughout his entire monologue, but as he pressed the urgency of his cause, the one on the right glanced at the macrokinetic, and she nodded. He smiled at her and stepped closer to read her designation.

"What's the plan?" KD-7921's voice was low as she replaced her visor.

It took Scraps only a few seconds to explain that they needed to round up the others and meet the bus that would be parking at the corner of the block. The macrokinetic agreed to go to the next building on her own while her partner, a remote-viewer, said she would go along with Scraps so that the others believed him quicker. From there, they could use the next pairs each encountered to split up and find the others. There were twenty-two Registereds left, and if everything went off without a hitch, they should be able to make it to the corner just in time to meet TB-219.

With the plan set, the three Derivates left the first building and made their way to the street. They split up as they traversed the concourse between the next row of buildings and went their sepa-rate ways. There was little room for discussion or hesitation, but with the remote viewer at his side, Scraps was able to convince the next lot of Derivates in a matter of seconds.

Even though everything appeared to be going smoothly, Scraps did not let himself relax. He kept alert as they travelled through the city blocks and collected pair after pair. With the extra assistance, they were able to move quickly through the mission.

Scraps checked the time as they approached the final building, and was pleased to see that they were a few minutes ahead. Then, he looked up to see that there was a line of the Registereds now making their way through the alleys between the buildings.

The remote viewer who had been helping Scraps agreed to gather the final pair so Scraps could help organise those waiting.

It was still so dark as Scraps made his way through the alley between the buildings that the glass walls almost looked like mirrors of the black sky and neon lights above. The doors that spotted the walkway were the rear exits of various restaurants, shops, and service rooms, as well as emergency exits that would have come from higher levels. Whilst the Government had seemed keen to guard the main streets around the city, the alleys were thankfully clear of added in-person surveillance.

Scraps was not naive enough to believe that there were no security cameras in the area. Even if he couldn't see them, they had to be there, and they were likely being controlled by AI algorithms with facial recognition. It was the reason he had asked Andy to watch over him, and he was sorely hoping that she still was. With each new Registered that joined the marching group, he felt his sense of responsibility increasing. He had made a promise to himself, Flit, and the people around him. He needed to get them out safely.

"That's far enough for now," Scraps said in a low voice that carried further in the alley than he would have liked. It was enough to stop the group, and he carefully squeezed past those at the back so he could get to a midpoint. He glanced at his watch again and then at the building the remove viewer had disappeared into. "The escape vehicle will be on the corner in three minutes. If we go out too early, it will be suspicious. Please, remain here and follow my lead. When we leave the alley, resume your assigned pairs. If we are stopped, please let me speak to them while you continue onto the bus."

Time trickled by. When there was a minute left, the bus pulled up on the assigned corner. It was larger than the usual medium-sized transport shuttle that the Government used. It was a full-scale public transport bus similar to the ones running across the diagonal axes that made up for gaps in the maglev grid layout.

Doing a quick headcount and noticing that everyone was present and accounted for, Scraps gestured for the attention of the group and then led them out of the shadows of the alley. One of the nearby officers assigned to guarding the street turned to watch the group. They seemed content to let the process continue until the Derivate at the next interval with a red captain epaulet on their uniform turned and called, "Halt."

Scraps gritted his teeth and considered his options. He was trying to figure out whether to pretend he hadn't heard the order when TB-219 emerged from the bus and intercepted the man. The sound of clipped and increasingly heated words sailed over to Scraps, but he just focused on leading the group to the bus and getting them on board efficiently.

"Do you want me to report to my superiors at Centre One why my entire shift was delayed due to your insolence?" TB-219 barked at the captain.

The captain's head shifted back and forth as he undoubtedly took in the Derivates filing past him onto the bus.

"I will be checking in with my own superiors, TB-219. Consider yourself reported," the captain said, looking between the designation on TB-219's uniform and the registration plate on the vehicle.

"Fantastic. I look forward to writing my counter-report," TB-219 informed him as the rescued Derivates streamed onto the bus.

Scraps stood by the door, making sure everyone boarded before TB-219 joined him.

As the door closed and the bus pulled away from the curb, Scraps peered deeper into the vehicle and was surprised to see there were an extra twenty or so people on board, beyond the ones he had just gathered.

"I did not want to waste the opportunity to get some of my own out," TB-219 informed him, her voice gravelly after the heated exchange with the captain. "However, we will be in a lot of trouble if that captain does report me. Hopefully you have got a few change points set up so we can cover our trail."

"Better," Scraps said, catching his breath after the tense mission. "I have hackers on overwatch. The security footage has been looped. They won't be able to track us unless there is a beacon in this vehicle."

"We already took care of that." TB-219 retracted her visor and looked him right in the eyes, her deep crimson ones as serious as he had ever seen them. "Hopefully we are in the clear, but I will not celebrate until we have found refuge."

"I agree." Scraps let out a sigh and leaned back against the closed door of the bus.

Scraps glanced at the driver, wondering if they knew where they were going.

"Don't worry. I briefed him properly," TB-219 said. The driver turned and tipped their narrow-rimmed uniform hat. Scraps grinned as he recognised CC-9832.

Scraps returned the gesture with a small salute and looked at his watch. He hoped the next part of this mission would be quick. He still had to get back to Nightmix before Adam became suspicious.

TEN MINUTES LATER, the commandeered bus pulled into a parking garage beneath a run-down block of apartments on the edge of the city. The area and condition matched what he had seen of Flit's image before she had translocated to see Layla's contacts. It was definitely the address she had given him, so he hoped they were still there. The only place he could take the group if they weren't was the Underground, and that did not seem like a good idea.

"This is the place?" TB-219 asked as CC-9832 set the engine to idle.

Scraps nodded. "I will go and speak to the contacts before bringing this group in." He looked back over his shoulder at the people seated in the many rows of the bus, peering around anxiously.

"That's a good idea." CC-9832 pointed to the dashboard of the bus. "I'll keep us running just in case. If you're not out in ten minutes, we will have to move elsewhere."

"Copy that. With any luck, it won't take that long." Scraps

stepped towards the door and CC-9832 pressed the button to release the lock.

The garage smelled like damp cement and week-old garbage bins. It was sparsely populated with older model hovercrafts that were parked over the guidelines. Between the poor parking and the stacks of boxes and crates in many of the car spots, Scraps got the impression that not many people in the building owned their own vehicle. The overhead lighting flickered and buzzed as Scraps walked across the deserted space towards the stairwell entry. He preferred climbing stairs versus possibly getting stuck in another elevator. He'd had enough of that for one week.

It was easy for Scraps to find the level as he ascended. He wasn't so sure when he had entered the stairwell, which smelled faintly of urine, but the signs were probably in better condition than the rest of the place he had seen thus far. It was always a jolt to his system to travel out to this part of the Hub. It was a stark reminder that the shiny, pristine buildings and breezeways of the inner city were definitely not representative of the entire population's living conditions.

When Scraps was a few stairs away from the right landing, he reached out with his telekinesis to tug at the door handle, guessing that if he triggered any alarms, then he would have a head start on retreating back down to the garage.

The door clicked open without a fuss, and Scraps figured he should have known better than to think it was alarmed based on the condition of the rest of the building.

Scraps was pleased that the apartment he was looking for was only one door away from the stairwell. When he got there, he remembered Flit's instructions that it was an empty safe house, so he put his hand on the door and *pushed*. There was a crack as whatever weak mechanisms were holding the door in place broke. He stepped into the room all the same, knowing that this part of the building at least was monitored.

The rest of the space was as run down as the image Scraps remembered on the screen of his apartment. He took time to wander around, noting that it was, for the most part, abandoned.

There were very few signs of recent life, and even then, it was just in the thickness of the dust or displaced pieces of furniture.

Footsteps scuffed against the floor behind Scraps a split second before a voice growled, "Don't take another step, or you'll have more holes in you than a cheese grater!" There was a low, almost imperceptible and muffled pounding of music that accompanied the low voice.

Scraps had no idea what a cheese grater was, but the meaning of the message was loud and clear.

Raising his hands slowly, he kept his eyes ahead to give the newcomers a greater sense of security. "My name is Scraps. I would like to speak to Mitch or Iris, please."

"Keep talkin'," the same gruff voice demanded.

For a moment, Scraps considered asking to speak directly to Mitch or Iris, but there was no time to waste, and the sound of skin sliding against the matte metal of a firearm told him that his assailants wouldn't be interested in negotiating. "I was sent by Flit and Layla. I have proof. They told Mitch and Iris they would get a friend to do something for them. I am that friend, and that task is complete."

"What is your proof?"

"I have it hanging around my neck. Will you let me reach down to get it?"

"Yes, but no funny business."

Once more, Scraps was left confused by the word choice. He did not see anything remotely funny about the situation, but he slowly moved one hand down to tug at the chain around his next. He then held it up, the dull silver metal coin.

"See!" an excited female voice Scraps hadn't expected exclaimed. A slapping sound made Scraps wince. "I told you it was him!"

"You can turn around now."

Scraps did as he was told, seeing a pink-haired individual lowering a rifle as a woman beside them grinned. He noted that the music seemed to be coming from the headphones covering her ears. He wondered if—

"Yup, we're Mitch and Iris," she said. "Well, I'm Iris. This is Mitch."

It was then that Scraps remembered Flit mentioning Iris was a telepath. That made sense, although he wasn't sure if music would be an adequate strategy to prevent the disruption of mind-reading.

"It works just about as well as anything else." Iris shrugged. "So, Flit said you'd get our people out."

"I did," Scraps said, "as well as a few extras."

Mitch frowned. "A few extras?" They didn't seem impressed by that revelation. "We're not some sort of charity. We don't have endless space or resources."

"One of the contacts who helped pull off the escape plan brought them. It is not negotiable," Scraps said, not impressed by the open hostility in Mitch's tone. He understood that resources were scarce, but this was war, and they were all Derivates.

"Oh... they're Drones too. That's fine."

Scraps was about to question what a drone was, but after a moment, he paused. He was able to deduce that for himself. He pressed his lips together and nodded, figuring arguing about respectful terminology was useless.

"Sorry, didn't mean to offend. We just get used to certain words, you know?" Iris scrunched her nose.

It took conscious effort for Scraps to keep his mind clear of a response, and even then, the expression on Iris's face told him that she sensed his discomfort.

"We can take them," Mitch said, cutting through the growing tension, "although we'll need help with removing the chips. I don't know how long we have before the Government will start trying to track them, and we don't have the resources to deal with the twenty-four we knew about, let alone however many you brought along."

Scraps frowned. That wasn't good. If they were tracked here, then the rescue mission might have made things worse.

"I know someone who can help," he said. He reached down his shirt and walked over to a nearby end table. He tugged the necklace to snap the chain and then, with a pound of his fist and some added telekinetic pressure, crushed the beacon.

"Oh, he's got one like yours!" Iris said, sounding excited. "Does that mean we'll get to see Layla again?"

"I'm not sure who it will be, but someone from the Underground will come to help." Then, the time on his watch caught his attention, and he frowned. "I need to get going before my absence becomes remarkable. If someone wants to come down to the garage with me, I will introduce you to the refugees."

Mitch went to speak.

Iris held up a hand and shook her head. "The last thing they need is your crankiness and that damned gun in their face. You wait here for whoever comes to respond to that." She jabbed her finger in the direction of the broken charm.

Iris turned and led the way out of the apartment. Scraps followed her, keeping his eyes peeled for any signs of surveillance.

"Don't worry. If anyone tries to sneak up on us, I'll hear them coming." Iris tapped her head.

Scraps wondered what her power level was, although given the fact she was a Citizen Derivate, the usual Government classifications might not be able to cover the nuances of her situation.

"Thanks for getting that group out. I know Mitch was a grumpy jerk about it, but it's nice to know we can help others."

The contrast between Layla's two contacts was not lost on Scraps. He didn't mind Iris, though. She had the same kind of chaotic energy Flit did.

As Scraps' mind veered to Flit, he frowned. "Iris, when the Underground person comes to—"

"You want me to ask them to let lover girl know that you're okay?"

Scraps frowned. He didn't even know that thought was complete in his own mind yet.

Iris waved a hand and chuckled. "Oh, please. You spend enough time in peoples' heads, you get an idea of how thought patterns go. Don't worry. I'll ensure Flit knows you're alive."

Thanks, Scraps thought as they reached the bottom of the stairwell.

From there, Scraps guided Iris to the bus and made the necessary introductions. As it turned out, CC-9832 and TB-219 were planning to dump the bus somewhere and return to Centre One. Scraps was not sure it was the wisest choice, but TB-219 ensured him they were safe and that they had more work to do before they felt okay with escaping themselves.

Scraps could only trust everyone involved to do their part. He was tempted to return to the Citizen Derivate refuge to see if Flit had come with whoever the Underground sent. He wondered if Flit had been back to the apartment yet and was concerned about her reaction. If he had to face her and see the relief he knew would be in her face, he would never want to leave her side again.

It was much easier this way, Scraps told himself, even though he wished otherwise.

46

FLIT

AN OBNOXIOUS ELECTRIC tone pierced through Flit's sleep.

Someone was trying to call her.

"No, fuck off," she grumbled, face half buried in her pillow, cheek suspiciously wet due to the way her mouth was hanging open.

The wailing continued.

Just before Flit could throw something hard at the comms screen, the events of the past few weeks cascaded over her, and she realised the call might be important.

Teleporting over to the door and tripping over her own feet upon landing, Flit pressed her hand against the panel to answer the call. "What is it?" she asked, voice slurring slightly as she wiped her mouth. Her eyes were gritty and dry, and she could swear from the way her head spun that she had only just fallen asleep.

"I got a call from Cogs. Scraps' emergency beacon went off."

Hawkeye's voice was annoying clear and calm despite the fact it was—Flit squinted at the time in the corner of the panel—five in the morning. Flit was about to ask how that was possible when her brain finally processed what he had said.

"Wait. What?"

Suddenly, she felt very awake.

Over the past two days, Flit had been wrestling with the terrifying possibility that Scraps had been captured by the Government. Fortune had encouraged her to be conservative with her concerns and reminded her that they rarely killed important assets. If they had captured Scraps, they would apparently be far more interested in the information he possessed than wastefully killing him. Flit knew Fortune was trying to be supportive, but it was not as comforting as it should have been. All the same, Flit was unsure when she was going to see him again, and it was tearing her apart. To hear that he was able to activate the beacon...

"Exactly what I said." There was a hint of urgency in Hawkeye's tone. "We need to get over there as soon as possible."

Flit teleported to her wardrobe and pulled cargo pants and a tank top on over her boxer shorts and chemise. "Do you know where he is?"

"Yes, I'll give you the coordinates when you get here," Hawkeyes hedged.

Flit frowned. She assumed he wouldn't let her go without him.

She retrieved the flame grenades she kept hidden in her own room and tucked them into her pockets. "Do we need to stop by the armoury to get extra gear?"

"No, I've got some stashed in here."

"Great. Whereabouts in your room are you?"

There was a pause on the other end of the line.

"Uh, by my door?"

Flit finished dressing by tugging her jacket on. Hawkeye's studio apartment was so familiar to her that it easy to picture it. She set her intention. Then, a moment later, she appeared in his room.

As promised, Hawkeye was beside his door when Flit arrived, so she was completely unprepared for the shocked yelp and the rustle of fabric from behind her. Flit whipped around, ready to fight, but her body sagged with relief when she saw Layla on the bed, the sheet tugged up around her armpits.

"Ah, shit. Not again." Flit turned away to give Layla privacy and rubbed her eyes. First Sway, Link, and Clarity... now Hawkeye and Layla.

"Again?" Hawkeye cocked an eyebrow at her as he grabbed her shoulder and pulled her closer, away from the middle of the bed and from Layla as she gathered her clothing, if the continued rustling of fabric was anything to go by.

"Not important." Flit shook her head. "Where is he?"

Clearly more than happy to not have to discuss the situation in his room, Hawkeye steered Flit over to his wardrobe, where he retrieved an aged metal trunk. He opened it and pulled out two fully stocked weapons belt and handed her one.

"Same place you and Layla have been meeting Mitch and Iris."

Hope flared in Flit's chest, and it must have been radiant enough for Hawkeye to notice. His frown deepened as he buckled his weapons belt.

"Flit, we don't know what happened. We need to prepare for the worst. If Scraps was compromised, we have to assume—"

"I'm not an idiot," Flit snapped, holding up her hand. "I know we could be walking into an ambush. I'm happy to do this alone."

"Not a chance." Hawkeye glanced at Layla. "But this will be easier and quicker if it is just Flit and I who go. Taking both of us for translocation in a possible combat situation—"

"I get it," Layla interrupted, holding the sheet around her tighter. "If you're not back in an hour, I'll let Cogs know."

"Thank you."

Flit was not only grateful for Layla not arguing, but for the initiative it took to consider a search and rescue time without prompting.

Knowing there was no time to waste, Flit waited for Hawkeye to get his belt properly situated before she stepped closer and put one hand on his lower back, the other at the base of his neck. "Quick breath, and we'll be there."

True to Flit's word, there was a matter of milliseconds between Hawkeye preparing himself for the inevitable tugging sensation he hated so much and their arrival in the now familiar shelter living room. Flit let go of Hawkeye and whirled around to immediately survey their surroundings while he gathered his senses.

"Mitch?" Flit paused as she saw the pink-haired, rifle-toting Derivate in their favourite place in the doorway. She was immediately wary.

Maybe this really was a trap.

For once, Mitch seemed to sense the unease now in the room, and they set their gun aside.

"Your man brought in a bus load of nearly fifty Drones. I've got two micros down there working on the chips, but if we don't get them out ASAP, the whole rescue might have been for nothing," Mitch informed them.

Flit blinked. "My man?"

"Yeah. Tall, stoic, and concerned about you thinking he was dead?"

Scraps is alive!

"Where is he?" Flit demanded, looking around with renewed interest.

Surely, if he had summoned Flit using the emergency beacon, he would have waited to see her.

Mitch sighed. "Said he had to get back to wherever it was he was hanging out before they noticed him missing."

There was a suspicious part of Flit that was desperate to challenge Mitch's assurances, to push for proof. But... they were supposed to be building trust, and trust went both ways.

"Look, as much as I enjoy catching up with you," Mitch begun, voice laced with sarcasm, "we are in a hurry. I either need a microkinetic or an escape plan. Which will it be?"

Flit turned to look at Hawkeye. "Cogs?"

He shook his head. "She's too heavily monitored. She can get away with a bit of micro manipulation here and there, but busting down her door at five o'clock in the morning and trying to extract her would be too suspicious."

Then, as much as Flit knew it would cost her later, she hung her head. "I know who we can ask." After gathering her courage for what was potentially the most intimidating thing she had done in her life, she turned to Mitch. "I'll be back in a few minutes with help."

Hawkeye stepped closer to Flit without prompting. She wrapped her arms around him, and then they were back in his room.

Poor Layla jumped again as she was pulling a shirt over her head. "That was quick. Everything all right?" she asked as she tugged the fabric into place. Flit was pleased she put her pants on first.

"Yeah. Flit's got some sucking up to do," Hawkeye said. He squeezed Flit's shoulder. "Remember, go in humble and own your crap. It's the only way it won't turn into a shit fight."

"Oh, it'll be a shit fight either way." Flit shook her head.

She didn't bother saying goodbye before she teleported back to her room. The instant her feet hit the floor, she started running towards her parents' room.

It took two rounds of impatient knocking for her parents' bedroom door to open to reveal her father in his pyjamas, rubbing his eyes, and her mother sitting up in bed yawning.

"What the hell is going on?" Stride half yawned, half groaned.

Flit patted her father on the shoulder and walked past him to sit on the foot of the bed. "Mum, I know this is going to piss you off, but I need you to listen to me before you bite my head off."

Immediately, Tinker's mouth set into a firm, unimpressed line. There was a sharpness to her glare that let Flit know that she was listening, but she wasn't happy about it. It threw her right back to her teenage years. She could only hope her mother would have a slightly more open mind this time.

"I promise to explain more fully to you later, but the short version is that I have been working with Scraps and some others on the surface to organise the rescue of some Registered Derivates who were looking to get free from the Government's grasp," Flit said, diving right in and barely pausing to take a breath. "The fact is, the Government is getting ready for a war against the Free Citizens, and we thought it was important to get the Registereds out before they were forced to do unspeakable things. The only problem is, the group that offered them refuge does not have enough micros to get the tracking chips out as fast as they need to."

The gears ground into place, and her mother, far more alert than Flit would have been for being woken at a stupid hour of the morning, held up a hand. Flit fell silent. Tinker turned and slipped out of bed before padding over to her wardrobe. She did the same thing Flit did and pulled her clothes on right over her pyjamas.

"Mum?" Flit followed after her. "I'm aware this goes against everything happening down here, but I need you to understand."

Flit felt her father's hand on her shoulder, and her heart skipped a beat. She couldn't help but feel she was just digging a deeper hole for herself.

"Please. I know I sound crazy, but if Harmony and Divvy find out—"

Tinker turned around as she buttoned her blouse. "The only thing that's crazy is that you think I would tell Harmony and Divvy about this."

Flit paused, pressing her lips together to keep her hope contained. She didn't want to speak and ruin whatever potentially positive tangent her mother was on.

"Am I happy you burst in here at five in the morning to tell me this instead of keeping me up to date?" Tinker grumbled.

"No," came Flit's father's voice from behind her. "Are you going to have to explain yourself fully later?"

"You bet your arse," Tinker completed.

As old as they were, Flit had assumed her parents were well past the "finishing each other's sentences" phase, but she rolled with it.

"But there is no way I am going to let the Government have those people back when they managed to escape." Tinker turned her attention to Stride, who was still standing behind Flit. "If we're gone for a while, you may need to take Flit's classes. Just tell them she's sick with something contagious like gastro."

"Copy that. Stay safe, you two," Stride replied.

There was a kind of disappointment in his tone that Flit could empathise with. She had no doubt he would want to come along, but they all knew his limitations, and it was also critical that he remained behind to cover for the two of them.

Brushing her clothes down flat and meeting Flit's gaze once more, Tinker said, "Now, where do we need to go, and how do we get there?"

Flit couldn't help but grin. "You stay right there, and I'll do the work." Flit stepped closer and gave her mother a hug. The moment she felt Tinker relax, Flit whispered, "Okay, translocation time."

Before Tinker could express her shock, they were gone.

"SO, you make sure that you're holding both switches on the circuit down. Then you disconnect the electrodes. When the electrodes are disconnected, you can safely crush the chip."

Leaning back against a wall in an abandoned restaurant in the same block as Mitch's and Iris' safe house, Flit watched as her mother spoke to a pair of Registereds who had already had their own chips deactivated. As microkinetics with a rating of B, Tinker had expressed complete faith in their ability to do the procedures. Given the cruelty of the Government, forgetting to hold down the switches on the circuits could lead to the kill-switch being activated. However, Tinker invited the pair to hover close and rest their hands on the shoulders of the next patient as she worked.

A trio of the Citizen Derivate micros were already working on the chips, but there were a lot to get through and little time in which to do it. Tinker was making sound progress, though, and no one had questioned her when she had come in with Flit to help. As her mother had surveyed the place, Flit could see the questions in her eyes, but she was a professional. There were people to help, and she did not need to be told what the priorities were.

"You're mother's quite impressive."

The sudden voice at Flit's side made her jump, and she turned to see Iris come and lean back on the wall beside her. The telepath had been busy since Flit arrived, so this was their first real chance to check in. Not that they knew each other well, but Flit did like the woman. She got a good vibe from her. Well, except for the whole "Drone" thing.

"She is." Flit couldn't resist smiling as she resumed watching her mother working.

"Much more business-like than you, though."

Flit snorted. "Yeah, you're right about that. I definitely don't get my sass from her."

"I don't know about that." Iris shrugged. "It sounds as though she's just gotten better at keeping it to herself."

That caught Flit's attention. She raised an eyebrow at Iris.

"I'm clearly not as in control of my powers as the people you're used to dealing with." Iris raised her chin but couldn't hide the blush on her cheeks. "For me, being in this city feels like having a thousand people screaming in my head constantly."

"Wouldn't the music add to that?" Flit asked, genuinely curious. She couldn't imagine what it felt like to have that many voices in her head. Her own mind was busy enough, without having to deal with others as well.

Iris shook her head. "I suppose it'd be easy enough to assume that, but the music actually helps. If it gets overwhelming, I focus on that. I listen to the beat, feel the rhythm... Then, when I feel I can think again, I can focus on the different voices."

Throughout her time in the Underground, Flit had heard plenty of other telepaths say similar things. It was well known that raising a telepath came with its own unique challenges from keeping careful control of your thoughts and your words to finding ways to calm the overwhelm. It was a challenge Flit truly admired.

Not that her own parents had it easy, of course. She had been teleporting around the place from far too young an age and had been very cheeky about it. Teleporting and telekinesis allowed for quite a fair bit of mischief in the younger years.

And older years, for that matter.

Then, there was the telecoercion...

"Damn, it's dangerous being us, isn't it?" Iris let out a low whistle.

With a heavy sigh, Flit nodded. *"That's not even considering the Government,"* she thought, figuring that there was little point talking when Iris was in her head anyway. *"So, will they be safe with you guys for a while?"*

"I'm not going to lie. We are low on resources," Iris admitted, her voice uncharacteristically gritty.

"With any luck, you won't need to worry for long. The Free Citizens will probably be ready to move in about a week. I'm hoping we can figure out how to get the Underground up and ready to join them in that time."

Iris was silent for a good few seconds as she considered that. "I didn't get the feeling that Layla or her hunk knew much about the Free Citizens."

"No one really does beyond myself and Scraps," Flit admitted, *"and the Free Citizens know nothing at all about the Underground. We need to figure out how to make the official introduction, but I'm hoping the giant common enemy we face will be enough to unite us."*

"At least until we get the Government out of the way?" Layla asked, finishing a thought Flit hadn't wanted to express.

With a grim frown, Flit nodded.

Even if the Free Citizens accepted their help and they fought together, there was nothing to say that they wouldn't turn out to be a bunch of bigoted arseholes. She was pleased that at least a few of them were decent people, but given Adam was the leader...

Flit paused that train of thought. It was a rabbit hole she didn't need to go down.

"So, I got a quick chance to speak to Scraps before he left," Iris said.

Immediately forgetting about everything else, Flit raised an eyebrow in question.

"He's very much alive and probably as safe as any of us are for now. He wanted me to let you know that. He seemed genuinely disappointed that he wasn't able to see you—" Iris then paused, biting her lip as she leaned in. "I probably shouldn't tell you, but... What the heck."

Flit turned to face her, finding it hard to hear her lowered voice with all the chatter in the room and the growing noise from the morning traffic outside of the window. "What is it?"

"He said he had to get back, but he probably could have stuck around, as he knew you'd be here soon. He chose not to because he knew that if he saw you again, he wouldn't want to leave," Layla whispered.

Tears prickled Flit's eyes, and she blinked back her emotions. Her heart warmed at those words. She licked her lips as she tried to find words to show her gratitude before settling on a silent but genuine, *"Thank you. You have no idea how nice it is to hear that."*

Iris patted her shoulder. "I don't know your story, but I can sense this is part of what has been a rocky road. Hopefully it'll get smoother for you—for all of us—really soon." She pushed herself off the wall and walked over to one of the newly de-chipped Registereds. Iris helped the person off the couch and walked them to a different location for their recovery.

TWO HOURS LATER, Flit and Tinker arrived back in their underground apartment. As they had predicted before leaving, they were gone long enough that Stride had left and started Flit's day on her behalf. Flit was grateful to know he was on top of things, but the moment Tinker gathered her bearings and rounded on her, she had a feeling she would be begging for Stride's equalising presence very soon.

"Sit." Tinker gestured to the couch in the living room, and Flit sank down onto the soft, worn cushions without argument. "Talk."

Flit let out a heavy sigh. She almost wished her mother would just ask questions. She knew she had to have plenty. Instead, she left the direction of the conversation wide open, and Flit wasn't sure where to begin.

"What do you want to know?" Flit was stalling for time.

Her mother saw right through it. "Everything. Start with what happened when you got back down here."

So, Flit spoke.

She told her mother about the fact she had been dragged back to the Underground against her will, whilst Scraps had thrown himself at the Government to give them time to get away. She spoke about the strange feelings of betrayal she'd had when she had first arrived and then slowly discovering that Harmony had been coercing her to believe so many lies. She then explained that she had been able to reach out to Scraps with the intention to bring him back and how he'd decided to stay with the Free Citizens to ensure they had eyes on what was happening there. She then had to explain how they knew the Free Citizens but stopped short of explaining her role in freeing the Citizen Derivates. Her mother sensed her hedging around the issue. By some miracle, she did not insist Flit explain. Instead, Flit told her that there were some things that even the people involved had forgotten and that it was safer that way. Then, she talked about the Blue Team's plan to train up the Underground so that, when the Free Citizens were ready to attack, they could join in and hopefully help win freedom for everyone.

After the long and, at times, emotional story, Tinker stayed silent for long enough that Flit started to worry about her ability to process the information. Just as Flit was about to ask if she was okay, Tinker let out a heavy sigh and squared her shoulders.

"So, what can I do to help?"

Flit almost choked. "You're not going to lecture me?"

Even though Flit had surpassed young adulthood, it seemed as though her interactions with her mother were still characterised by certain lifelong patterns.

"Would it change anything?" Tinker crossed her arms. "Please don't think I'm not angry. I am. Very much so. However, I understand why you thought you had to keep this secret. I think you're right about this being a chance to fight, but I do not want you thinking you can leave your father and myself out of it. If you're in, we're in too."

It was not what Flit had expected, but it was what she desperately needed to hear. She reached out, taking her mother's hand and squeezing it. If her mother wanted to help, then she would let her.

"Right now, we're just watching our backs. Harmony and Divvy were pissed that we messed with whatever plan they had to get us all using inhibitors. I have a feeling that they're not going to let that go easily."

"I always knew Harmony was a bitch," Tinker said, shaking her head.

That comment made Flit think that, just maybe, Iris had been right. Perhaps she was more like her mother than she knew.

47

————

SCRAPS

AS IT TURNED OUT, Scraps need not have rushed back to Nightmix.

When he returned two hours later, it was to a new type of chaos.

From what Scraps gathered over the hours that followed, Andy's estimate of around twelve hours had been woefully inaccurate. Even with the new additions to the team, the group were fighting tooth and nail to remain ahead of the Government's hackers and micros.

It was close to midday when an irate Adam pulled Andy aside and called Scraps over.

Andy looked exhausted. She had dark circles under her bloodshot eyes, and her posture was slumped. The other hackers all seemed to be showing signs of wear too. Scraps could see why. They had been working nonstop for so long. The mental toll of constant problem solving combined with looking at screens for hours on ends had to be making them feel incredibly uncomfortable and reduce their competency.

"How much longer, Andy?" Adam snapped, not even bothering to hide his aggravation.

"At our current capacity?" Andy looked back over her at the team, and her shoulders slumped. "Less than an hour. They are throwing everything they have at us now, and we're fatigued."

"Then have energy supplements—"

"We've already had the damn supplements!" Andy threw her hands up in the air. "We've done all we can for as long as we can. We've got nothing left up our sleeves."

Adam stepped towards Andy, rage flaring in his eyes at her tone. Scraps also figured it had something to do with the fact he had lost control of this situation. He paused, nostrils flaring. "Do you still have the capacity to access the network? Or have we lost the chance to broadcast, too?"

"We've been able to broadcast at any time. We could do it right now if you wanted," Andy replied with a shrug, making the point that the only reason she was fighting was because Adam had demanded it.

"Is there any way they can interrupt it?"

"It's unlikely but not impossible."

Scraps frowned. "But we can't broadcast now. We're not ready to lay siege."

Crossing his arms over his chest, Adam raised an eyebrow. "Perhaps you should have considered that before you failed the server mission so spectacularly. All you had to do was get in and out without notice. Now, we may lose the most important part of our plan."

It took a great deal of self-control for Scraps to see past the insult in Adam's words. Scraps knew that he and the strike team had done their best with difficult parameters. Adam just did not like things not going according to *his* plan.

"With all due respect, Adam, I see no need cancel the entire plan," Scraps said, keeping his voice low and tentative. Calming, almost. It was a tactic he used to use with the supervisors he had in the Department of Law Enforcement to make suggestions to Citizens he knew would not receive them well. "Why don't we broadcast what we can for as long as we can? That will give people time to think so that, when we do attack next week, they will be ready to join."

"It should be easier to hold the network once the broadcast is out," Andy agreed. "They'll probably be distracted trying to do damage control."

Adam considered it. He rubbed the stubble on his chin as he looked at Scraps.

Scraps was just about to mentally congratulate himself for a plan well-reasoned when—

"Harry" Adam turned his back on Scraps and looked over at the man who had stolen the last shipment of weapons from the Government. "What news from Eastbay? Are they ready to move?"

Harry grinned and nodded. "They are. We've got green lights from all satellite bases."

Scraps was immediately wary. "Adam, I don't think this is the best way to go about starting the war. We don't have to drag every city into this right away."

"The war started decades ago, Brian." Adam turned his laser focus on Andy. "Get the broadcast up and running immediately. Do everything you can to keep it on the air for as long as possible. If you start to lose control of it, let me know. No sense leaving the system up for them to reclaim."

Blinking, Andy took a moment to process the change in plans. "But I can't bring down the system. I told you before this all started that the most I can do with the access I have is to broadcast."

The spark of smugness in Adam's expression was truly sickening. "Then I'm glad I had Tai leave behind some insurance while they were in the server farm. You just worry about your part. I'll take care of the rest."

Scraps' eyebrows furrowed with concern at the very clear threat in Adam's tone. He thought back to that building, to how many innocent people worked there, and to how many levels there were above and below the one holding the server farm.

If Adam wanted carnage, he was going about it the right way. Scraps only hoped he could talk him out of it in time.

"ALL STATIONS, READY?" Adam called out. He was wedged between Andy and the hacker at the desk next to her, hands resting on the edge of the table, skin on his face pulled taut with concentration.

In the past twenty minutes, the leader had notified the Free Citizens who would be using Nightmix as a base that they should immediately make their way to the building. They were not sure what the Government's immediate response would be, so they wanted to get as many people as they could while they could. A few of the ones living closer by had started to trickle in, but Scraps could only imagine others were still trying to extract themselves from their daily life. Every time the door to the bunker opened, he looked up, hoping to see Chris and Liana. In reality, though, he knew they might not make it in time for the broadcast.

Andy tapped a button on the keyboard in front of her, and the image that was on the screen she was working at was beamed to a dozen wide-screened monitors that the Free Citizens had set up. The one in the middle was a feed of what the Hub networks were rolling, and the other eleven were copies of the Government broadcast channels in the satellite cities. There was a mix of weather, stocks, local news, and advertisements for Government initiatives.

"All stations ready," Andy announced.

Standing as part of a growing crowd of Free Citizens, Scraps watched as Adam straightened, crossed his arms over his chest, and ordered, "Begin the broadcast. Set it to repeat. Do everything you can, for as long as you can, to stop the Government from shutting it down."

There was a split-second delay, and then all of the screens turned black. There was absolute silence in the room as a bold white "ten" appeared on the screen, then replace by a "nine", then an "eight", and all the way down to "one".

Before a "zero" could take over, the screen exploded with into footage of flames. They roared, the sounds blaring from the speakers so real with the hisses and crackles that Scraps could almost imagine the fire right there before him. Slowly, a shadow danced over the flames, curved and shifting, then forming in the middle into the Free Citizens' logo of two people standing with their clasped hands raised.

"Greetings, Citizens of the Government," came a warbling, distorted version of Adam's voice as the logo pulsed on the screen. A quiet yet rousing tune started behind Adam's voice, the solid drum backing it resembling that of a pounding heartbeat. "This is the leader of the freedom seeking movement known as the Free Citizens. It has been six weeks and six days since our last broadcast when we called the Government out for its atrocities."

Everyone in the room stood, transfixed by the message on the screen and the way it was being presented. Even Scraps had not seen the full thing, and he couldn't help but be impressed by the drama Adam had added to it. Just like last time, this was about more than just showing the Government's flaws. It was about inspiring people to rise against them.

"That is almost seven weeks that the Government have had to consider the way they subjugate the very people they purport to protect, but... that was not what they did. Instead, they chose to spend their time doing this."

The screen abruptly changed to a slideshow of documents and images, calling out the Government for continuing to restrict the freedom of its peoples. There were pictures from what must have been law enforcement body cameras of people being violently arrested, candid shots from medical testing labs, and screen captures of new policies being pushed through to further force certain medical procedures or movement restrictions.

"The Government had an opportunity to do the right thing. Instead, it spent time trying to hunt us down, to take away our voice, and to shut down the only access you had to the truth." Adam's voice-over resumed as the images cascaded. "So I put it to you now, Citizens. Will you sit idly by and allow these dictators to rule your life with impunity? Will you allow them to treat you as if you are mindless drones? Or will you join us in our quest for freedom?"

At that last word, the image on the screen caught fire and burned away, the ashes collecting along the bottom. Then, there was a great, bone-chilling whooshing sound as a wind swept up the ashes and swirled them into one word:

REBELLION

A spark spluttered to life at the start of the "R" and began burning its way through the word. The music in the background swelled, the drums in the background getting louder and faster until Scraps found his own heart sped up to keep pace.

Then, as the spark reached the end of the "N", there was an explosion on the screen that showed zoomed-out, slowly spinning bird's-eye drone footage of the city. The Hub looked almost like a toy city from the aerial view, made of building blocks that shone in the midday sun.

The view slowed, and when it stopped, the voice-over resumed. "Government, take note. As of midnight, your cities will belong to the Citizens. If there is anyone who is unable to muster the courage to fight, you will have until eleven fifty-nine to evacuate. Following that, we will reclaim the streets that were built on our backs and are maintained by our sweat."

The voice-over stopped to let that warning settle, and the image of the Hub was replaced by other cities on each relevant monitor. Another countdown appeared, this time it was ticking towards midnight. In the corner of the frame, a video reel continued to expose all of the appropriate documents and images.

A slow clap from the back of the room made Scraps jump, pulling his attention from the broadcast. The applause gained momentum until it was a roar of constant thunder.

Adam peeled away from the desk and turned his back on Andy and her crew to face the gathered Free Citizens. A broad, smug smile was on his face, as if he had won an award rather than started a war. It made Scraps' gut twist with disgust.

Adam raised his hands, calling for silence, and had to wait a minute for those gathered to stop. "Free Citizens, thank you," Adam said, voice deep, sincere. Somehow, it sounded even more menacing to Scraps now after listening to the twisted, edited voice-over. "Getting to this point has been a battle in and of itself. It would not have happened without the bravery and hard work of so many people, not to mention the sacrifice of the brave souls who ensured our success in previous missions."

The leader paused, bowing his head for the count of twenty before looking up. There was a shine of emotion in his eyes that

Scraps felt was so entirely false. He did not mourn those they lost. He only cared about what he had gained.

"As well as that broadcast went, we cannot afford to become complacent. Unfortunate circumstances have meant that we need to move our attack forward a week. Luckily, we have all of the resources we need, even if we have to cut our training short. However, I have every faith that you are all ready. That you are all capable." Adam turned slowly as he surveyed the room. "The next ten hours will be hours of preparation. We will fortify ourselves and our outposts, and at midnight... we rise!"

The cheer that accompanied Adam's final words was deafening. Scraps found himself cheering along, his heart hammering in his chest, as a sense of dread washed over him. Adam's leadership up until this point had glorified needless sacrifice and dangerous risks. Scraps thought he would have more time to help with the planning to ameliorate that, to reduce the collateral, but any chance of that was gone now.

The people around him had no idea what they were getting themselves into.

48

FLIT

FLIT AND TINKER caught up with Stride at lunch time. When he first saw them, his entire body seemed to melt with relief, the worry and tension of the morning sloughing off in an instant. Then, a smile crept onto his face, and he straightened, his shoulders square and proud as they approached. He pulled Tinker in for a hug and reached out to pat Flit's back before they all sat at the table in the Mess.

"Your morning groups went well," Stride reported in a low voice. "They've taken well to their pairing with different abilities, and the sparring is really teaching them a lot."

It had been a long time since Flit's father was pleased by an achievement. It was refreshing seeing him glowing with pride now. She had always thought his personality and knowledge of teleporting were wasted in Supply, but his injury had meant that the Underground had been conservative with his placement. As Flit considered it, she realised how problematic it was that he was excluded from certain roles purely based on the fact he'd had an accident so many years ago. It was something the Government would do, not a group of understanding, progressive rebels.

"Thanks for that, Dad," Flit said. She patted her stomach. "I'm feeling a lot better now though, so I appreciate being able to sleep in."

"Good. I'm glad I could help." He grinned. If Flit hadn't seen the concern creasing his features when she and her mother had arrived, she might have thought he'd forgotten the true reason he had to take over based on his tone. "Did you want me to hang around this afternoon?"

Flit shook her head. "I woke you and Mum up way too early this morning with my vomiting. You guys should head back to the apartment and get some rest."

Whilst Stride deflated, the purposeful look Tinker gave him had him sighing in resignation. Flit and her mother had already talked about it, and they needed to let Stride in on what was happening. Now that her plans and her secrets were out, and they were marching towards something bigger, her mother wanted to make sure they were all on board as a family.

They sat and ate lunch, making small talk about shows they had seen or old memories. So many conversational topics had grown stale over the past weeks. Without any new information or upcoming events, there was little to really talk about in the Underground. All of the days, save for the ones with critical incidences, melted into a garbled, glutinous mess in Flit's mind.

When the trio finished their meal and stood to go their separate ways, Tinker surprised Flit by pulling her into a tight embrace. Before she let go, she whispered, "I don't say it often enough, but I'm proud of you."

The unexpected praise had Flit blinking as she pulled back from her mother. Tinker met her gaze and held it, letting her know she was entirely serious.

"Thank you," Flit said softly, conscious that the Mess was getting busier by the second. "I love you."

Tinker's face twitched with emotion, but before it could get the better of her, Flit saw her mother pull on that hard-arse armour she wore every day. She gave Flit a final nod before she took her husband's hand and led him out of the Mess.

Flit waited for her parents to leave before she wove through the tables and found her way to the back corner where Hawkeye, Layla, and Fortune were sitting. They looked up at her as she approached, and there was a certain tenseness in all of them that Flit recognised. It was so easy now to tell when someone she knew was trying to keep their thoughts under tight control. It was a difficult task at the best of times, but recent events had everyone worrying that Harmony and Divvy had asked the telepaths to spy on them.

When Fortune reached over and patted the bench on her left-hand side, Flit sank onto it. She had no doubt Layla and Hawkeye had filled her in on the goings-on of the day.

"How are you feeling?" Fortune asked. "I saw your father taking your class earlier, and he said you were unwell."

"I'm much better now, thank you. Mum stuck with me, and you know how good she is at her job," Flit said, her words letting them know that things went well in the Hub.

Hawkeye's posture sagged a little, and he let out a sigh. "Good to know. We're just about to head to the training rooms for the afternoon sessions. Will you be taking your class again?"

"Yes. I was going to make my way over myself, but then I saw you guys were over here so I figured we could go together instead."

Fortune checked to see that Layla and Hawkeye's plates were empty before she rose. Everyone followed suit, and the group left the Mess and walked towards the training room in silence. They had just about left the hallways for the main living areas when Hawkeye's name being called out made him stop.

As they passed the white walls that led to Control, Flit spotted Cogs running their way, her red braid bouncing on her shoulder. It was a rare treat to see her outside of the tunnels dedicated to the leadership of the Underground, but she gestured for them to follow her into a nearby multi-purpose room.

"I don't have long," Cogs panted as she shut the door behind them, digging her hand into the pocket of her cargo pants and pulling out a wafer-thin microchip. She stepped closer to the screen by the door and held her hand over it. After a moment, the screen sprung free, and Cogs caught it in one hand while slipping the chip into a slot behind it. She then replaced the screen and pressed her fingertips against it.

Curiosity was getting the better of Flit, and she was just about to ask what was going on when the screen flared to life. An aerial image of the Hub played on it, with a countdown over it and a small inset panel on the image running a reel with pictures of... documentation?

Understanding hit Flit like a bucket of ice water over the head. She was gawking, transfixed, as she asked, "Was there anything else? Or just this?"

Cogs raised an eyebrow at her, but her fingers shifted on the bottom of the screen, and images and code flickered on it faster than Flit could follow.

"What is this?" Hawkeye asked, frowning.

"The Free Citizens," Flit said, just as the voice-over begun and the logo on the screen left no doubt about which group was responsible. She turned to Cogs. "When was this?"

"Around twenty minutes ago. I was able to slip away because Control is in chaos at the moment."

"What does it—"

Cogs held up a finger. Before Hawkeye could finish the question, an audio track kicked in, and Flit listened as a heavily distorted version of Adam's voice explained exactly what was going on.

Hawkeye's attention snapped to Flit.

She raised her hands in front of her. "Hey, don't look at me. They were not meant to be doing this for another week."

Fortune hummed with dissatisfaction. "Well, it seems they have moved their plans forward. I am guessing Scraps did not mention that to you?"

Flit shook her head.

"And Mitch or Iris didn't say anything?" Layla added.

Once more, Flit shook her head. "Perhaps they didn't know?"

"How bad is it in Control?" Fortune asked, her expression all business.

Cogs scrunched up her nose. "It's pretty bad. They're scrambling to ensure no one is able to hack into the system to retrieve this, and they are planning to cut—"

All lights in the room failed. The screen Cogs had been working on spluttered off, and they were plunged into dark, warbling shadows as the lights reduced to the unstable emergency setting. A loud klaxon siren blared through the room.

"Emergency. This is an emergency. Initiate lockdown procedures

immediately," an automated voice chimed, interrupting the siren for a blessed moment.

Flit groaned. "Another fucking lockdown?"

Cogs worked quickly to retrieve the thin chip from the behind the screen. "I need to get out of here. I can't be seen helping you."

So many thoughts competed for attention in Flit's mind, but she ignored them and focused on the most important and practical ones. She did not want to compromise Cogs, but she also knew that the lockdown was complete. If the power was out in this room, it would likely be out elsewhere. She would have offered to return Cogs to her apartment, but without being able to access some sort of visual aid, she would not be able to get her out.

Instead, she leaned in closer to Hawkeye, Layla, and Fortune. "I can teleport you three back to my apartment," she offered, figuring they had to be the ones to move, not Cogs. "That will get us out of here, and if Control does find you, then you can just say you took shelter in here as you were walking past."

"What about what's happening in the Hub?" Layla asked. In the darkness, it was hard to see her expression, but Flit could hear the worry in her tone.

The knowledge Scraps was on the surface with the Free Citizens and she was unable to back him up settled over Flit. She did not like the idea at all, and she just wished they'd had more time to get things sorted in the Underground so they could help them.

"We'll get to that," Flit said without hesitation, "but I have a feeling we'll only get one shot at this. We need to do it properly."

Cog nodded. "If this battle is starting, we can't fuck around, which means I can't get caught with you yet. If they realise I'm helping you, I'll lose all access I have to our systems."

"We can't let Harmony and Divvy know that you told us anything, either," Flit said. "We need to play it cool. If anything new comes through, please let us know, Cogs."

"I'll do my best," Cogs promised. "Keep an eye on your comms systems. I may be able to get messages across if I have the right opportunities."

"Thank you." Fortune's voice was grave.

Flit sighed and looked in the direction of the siren, the sound still blaring over their conversation. "I'll take you guys back to my apartment. It'll make sense if they come and find us there. No one should question that."

Flit took Fortune's hand and teleported with her first. Fortune seemed to take the translocation well, but Flit didn't have time to study her properly as she returned for Layla and then Hawkeye. She could have taken them together, but the low emergency lighting made it too risky.

When everyone was safely in Flit's family apartment, the alarm was still blaring obnoxiously. Flit was not sure where her parents were, but she sincerely hoped they were close and safe.

The sirens and warning continued for well over half an hour. By that point in time, Flit had been able to give the others a good rundown of everything that had happened with the Citizen Derivates. Her concern for the fact the Free Citizens were starting their rebellion that night grew. She racked her brain to figure out a safe place she could translocate to in order to find Scraps. Even then, she was unsure if that was a good idea. If she returned to the Free Citizens right now, she would have a lot of explaining to do.

As much as Flit tried figure out how to get back to the surface, the blaring of the sirens made it nigh impossible to fully process a single thought. She figured that was on purpose, a move by the leaders to make it hard for people to do anything other than lockdown. She was just about to hunt down the speakers and destroy them when the sound stopped.

Static crackled, and then a voice burst into the apartment through the speakers. "Good afternoon." Flit gritted her teeth as Harmony continued, "As you know, we recently had a critical incident that led to the death of one of our own. We implemented an ability-training program in hopes to reduce further incidences. However, it has not been successful."

"It's been two fucking days!" Flit spluttered, even though she knew there was no way the woman could hear her.

The broadcast continued without pause. "It has happened again. Unfortunately, one of our members lost control, and their outburst hit key power and resource lines. Thankfully, no one was hurt in the initial incident, but until we can get the system up and running again, every single one of us is at risk. This facility cannot operate without the critical technology to keep our oxygen and water running."

The hairs on the back of Flit's neck prickled. She couldn't help but think it all was too convenient for her liking. She balled her hands into fists and shoved them into her pockets and kept her mouth shut in hopes she would not say or do anything stupid.

"The loss of power is an example of what can happen if we are not careful. As we work to repair the lines, we must be aware that the outage may start to impact the food, water, and oxygen supplies. It is a risk we simply cannot take. Therefore, we are now issuing emergency orders. All Underground members below a specific clearance level must wear inhibitors. We understand this is an inconvenience, but good intentions and promises are not enough to keep our systems safe. We refuse to allow you all to suffer or to put your lives at unnecessary risk, and this infraction was a timely reminder of just how much we stand to lose if powers go unchecked."

"Oh, for fucks' sake." Flit rubbed her face with her hands.

"Given the urgent need to ensure your safety, we ask that everyone remain where they are. We have members of Control walking the halls, corridor by corridor, seeking out people and installing the inhibitor cuffs," Harmony continued.

Everyone in the room knew that would not go down well with the general population. Flit couldn't help but marvel at the fact that someone in Control had just happened to lose it, giving Harmony and Divvy the exact outcome the had been trying to push for earlier. It was far too convenient.

"We need to hide somewhere. We can't have those cuffs," Flit said, voice low. "We need to get back up to the surface and figure out what the fuck is going on."

"They said they're only cuffing people below a certain clearance level," Hawkeye said, not looking as confident as he sounded.

"Yes, but what are the chances we're those people?" Layla asked, pointedly gesturing between herself and Fortune. When Hawkeye frowned, she added, "Or anyone on our side, for that matter?"

Fortune sighed. "I will handle that when they get to us. Don't worry. For now, let's just take a seat and relax. If we try and make a run for it, it will only look more suspicious. There's no point. We cannot act until we know what is happening on the surface."

Tense silence sucked the desire for conversation right out of the air as the minutes ticked by. As tempted as Flit was to just leave, Fortune was right. Given the state of the surface, they couldn't just go up there.

It was a good hour before there was a knock at the door. Flit teleported over and opened it. "What can we do for you?" she asked the two Control workers that were standing there. They each had a black duffel slung over their shoulder.

"We're here to install the new inhibitors, as per the order from Control," one said, sounding as though he was expecting argument.

Flit was tempted to deliver a quick couple of punches to knock them out then destroy the devices, but Fortune's words rang her ears. She would take care of this, so Flit tried to do her best to calm her outrage at the situation and stepped back to let the workers walk past.

Just as one approached Fortune, the older woman held up her hand. "When you put the inhibitors on myself and the others in this room, you will not close them fully. Nor will you activate them. When you are done, you will forget that I ordered you to do this and assume the inhibitors were correctly installed." Her voice was firm and held a note of command that Flit found herself wanting to follow, even though she was not the one putting the inhibitors on.

The workers paused for a moment, as if registering the order, and then looked around. "I will put the devices on. My colleague will check for more people. Is there anyone else in this apartment?" the man asked.

Flit shook her head, and he put his bag down, pulling out the first device. He approached Flit first.

"Are you not even going to ask our clearance levels?" Flit asked. "Didn't the announcement say certain clearance levels would be spared?"

The man raised his eyebrows at her as if she was stupid. He didn't even bother answering her question. "Arm, please."

As much as it grated against everything in her, she held out her arm. He wrapped the cuff around her wrist and joined the two ends together but didn't twist it or press the small button on the clasp. He nodded, apparently satisfied with his work before moving to Hawkeye, Layla, and Fortune.

The other team member came out of the bedrooms. "All clear. You done?"

"Yes. Let's move on," he stated.

His companion took out a small datapad and scanned each of their faces. Then the pair left.

Once the door was closed, Flit's first instinct was to rip the damn inhibitor off her wrist. She hated the feel of it and the tension in her shoulders that came with knowing that the device could be activated so easily and take away her favourite thing about herself.

"What do we do now?" Layla asked, frowning at her own wrist even though her device wasn't fully connected, either.

That, Flit thought, *is a good question.*

49

SCRAPS

GLOWING white numbers loomed on the screens, casting a cold light over the swelling population of the bunker beneath Nightmix.

Following the release of the announcement, Adam had put a call out to all members of the Free Citizens to gather their supplies and head to their nearest base. Scraps had been relieved to see Chris and Liana arrive within half an hour. He was worried that the Government would stop people moving about, but the hijack of the network had prevented the Government accessing their usual communication channels and issuing orders remotely.

The footage Adam had of the Hub that was projected on the screen was, apparently, not live. From what Scraps could tell from the security cameras that Andy's team had hacked around the city, people had started to flee. So far, it was going peacefully, but from the reports of the member who joined them over the next few hours, the Derivates and officers on duty were losing patience as the tension increased, and more weapons were being drawn. So far, it appeared to be all empty threats, but that might not last much longer.

Scraps stood by one of the monitors, watching a swelling stream of refugees from two streets over, when Andy walked past. She was clutching a meal pack like the ones Petra and Trey were handing out in the corner. Scraps gave her a smile as she approached, feeling sorry for the way that Adam seemed to snap at her any time she wasn't at her computer.

Andy leaned in closer as she passed. "I've got your reel loaded up. Closer to midnight, yeah?"

Scraps nodded. "Yes, I believe that will be best."

With any luck, the streets would be full of Derivate officers at that time. Scraps hoped they would all be able to see the feed on the screens plastered across the buildings. Would it be enough to have them turn on the Government? What would the Government do if they did?

Just as Andy stepped away, something on the screen Scraps had been watching caught his eye.

The sea of people walking down the middle of the road, arms full of bags and clothes and whatever they could carry, all looked over their shoulders and jumped off the asphalt. They parted like a curtain as a convoy of sleek, chrome-coated Government vehicles zoomed down the street, siren lights flashing at their fronts and rears.

"Adam?" Scraps glanced around. The leader was on the other side of the bunker, speaking to a group of people pulling on body armour. "Adam!"

The volume and urgency in Scraps' tone caught the attention of some of the people between him and Adam, and with a few passed messages, Adam looked up.

"Hurry!" Scraps beckoned him over as the cars reached the barricade.

Adam ran over and stopped beside Scraps as the vehicles waited for the teams guarding the street to shift the barriers aside. Then, they hooked a ninety-degree right and resumed their race in the direction of Nightmix. Scraps thought it could have been a coincidence, but then again, the Government had an idea that the Free Citizens were based in this block.

"We need a lockdown," Scraps said.

"Attention!" Adam jumped up onto the table and waved his arms. "We are calling a total lockdown in the bunker. All non-essential tech is to be completely switched off, and everyone is to sit against the walls. The lights will be turned off, and complete silence is expected."

"Want me to let them know up there?" Scraps asked, pointing up to the club.

"Yes, we need the entrance to this bunker concealed."

Scraps didn't wait for further commands. He turned and ran over to Petra and Trey. "We need to seal the entrance to the office."

Trey put down the meal pack he had been holding and straightened up. "I can do that now."

"It has to look like business as usual up in the club or at least as though you are preparing for whatever is to come tonight. Get up there, and ensure the day staff are still doing their thing. Don't tell them anything, and if you see any Derivates with the letter T at the front of their designation, do not think of this place. At all."

Petra's eyes widened. "We... we need to stay up there?" She glanced at Andy, biting her lip.

"The more normal we can make things look, the better." Scraps reached over and patted her shoulder. "This is the best chance to keep *everyone* alive. Go!"

After another moment of hesitation, the pair nodded and turned to leave.

Scraps followed them up, jogging behind them. As they reached the exit of the bunker, he retrieved a couple of errant crowbars they had used for previous missions and brought them along with him. At the end of the passage, he let Petra and Trey go back into the office before he reinforced the doors by propping the crowbars up against them. It was not ideal to prevent re-entry to the space, but if it meant keeping the Government away from the people hiding in the bunker, it would be worth it.

When Scraps returned to the main space, people were turning off their devices and moving to the outer walls of the room. There was not enough wall space for them all, so they spilled out onto the main floor.

"strike team, with me," Scraps called out.

The people who had raided the server farm with him rose to their feet and picked their way across the legs of those seated on the floor.

"We need firearms. We do not enter the passage, but we guard the entrance with our lives. Understood?"

Each one of the strike team members nodded.

Scraps returned to the main desk where Adam was and looked at the monitors. Adam was tapping at the screens and managing to follow the security cameras to see that the Government vehicles were pulling up right outside their building. Dozens upon dozens of uniformed and armed agents spilled out of the vehicles.

"Can you please copy that feed to my datapad?" Scraps asked, reaching over and retrieving his own device. "Then turn the brightness down on these screens, but keep them running. We need to know what is going on."

Even though Adam was the one in charge, he responded to Scraps' orders without delay.

Scraps picked his way through the seated Free Citizens and turned, motioning for Adam to ensure the lights were down. In the darkness, he also dimmed the screen of his datapad as he retrieved a weapon from a crate by the door and went to join his comrades guarding the exit. Tai, Leo, and Nick were on one side, and Elise was on the other. He sank to a knee beside Elise, his gun resting over his lap as he held up the datapad and watched as the screen filled with armed officers falling into formation on the sidewalk outside.

Scraps' heart sped up, but he felt the familiar calm of a mission washing over him. His head cleared, and all that mattered now was protecting the people in the bunker.

From across the archway, Tai raised their hand. Scraps frowned and squinted as he tried to see what was in it and noted that they were clutching a palmful of explosive putty.

"No," Scraps hissed, shaking his head for emphasis.

As good as it would be in stopping the Government from making their way down into the bunker, it was also possible it would cause enough damage to seal them in this underground tomb. They would stand a better chance of surviving even if they were captured by the Government.

Tai looked disappointed but shoved the putty back into a container at their waist. Scraps would have to talk to them about their explosive preferences later, but for now, he retrained his attention on the issue at hand.

The anticipation made sweat bead on Scraps' skin and roll down the back of his neck. He watched as the Government workers approached the front door of the shared building space. Nightmix did have its own private ground level entry, but seeing as that could be observed from the street, they probably figured it was safer to work from the inside instead. It would be easier to flush people out of what they thought would be a clear exit onto the street rather than risk them delving deeper into the building or going to one of the higher levels.

Two of the agents surged out from the group carrying a long black log-like structure that Scraps knew was a battering ram. They were able to bust through the front doors of the building without any issue, and the team rushed in.

The footage Scraps was watching changed to that of the club itself. It flicked through a few different views, showing that Petra and Trey had corralled the staff onto the main floor, having them move around some chairs and tables. They seemed oblivious to what was going on, and Scraps was pleased that Petra and Trey were keeping cool heads. The camera then finally settled the internal doors at the rear of the kitchen that were only every used by staff. It was the entry point the Government would be using based on their approach, and Scraps watched them with undiluted interest.

As the minutes ticked by, the doors remained unassailed. Scraps shifted uncomfortably on his knee but not because of the position. What were they waiting for?

Scraps turned towards Adam. He waved a hand at him and shrugged. Adam's forehead was creased with confusion as he tapped the screen in front of him. The one view on Scraps' datapad flicked from one camera to another until they settled on the corridor in front of the doors that led to the emergency stairs.

An agent held the door open while their colleagues filed through, weapons raised and at the ready. It was hard to see at first from the angle, but judging by the way they all moved, Scraps deduced that they were going up.

"Andy, can we get the—" Adam started.

Andy, who was already sliding out of her seat, said, "Yep, on it," as she ran over to Adam's desk.

Adam stepped aside and let Andy do her thing. The screens now had a somewhat translucent overlay that she was using to access the network and hack through the building's systems.

"They must have some micros working on their own surveillance. I have to be careful. Sorry. This may take a minute." Andy's fingers flew over the surface of the screen until she gave one final, aggressive tap and said, "Ha!"

The new view was a split screen with four camera angles. One was the internal ground floor stair well. Another was the corridor of the first floor, and the next two showed footage inside of—

Char!

Pressing his lips together to prevent a gasp from escaping, Scraps blinked. His mind whirled back to when Hector had been pressing him for information about the Free Citizen's base. Scraps had told the agents that the Free Citizens were using the restaurant on the level above the club.

Dark-uniformed agents lobbed smoke grenades into the kitchen and dining room. Scraps watched with horror as they rounded up all the workers. The poor people on that level probably didn't even know that the Free Citizens' base was right beneath their feet.

Over the next half hour, the Government Agents ransacked the restaurant, looking for any sign that there was a rebel headquarters in the space. When the agents had the people on their knees, the laser scopes of their weapons visible in the smoky aftermath of the grenades, Scraps was worried. Not for himself, but for the people that the Government now thought were rebels.

Out of sheer curiosity, Scraps wanted to ask if Andy could get the audio for the restaurant as well, but he stopped himself. If anyone in the room said that there was an informant, it would throw a flame grenade of chaos amongst the Free Citizens.

"I can't hold this much longer. I'm going to retreat from the restaurant and just keep an eye on the corridors around us," Andy said.

Two quadrants of the view turned black, and the screen moved into a dual split instead.

"They're not coming?" Tai asked from across the way, their face alarmingly disappointed.

"Not right now," Scraps said, "but... they might."

"We can't be complacent," Adam agreed from across the room. Everyone crammed into the space listened to the exchange with interest. "If they don't find what they are looking for up there, then they may search other parts of the building. We remain here, in lockdown, for as long as it takes for them to leave."

As long as it takes happened to be a good four hours. In that time, a group of agents escorted their captives out of the building and towards some of the vehicles waiting on the street outside. Then, they went, level by level, clearing the spaces and trying to finds signs of the Free Citizens.

When they reached Nightmix, Scraps noted Andy's tired, hunched posture stiffen as she watched the security footage of the club. Dozens of agent spent a full hour combing the club and looking for guilty parties or signs of rebellion. It was a tense time for the bunker, which had fallen to a surprising new level of still silence as the agents hovered overhead. There was not even a cough or the sound of a shifting body.

The countdown clock crept ever onwards, and towards the end, the captains of the agents appeared to become more and more impatient and agitated. They finally called it a night and drew all of their people out and back to the street. As Andy followed them on the street footage, it seemed they were moving on to try and find their quarry in other places.

"They're hitting anywhere we tagged with graffiti," Adam finally said.

From memory, the Free Citizens had been prolific in their tagging, so Scraps only hoped that meant the Government would be chasing those leads for quite some time.

Sensing that the immediate danger was over, Adam finally released the lockdown.

Scraps walked up the passage and remove the crowbars so that Petra and Trey could access the space again if they needed to.

When Scraps returned to the bunker, Adam gestured for him to come over. "We lost several hours of planning from that. I'm just getting reports from the other cells around the city, and they seem to be going well. Everything is in place for setting up the barricades tonight come midnight. There have been some Government raids in other cities, but none have been successful."

Yet, Scraps thought, but he kept his concern to himself. It wouldn't do to antagonise Adam while he was in action mode.

"Will they be able to roll out the barricades whilst the Government blockades are in action?" Scraps asked. It was one part of the plan he had been hoping to learn more about over the next week.

Adam grinned. "That won't be a problem."

Something told Scraps that he would not like Adam's plan in the slightest.

50

FLIT

THE LOCKDOWN LASTED FOR HOURS. Flit, Fortune, Hawkeye, and Layla had ran out of topics to talk about, and the latter two had fallen asleep on the couch across from Flit and Fortune. Flit couldn't help but think it was their own fault as the compromising state of dress she had found them in that morning likely indicated that they had spent the night awake rather than sleeping. Not that Flit blamed them, of course. As tired and on edge as she was because of the situation in the Underground, she still would have sacrificed sleep to spend that time being intimate with Scraps.

"They seem to have gotten close," Fortune whispered, jutting her chin in the direction of the sleeping lovers.

Flit smiled and nodded. "It's good. I'm glad they have each other. Layla seems lovely, and Hawkeye deserves to be happy."

"You know, for the longest time, I thought he was jealous of you and Rook."

Flit found it impossible to resist the urge to roll her eyes. "Yeah... Apparently you and the rest of the Underground knew it. I didn't, though. Things got a bit messy when Scraps and I got together, but we resolved it."

"I'm glad to hear it. You two are such good friends. It would be terrible for that to be lost." Fortune shifted so that her body was angled towards Flit's. "How are you going, knowing Scraps is up there and you're not?"

"I don't like it." She sighed and slumped against the couch. "But he made the right decision, and it won't be for much longer. Regardless of whatever plans Harmony and Divvy have, we're going up there to join that fight."

"It's a pity we only just started training everyone." Fortune leaned in closer, her gaze holding Flit's. "Is it wise to take them up there in this state?"

Raking a hand through her hair, Flit knew Fortune had a point. "We can't afford not to. The Free Citizens are up there making a stand. The Citizen Derivates will join them but only if we do. If the Free Citizens lose the uprising, it could be another century before anyone else dares to try."

"It's now or never, huh?" Fortune asked.

Flit nodded.

"Then we just need to make sure we do this right."

The lights in the room suddenly flicked from lockdown reserves to full power, and the screens around the room flared to life.

Harmony and Divvy appeared on the monitors. It looked as though they were seated in one of the Control meeting rooms. All of the heads of departments stood behind them. Everyone looked solemn and far too drained for Flit's liking.

"Good evening, Underground residents. Apologies for the extended lockdown, and thank you for your patience during this dangerous time," Divvy begun, looking directly into the camera. "We have asked the various leaders of the Underground here to give reports on the status of their departments, so that we are transparent in our sharing of information."

Divvy gestured to a man named Wrench, who was the micro in charge of Maintenance. He stepped forward, wiping a sheen of sweat off his wrinkled brow and pulling a datapad out of his pocket. He cleared his throat, eyes darting up to the camera and back down to his datapad several times before he spoke.

"We have been unable to repair ruptures in the power, water, and life support systems fully," he said, his voice more gravelly than Flit would have thought given the softness of his cheeks and posture. "At this stage, we are working on emergency reserves. As such, we have cut service to all non-essential areas, including many thoroughfares, until we can get the lines back up and running."

Flit leaned forward, pulling a pillow from behind her back and throwing it at Hawkeye. "Oi, Loverboy, wake up!"

With a groan, Hawkeye rubbed his eyes. He leaned forward, whispering something to Layla who had fallen asleep on his chest, and they both sat up. Hawkeye glared at Flit, as if asking why she'd woken him, and she jabbed her finger in the direction of the screen.

"In order to ensure that there is enough life support to sustain us for an extended period of time if we need it, we are putting restrictions in place." Wrench went to step back, but Divvy shook her head ever so slightly and he let out a sigh before continuing. "To keep everyone safe, the following orders have been made. Access to full lighting shall be restricted to between the hours of seven AM and nine PM. Outside of this time, only emergency level lighting will be accessed in all areas save for the Medbay and the kitchens. So that we can reduce oxygen distribution and keep more in reserves for later, all extraneous activities have been cancelled. Residents are asked to remain in their designated living quarters. They may only leave if they have been given approved duties or are seeking urgent medical attention."

As much as Flit wanted to say that she couldn't believe what she was hearing, she could. If she was completely honest with herself, this was where she'd feared the restrictions going all along. It was one of the few times in her life that she wished she had been wrong about something.

Awful as Flit felt about the restrictions, she felt worse for Wrench. She watched him shrinking further into himself as he became the public face for orders that the entire Underground population were going to hate.

"This is crazy," Hawkeye muttered, shaking his head.

As the only person who had been stuck in hiding his whole life, Flit wasn't shocked that he was the only one in the room who seemed blindsided by this outcome.

Wrench continued, "Connection to all but the basic Underground network sites will be restricted. This is to ensure that our communication lines are free of clutter for urgent matters. All necessary supplies will be delivered to your living quarters. This includes meals, three times a day. If there is anything else you require, you must put in an order with our Supply team."

Shoulders sagging with relief, Wrench stepped back, and the leader of Supply stepped forward.

What followed was a report of the situation at hand. They got a full explanation of how their food and other supplies would be running low soon. They learned that the security of the Underground would be in question if they had to do too many repairs close to the surface. They were told that the best way to survive, for now, was to follow orders for the sake of their safety.

Just before the broadcast ended, Divvy reminded them that they were all to return to their apartments to await further instructions. Those required to work would hear from their supervisors as soon as new schedules had been sorted, and anyone else would be free to engage in whatever appropriate leisure pursuits they saw fit within the new guidelines. From the way Divvy said it, it sounded almost as though she was granting them a holiday. A reprieve from work. Some extra time to spend with their families.

Flit and the others were not naive, though. It was nothing more than an extreme attempt to control them and to keep them from finding out about what was going on above their heads.

AN HOUR LATER, when Fortune, Hawkeye, and Layla had returned to their room, Flit's parents arrived home. Instead of coming in and complaining about the current circumstances, Flit's father walked straight over to her and pulled her into a tight hug.

"What's that for?" Flit chuckled, hugging him back. "Not that I mind, of course."

Stride stepped back and held her at arm's length. "I've spoken with your mother about this morning. I'm not happy about you keeping us out of the loop, but I'm so damn proud of you."

The tension Flit had been feeling only partially melted away.

"Are you still going to be proud of me when I expose whatever bull-shit Harmony and Divvy are up to?"

Stride let go of Flit and glanced over at Tinker. The look they exchanged told Flit that they had probably already discussed this outcome.

"Because of my job in the Medbay, I should have a fair bit of freedom of movement," Tinker informed Flit. Then, she held up her wrists to show that neither held an inhibitor. "Clearly they want my abilities at their disposal too."

On one hand, it made complete sense. Tinker needed to be available and ready for any medical emergency. The time it took to get someone to release an inhibitor could mean the difference between life and death for a patient. However, the fact she was Flit's mother surely should have triggered some level of concern for the higher ups.

Unless they thought Flit was still completely brainwashed.

"I wasn't so lucky, so I'll have to find some other way to help you." Stride sounded disgruntled at not being able to offer anything immediately, but Tinker gently squeezed his shoulder. "Although, if you happen to want to translocate me somewhere, I wouldn't complain."

"Where do you want to go?" Flit asked, amused by his suggestion.

He scratched his head. "I mean, the next room would be fine. I'm not picky. I just want to see what it feels like."

Flit could understand the interest. Translocation was an end goal for most teleporters. She still remembered the first time Shadow had taken her along. It had been such a rush to experience that kind of power.

"Too bad she's got an inhibitor on. I could try and take it off, but they aren't my specialty," Tinker offered, taking Flit's wrist in her hand.

"Oh, yeah. That's not connected." Flit pointed to the clasp to show that it was closed, but as she shifted her hand, it was clear it wasn't active yet.

Tinker blinked. "That was... stupid of them."

"Not really. Fortune was in here with me, so she just told them not to activate it then to forget the order." Flit took her hand back and slipped it into her pocket. "We also happened to hear from someone in Control that the Free Citizens have started the countdown to their rebellion. It should begin at midnight."

Both of Flit's parents' eyes widened.

"Will they be able to hold their own?" Stride drummed his fingers against his prosthetic leg, the faint metallic sound rhythmic and anxious.

"They should be able to, at least for a while. Adam may be unhinged, but he wants this. I have no doubt he has some decent plans laid out for whatever they are attempting. I also know that they will be better off if we are up there helping them," Flit explained, leaning against the back of the sofa.

"And the people we helped today... are they accounted for in your plan?" Tinker asked.

"That is up to the Citizen Derivates. I don't want to tell them how to run their show. I will need to reach out to them, though. I don't know how safe they'll be if the city plunges into chaos."

"It would be worth checking but not tonight," Tinker said. "You were woken early. You've had a long day, and you could probably do with some rest. I wouldn't put it past Control to put someone on patrol to make sure everyone is in their home."

Flit agreed with her mother. Well, at least so far as rest and patrols went. Not so much the implication that she shouldn't go anywhere. After all, Control would probably assume that all of the inhibitors had been installed correctly, and all they would need to do to ensure Flit and her family were home was visit their apartment. Once that had happened, they probably wouldn't bother checking again.

Later that evening, three meals were delivered to their apartment by workers from Control. They insisted on scanning the faces of all the family members before leaving. Following dinner, Flit yawned and wished her parents a goodnight. When she got to her room, she checked the time. There was still several hours to go before midnight. She bit her lip as she set an alarm on her comms system for fifteen minutes before the Free Citizens deadline and then had a shower. She dressed in dark, warm clothes and lay down in her bed to get some rest.

THE ALARM WENT OFF FAR TOO SOON. Flit felt as though she had just fallen asleep when the beeping startled her awake. Just in case her parents were still up, she teleported over to the door and switched the alarm off. With a yawn and a stretch, she wrote a message to Hawkeye.

To: Hawkeye
From: Flit
Subject: Please tell me...
Please tell me you're still awake?

Not even a minute passed before Flit received a reply.

To: Flit
From: Hawkeye
Subject: RE: Please tell me...
I am. Can't get to sleep. Just chatting to Layla on the vid system, but thinking of watching a movie or something before bed.

Flit grinned to herself as she translocated to just in front of Hawkeye's closet, the place he was least likely to be given his response.

"Yeah, I think we—" Hawkeye's casual, conversational tone was interrupted by a yelp of surprise at Flit's appearance. "For the love of..." He stopped, shaking his head and running a hand through his hair.

"Everything okay, babe?" Layla asked.

Flit cocked an eyebrow at Hawkeye and mouthed, "Babe?"

He shot her a glare that was sharp enough to cut, and she held up her hands.

"Yeah, all good. I just realised I forgot to file a report earlier. Catch you in the morning?"

"Sounds good. Sleep well."

The call ended, and Hawkeye rounded on Flit. "What the actual fuck?"

Ignoring his outrage, Flit gestured to the door. "I assume they've checked on you already?"

Hawkeye leaned back on his unmade bed and nodded. "Why?"

"It's almost midnight," Flit said, holding her hand out to him. "I can't be down here when things begin."

There was a flicker of hesitation in Hawkeye's features before he sighed heavily. "If they catch us, they're going to make sure we never leave these tunnels again. You know that, right?"

Flit rolled her eyes. "They'll have to find out first. We should be clear for at least a short time. C'mon. I don't want to miss this."

Hawkeye didn't take much more convincing than that. He got off his bed and walked to his closet to retrieve a long black coat. After pulling the coat on, he stepped closer to Flit and wrapped his arms around her.

"Come on then, you little chaos goblin. Let's go watch the world burn."

"Now you're speaking my language." Flit settled one hand on the back of his neck and the other on his lower back.

Closing her eyes, Flit recalled the last time she had seen the apartment she had shared with Scraps. The image of the broken furniture and strewn items was still as clear in her mind as it had been that first day. She knew it was a risk to go back there, but she figured that the Government would be far too busy trying to root out the Free Citizens before the deadline to keep an eye on an apartment they had probably already written off as a lead.

Putting all of her concentration into the jump and hoping the main thoroughfare through the living room was still as empty as she remembered, Flit willed herself and Hawkeye there.

When Flit and Hawkeye arrived, the living room was darker than Flit had ever remembered it. Hawkeye's arms tightened around her, and she held her breath until he muttered, "All clear."

Blinking and trying to adjust to the lights, Flit noted that the reason everything was so dark was because she was used to the light streaming in from the city beyond. Dodging the shattered crockery and cushion stuffing strewn over the floors, she made her way to the control panel. Flit tapped it to remove the light filtering from the window, only to find it was gone. The only light in the space was coming from the countdown in the corner of the control console screen. The broadcast from the Free Citizens.

5:24

As her eyes adjusted the faint glow of that eerie doomsday clock, Flit glanced around. "What the..." Flit trailed off as she teleported to stand in front of the floor-to-ceiling window, and her eyes widened. "Hawk, check this out!"

Beyond the glass panes, the entire city was nearly black. As the clouds moved over the crescent moon high in the sky, the reflection on the buildings made it looks as though the Hub was made of water, like the dark, fathomless depths of the ocean.

"They must have ordered power off. They're probably fearing overhead bombing if that's the case," Hawkeye said, his voice hushed to what felt an appropriate level given the way the city seemed to be sleeping all around them. "Do you know what this first stage is going to look like?"

Flit shook her head. "We didn't get a chance to discuss the details. All I know is that it will be a siege of some sort."

Hawkeye walked over to the window, resting a hand against it as he looked up. Flit watched him with interest. She couldn't see his face, but from the way his posture tensed, she knew he was using his powers.

"They've got some stealth craft in the air, I think... but apart from that, some barricades in key zones, and Derivates on the streets, it's dead out there. No Citizens at all," Hawkeye reported.

"They wouldn't have had a chance to issue a warning if the Free Citizens still have control of the airways. Not as a broadcast, at least."

Flit leaned against the window and looked down. The advertising screens on each building were plastered with the same network message that had been on the one in the apartment, and the light occasionally flickered over the scene below. However, it was impossible for Flit to get a full gauge of what she was looking at beyond some human-shaped shadows and the matte black void of body armour.

Flit stepped closer to Hawkeye, reaching out and holding onto his forearm as they stood there. She glanced over her shoulder.

3:39

Time slow to a crawl, and Flit thought back to the last time she had been peering out of this same window with such anticipation. She seriously hoped the Free Citizens had learned their lesson from the maglev attack and would be more sensible about this one. And more respectful of life. She shuddered at the thought of the family members who would have been in mourning following those "sacrifices", as Adam had called them.

3:01

Taking a deep breath, Flit bounced on the balls of her feet.

"This is—"

Flit was interrupted by a spurt of static, and she spun around to see the screen change back to the view of the flaming Free Citizens Logo. A voice-over begun, but the depth of the garbled tone was gone, and it was clear it wasn't Adam behind it.

"The Free Citizens want the Government to be aware that we will declare war within three minutes if there is no surrender offered," the voice stated.

It was hard for Flit to tell who it was with the audio manipulation on it, but it made her tilt her head to the side and close her eyes as it was so very familiar.

"However, before we do, we have more information to share. We have shown evidence of the Government's crimes against Citizens, but we also wish to bring to light other crimes, ones that have gone unaddressed for nearly a century."

Eyes snapping open in surprise, Flit watched as the flame logo dissolved and a picture of the Derivate Training Facility appeared on the screen.

"Oh, shit..."

Hawkeye pulled his arm closer to his own body, squeezing Flit's hand against his side. "What is it?" he asked, suddenly wary as he returned his attention to the world outside, clearly preparing for whatever threat there might be.

"For as much as we stand for the Citizens, we would not be a movement geared towards freedom if we did not acknowledge the suffering of the Derivates."

The footage of the training facility was replaced with a rapid reel of images from the medical facilities where Derivates were tortured. Tables with an analysis of the work hours and conditions of Derivates were also included, from the strict education routines starting in toddlerhood to the military assignments of mere children. Accompanying these documents were photos and short clips of what life was like inside the residential areas for the Derivates, and, as midnight approached, images of the drab, white, loveless nurseries with rows of dozens of cots and babies lined up.

"So, Citizens and Derivates, please take off the rose-coloured glasses the Government have forced on you. It is time to see the world for what it is. It is time to fight for your humanity. For your freed—"

The Free Citizens logo started again, with a large "ten" over it.

9... 8... 7... 6...

"What are they going to do?" Hawkeye whispered, his face moving all around as he tried to keep track of everything going on around them. Flit remained plastered to the window too.

3...

2...

1...

Then, the whole city shook as fire exploded to life outside, turning the deep night into day for a terrifying, glorious moment.

51

SCRAPS

"WHO AUTHORISED THAT?"

Adam's roar drowned out the deep, ominous rumbling that shook the very foundations beneath their feet. Scraps had to peel his attention from the bird's-eye view of the Government's key cities on every monitor as their metropolises became rings of fire.

The low buzz of conversation that had rippled through the room ceased, and the only sound was shifting feet and the creak of body armour. Whether in response to Adam's demand or the carnage on the screens before them, Scraps wasn't sure.

Clearly enraged by a lack of response, Adam pushed through the crowd between him and the tech station. He slammed his hand down on Andy's chair and turned her to face him. She yelped at the sudden jerk, jumping under his touch. Petra and Trey, who were standing nearby, surged forward but were held back by a couple of Free Citizens before they could reach her.

"Who authorised that broadcast?" Adam seethed, leaning in closer, face reddening and contorted with hard lines.

Andy gulped, but her lips remained pressed together.

"Stop!" Scraps launched through the still-parted crowd and grabbed Adam's forearm. His grip on Andy's shoulder was so tight Scraps didn't dare move it for fear of hurting his friend and ally.

The leader of the Free Citizens attempted to shake Scraps off, but he held on.

"What was that, Adam? What were those explosions?" Scraps asked in a low voice, directing attention to where he thought it really needed to be.

"We needed barricades. I made barricades... and destroyed any maglev station exits that would lead to the streets beyond them," Adam said with a dismissive wave of his hand. He turned back to Andy. "Tell me right now who authorised that fucking broadcast."

Andy tried hard, too hard, to keep her eyes on Adam and Adam alone. It was clearly suspicious, but Scraps had a lot of respect for her. It would have been all too easy to look his way.

With a low growl of disgust, Adam threw Andy against the back of her seat. "Get away from your station before I crush you." His voice was quiet but sharp enough to show the threat was real.

Stumbling as she got to her feet, Andy backed away. The people who had been holding onto Petra and Trey released them, and they took Andy into their arms, glaring at Adam.

"Free Citizens!" Adam turned his back to the computer station and the dozen programmers still working through the drama to keep dominion over the networks. "I intended to make this moment one that belonged to all of us, to congratulate you all for getting the movement this far, and to urge you forward with bravery and purpose." He opened his arms in a sweeping gesture, the sneering, threatening expression of a few seconds ago superseded by one full of charisma and hope. "As the dust settles on the start of our uprising, take a moment to look at those around you. Breathe in the anticipation in the room. Take strength in each other, and fortify yourselves for tonight, we fight!"

Adam pumped his fist into the air, and a communal cheer rung through the bunker. Scraps raised his arms like those around him, but even as he opened his mouth, no sound came out to join the celebration.

"Form ranks, Free Citizens, and prepare to strike. Everyone, find your team for the first wave and claim back the streets!"

A flurry of action erupted in the bunker as people shifted about and moved into the groups Scraps had trained them in over the past few weeks. He was pleased to see how swiftly they formed up, but he couldn't help wondering how enthusiastic they would be when the morning light washed away the veil of excitement and shone on a cold dose of reality.

"Brian, remain in the bunker with me," Adam said, coming up beside Scraps. "I will keep the strike team here and rested, just in case you need to move out with them."

Scraps moved away from the computer console and gestured for Adam to follow. "Do you want me to just ignore the fact that you set bombs in dozens of buildings around the city?" he asked in a low, firm voice.

"No, I want you to thank me for it." Adam raised an eyebrow at Scraps, seemingly tolerating this line of conversation because it appeared to amuse him. "I restricted the fireworks to the upper levels of buildings that were less likely to be in use at this time of night. The debris should have settled on the streets now, and some charges I had Tai set over the past few days have ensured that vehicles strategically parked around the streets also exploded and damaged the structural integrity of the thoroughfares. It is similar in every other city. The Government are now penned in like the animals they are."

"What about casualties?" Scraps demanded through gritted teeth as he struggled to control his anger. They were supposed to be freeing the Citizens, not slaughtering them.

Adam shrugged. "That's the Government's problem."

Scraps took a deep, steadying breath. "This is not what I agreed to."

"No, it isn't," Adam conceded with a dip of his chin, "but it's what the Free Citizens need. I expect you to get on board. We have the element of surprise whilst the Government tend to the casualties. Can I trust you to keep an eye on the team and act with the tactical mind I know you have, or are you too much of a coward?"

Oh, how Scraps wished he could punch Adam.

Instead, he straightened his shoulders and nodded curtly. "Show me where you need me," he said, hoping it wasn't too late to salvage the situation.

Scraps wished he had given up work earlier. As he stood in the bunker watching Adam's most trusted personnel moving between screens and communicating with those in the streets, he realised he had missed too much. Beyond helping to train the Free Citizens and being part of the strike team, Adam had not confided nearly enough in his second-in-charge.

As the early hours of the morning dragged on, each feeling like a month itself, he spent time with the different people Adam seemed to trust. With some well-pointed questions and a few white lies, he managed to gather more information about Adam's plans.

The most important thing Scraps had to remember was that the outer cordon that had been established by Adam's rash actions was not going to stay the outer cordon. The plan was to take more and more of the city, tightening the noose around the Government until they were within a good enough distance that they could move to seize Centre One.

Despite the fact Scraps disagreed with Adam's methods, a siege was a good plan. An invasion starting farther out would have meant the Free Citizens would have been vulnerable to air attack. At this point, if the Government wanted to use their aerial drones to launch an assault, they would be destroying a significant amount of their own infrastructure, and the human collateral would be huge. Scraps wasn't entirely convinced they wouldn't try as time went on. If the Free Citizens got close enough to Centre One or to other main areas of control in the other cities, the Government would probably be desperate enough to try it. It would all just depend on when they decided enough was enough.

"So, are there any other explosives placed throughout the city?" Scraps asked Tai as he leaned against the console the explosives specialist was working on.

Tai glanced at Scraps as they manipulated a wireframe map of the city on the screen. "There are some here and there. Adam wanted insurance just in case."

"Is he going for maximum impact in high-traffic areas?"

"Well, yeah," Tai said, frowning as if Scraps was being foolish. "There's little point blowing up shit that doesn't matter."

Scraps happened to think there was never a point for blowing up anything that would kill innocent civilians, but he kept that thought to himself.

"The ones that we let off tonight were in the highest levels only." Tai glanced at him between taps on the screen. "The charges were set strategically so we could ensure that enough debris would fall onto the streets to block them. It was pretty efficient, really. Probably some of my best work."

The way Tai spoke about the explosions made Scraps think that, perhaps, their interest in the Free Citizens might have been less about freeing people and more about having an opportunity to blow things up with impunity.

"Right, well... that is good to know. Thank you." Scraps stood and rolled his shoulders.

Scraps looked around, noted that Adam was not in the bunker, and decided to use the time wisely. He walked over to where Andy was sitting on a stool from upstairs, away from the rest of her team. She was still working away on a datapad, apparently not able to stop even with the way Adam had treated her.

Andy looked up as Scraps approached and then peered around, no doubt checking for Adam.

Scraps stopped when he was beside a nearby stack of crates, so he was somewhat sheltered from view. "I just wanted to say that the broadcast was perfect. Thank you for making it and for taking the risk to push it out," he murmured, not wanting to be overheard.

The worry creasing Andy's brow smoothed somewhat. "You were right. It needed to be done. I didn't realise Adam would be so mad, but I'm glad we did it. It's so important."

"But not mad enough to keep you off the network?" Scraps gestured between Andy and her team.

"He told me to work on ensuring our supply spreadsheet is up to date," she admitted, scratching her neck and shrugging. "But that was boring. I've remoted back in, and I'm still helping the team. I know it's not what he said to do, but he's acting like a fucking toddler throwing a tantrum. Our top priority has to be keeping control of the information highway, and taking me off that task is just plain stupidity."

Scraps agreed with Andy's assessment. "Where are Petra and Trey?"

The corner of Andy's lip twitched down, and she let out a sigh.

"They've been assigned to the team going around planting remote security cameras on the buildings around here."

It was a good idea given the fact their hackers were bound to succumb to the Government at some point. Well, at least they would if they didn't get more skilled hackers or some micros of their own.

"Good. Thank you again for the broadcast but also for the work. You must be exhausted."

Andy chuckled. "I'm in a relationship with two nightclub owners, Brian. Trust me, I've had my fair share of way too many days and nights melting together. We'll be starting a rest rotation soon, though."

Pleased to hear that they had considered a sustainable approach to the matter, Scraps noted Adam had just walked back into the bunker and was making his way to his desk. Scraps moved in that direction too but arrived faster than Adam did. While Scraps waited, he looked down at the screen. It was split into thirty-two quadrants monitoring the streets that had been barricaded. In addition to the various crumbled building debris, Adam had ordered some of their teams to steal service vehicles from nearby garages and drive them up to block the roads. On the Free Citizen side of the blockade, their people waited with weapons at the ready, out of view and around corners.

"I would like to get out there at some point myself. It's different when you're on the field," Scraps said.

Adam shook his head. "All in good time. For now, you should rest. We'll need to take it in shifts to supervise the efforts. I suspect the Government will try and use the dark of night for all manner of things, so I will cover nights, and I want you working days."

Theoretically, Scraps knew he should be tired and hungry. However, the sequence of events meant that he felt neither. He wanted to argue, to claim that he wouldn't be able to sleep, but that was not true. Despite how he felt, he would fall asleep the moment his head hit the pillow.

Scraps looked over at the little room he had made for himself in the corner by piling up crates around his blanket. It was a great space for just him, but there would be a lot more people needing a place to sleep soon. "Before I go to bed, I will expand the sleeping corner. There are going to be many people staying here now. Even though there is plenty of room upstairs, I think it is safer if we remain down here," Scraps said.

"Ah, and this is why I want you at my side." Adam gestured to some of the older members of the group who had decided to remain behind rather than participate in the active duties. "Ask for some help from those taking stock levels. You can bring down some of the cushions from the couches upstairs to put on the floor down here. No sense having them go to waste when we can all sleep more comfortably."

The thought of some light physical labour to help wind down before bed was a comforting one.

Scraps did as Adam asked and was grateful there were no telepaths around. He needed time to think without people getting into his head. The prospect of having control of the bunker during the daylight hours meant he would have some much-needed time to play with.

52

———

FLIT

WATCHING the outskirts of the Hub explode in a chaotic ring of fire had simultaneously been one of the most alarming yet gratifying moments of Flit's life. The way the night sky flared to life as the flames rippled through the air had burned itself into her memory.

Following the declaration of war and the first acts of violence, Flit and Hawkeye had spent another half hour in the apartment, with Hawkeye using his remote viewing to report the goings-on around the city to her. As much as Flit wanted to find Scraps, it was too much of a risk. The communication network seemed to be down, and the nearby streets were dark and being patrolled by Government officers with top-of-the-line night vision tech.

When she and Hawkeye returned to the Underground, the last thing Flit wanted to do was sleep. She was so fired up by what they had seen, by the way the Free Citizens had made such a blatant statement, that she wanted to wake the Blue Team right away and to call the Underground to action.

Hawkeye, as always, was the voice of reason. If the battle were to continue, a full night of sleep would become a luxury. The best way to fortify themselves, he told Flit, was by getting rest now while they could and putting together a solid plan with the Blue Team in the morning.

Of course, it was far easier to talk about sleep than it was to do it. As Flit lay in her bed that night, she tossed and turned until her limbs were tangled in the sheets, and she figured she had done more cardio in a few hours than she had in months. And that was just her body. The resonant rumble of the explosions and the glimmer of flames against glass haunted her mind, refusing to let her properly rest.

Then, there were her thoughts of Scraps. They danced between missing him sorely and wondering where he had been when the world had been set alight. Thanks to Iris' message, she was confident he was with the Free Citizens, but doing what? Regardless of the answer, Flit wished she was by his side.

In the morning, when her alarm finally sounded, Flit was eager to rise and get ready for the day. She was tired but not in the way most people would think. She was mentally fatigued by her own inaction. By the pressure to *rest*.

She had been resting her entire life. Now, it was time to *fight*.

"Good morning." Stride looked up from where he was sitting at the dining table and holding a mug. He tilted his head to the side as Flit teleported into the living room. "You look extra... perky this morning. I take it you don't need a coffee to wake you up?"

Flit shook her head. "I don't," she admitted. She walked over and pulled out the chair beside him, sinking down into it and leaning in close. "I went to the surface last night—"

"Flit!"

"It was incredible," Flit continued, unperturbed by her father's exasperation. "The Free Citizens broadcasted a message exposing the things the Government had done to Derivates right before midnight and then lit the city up with explosions."

Her father's surprise that she had left the house was now surpassed by what she was telling him. She gave him a rundown of everything that had happened.

Just as she finished explaining, she looked around. "Where's Mum?"

"She got called to do a shift in Medbay an hour ago. Looks like she'll be lucky enough to leave this apartment once in a while. I've yet to hear about my own shifts," Stride said, looking somewhat green with jealousy.

Flit let out a huff. She hadn't gotten any messages, either. She had a feeling some of the other teams might be called to duty but not her own. It would be stupid of Control to let the Blue Team gather in any number and have any measure of freedom. Not that a lack of patrols would stop them, especially when Flit was able to translocate.

"Well, I might go and sort some stuff out. I don't want to waste any time," Flit said.

Stride looked concerned. "Just wait until they've delivered the first meal. If they show up and you're not here, then we could be in trouble. Once that's sorted, no one would have any reason to drop by for a couple of hours."

As much as Flit wanted to get going, her father was right. Waiting would be frustrating in so many ways, but it was better than getting caught. She was walking a fine line, having an inhibitor that wasn't connected and being a known anarchist. It would suit her far better to be smart about things, like she had no doubt Scraps would caution her to be.

It felt like forever before there was a knock on the apartment door. She teleported right over as her father sighed from the table. When she opened the door, she realised in hindsight that tele-porting over was foolish. Luckily, the person outside with a trolley full of dome-covered plates didn't seem to want to barge in. The person in control of the trolley explained that she had to see the people the meals were going to, so Stride came over to join Flit. Flit then asked for one for her mother, and after a bit of back and forth on the datapad, it was confirmed that she was at work and the meal would be given to her there instead.

The moment the door was shut, Flit turned to her father. "I'll take my datapad with me. If you need me to come back, send me a message, and I'll return right away," she said. She barely stuck around long enough to hear his hum of agreement.

When Flit was back in her room, she went to the control panel beside her door and tapped out a message to Hawkeye asking if he was awake. After a moment she received a reply confirming he was. She told him that it was a good time to go to the bathroom, gave him a few seconds to move, then teleported into his room.

"I had a feeling you'd be up bright and early." Her best friend was leaning against the bathroom door frame. "Are we going to get the gang together?"

"Yep. Which room is best to meet in?"

"Probably here. I'm the least suspicious of you lot given I've been working in Control for a while now." Hawkeye walked over to his bedside table and retrieved his datapad. "I'll send some messages and see who is awake."

Five minutes later, Flit and Hawkeye had ascertained that Layla and Fortune, like the other refugees, were being kept under strict watch. Given that their sleeping quarters were more like closet-sized cells, they were moved to a common space for their meals and to give them some socialisation before returning them to their rooms. Even though no direct messages about meeting up were sent, Fortune and Layla indicated that they did not think it wise for them to join in any "VR Games" from their small spaces.

That left the rest of the original Blue Team. Once it was established that everyone but Tweak was awake, Flit went to get them and bring them into Hawkeye's apartment. Getting Swipe, Link, Clarity, and Sway was easy. Retrieving Tweak was another matter. The last thing Flit wanted to do was go into his room when he was sleeping, but she had little choice. When she woke him, he had drool running down his cheek and was muttering something about golden mushrooms. Flit didn't ask what the hell he had been dreaming about, and he did not offer the answer. Instead, he begged for a minute to go to the bathroom before she teleported him to join the others.

Hawkeye had left explanations for Flit's return, for which she was grateful. Then, together, they shared their side of what had happened over the past twenty-four hours. A ripple of shock went through the group when Flit and Hawkeye described the broadcast and the explosion.

"We need to get up there," Sway said into the stunned silence that had settled over the room.

"The question is, how? We're under such tight restrictions. We can't do shit without getting caught," Tweak muttered, shaking his head.

"We can't do this on the sly." Flit drummed her fingers against the desk she was leaning back on. "We don't have the time for lengthy, slow-burn plans."

"What are you suggesting?" Swipe asked, leaning forward as she sat on the edge of Hawkeye's bed.

Flit glanced at Hawkeye whose brows creased with concern, but he nodded all the same.

Flit cleared her throat. "I'm saying we need to strike hard and fast before they have a chance to fight back." She gestured to the others. "You've all got your inhibitors working, but Hawk, Fortune, Layla, and I don't."

"Do you think Layla can get mine off?" Tweak turned to Hawkeye, holding up his wrist. "I haven't had much experience tampering with them, but surely it won't be too hard?"

"Unfortunately not," Hawkeye conceded. He scratched the back of his neck. "However, if we can get to Cogs, I know she'll be able to do it."

"Will she be okay with that?" Link asked. "She's been helping with certain things, but we can't just assume she will stick her neck out for us."

"I think she will be if it is worthwhile," Hawkeye said. "Which means we need to make a solid plan."

Those gathered turned introspective as they considered the information they had heard and what they were dealing with in the Underground.

It was a good couple of minutes before Clarity spoke. "It sounds like the Free Citizens kinda took the Government by surprise. We could follow that kind of approach?"

"What do you mean?" Hawkeye turned his keen gaze on her.

She shrugged. "The broadcast thing. Like, given we're all restricted to quarters, we'll need a way to get the message across to everyone. I think that if the others know what our plan is, then we can recruit them. I'm sure there are plenty of people willing to fight."

"But how do we handle Harmony and Divvy? Harmony's shown she is a total boss when it comes to that coercion," Tweak pointed out.

Having Fortune at their side at the right time would nullify the possible impact of any telecoercion, but Flit's main concern was the fact that so many people still loved and respected their leaders.

"We need to discredit her," Flit said. "If we can get evidence of all the shit they've done, including this supposed maintenance issue from yesterday, then we can probably turn enough people against them to make this work."

"Would there even be any evidence, though?" Sway slumped back against Hawkeye's well-made bed. "Surely she would have been careful."

"She wasn't careful enough with me." Flit shrugged. "Hawk, any chance you can get back into Control for a bit? Or contact someone else who might be able to help?"

Hawkeye appeared to consider it before nodding. "I should be able to. I think the best way to go will be to get to the bottom of what happened yesterday. The excuse of yet another person losing control just seems too convenient. People will buy that easier than some of the other stuff she's done."

"That's a good start, but what comes next?" Link asked, looking between everyone but pausing to stare purposefully at Flit.

"We need to get ready to march on the surface. We should pre-emptively create teams to ensure abilities are well spread. Thank-fully, the data from our training sessions will assist with that. Assuming everyone did their pretest stuff correctly?" Flit asked, the plan already formulating so clearly in her mind. She had been waiting for this moment for so long. She wasn't about to let it slide by.

Everyone nodded or hummed in assent.

Tweak said, "We'll need to formulate a safe escape route too, given the tunnel closures."

"Oh, I can get the map of that. It was sent through the night before last for the Security team leaders." Swipe grinned.

"Not everyone will be good at navigating the tunnels via map. Most of them have been stuck in the residential areas their entire lives," Clarity pointed out. "We'll need some way to make the route abundantly clear."

Flit's mind danced back to the Free Citizens and how she had criticised their juvenile graffiti. The irony of her own sudden appreciation for the idea was not lost on her as she said, "I'll ask my father where they keep the spray paint. I can teleport around and mark the tunnels once we have the map. It won't take me long if I go alone."

From there, the rest of the plan flowed smoothly. They were counting on the fact that Harmony and Divvy would need to make an Underground-wide announcement at some point, so they would just have to be prepared to hijack it. When they had everything they needed, Flit could teleport the team in there to handle it live.

There was still plenty to do before then, though. Hawkeye had a shift in Control later that day and still had his armoury keys. He would be able to access weapons without too much trouble, and he would work on ensuring Cogs was on board and could get evidence against the leaders. Tweak would hack the comms network to ensure it remained open. Link and Clarity volunteered to go through the ability and demographic data to put some teams together, and Swipe and Sway pulled out the maps to get started on the best route to the surface for those wanting to fight, given the new tunnel closures.

About an hour before lunch was due to arrive, everyone knew what they were supposed to be doing. There was a buzz of anticipation in the room when they all sat back and looked at the plans they had made. It was exciting for Flit but also intimidating because once they started down this path, there would be no taking it back.

Flit loved the Underground, but over the past few weeks, desperation had turned it into something she didn't recognise. Her persistent, life-long desire to see her people free of the darkness reared at the news of the battle being waged overhead. It felt as though all the pieces of what she'd thought her life would lead to were finally falling into place, and she knew she had to run with the momentum while it existed.

The attitude of Flit's fellow Underground dwellers had always been somewhat sceptical when she'd spoken of her desire to fight back against the Government, so the Blue Team's support meant a lot to her. She was also fully aware that their relationship with Scraps had a lot to do with it too. The knowledge he *chose* to remain behind and fight made Flit's heart swell with pride, and it showed that there was real hope for the cause. After all, it wasn't just Flit being chaotic and rebellious. If the most logical and sensible of them could see the merit in it, then it had to be worth something.

"So, everyone knows what they have to do?" Flit asked, looking around.

She was met with a variety of nods, salutes, and hummed acknowledgements.

"Ooh, that's a good question," Link said, turning to Clarity and giving her a warm smile. "You should definitely ask."

Flit rubbed her face to hide her own smile at the tenderness in Link's tone and the fact she was clearly in the other woman's mind more than would be normal for just a regular teammate.

"Well, let us all in on the secret." Tweak leaned closer.

Clarity sighed. "I think this plan is great and all, but from what I can predict, it is almost certain they will do a lunchtime broadcast. How do we handle that?"

The excitement that had been buzzing in the room at the plan deflated somewhat, and Flit's foot bounced on the spot as she considered it. Clarity had a point. As good as her predictions were, they needed some level of information to go off. It was easy for Clarity to see when Control would make an announcement, but there were simply too many variables for her to determine what the Blue Team would do about it, especially as they hadn't considered the obstacle yet. Flit wasn't the best at wrapping her head around the whole precog thing, but she knew that there had to be some level of contemplation of a course of action before the outcome could be predicted. Luckily, Clarity had initiated just that with her question.

Hawkeye looked just as concerned by Clarity's question as Flit felt. His brows creased. "We need a good couple of hours to get all of this together."

"Maybe we need to make sure that there can't be a broadcast until we want one," Tweak said in a tone that was far more devious than usual.

Hawkeye cocked a brow at the micro. "What are you suggesting?"

"Well, if they can't access the network, they can't make a broadcast, right?" Tweak gestured to the communication panel on the wall then Hawkeye's datapad.

"But if we bring down the network they use, that means we won't be able to do what we need to do... right?" Sway muttered, sounding as though he did not like that option in the slightest. He glanced over at Link and Clarity.

Flit knew that look. She felt it in her bones. It was one thing to spend time away from the people you loved, but it was another matter to know they were out of communicative reach.

Tweak shrugged. "Not necessarily. If our talented translocater can get me into the network room for the Residence, I may be able to make a few... tweaks."

Everyone groaned, but the point he made was enticing enough for Flit to let that terrible pun go. "Is there any way you can get me a picture of it? A live feed would be preferable."

"I'll work on it. With any luck, they should only be watching their own network vulnerabilities. It doesn't make sense for anyone to be messing with the connections here, not when we know people will get bored out of their brains without it."

Swipe leaned closer, her braid falling over her shoulder as she shifted. "Will we still be able to access the documents and maps we need?"

"You'd be best off saving them to your devices just in case."

"How will we communicate with each other?" Flit asked, voicing a question that everyone would be thinking.

"If I'm careful about it, I should be able to keep the messaging system intact. The benefit of disconnecting from the Control server means we will also be protected for a short time as they won't be able to monitor our messages," Tweak explained. The more he spoke, the more serious he got.

Flit had seen him like that before. He presented as a joker a lot of the time, but when he started talking about his areas of interest, his true cleverness shone through.

"That could be useful," Flit said encouragingly. "How long will it take them to notice and come in to fix it?"

That was enough to earn a heavy huff from Tweak. "Honestly?

I'm not sure. They could notice it right away. They could notice it in an hour. We just don't know."

Everyone took that information and seemed to chew it over.

When the worry in the room turned thick and counterproductive, Flit clapped, snapping everyone from their musings. "Well, sounds like we have a plan for now. We may have to adjust on the fly, but if we don't start now, there's no point to any of it." She looked at Tweak. "I'll teleport all these knuckleheads back to their rooms and then come and get you last. Think you can find me that reference video in the meantime?"

Tweak sat up straighter and nodded. "I'll get onto it right away if Hawkeye lets me borrow his datapad."

Hawkeye handed it over without hesitation.

Flit approached Swipe. "I'll get you back first," she offered.

Swipe didn't argue as Flit stepped in close and got in contact to translocate her.

When they arrived in her room, Swipe asked, "What about Fortune? When will you get her?"

"I think we'll have to wait until right before we bust into Control. If she is as heavily monitored as Hawk said, we need to be careful. She will be on board, though," Flit said, knowing enough about Fortune to be confident she wasn't overestimating her support.

"Just as long as we take her with us," Swipe confirmed with a resolute grimace. "Because if those bitches in leadership really were involved in getting her, Vector, and Rook caught, then she deserves to be there when we bring them down."

"I couldn't agree with you more." Flit squeezed Swipe's shoulder before she translocated back to Hawkeye's room to get the others sorted out.

53

———

SCRAPS

BETWEEN THE ACTION of the night and the busyness in the bunker, Scraps found it difficult to stay asleep. He drifted in and out of awareness for what felt like an eternity. At some point, he decided that sleep was probably out of the question and rest would have to be enough. Once he let go of his expectations and just let his body relax, his mind settled enough for him to feel some benefit from the process.

Scraps knew it was time to get out of his makeshift bed when the sound of excited chatter filled the room. His curiosity got the better of him as he rose, pulled a shirt and pants over his sleep shorts, and stepped outside of the crates stacked around him.

Adam was standing at his usual place behind his desk, surrounded by a variety of Free Citizens who were part of the command team. Well, some of them. From what Scraps could tell from a cursory glance around the bunker, it seemed they had worked themselves into shifts too. Others were resting in sleeping bags around the edges of the room or on some of the cushions Scraps and the others had brought down before he had gone to sleep.

The people who were awake, with the exception of the tech team who were still hard at work at their consoles, gathered with Adam, watching the screens before them with expressions more aligned to watching a comedy film than a live feed of a rebellion.

Scraps needed to use the restroom but decided to detour past Adam's desk as he walked.

"Morning, Brian," Adam said, tearing his attention away from the screen for the bare minimum.

The others made their own greetings, but they were distracted by what they were watching. Wanting to know what was so interesting, Scraps leaned over. His eyes widened. On the screen, the live feed of dozens of large, old, weatherworn vehicles drove down the middle of the streets behind the Free Citizen's debris barriers. Scraps tried to figure out where he had seen the odd vehicles before. They had tracks instead of wheels or hover bases, as well as appendages shaped like open containers or massive pincers. One even dangled a heavy-looking ball from the end of a chain of its arm.

A low chuckle tore Scraps away from the screen.

"Bet you didn't think we had anything like these old girls lying around," Adam said, a smug grin on his face.

Scraps shook his head. "What are they?"

"I forget how young you are sometimes." Adam shook his head as he gestured to the screen. "We don't see them around much anymore, but these are some of the vehicles that were used to build and expand the Hub. They have a range of functions, but once the city stopped expanding, these older, bigger ones became redundant. There is a vehicle graveyard on the outskirts of Old City. I had some of our team go and resurrect these. Figured they could help us keep the siege moving closer to Centre One. Tightening the noose, so to speak."

Scraps watched, astounded, as the vehicle with the large open container on the front barged forward, gathering debris in the scoop and pushing it forward. The Government Agents stationed on the other side all let out horrified yells as the stationary barrier suddenly started moving.

As the main vehicle crawled ahead, the one with the large ball swung its arm and smashed glass and steel from the building to the side, sending Government Agents scattering. The same scene was repeated on ten other feeds, showing similar vehicles adding debris to the partition as they pushed it forward.

On one of the screens, a group of three Registereds stepped into the path of the vehicles. Scraps couldn't see their designations, but the moment they raised their arms and their faces set in determination, he knew they were like him. Well, they were like him before he had joined the Underground.

As a macrokinetic with a ranking of C, Scraps had been able to move quite a few large things but nothing near what he could do now he was uncapped. As he watched the trio that were now trying to fight back against the massive machines, he knew the Government was not prepared for this. The Derivates were barely able to make the rubble shake.

Seeing that they were outmatched, the Registereds retreated, probably calling for backup.

Scraps frowned as he noted that shifting the debris forward a block meant that the blocks on either side would be left vulnerable.

"Adam, we're leaving the sides exposed along the diagonal." Scraps tapped the screen in the areas in question at either end of the push.

The smug expression on Adam's face faltered for a second before he got control of it. "I'll redistribute our forces to cover the gap."

"Who have we got, and where are they?" Scraps asked.

Adam pulled up a neon blue wireframe map of the city that had red dots indicating tracked Government forces and green dots and designations indicating the Free Citizens forces. He pointed out another three locations on the map that were marked yellow, indicating that each cardinal direction of the Hub had its own construction team working to push the barriers closer together in tandem.

As it was, the Free Citizens were scattered sparsely along the barriers. The only reason Scraps thought they hadn't been taken over was because the Government had to be preparing their attack for a time when their enemies were in closer proximity to one another. At this point, the cost of taking them out whilst so separate would be greater than the benefit they would gain from it.

Unless, of course, they found a weak spot to exploit.

"We are going to need to rest those teams soon, and they are already spread so thin," Scraps said, looking up at Adam. "I think we should put together teams dedicated specifically to protecting the gaps while the vehicles tighten the noose." Scraps decided to use Adam's word for this tactic of shifting their boundaries, finding the metaphor appropriate.

Adam tilted his head to the side as he considered it.

"We also need to ensure they are skilled at fighting. If I were the Government Agents, that would be where I would attack," Scraps added, not wanting their rebellion to fail because of such a foolish, easily remedied oversight.

"Very well." Adam stepped back from the console. "Give me a list of the best fighters from the units you've trained. Take some from each group to form the ones you need. Just be sure to leave the other areas with decent fighters as well."

Scraps couldn't help but think that this would be a great reason to join with the Underground, but he kept that thought to himself. For now, at least. He still had to find a way to get to them.

Adam tapped the communicator tucked against his ear, the beeps indicating he was turning the sound down. He reached into his pocket and retrieved a similar one for Scraps. "This is for you. I am going to get some rest. You sort out these teams and give them the orders to move out."

"Copy that." Scraps took the communicator and watched as Adam walked over to a small, crate-stacked-walled room that was in the corner of the bunker and disappeared behind a tarp strung between two weapon vaults on either side of the makeshift doorway.

There was a part of Scraps that wanted to leave the bunker the moment Adam was out of sight. He wanted to head back to the Underground and seek out Flit. It would be a step towards getting the Free Citizens the help he knew they would need in the coming days.

As tempted as he was to leave, Scraps had to be careful. Patience was a virtue, and there was little point in seeking help if he was unable to ensure the safety of the people already under his charge, so, with the assistance of the members of the strike team, Scraps worked on reorganising the teams.

The sheer amount of ground they had to cover in the Hub meant that, even with the significant force they had amassed, their foot soldiers were still too spread out. Scraps was grateful that Adam's plan for the other cities was mere sieges rather than the choking of the Government like they had to achieve in the Hub. The different tactics did not make things easier in their main city, though, and it had not been more transparent to Scraps until that moment.

"It won't be permanent," Elise said, her forehead etched with deep creases of concern as she looked at the chart with the new team assignments. "As the days pass, we'll take more blocks, and the teams will get closer together. When we have good coverage, we can start dissolving groups."

"So, we are agreed this is the best arrangement?" Scraps zoomed out on the screen, showing the tables with the new team assignments.

There was a murmur of agreement from Tai, Leo, and Nick as they all stood around Adam's desk with Scraps and Elise.

"So can we just send the group reassignments out?" Nick asked, glancing back at the part of the room that had been turned into makeshift sleeping quarters.

Now that the initial push was over, fatigue tugged at the faces of so many of the Free Citizens. Whilst Scraps could understand why so many people had been present to watch the clock tick past midnight, he now saw the folly in not asking some to return to sleep.

"I do not think that is wise." Scraps gestured to the many names. "It would be chaotic if they all just decided to start moving. It would be better if it was a guided process."

The team didn't have to groan for Scraps to know that was not what they wanted to hear.

Elise was the only one whose shoulders didn't slump at the news. "So, we need to get on comms and start issuing orders?"

"Yes, but I think redistribution of assignments should be handled in person. We need to be able to guide the people assigned to the gaps under cover," Scraps suggested.

"Right. In that case, Tai, you take north. Nick, you're on west. Leo, south. I'll handle east," Elise ordered.

Even though Scraps was technically in charge, he let it go.

"Please order everyone to meet back at the central block of their cardinal direction. When they arrive, we will escort to the gaps. Tell them this order is a priority, and we expect everyone to be on site within forty-five minutes," Scraps said.

Everyone took their orders and moved on, and he swapped the view of the screens to focus on the heavy machinery moving their blockades forward. It was a slow process but one that filled Scraps with awe as they used such outdated technology amongst the soaring buildings to impressive effect. Scraps was transfixed by the happenings outside as he kept an eye on the unfolding situation.

A short time later, he was approached by Petra with a cup of water and a roll for breakfast. He took it with a word of thanks and a grateful smile. He thought she would return to where Andy and Trey were seated over in the hacker's area, but she hung back.

"Andy wants to let you know that they are going to lose the network soon," she whispered as she leaned closer to him. "Following that, Adam's plan is to blow the network hub. That will destroy the servers and leave the Government—and us—without a way to communicate."

This was something Scraps had been anticipating based on what he had seen Tai doing in the server farm. Even though he did not want more needless destruction, he was coming to think it might be necessary. In his mind, he weighed the benefits of keeping the communication lines versus the problems. When it came down to it, both the Government and the Free Citizens were dependent on the networks to manage their efforts. However, the Government, being the larger organisation, would be relying on it far more than the Free Citizens were.

Scraps' mind went once more to the Underground and the heavily wired networks they had to use to communicate with the barrier of concrete, rocks, and steel support between them. Then, his attention caught on the vehicles on the screen as they pushed tonnes of glass and asphalt as though it weighed nothing. He wondered what other kinds of communication technology would be available if they delved into the methods of the past...

"If we need to blow the network, we need to blow it. We cannot afford the Government taking control of it again," Scraps said, hating that he was agreeing with Adam on this but knowing it was the best option. "We will figure something else out."

Petra gently squeezed his shoulder and smiled before moving away. She went straight to Trey and Andy, clearly communicating the message with then. Andy looked back over her shoulder and nodded at Scraps, and he knew they would allow it to happen.

"Hey, boss, looks like the fighters are en route to the gaps."

Scraps turned to see Nick approaching.

"You gonna call the guys in the area to let them know they have escort duty?" Nick continued.

"No, I'll do it myself," Scraps said, surprising himself with the unexpected nomination.

It would be a perfect chance to hit the streets himself and to see if he could find the Citizen Derivates. They weren't Flit, but at the very least he knew where to find them.

"Uh, you sure that's a good idea? You're supposed to be boss around here while the big guy is snoozing," Nick said, brows knitting together.

"Of course," Scraps said with an unwavering tone of confidence that was only partially false. "Andy will be in charge of watching over things while I'm gone, and I'll have the earpiece if there is anything urgent."

Nick looked as though he still was not pleased, but he nodded and returned to where he was seated with Tai, who was still hunched over their own datapad.

FIFTEEN MINUTES LATER, Scraps was dressed in his body armour and buckling a pistol into a leg holster. He checked that everyone knew their planned directions and then went to let Andy know that he was handing over command.

"Hey," she said as he approached, not bothering to look up as she tapped away on her keyboard.

Scraps thought that her fingers must be screaming in agony after so many hours at the desk, but she was still going strong. As Scraps watched her, it was almost as if she wasn't even blinking.

"I have to step out to escort some team members to their new assignments," Scraps informed her.

"You sure Adam will be okay with that?"

Scraps shook his head. "He won't be, but he is sleeping so it is not up to him."

In profile, Scraps could see the way Andy's lips curved in a smirk. "You'll be taking a datapad with you, right?"

"Uh..." Scraps looked down at his body which currently carried armour, a pistol, a knife, and a few grenades, but no datapad. "I wasn't planning to. I will be on comms."

"Take one of the smaller datapads. There should be a belt clip over with the other tactical gear. Comms are great, but if there is something we need eyes on, you're going to need a datapad."

"Copy that," Scraps conceded.

At that moment, he longed for the visor he had to wear every time he had left his barracks as a Registered. It was the perfect tactical accessory, with a mixture of functions that would negate his current need for an earpiece and a separate, awkward-to-carry datapad.

Scraps returned to the crates full of tac gear and managed to find a belt clip that would do the job. He then took a smaller datapad from the pile, tested that he could access it and that it had plenty of charge, and then walked towards the exit to the bunker.

A couple of people sitting by the tunnel entrance looked up at him and the others as they passed but made no attempt to stop them. The walk up the tunnel felt almost like taking a breath of fresh air. He had been in the bunker for what felt like far too long. The feeling did not last long, as the Club above had been trashed from the Government's search and utterly abandoned. It felt odd to walk through it, and this was only exacerbated as Scraps stood on the street.

The Hub had never felt so quiet as it did when he parted ways with the other strike team members. There wasn't a single person on the street. He swore that he could hear the wind whistling through the streets. The ominous grey of the sky above was not helping the situation. As eerie as it was, the streets being clear was a blessing for Scraps. It allowed him to stick to the shadows cast by the buildings as he made his way towards the rendezvous site.

Each step away from Nightmix felt like a step away from the mask he had to keep on around Adam. Even though he was walking towards danger, Scraps almost relished that compared to the frustrating social dance he had been doing for far too long now.

Keeping his eye peeled for threats, Scraps made his way through the city. He made a note to himself that he would have to ask Adam if there were any vehicles available to the Free Citizens. Not that this would be a wise choice, of course, as they would be far easier for the Government to target by air strike if they finally decided to bring drones into the mix. Not *if*, Scraps corrected himself, but *when*.

Thankfully, the trip to the rendezvous point was uncomplicated for Scraps but also for the Free Citizens in general, if the lack of comms chatter was anything to go by. Still, Scraps removed his pistol and kept it in his hands as he waited for the transfers to approach.

The people he was waiting for arrived in dribs and drabs. The training sessions he had held over the past week meant that he was easily able to identify the ones he had reassigned, but they were far more suspicious of each other. His first course of action was to have them introduce themselves to one another. Generally, the Free Citizens in different cells or training groups were reluctant to use names, but he encouraged them to get familiar with one another, as they would be working in close and dangerous quarters together.

When the introductions were finished, Scraps then relayed the new orders to them and explained the reason that they were required. They all seemed to get renewed sense of purpose in them, a new glint in their eyes, as they learned about their special responsibilities. He gave them the opportunity to step back, and only one man did on account of the family he had waiting for him at home. He was happy to fight, he said, but in more of a reserve capacity. Scraps used the datapad he had with him to send a message back to base that the man was approved to return to his originally assigned unit, and then Scraps had the rest move out.

What felt like a silent city turned into something entirely

different as they neared the blocks where the heavy earth-movers were working. The squeal and grind of shifting concrete and steel was a sound that made Scraps wince. From the videos, he would never have guessed at the sheer volume of the bone-crunching sounds. The closer they got, the harder it became to ignore the way the ground shook.

Gesturing for the Free Citizens to fall in behind him, Scraps led the group to the gaps. When they were close enough that the area they needed to cover was obvious, he paused. He let them know that he would send their replacements at the same time they were scheduled to be relieved from their original postings. He encouraged them to remain hidden and to avoid combat at all costs. They were only to engage if there was a threat to their own lives or those of the people sitting high in the cabins of the construction vehicles.

Satisfied that everyone knew what they were supposed to be doing, Scraps slipped away. Instead of returning to Nightmix, he jogged back under the cover of the buildings and wound his way through the deserted city. Luckily, his choice of team to escort had kept him in the right direction for him to go and speak to the Citizen Derivates. At least, he hoped he could. He was not sure if they would still be in their hideout. If it was him in that ramshackle excuse for a safe house, he would have led his people out the instant the Free Citizens made their announcement. Except... where would they have taken them?

Shaking himself out of his thoughts, Scraps returned his attention to the streets. As he got farther away from the club and the centre of the city, he noted that this area had not escaped the lockdown well. It was clear that the residents had attempted to loot what they could in preparation for what was to come, and that observation had Scraps watching the shadows more closely.

A few minutes later, Scraps reached the apartment building without being noticed. He slipped in through the front door, which was hanging off a hinge, and followed his way through the corridors until he reached the apartment he was looking for. The door was closed, but he used some of his powers to force it open. Inside, it was dark, lit only by streams of light coming through the worn curtains in piercing shafts. He shut the door behind himself and walked into the living room. He frowned as he waited, wondering if he had made the wrong decision.

Ten minutes later, when Scraps was about to leave, the sound of the door opening made him turn and hold up his hands.

He was met with the familiar face of Mitch as they held a gun in Scraps' direction.

"Oh." Mitch let out a groan and relaxed as they entered the room and kicked the door shut behind themself. "It's only you."

"Uh, thanks," Scraps said, not certain what else would suit the situation. "I am sorry to intrude, but I do not have long. As you can see, the Free Citizens launched their assault earlier than expected."

"Yeah, no shit," Mitch muttered warily.

Scraps had heard the expression before and realised it was more of a rhetorical vocalisation, so he continued on unperturbed, "I am not sure if you have moved your forces yet, but it would be wise to get out of the city. The farther away the Free Citizens' barrier gets from here, the more prone it will be to lawlessness."

Mitch lowered the weapon and ran a hand through their hair. "We had to split up because we had too many people. We have more than half of our numbers four blocks thataway." Mitch gestured in the direction of the outskirts of the city.

"Ah." Scraps frowned. That was not ideal. "Well, if you need to move, the time will be soon."

Crow's feet appeared on either side of Mitch's eyes showing their confusion, but they kept their mouth shut. "But where are we supposed to go?"

"I know a place that could help," he said, smiling. "There is an abandoned train shed on the outskirts of Old City. If you head East from here and follow the train line south, you should be able to find it."

"So, what? We hide out there and wait for the radiation to get us? I'd much rather die fighting." Mitch adjusted their hold on the rifle so they could cross their arms and lean against the wall behind them.

"You can do that later," Scraps said dismissively.

Mitch choked on an exclamation.

Scraps surged onwards, "For now, though, it will house you. If you go downstairs, you'll find a well-stocked emergency bunker that the Underground set up."

"And what? They'll let us in, just like that?"

Scraps shook his head. "You may need to get one of your micros to bust in, but it will be worth it. I am unable to get word to the Underground that we need them up here. However, your arrival will send a message loud and clear. If you can't get into the bunker, use that." Scraps pointed to the charm Mitch had around the wrist they were still holding onto the gun with.

"Flit said that the Underground wasn't really the best place to mess with at the moment," Mitch said, frown deepening.

Mitch had a very good point.

"Then ignore the bunker, stay in the train shed, and just use the bracelet. That will alert only the people we want to know. I'm sure that the Blue Team already has a plan to get up here... They may just need to enact it a little early."

Scraps' suggestion was met with a sarcastic laugh from Mitch. "Ah, yeah, just like the rest of us, huh?"

"Yeah, right." Scraps let out an awkward guffaw before nodding.

"So, you don't want my people to act until then? What if we marched to your aid while you waited for the Underground to get their shit together?"

Scraps blinked, surprised at the offer. "I appreciate the thought, but no. I think we need the numbers to convince the Free Citizens. Stick with the Underground because, if things go poorly with the Free Citizens and the Government, they will protect you."

"Still not sure the Free Citizens won't turn on us?" Mitch asked, voice more discontented than Scraps had ever heard it before.

It was unfortunate, but Scraps did not wish to lie. "I am still not certain. If I were in your position, knowing what I know, I would rather put my faith in the Underground."

Mitch stared at Scraps for what felt like an eternity before they nodded. "Thank you. I appreciate your honesty." Then, they gestured towards the door. "Do you need an escort to the Free Citizens?"

"I will move quicker on my own." Even though he declined, the offer still warmed his heart. "I wish you all the best with moving your people safely, though, and look forward to seeing you and the Underground joining the fight. I will ensure that the reception from the Free Citizens is as warm as it can be. Whatever happens, please do not fire first."

The way Mitch chewed on their lip told Scraps they did not like his final words of wisdom, but they nodded all the same. "See you soon."

An unexpected sense of relief washed over Scraps as he walked out of the apartment. Even though the rapport he had with Mitch was tentative to say the most, he had every faith that they would keep their word. The knowledge that Flit and the Blue Team would be aware of what was happening in the Hub shortly gave him hope. The Government had not come out to play yet, and Scraps had a feeling it was a bad sign. Whatever they were planning that was taking extra time did not bode well for the rebels.

54

——

FLIT

NOXIOUS, black-hued fumes clouded around Flit's head. Even though she had her mouth and nose buried in her elbow, the odour was enough to make her eyes water and her brain throb painfully against her skull.

Even with the headache, she had to admit she was having fun.

Flit sprayed the final section of the stencil she had made from an emergency exit sign in her parent's apartment. She repressed the urge to cough. She was still too close to the residential tunnels to dare make a noise.

Ripping the stencil away, Flit teleported back to observe her handiwork. Before her, on the wall, was the U-shaped logo of the Underground with an arrow in the gap, the tip of which was pointing in the direction of the escape path Swipe and Sway had put together.

The black paint blended into the tunnel walls probably a little too well, but she and Sway had agreed it was better than the alternative, which was a luminous fluorescent orange. As much as they wanted people to be able to see the exits, if any of the people on patrol around the Residence sighted them too early, it would ruin the Blue Team's plans.

Flit spent the next hour and a half following the path assigned by her friends and spraying logos at every junction. Holding down the nozzle of the spray cans slowly turned her fingertip black, and she couldn't help but think that they had better start their mutiny soon because there was no way she would be able to explain the sudden change in the colour of her fingers if someone from Control came in to check on her.

By the time she reached the Surface-level tunnels, the novelty had well and truly worn off. Her head was swimming from the paint fumes, and she was ready to just crawl back into bed for a nap.

Still, as she teleported into the tunnel where she would spray her final logo, she looked up the incline that led out towards Old City. The sun peered in, just a razor-thin crescent at the top of the arch. It was impossible for Flit to resist the urge to teleport to the very end of the tunnel.

As if it would counteract the impulsiveness of getting so close to the surface during the day, Flit pressed herself against the edge of the stone and took a deep breath of fresh air. It helped to chase away some of the graffiti-induced fog in her mind, and she bit her lip as she surveyed the world beyond.

The crumbling buildings of Old City formed an almost thorax of brick and mortar around the ancient subway outlet Flit was standing in. Thanks to the ruined tracks at her feet that continued through the destroyed metropolis, she was able to see much farther than she would have been able to from another nearby vantage point. The distant glittering heights of Hub were barely visible from where she stood.

Even though she knew she probably shouldn't, Flit looked up and around. She couldn't see any Government drones and assumed they were all probably tied up with what was going on in the Hub.

She focused on the roof of a nearby building that held what looked like a broken arbour that was now bowing under the weight of wild vines. Figuring it was probably a rooftop garden, Flit concentrated on the space about five feet above it then willed herself there.

The exhilarating sensation of falling lasted only as long as it took Flit to find a safe landing space on the roof and teleport there instead. She bit her lip as her feet hit the concrete and she checked her surroundings again, just in case she had missed any Government drones that might mark her as a threat. Satisfied that there weren't any flying surveillance drones getting all her best angles on camera, Flit turned her attention towards the Hub.

The familiar glittering skyline looked different.

Wrong.

It reminded Flit of when she had been younger, and she had smiled at herself in the mirror after losing a tooth. Sure, it was still her, but the absence of one tiny bit of bone had completely changed her own perception of herself.

Likewise, the way that the upper levels of the outer buildings had crumbled around the edges of the city drew her attention. It was impossible to look past them as they snagged her gaze with the sheer *wrongness* of them.

"Well, I'll be damned."

Flit shook her head as she saw the destruction the Free Citizens had wrought the night before. She couldn't help but wonder how many people had been hurt in that attempt, and it worried her that she could not see vehicles crawling through the outer streets, going through the debris, and looking for survivors. Although, she reasoned, it would be hard to see that kind of thing through the blue of the electrostatic fence that was still powered up around the city.

Seeing the previously immaculate city at the start of what could be significant destruction really drove home the reality of the situation. Any excitement stirring in the pit of Flit's stomach at the thought of an uprising was now quelled by caution.

How many people had been hurt—or worse—in the Free Citizen's explosions? How many more were now risking their lives on the streets of the Hub? How many of her friends, family, and fellow Derivates would die in the name of freedom?

With a heavy sigh, she took a final deep breath of fresh air. She closed her eyes, conjured the very familiar image of her bedroom in her mind, and teleported.

Flit didn't even need to open her eyes to know she had succeeded. The familiar dark, dank, mildew smell of the Underground hit her, and her shoulders sagged. She took a moment to gather her feelings before she opened her eyes, and she walked out into the main living area.

When she stepped out, she noted that her mother was home.

Both Stride and Tinker were sitting on the couch in the living room, knees together, heads close as they discussed something. They jumped as she walked in, but their shock quickly dissolved, and Tinker started to smile. Then, she saw the black paint on her fingertips.

"What the heck?" Tinker jumped up and ran over.

Flit held her hands up in what was supposed to be a placating motion, but it only seemed to exacerbate her mother's concern. "It's just paint," she said quickly, pulling her hands back again before her mother could grab them. "I was working on marking an exit route."

A million questions flashed in the hazel of Tinker's eyes. "Should I ask?"

"The Free Citizens have launched their attack as promised. It started at midnight with quite the bang. We need to work on getting up there to join them as soon as possible," Flit explained, not bothering to hide anything from her parents.

"Is that wise?" Stride stood, stretching his limbs a little before teleporting over to join them. "We've barely got any training in."

"It's not like we can do any more training in the current climate anyway." Flit shrugged. "Besides, if we are too late to the fight, then it might be lost. It would have been good to have extra time to prepare, but we didn't get it. We need to just do our best with what we've got."

Tinker and Stride both took the news as well as Flit could have hoped.

"Is there anything we can do to help?" Tinker asked.

"If you could work together on a list of supplies that we would need to create field medic stations and where to get the stock, that would be great." Flit paused as she tried to figure out if there was more. She couldn't think of anything else, so she shook her head. "Apart from that, just be prepared to back us up if we need it. We are waiting for Harmony to make another announcement before we can move."

A ping on Flit's datapad made her look down at the device buckled to her belt. She unclipped it and tapped the screen to bring it to life.

To: Flit
From: Tweak
Subject: Yes, being this clever is painful
So, I'm pretty much a genius (obviously).
The Residence network is now disconnected from the Control network.
Also... prepare to be really impressed...
I managed to loop some feedback into an AI I've been messing around with, so they will get some bullshit responses if they try and send messages our way and notifications that we are all engaged on other calls if they want voice or video.
You're welcome, by the way.
Looks like that's my part done. I'm gonna take a nap while the rest of the shit gets figured out. I don't know that we'll get much of a chance to sleep once everything starts.
Wake me up if you need anything (although this will be at your own peril).

Flit snorted at Tweak's message. Regardless of whatever situation the team had found themselves in, his sense of humour and unabashed self-love never failed to lighten a situation.

Her parents looked at her curiously, and she teleported over to the entertainment unit on the wall in their living room. She played with the settings and tried to access the network beyond the regular Residence databases and was pleased to find that any attempts to message any site other than the Residence was blocked.

"Ah, Tweak, you've outdone yourself," Flit muttered, turning the screen off.

"Wait. We can't connect? What are we supposed to do now?" Stride groaned in the way a small child might when their favourite toy had been taken from them.

Flit teleported back over to him and patted his shoulder. "It's a good thing. It means we have a little more control over when we start our mutiny."

"Mutiny?" Tinker's eyebrows rose almost into her hairline.

Flit ignored her surprise and decided to teleport over to Sway's room to see how the list of assault teams was coming along.

ALMOST FOUR HOURS LATER, Flit had spent so much time translocating from room to room that even she was over it. She had been able to check in with Swipe and Sway who, from their own apartments, had worked together to collate a well-thought-out list of teams. Instead of randomly assigning people, they had used the various classifications to create elite strike teams, teams for covert operations, suitable medics, and then general-purpose units that were well balanced in ability. The only real question had been what the interpersonal dynamics were, but they did the best with what they remembered from their time in the Mess and around the Underground to keep any people who might have issues apart and to keep family members together.

As Flit looked through the lists, she was pleased to see that her parents had both been assigned to a field medic team that would remain far from enemy lines. Her mother's skills were incredibly well developed, and sending her out into the battle itself would mean people wouldn't be able to access her healing quite as easily. Far better she remained behind for any of the more involved operations that might be required.

Stride's ability to organise resources would be a great benefit to the people working at the field medic station, and his teleporting was still good enough that he could assist with emergency retrieval and restocks as needed.

The Blue Team would remain together, too, with Layla and Fortune added to the mix. Layla was still developing the control and breadth of her abilities, but Fortune was a veritable powerhouse of telecoercion, and then, there was her unique nullification powers.

When Flit arrived back in her own apartment, she was looking forward to crashing onto the couch and taking a nap, but Hawkeye was standing in the kitchen, talking to her parents. He looked up when she entered and gave her a grim smile. Even before he spoke, Flit knew that he was prepared.

"I guess everything is in place, huh?" Flit asked.

Hawkeye nodded.

"You've got the evidence we need?"

"It's with Cogs now. She's prepping it for transmission." Hawkeye's voice was flat. Defeated.

Walking over to stand before him, Flit reached out and took his hand. "Are you okay?"

Tinker and Stride retreated from the space, and a few moments later, Flit heard the door to their room close. She appreciated the gesture of privacy.

"Yes? No?" Hawkeye shrugged. "I don't know. I know you've always had a bit of a chaotic side, but it still feels wrong to be plotting this."

"Hawk—"

"I'm not saying that I'm getting cold feet. Just that it feels so underhanded."

Flit put her hands in the pockets of her pants. "Look, I agree. If we could go back in time to a year and a half ago and tell me that we'd be plotting this today, I'd be the first to tell you you're fucking crazy."

She wished she could say more to put him at ease, but anything else would just be buttery bullshit. He knew what they needed to do and why just as well as she did.

"Control is in a huff at the moment trying to reconnect to the Residence," Hawkeye told her. "I told them I was taking my break just as they started trying to hack it. I think it's time we get some weapons and tell Tweak to drop whatever it is he did to keep them blocked."

Flit's head spun for a moment. "So, it's really happening, huh?" she asked, the reality bearing down on her once more.

Hawkeye nodded. "This is how the mutiny beings."

"Mutiny?" Shaking out her shoulders and releasing a slow, measured breath, Flit looked up and grinned. "This, my friend, is not mutiny. This is a revolution."

Despite the reservations Flit knew Hawkeye had, he smiled back at her after her declaration. She reached both hands out to him. He took them and gave them a firm squeeze before he pulled her into a tight embrace.

"I don't care what happens up there. You make sure you walk out the other side of this alive, got it?" he whispered.

Flit nodded, her head against his chest. "Likewise. You're a total dipshit, but I don't want to imagine a world without you."

They remained in the embrace for another few seconds.

Flit moved her arms into teleporting position. "To the armoury?"

"To the armoury."

FLIT AND HAWKEYE were so used to getting ready for missions that it took almost no time at all for them get all armed up. It was also far too easy for them to grab a few duffle bags and empty the shelves, lockers, and crates.

When they were done, they each looped their arms through a bag and teleported back to Tweak's room. As he had told Flit, he was indeed napping when they arrived. It was quite the rude awakening, Flit imagined, rousing to the sight of two heavily armed people. Tweak did well to process it, though, and then went about the business of arming himself as Flit and Hawkeye made a few more return trips to empty the Security department's cache of weapons.

There was no doubt that the Underground had other weapons lying around, but what they had would have to do for them for now. Hiding it all in Tweak's room also meant that any other Security teams that tried to intervene would only be able to rely on their powers, and, as Flit cockily pointed out, the Blue Team was the best team around.

By the time Flit and Hawkeye finished retrieving all of the weapons, Tweak was alert and ready to go. "Are you going to get the others?"

"Yep. I'll bring them back here."

As much as Flit thought her parents' apartment would be a much better size, she had no doubt that she would be the first one

Control came after. Despite his sass, Tweak was often seen as a relatively compliant member of the Underground in general. They would knock down a few doors before they went to search his apartment.

"What's our—"

Tweak's next question was interrupted as the communication screen flared to life in his room.

"Fuck. Control is broadcasting." Flit glanced at the two men with her. "Back up to the walls. This is gonna be fast."

Both Tweak and Hawkeye scrambled to comply, and by the time they were pressed into the walls and were watching Harmony, Divvy, and the department heads greet the Underground, Flit was already depositing Swipe in the room with them.

Flit had never worked as quickly as she did then. She teleported from place to place, snatching up her friends and returning them to Tweak's room.

"Apologies to everyone for the temporary communication outage," Harmony said as Flit completed the final translocation that had Clarity in the room with the rest of the Blue Team. "It was, sadly, another symptom of the degradation of our networks that we are trying so diligently to repair and protect."

"Fucking liar," Flit muttered. She turned to Hawkeye to ask where to next.

He was already opening his mouth to speak. "Can you get us all to the tunnel outside of Control?"

Flit looked around at the six sets of eyes all focused on her. There was a mixture of hope, worry, and outright fear in the group.

"I can do it," she said, confident she knew that particular tunnel well. She'd been in trouble so many times and spent more than enough time to visualise it with ease. "I could probably take you two at a time, but I don't want to risk more than that."

It was better to be comfortable than to push.

"Two at a time will do," Hawkeye said.

"Just let me make sure I've got the image right in my mind, and then I'll be back," she said, glancing at her friend. "Get your arses into pairs. I'll be a second."

After taking a deep breath and recalling the details of the tunnel outside the door to Control, Flit set her mental intention and jumped. Her feet hit the ground, and as she looked around and winced, realising she was a little too close to one of the walls. She was glad she had practised, as doing it blind with two passengers would have ended in disaster.

Flit returned to Tweak's apartment. "Changed my mind. One at time. When we get there, I need whoever I've taken to move ten feet back down the tunnel, away from the door, and to stay there."

There was a general murmur of acknowledgement in the room, and Swipe stepped forward.

"Let's get this party started," Flit muttered as Divvy droned on in the background about the emergency supply of water.

Flit teleported back and forth, and the team moved just as they were asked. When she got the last of her friends in place, Hawkeye beckoned her over. "We need to get Layla and Fortune—"

"On it," Flit replied.

Then, she was off.

Thankfully, the tunnels where the refugees were being kept were far closer to Control than the Residence. She managed to cover the distance in under thirty second. There was a guard standing outside in the hall, but Flit appeared in front of Fortune's door and knocked on it before he even realised she was there.

Fortune opened the door immediately, and just as the man held up his hand to do whatever it was his powers would allow him to, Fortune said, "Stop. Put your hand down. Do not alert Control. When we are gone, you will forget you saw us."

While Fortune was using her telecoercion on the guard, Flit teleported to Layla's door. As she raised her hand to knock, it slid open.

"I was wondering how much longer you'd be." Layla zipped up her jacket and stepped out of her room.

"Eager for some action, huh?" Flit asked as Fortune jogged over to join them.

Layla nodded and stepped closer. "Something like that."

Flit wrapped her arms around the women and translocated. When they arrived at Control, the door was opening, and Cogs was standing inside the main room beckoning the team in.

"Talk about good timing." Fortune wobbled slightly as she found her feet.

They joined the end of the group walking into the main hive of authority for the Underground.

Cogs shut the door behind the team and swept some loose strands of red hair behind her ears. She walked over to Hawkeye and put her hand on his inhibitor. "You guys don't have long to get in there. I have the broadcast ready to go, and I can get the doors open for you, but I don't know how much longer they are staying on the air."

"That's okay. We won't need long," Hawkeye promised as the inhibitor unlatched with a click and fell to the ground.

Several more inhibitors joined Hawkeye's on the ground as Cogs freed the group. Flit focused on helping Layla and Fortune arm themselves.

When they were ready, Cogs pointed to the doors that led to the conference rooms. "Good luck," Cogs said, standing tall and giving the group a nod of respect.

"We don't need luck," Flit promised her. "We have the truth on our side."

55

SCRAPS

IT WAS a matter of great relief to Scraps that he managed to return to Nightmix before Adam woke. He also managed to return before anyone had noticed he had been gone for too long. It was a bit of a problem, considering he could have been taken by Government Agents and questioned, but he was grateful for the oversight. He did, however, make a mental note to address it with Adam and his team because setting search and rescue times should be a critical task of every operation.

Once he was back in the bunker, Andy was pleased to be handing the reins back over to him. Her eyes were underscored by bags so dark they could have been confused for bruises, and her voice was stilted and croaky.

"How much longer can you hold it?" Scraps gestured to the screen she was still tapping at.

Andy sighed. "It's going to slip through our fingers at any moment."

Scraps drummed his fingers against his thighs as he considered something then leaned closer to whisper, "Any chance you could run the broadcasts one more time each as a kind of send-off?"

Fingers stalling for a moment, Andy glanced at him over her shoulder. "Both of them?"

The waver in her voice echoed the concern Scraps felt about

Adam finding out. All the same, he nodded. "Could you attribute it to a glitch?"

Andy licked her lips. "I can try."

There was a renewed sense of determination in her as she lowered her head and locked her focus on the screen.

Scraps returned to the main console where the view was split in quarters and honed in on the earth-movers shifting the barricades. He was impressed with how quickly the machines were working. He hadn't expected much, but the crew were getting their jobs done, and the Free Citizens reassigned to guard the gaps were doing exactly what they needed to do.

Just as Scraps was about to ask for updates on the other cities, the screens in the room went black. Adam's broadcast started playing again with the exception of the countdown. Everyone in the bunker fell silent as they watched. When the view switched to the Derivate-oriented announcement, some of them turned away and muttered to each other, but others continued to watch, as if committed to giving the message the same respect as the one for the Citizens. Scraps noted each and every one of the latter for when the time came to plead his case with Adam. He would need all the support he could get.

Following the broadcast, Andy gave her screen a final tap. After a few seconds delay, the sound of a distant rumble vibrated through the bunker.

"Now, no one can use it," Andy half-said, half-yawned. She got to her feet and gestured to a few of the hackers who had been awake and working with her. "Time to sleep, guys. I'm sure we'll have plenty to do when we wake up."

Petra, who had been opening some crates nearby with Trey, walked over and slipped her arm around Andy's waist. She leaned in closer and said something to Andy that Scraps couldn't hear. He watched the pair walk back towards the sleeping area and felt a twinge of longing for a moment like that of his own.

Instead of getting caught up in his thoughts, Scraps walked over to see what Trey was up to. When Scraps peered down into the crates, he saw a heap of devices around the size of his palm, with plastic-looking grates on the front, two dials, one button, and short, thumb-length antennas. Trey reached in and pulled one out.

"What's that?" Scraps asked.

"Radios, apparently," Trey said with a brow-furrowing frown. "Adam said he dug them up from some antique shop. They're apparently connected to a tower outside of Old City. We charged them all a few nights ago, but he said they won't last all that long."

Scraps picked one up with a heavy sigh. He looked down at it and shook his head at yet another plan Adam had left him out of. He couldn't help but wonder if Adam actually knew what the word teamwork meant.

"Do you know how they work?" Scraps asked.

Trey nodded and spent the next few minutes giving Scraps a crash course. Scraps and Trey then went and showed the other Free Citizens. Soon, the bunker was filled with the hum and static of the devices.

Despite his annoyance at Adam, Scraps had to admire the radios. The Government, in their foolish attempt to be the sole controllers of the flow of information, had not allowed any third party or private operators to hold their own networks in their cities. Destroying the Government's server farm meant that there was no other way for them to communicate. Scraps had no doubt the Government would find a workaround, but until they did, they would be forced to operate without any way to communicate remotely.

The Free Citizens, however, had radios.

"We need to get these out to the teams ASAP," Scraps said, looking over at the strike team. "Let's get the next shift to start a little early. Get these radios to whatever shelters those teams are hiding in, and get them to take them to the front."

The strike team all found bags to fill with the devices and then made their way out into the city. Scraps hated being left behind, but he knew it was the best plan. He needed to be in place to receive the radio calls when they started coming in because he was absolutely certain that the Free Citizens had no concept of radio protocols. He wished he had thought to drill them on it, but if he was honest with himself, there really had been no time.

Scraps wished that the Government had allowed better access to historical archives. Unfortunately, the history of the world prior to their dominance had been classified as restricted and had been forgotten by the general populace. It was impossible for Scraps to know whether previous wars had been fought and won by sides who had been as disorganised as theirs. He would have completely understood if the answer was no. To the winning, at least, not so much the fighting. He had no doubt many fights had been fought by people who were not ready or equipped.

Just as Scraps was wondering how they would communicate with the other cities to see how they were faring, the radio in his hand flared to life. The quality was crackly, spluttering, and atrocious compared to the perfect sound he was used to on his headset, but it was better than nothing.

"Uh, Brian? Tai told me to call you on this thing," a voice warbled.

Scraps winced at the information he'd given away. "Greetings, officer. We're going to have to work on radio protocol, but for now, just let me know your location."

The person replied and was the first in a cascade of check-ins. Scraps was using a note-taking app on his datapad to keep track of them all, and he assigned team names to each of them. When he had received about half the number of check-ins he was expecting, he was about to start a quick verbal briefing on how and when to use the radios when an incoming call interrupted him.

"Uh, Brian. Leo's been shot. We need urgent medical assistance."

The voice was full of panic, and Scraps stiffened at the words.

He was about to reply when one of the older women in the bunker rushed over. "I'm a medic. I can help them with first aid," she said.

Scraps nodded. "What's your location?"

Taking note of the coordinates, Scraps handed the radio over to the woman who started asking diagnostic questions.

"Should they move him?" Scraps asked.

The woman shook her head. "Better not. Carrying him could cause more damage."

Scraps looked around at some of the equipment in the bunker and saw a hover stretcher packed up over to the side behind some first aid gear. "What if I can get him on that?"

A quick nod between instructions was the confirmation Scraps needed. He ran over to retrieve the stretcher and tucked the main part under his arm before running for the door.

"Brian! Where are you going?"

Adam's voice made him pause, and he turned around. "Man down near the barrier. I'm heading in for retrieval."

"Let someone else do it. I need you here on radio," Adam said.

Scraps gritted his teeth. "We don't have a medical response team set up. I'll handle it this time. You can sort out the radios. It is simple enough."

Before Adam could argue, Scraps grabbed a spare radio and tucked it into his pocket, hitched the folded stretcher up under his arm, and ran.

WHEN SCRAPS HAD VENTURED out earlier, the streets he had travelled through were quiet. The low-rent, relatively rundown area had been completely void of foot traffic. Even though he had had a sense that people had been watching from various windows, they had not made their presence known. There had been a definite undercurrent of tension that hummed around the place.

The streets that took Scraps to retrieve Leo were a different story altogether.

The buildings in this part of town were far better kept than the ones near the Citizen Derivates' hideout. Even with the debris scattered around and dusting the asphalt, there was a sense of order here missing in the other area.

Another thing Scraps couldn't help but notice was the way that there seemed to be hastily drawn Government symbols of two hands cupping intertwined links taped up in various windows on all different levels of the buildings. The signs instantly put him on edge, and he stuck closer to the shadows that were forming due to the late afternoon sun dipping behind the skyscrapers.

Keeping his attention on his surroundings and moving with caution meant it took longer for Scraps to get where he needed to be. From his training, he knew it would be well worth it. As much as Leo needed help, Scraps would be of no assistance if he was riddled with bullets himself.

Despite his decision to remain alert, Scraps couldn't help the way his thoughts returned to the symbols in the window, to the very clear statement that the Free Citizens were not welcomed by whoever lived in those apartments.

As much as Scraps wanted to be outraged by it, he understood. Had he not met Flit and been dragged to the Underground, he was certain he would have been outraged by the actions of the Free Citizens. As a matter of fact, he still was, and he was part of the group.

"Brian, over here!"

Scraps turned to see a small group of people sheltered under the awning of a building across the way. He paused and took time to observe the buildings around them for signs of movement before racing across the street.

The first thing Scraps noticed was that Leo wasn't the only one injured. Even though the man was lying on the ground pale and surrounded by a pool of blood, there were others with fresh bruises blooming, nursing sore arms or grazed fists.

Scraps unfolded the stretcher but kept it turned off, so it remained on the ground. "What happened?"

"We've had people coming down and telling us to leave for an hour or so," a woman told him. Her hands were covered in blood as she held a wadded-up piece of fabric against Leo's stomach. "When they saw Leo approach, they lost it. A group of about five randoms came up, and one had a gun..."

"We managed to scare them off when we took out our own weapons," a man beside her added, his hand still wrapped around the handle of a gun holstered at his hip.

"Grab his legs for me," Scraps said, directing yet another man who was standing at the end of the stretcher.

The man looked reluctant to let go of his weapon but complied after someone else hissed something Scraps couldn't quite make out.

"Lift on the count of three," Scraps ordered. "Be gentle, though."

Scraps slipped his own hands under Leo's shoulders. He knew he would be able to transfer him safely to the stretcher on his own, but it would look awfully suspicious if he managed to do so without any assistance. The last thing he needed was to see what these particular Free Citizens would do if they found out he was a Derivate.

After the required countdown, Scraps forced a groan and helped get Leo settled onto the stretcher. He reached over, pressing the control that rose it to waist height with a soft electric hiss. He then gently opened the bag at Leo's hip and frowned to see there were still two radios left there.

"Do you know where the last two teams are?" Scraps asked the man with the gun.

He nodded.

"You need to take these to them so they can communicate. You probably know the network is down already. They can't remain out of contact." Scraps retrieved the radios and handed them to him. "Did Leo have a chance to explain how they work?"

"We got most of it, but I'm not confident." The man tucked the radios into his pockets.

"As long as they don't change the frequency, they'll be able to figure it out." He turned to the other two. "Your replacements will be coming out within the next hour or so. When you swap over, make sure you watch your tails on the way back to base. If you get followed, take a twisted, scenic route." He gave them a stern look. "Do not under any circumstances enter the building if you have a tail."

The pair shifted uncomfortably but nodded in understanding.

Without wasting further words or time, Scraps put his hand on the control for the stretcher and ran.

Everything went well for the first few blocks, but just as Scraps rounded a corner that took him in the right cardinal direction to reach the club, a group of people dressed in practical but dark clothing stepped out of an alley nearby. Scraps skidded to a halt, and the people froze as they turned to face him.

In that instant, Scraps realised he had no way to tell friend from foe.

They hadn't even thought to create markers or symbols for the Free Citizens to wear to identify one another. Sure, it would mean that they would stand out to any Government or Citizen attackers, but it also meant they would know who to run from and who to run to.

The radio at Scraps' hips erupted with static. "North Four-West Four checking in... when are our replacements coming? We're falling asleep out here."

Several streaks flew towards Scraps, and he raised his arm to cover his face, throwing some power into the motion and bouncing whatever projectiles were lobbed at him back in the direction of his assailants. Their cries echoed through the streets as the glass bottles they had thrown hit the ground at their feet and exploded into flame and shrapnel.

Whilst the Citizens were distracted by the injuries they were getting from their own improvised explosives, Scraps grabbed the stretcher controls again and darted around them. He was tempted to remain behind to incapacitate them properly, but he knew they were just Citizens doing the best they could to protect the lives they had come to know. He hoped they would have learned their lesson from this interaction and that his choice did not haunt him, but he had not joined this rebel group to hurt Citizens. He wanted to protect them.

BY THE TIME Scraps rolled into the club with Leo, he was genuinely concerned for Leo's health. He had lost enough blood that it had taken all his colour with it. Five minutes before they had arrived at Nightmix, he had been shaking so violently Scraps had to hold him down on the stretcher.

The medical team that Adam had roped together in Scraps' absence took over right away, and Scraps leaned back against the wall as he caught his breath. It wasn't until he slid his fingers through his hair that he realised his hands were coated in blood from holding Leo in place. He stared at them, blinking.

"You should go and clean up."

Scraps jumped at the sound of Adam's voice. The last time he had seen Adam, he had been standing over by his desk in deep conversation with Tai.

"Yeah, I probably should," Scraps agreed, pushing himself off the wall. He went to walk past Adam, but Adam put a hand on his shoulder.

"There was another broadcast before they blew the network." Adam's voice was a low, almost deadly whisper.

Scraps nodded but didn't flinch or even tense as Adam's fingers tightened on his shoulder, tips pressing painfully against his collarbone. "There was."

Adam leaned in. "Please know that you are walking a dangerous line here. I appreciate your experience but not so much that I will allow you to sully this mission with whatever agenda you're pushing."

Unsure of what to say, Scraps chose to keep quiet. He worried that his silence incriminated him, but arguing would only inflame the situation, and Adam was clearly trying to maintain a low profile.

Interesting, Scraps thought as he looked around. The people in the bunker were so busy fretting over Leo that they didn't seem to see the interaction between Scraps and Adam. However, even with a lack of observers, Adam was making a point of being quiet.

"While I was out there, it was clear some of the Citizens were revolting against us. I almost got shot. We need a way to identify ourselves whilst we are on the streets. Did you want me to figure something out, or will you handle it?" Scraps asked.

Adam stared at him for so long Scraps wondered if he heard the question. Then, the leader regained that arrogant, superior smirk he got when he used his control. "You do it. I have more important matters to attend to."

"I'll sort it out when I'm cleaned up," Scraps said, already knowing he was going to delegate the task to the support personnel in the bunker.

Even with a new task to complete, Scraps was still stuck on

Adam's comment earlier and the discrete way in which he had chosen to deliver it. There was a threat behind the words. Scraps was observant enough to understand that much at the very least. However, the delivery was confusing. Adam had no trouble tearing Andy to shreds in front of the bunker earlier. Why was he any different?

56

———

FLIT

"READY?" Flit asked the Blue Team, plus the honorary members Fortune and Layla, as they stood at the door to the conference room. The soundproofing was good enough that they couldn't hear what was going on inside. If it weren't for the broadcast playing on all of the screens around them, they wouldn't have known Divvy was harping on about the importance of unity during times of strife.

"Time to show them that unity is not real if it's coerced," Swipe said, flipping her hair over her shoulder and then flexing her fingers. She looked far too eager to throw shit around, and Flit was totally there for it.

Flit gestured to the control panel, looked over her shoulder at Cogs, and nodded solemnly.

As the door to the meeting room opened, the reality of the situation hit Flit in the face like a hovertruck. Time ground to a crawl as Harmony, Divvy, and the other leaders of the Underground all froze and, in slow motion, turned to see why the door had opened.

A quick survey of the room told Flit that Harmony and Divvy were flanked by Shadow, Posthoc, and the leaders for Supply and Maintenance. Acumen stood over in the corner, outside of the view of the camera. He caught Flit's eye, and his lips curled in the barest hint of a smile before his face returned to its previous stone-like state.

Fully aware that every nanosecond of this mutiny would be on camera, Flit surged in the room and walked right up to stand beside the leaders. The others followed her, making sure that there wasn't a single part of her back exposed to the women.

"What is the meaning of this?" Harmony's shout brought time reeling back into perspective.

Wrench, the only person in the room with physically active powers, raised his hands in their direction.

"I wouldn't do that if I were you." Flit shot him a warning glare. "We're not here to fight. We're here to speak to the people of the Underground."

Getting to her feet, the chair skidding noisily as she rose, Divvy slammed her hands on the table. "All of you get out of here before I am forced to have you escorted out!"

Every person in the room, and probably all of those watching, knew that was a lie. There was no way the Blue Team were walking out of this room without cuffs on.

"What happened to their inhibitors?" Wrench muttered, thick bushy brows knitting together.

Fury flashed in Harmony's eyes as she got to her feet. She pointed to the Blue Team. "All of you are to move back into the hallway immediately. When you are out there, you are to put your hands on your heads and to keep your powers to yourselves and mouths shut."

The coercion in her voice was as strong and direct as Flit had ever heard it... yet she was not inclined to obey. Flit had to resist the urge to smirk at Fortune over her shoulder.

When the team didn't immediately comply, Harmony's eyes widened.

The door to the room slid shut, and Flit smiled at the leader of the Underground, pearly white teeth and all. "Yeah, nah." Flit gave Harmony a lazy, sarcastic salute. "Thanks for the order, Harmony, but we won't be complying."

The baffled telecoercionist looked between Flit and the other members of the Blue Team and then turned to Shadow and Wrench. "Restrain them!"

Before either of the men could move, Swipe held up her hands in their direction. "I strongly advise against that," she said in such a way that even Flit knew it would be utter madness to tempt her.

Layla and Tweak stepped up to Swipe's side.

"We came here to talk to the people. We'd hate to lose the opportunity because you were feeling selfish. Plus, I'm sure everyone is super curious about what we have to say now," Tweak said in an almost sing-song voice.

Before any people watching who wished to act as reinforcements arrived, Flit returned her attention to the screen at the front of the room, which she knew would have the camera equipment integrated.

"Acumen, I don't want to fight you. Please don't try and shut this down," she thought before plastering a grimace on her face. "People of the Underground, we apologise for interrupting this important message from Control, but we have one of our own, and we believe it is something you all need to hear."

Flit gestured to the team of people behind her and hoped the weapons and body armour would not turn the viewers off their message.

"The Blue Team and I regret that we have to come to you in this manner, but we feel as if we have been given little choice. You see, we have all been lied to." Flit paused to let that sink in. "Over the past few years, the Underground has been subject to underhanded, unethical manipulation. Not by the Government, mind you, but by our very own leaders."

Flit cast a hand to the side and pointed at Harmony and Divvy.

"Flit, that is enough. Stop this immediately." Harmony was close to yelling. The command in her tone hit Flit, but instead of her brain reacting to it and holding her silent, it washed over her and away, just like waves lapping at the shore.

"Harmony, it's rude to interrupt," Flit told her with a poisoned, honeyed smile. She returned her attention to the front. "From fake tunnel explosions caused by coerced Underground members and pinned on innocent scapegoats to outright manipulation of each and every one of us, Harmony, Divvy, and the team in Control have been slowly taking away your freedoms."

Harmony turned to Shadow. "Stop this. Stop this immediately."

Once more, her powers failed. Alarm flashed in her eyes.

"Don't you dare," Fortune snapped.

Shadow froze in place. He let out a low hum of disapproval and shook his head.

"Wrench! Abacus!"

Without a word from Fortune, the other two leaders looked between Harmony and the Blue Team and also shook their heads.

"As you see, the leaders are clearly concerned about what we have to say. I hope that shows we are right in our reasoning. However, we are not asking for blind faith. That is a mechanism of those who abuse power." Flit tilted her head in Harmony's and Divvy's direction suggestively. "So, let me make the situation at hand abundantly clear."

Flit pointed at the screen on the back wall, and it flickered on. A reel of the Free Citizens announcement as well as the footage of the city exploding in a ring of fire played. Flit let it go until it was clear that there was significant destruction. Somehow, Cogs had also managed to get some footage of Free Citizens and Government Agents standing on opposite sides of tall mounds of debris.

"This is what is happening above our heads. In actual fact, the start of the uprising coincided so very conveniently with our own increased lockdown." Flit let her hand fall as she squared her posture so she was facing the front again.

"Flit, that's enough," Divvy growled, getting up from her seat.

"Sit back down," Sway ordered.

Divvy fell back into her seat, and there was a mixed round of protests from her and Harmony.

"I imagine many of you will be wondering why we marched in here for a mere coincidence, but please, let me tell you, there was nothing coincidental about it."

Another wave of Flit's hand at the screen had new footage coming into view. This time, it was the inside of Control headquarters, and sound came along with it. There was a clear image of Harmony walking closer to one of the staff members and leaning in. What Flit assumed was a low murmur was amplified by the recording as Harmony ordered the microkinetic to shut down the system. The force of the order and the work it took to close the systems down in one go had a thick trail of blood leaking from his nose.

Of course, the moment the man fainted, Harmony slipped in to catch him and called for help. It was a perfect plan, as people in Control were thrown into chaos thanks to the way the lights suddenly failed and their workplace went dark.

The footage continued behind Flit, but the volume lowered as she resumed her speech. "Not only did our leader force a person to destroy our network, but she lied about the causes of the tunnel collapses several weeks ago, coercing me to believe that Scraps was the culprit. Prior to that... she had Heft collaborate with Citizen bounty hunters and cause the tunnel collapses that killed several of our comrades."

"Lies!" Divvy cried out.

Fortune stepped forward besides Flit. "I wish this was not true, but I had suspicions about Harmony's deceit years ago. When I got too close, she had myself, my husband, and my son captured by the Government. Her trail of destructive rot goes deeper than that, but her betrayal is not what we should be focusing on right now."

Flit put a hand on Fortune's shoulder and squeezed it gently. The mention of Rook cut Flit deeply today, knowing he would have wanted to be here to see this moment.

Still, she surged on. "Fortune is right. What we need to think about is the war that is being waged above our heads. A war for freedom. A war that might finally disrupt the balance of absolute power the Government has held for a hundred years."

Hawkeye stood up beside Flit as well. She held the hand that he settled on her shoulder and stood a little straighter.

"We have an agent who has infiltrated the Free Citizens. He is there waiting, ready for us to join him, to join *them*, so we can bring down the Government together," Flit announced. She wished she was able to see the reactions of those listening to gauge how her message was going down. "We know this is a dangerous endeavour, but we worry that if we do not act bravely and decisively now, we will be stuck in these tunnels, buried alive, and lose this once-in-a-century opportunity."

"Given the danger," Hawkeye said, picking up when Flit

paused, "we do not wish to force anyone to fight—"

"Hawkeye, stop this nonsense," Harmony hissed. She then looked around at the others, a silent command in her expression.

"It's not nonsense."

Everyone froze as Shadow stepped forward. He moved out from behind Wrench and Abacus.

"For years, Control has consistently ordered Intelligence to squash evidence and cover tracks. It started even earlier than Fortune mentioned and went right back to the fall of Longbeach," he continued.

There was a gasp from a couple of the members at the Blue Team. Flit didn't want to turn around to see who it was, but she understood the sentiment. Even though she had an idea of how insidious it was, hearing it out in the open made it that much more real. That much more devastating.

"You say that, Shadow, but you did everything we asked!" Harmony's tone took on an edge of hysteria.

Shadow turned to face her, his expression as deadpan as Flit had ever seen it. "Yes, Harmony. I followed the orders that were telecoerced into me by you. I will suffer whatever punishment the Underground sees fit, but I will not..." He held up a hand between them, a physical reinforcement of the sudden hardness in his tone. "...sit idly by while whatever fear and madness drives you ruin the one chance we might have to leave these tunnels."

Flit blinked. If she was honest, she didn't completely believe him right now. He had been the one shutting her and Scraps down while they were on their covert mission. However, she was not about to let the opportunity go based on her suspicions. He was helping, and they desperately needed the weight his words would bring. She would deal with any possible betrayals later.

"Why aren't you doing anything?" Harmony hissed, leaning ever so slightly towards Divvy.

"I can't see anything," Divvy whispered back, forehead creased with confusion. "It's all just... blank."

"No!" Acumen and Link cried out.

At the same time, Harmony yelled, "Get Fortune!"

There was no coercion in the order, but with the space left

behind by Shadow stepping forward, Wrench had enough room to launch towards Fortune.

The Blue Team were packed in so tightly that it was near impossible to avoid tumbling over each other. Swipe threw her arms up, and Wrench was thrown back against the wall and pinned to it, legs dangling. Abacus attempted to attack.

This time, Sway stepped forward, yelling, "Stop!"

Whilst all of this was going on, Flit noticed Harmony whisper something to Divvy, and a sliver of metal flashed as the latter reached out and snatched a gun from Sway's belt. She held it up, hands shaking as she pointed the weapon at Fortune.

Before anyone could do anything, Divvy pulled the trigger.

"No!" Swipe cried, her arms slicing through the air to knock the bullet off its trajectory.

Flit leapt to the side, pushing Fortune out of the way, but there was a wet thunk as the bullet veered off and found a new target.

"Acumen!" Everyone turned as Shadow teleported across the room and caught the telepath as he fell.

"See what you've done! Murderers!" Harmony hollered, pointing at Flit as she jumped to her feet. Horror contorted her features.

"Medic... We need a medic." Shadow's calm voice was tainted by a growing stain of concern.

Without even considering any other option, Flit teleported back to her parents' apartment. She could hear the chaos of the meeting room playing out over their comm screen and noted her mother and father standing in the living room.

Tinker turned and rushed right over. Flit didn't delay, wrapping her arms around her mother and translocating her back to the meeting room.

When they got back to the meeting room a second later, Tinker disengaged from Flit and rushed over to where Shadow was kneeling beside Acumen, putting pressure on the wound in his shoulder. Acumen's skin had gone worryingly pale.

The Blue Team worked to hold Divvy down as tears streamed down her face. Swipe used telekinesis to remove the gun from her and then held Harmony at bay.

"Don't say a single word. Don't make any verbal sounds," Fortune ordered Harmony.

Unfortunately, even Fortune's power wasn't enough to stop Harmony from gritting out, "This. Will. Not. End. Well."

"Guys, we're taking Acumen to the Medbay. Clean up in here," Tinker called out.

Shadow let her take over applying pressure, scooped Acumen into his arms with a grunt, and then translocated the three of them from the room.

Panting and knowing the situation was still tenuous, Flit turned back to the camera. "For those of you wanting to fight, wanting to escape the prison the Underground has become... meet us in the Residence foyer in twenty minutes."

Then, Flit made a "cut" motion to the camera and had to hope that Cogs ended the feed that had turned into a complete and utter clusterfuck.

The instant the feed ended, Flit turned to where Harmony was seated, being held by invisible bonds Swipe appeared to be straining to keep her under. She looked down at the white-haired wench, and her face hardened.

"This, Harmony, is where it ends," Flit whispered. "You've been complicit in keeping your own people enslaved and in the dark for too long. We're going to make this right."

"Good... luck..." Harmony spat out, fire in her eyes. "You'll...need... it."

It took a great amount of restraint for Flit to resist the urge to punch the bitch.

The door to the room slid open, and several Control workers rushed in, heading directly towards the now usurped leaders. They wrestled them into inhibitor cuffs and then dragged them from the room.

Worryingly, neither Divvy nor Harmony put up a fight as they were taken out.

Flit looked over at Fortune. "Do you want to make sure they get where they are going?" Flit whispered.

"It would be my pleasure," Fortune replied. She pulled Flit in for a quick embrace before walking out of the room.

Finally, as a shaken silence overtook the space, Flit took stock of her teammates. Poor Link was pale and shell-shocked as she stood by Clarity's side. The precog didn't waste any time, pulling her girlfriend into a warm embrace. Sway, who had been standing closer to Flit, moved over and wrapped his arm around their shoulders.

"Will Acumen be okay?" Layla asked, looking over at Hawkeye and Flit.

"Mum will do her best," Flit replied, knowing that Tinker's *best* wasn't always enough. "For now, we need to keep moving. I know we're all worried, but if we lose this momentum, it would all have been for nothing."

The statement earned a series of wary nods, and Flit took that as permission to lead the Blue Team from the room. They had to prepare to see how their fellow Underground residents had taken the coup.

"HOW IS ACUMEN?" Flit asked as she entered the Medbay and saw her mother standing at one of the consoles nearby. There were quite a few curtains drawn around various beds, and another two medics were moving down the aisles.

Flit was on her way to the Residence to meet up with whoever decided to join the uprising, but it didn't feel right to do so without stopping to see if Acumen was all right. She was so relieved she was able to get her mother on the scene as quickly as she had, but even with that speed, there had been so much blood on the floor when Shadow had teleported them out.

Tinker's fingers paused over the console as she let out a slow breath. She took some time to close whatever she was working on and then walked over to where Flit was waiting by the door.

"The bullet didn't hit anything critical." Tinker's voice was low, quiet. No doubt to protect Acumen's privacy. "He did lose a lot of blood, though, and it's going to take a while to recover the use of his arm."

A sigh of relief slipped from Flit. She was not glad that Acumen was injured, but being injured was better than being dead.

"Did Shadow come to see you?" Tinker asked, glancing around warily.

"He came back to Control. He is working with the team there to restore the power and resources that had been blocked. He asked Link to stay with him to monitor the thoughts of the workers, just in case someone tries to snatch the leadership while everything is unsettled."

"Good." Tinker looked back over her shoulder towards Physie, who was restocking a supply trolley. "I'm going to head to the meeting with Flit. Are you all right here?"

Physie waved a hand. "Don't fuss over me. I've handled more than this before," she said with a low laugh. Then, she smiled at Flit. "Please consider me part of an emergency medical response team for whatever it is you plan. I helped that Scraps of yours before, and it is horrible to think of what they did to him." She shook her head. "Also, I think I would look good with a tan."

Despite the seriousness of the day, Flit laughed.

She wasn't sure what to expect from the other Underground residents. They had all been living in the tunnels for so long she imagined many of them had no interest in changing that even if it would be better for them. People were often resistant to change due to the sheer unknown. She would have counted Physie amongst that group, but the woman had pleasantly surprised her.

"Thanks, Physie. I'll be sure to count you in. I hope we don't need it, but your skill and experience is certainly appreciated. I'll make sure someone fills you in on the details once we have them sorted." Flit then turned to her mother. "Might as well do this the quicker way, huh?"

She offered Tinker her hand, and Tinker took it immediately. The two reappeared in the apartment just in time to see Stride getting ready to go down to the meeting in the Residence foyer.

When he saw Flit, he walked over and pulled her into an embrace. "I'm glad you're safe," he muttered, squeezing her before letting her go and stepping back. He turned to face Tinker. "Acumen?"

"He'll pull through."

That seemed to be enough for Stride, who opened the door and led the way towards the staircase. When they reached the stairwell, he offered Tinker his hand and called out, "Teleporter going to ground." He waited a beat for any protests and then teleported down.

Flit moved closer to the edge of the railing and watched as her parents appeared on the ground floor then moved away from the void. "Another teleported aiming for the ground floor."

When there were no shouted warnings, Flit teleported down too. Her parents were waiting for her by the door to the stairs. A few people were filtering off the staircase who all seemed a little wary as they saw her. She wasn't quite sure what to say, so she just gave them a grim smile as she walked out of the stairwell.

Emerging into the foyer, Flit was surprised as she saw just how many people had shown up. A few at the back turned to see her and stepped aside, making room for her and her parents to get to the space near the front door where the other members of the Blue Team were waiting.

Cutting it so fine to the twenty-minute deadline meant that Flit was the last one to arrive. Her parents stopped at the front of the group as she went to stand beside Fortune and Hawkeye. Swipe, Sway, Tweak, Clarity, and Layla were already with them. Link had even taken a break from Control to join them. Everyone was quiet as they shifted on their feet and glanced at the crowd.

"Acumen is in recovery now, Mum said he should be okay," she announced before even launching into any business. They seemed relieved to hear that at least. "Swipe, Sway, do you have those groups handy?"

Sway pulled a small datapad out of his pocket and waved it in the air. "Everything's on here and ready to distribute as needed. "

"Good. What's the vibe been here so far?" She looked at Link for the answer to this.

The raven-haired woman sighed. "Mostly wary and anticipatory. There is a lot of alarm about what we did, but they are all so fed up with the restrictions that they're willing to listen."

It wasn't really the reason Flit wanted people to be receptive, but she had to work with what she had. It was better than nothing.

"So, how do we do this?" Hawkeye shifted his stance to allow

Flit to see past him to the group filling up the area.

Tweak smirked. "Flit, you got another one of those rousing speeches you can pull outta your arse?"

"You'd be surprised what I can pull outta my arse." Flit winked at him, and a couple of the others groaned.

"You really do not have any boundaries, do you?" Swipe shook her head. "If that is the kind of thing you'll be saying, maybe someone—"

"Lighten up." Flit rolled her eyes. "This is a shit situation. Sometimes, you just have to take a moment to laugh so you don't break."

Swipe's featured softened somewhat, but she still crossed her arms over her chest.

"Am I the best person to address the group, though?" Flit turned to Link. "With everything that happened with Scraps, I don't want to jeopardise things. If someone else is better suited, then that's fine."

"No one else has the same experience with the telecoercion as you do. They may be suspicious, but you speak with conviction. They are bound to understand." Link gestured to the rest of the group. "We'll all be here together. Others can jump in as needed. We need to present a united front for this."

Letting out a soft sigh, Flit knew Link was right. She reached across, squeezed her hand in thanks, and then turned to face the waiting group.

Standing in the back of the crowd and calling out comments here and there felt very different to standing in front of a crowd with all eyes glued expectantly on her. However, Flit was not about to let so many dubious or wary expressions get in between her and marching her people up to fight for their freedom.

Flit cleared her throat to get attention of those remaining chatters around the room, even though it was already fairly quiet in the lobby. "So, before even saying anything else, I want to begin by thanking everyone for coming to hear us out. I know that this is... unorthodox." Flit gestured around and back to her teammates. "It's not something we wanted to do, but given what we knew about what is happening on the surface, combined with the increasing restrictions to our freedom down here, we felt like we needed to act."

"How do we know that's true?" someone called out from somewhere in the middle of the group.

Flit couldn't see who it was, and the people around whoever spoke didn't shift or turn to look at them. Maybe because they didn't want to identify them. A lot of people probably felt the same way.

"Tweak, can you get that screen working and connect us to Cogs?" Hawkeye asked, gesturing to a screen above the door that was currently just saying "Exit".

With a lazy salute, Tweak walked over and put his hand on the wall. After a few seconds, the text on the screen disappeared, and Cog's familiar face appeared on it.

"Cogs, we're just in the Residence lobby with the people who wished to join us. They wanted to verify that the footage they saw this afternoon was real," Hawkeye explained.

"Sounds fair." Cogs leaned in. "Before we get into it, does someone want to ask me some random questions? Gotta verify that this feed is real before we jump in and talk about the evidence."

There was a resounding silence in the room as people seemed to not want to be the one to speak up, so Flit asked a basic math question that Cogs answered with ease. Another couple of people cropped up to ask about what meal was served at lunch or to see who else was in Control with Cogs. Eventually, everyone seemed a bit more interested in her as they verified that it wasn't a recording or an AI, and the question about the data came up once more.

"I can confirm that all of the footage shown by the Blue Team was legitimate," Cogs said through the screen. "I also have some updated images that myself and the other Control micros have been able to locate. Please be aware that it is graphic, but some of it is as recent as half an hour ago."

Cog's face was replaced by a nine-way split screen showing parts of various cities. It was hard to tell which was which at first, but Flit knew they weren't all the Hub. Whilst she might not have been able to identify all the locations, there were some whispers that danced through the room and let her know that some of the returned agents who had chosen to join them knew the locations.

All locations were equally decimated, with ruined buildings, scattered vehicles, and debris on the streets. Some of the screens had people on them, and there was a mix of Government uniform and regular clothing.

"This is recent?" someone called out.

"That is correct. The battle for the surface is well and truly underway," Cogs confirmed, her voice overlaying the videos behind it.

The footage only made Flit want to get up there faster. She faced the group again. "So now you've seen what is up there, and you've seen how we are also being trapped and lied to down here... We need to fight. We need to fight not only for our freedom but for the freedom of every Derivate in the future. Will you join us?"

There was a murmur of agreement, but it was not nearly as enthusiastic as Flit had hoped. She was about to continue when Hawkeye's datapad buzzed in his pocket. He pulled it out, and his eyes widened as he looked at the screen.

Sensing the gap in conversation, Swipe stepped up beside Flit and held up her own datapad. "There are a lot of unknowns for now, but the Blue Team has put together some ideas for strike teams. We have access to weapons, a safe passage marked to the surface, and plans to join up with the forces already fighting the Government. This will be our victory, so I ask again... will you join us?"

The cheer that Swipe managed to earn was drowned out by the noise in Flit's mind as she looked down at the datapad Hawkeye was subtly holding out to her. She gulped as she saw that a second emergency beacon had been activated.

"Can you zoom out, please?" Flit whispered to Hawkeye as Swipe continued gearing the crowd up. Hawkeye did as asked, and Flit's head tilted to the side as she saw the wider scope of the landscape around the beacon.

"Looks like someone knows about our safe house," Hawkeye whispered. He grabbed Flit's arm and pulled her behind the others.

Flit frowned at the deserted train garage and surrounds just on the outskirts of Old City. "Who do you think it is?"

Hawkeye sighed. "There's only one way to find out."

57

SCRAPS

SCRAPS SAT in a production line with half a dozen Citizens, all tearing strips of red fabric from some banners Adam had made with the Free Citizens logo on them. Adam was not pleased about the symbolism of tearing up their own banners, but when Scraps had, in front of others, told him that it was either that or tearing clothes off dead bodies, Adam had conceded.

The red would work well too. The Hub was a sea of silver, grey, and reflective glass. Colours usually stood out well enough in the streets, and they would be able to see each other easily enough from a distance with the red.

Once the strips had been torn, they were stacked into piles that would be distributed to each of the bases located around the city. Even though Scraps knew he could have been doing other, probably more critical work, he was grateful for the chance to get away from Adam for a while.

The people Scraps was working with were not fighters, but they asked a lot of questions about how the next few days would progress. Scraps did his best to answer the questions they had honestly and with a sense of hope, but he couldn't hide the fact that a lot of the future would be determined by the Government's response to their attacks.

The world outside had been eerily quiet as the Government hid within the heart of their city. The barriers were successfully being moved forward a block at a time. Reports from the gaps had been positive so far, with minimal interactions between Government Agents and Free Citizens. Really, the skirmishes with regular Citizens had been the most problematic thus far.

A few of the Free Citizens, Adam included, were smugly proclaiming that they had done an excellent job of catching the Government off guard.

Sure, they were probably surprised that the Free Citizens had taken the communication networks offline, but Scraps thought it was grave foolishness to assume that they were not using this time to regroup and plan.

Either way, as the piles grew and they ran out of fabric on the banner they had been tearing, Scraps got to his feet and stretched. He reached down, taking the top five off a pile. He kept one for himself and handed one to each of the people who had been working with him. He tied his scrap around his right arm.

The woman who had been seated across from his tied hers around her left. The man next to her was trying to tie his own on his right, but she shook her head. "No, keep ours on this side. I think Brian and the others in charge should have theirs on a different side. Much easier to identify them in a pinch."

Scraps smiled at the woman and the wisdom in her words. He stood up, taking two more pieces of fabric and walking over to where Adam and Elise were leaning over Adam's desk. "Right side for leadership," he said, holding them out.

Adam tore his attention away from the screens on his desk and looked at the rag. His nose crinkled up as he sneered at it. "What do I need that for?"

"We've torn enough for all the Free Citizens in the Hub," Scraps said.

"I'm the leader. If anyone shoots at me, they can march themselves back to the Government for the sheer stupidity of it."

The arrogance in Adam's statement made Scraps blink. The leader's sneer slowly transformed into a smile and then a hearty laugh. Then, Elise started laughing. Scraps was sure he was supposed to be laughing, too, but he had no energy to pander to the psychotic leader's whims.

"Oh, for goodness sake, Brian. Lighten up." Adam clapped Scraps on the back and took the pieces of fabric. He tied one around Elise's right arm but left the other on the table, leaning on it as he pointed to the map on the screen with a free hand. "If you're going to distribute those, you might as well take some other supplies with you. I've got a couple of things for West Four-North Five."

Adam had been cagey about the locations of the other bases up until this point, so even though Scraps thought that Adam would have put someone in a lower position on the run, he was pleased to be assigned. He was also, secretly, keen to get away from Adam for a while. After everything, Scraps did not enjoy being around the man. Additionally, speaking to others without Adam around meant there was a better chance of getting useful information that he might not otherwise be privy to.

"Sounds like a plan. Let me know when you are ready. I will suit up." Scraps made to step back, but Adam's hand on his shoulder held him in place.

"I'll need you to take Andy with you. She's got a new assignment there to handle." Adam let go of Scraps and turned back to Elise.

Scraps pressed his lips together. "But Andy is here with Petra and Trey." He looked over to the corner where the trio were sleeping soundly on some cushions from the couches upstairs.

"Oh, please." Elise sighed. "She's a grown-arse woman. She can be away from her lovers for a little while."

Adam chuckled. "I have a job there for her. It's critical. Non-negotiable."

His tone was so dismissive of Scraps' concern that it made Scraps frown. It felt like the way his superior Citizen officers would give him orders when he had been a Registered, as though he was unworthy of any opinion or explanation.

"Well, let me know when you have issued her that order. I will be busy getting ready," Scraps said.

Scraps slipped out of Adam's grip and walked away without waiting for further response. When he reached the small space he had been using for his sleeping quarters, he took his time to strap on the tactical gear he had acquired.

AN HOUR LATER, Scraps and Andy were standing at the entry to Nightmix, looking out into the city. Night had fallen in the streets, and the city was eerily dark. Even beyond the barrier, the Government had reduced the lighting to emergency reserves only. Scraps figured it was probably a good idea. He had no doubt their night vision tech was far superior to anything the Free Citizens had.

The darkness did not worry Scraps too much. He was not going in that direction, so the only people he would have to watch for were the general Citizens who were unlikely to have any darkvision tech at all.

"This isn't very comfortable," Andy muttered as she shifted the visor on the narrow bridge of her nose for what had to be the twentieth time in the past minute.

Scraps shrugged. "It isn't supposed to be. It is designed to be functional."

Andy just raised an eyebrow at him. "Could they not have made it both?"

"We are getting off task," Scraps noted, not giving in to the conversation, even though he was actually interested in having it. He wouldn't have minded discussing the various comfort accommodations that had to be sacrificed to make various tactical items functional.

"Right," Andy huffed and tugged at the straps on her shoulders. "Are you sure you don't want a hand with that?"

Hitching the crate he was holding up higher, Scraps shook his head. It was heavy, probably more of a two-person job, but he wasn't a regular Citizen. He would much rather carry it on his own than let Andy weigh herself down with it.

"I am fine. Are you ready to go?" He gestured back to the club. "You do not have to do this, you know. Just because Adam gives you an order does not mean you have to follow it. I will back you up if you need to say no."

The worry that was causing crow's feet on either side of Andy's eyes softened, and she smiled at him. "Thank you, but Adam is right. The other shelter has access to some servers that I may be able to use to get us better communication. It's the best place for me."

"I am happy to escort Petra and Trey as well—"

"No!" Andy's response was surprisingly loud. She winced and repeated herself, but quieter. "No, it's okay. I'd rather them be here. It's much safer for all of us, and Adam needs a reminder of the fact he doesn't own everything and everyone."

Scraps couldn't have agreed more.

Seeing that there was little left to discuss, he stepped out onto the dark street. If Flit had been beside him, he was sure she would have made some comment about how pretty the stars looked as their reflections splattered across the glass or something similar.

The stars would not help them tonight, though. Scraps shrugged his shoulder high enough that it nudged his ear and activated his night vision visor.

"Very well. Let's go. Stay close. Stay alert. If you see anything suspicious tell me immediately… and do not be afraid to use that gun at your hip. We are armed for a reason," Scraps advised.

"Are you certain I can't take that crate?" Andy whispered as she followed him out onto the street. "You're a far better shot than I am."

"If we get attacked, I can drop and draw quickly enough," Scraps said, leaving out the fact that he could use his powers with a flick of his fingers, and it would be far more effective than fighting, anyway.

Silence fell between the pair as they travelled down the wide, now dusty avenue that Nightmix was on. Scraps kept his head on a swivel and ensured Andy remained behind him every time they reached a junction, corner, or alley.

Thankfully, the streets in this part of the city were quiet save for a few people who seemed to be scurrying between neighbouring buildings and doing the best they could to avoid even looking in the direction of the Free Citizens. Scraps didn't allow himself to become complacent, though, particularly as part of their route meant they had to cut a diagonal across a wide intersection, bringing them closer to the edge of the barricade.

Off in the distance, the rumbling of the construction vehicles could be heard, but the emptiness of the streets made the sound echo so much it was nigh impossible to tell where they were. Scraps didn't care so much, as long as they were still working. Getting the noose of the barrier tighter and tighter around Government headquarters was imperative for ensuring the Free Citizens would be able to make a proper final stand when the time came.

A low rumble was the only hint before a flicker of brightness sent a painful jolt of adrenaline through Scraps.

"Duck!" Scraps cried as he dropped the crate and leapt towards Andy, pushing her to the ground and covering her body with his own. He didn't have time for anything else as a missile exploded against the nearby barrier, sending shards of glass, steel, and concrete flying through the air in a deadly spray. Without a second thought, Scraps held up his arm and sent out a push of telekinetic force to repel the shrapnel.

Andy groaned. "What the fuck?" She remained still under him, but he rolled off her as another flicker of light caught his attention. He gritted his teeth and pushed his palms in her direction, sending her flying back under the cover of a building awning nearby.

Because he had helped Andy, he was unable to run for protection himself, so Scraps raised his arms above his head again and fended off another wave of deadly spray as a second missile hit the barrier.

Ears ringing from the blasts, clothing covered in dust and a fine layer of glittering glass, Scraps got into a crouching position. He ignored the way his palms sung with pain as he pressed them into the concrete to get his balance and looked over his shoulder as he ran for cover. As he did, a dozen drones flew in and peppered the streets with fire.

"Are you okay?" Andy shouted.

Scraps could barely hear her. Instead of answering with words, he gave her a thumbs up as he stumbled under the shelter. A warm trail of blood trickled down his hands, and when she saw, it her lips moved in what he was certain was a curse. She tugged the red band off her left arm. She pulled him close, tore it in half, and wrapped a strip around each of his hands.

The bombing of the barrier turned into a worrying beat as they turned to watch the fireworks.

Even though the Government was only targeting the barrier, Scraps didn't want to be complacent. He held up a hand to get Andy's attention, and she winced, recoiling from him. Her eyes were wide, and she immediately bit her lip as their gazes met.

"You... you're..." She leaned back in because there was so much noise it was the only way they would hear one another.

Scraps' body tensed. "Yes."

Andy blinked. "But... how?"

"It is a long story." Scraps hated how he had to raise his voice to be heard, especially when discussing something he had worked so hard to conceal for so long.

Chest rising and falling rapidly, Andy bit her lip. She seemed to consider her options before she nodded. "Well, you left that out there. We may need it!"

Scraps followed the line of Andy's finger as she pointed out into the street at the crate he had dropped.

Despite everything, Scraps chuckled. It was completely inappropriate in the situation and not his usual reaction, but she was right, and she had chosen to bring it up at a most amusing time.

Reaching out one of his bandaged palms, he summoned the crate closer. As though weighing nothing, it zoomed under the shelter and settled behind him.

"Oh, now that's fucking cool," Andy said. The only reason Scraps could hear the awed whisper was because the bombing had stopped for a moment and the drones seemed to turn and move away, back to the dark fathoms of the skies above the city. "Is Ava one too?"

Figuring there was no point hiding it, Scraps nodded. "She's a teleporter."

"Seriously?" Andy's eyes widened with excitement. Then, her eyes creased in the corners. "But... why are you helping Adam?"

With the earth-moving machinery stopped or disabled, it was far too easy to hear the light hum of the drone engines as they descended on the city again.

Scraps frowned. "Because we all deserve to be free." He

gestured to a door nearby that led into the building. It looked to be shut, but he felt it would be better to get more reliable shelter than the awning they were under. "For now, though, we should concentrate on getting better cover."

Given that Scraps' own cover was blown, he didn't bother hiding his gestures as he rose, forced the doors open with his powers, and pulled Andy inside. They got there just as the Government drones came down for a second attack on the barriers the Free Citizens had created.

There were three more rounds of missiles before the air cleared and the night went quiet. Any conversation between Scraps and Andy had stalled as they watched the destruction outside with a sense of dread. When there was a break, Scraps wished he had Hawkeye or another remote viewer with him to get a better idea of whether there were more drones nearby. Instead, he led Andy out so they could move together and just kept his wits about him.

By the time Scraps and Andy tumbled into the subterranean parking lot that was being used as a Free Citizens stronghold, Scraps' hands where aching and burning from where he had pressed them to the ground to get to his feet. The red fabric Andy had torn for him was an even deeper shade of crimson, and he was grateful when someone immediately led him to a first aid area to clean and tend to his wounds properly.

As Scraps left the First Aid area to find Andy, he walked past a group of Citizens who had taken the crate he'd brough them and opened it. They removed the red fabric strips and distributed them around the bunker, and for the first time, Scraps saw what was beneath them. He suppressed a groan at the sight of plastic explosives.

He walked over to the woman unpacking the items and gestured to the fabric strips. "May I please get one of those for Andy? She used hers to bandage my hands."

"Absolutely." The woman gave him one right away and stood a little straighter. "So, you're Brian, huh? Adam spoke a lot about you. I was disappointed I couldn't get to the training you were offering. Hopefully, I won't miss it."

Given the Government retaliation on display outside, Scraps

was certain her hope would soon be dashed. He chose not to disillusion her right now.

"I hope so too," he said instead. It wasn't a lie. "I was wondering if you needed any assistance or advice with that." Scraps gestured casually to the C4.

"Oh." The woman waved a hand dismissively as she leaned against the crate. "This is just for the maglev stations Adam wants us to clear as the noose tightens around the city. Can't have the Government using the tunnels to pop up behind us."

"Ah, of course." Scraps wiggled his fingers and shifted on his feet, trying to make out as though he was distracted by his injuries. "Well, thank you for the extra bandana. I'll get it to Andy. Let me know if you need anything from me before I leave."

With a polite nod, Scraps extracted himself from the situation and walked towards the parking security room, which had been commandeered for a technology station. He saw Andy in there in a passionate conversation with the other Free Citizens who all held their own datapads.

"Will that really work, though?" one of the men asked, frowning at Andy as he looked at some sort of network map on his screen.

"That's why Adam insisted on this building." Andy gestured around them. "This company has always had tight systems and security. I worked on it myself well before everything started. If we can get into this one now, when the Government get a new network up, we should be able to take hold of it for ourselves."

The others grumbled between themselves, but as Scraps walked over and tied the scrap of red fabric onto Andy's right arm, they all looked at the ones they had been told to wrap around their lefts, and they capitulated. Andy gave Scraps a wary look, but he just winked at her.

Over the next few hours, Scraps moved up to the entry of the garage and watched the city outside. The drones were coming in for sporadic attacks, hitting any sort of vehicle, cart, or accessory that had been left in the streets. It was evident the Government was only interested in reducing useful items in the city, not destroying infrastructure.

At least, not yet.

Due to the ongoing bombardment, Scraps radioed base and insisted that he and Andy remain for several hours. It was well after midnight when the Government finally finished their rampage, and he let out a heavy breath as they were finally free to leave. Scraps and Andy made their way back through the streets, and Scraps' mind flicked back to what it had been like in Old City, to be surrounded by so much destruction. Only, this time, it wasn't nature reclaiming the site. It was the battle between the denizens of the city itself.

Just as they reached the block Nightmix was on, Andy tugged Scraps' sleeve and pulled him to a stop. "I'm not going to tell anyone about, you know…" She pointed to his hands and then wiggled her fingers. "That. I just want you to know that I've given it some thought over the last few hours, and you're right. The fact you wanted that video played makes sense, and I, for one, hope we will be able to get more Derivates to join us. We Citizens may be complaining, but our experience is nothing compared to what you guys must have been through."

The heaviness of the night felt a little less weighty on Scraps' shoulders at Andy's words, and he gave her a sombre yet genuine smile of gratitude. "Thank you for that. It means a lot. Flit— Ava— promised she would have some of them up here to join us soon, so I hope I can count on your support when that happens."

Excitement flickered in Andy's eyes. "Are you kidding? Of course you can. Can you imagine how kick-arse it'll be to have you fighting by our sides?" Then, she paused and let out an awkward laugh as she scratched the back of her neck. "Well, I suppose *you* already are. Either way, I'm here for it. I'll try and make sure everyone else is too."

With that, Scraps gently squeezed Andy's shoulder and then resumed his trek back to the bunker and back to Adam. He wasn't looking forward to reporting the amount of damage the Government had wrought and the inevitable truth that their earth-moving machinery would be spare parts by now, but at least he and Andy had completed their mission successfully.

58

———

FLIT

DIRT SHIFTED beneath Flit as she leaned in closer to Hawkeye. "Can you get any angles to see inside?" she whispered.

Hawkeye was lying beside her on rough gravel, underneath an old rail carriage fifty metres away from the train shed. It was dark, with only the haunting silver sliver of the moon and the eerie blue of the distant electrostatic fence lighting the night.

With a heavy sigh, Hawkeye's posture relaxed against Flit's side. "Yes, but they aren't using any lights, so it is near impossible to get anything useful." He drummed his fingers then pressed his palm flat against the ground.

"Well, someone is there. At least they didn't activate the beacon and go." Flit pulled back and rested her chin on her hands.

"We're just going to have to go in and hope for the best." Hawkeye rolled onto his side so he could look at her properly. "Although we need to avoid being heavy-handed with the weapons. Flame grenades included. We can't afford to draw any attention from the Government. They have drones hovering around the Hub that might be able to pick that kind of thing up."

"Me, heavy-handed with weapons? I don't know what you mean." Flit's eyes widened in an expression of faux innocence. Then, she grew serious. "Where do you want me to get us to?"

"There's a broken window on the south side. You can see it just over there." Hawkeye pointed to a spot that was just in sight. It was a window on the east side of the shed, with some panels dangling off a nearly disintegrated sill.

Flit and Hawkeye shimmied out from under the train car and rose on the side opposite of the train shed. She stepped closer to him and wrapped her arms around him. Flit teleported them so they were standing beside the window.

Hawkeye leaned closer, peering through a gap in the shutters. When he pulled back, he let out a breath of relief. "Mitch just stepped into a beam of moonlight."

"Thank fuc—"

"It would still be good to approach cautiously," Hawkeye whispered, cutting Flit off. "Let's just take the front door."

Hawkeye had a point. Mitch was jumpy at the best of the time, and if Iris wasn't there, they would be in trouble.

Flit nodded and led the way around, taking care to tread lightly and stick close to the shadowy shelter of the building walls. When they reached the front door, they rapped on it lightly and announced their names. There was a soft scuffling before the door opened. True to Mitch's form, a rifle was pointed in their direction.

Both Flit and Hawkeye raised their hands into the air and waited for Mitch's eyes to adjust so they could identify the newcomers. Then, to Flit's surprise, Mitch let the gun go, the weapon swinging on its strap as they grasped Flit and Hawkeye's sleeve and dragged them into the building.

"We saw Scraps. He told us about this place and promised you would get us either safety or supplies," Mitch said.

Clearly, they were in no mood for foreplay.

Leaning past Mitch, Flit saw a huge group of people dressed in a mix of Government uniforms and civilian clothes. They all appeared to be waiting nervously. She was about to ask for more detailed information when a familiar figure stepped forward from behind some crates, yawning and stretching.

"Lucky I was sleeping, or I would have caught your creeping arses way earlier," Iris called out as she walked over.

Flit smiled at the sight of her. "Nice to see you again too."

"We've got more of us downstairs, mostly the young, old, and those who aren't able or willing to fight." Iris stood beside Mitch and slipped her hands into the pockets of her black cargo pants. For once, the woman wasn't accompanied by the constant hum of music. "It's quieter out here. I don't need it as much. Plus, better to be safe than to be comfortable, apparently."

Mitch rolled their eyes.

Flit was too busy thinking about what Iris said to be amused by the relationship between the two. "Wait... you said those not willing to fight?"

The grin on Iris's face was wide. "Yep. We've already figured out who wants to help the Underground. You're still planning to join the fray, right?"

Once more, Flit found herself feeling relieved. "We are. We've got a few people forming teams back at our base. Everyone will need rest before we launch our attack, so we will be ready to rise come morning."

Flit hated the fact they would still need to wait several hours. It was already difficult to think about the fact that Scraps and the Free Citizens had been going it alone for twenty-four hours. She hoped the Underground and the Citizen Derivates weren't going to be too late to make a difference.

"Will you be able to shelter the people we have who can't fight?" Mitch asked.

"Of course," Flit said without hesitation. "We'll move them while we're marching on the city. That should keep the Government distracted and give them a chance to get to safety."

Iris perked up. "Great! What time do we need to tell our crew to be ready by?"

"An hour before dawn?" Hawkeye suggested. "I think we should be up here and ready to charge past the fence line at sunrise."

Iris, who had been watching Flit closely, nodded. "That sounds like a plan. We don't have much in the way of weapons and armour, though."

"I don't know if we have enough, but we'll bring everything we have," Hawkeye said. "With any luck, the Free Citizens can supplement anything we don't have."

Mitch snorted. "I'm sure they'll share some of their bullets by putting them in our chest. I hope your people will lead the charge if that's the level of faith you have in them."

Flit could totally understand Mitch's cynicism. "We'll do our best to ensure it doesn't come to that."

She bit the inside of her lip as she thought of Scraps. Her heart ached at his continued absence, but she knew she could trust him.

"Do you guys need any other supplies?" Hawkeye made a wise attempt to change the discussion.

Iris perked up. "Food would be good. We're surviving on shitty, expired protein supplements. Any other clothing or whatever you can spare would be helpful too."

"We'll make sure people are taken care of," Flit promised. "We'll probably also use this place as a safe house as well. We still have a bit of planning to do, so we will have more information when we get back in a few hours."

"Stay safe until then." Hawkeye stepped closer to Flit.

She wrapped her arms around him and teleported him back to the Underground. When Flit and Hawkeye returned, it was to find that the Blue Team members were working with various Control, Intelligence, and Security operatives to make plans for their assault on the surface. As the team had postulated, there was a cache of hidden weapons, and it was rather impressive. Given the fact Harmony and Divvy had no intention to let them go to the surface, Flit shuddered to guess what they had been planning to use them for.

Everyone was surprised to hear that they would be meeting a new team of Derivates on the surface, but the news sent a thrill of excitement through the group making the plans. The Underground community was so insulated that newcomers always caused a fuss. The fact they were fighting for a chance to live in the world above was a stark reminder that they were also fighting to live in a place that would have so many opportunities they had been denied for decades upon decades.

Although they knew better than to get ahead of themselves. The first order of business was to figure out who would go where and when. It was difficult given how little they knew of the Free Citizens' intentions. All they could plan for really was their rise to the surface and their approach to the city. For this, they knew it would be critical to have their tech-oriented micros and their macros in the frontline. There wasn't a single person in the planning group who believed that the Government would sit idly by and watch an army of Derivates march on their city. That was where the remote viewers would be in their element. Up above, their range of view would provide them with advanced warning of any incoming concerns.

As the majority of the Blue Team worked with Control and Intelligence, Flit liaised with her parents to ensure planning for the field hospitals was on track. She was pleased to see them both hard at work organising supplies and people and working with Shadow to find locations where they could realistically set up.

Pleased with how that was progressing, Flit returned to the Blue Team and pulled Hawkeye and Fortune aside. She let them know that, even though she was going to go up in the first wave at dawn, she would be leaving once the action started to find Scraps. His help would be critical in ensuring the Free Citizens welcomed them rather than attack them.

Once all of the important decisions were made, everyone was encouraged to get some rest. Flit returned to the apartment she shared with her parents. They sat together and shared a light snack before they went to their rooms. Flit showered, got ready for bed, and lay down under her blanket. Her mind raced with the knowledge of what was to come.

FLIT WAS up before her alarm. Well before. So well before, in fact, that she was able to give herself a minute-by-minute count down for an hour before it went off.

Even though Flit should be tired, she had never felt more energised as she jumped out of bed and pulled on the same gear she had worn for her Security patrols. She was ready in record time, and when she got out into the living area, she found that her mother was just putting three bowls of breakfast onto the table.

After eating their meal, the whole family went to assemble in the Residence foyer as planned the night before. Fortune approached them and pulled Flit into a hug. As she did, she whispered to Flit that Harmony and Divvy were still safely locked away and under supervision. In the rush to get things sorted, Flit hadn't even considered what to do with them. Thankfully, they were sorted for now.

It wasn't long before everyone who had signed up to join them was present. As Flit stood amongst the Blue Team, she sought Hawkeye's gaze. He caught her attention and nodded, as if to say, "It's time."

Flit walked over to a nearby side table and teleported to stand on top of it. "Thank you to everyone for assembling today," she called out.

It took a few moments for the conversations to die down and for her to have undivided attention, but the silence that followed was the most complete she could have hoped for given how many people were present. She was surrounded by so many familiar faces that her heart became swollen with hope.

"Your team names were sent to you a couple of hours ago," she continued. "Beside that name should also be the name of your team leader. We are going to the surface in waves. Your team leader will be your first point of contact. Please listen to them closely. It is their responsibility to give you the conditions needed to survive."

Flit let her words settle over the group as she gestured to the small group of people to her right who the Control and Intelligence informants had nominated as team leaders. They all looked suitably serious.

"In ten minutes, we will form our teams. We will then travel to the surface and move through Old City until we reach a building where we will be able to gain new allies. There will be a team assigned to escort some of their people back to the Underground for shelter. The rest of us will march towards the electrostatic fence." Flit stopped at the ripple of worry that passed over those gathered.

"All of this has suddenly become very serious. I know it feels like a lot… but this is an important and necessary first step in what is hopefully a short walk to freedom. I know the Government will try to intimidate us, but… we are the Underground. We do not run from darkness."

A cheer rose around the space.

Flit's heart hammered against her ribs. "Enough is enough. We will no longer allow the Government to force us to hide in these tunnels for a chance to escape their cruelty. When we arrive on the surface, we will rise like the sun and fight through the day and night until we can bring down a new dawn down upon them! The Derivates are rising!"

The second cheer was nothing short of riotous, a chorus of voices echoing, "The Derivates are rising!"

The team leaders stepped forward and called for everyone to arm up.

Flit teleported off the table and stood beside the Blue Team, where Swipe handed her a fully stocked weapons belt, some body armour, and a datapad.

Shadow walked over to her as she strapped everything in place, his face pulled taut. "What is your plan if the Free Citizens do not ally with us?" he asked in a low voice meant only for her.

"There is no plan," Flit admitted. Anyone else might seem contrite in such a response, but Flit was confident. "We won't need one."

It was clear Shadow did not like that, but Fortune came to stand beside them, and he was distracted by her arrival. "I assume your new skills may come in handy in this uprising," he noted to Fortune.

"I was wondering if you would have picked up on that," Fortune said, her voice stiff.

"I notice a lot more than people know," Shadow replied. Then, he offered her a hand. "I believe we need to get a head start to set up the command station."

Flit bit her lip as she looked at Fortune. Someone needed to keep an eye on Shadow, who had volunteered to oversee the command station. It was a natural position for him to fall into but not one Flit wanted him in alone. Sending Fortune with him would hopefully keep her out of harm's way for the early stages of the fight and allow them to determine whether Shadow could be trusted. He had helped them in overthrowing Harmony and Divvy, but that could have been a move of sheer convenience.

Before accepting Shadow's hand, Fortune pulled Flit into a tight embrace. "You watch yourself up there," she whispered fiercely in her ear. "I might have lost my son, but there is no way I will allow them to take my daughter from me too."

The words brought tears to Flit's eyes, but before she could say anything, Fortune stepped back, took Shadow's hand, and was gone.

Blinking back the emotions, Flit moved to find her parents, who were standing with a group of medics who would be working the first shift. Flit described where to find the markers she had painted for the route to the surface and encouraged them to move ahead. She got the members of the Blue Team to go with them to act as guards.

When only Flit and Hawkeye remained, they approached the team leaders and had them form ranks with their new teams. They gave them five minutes to chat and then started sending them along the evacuation route one team at a time.

Finally, the last team left the Residence, and Flit was alone with Hawkeye in the foyer.

He turned and looked at her, an unexpected smile on his face. "You were right."

Flit blinked. She wasn't sure what was more shocking—his words or the setting. "What?"

"All our lives, you've been harping on about taking the fight to the Government. Now, we're really doing it." He rested his hands on the weapon belt he was wearing. "You were right."

"Well, obviously. I'm always right." Flit playfully elbowed him.

"Now that I've buttered you up with a compliment, I hope you're not going to argue when I tell you that I'm not letting you find Scraps alone. You have no idea what you'll face up there, and there is no way you're doing that without backup," Hawkeye said.

Flit should have known his concession was too good to be true. Her natural instinct was to tell him she didn't need backup, but as she took in the concern stretching his features thin, her posture softened. "Fine, but joke's on you because we're going to be doing a shit-load of teleporting, and you're gonna have your boots covered in puke before the battle even begins."

Hawkeye rubbed the back of his neck and shook his head. "Why do I get myself into these situations?"

59

SCRAPS

"WHAT DO YOU MEAN, it's all gone?" Adam's booming voice echoed through the bunker and had everyone wary and finding whatever reason they could to get out of his line of sight. "Are you trying to tell me we don't have a single fucking piece of heavy machinery left?" He rounded on the person who was flicking through the camera footage on the new network Andy had activated.

In all the yelling about the machines, Adam did not once mention the lives of the people who had been operating them. Scraps found that far more concerning than Adam's anger. The ranting and raving was old news by now.

"Y-Yes, Adam." The man's fingers shook as he stepped back and hung his head.

"Impossible." With a rough shove against his shoulder, Adam pushed him back to the console. "Check again!"

The approaching dawn provided enough light for their cameras to pick up the precise details of the destruction wrought by the Government drones. Even though most were fitted with night-vision technology, nothing could replace the illustrative value of proper lighting and colouring. As the feeds the man was flicking through came up on the screens all around the bunker, everyone watched with rapt interest for some sign of, well, anything.

Scraps was glad that some of the Free Citizen in the machines had been able to take shelter when the attack started, but others had not been so lucky. There were six operators who had yet to check in. The most logical assumption in this situation was that they had not survived.

The security screens panned over the noose of rubble the Free Citizens had been using to create physical barriers around the city. The previously high piles were now scattered up and down all of the wide streets, essentially flattening the barrier and making it rough, yet passable, terrain. The antique earth-movers had been blown to smithereens, the yellow metal shells shredded into ribbons that now adorned the streets.

Camera after camera revealed the same level of absolute destruction. With each new location that passed, Scraps could feel the tension growing in Adam. His rage was so strong it was heating the air around them.

Just when Scraps thought the man would boil them both alive with his anger, the sound of a clearing throat drew his attention.

"Uh, Adam... you need to see this," Andy called, her eyes wide as she stood in front of her console.

"Can't you see I'm busy?" Adam snapped.

Frowning, Scraps used the request from Andy as an excuse to step away from Adam. He walked over to see what was worrying her and stopped dead in his tracks as noticed the formations on her screen.

"Where is that?" he asked.

"Looks like they are assembling around Centre One," Andy said, zooming out the footage she had on her screen.

Scraps' blood ran cold, and his mind snapped into sharp focus, the same way it did whenever a new mission began.

On the screen, there were thousands upon thousands of agents amassing outside the Government's stronghold. Made up of what had to be a combination of Derivates and Citizens, they were all fully armed and armoured.

"Adam, the Government is preparing to march on us." Scraps' words fell heavily in the silence of the bunker.

Adam's shoes creaked as he shifted his weight and turned to look at Scraps.

"Andy, on the main screen, please," Scraps said calmly.

When the new footage hit the screens, the wariness that had been suffusing the air snapped into outright fear. Terrified whispers rippled through the room, and even Adam looked frozen on the spot as he assessed the situation.

A whispered, "There's too many of them", made Adam snap out of his catatonic state. Scraps frowned over at Liana as she pressed up against Chris' side, her eyes wide with horror.

Even Scraps was shocked that the Government had pulled out what appeared to be their entire force so early. He had expected a few more days of dancing back and forth in attempt to minimise the collateral.

"They want to squash this uprising right here and now," Elise said as she rose from where she was sitting with Tai and Leo. "They are done messing around."

"And so are we." Adam's voice had a bite to it that made Scraps stare at him. "Brian, get on the radio, and let our teams in other cities know what is happening. Elise, message all Hub bases. We need every fighter we have on the streets."

"How long do you think we have?" Andy called over, zooming the view farther back to give them all a better bird's-eye-view of the city.

Scraps watched as the force slowly came together. So far, the agents were on foot. There would undoubtedly be some vehicles waiting in the garages, but they had yet to release them. A force like that would take time and coordination to move, though.

Adam's brows creased. "A couple of hours, perhaps."

"I would not discount the possibility that they have put together some advanced strike teams to try and catch us unaware. They do have teleporters amongst their ranks." Scraps frowned as he tried to spot any other movement on the screens.

"Then we don't have any time to waste," Adam announced. He looked around at the people who were all staring at him. "Move!"

The bunker of Nightmix erupted into a flurry of activity as the Free Citizens got ready for their first real call to battle.

60

FLIT

"I'M SORRY, Flit, but in what world is 'I think I know where they are' supposed to fill me with confidence?" Hawkeye asked as they stood beside the ruined train shed once more. He held his hand to his mouth as if worried he might be sick if he moved it away.

In the dwindling moonlight before dawn, Hawkeye looked pale and drawn. It was too hard to tell, but Flit would have put a good bet on the fact that his skin was also tinged green. She had a feeling that his nausea was probably the reason he was such a cranky jerk.

"I haven't seen Scraps since he went undercover, have I?" Flit rolled her eyes. She gestured towards the Hub, looming like a dark, still sentinel in the distance. "From what Layla said after he helped them free the Registereds, it sounds as though he was in a rush to get back to the Free Citizens. I can't say for certain where they are, but Adam was setting a club called Nightmix up as their base of operations. That's our best bet."

"And you want to just teleport us blindly into the club without taking time to confirm it first?" Hawkeye asked.

"Well, I can hardly translocate to any old street in the area, can I?" Flit scoffed. "I only have enough of a memory of the club, the apartment, or my office in Centre One. Which do you prefer?"

"There are a billion other options between here and there, dumb-arse!" Hawkeye threw up his hands in the direction of the city. "Just because you *can* translocate doesn't mean you *have* to."

"So, what? Do a dozen line-of-sight hops and just hope we don't get shot along the way?" Flit put her hands on her hips. "That's a fucking bright idea when both the Government and the Free Citizens are likely to blow our heads off without warning."

"For fuc—" Hawkeye stopped, letting out a groan of frustration as he pinched the bridge of his nose. He took several long, exaggerated breaths.

Concerned he might breathe himself into hypoxia, Flit put a hand on his shoulder. "Gee, if only we had a talented remove-viewer with us."

Hawkeye glared at her. "It's a big city, Flit. We don't have that much time."

Flit turned towards the city and frowned "Well, why don't we start with the streets outside Nightmix, then? It should be easy enough for you to get a vantage point for that with the grid layout of the city. I can tell you where to look."

Even though he looked like he might argue, Hawkeye signed and nodded. Flit took his hand and dragged him over to a patch of dirt alongside the train tracks. She dragged her finger in the dirt to draw a rough grid pattern.

"Nightmix is on the ground floor of North Four-East Three." She drew a circle in the dirt then pointed to the city. "Come in along that street there, and you should be able to bounce your view around just right."

"Fine." Hawkeye walked back to stand against the wall of the train shed, ignoring the noise of the Citizen Derivates preparing to leave inside. "Just keep an eye out for trouble while I'm looking."

"Copy that, Captain Bossy." Flit gave him a mocking salute as his gaze turned vacant.

Leaning back against the shed, foot tapping on the dirt and fingers drumming against her forearms, Flit waited for Hawkeye to do his thing. She was quite impressed that he had been able to stretch his range over the past few months in his training. It seemed like Layla and Swipe had done well, with the former getting a good handle on the idea of manipulating tech with her microkinesis and the latter lifting eye-watering weight with her macrokinesis.

"So, I've found the street you mentioned," Hawkeye said,

posture still taut with concentration. "There's a lot of people on the streets nearby, with a tickle of foot traffic between their mustering point and the club..."

Flit smirked to herself.

"Stop smirking."

"You should be concentrating on the city, not me."

"I don't need to see you to know you're smirking."

That made Flit chuckle.

Hawkeye fell silent for a few more moments before his shoulders sagged and he rubbed his eyes.

"So, what's the verdict? You didn't happen to see Scraps, did you?" Flit asked, leaning sideways against the shed wall.

"It's too dark for that, unfortunately," Hawkeye said, scratching the back of his neck. "I did have a look around some of the other streets. The concentration around the club is the highest. That probably is their headquarters—"

"What a surprise!"

"—but that doesn't mean Scraps is there."

"As much as I hate to say this, we need to be where Adam is," Flit told Hawkeye. "I am hoping Scraps will be with him or, if not, at least somewhere nearby. However, if we want the Free Citizens on our side, Adam will be the key."

That seemed to satisfy Hawkeye as he stepped away from the shed and let out a heavy sigh. "I guess this means we're translocating to the club."

"I mean we *can*, but we don't *have* to." Flit shrugged. The sense of satisfaction she got from turning his earlier comment on him was immense. Hawkeye prinched the bridge of his nose. "However, I'm happy to do whatever will keep your stomach settled. Need you on your best game when we get there, just in case. So, several long hops across risky enemy territory or one translocation? Which would you prefer?"

"Just get us there," Hawkeye said through gritted teeth.

"It would be my pleasure." Flit stepped closer and wrapped her arms around him. "Tell me when you're ready."

Hawkeye took a deep breath and nodded.

When they arrived at one of the booths in the club, several

people were walking past, carrying crates and muttering to one another in quiet voices. They jumped at the sudden arrival of two new people in the room, cries of alarm sounding over the oddly quiet dance floor.

"Don't mind us!" Flit said, smiling in what she hoped was a completely non-threatening manner and holding up her hands in a gesture of peace. "We're friends of Adam and Brian. Just popping in to say hi."

"Er, go about your business," Hawkeye added.

The people stared at Hawkeye and Flit and then at each other. One of them started stuttering something to the other.

Flit just took Hawkeye's forearm and dragged him out of the booth. "C'mon, I know where he'll be."

Flit led the way to the back of the main area. The door to the office was open. So was the panel on the back wall. Thankfully, there was no one else in the narrow tunnel as she led Hawkeye down to the bunker. When they entered, Flit couldn't help but be impressed at just how many people and tactical stations they had squeezed into the space. She noticed they all had red scraps of fabric tied around their arms too, and she figured it was probably a good way for them to figure out who was who on the street.

Oddly enough, no one was guarding the door. Nor did anyone seem to notice there were intruders in the space. Flit was just about to mutter something to Hawkeye about the alarming lack of security when she spotted Adam at his desk. Well, the desk that he had used when she last had seen him. It had clearly been upgraded since. She spotted a few other familiar faces in the room, too, like Andy, Petra, and Trey, but she was on a mission.

"Over there," she whispered, pointing Adam out to Hawkeye.

"Let's go."

Just as Flit and Hawkeye started to cross the floor, footsteps echoed down the tunnels behind them.

"Derivates!" a voice cried. "A Derivate teleported into the club!"

Chaos erupted in the bunker as people either tried to hide or find the intruders. Flit and Hawkeye seemed to be immune to their searching, though, and Flit realised that everyone was probably expecting the intruders to be dressed in Government uniforms.

"Woah, woah, woah!" Flit called out above the ruckus. "Teleporter here, and I promise we come in peace."

Adam, who had been hurriedly shutting down the screens around the room, looked up at her, eyes wide and calculating.

"Don't even think about it!" Hawkeye's head snapped around, and he pointed to a tall woman wearing her red sash on her right arm. She froze, keeping her weapon raised, but her finger off the trigger.

"Elise, stand by," Adam said, stepping out from behind the desk and walking closer. The Free Citizens parted in front of him. "Who the fuck are you, and what are you doing in my bunker?"

At this stage, Flit figured that Scraps must have been elsewhere. Otherwise, he would have shown himself already.

She frowned, tilting her head to the side. "You don't remember me, Adam?" Flit asked, pouting. "A girl changes her hair and eyes, and suddenly she's unrecognisable."

Adam's lips pressed together in a hard line as he stared at her. A full five seconds passed before his eyebrows rose. "Ava!"

"Ava?" Andy's excited call from off to the side made Flit smile, but she didn't allow herself to become distracted.

"Brian's wife?" the woman with the gun scoffed.

"Ah, there we go! Yes, it's me, although my name's not Ava. It's Flit." She winked at Adam then turned to the woman with the gun. Elise. "And I'm his girlfriend, not wife, but... same same, right?"

One of the people who had seen Flit and Hawkeye arrive in the club burst through the crowd. "That's the teleporter!"

"Heck, can't a Derivate have any secrets around here?" Flit sighed, shaking her head. "Yes, I'm a teleporter. I also happen to have a huge group of unregistered Derivates sitting at the edge of Old City, ready and willing to ally with you and bring the Government down. What do you say, huh?"

"Woah, shit. Adam, get a look at this!" Andy said.

The monitors around the room that Adam had just turned off came back to life, all filled with the same view of Old City. At first, it was hard to see the people scattered out along the edge of the crumbled metropolis, but the longer Flit looked, the more of her people she could see standing at the ready.

"They're all Derivates?" Elise hissed.

Flit sighed "Yes. All Derivates who want their freedom just as much, if not more, than you guys do. I know it's a novel concept, but I think we can help each other out."

Everyone in the bunker looked to Adam. The tension in the air grew so thick that Flit was tempted to tug at the collar of her shirt to breathe a little easier.

"Get that off the screens!" Adam glared at Andy. "And get Brian on the line. Now!"

Andy turned the screens off again, pulled out some weird, black plastic contraption, and spoke into it.

"And you, don't move. If you try, they'll shoot," Adam said.

At his words, several of the people surrounding Flit and Hawkeye raised weapons.

"Oh, come off it." Flit rolled her eyes. "If we wanted to hurt you, we would have done it already. Besides, what's that old saying? The enemy of my enemy is my friend, or some shit like that."

Adam watched Hawkeye more closely than before. He already knew that Flit was a teleporter, but he had to be wondering what Hawkeye was capable of. Adam was clearly trying to be calculated about his decisions.

When Flit and Hawkeye stayed in place, Adam reached down and plucked a similar plastic device to the one Andy had used off his belt. "Time to call Brian back to base. He has a lot of explaining to do."

61

SCRAPS

THE ANGLE of the rising sun dragged the shadows of the buildings and debris in the Hub far across the streets. The dark, wavering tendrils of shade wrapped around everything they touched and were a stark reminder that the Free Citizens had yet to learn the full reach of the Government's destruction the night before.

As hundreds of wary Free Citizens formed ranks on their side of the broken barriers, Scraps looked around. It was hard to truly tell their numbers with the partially shattered skyscrapers blocking their view. As the dawn approached, some Citizens had crawled out of the cracks in the city to join their ranks. However, one glance down at the datapad Chris was holding beside him was enough to confirm one of his greatest worries—they were severely outnumbered.

Of course, the Free Citizens knew numbers were never on their side, but they had planned to be closer to Centre One before they were forced to take the streets.

Scraps thought back to the conversation he had with Adam weeks ago about the problems with a siege approach. If the situation was not so dire, he would have been tempted to say, "I told you so."

"This doesn't look promising, does it?" Chris muttered, shifting from foot to foot beside Scraps. He and Liana looked distinctly uncomfortable with the weapon belts around their hips and the armoured vests they were wearing.

Scraps had tried to get his friends other roles back in the bunker, but Adam would hear nothing of it. Adam had asked Scraps to stay as well, but as much as Scraps wanted to keep overwatch, he did not trust anyone else in the Free Citizens to have eyes in the field. As it were, he and any Free Citizens who could fight had left the club and made their way onto the streets. Even though there was nothing for them to fight yet, it would be good for them to become comfortable being in view, and the more people who were there to look around, the higher the chance someone would notice something useful or helpful.

"The odds are not the greatest." Scraps kept his voice low so that his words did not travel farther than intended. "However, I have fought against worse odds and won."

"That's, uh, really reassuring. Thanks." Chris cleared his throat and glanced warily at his fiancé. "So, what's the plan? Do we wait here for them to come to us?"

"No." Scraps gestured around them. "I've got some people scouting the streets to find better vantage points to fight from. Hopefully, there are some areas that will be easier to fortify than others."

"Do we have to stay on the streets?" Liana stepped closer to Chris, her fingers fluttering over the hilt of her gun on the way to rest on her belt.

Scraps tilted his head to the side as he looked at her, considering his words. Even though it wasn't what she meant, he looked around at the buildings surrounding them. Many of them were now structurally questionable after the Free Citizens bombings. However, they were not really any worse for wear than they had been the day before.

"The Government didn't attack the buildings..." Scraps turned in a slow circle as he kept his eyes glued higher. Then, he made an executive decision. "I'm going to take a team to see if we can break into some of the buildings. We should scatter our people across all different heights to give us an advantage. The Government are less likely to attack if they think they might kill too many civilians."

Chris and Liana perked up at Scraps' suggestion.

"Everyone, listen here," Scraps called out. "I need four volunteers to come with me on a quick mission. Everyone else will stay here. Take shelter under the awnings and keep watch in the meantime."

Chris and Liana were the first two to volunteer. As much as Scraps thought the street might be the safer option for them, he also felt more comfortable having them close to him. He selected them as well as two younger members of the Free Citizens he had tutored in his combat lessons and knew to be quite fit.

Just as Scraps was about to lead the small team to barricaded revolving door of the nearest building, his radio flared to life.

"*Uh, Brian?*" Andy's voice came through the coms, quiet and uncertain. "*Have you looked east lately? You need to check it out ASAP.*"

Scraps frowned at Andy's cryptic words, but he turned around all the same. Some of the broken and bent construction vehicles were blocking his view down the long street that led out of the city.

He issued a low order of, "Wait here," before he sprinted to the tall machine with a long arm and a heavy ball swaying in front of it. He started to climb the precariously rickety tracks and onto the main frame of the vehicle. As he got high enough to stand beside the cabin, he could see past all the wreckage.

The distant horizon, painted all shades of blue and orange as the blazing sun rose, burned his eyes. He raised an arm to shield his view and blinked rapidly to clear away the dazzling brightness. When his vision cleared, his attention was drawn to the bluish, hexagonal grid of the electrostatic fence surrounding the city or, more precisely, the thousands of people standing on the other side of it, stretching across the distance. There were no flags and no banners, but Scraps had no doubt who it was.

"The Underground," he breathed, his heart skipping a beat at the sight of the reinforcements. Despite the seriousness of the situation, a grin spread across his face.

"*Brian... you need to get back to the bunker. Now.*" Adam's voice was sharp enough, even through the radio, to tear Scraps' attention away from the reinforcements. *"It seems your wife is back, and we all need to have a nice little chat."*

Scraps almost slipped as he stood on the vehicle. "Fl—Ava's there?"

"That's right." It was Adam again, and there was something about his tone that did not sit well with Scraps. *"Better hurry. I would hate to keep this lovely wife of yours waiting."*

Not liking Adam's comment at all, Scraps turned and scrambled back down off the side of the machine. When his feet hit the cracked asphalt, Chris and Liana came over to him.

"Did we hear that right? Was that Ava?" Liana's smile was the complete opposite of how Scraps felt inside. "Can we come see her too?"

"I don't think that's wise," Scraps muttered, already starting to walk away.

Despite the fact he was already moving, Chris and Liana ran to keep pace with him.

"Brian, what's going on? What's wrong?" Chris put a hand on his shoulder.

Stopping and turning to face his friends, Scraps frowned as he considered his options. "Things are about to get... complicated. As much as I want to bring you with me, it is far safer if you two remain out here and keep an eye on the situation. If I don't make contact within an hour... run. Hide somewhere, and wait this out."

The mild intrigue on the faces of his friends soured with concern. He didn't hang around long enough to hear their complaints.

Scraps powerwalked the rest of the way back to the club, knowing running might draw too much attention. It was far too long, at least in his opinion, before he reached Nightmix. The club itself was quiet as he entered, and the bunker door opened without resistance. Over the past few days, he had been able to hear the buzz of conversation the moment he had stepped into the roughly cut passage that led to the Free Citizens headquarters. This time, however, it was quiet down there, with only the occasional shuffle or cough breaking the silence.

Taking care, Scraps slowed his steps and stood closer to a wall as he walked farther and farther down the path. He turned the slight corner and immediately raised his hands. Not in surrender, but in a position ready to tear people apart if needed.

In the middle of the room stood Flit and Hawkeye, surrounded by a dozen Free Citizens with guns out and trained on them. Adam lingered by his desk, an expression on his face that Scraps had never seen before but set alarm bells blaring in his mind. The screens lining the walls cycled between locations, casting an almost strobe-like effect over the scene.

"Interesting... If that was my wife in the middle of a circle of well-aimed rifles, my first instinct wouldn't be to raise my weapon-less hands." Adam sagged back against his seat and crossed his arms over his chest.

"This wasn't quite the welcome I was hoping for," Flit said, casting a glare back over her shoulder at Adam. Her shoulders were relaxed, and her hands were dangling by her sides.

Normally, Scraps thought she would have them in her pockets at this point, but she was clearly being careful despite her seemingly relaxed posture. Beside her, Hawkeye stood a little straighter than usual, and Scraps couldn't blame him. He had no reason to trust anyone in the room.

Scraps stepped closer. The people surrounding Flit and Hawkeye shifted, and the metallic clink of their weapons made him pause. "Adam, I don't know what Ava—"

"Oh, cut the shit, you traitor." Adam pushed himself off the desk. "What's her real name... or yours, for that fact? Are you one of the Government appliances as well?"

Twitching at the accusation, Scraps let out a slow breath. "I was..." He paused as a collective buzz of gasps and exclamations rippled through the room. "...until Flit and the Underground found me. They undid the brainwashing that the Government had forced on me for my entire life and taught me that freedom was worth more than any false sense of order the Government offered."

A quarter of the gun barrels shifted towards his direction, but he ignored them. Between Flit, Hawkeye, and himself, they could get out of this room without any trouble.

"He didn't have to help any of you," Flit snapped, the casual set of her shoulders gone the instant weapons were aimed at Scraps. Her fingers twitched by her side, and Scraps would have bet anything that she had some flame grenades hiding under the black jacket she was wearing. "Luckily for you, though, we believe in freedom for everyone, not just our own kind."

Adam sneered at her. "No one asked you, *Flit*."

"That's lucky because I don't give a fuck. I don't take orders from you," she fired back.

Hawkeye put a warning hand on her shoulder.

Scraps cut into the conversation in hopes to stop it from deteriorating. "She's right, Adam. I could have gone back to be with the Underground Derivates weeks ago. Instead, I wanted to stay up here and get information for the Free Citizens. I wanted to help because I believe in your cause."

Before Adam could respond, the screens that had been flickering between different vantage points around the city turned black. After a second delay, they started showing highlights from the reels about the Government's atrocities against Derivates. It was the same one Scraps had had Andy play at the end of the Free Citizen's countdown at midnight. Then, it showed images of Scraps from inside the bunker, training the Free Citizens how to fight or bending over Adam's desk and working on strategy with him. The extended footage had everyone enthralled. Scraps marvelled at it, not sure how Andy had managed to pull it all together in a few hours, but he was so grateful.

"Stop it! Cut the feed!" Adam turned around, glaring at Andy. She just raised her hands innocently and winked at Scraps.

The people who were holding the weapons faltered in their conviction, looking between Scraps and the undeniable evidence of what he and other Derivates were willing to do in the fight against the Government.

"Right now, we have a veritable army of Derivates waiting outside of the electrostatic fence," Flit said, keeping her voice low. The people around her took a step closer so they could hear her better. "From what I saw on the screens when we walked in here, the Government will be here by the afternoon, and this uprising will be over."

Pressing his lips together to stop himself from talking, Scraps watched as everyone in the room was held captive by Flit's words. There was a brutal truth to her tone, a level of honesty and transparency that they never got from Adam.

Flit held her hands out, palms up. "We came here to join the cause. With our help, I have no doubt we can take this city. If we work together, they will not be able to stop us. What started as a rebellion will end with a revolution."

It would have been possible to hear a pin drop in that room. The walls were lined with people who were standing, enthralled. Others were still lying warily in sleeping bags. The entire bunker was full, but not even one moved as they waited for Adam's response.

"That's rubbish. The moment we're distracted, the Derivates will turn on us and destroy us," Adam said, eyes narrowed, tone razor sharp.

"With all due respect, Adam," Hawkeye said, speaking for the first time since Scraps had arrived in the bunker, "we could have ended this whole situation the moment you turned weapons on us. If we wanted to take over your movement... we would have."

The tension that had been winding itself so tight in the room snapped as Adam shouted, "Fire!"

Several things then happened at once. Half of the armed Free Citizens shot their weapons. Flit teleported behind Adam and knocked him to the ground. She put her boot on his cheek to keep him down. Hawkeye dropped and swung his leg in a wide circle, knocking several Free Citizens off balance. Scraps threw his hands up and sent a push of telekinetic energy around his girlfriend and friend.

"No!" Adam's cry came at the same time as the bullets hit the telekinetic shield and hailed harmlessly onto the ground.

Flit growled and pressed her boot harder against his cheek.

Scraps had a feeling she was enjoying the position of power a little *too* much.

"Please," Scraps called out, keeping his hands up. "Please do not waste this opportunity. Every second we argue in here is another second the Government gets closer. The Underground Derivates are waiting just at the outer limits of the city. Let them in. Let them help us win this war."

Rising from their spot at the back of the room, near Andy and her console, Petra and Tray stepped forward.

"Brian has done nothing but help us. Adam asked people to needlessly sacrifice their lives. Brian has been trying to preserve them from the beginning," Trey said. He and Petra skirted around the loosely formed circle of armed people to stand by Scraps' side.

"And Ava was one of the people who helped us get weapons and plan raids," Andy added, rising from her own seat and smiling at Flit.

Slowly, people started to lower their weapons and walk over to join Scraps. The time he had put into getting to know them over recent weeks, in training them, in learning about them, had clearly paid off.

Hawkeye rose to his feet and brushed his pants smooth.

Flit looked down at Adam.

"Lemme up," he muttered, voice almost indecipherable because of the way she had his jaw pressed to the ground with the heel of her boot.

"Try and fire at my friend or boyfriend again, and my boot will go through your skull," Flit hissed.

It was just loud enough for Scraps to hear, and he winced. Probably not the right moment to make a threat, but when she gave his face a final shove and teleported to Scraps' side, everyone let out a breath of relief.

Flit's familiar scent hit Scraps, and he spun to face her. The heat that radiated from her warmed his skin, and he couldn't help but smile down at her. He raised a hand to cup her cheek and looked into her eyes.

Flit grinned. "Seeing me all tough gets you frisky, huh?"

With a roll of his eyes, Scraps closed the distance between them and kissed that smug grin right off her face.

Hawkeye cleared his throat, breaking Scraps from the moment.

"As sweet as this is and all, there's a literal war going on outside. Do you think it can wait?"

Scraps blushed as he stepped back, but he didn't mourn the loss of contact as Flit grabbed his hand and threaded her fingers through his. He nodded towards Hawkeye. "You are right. What do you need me to do?"

62

FLIT

TELEPORTING out of Nightmix and back to the fence took far more willpower than Flit would have imagined. After spending the better part of an hour trading information and strategising with Scraps and the Free Citizens, she hated the fact that they had to split up again. Of course, she knew it was for the best, but that didn't stop the bitterness from eating at her insides as her feet landed on the grass and the buzz of conversations filled the air around her.

"We were about to send in the search parties. What the hell took you so long?" Swipe snapped, breaking up a conversation she was having with someone who worked in Intelligence. "Blue Team, form ranks!"

The rest of the Blue Team, plus Layla, came at Swipe's call.

"What's the situation out here?" Hawkeye asked, looking around.

Very little seemed to have changed whilst they were gone.

"We've had a few drones out this way," Link told him, crossing her arms over her chest. "However, they haven't fired. It looks like they were more trying to suss us out."

"They probably can't figure out whether we're the Free kind of Citizens or the regular ones," Layla added. "They stayed too far out of range for Tweak and me to get a read on them."

"What about you guys? We're batshit boring. What did you find out?" Tweak was almost bouncing from one foot to the other in his eagerness to get an update from Flit and Hawkeye.

"Well, we've got the Free Citizens on our side—"

Flit's announcement was interrupted by a cheer, and several of the Blue Team members pumping their fists into the air. She held up a hand to stall them.

"—but the tactics they were using to keep the city under siege failed last night when the Government bombed their heavy machinery." Flit let that settle over the group. "They were using debris to create physical barriers and pushing them towards to the core of the city."

"We've got a heap of macros out here. We can probably help," Swipe offered, gesturing to the people scattered all up and down the fence line.

Hawkeye shook his head. "There are just too many blocks, and it is too far spread out. By the time we got in there to clean it all up, you'd all be spent. We should conserve our energy."

"So, the siege is over?" Sway asked, looking thoroughly disappointed.

"Not quite." Flit smiled as she turned her attention to Tweak. "While we can't get the macros to brute force the barrier... I have a feeling you and the other micros can help us find a more elegant solution."

"Oh?" Tweak's grin was wicked as he tilted his head to the side. "Please, tell me more."

HALF AN HOUR LATER, Flit was standing with Cogs and Swipe several meters away from one of the posts that powered the electrostatic fence surrounding the Hub. The sun was rising behind them, warming their backs and dragging their shadow through the long grass at their feet. Other teams of Derivates stood behind similar posts as far as Flit could see to her left and her right, all bathed in the blue glow of the fence.

"*Uh, guys... we have drones incoming,*" Hawkeye said through the comms unit Flit nestled into her ear. He was standing a hundred meters back from the fence with anyone who wasn't a micro, macro, or teleporter.

"Copy that. Macros, take care of the drones if they get within firing range," Flit ordered. *"Micros, begin your work now."*

All along the fence lines, microkinetics held out their hands and pushed through the painful crackle of power near the fenceposts. Some of them had to touch the posts to work, but others, like Cogs, could stand comfortably outside of the static range.

Flit glanced between the drones peppering the sky above the Hub and the progress of the microkinetics. Her goal was to get the telekinetics to pull apart the fence guarding the city, so they could drag the pieces into the streets and set it up around the Hub instead, essentially using the Government's own protection to trap them.

The irony amused Flit far more than it should have.

"These are so old. They must be damn complacent if they thought they would hold up to anything worthwhile," Cogs muttered, her face twitching. The projected barrier on either side of the fence flickered. "Not that I'm complaining, of course. It's good for us."

"Not if these drones have anything to say about it." Swipe stepped forward instinctively, raising her arms in the direction of the incoming swarm of drones.

The flying machines spread out, passing the outer city limits and approaching the fence. Flit frowned as she watched them. "Well, how about you help us solve that problem, huh?"

"My pleasure." Swipe's lips curled into a wicked smile. She made grabbing motions with her hands and then slammed them together.

Two of the drones that had been headed their way seized mid-flight and then smashed into each other just as Swipe's fists had.

A raucous cheer roared behind Flit, and the rest of the drones answered by firing a volley of artillery.

As much as the Government liked their technology, it was no match for the furious Underground and Citizen Derivate macrokinetics. The bullets zooming in their direction were deflected, some cast back on the very vehicles that had launched them.

The noise and explosive flames were almost enough to distract

Flit from Cogs' whoop of success. The fence on either side of the post they were working on fizzled out, and another cheer rose behind them.

"Let's go to another one!" Flit stepped towards Cogs and wrapped her arms around her.

The next instant, they were standing by the fence post closest to their left where Layla and one of the Citizen Derivate macros were working. Cogs stepped in to help her fellow redhead, and Flit kept an eye on the battle.

Metal drone carcases fell to the ground all around them, and other panels of the fences started to blink out of existence. Seeing the teamwork on display, the others ran across the distance between fences to help each other get the posts down faster. Teleporters from the line behind them joined the fray, picking up people and moving them around faster.

Flit was momentarily stunned by the scenes around her. She felt as if she was in a waking dream. The knowledge that the day had finally come suddenly rushed in and hit her, and her sense of exhilaration only grew.

"Hawkeye, how are we looking? Are we close to target?" Flit asked through the comms, not able to count how many posts they had deactivated from her vantage point.

"About half-way there," Hawkeye replied, sounding distracted. *"Looks like the Government is concerned. Second wave of drones incoming. I'm sending more macros to the front."*

Footsteps pattered through the long grass as the last few drones from the first wave exploded, and the pieces rained to the ground. The reinforcements arrived just as the second round of drones started to send a deadly spray of bullets in the direction of the Derivates. The extra macros ensured that any gaps were protected whilst the micros and teleporters moved on. Between jumps, Flit watched the carnage as incredibly expensive machines, and valuable Government resources, were smashed against one another, crushed like tin cans, slammed into the ground, and riddled with their own ammunition. Every single aircraft that came their way was destroyed before it had a chance to hurt them, and Flit enjoyed every moment of it.

"That's it. We've got enough!" Hawkeye announced through the comms. *"We're coming. We'll march these to the city. Flit, alert the Free Citizens."*

"Copy that," Flit said through the Underground Comms. Then, she tugged an antique radio off her belt and looked down at it. This was the part she had been waiting for. *"Scraps? Fence is down as promised. We could do with a hand getting these posts in."*

"Flit, this is Scraps. We've got thirty vehicles headed in your direction. Please don't dispose of them as effectively as you did the drones. Over." There was a hint of amusement and pride in Scraps' voice.

"So long as they are here to help, we'll play nice. Over and out."

Flit clipped the radio back onto her belt and watched as distant specks of movement slipped out from under the shadow of the city and zoomed their way. Whilst she and Hawkeye had planned this endeavour with Scraps and the Free Citizens, Scraps had revealed that one of the other Free Citizens' bunkers was in a car park. It had apparently been easy enough for Andy and a few other technologically oriented hackers to crack into the navigation system of the vehicles.

"All right, Derivates. Vehicles incoming. They will disperse to the farthest fence posts. The cars will loop back around once they have delivered their first round of cargo. If your posts are in the middle, start moving the posts yourselves. Everyone else, form ranks and start the march. Watch each other's backs, and keep your chins up." As Flit gave the orders, she nodded at Cogs who began the march as promised.

All around them, macrokinetics tore the fence posts out of the ground, sending grass and dirt clods flying through the air.

Flit changed the channel on her comms so she was speaking to Hawkeye only. *"Okay, I'm going to check in with Scraps. Want to make sure the Free Citizens are going to behave when you all arrive. See you shortly."*

"Stay safe."

Flit sighed with relief as she closed her eyes, pictured her old booth in Nightmix, and teleported back to the Free Citizen's headquarters. When the surface beneath her feet changed to smooth flooring instead of uneven grass, she opened her eyes. She doubted she would ever get used to the sight of the club during the day. Without the strobe lights piercing the darkness and the music pounding in her ears, the place that had been full of life, sensuality, and freedom just felt... ordinary.

Shaking her head to loosen the disorientation at seeing behind the curtain of the club, Flit slipped out of the booth and made her way to the office. Then, she took the familiar path through the panel at the back. She hoped Scraps' calm tone on the radio call was a good indication that no funky business had gone down in her absence.

When Flit arrived in the bunker, it was a hive of activity. Scraps was standing over the desk Adam normally haunted, with a group of Citizens she hadn't met before hovering around him. He was giving them instructions and pointing to the map of the Hub on the surface of the desk. They all seemed to be nodding and agreeing with him, and it wasn't until one of them cleared their throat and gestured to the door that he looked up. The smile on Scraps' face was instantaneous and wholesome.

Following their little takeover, Scraps, Flit, and Hawkeye had spent the time planning how to best get the Free Citizens and the Derivates to work together. The first part of that was getting the Derivates into the city, and then they knew they would need to find a new way to rebuild the barriers they had been trying to maintain in the streets. It had come to Flit pretty quickly that they could address both obstacles in one go, and she was pleased it worked out. Judging by the look on Scraps' handsome face, he was every bit as relieved as she was.

Extricating himself from the group, Scraps wove his way through the people between them and stopped in front of her. He rested one hand on her hip and brushed a smudge of soot off her cheek with the other. "I am sorry I could not be there with you. I should have been."

Flit shook her head. As much as she wanted him by her side, they both knew it wasn't possible. With Adam now sitting in a cubicle of boxes in the corner of the bunker, Scraps had to step up for the Free Citizens.

"I have a feeling that wasn't the last time we'll need to split up," Flit whispered, even though she hated the truth in the words, "but it's okay because once we get this shit sorted, we've got the rest of our lives to stick together, right?"

"I can think of nothing I would like more," Scraps said, with a husky edge to his voice that made Flit's heart race. He took her left hand with his own and threaded their fingers together. They were both still wearing the wedding rings they had been given for their cover story. "I guess we both feel the same way about that."

The smile on Scraps' face stretched wide as he leaned down and kissed her. She let out a soft moan and stepped closer, wrapping her arms around him. She would never tire of the feeling of his lips against her own. However, as much as she wanted to linger in this moment with him for an eternity, they still had work to do between now and the rest of their lives..

So Flit ended the kiss. Not because she gave a crap about anything else, but because she would beg him to make love to her then and there if they didn't stop. They had too much to do before they could think about sleep, let alone more.

"Are the others on their way?" Scraps asked, straightening up and trying to look as though he hadn't just been super invested in kissing her.

Trying to get her head back in the game, Flit nodded. "They all have their orders and will be reaching the city outskirts soon. I should probably get back there. I'm a little worried that the official introductions won't go too well, even though we are here to save their arses."

Scraps chuckled. "I think you are right."

"That isn't really funny, though," Flit said, looking up at him.

He reached out, brushing his fingers over her cheek. "It isn't, but I have missed the way you describe things. It makes life far more entertaining."

Turning her face to kiss his hand, she muttered, "Well, I'm glad I can entertain you again. Life must have been pretty dull without me."

Scraps frowned as he stole a look around. "Not dull, just... lacking passion."

To avoid the temptation to ask what sort of passion he would really like, Flit stepped back. "Can you come along? I'm not certain the Free Citizens will listen to me."

"That is probably a good idea. I can leave Andy in charge of things here." Scraps turned around and led the way over to where Andy was at a console with Petra and Trey.

The teal-haired woman's eyes lit up when saw Flit. "So, I might have already had a crush on you from when we were dancing in the club a while back, but now..." She imitated wiping some sweat away. "You're a total badass. That was amazing, Ava. No, Flit. It's Flit, isn't it?"

Flit's cheeks warmed at the compliment. The clear appreciation made her feel pretty darn good. Still, she shrugged it off casually as though it was nothing. "I'm just ready to see this fight taken to the next level. It's time we bring the Government to their knees."

"So, when you were away, you were back with the other Derivates?" Trey leaned closer. He had seemed the most surprised by hers and Scraps' real identities.

"Not by choice, but yes. I've lived between the Underground and the Hub for most of my life," Flit explained, "but this is all something we can talk about later. Right now, Scraps and I need to get back out there. The Free Citizens and Derivates are due to meet up soon, and we don't want any misunderstandings."

"Who will be in charge down here?" Petra asked, her posture stiff. She was clearly trying to avoid looking in the direction where Adam was being kept. "The strike team members are probably next in rank, but I don't know we can trust them not go to Adam and get him to undo everything you've worked towards in the last few hours."

"Agreed." Scraps gestured to Andy. "That's why I'm asking you. You've had our back this whole time, and we need someone we can trust. As much as I do not want to cut Adam out of the movement he has created, we need to think about the best chance of survival for everyone involved, and that means working together."

Andy blinked. She opened her mouth and blurted out a garbled mess of words.

Trey put his hand on her shoulder. "Hey, don't freak out. You've got this."

Andy's posture softened, and she bit her lip then took a deep breath.

"We'll be on radio," Flit promised, giving her an encouraging smile, "and if you desperately need either of us back, then we're just a quick teleport away." To illustrate her point, Flit made several short hot teleports around the room before settling back into the spot she first left. She winked at Andy. "See?"

The show of powers was enough to knock Andy out of whatever anxious thoughts she was wrestling with. Her face set with determination. "Right. Of course. You two go. I've got this down here. I'll call if I need anything."

"Excellent. I knew I could count on you." Scraps beamed at her as he stepped closer to Flit.

Flit turned to him, and she wrapped her arms around him.

"Hey!" Andy called out, perking up.

"Yes?" Scraps put a hand on Flit's shoulder.

"Flit, can you take like anyone along with you on a teleport?" Andy asked, tucking some short-cropped hair behind her ear.

Flit smirked. "Haven't met anyone I couldn't take yet. Why? Want an excuse to get up all close in my personal space?"

Andy chuckled. "Sure... something like that."

"Then consider it a promise. Once we get shit sorted out there, I'll come back here and give you the ride of your life."

Flit winked at her again and wrapped her arms around Scraps to the sound of a half-cough, half-choke. His hands tightened against her jacket, and then, they were gone.

63

SCRAPS

SEEING the Underground and the Citizen Derivates on the horizon at sunrise had inspired Scraps in ways that nothing else had before. Despite decades upon decades of repression, torture, murder, and denial of their humanity, the Derivates had finally risen. The sheer number of people spread along the edge of Old City was a show of strength but also an alarming reminder that their numbers were limited. Between the population of the Underground, the number of Citizen Derivates, and the nearly ten-thousand Registereds in the Hub, their population was barely a drop in the ocean compared to how many Citizens there were. The Government's other cities had low Derivate populations as well, so the reinforcements they had with them now were all they could really count on.

Those reinforcements were marching closer to the Hub as Flit and Scraps made their way to the outer limits of the metropolis. The Government had paused the drone assault, probably because the Derivates had made such quick work of them. The few drones that were sent their way, most likely for surveillance reasons, were dispatched by the marching Derivates easily enough, even at a distance. The ruined husks of the drones rained down on the streets and buildings at the edge of town, just as Flit and Scraps joined the Free Citizens lined up there.

"Well, it's been a day of warm receptions all around, it seems,"

Flit muttered beside him, her hand still in his as they approached the Free Citizens.

Dozens of pairs of eyes stared back at them warily. Scraps kept his face neutral and nodded in greeting at the people he had been training and working with for the past few weeks. Most of them looked at him as if he was a stranger. He hated the fact that one small piece of information about him had them so guarded, but he supposed it was to be expected.

"Oh my goodness. Ava?"

The excited question broke the tension in the group as Liana burst through the line of people. Scraps had never seen her move so fast, even in training, as she catapulted towards Flit.

Flit spluttered as Liana skidded to a stop in front of her. Liana's eyes were wide as she reached out, grabbing Flit's shoulders. "That is you, right? You look..."

"Gorgeous?" Flit supplied.

Liana laughed. "I was going to go with different, but gorgeous works!" She pulled Flit into hug so tight it made Flit groan.

Despite the enthusiasm of the greeting, Flit was laughing as she hugged the other woman. "It's good to see you too, Li."

"What happened to you? Where did you go?" Liana pulled out of the embrace and held Flit at arm's length. "And how did you get back? What happened down there—"

"Woah, Li, give the woman a chance to answer." Chris was still puffing as he pushed through the crowd to stand beside his fiancé.

Flit cleared her throat. "How much do you guys know about what happened in the bunker this morning?"

"Apparently you and Brian are Derivates, and Adam lost it when he realised. There was a shootout because Adam tried to hurt you. From what we've been told, Adam was trying to lock us in a war with both the Government and the Derivates, even though you came to him with the offer of an alliance." Liana blurted it all out without hesitation.

"Hmm." Scraps nodded with approval. "For once, the rumour mill is correct."

"It's all true?" Liana asked, eyes wide.

"Yeah, pretty much." Flit teleported a step to the side and then back again.

Scraps laughed softly to himself. The response was so typically Flit.

Both Chris and Liana gawked at her.

Flit grinned. "Sorry, I should probably introduce myself properly, huh?" She was about to speak, but something stopped her as she turned to Scraps. "Actually, we should both probably introduce ourselves properly before the others arrive."

Given the way everyone was watching them with either open distrust, barely hidden curiosity, or outright confusion, Scraps thought she was right.

Clearing his throat, Scraps raised a hand into the air. A few people nearby flinched, but he didn't put it back down. "Free Citizens, I would like your attention for just a few minutes before we are joined by our new allies," he called out, letting his voice carry through the quiet streets. "Please, gather around."

It was a minute or so before everyone made their way over, and people who looked tired, were dusty, and had red strips of fabric tied around their upper arms surrounded Scraps and Flit. They shuffled on their feet and went between glancing over their shoulders towards the group of Derivates they could see marching closer and the two Derivates in the middle of the circle they had formed. Despite the clear tension that had rebuilt, Scraps felt confident there amongst the people. Even if he was misreading the situation, Flit would have them out of there in an instant.

"Thank you, everyone," Scraps begun, stepping closer to Flit once more and resting his hand on the small of her back. "I understand that there have been many rumours floating around about what happened in the Nightmix bunker this morning, so I wanted to take a moment to address those. Before I do, however, I believe we should introduce ourselves properly." He paused, gently rubbing Flit's back.

She didn't miss a beat. "I have met some of you before, but I have been away for a while, and the numbers have grown. It's good to see so many new faces, but I don't want you all looking at me and wondering who the heck I am." Flit spoke clearly despite the obvious suspicion of the people staring at her.

Scraps had always admired her ability to speak truly no matter the audience.

"The people who know me believe me to be Ava Parkes. My real name is Flit. I am a teleporter who was raised in the Hub by day and in the Derivate safehold known as the Underground by night." Flit paused to let that settle. "I took on the name of Ava Parkes recently as part of a plan to help the Underground fight back against the Government. It was living as Ava that I became involved in the Free Citizens, but recent event in the Underground meant I had to return there. Regardless of where I have lived or what name I have been using, I have always had one goal... to bring the Government down."

Whispers whipped through the crowd at Flit's enthusiastic and open declaration against the Government.

When it was clear the whispers were only going to grow the longer he remained silent, Scraps raised his hand again to call for attention. "As with Flit, I was introduced to the Free Citizens under the alias of Brian Parkes. Prior to that name, I had chosen to call myself Scraps. Before that? I was known as KC-847."

It took a moment for the revelation that he had been a Registered to hit, but when it did, Scraps heard gasps of surprise through the crowd.

"Unlike Flit, I was born in the Hub, trained in the Hub, and I worked in the Hub. I was just like the Registered Derivates in the middle of the city now, brainwashed to think that my sole purpose in life was to carry out the Government's orders." Scraps slid his hand farther around Flit's waist and held her closer. "That was, at least, until I was on a mission to retrieve a runaway Derivate, and I ran into Flit. Instead of killing me, like I was planning to do to her, she took me down to the Underground and showed me that I was worth more than the slavery I had been born into."

Flit covered Scraps' hand with her own. The love on her face had a low burning hint of righteous fury to it.

"I was eager to return to the surface with Flit, knowing that my role as Brian Parkes would help me find information that the

Underground might be able to use to free themselves. Little did I know that I would have the opportunity to meet some incredible Citizens." Scraps gestured to Chris and Liana. "They introduced me to a group of people who were chafing at similar restrictions to the ones I was living with. It made me realise that freedom for Derivates was not enough. We need freedom for all."

An unexpected cheer rose from the group. It wasn't nearly as loud or as enthusiastic as the one Adam had received when he had started the uprising, but it was still a cheer.

With a wave of her hand, Flit gestured to the street beyond the crowd, the direction the Derivates were coming from. "Marching towards us right now are the people I grew up with and some others who grew up in this city being treated as nothing more than mindless slaves," she called out. Fury made her voice waver. Instead of the trembling quality making her sound weak, it only highlighted her passion and made her seem more human. "We have come to the surface because we saw the battle you started. One we also need to fight. Please, rest assured, we have no intent or desire to harm you. We just want a world where we can live, peacefully, side-by-side and unrestricted by the harsh control of the Government."

A second cheer rippled through the crowd, and Scraps knew they had said the right things. At least, for now. He was certain there were people within the group who disagreed with them or would want to see them disposed of, but the majority were with them, and that would have to be enough.

"The Derivates are approaching now. This will be new territory for both Citizens and Derivates alike," Scraps called out over the voices around him, and the Citizens turned back to him, the weight of their gaze a reminder of just how much everyone had to lose in this battle. "We know you have been lied to about Derivates for your entire lives. We have been lied to about ourselves too. Please just know that we are human all the same. We love, we laugh, and we grieve our losses the same way. As we join forces to fight together, I ask that you approach one another with curiosity and openness rather than suspicion and hate. If you have any questions or worries, please come and speak to Flit or myself. We are here for you."

Scraps stepped back to indicate he was finished speaking.

Conversation immediately erupted, but so many people stepped out of the crowd to walk over and shake his or Flit's hands or to thank them for their stories. They were not able to stay and talk for long, though, as the sound of marching feet echoed down the street, and the vehicles carrying the fence posts started to arrive.

Flit told Chris and Liana to keep the Free Citizens calm and then teleported herself and Scraps to the frontline just as the vehicles came to a stop. People poured out.

Scraps barely had time to register the faces of his friends and chosen family before he was surrounded and pulled into a dizzying sequence of bear hugs and pats on the back. The voices of the Blue Team members rained over him in an enthusiastic chorus.

"Bloody hell, guys, give the man a chance to breathe!" Flit called out, laughing as the others finally released him.

"Damn. So many months living the pampered city life, and you're still packing," Swipe teased, brushing her hair off her face. She gave him a wink that he now knew meant the flirting was harmless.

Scraps smiled. "You're not looking too bad yourself."

"Oh, and the comebacks are quicker now. That's my man!" Sway patted Scraps' shoulder.

"Can't believe you managed to pull all that together!" Tweak gestured farther down the street where the Free Citizens were watching the exchange.

"I only supervised. Other people did most of the hard work," Scraps said, brushing it off. He pointed to the vans the team had driven up in. "I am interested in those posts, though. As much as I would love to stay here and catch up, we need to get the city secured. We only have an hour or two before the Government forces will be upon us."

That was enough to stall any social conversation, but he did still get a second hug from Clarity and Link, before Layla greeted him. Hawkeye stepped up behind the red-headed woman who had been rescued from the medical facility and draped his arm around her shoulder.

"Well, looks like we have work to do," Hawkeye said, smiling at

Scraps. "Why don't you tell us where you need us to go, and we'll get these posts set up."

From there, Scraps and Flit were caught up in a whirlwind of activity. Andy radioed through from the bunker to let them know that the Government had increased their pace. It was concerning, but Scraps and Flit worked with the Free Citizens to commence the distribution of the fence posts. As soon as a post was dropped off by some Free Citizens, a team of Derivates would help get it set up in the ground and turned on. Soon, a line of blue electrostatic energy lit the streets between the fourth and fifth blocks from Centre One in each direction. It created a barrier between the rebel forces and the Government who had been using the fence to protect themselves for so long.

With the new siege walls in place, Scraps ordered their forces to fan out around the barrier they had created and then had Flit teleport them both back to Nightmix. The news of the alliance between the Free Citizens and the Derivates had reached the other cities to mixed review. However, everyone agreed on one thing. Together, they had a chance. Even though other locations were currently locked in sieges of their own, the one that would determine the outcome of the battle was the Hub. If they could take the Government in their own capital, every other city would follow.

"Shit. You weren't kidding when you said they were gaining speed." Flit let out a low whistle as she kept a hold of his hand and dragged him over to the console where Andy was working. Petra and Trey were seated beside her, keeping on top of communications.

The views of the city Andy had on the screens showed them that the Free Citizens and Derivates had followed their orders well. They were still spread thin compared to the force amassed at the core of the city. What had been a steady build of officers now had become a slow march.

"What's the plan from here?" Andy asked, turning to Scraps as if he had the answer.

Given the speed with which the Government force was approaching, Scraps could only see one option. "We will need to fight."

Petra's brows furrowed with concern. "When was the last time you slept? And what about the people on the streets?"

"That is a very good question," Scraps said, stalling for time as he tried to figure out the answer. The last few days had blurred together into one big mission in his mind. "I, uh, I am not so sure."

"Then it was too long ago." Flit turned to face him and reached up to brush her fingers over his jawline tenderly. "Why don't you try and get some sleep? Even if it is just an hour, it's better than nothing."

Scraps shook his head. "That will only make me more fatigued."

"Oh, I have you covered." Trey reached under the desk Andy was working at and held up a couple of fluid packs that Scraps had seen people drinking in the club. "This will keep you awake for a good long while. It'll fuck up your sleep cycle for a few days, but it'll do the job in a pinch."

"That sounds healthy." The sarcasm and amusement in Flit's tone were evident. Still, she reached over to take the packs from Trey with a word of thanks and turned to Scraps. "Get as much rest as you can, and I'll hold onto this for you when you wake."

Scraps yawned and his shoulders sagged with defeat. A nap did sound appealing. He tightened his grip on Flit's hand and was about to go to his makeshift sleeping quarters when Andy's voice stopped him.

"Actually... we may not need that." She took her constantly typing fingers off the keyboard and smiled tentatively at Scraps and Flit. "The people who took down the fence posts... can they fuck with other tech?"

"Most likely," Scraps said, not needing to look at Flit for confirmation. "What are you thinking?"

"Well, I have been toying around with the self-drive navigation grid. I worked on it a few years ago for the Government when it needed some tweaking. I've been able to slip back into the network. I think we could probably wake up the vehicles around the city and cause some mayhem. Only problem is, me and the others can't do it in time to make a real impact."

"But with our micros helping..." Flit trailed off, her lips curving into a wicked grin.

"That should buy you all an extra few hours of sleep. What do you think?" Andy sat up a little straighter as the excitement in her tone became contagious.

"Then let's get it set up. I think we could all do with some rest." Scraps turned to Flit. "Think you can get them all here?"

"Yes, sir." Flit winked at him and pulled him down for a quick kiss before she teleported away, leaving Scraps to stumble forward a little when the space she had occupied was empty.

"Do you ever get used to that?" Trey chuckled as Scraps caught his footing.

Scraps laughed to himself and shook his head. "Every time I think I am used to it, she does something to prove me wrong."

"Ah, a hallmark of a successful marriage, I'm sure." Petra bumped Andy and Trey with her hips.

"Oh, we're not married," Scraps said sheepishly. "That was just for the cover."

"Fooled us pretty damn well." Trey's comment came with a warm smile. "So, when will the Derivates arrive? We don't have long."

"Oh, don't worry. Flit will have them here in a flash."

Sure enough, it was only another minute before Tweak, Layla, and Cogs arrived. Scraps rushed over to greet them and did the introductions before another pair arrived. For the next ten minutes, a steady stream of micros walked down the tunnel that led to the main bunker. Scraps helped them all set up around Andy, and they got to work without so much as a single disagreement or sharp word. Flit arrived five minutes after the last of the micros and stated that she had checked on the field hospitals and other teams. Everything was going smoothly.

So far, at least.

The other Free Citizens in the bunker watched the newcomers warily, but after half an hour, when reports were coming in on the radio that those on the streets had the frontline of the Government forces in visual range, Andy changed the view on the screens away from the fence and to the Government army.

Andy stood, called for attention, and then gestured to the

screens with a dramatic wave of her arm. "Free Citizens, I introduce you to what I have humbly named Project Chaos."

With that, all hell broke loose.

Scraps watched in awe as garage doors around the city opened, and vehicles previously parked below buildings filed out. The Government forces stopped at the unexpected twist, and the vehicles wove through the streets, slowly but surely corralling the army back in the direction it had come from.

At first, the Government forces were wary, looking to their commanders and backing away as the vehicles approached. At one point, some of the ones headed for the streets closest to Nightmix opened fire, but the vehicles charged forward without pause. It was then that the combatants seemed to realise that there were no people in the vehicles. However, the more they fired at them, the more vehicles came. It was like every car in the city was determined to be on the streets, and the sea of Government Agents had no choice but to part for the incoming tide.

"Well, that was a fucking brilliant plan," Tweak called out, jumping to his feet and thumping Andy on the back.

"How many cars are there in the city?" Scraps asked.

Andy grinned and shrugged. "More than enough to chase these bastards around well into the night."

Flit laughed and then looked at Scraps. "Guess we can skip the drugs, huh?" She gestured to the drink pack she had left on Andy's console and then offered him a hand. "What do you say we get some rest?"

Scraps took her hand and looked down at that point of contact. He wasn't sure that rest was the main thing on his mind. He raised her hand to his lips and brushed a kiss over her knuckles. "Sounds good. Let's get everyone on a rotation roster for sleep, and then I will show you my very fancy accommodations."

Whilst Flit did not seem happy about delaying their own rest, it was clear she understood the need. She worked with Tweak and the Underground micros to send a message to Swipe and Sway, who were apparently on top of the different Underground teams. They distributed their people between various Free Citizen bunkers throughout the city for rest. Hunkering down with the Free Citizens meant the Derivates would not need to go back and forth across the vast expanse of vulnerable land between the Hub and Old City.

Scraps and the strike team worked together to get a similar rotation for the Free Citizens. Scraps made sure Andy stepped away from her console too. For the first time since the battle had started, she seemed content to leave the hacking and tech work in the hands of someone else. It warmed Scraps' heart to see how easily she had taken to working with his fellow Derivates.

Free Citizens and Derivates filed into the bunker, the lovely people who had helped Scraps tear up the red pieces of fabric guiding them to the makeshift sleeping pallets set up around the edge of the room. Scraps and Flit were joined by Hawkeye, Layla, Swipe, Sway, Tweak, and Link. They all spent a short time sharing highlights from the past few hours before Flit warned them that they needed to rest. Then, she and Scraps peeled off, and he was finally able to show her where he had been sleeping.

"I bet you're both feeling mighty smug right about now," a low, cynical voice crooned.

Scraps paused and looked over at the stack of crates Adam had been secluded behind. The man peered at them over the shoulders of the two Free Citizens assigned to guard him.

"There's nothing to be smug about." Flit stopped walking. "We might have had a few successes, but we still have a revolution to pull off. I have to say I am rather pleased things are working well between the Free Citizens and Derivates thus far. Bet you didn't see that coming?"

Adam laughed, a deep, genuine chuckle that bubbled all the way up from his stomach. "Oh, of course it is going swimmingly right now. It's the honeymoon period, and they haven't faced anything life-threatening just yet. You wait. Once you get into the real fighting, they'll be climbing over one another to reach safer ground."

The way Adam spoke made Scraps' lip curl as he forced himself to maintain eye contact. "It is sad that you have so little faith in humanity, Adam."

"I have faith in humanity." The man merely shrugged. "But

Derivates aren't human. They're also the reason we have the Government in the first place."

"You're disgusting." Flit tugged on Scraps' hand. "C'mon. We've got better things to do than listen to him."

Flit was right, of course.

Scraps didn't bother with any farewell as they resumed their short walk to the small room he had made for himself. It was not much more than his bags of personal effects beside a few cushions pushed together to make a bed, but it was a bit more private than the sleeping positions the others had been offered. Scraps allowed Flit to step into the space first and then followed behind her. He pulled the coat he had been using as a makeshift curtain to cover the open "doorway" and then turned to his girlfriend.

"You weren't kidding about this place. It's the swankiest I've ever seen." Flit stepped closer to him, the front of her body pressing against his.

A low rumbling groan vibrated in Scraps' chest as he embraced her. He leaned down to kiss her. It was a loving but tired thing. When it ended, he rested his forehead against hers and said with regret, "As much as I want to do more, I do not think this is the time or place."

Flit tilted her face to steal another kiss. "I know, but I hope we can at least curl up on that little bed together. I want nothing more than to be in your arms for as long as I can."

Even with the constant hum of chatter and the shuffle of feet outside of their little oasis, Scraps nodded. How could he deny her that simple point of connection after so long apart?

He stepped out of his boots and then sank to his knees to help Flit unbuckle hers. When she was able to get out of them, he sat back on the mattress and pulled her down against him. He kissed her once more and then laid her down so that he was curled around her, holding her tight.

"I missed you so much," Flit whispered, voice suddenly sounding so small

Scraps gently kissed the top of her head as he held her. "I missed you too, Flit."

64

———

FLIT

THE CONSTANT CHATTER and hum of the radios became the backdrop for Flit's restless dreams. She dipped in and out of consciousness, unsure of whether it had been hours or minutes since she had first closed her eyes.

At some point, she turned towards Scraps and buried her face against his neck. He groaned but draped an arm over her. It was a good tactic to block out the light, but when the hum turned to a rumble, she squeezed her eyes shut tighter and took a deep breath.

What started as a low rumble turned to a genuine shaking, and Flit held Scraps' shirt tighter. She'd been tired before and she often felt dizzy if she woke too early, but this was something else entirely.

Then, the conversations in the rooms turned to shouts.

"Flit! Scraps!"

The jacket Scraps had strung up to protect them from view was torn down. Light streamed in.

Suddenly awake, Flit teleported to her feet. The sheet that had been covering her deflated where she had been a moment ago.

"What?" Flit spluttered as Hawkeye grabbed her hand and dragged her into the main space.

There was a groan and a shuffle of feet as Scraps rose to join them.

Flit had to blink several times before she was able to see the screens properly. Even then, she rubbed her eyes in disbelief. The buildings on the surveillance cameras were all destroyed. The Hub had turned into a crumbling ruin.

"What's going on?" Scraps asked as he stepped up behind her and slipped his arm around her waist.

Flit's head tilted to the side as she watched the screens. That wasn't the Hub. That was Old City.

She turned to ask Hawkeye what the deal was when an alarming rumble shook the bunker. The sound was ten times more powerful and infinitely more concerning than thunder. As Flit watched the screens, the buildings just crumpled and sank down into the crack forming beneath them.

With her mind still trying to wake, it took Flit several seconds longer than it should have to make the connection between what she was seeing and why she would be seeing it.

"Oh, shit!"

Flit slipped out of Scraps' arm and ran back into their little alcove. She snatched the communicator she had taken out before sleeping and shoved it into her ear.

"Flit to Control... Can you read me, Control?" Flit asked.

Even though it was difficult to communicate within the tunnels of the Underground, they no longer had to worry about hiding their communication from the surface. Cogs and the other micros had set up a relay that had allowed them to communicate with Control earlier in the day.

Right now, though? There was no answer.

"Control, this is Flit. Respond immediately!" she shouted. Hearing the panic in her tone, other Blue Team members got up from where they must have been sleeping around the room and ran over to join her. *"Shadow? Fortune? Anyone, come in!"*

A hand settled on Flit's shoulder. "If the Underground has been compromised, our communicators won't reach them," Tweak said, voice low and as serious as Flit had ever heard it.

"Then we need to—"

Another rumble interrupted Flit. This time, dust trickled out of cracks between the concrete ceiling panels and rained over the Free Citizens. Shouts echoed through the room as people scrambled for cover.

"—check on them."

The screens flickered to a wider view. A second building crumbled, falling onto another and knocking it down like a domino.

Flit was about to teleport to the streets of the city.

Scraps grabbed her hand. He reached out with his other one and summoned an old radio off a nearby table. "You're not going alone."

As heart-warming as it was, Flit didn't have time to appreciate or argue with him. Instead, she turned to face him and wrapped her arms around him. "I'm taking us straight to the train shed."

"That's in Old City." Scraps' forehead creased as he glanced over her shoulder at the screens.

"It's in the outskirts. It will be fine for now. We just need to get everyone out of there," Flit said dismissively. Then, she turned to Tweak. "Any chance you can help Andy get the Project Chaos vehicles over to the train shed? We need to evac, fast."

"Copy that, boss. You go warn them. We'll take care of things here," Tweak replied.

Then, Flit looked up at Scraps, giving him one last chance to change his mind about coming with her. She was met by a steely nod.

Just as she was about to teleport out, she heard Adam call out from behind her, "Careful out there. You never know who you can trust."

THE GROUND SHOOK MORE VIOLENTLY in the train shed. The old building creaked ominously, and somewhere farther away, the high-pitched tinkle of glass rained over the broken streets. Flit was relieved to see her parents in the corner of the shed at their field hospital, and she rushed over to them. Of course, they were already packing up and issuing orders to evacuate. By the time they had most of their supplies ready to go, an army of vehicles on auto-drive arrived from the Hub. Scraps, Flit, and her parents led the group of Derivates out of the shed and herded them towards the vehicles as Old City continued to topple behind them.

"Flit, wait!"

Flit whipped around toward the warehouse she thought they had emptied. Standing there, covered in soot and worse for wear, were Shadow and Fortune, Acumen slung between them. Flit's knees almost buckled with relief. She teleported over and nearly tackled Fortune in an embrace.

"What happened?" Scraps asked, not even a little out of breath as he jogged over to join them.

"Harmony... broke free..." Acumen wheezed, his already pale skin tinged green with the effort of remaining on his feet.

Scraps held out a hand, and Shadow stood a little straighter as Scraps must have used telekinesis help support Acumen.

"I went to check on her in her cell. The next thing I knew, I was waking up to Fortune shaking me, with the two guards who had been watching Harmony dead on the floor and the cell wide open," Shadow explained, frown creasing the crow's feet at the corners of his eyes.

Flit's hands balled into fists at her side. "Why didn't she have an inhibitor on?"

"She did when we put her in the cell," Fortune said. "Regardless, she was gone. Before we could look for her, everything started going off. She must have had explosives set up in the tunnels. We barely had time to get out. The others..." Fortune stopped, choking on the words.

Flit's eyes widened with horror. "No."

All the people left in the Underground. Their most vulnerable population. Children, pregnant people, the elderly...

Flit pulled away from Fortune and pressed a hand to her mouth as bile rose in her throat and threatened to splutter from her lips. Scraps settled a hand on her shoulder, but even his usually steady fingers shook. Eyes blazing with tears, Flit looked between the trio in hopes one of them would contradict the horrific conclusion her mind had drawn.

"I'm not sure how much of the Underground was destroyed. We got out before we could assess the damage. We needed to let you know," Shadow said, voice cool and collected.

The world spun, and Flit reached out, grasping at Scraps' arm.

Her stomach heaved, but she used all of her willpower to keep the contents down. The conversation continued, but a low buzzing in her ears made it impossible to hear it properly. Scraps' arm draped around her shoulders, and she shook her head, hoping to dislodge the vertigo that had settled over her.

"—too many people. You need them up here to fight. If we split our forces, then even more of us will die," Shadow said.

Scraps pressed his lips together and held her a little tighter. "There has to be some way—"

"There is but not now." Acumen frowned at his own words. "Look, I hate it as much as everyone here, but we can't afford to get distracted."

Holding up a hand for silence, Scraps took the radio off his belt.

The ground rocked beneath their feet as another explosion hit. The destruction was still in the depths of the city. No tunnels ran directly under this part of the city. Thankfully, all the train lines around here were above ground, and the roads and highways didn't delve underground in the area either.

"What's the holdup?" Tinker yelled as she slammed the door on the second last vehicle that had come their way. She ran over to join them whilst Stride teleported to Flit's side.

Scraps lifted the radio to his mouth and pressed the rubber button on the side. *"Free Citizens, this is Scraps. What's the read on the Government? Is Project Chaos keeping them occupied? Over."*

"It is, but not for much longer," Andy replied.

Whilst Scraps might have given everyone a bit of basic combat instruction, Flit noted he had not had a chance to brief them on radio etiquette.

"There are Derivates—sorry, Cogs is specifying that they are micros—disabling some of the vehicles, and their agents are using EMPs to deal with others. It was a good plan, but I think we've only got a few more hours of protection left."

"Thanks, Andy. Looks like we're out of surprises. Over and out." Scraps' shoulder sagged, and he turned to Flit. "Shadow doesn't think we have enough resources to launch rescue efforts into the Underground and face the Government at the same time."

Flit winced. "Is there nothing we can do? There are kids down there—"

"Don't you think I fucking know that?" Shadow snapped, throwing his hands up into the air. Acumen rested a hand on his shoulder, but Shadow shrugged it off and took a deep breath, burying the uncharacteristic outburst. "We've got a snowball's chance in a volcano of making it out of this battle alive as it is. The search party would have to be huge, and if we let go of that many people, we can kiss any chance of success goodbye. On top of that, we don't know if Harmony set any other traps down there for us. Please trust me when I tell you that I do not say this lightly, but we cannot afford a rescue mission right now."

The conviction in Shadow's words and the twist in Flit's gut told her he was right. The fact that the Underground Derivates had spent so many days restricted to the habitable tunnels finally made sense. It wasn't just about keeping them in one place. It was about ensuring the tunnels were clear so Harmony could set the charges for the explosions that were only just now slowing down.

"Fine," she said, "but we—"

"*Uh, guys?*" Andy's voice sounded through the radio, interrupting Flit.

Looking pleased to have a chance to interrupt the discussion, Scraps cleared his throat. "*Andy, this is Scraps. Go ahead. Over.*"

"*So, I know I said we've only got a few hours left, but... Adam has a plan. You might want to hear it.*"

Rage surged in Flit. She reached over, snatching the radio off Scraps. Her fingertips turned white as they dug into the soft button and opened the channel. "*You can tell Adam to dip that plan in ethanol, shove it up his arse, and light the fucking thing on fire. We don't—*"

This time, the hand on her shoulder belonged to her mother. Tinker stepped in front of her daughter and cupped her cheek, looking into her eyes. Flit wanted to turn away. She didn't want to see the quiet, calm empathy in her mother's gaze. Not here. Not now. "Flit, we need every idea we can get."

As much as Flit wanted to rage, she let Scraps gently remove the radio from her pale, shaking fingers. *"Andy, we will make our way back now. Ensure Adam holds onto that idea, please."*

Silence fell between the group as they stood in the dying sunlight. The sky above their heads turned beautiful shades of lilac, peach, and fluorescent pink, with silver clouds and plumes of dust painting it with more character. It was far too pretty to be sitting in the horizon above such destruction on the ground, but Flit supposed nature was full of contrasts.

"Come on. There's one car left. Flit, if you're okay to translocate yourself and Scraps back to the bunker, the rest of us should fit in there easily enough," Stride said gently.

The thought of the new task shook Flit from darker musings. She looked over at her parents and shook her head.

"No. I don't want the Government sending drones over and shooting you guys down while Scraps and I go back to the club. I'll translocate you over, but I'll take Scraps and Shadow first. Once Shadow knows where it is, he can help ferry you back and forth safely," Flit said, knowing that she could carry a max of two people with her safely.

65

SCRAPS

AS SOON AS SCRAPS, Shadow, and Flit arrived in Nightmix, Flit and Scraps pointed to where the office was and explained how to access the bunker. Shadow took a good look around, nodded in approval, and then disappeared.

Scraps and Flit used the opportunity to make their way back to the bunker. Scraps was still sitting with the uncomfortable knowledge that they were not able to spare resources to search for survivors in the Underground. He understood the decision, but as he walked into the basement of Nightmix, it stung to see how many people were down there, safe, while the fate of his own kind was in question. The space was more full than before, even with some of the people apparently out ferrying the new refugees across different bases. It wasn't ideal to be splitting up, but there were simply not enough resources in any one of the bases to sustain such populations for long. It was already becoming hard to find space to walk. That would change, of course, when the fight truly started. For now, Flit and Scraps just had to pick their way across the room the best they could.

Andy and Hawkeye were already waiting by the little cell they had set up for Adam. Andy gestured Scraps and Flit over. Just as they stopped by their friends, Tweak's voice calling out from the console a short distance away alerted them to the first arrival from the train shed—Fortune. Hawkeye pointed towards the older woman and then at Tweak, and the micro left his station to go and check in on her. With him looking after Fortune and the other new arrivals, Scraps and Flit were free to focus on Adam, who looked thoroughly smug.

Scraps felt the tension in Flit immediately as she shifted closer to his side. He wrapped an arm around her waist, hoping she would wait to see what Adam proposed before telling him where to shove it again.

"You should send a strike team to Centre One."

Adam dropped those words like the Government drones had dropped their missiles. He hovered there, leaning against the wall of his cell, as he watched for the idea to explode amongst them.

"As in... the headquarters of the Government?" Hawkeye asked with as much healthy scepticism as Scraps felt.

"The very same." Adam pushed himself off the makeshift wall and walked over to the doorway of the cell.

Scraps shifted, glancing to the side to find the two guards had stepped a few feet away but were still armed and vigilant.

Andy snorted. "Yeah, right. Sounds like a grand old plan. Why don't we take them some wine and cheese as we waltz on into their stronghold."

"You can if you want. We do have some catering uniforms in the storage trunks." Adam shrugged nonchalantly.

Scraps frowned at his casual, almost amused attitude.

Hawkeye didn't seem overly impressed, either. "Thank you for the suggestion, but—"

"No." Flit reached over and placed a hand on Hawkeye's. She jutted her chin at Adam. "What else do you have?"

Head tilting to the side, almost like a predator who knew it was cornering its prey, Adam shrugged. "You should ask that husband of yours—Oh, wait. Brian and Ava were married. Not you two. Right, Scraps?"

Scraps' shoulders tensed, and he glanced at Andy. She shook her head, as if to say she hadn't shared the information.

Of course, Flit was too clever to fall for the bait and remained silent.

"We have some Government Agent uniforms too," Scraps said. "I am assuming you kept those after you used them?"

"It would have been foolish not to." Adam leaned in closer, sticking his head beyond the small opening that had previously been the invisible edge of his cell. He was pushing the boundaries. "Between Andy's teem and your micros, I bet you could reprogram some of the chips in the uniforms to get access to the building or at least the areas around it."

"Why would we do that when the Government is marching this way to meet us? We have the location advantage," Hawkeye said, shaking his head.

"A whole army marching this way," Flit said slowly, "which means... that the bulk of the Government forces will be away from Centre One."

Then, Scraps understood. A thrill of recognition at the true genius of Adam's plan ran through him. "If we wait until they are here, engaged in a fight, then—"

"We will have a decent amount of time before reinforcements can get back to Centre One," Flit added, finishing Scraps' sentence.

"Oooh, especially if we can get the remaining vehicles we used for Project Chaos in the area." Andy sounded far too enthusiastic about adding her own personal flair back into the battle.

The way Adam smiled and nodded reminded Scraps of the tutors he had had a child who would pretend to be encouraging when the class finally grasped a basic concept. It was condescending, but Scraps chose to ignore it for the sake of progress.

Hawkeye scratched the back of his neck. "This all sounds very promising, but no one knows the way around those upper levels, right? Only the Ol—"

"Oligarchs know their way around there?" Adam asked with a wicked smirk. "I've got you covered there too."

"No. Absolutely not. There is no way you are coming with us." Flit crossed her arms and shook her head.

Scraps gently pulled her against his side. "Adam wants to bring the Government down, just like we do."

He couldn't believe he was defending the man, but it was the truth. If there was one thing Scraps was sure of, it was that Adam wouldn't ruin the best chance he was going to get to infiltrate the heart of the organisation he was seeking to destroy. He wouldn't be a risk to them until *after* they had ensured the Government would fall.

A chain of swear words that were more colourful than Scraps had heard in a while fell from Flit's mouth. Then, she sighed. "Fine, but we pick the members of the strike team."

"Oh, I wouldn't dare presume otherwise." Adam's tone was saccharine enough that even Scraps felt uncomfortable.

Flit shifted at Scraps' side, and he could only imagine the glare she levelled at Adam.

"Petra and Trey should be able to get the uniforms for me. I'll talk to Cogs and see if we can get the ID chips sorted while you put together the team," Andy offered, smiling at Scraps.

"Sounds like a good plan." Scraps let his hand fall from around Flit's waist.

Stalking over to the corner of his makeshift cell, Adam sank down to sit on a cushion and smirked up at them. "Let me know when you're ready to leave. I'll be waiting here. Might catch a nap in the meantime." He made a show of making himself comfortable.

Flit rolled her eyes as she walked away, leaving Scraps and Hawkeye with no choice but to follow. As the trio made their way around the bunker, there was no question about the people they were going to include on their team. It was an easy matter to find the Blue Team members scattered around the space, especially with Layla and Fortune hovering around Tweak.

In the time it had taken Scraps, Flit, and Hawkeye to speak to Adam, it appeared Shadow had gotten everyone from the train shed to safety. Scraps suggested that Tinker and Stride could set up a better first aid station in the area.

When the Blue Team were all together, they had Fortune and Layla join them before Flit led them out of the bunker and back up to the office. She showed Tweak the console Andy had told her about hidden between the surface of the desk, and he deactivated the security cameras in the area before anyone spoke.

"So, this looks like a reunion, and I gotta admit... I'm here for it." Tweak sat on the edge of the desk and smiled.

"It is a reunion, I suppose," Scraps conceded, "but not of the partying kind. We have a request. It is not something you need to feel obliged to do, but we would appreciate your assistance."

The seriousness in Scraps' tone had everyone leaning in. Out of all the people gathered, only Link looked worried. Scraps could only figure she had caught wind of the plan in his, Hawkeye's, or Flit's mind. Swipe, Sway, and Tweak looked interested. Clarity and Layla were a little more wary, and Fortune just seemed to be waiting for the hammer to fall.

"It's more of a call to action than a favour," Flit conceded, "and nothing any less worthy than things we have done before. It feels like forever ago that we all sat in the Underground and debated whether or not to go to Old City to track down the leads after Heft's betrayal, but it seems that is where we are at again."

There were no whispers of surprise amongst the group. Scraps supposed that was to be expected. Still, he wanted to ensure everyone knew exactly what they were going to get themselves into.

"Adam and the Free Citizens set this rebellion up as a siege approach," he said. "The idea was to barricade the Government in and fight until they had no choice but to give in."

Sway hummed. "Generally how a siege works."

Ignoring the jibe, Scraps continued, "Adam has suggested another plan, something that could end the battle almost as soon as it begins. It is a risk, but we could save many lives by cutting it off early."

"We don't really want people to die. That isn't the goal," Clarity whispered under her breath. Her dark eyes were wide. Always one of the most wary of the group, she might be the hardest to convince.

"Right, and if we do what Adam is suggesting, we may be able to avoid that outcome." Flit gestured back towards the bunker. "He's a crazy fucker, but he'll do whatever it takes to bring the Government down."

"What he proposed has merit," Hawkeye conceded. Everyone turned to him, apparently more invested seeing that even a more conservative member of the team was on board. "We send a strike team right into Centre One when the battle begins. Even if they do notice we're there, they will be limited as to how quickly they respond. We could have this battle over in hours rather than weeks."

Swipe sighed. "And let me guess." She leaned back against the wall and crossed her arms. "The Blue Team reunion is really a cover for 'strike team slash suicide squad'."

"We're kick arse together," Tweak said, breaking a quiet tension that was brewing, "but we've never been in Centre One before. Are there maps? Do we even know what we're looking for?"

"We don't, but Adam does." Scraps didn't like this part of the plan any more the second time around.

Link stiffened. "Isn't he a... completely unhinged fucker?" The way she tilted her head when she looked at Flit made Scraps realise that the reference to Adam was pulled straight from Flit's mind.

"Well, yes," Scraps conceded, shaking his head at what had to have been some very loose thoughts from Flit. Still, he couldn't help but smile a little at her very accurate assessment. He had missed her forthrightness. "But he has information we do not. What is it you would say, Flit? I do not trust him any farther than you could kick—"

"Throw."

"—him, but I would rather take that risk to try and end things early than to lose more innocent people." Scraps pressed his lips together as his mind automatically went to the horrible shaking and the admission from Shadow, Acumen, and Fortune about what had happened with Harmony.

"Oh my!" Link gasped and reached out, grabbing at Clarity's arm as her face fell. "Oh... I was hoping that was just... Oh..."

The air in the room grew thick with worry.

"What?" Sway stepped around Clarity and took Link's hands. "What is it?"

Fortune cleared her throat. "That rumbling from before it was the Underground being destroyed. Harmony set off bombs down there. We have reason to believe—"

"No!" Link covered her mouth with her hand and fell to her knees. "Patch! Mum!"

Scraps closed his eyes as Link started sobbing. Clarity and Sway took her in their arms as reality dawned on the rest of the team.

"What the fuck are we doing up here?" Tweak snapped, throwing his arms in the air. "We need to get down there! We need to help."

"If we go down there, then the battle up here will be lost," Flit said, her voice so quiet that she had to repeat herself to be heard.

"Fuck the battle!" Tweak argued. "We can't just leave them."

Hawkeye stepped between Flit and Tweak and spoke over Link's sobbing. "This is why we need the strike team. If we can get this sorted tonight, then we have the best chance of survival for everyone up here. Then, we can send a team to look for survivors in the Underground once that is done."

"This is bullshit! If we weren't up here in the first place, none of this would have happened." Tweak stepped closer, jabbing a finger in Flit's direction.

"If we weren't up here, then where would we have been?" Flit hissed, glaring at Tweak and then looking pointedly at where Link was still sobbing.

Fortune raised her hands, as if to ward off the impending argument. "This is not a productive discussion. We need to focus on what's really important right now."

Tweak's face reddened and his shoulders tensed as his hackles rose further. He ignored Fortune's response. "Maybe if we hadn't fucked around, then we—"

"I'm in."

Those two words were perhaps the smallest and quietest ever uttered, but there was such power in them that the argument stopped.

Pulling away from Clarity and Sway, Link straightened. Her face was wet with tears, but she sniffed back her emotions, and determination shone in her eyes.

"Link, hun, you don't have to do this," Clarity whispered.

The telepath straightened and puffed her chest out. "Yes, I do." She pointed to Flit. "They are right. We need to end this. If that means we have to be the ones to do it, then... I'm in."

"I am sure there would be other volunteers for the team," Fortune offered.

Scraps knew it was true, but part of what made the Blue Team the best option was that they had worked together for so long. They knew each other. They trusted each other.

"No." Link remained adamant. "It has to be us."

"She's right. Everyone else sucks."

Flit's response was so out of the blue, so irreverent, that everyone froze.

Slowly, Swipe snorted a laugh. The sound was followed by a splutter from Sway. After that? The whole team was chuckling. Scraps, utterly confused, let out an awkward laugh too, just to remain in keeping with the mood. He wasn't quite sure what was happening, but Flit winked at him, and he trusted her enough to roll with it.

If there was one thing Scraps could say with certainty, it was that some of the heaviness in the room had dissolved with Flit's quip, enough so that Tweak had backed down, and Link was wiping away her tears.

"So, what do we say? One last hurrah for the Blue Team?" Flit asked, biting her lip as she looked around.

"Hey!" Swipe stepped closer and playfully nudged Flit with her hip. "Back off, bitch. You're not the leader of this team. I am."

Flit rolled her eyes but made a low, sweeping bow towards Swipe.

"So, what do we say? One last hurrah for the Blue Team?" Swipe asked, stealing Flit's question.

The cheer that followed wiped away any uncertainty about whether or not the group was ready for this.

As much as Scraps wanted to let them all revel in the newly rekindled camaraderie, they were already operating on borrowed time.

"If we are doing this, we have a lot of work ahead of us. Come on, we cannot afford to waste another minute."

And with that, the Blue Team, plus Fortune and Layla, got to work.

66

FLIT

BY THE TIME the new strike team was assembled and ready to go, the Government Agents and Registereds were close enough that the Free Citizens could see the city lights reflected off their mirror-like visors through the blue glow of the fence. A scan of their designation patches told Flit there was a wide range of ability types and levels across from them and that the Government had pulled Registereds as young as fourteen to the frontlines to fight. Even if Flit had endured nothing else from the Government, she would have wanted to bring them down for that alone.

The team stood on the street, amongst their fellow Derivates and mingled with Free Citizens. There was a tense calm charging the spaces between the rebels, almost like the electricity that sizzled through the humidity before a thunderstorm. With the number of weapons in the area, firearms and Derivate abilities alike, there was no doubt this space would soon become a killing field.

Scraps was liaising with the Free Citizens a few feet away, whilst Flit watched a hunched over Acumen speaking rapidly with Posthoc. Posthoc and Hawkeye had spent the last little while talking strategy for the different Underground and Citizen Derivate teams and had come up with a plan to ensure powers were spread effectively across the wide barrier that had been set up. Acumen being involved had to mean he was planning on helping out despite the fact he was still injured. Flit had no doubt the micros had done their best to heal him. Sometimes, though, there were certain parts of the healing process that only nature could take care of.

As much as everyone tried to plan for what was to come, there was no certainty as to how things would turn out. The past few days showed that the Government was willing to pull some moves the Free Citizens hadn't anticipated, such as the night-time bombings that had destroyed their earth movers.

Flit watched, teeth gritted and brows creased, as the Government Agents slowed to a stop on the other side of the fence.

"Oh, there you are!"

Flit turned around fast as a whip when she heard that voice. She frowned, running over to her mother and father as she narrowed her eyes at them. "What are you doing up here?"

"We came to wish you well for tonight," Stride said, pulling her into an embrace.

"You're supposed to be in the club," Flit muttered against his shoulder as she squeezed him back.

Tinker chuckled. "Oh, so you spend your life not doing what we tell you to, and you expect us to suddenly obey *you*? That'd be right." Flit's mother joined the group hug. "We had to tell you to take care and to come back to us alive and in one piece."

There was a medical clinic set up on the main floor of the club that Flit's parents were supposed to be manning. Knowing they were there, out of harm's way, was one of the few things that made it easier for Flit to focus on the night ahead.

"Oooh, are these your parents?"

Chris and Liana worked their way through a nearby group of Citizen Derivates and joined Flit.

"Ah, Mum, Dad, this is Chris and Liana. They have been great friends to Scraps and me since we started up here undercover."

Everyone introduced themselves with handshakes or waves.

Flit looked between them. "Mum, I need you to take good care of these two if they wind up with you."

"Of course." Tinker gave Chris and Liana a warm smile. "Although I'd much prefer not to see you until this is over."

"No offence, but I totally agree," Liana replied.

There was a tense chuckle, and Flit turned to look at the

Government Agents off in the distance. They had all stopped in place, and an order seemed to ripple through the group as their faceless army's shoulders tensed and hands settled on the weapons at their hips or across their backs.

"Guys... I'm taking you back." Flit stepped in and embraced her parents before they could argue. She teleported them back to the club and kissed them each on the cheek. She let out a soft breath as her heart hammered in her chest. "Stay here. Stay safe. I'll see you in a couple of hours."

"You too, Flit. Please, don't take any unnecessary risks," Tinker said, face creased with concern.

Flit stepped back. "Me? Pfft, never!" Flit winked at her parents before she blinked out of the room and reappeared on the street just outside the club.

She wasn't sure if the rebels had shifted positions at the obvious order to prepare for engagement from the Government, so she couldn't risk translocating back to where she had just been standing. Instead, she made several rapid hops to get her back to where she needed to be. The tension had tripled when she got back to the group.

She approached Chris and Liana. "Sorry. I just wanted to get them out of here. Are you sure I can't take you guys somewhere? Maybe a nice, tropical beach? Or snowy alps? It's been a while since you've had a getaway, right?"

"So you offer your new friends a safe holiday but volunteer us for a suicide mission? Guess we know where we stand, huh?" Sway's voice cut through Flit's attempt to coax Chris and Liana away from danger.

"Who said you were my friend?" Flit raised an eyebrow at him.

Sway just rolled his eyes. "We need to consider getting out of the front line before it gets too—"

Before the telecoercionist could finish, the low buzz of drones sounded overhead.

"Take cover!" The warning from a Citizen Derivate a few feet away made people scramble.

There was a counter command from Posthoc. "Macros and Micros at the ready!"

Flit gestured for Chris and Liana to run. She found Scraps and Swipe not too far away and watched as they threw their hands up. Just as dozens of drones smashed together overhead, the Government Agents sprayed a round of bullets over the barrier towards the rebels. A group of Free Citizens raised their weapons and fired a rain of bullets over the barrier.

The macros were on it. They threw out bursts of telekinetic energy that either knocked the bullets off their trajectory or directed them back over the fence.

"Flit, get under cover," Scraps said, not even looking at her.

"Not a chance, love."

She watched as he sent the next round of bullets flying towards the drones. Several took damage and let out high-pitched whines as they crashed to the ground. Swipe directed her energy in their direction and caught them as they fell, hurling them against the fence and causing them to fry with a satisfying sizzle.

Flit was about to congratulate her when her attention snagged on movement by the nearest fence posts. She activated her comms. *"Registered micros attacking the fence posts! Protect the posts!"*

At her command, the micros who had been assisting by decommissioning the drones all focused their attention on the uniformed officers at the fences. Muffled cries sounded around them as bullets from the drones found new homes amongst flesh.

"Bastards were distracting us," Swipe hissed through gritted teeth.

Before anyone could reply, a voice pierced through the staccato of weapons fire. "Free Citizens, this is your first and only warning. You are in violation of the Government's Mandatory Safety Directorate section One-A."

"Only One-A?" Scraps muttered seemingly to himself.

A snort escaped from Flit. She fondly remembered when Scraps would quote policies and the like to her.

"If you surrender now, you will be treated leniently. You have thirty seconds to lay down your arms and deactivate the fence." The voice seemed to be coming from everywhere—the drones that were hovering above them, weapons armed but not firing, and from the

Government officers, and even from some of the buildings behind the fence.

"We don't need thirty seconds. We will never surrender!" Flit yelled, not needing to rely on technology or microphones to make her voice heard. She turned to face the Citizens and Derivates around her, scanning the ones out in the open as well as under the shelter of nearby building awnings. "What do you say, Revolutionaries?"

Cries of "Never surrender!" went up around her.

She turned back to the Government Agents. "Scraps, which one is in charge?" she hissed.

Scraps considered the crowd for a moment. "Three feet back from the fence post. Blue bar above his nametag."

Flit spied the person and grinned. "Great. Thanks!"

Just as Flit was about to teleport past the fence and take down the officer in charge, the sound of a weapon being fired pierced through the dusk. The man Flit was about to take down convulsed and clutched his chest. A blot of deep crimson spread across the light grey fabric of his shirt, and he coughed. Blood spluttered from his lips, and he fell to his knees.

Behind him, a woman who was wearing a Citizen uniform and was flanked by two visored Registereds saluted across the fence.

"Agent Greene!" Scraps whispered, shocked. "TB-219. CC-9832."

The woman raised her gun in the air. "Derivates, execute order twenty-one!"

On the other side of the fence, Registereds peppered through the ranks of the Government's forward force turned on their Citizen counterparts. Those remaining loyal to the Government quickly huddled together and started to fight back. Acumen and Posthoc moved around, calling for teams to gain higher ground by entering the buildings so they could fire into the fray, and the macros and micros continued focusing on clearing a new wave of a seemingly endless stream of drones.

"We need to leave." Scraps put a hand on Flit's forearm.

Scraps was right. As much as she wanted to have her eyes on this scene, their presence would be far more valuable elsewhere.

"Swipe, let's get back to the bunker," Flit called, shifting to the side so she could see the other telekinetic.

She waited for the pair to join her, and she teleported them back to the empty booth space she had been using as a landing pad.

When they walked into the office, the Blue Team, Layla, and Fortune were already waiting for them. Shadow was there too, talking to Adam about a map on a datapad on Petra and Trey's desk. Everyone was wearing Government uniforms from storage, and Hawkeye handed some to the newcomers. Flit was stepping into the pants as she heard raised voices from Shadow and Adam's vicinity.

"She needs images or, preferably, a live feed," Shadow argued, jabbing his finger toward the map.

"Well, this is all we've got." Adam shrugged. "Take it or leave it."

Flit walked over to them. She pulled the grey Government Officer shirt on, hating the fact she was wearing the enemy's colours. "What's going on?"

"I'm just explaining to Adam that translocation requires more than a wireframe map if you want to arrive safely at the other end," Shadow said, his cool tone holding a sharp edge.

"Shadow's right." Flit gestured to the map. "I need more than that. Is there a reason why you want that particular location?"

Adam cocked an eyebrow at her, as if to say it unlikely he had picked at point at random. "It's a surveillance dead zone."

"Which is great for avoiding the Government's notice but not so great for getting footage." Flit was about to say they would have to come up with somewhere else when she did that very thing herself. "I think I have another location. We'll need to get moving, though. It will be a bit of a walk to Centre One."

"I'll retrieve Acumen, and then we can be on our way." Shadow immediately teleported away.

Flit was about to ask Adam for more information about where they were headed when Fortune rushed over. She was glancing around warily as she put a hand on Flit's shoulder and leaned in. "There is something about Shadow's story earlier about Harmony's escape that felt... *off*. Acumen just bought it, though. I don't know what's going on, but I have a bad feeling about those two."

When Fortune pulled back, Flit noted the genuine concern on her face. After everything Fortune had been through, after everything Flit had learned about her... she couldn't ignore the warning.

Clapping her hands together and turning to face the team, Flit called out, "All right, you lot. I've got a location to teleport to, but we need to hustle. Line up. Let's make this quick."

"Not going to wait for Shadow to return?" Adam asked, stepping around the desk.

Flit reached out, snatching the front of his uniform shirt, and tugged him closer. "Shut up, and don't forget to breathe." Then, she turned to the other side and made grabby hands for Scraps. "You're up first. After that, everyone, form pairs."

Scraps joined her without hesitation, and the next moment they were in the living room of the apartment they had shared. It was still an absolute mess of shattered glass, broken furniture, and fractured wall panels. She only hoped it was also still outside of Government surveillance.

"Ah, good choice," Scraps said as he looked around.

"Your girlfriend's able to make those from time to time." She leaned in, stealing a kiss.

"This is still a war, you know," Adam said, his skin tinged green from the teleport.

The sheer visibility of his queasiness was enough to satisfy Flit and allow her to forgo a comeback.

She returned to the club. Luckily, the Blue Team didn't waste any time following her orders. She conducted a series of rapid hops back and forth, taking two people at a time, until she was down to just Layla and Hawkeye left in the office. Just as she slipped her arms around them, Shadow and Acumen phased into the space he had left at the desk minutes earlier.

"What—"

Before she could hear the rest of the question, Flit teleported out of the room.

When they landed back in the apartment, Hawkeye frowned at her and whispered, "I assume you have a good reason for leaving Shadow and Acumen behind?"

Flit shrugged. "It depends. Who do you trust more, Shadow and Acumen or Fortune?"

"Ah," Hawkeye hummed.

It wasn't an answer, but Flit assumed she wouldn't get one. There was no easy way to pick. Sure, they had held Acumen as a friend and companion and Shadow as a respected leader, but they were both secretive and transient members of the Underground. They had also been closely involved with Harmony and Divvy. Even if they hadn't done anything dodgy, they had to have been tolerating suspicious acts for a while. Fortune, however, had been tortured and almost killed for her determination to clear the Underground of rats.

Patting Hawkeye on the back as she walked past, Flit turned her attention to the rest of the team. Usually, the group had no problem filling in-between moments with small talk, but this time, they were all standing about, shuffling their feet, and keeping conversation to a minimum.

Adam appeared smug and unaffected as he clapped his hands together. "Well, that was a fun bit of drama," he said, squaring himself towards Flit. "I guess the Free Citizens aren't the only ones who felt the need to usurp their leaders. It's a pity. Hopefully it doesn't come back to bite them—or you—later."

There was little more to do than ignore the comment. Flit didn't have the time or energy to waste indulging his shit-stirring. "Let's get moving. Every second we waste here is another second someone could get killed in that shit fight." Flit caught Scraps' gaze. "We're only a few blocks away, but we need to look like Government workers, not a bunch of rebels in disguise."

Scraps stood a little straighter and nodded, his face setting into that all-business, soldier-mode. "I can help with that," he said with total confidence.

Flit grinned to herself. Not only had they used the Government's fence to pen them in. Now they were going to use the skills they had taught Scraps to keep him compliant against them.

67

SCRAPS

GETTING the Blue Team into formation and ready to leave was far easier than trying to sort the Free Citizens into any type of order. Even though both factions were more into the guerilla approaches, Scraps' friends from the Underground had known each other for decades and had worked together hundreds of times. Their training showed as they formed rank and managed to wrap their team around Adam, Layla, and Fortune without needing to be told what their priorities were.

Whilst the team was moving into position and doing a final arms and armour check underneath their forged uniforms, Scraps stepped towards Flit. "What happened back at Nightmix?" He kept his voice low to avoid drawing the attention of the others.

Flit leaned in closer, resting her hand on his arm. "Fortune said she felt as if Shadow was hiding something in his account of Harmony's escape. I'm not sure what happened or if he and Acumen would be liabilities, so I figured it was better to leave them behind."

As much as Scraps wanted to think all the denizens of the Underground were honest, recent events had proven otherwise. It was unfortunate, but he had to trust Flit on this. "Then we should move out. I don't think it will take Acumen and Shadow long to figure out where you might have brought us."

With that, Flit took her place at the rear of the group, and Scraps moved to the front. Even though they worked better together, they had the whole team to consider. With Layla in the middle of the formation, it meant that, if they were split up, there was a good chance someone who knew the layout of the city would be within any one group.

"Let's move out," Scraps ordered. With Link at his side, and Clarity and Hawkeye right behind them, Scraps was confident he would get advanced warning of any potential threats. "Do not forget agents do not get distracted. We have a job to do, and we have every right to be marching right up to Centre One. If we are stopped, allow me to do the talking."

A flick of his hand was all it took for Scraps to open the front door. As he led the way out of the apartment he had shared with Flit not all that long ago, he wondered if he would see it again and, if he did, what the rest of the city would look like at the time.

Deciding that it was safer even if it would take longer, Scraps led the team towards the emergency stairwell. Given the fact that the city was under siege, he was not too concerned about triggering any alarms. He had a feeling Citizens had been sneaking about all sorts of ways and places to get urgent supplies or to find safety in other parts of the building.

The clatter of their boots on the concrete stairs echoed through the space and became almost a constant drumming as the team wound around and around down towards ground level. When they reached the exit, Scraps had them pause for a moment and gestured for Clarity and Hawkeye to check the area beyond. Hawkeye opened the emergency exit door just a crack and, within seconds, was able to verify that they had the all clear. Clarity nodded in confirmation, and Scraps was confident that they would not have any nasty surprises.

"Having it this easy feels almost like cheating," Adam said.

"Please, only speak if you can improve upon the silence. We're all trying to work," Tweak hissed back.

Scraps heard a couple of quiet chuckles at the rebuke, and he was surprised Flit wasn't the one to call Adam out. Then again, the version of Flit he had seen today was a far more serious one than he was used to.

Just as Hawkeye and Clarity had confirmed, the group was able to move safely through the deserted foyer of the building and out on the streets beyond. It was not all that long ago that Scraps had thought the streets were eerily quiet. Now, he realised he was wrong. Back then, with Derivates posted at frequent intervals and Citizens scurrying from place to place, it was infinitely more lively. From what the Free Citizens had told him, few Citizens had taken up the advice to evacuate. The population had to be around somewhere. However, the street was not one of those places. He was certain there were hundreds of eyes on them as they made their way in tight formation to the centre of the town. The reflective glass windows and the dark sky above made it impossible to discern where their watchers were. It was unnerving, and it was difficult for Scraps to resist the urge to tell everyone to put their hands on their weapons.

That would only make them look suspicious.

For all intents and purposes, the team had to have the confidence of Government workers. People who would know this part of the city was not only under their control but completely safe for them. It was a trick that Flit had taught him when they had first started sneaking around in the Underground, and he hoped it worked just as well up here.

As they approached Centre One, there were intermittent patrols of armed Citizen Officers with one or two Derivates. They all seemed to be on watch but not with any real level of vigilance that led them to question the Blue Team or make Scraps feel as if they thought the rebels on the outskirts of the city presented any real threat to them.

The feel of Link's hand on his arm made Scraps glace over at her. "Adam wants you to know there's a service entrance down an alley on the East side that will take us to their waste management station."

"Copy that." Scraps should have figured their entry point would be somewhere less than desirable.

He glanced over his shoulder to nod at Adam to let him know the message was received and was pleased to see Flit still bringing up the tail. She winked at him, and his lips curved in a slight smile before he turned back around.

Bolstered by the team at his back, Scraps kept their march steady and strong. Without the city lit up to its usual standards, the buildings turned their surroundings into a glossy whirlpool of darkness. Occasional bursts of light flared from headlamps or the reflective panels on the armour of those assigned to the streets, but overall, the team was trespassing on what felt like an odd, mirrored reality of the city Scraps had grown up in.

When the team turned a final corner and Centre One loomed up overhead, there was a muffled curse behind Scraps. He wasn't sure who said it, but he was in such agreement with their awe that he didn't feel the need to silence them.

Neck aching, Scraps took in the very top of the skyscraper he stood before. Whilst the city around him was a sea of black, Centre One stood like a lighthouse amongst the darkness. The very top level was illuminated all the way around with brilliant, retina-burning lights. Standing up so high, it was a beacon, a symbol of the Government's power, the heart of the decrepit faction, throbbing over a quiet, waiting city.

"The bastards aren't even trying to hide," Flit whispered.

The group had compressed when Scraps had stopped at the front of the line.

"It's almost like they're waiting for us." Fortune spoke slowly, a frown dragging at her lips as she watched Adam closely.

"Or," Adam started, returning the older woman's look with a steely gaze of his own, "they are using the light as a decoy, hoping to lure in idiots who think they are foolish enough to remain up there."

Suddenly tired of the riddles and lies, Scraps wheeled around and glared at Adam. "What are you saying?" He reached out, using his powers to grasp the front of Adam's shirt.

It was a little too satisfying when Adam made a choking sound. Adam looked around, as if to see whether any of the patrols in the distance saw. However, the Blue Team crowded around closely enough that no outsiders would be able to see Scraps' subtle gesture.

"The top of the building isn't our target. We need them to think it is, but what we are really after is below basement level," Adam wheezed.

Scraps loosened the grip somewhat. The Government was all

about grand shows of confidence obfuscating petty, tenuously held control.

"What are you proposing?" Scraps asked, keeping close to Hawkeye and Clarity in case they had any warning for them.

"We send a decoy team to the top. That should draw the security forces." Adam gestured to the members of the Blue Team. "Then, a smaller force should be able to go to the bunker to topple the Government from the ground up." Adam gave Scraps a pointed look, letting him know just who he thought should be the smaller force.

"You want us to split up?" Tweak scoffed. "What is this, some F-grade fucking horror movie?"

Adam shrugged. "Alternatively, we could take this whole damn circus right to the basement and bring the entire security force chasing after us. You pick."

Once more, Scraps had the uniquely infuriating feeling that Adam had played him. "Did you not think this information would have been helpful before we started out?"

"Of course, he did," Flit said in a low, annoyed voice as she shook her head. "He just needs to keep himself relevant. I suspect there is a lot more information he should be giving us."

"I can confirm that," Link said quickly, her eyes darting between Adam and the others.

Flicking her braid over her shoulder and stepping forward to stand over Adam, Swipe growled, "Perhaps we should just have Link extract it and be done with this dickhead."

"We don't have time for this." Hawkeye put his hand on Swipe's shoulder and pulled her back. "There's a patrol that will come around the corner in twenty seconds."

Stepping between Swipe and Adam, Clarity said, "Agreed. If we don't move now, there will be trouble."

The terse warning in Clarity's words and tone was enough to have the team scramble back into position. Scraps took the lead but not before he noticed the smug grin on Adam's face. He just gritted his teeth as he resumed the march and cleared his own mind. If the patrol had a telepath with them, they would all need to have their heads clear.

All Scraps thought about was bypassing the side of the building he had approached so many times for work and moving to the service entrance. The team had just slipped into the alley when the muffled stomps of the patrol Hawkeye had spotted marched past the entrance.

There was a collective breath of relief from the team as the patrol passed, and they turned their attention to the wide double doors beside the service vehicle entry.

"Andy, Cogs, and I anticipated this," Tweak said, tapping his finger against the fake nametag on the chest of his uniform. He tugged it off and slapped it against the sensor. It stuck, as if by magnets, and Tweak nodded with satisfaction.

"Did you hijack some ID codes?" Hawkeye asked as the green light in the sensor flashed, and the door lock clicked open.

"No, it's more of a virus. Cogs and Andy should be working their way into their network as we speak," Tweak replied with a roguish wink as he pulled the door open and gestured for everyone to enter. "Pretty soon, their security and surveillance system will be suffering from catastrophic oversights."

"Isn't their network too strong for that?" Sway asked, gawking up at the tower.

"It would be if they didn't need their micros out by the siege fence. We're hoping their skeleton crew won't be a match for our own." Tweak shrugged as Scraps led the team past him. "We also put a message in there for their micros—amnesty in return for looking the other way while our team slips in. That should convince them."

Scraps smiled to himself as he stopped just far enough into the building for the team to follow. He was fairly confident the Government would not be expecting an incursion when the rebels were putting so much effort into the siege. He also knew that the Government had come to rely on their Derivates for far too much and that they weren't all brainwashed as Scraps had been. Tweak, Cogs, and Andy had made a sound gamble. He hoped it would pay off.

Once the service doors were shut and the team was inside, all attention turned to Adam.

"How are we supposed to get up to the top?" Scraps asked, figuring he would be willing to share the next part of the plan.

"*You* aren't," Adam said, jabbing his finger in Scraps' direction. "*They* are." He tilted his head towards the rest of the team. "There is a direct elevator from here to floor one hundred and fifty, but it would be too risky. There's only one reason someone would be going that high right now. They'd be on the lookout for that. The stairs would be better."

"You're joking, right? That's fucking impossible." Swipe threw her hands up in frustration.

"For an ordinary Citizen, maybe, but not for a teleporter who can translocate and has intimate knowledge of the office space on floor ninety-eight," Adam responded, turning to Flit as the true cleverness of his plan settled over them.

"Even so, they'll be watching for any elevator door to open up there." Swipe shook her head.

"Yes, but if some of us take the stairs and some the elevator, we might be able to catch them by surprise," Link said. She spoke slowly, clearly plucking the thoughts from Adam's mind. He glanced at her but did not seem annoyed by the intrusion. "Flit can get us all up there before coming back down to go to the basement."

Flit sighed. "Then we better get moving. We don't have time to fuck around." She looked at the others. "Who is going where?"

"Since we are the decoy, we will need numbers," Hawkeye said, automatically putting himself into that team. He looked at Fortune. "You'll need to go with whoever is headed to the basement. I'm guessing they'll have their best Registereds with them."

"Flit, if you come to the basement with Fortune, Adam, and I, you can get us out if we need to retreat," Scraps suggested, looking past his teammates at his girlfriend. "If the others have the combined powers of the team, they should be able to help themselves out of other situations easily enough."

If Scraps was completely honest, he also just wanted Flit by his side.

The others milled about, murmuring to each other before appearing resigned to the split.

"We should stay quiet on comms. We're not sure if they are

listening in, so mission-critical information only," Tweak suggested as he reached into his pocket. He pulled out several small strips that looked like the name tag he had been wearing. "If you guys get into a pickle, put these on a sensor and ask for Cogs or Andy to assist. I'll be a bit too busy with this lot."

Scraps thanked him and took the pile of strips. He was able to separate the six slips into three lots. He kept two strips for himself and then shared the others between Flit and Fortune.

As he handed the strips to Flit, he wrapped his fingers around her hand. "Stay safe up there. We'll be waiting for you here," he said, meeting her hazel eyes.

Even in anticipation of what might be the biggest risk she would ever take, there was a spark of mischief in her gaze. "Me, safe? Always." She winked at him before she teleported away to the opposite side of the group where Layla and Hawkeye were standing side-by-side. "Okay, lovebirds, you two first. You can get some canoodling time in before the others arrive."

The joke was enough to have Scraps' lips crack into the barest hint of a smile before the trio disappeared.

68

———

FLIT

TELEPORTING BACK into her pod on floor ninety-eight at night with only emergency lighting on the level was an eerie experience. However, given the way the last few weeks had turned out, nothing came as much of a shock to Flit anymore.

"Once this is over, I hope I never have to teleport with you again," Hawkeye muttered, raising his hand to cover his mouth as his skin paled. Beads of sweat broke out on his forehead.

"You're welcome." Flit gave him a bright, sarcastic smile before she translocated back to the basement.

On the next trip, she transported Tweak and Sway then Link and Clarity, finally following up with Swipe. Once they were all grouped together, Swipe ran a hand through her hair and looked around. Flit took the opportunity to catch her breath as her heart fluttered from the millionth rapid translocation of the night.

"The stairs are over there." Flit pointed past the seemingly endless sea of office pods.

"We still have…" Swipe paused, eyes rolling up a little as she whisper-counted to herself. "Fifty-two floors to climb. Any chance you can get us closer?"

Fifty-two floors was too much for anyone to have to climb and then to be expected to fight after. Not to mention the fact it would leave those taking the elevator up far too prone to attack. Flit did not fancy leaving her friends as sitting ducks.

"Yes. I think it's best to take the elevator from this level to make sure we don't risk triggering alarms on more floors," Flit said because while Cogs and Andy would be on the case, Flit didn't want to make their job any harder. "I'll take the group up to a higher level in the stairwell and then teleport back here to let you guys know so there's only one radio call needed when those in the elevator arrive. The less chatter about this, the better."

Everyone acknowledged Flit's suggestion. Hawkeye, Layla, Sway, and Link formed the group that would infiltrate through the emergency stairwell, as the combination of their powers leaned best towards covert operating. Tweak, Swipe, and Clarity would work together as the heavier hitters and destructive distraction the moment the elevator doors open. Thanks to Clarity's powers, they would have some idea of what to expect when they did, so they could plan accordingly while the others navigated their way from the stairs to provide reinforcement.

It was not an ideal plan. Flit had a feeling they all would rather stay together, but nothing about any of this was ideal. They just had to do the best they could and hope for a good outcome.

"First jump for everyone will be to the door to the stairs. You'll all wait there while I scope things out. Then I'll come back for you in pairs. Understood?" Flit said, clapping her hands together. Hawkeye, Layla Sway, and Link all nodded back at her. "Lovebirds first."

Hawkeye groaned but did not waste any energy on further protest as Flit took him and Layla in her arms. She had them over by the emergency exit in the blink of an eye. Before anyone in the group could count to ten, she retrieved Sway and Link, and the stairs team were together again. She rolled her shoulders as she pushed the door open. Her breath caught as she waited for some sort of siren, or flashing lights, or anything that would let her know she had tripped an alarm.

After counting to fifteen in her head, Flit figured there was no point waiting any longer. She gave the others a thumbs up before stepping into the emergency stairwell. Having always taken the elevator to work, Flit was relieved to see that the Government hadn't bothered with any pretentious, fancy architecture when building the stairs. Whilst the stairwell itself was a rounded shape, there was a platform for each story, with a clearly marked sign on the door leading to each, and perhaps more importantly, a void that ran right down the middle from top to bottom.

"Well, shit," Flit muttered as she leaned over the railing. Ninety-seven stories down, with the stairs disappearing into a dark abyss. It was the most dizzying drop she had ever seen, and she would be lying if she told someone it didn't make her clench her bladder a little tighter at the thought of teleporting into that void.

Flit had been called many things in her life, but quitter was never one. She swallowed the instinctive ball of *nope* and then teleported right into the middle. As the feeling of falling set off an explosion of adrenaline in her, Flit looked up and teleported again. She had to repeat the process several times because the top of the staircase was too dark to see from ninety-eight, but after ten free-falling hops, she sighted a landing with the numbers 14- at the front and teleported onto it.

Feet slamming onto the ground a little harder than intended, Flit doubled over as the wind was knocked out of her. She pressed her hand against the door as she wheezed and struggled to catch her breath. Then, knowing she couldn't waste time, she looked around as the shaking in her limbs lessened.

It took a moment for her brain to properly connect and to realise her hand was covering the rest of the number on the door, and she saw that she had landed on level one hundred and forty-six. Not bad, but given the way her heart was still racing and her mind felt foggy, she knew better than to push herself again. Between the adrenaline-inducing free fall and all the tagalong translocations, she was really pushing her own limits, limits she couldn't afford to bust.

Instead of using her powers, Flit took a deep breath and decided to work off the jitters in her limbs by climbing the stairs the good-old-fashioned, non-powered way. Things were going well, until she reached level one hundred and forty-nine.

The top of the staircase.

As much as she wanted to bust through that door and find a closer teleportation point for her peers, Flit knew that level had to have been far better guarded than ninety-eight. She used what was a rather new sense of restraint and caught her breath as she peered around, committing the landing to memory. The concrete floor felt as shiny and new as ever, and the handrails were so clean she wondered if anyone had ever touched them. There was the slightest build-up of dust at the bottom corners of the door, and there was also a soft light bleeding underneath from the main level.

"Got it," Flit whispered to herself before closing her eyes and willing herself back to the others.

The instant she reappeared near her friends, she swayed on the spot and a pair of soft hands gripped her to help her stand upright. Flit tried to shake off the dizziness. They had to hurry. They had a Government to topple.

"I can tell you want to keep going, but I think you should rest a second. You're not feeling great," Link whispered, brows creasing with concern as she looked Flit over.

Hawkeye turned away from a quiet conversation he was having with Layla and frowned. "Are you... sweating?" The confusion in his eyes was genuine. "I've never seen you sweat before."

On any other day, it would have been an amusing joke. It was no secret that Flit detested working out, and Hawkeye never seemed to tire of poking fun at her for it. However, he wouldn't joke in this context.

Layla stepped forward, resting the back of her hand on Flit's forehead and frowning. "You're cold and clammy, and your internal temperature is all out of whack."

Shrugging, Flit waved a hand dismissively. "It's humid in that stairwell. Get closer, and I'll let you see for yourself," she said, stepping towards Layla and Hawkeye, and pretending like it wasn't at least a little concerning that her body temperature was off kilter. "We can only go as far as one hundred and forty-nine. There isn't another level. You'll have to find another way in from there. I am thinking there may be another set of stairs behind a locked door, but—"

"We'll figure it out," Layla promised. "You just get us up there and then get back to the others."

The urgency in Layla's tone was something Flit felt in her gut. Without further ado, Flit recreated that landing in her mind and teleported them there. On the next hop, she took Link and Sway. Immediately, the team began to whisper a plan, but she cleared her throat.

Four pairs of blinking eyes turned to her, and a sudden wave of emotion overcame Flit. She leaned forward, pulling them all into a group hug. "No matter what happens in there, you idiots have to come out alive, you hear me?"

Everyone hugged a little tighter.

Flit teleported out of the huddle and took a deep breath. "Wait until you get the call from the team in the elevator, right? Don't go blowing your load too early. You need the Government to be distracted by them first."

"Copy that, boss," Hawkeye said with a teasing, playful salute.

That was all Flit needed to hear before she teleported back to her friends on floor ninety-eight.

Swipe, who had been in the middle of what looked like a heated conversation, jumped at the sight of her. "Fuck. Scared the shit out of me."

"I think we're all on edge," Flit said, choosing to empathise rather than poke fun at Swipe, who should have been expecting her back at any moment. She focused on the small team. "The others are on level one hundred and forty-nine, which is the highest the stairwell went. They're waiting for your signal."

Tweak bounced on the balls of his feet and expelled a long, slow breath. "So, this is it, huh?"

"Looks like it." Clarity squeezed his shoulder. "We've got this."

"Is that a prediction or a statement of hope?" Swipe snapped.

"Both," Clarity said, although it was clearly a lie, "but we won't know until we get into that elevator... and we can't afford to waste any more time."

"You're right." Instead of pushing the button to call the elevator, Tweak waved his hands, and it lit up.

Flit pulled the three into a hug. "I told the others to stay safe... so I suppose I should say the same to you lot. Come out of this alive, all right? We've got one hell of a party to throw once this shit is all sorted."

Clarity chuckled nervously and patted Flit's back.

"Same to you," Swipe said through gritted teeth, "and make sure Fortune and Scraps come out alive too. I can't lose them again."

"If nothing else, I promise those two will make it out alive," Flit said.

She meant every word.

That was enough for Swipe, who pulled away and broke the embrace for the group. Flit took one last look at them before she closed her eyes and brought the image of Scraps waiting for her in the waste management room to mind.

"You are back!" The pleased recognition in Scraps' voice was enough to distract Flit from the trickle of cold sweat that ran down her spine.

"Oh, fantastic." Adam's voice dripped with sarcasm.

Flit rolled her eyes. "When you're done acting like an immature dickhead, can you show us how to get to this basement? The grown-ups have a Government to topple."

Instead of biting back and proving her right, Adam led them past the rows and rows of trash compacters and turned a corner. At the end of a very plain but very well-trafficked corridor, there was door for what Flit would have guessed was a storage room. Both she and Scraps kept on their guard, watching their surroundings as Adam guided them forward. Fortune's sole attention was on the usurped leader of the Free Citizens, ready to use her powers on him at the first sign of betrayal.

When they reached the door, Adam looked down at the panel beside it and frowned. "You may need to get your micro—"

Before he could finish, Scraps threw up his hand and pushed the door clean off its hinges.

Adam gulped. "Or you could do that." He straightened his shoulders and looked like he was trying to shake off the worry that Scraps' decisive move had caused.

Flit smirked at Scraps. "Well done, love. Thank you." She then gestured for Adam to lead the way as she stepped closer to her boyfriend.

Inside the room was a series of crates stacked against a far wall.

"There are three entrances in total," Adam said, turning to face them. "One direct from an elevator that only runs between one hundred and fifty and the basement, another that tunnels under the surrounding streets and comes out in a maglev station—"

Flit frowned. "Why didn't—"

"We bombed it. This is the third and final." Adam gestured to the crates. "Brian, since you're clearly the muscle, why don't you do us the honours?"

Scraps pressed his lips together, probably at the use of his Citizen name, but he started moving the crates. Flit made sure Fortune had her eyes on Adam and then grasped the dagger at her own hip, ready to teleport somewhere and stab someone in the neck if this was a trap.

Adam sighed heavily. "We have the same enemy, remember? I don't like any of you, but I would rather bring the Government down with you than not at all."

"Uh huh." Flit kept her eyes on the wall that Scraps was revealing all the same.

It was only another few seconds before the crates were gone to reveal—

"An empty wall?"

Scraps looked between Adam and the wall in question. Adam walked over, slipped his fingers into a crease between the concrete panels, and... tugged. At first, nothing happened, but then the panel hissed and moved forward before the vent in the ceiling above it opened, and the panel retracted into it. They came face to face with another door. This one had a simple, blank screen on it.

"Now, this is going to be more complex. As much as your muscles are good, Brian, I think you need Andy for this. Don't want to trigger a full lockdown, hey?" Adam leaned against a stack of crates Scraps had just moved.

Grudgingly, Flit tapped her communicator and connected with base. *"Cogs, Andy? This is Flit. Over."*

"Cogs here. What do you need?"

"We have a door we need opened ASAP."

"Okay... Did Tweak give you one of the bugs?"

Flit blinked. Tweak? Bugs? Flit wasn't sure what insects had to do with it.

She was just about to ask as much when Scraps reached into his pocket and retrieved one of the small strips. He pressed it against the panel, and Flit cursed herself. Of course, that was what Cogs had meant. Tweak had given them the devices less than ten minutes ago.

Flit cleared her throat. *"Yes, the bug is on now."* She shook her head, trying clear the foggy headedness.

"Great, let me just—"

Cog's voice devolved into unintelligible muttering. Every now and again, Flit could recognise a curse word or some tutting, but mostly it was just the rambling of a very impressed microkinetic hacker.

Finally, an *"Aha, gothca!"* sounded through the comms, and the panel flashed green before the door creaked open.

"Cogs, you're a genius. Thanks!" Flit said.

She got her first sight of the space beyond the door, and her shoulders sagged. More stairs?

Flit made a promise to herself there and then to avoid stairs for the near future once this war was over.

The feel of Scraps' hand on Flit's shoulder made her perk up again.

"I'll go first." He turned to face her and leaned in to whisper, "You bring up the rear. Get Fortune out of here if anything happens."

"You really think I'd leave you?" Flit rolled her eyes. "You go first. I'll watch your back and worry about the rest of us."

For a moment, Flit thought Scraps might argue. However, he just nodded as he moved forward so they could get into formation. Flit wasn't terribly fond of Adam following right behind Scraps, but he had to be somewhere both she and Fortune could keep an eye on him. He had said that he was still on their side, but she wondered how long that would last once they came face to face with the Oligarchs. As arrogant as it might sound, she, Scraps, and Fortune would make great bargaining chips given the state of the siege.

The stairs leading down to the basement were a new level of dark that Flit hadn't seen since working in the lowest level of natural tunnels in the Underground. It was bad enough that Scraps tapped the datapad on his hip to activate the screen and give them some low light. The farther they descended, the more the odour of the musty, damp concrete messed with her senses. It made her think back to her home, and the fact that all those tunnels might now be destroyed.

Shaking herself out of the distraction, Flit refocused her attention on Adam's back. She wrapped her hand tighter around her dagger just in case.

Slowing to a stop after what felt like too long, Flit shuffled onto the landing with Scraps and the others. The door was a heavy-looking metal thing, with an old-fashioned, five-pronged vault handle on it. Flit figured that low-tech was a safe option if they were looking to guard themselves against different sorts of attacks.

"It's for containment, not security. It'll be heavy but nothing a macrokinetic can't handle," Adam whispered.

Scraps nodded, holding his hand on the round junction of the five-pronged handle.

Fortune put her own hand on his arm. "What should we expect on the other side?" she asked, the coercive force in her voice enough to make Flit flinch.

"An open-plan control centre," Adam replied, although the words weren't entirely forced. It made Flit think he would have told them without the coercion. "There will be eight leaders in there and probably a small guard detail made of elite level Derivates and Citizen Agents."

Fortune looked at Scraps and Flit pointedly. Then, she continued, "Would we have triggered any alarms to let them know we were coming?"

"Impossible to know. That door is normally alarmed, but with Andy on the payroll, I can't be certain." Adam shrugged as if it didn't really matter.

Flit supposed it didn't. "Either way, we're going in."

"Then, Scraps, can you please do the honours?" Fortune gestured to the door before she pulled a pistol out of her holster. Flit drew her dagger and retrieved a flame grenade.

"I can hit a target given the right weapon," Adam said, reaching for the spare pistol at Flit's hip.

"You can fuck right off." She shoved his hand away with the broad side of her dagger.

Raising his hands and stepping back, Adam shrugged. "Stupid decision if you ask me, but whatever. I'll let you guys handle this." He shoved those raised hands into his pockets and rocked back on his heels as if this were the most mundane situation.

Ignoring him, Flit jutted her chin towards the door. "No time like the present," she said to Scraps.

With a grim nod, Scraps flattened his palm against the centre of the handle, and it started to spin. Five heavy clunks sounded. Then it let out an awful creak as he pushed it wide open.

The sound of weapons firing was deafening, but Flit and the others were not surprised. Scraps threw up his arms, and a wave of telekinesis repelled the projectiles shot in their direction back towards the twelve grey-uniformed and reflective-visored officers standing on the other side of the door. One at the front waved their hands, and the bullets disintegrated.

"Micro," Flit hissed. She was about to teleport in when Fortune stepped forward.

"Government Agents, do not attack!" Fortune yelled.

The agents all froze, and Flit used the reprieve to peer past the wall of grey uniforms. Behind the guards, eight ordinary-looking strangers sat at a round table, people Flit would have never looked twice at on the street. With a spread of different ages and appearances, they were utterly unremarkable.

An odd sense of disappointment tugged at Flit as she looked at the people in the room. In the years of dreaming about this moment, about finally confronting the Government, she had been imagining some big, powerful people who looked like leaders surrounded by a faceless army of soldiers. But this? This was a group of plain people hiding like cowards in the basement of a veritable fortress.

She couldn't believe they had let these people control their lives for so long.

Just as one of the plain-looking folks was about to speak, there was movement to the right of Flit's view, and a person dressed in Government grey stepped out from behind the group of Registereds.

"Ah, Flit. I was wondering if you and Scraps would join us." The woman's blue eyes shimmered in amusement as she turned to face Flit and Scraps. She brushed a strand of grey hair behind her ear and smirked.

Flit's skin crawled. "Harmony?"

"That's not a name I go by here." Harmony inclined her head at Flit, half in acknowledgement, half in apology. There wasn't a single cut or bruise on her from her escape from the Underground. She brushed her hands down the front of her neatly pressed Registered uniform, complete with a designation patch. "Allow me to properly introduce myself. My designation is CAAA-671."

Then, Flit understood.

This whole time they hadn't been fighting against the Government.

They had been fighting against *themselves*.

69

———

SCRAPS

SCRAPS' mouth dropped open as he stared at Harmony. "CAAA-671?"

The mirth in the older woman's expression only increased.

He glanced at Flit and saw his own shock and wariness mirrored in her hazel eyes. Given that designation, she was likely the most skilled telecoercionist the Underground or the Government had ever seen. As the first born Derivate in the year 67, she would have turned seventy months ago.

"Yes, that's right. Never would have guessed that I started out like you, huh?" Harmony stepped forward.

"Stay back," Scraps warned, shifting one hand away from the agents and towards her. "You are nothing like me."

Raising an eyebrow, Harmony said, "I was born in the Hub, like you. Raised by the Government, like you. I went to the Underground after my training... like you."

Each time Harmony said "like you", Scraps twitched. He couldn't help but look at her in a new light now. Gone was the calm but calculated leader of the Underground, the woman who had agreed to take him in when he wanted to escape the Government. Instead, he was looking at a fellow ex-Registered. Or, Scraps though, perhaps she still *was* Registered. All he knew was that she was standing there with the Oligarchs, the leaders of the Government, and clearly on a different side of this fight.

"How?" Flit breathed beside him.

Harmony laughed. "Oh, it was far easier than you'd imagine. The Underground was in shambles when I joined." She sighed longingly, nostalgia warming the sound. "Divvy was the only real threat back then, even if she was a simpering fool. She was pushed into leadership because she was the best precog known to Derivate-kind. People were terrified to be around her because her predictions were so precise that conversations were a waste of time. It made her bored. Lonely. Desperate for a connection. It took hardly any coercion to stop her from reading my future and to turn her into my dearest friend. After that? It was just a simple matter of remembering my training, remembering my purpose to watch over the rebels and make sure they didn't get too big for their boots."

Scraps glanced at Flit and saw she looked just as horrified as he felt. Hearing Harmony talk of someone she had spent so long with made Scraps realise just how much of a liar she was. Her deception was alarming, and it appeared utterly complete.

"How could you do this? How could you work with *them?*" Flit practically spat that last word as she took her hand off the hilt of her combat knife and gestured wildly at the silent, altogether too comfortable-looking people sitting around the circular console. "How could you betray *your own kind?*"

"I have never been your kind, Flit." Harmony shook her head, taking another step forward.

"Move again. I dare you," Flit growled, holding up her flame grenade.

Harmony continued, unperturbed by the threat, "You've always been too instinctive. If you got your way, there would be chaos in the world. I have done my part for the last forty-six years to keep peace in the Underground. It was manageable, too, until you started snooping around. If you want anyone to blame for the way things have turned out, blame yourself."

"Keeping the peace?" Fortune asked from behind Scraps. She stepped up to stand behind his shoulder. "You mean, keeping us caged."

"You really think the Government didn't know about the Underground?" Harmony's eyes glittered with amusement. "You think the fake *radiation* signatures and raids on *abandoned* warehouses went unnoticed?"

There was a titter of amusement from around the console that made Scraps feel ill.

Flit turned then, her attention narrowing on Adam. Her forehead was creased in a pained expression, and her skin looked pale in the clinical, cool light of the bunker. "You weren't surprised when you saw me. When I told you about the Underground."

"Oooh, caught me there..." Adam shrugged and gave her a fake sheepish smile. "Although your lot was on Zane's portfolio, not mine." He saluted sarcastically at a middle-aged man with close cropped hair and deeply tanned skin. "All of the power and population control was beyond my purview."

The man responded with an annoyed grunt.

A choked sound spluttered from Flit's lips. "Population control?"

"What else would the Underground be?" Zane asked. He leaned back in his seat, and frown lines deepened on his brow. He gestured to Flit and Scraps. "Why waste resources chasing your lot when we can let you think you're free and just keep you contained in a different way? It's been highly efficient. It's taken over a hundred years for you all to try and fight back, but no matter what, you all belong to us."

You all belong to us.

Population control.

I started out like you.

The words buzzed in Scraps' mind as he put the pieces together. He glanced at Flit and could see her hands shaking as she stared, betrayed and dumfounded, at the woman she had previously respected so deeply.

With a flash of imagination, Scraps pictured himself in Harmony's position. If he had continued down the path of a Registered, he would have done anything the Government asked him to. Heck, he had even dragged Registereds who had run for freedom back to their oppressors, knowing they would be punished brutally and further stripped of their autonomy.

"Then I guess you fucked up. You lost control." Flit's smugness sounding forced, even to Scraps. "What about the Citizen Derivates? Population control only works if your bullshit breeding program is real. It isn't, though. Derivacy is a natural mutation. Even with your stupid genetic testing, there are still people falling through the cracks."

Harmony snorted a laugh. "You think we didn't know about that?"

Scraps looked up at the leader and noted the Government's logo on the shirt she was now wearing. His mind whirled back to the Government History Museum, to the similarities between the linked chain in the Government's insignia and the double-helix of the Helix Corp logo. The logo of the research organisation who apparently created the Derivates and started the war.

"They've known since the start," Scraps said, not taking his eyes off Harmony. "Since Helix Corp."

"We are Helix Corp." Zane gestured to the logo on his own chest. "The scientists didn't create the mutations. They just studied them. The Derivates were getting dangerous, causing chaos. People blamed them, so they rebranded and used their research to get the mutants under control."

"So... they broke the news, spread the propaganda and lies, and then rode in to be saviours?" Scraps asked.

"Sounds like an awfully fucking convenient way to grab power." Flit sounded equal parts disgusted and furious. "Luckily, we're here to end this bullshit once and for all. Guess you didn't consider that with your stupid little population control strategies."

With a dismissive wave, Harmony spoke again. "I knew you and the Blue Team were up to no good. I just thought I had a bit more time. The coup in the meeting room during the broadcast was very brave, but ultimately, all you did was bring our plans forward."

"Oh, you mean setting off bombs and killing innocent children in the Underground?" Flit raised the hand she was clutching a flame grenade in. "Give me one good reason I shouldn't do the same to you bastards!"

As far as Scraps was concerned, that was one of the best ultimatums Flit had ever made.

"Ah, no. That's not a good idea." Adam stepped forward and

grasped Flit's shoulder. She shrugged him off. "If bringing down the Government was as easy as burying its leaders in rubble, I would have done it already. Look closer, Flit."

Adam moved the hand on the back of Flit's shoulder to press against the base of her neck. She was about to slap him away when she froze mid-strike.

"Flit?" Scraps twisted his wrist and telekinetically grasped the back of Adam's shirt, pulling him away from Flit.

"Control chips!" Flit pointed at the back of one of the Oligarchs who was previously facing away from them, unbothered by their appearance.

Brows furrowed, Scraps looked where she was pointing and noted a narrow, straight scar at the base of the man's neck.

"The chips ensure that if more than one of them dies within twenty-four hours of each other, the whole system goes into hard lockdown." Adam sighed, shaking his head. "It's been the bane of my existence for decades."

"It's not the bane of my existence," Flit snapped, narrowing her eyes as she turned back to the people in charge of the Government. "I don't give a fuck about a hard lockdown. I won't hesitate to end them."

"I would advise against that," Adam said.

"Why? There's nothing you or they could do to stop me." She glanced at Fortune.

Harmony laughed. The sound bounced through the concrete bunker with all the irreverence and derision the woman could muster. "Ah, so those experiments did work." She turned to Fortune, a new flicker of menace in her eyes. "You must have hidden it all well for that not to be noted by the Department of Advance Human Research, but now I know—"

Without warning, Flit flashed out of existence and appeared behind Harmony. An agent yelled a warning as Flit kicked her ex-leader in the back of the knees. Harmony grunted and she fell forward, her hands coming out just in time to protect her face from smashing into the concrete. The surprise of the action meant Harmony was too slow to roll away and found herself pressed into the ground. Flit shoved the heel of her boot against the soft flesh between Harmony's shoulder blades to keep her down.

"Don't you dare fucking talk to her," Flit spat. There were beads of sweat gathering at her hairline that made Scraps frown. He was about to talk her down when movement flickered in the corner of the bunker.

Shadow and Acumen phased into the room. "Sorry. I lost them. They're on their way—" Shadow stopped mid-sentence.

The distraction was enough to draw the attention of everyone in the room. Without Fortune and Scraps watching them, several of the agents raised their weapons and fired.

Chaos erupted in the bunker. The Oligarchs ducked for cover beneath their console. Scraps raised his hands to protect himself from the onslaught of bullets, but one slipped through. The sick thud of metal burying into flesh sounded beside him, and Fortune cried out.

Flit flashed into place behind the shooter and took them out with a swift knock to the back of their head with the butt of her dagger. With the distraction of her revenge, she didn't notice another one of the agents raise a gun with a glowing purple chamber.

"Flit!" Scraps waved his hand just as the agent pulled the trigger. The gun tumbled from their hand as it discharged, and the purple energy slammed straight into Scraps' chest.

"Scraps, no!"

Scraps staggered back as agony surged through him. He felt as if every one of his nerves was zapped with electricity. He lost all sense of everything around him until a solid body pressed against his back and held him up, and a slick, sharp blade was pressed to his throat.

"Sorry," Shadow said. His voice was close enough to burst through Scraps' disorientation.

"Stop fighting!" Fortune's command made everyone freeze in place. She pressed a hand against her shoulder, which was bleeding profusely.

Technically, holding Scraps hostage wasn't quite the same as fighting.

The shifty leader of Intelligence pressed up against Scraps' back to hold the blade firmly. "Don't move. I don't want to hurt you."

Scraps wanted to fight him, but his limbs were still tingling with pain, and he knew better than to try and access his powers.

"You!" The cry was an accusation of the utmost outrage as Flit pointed at Shadow. "Let him go. Now!"

"Flit, remember what I said to you." Acumen, who had been in the corner of the room, shuffled closer to where Flit stood. He had a gun in his hand, but it was pointed at the floor.

She turned, pointing the tip of her combat knife in his direction. "You, of all people!"

Scraps felt the outrage in her tone to his core. He had trusted Acumen and Shadow too.

The pain of the situation was broken by a tired, irreverent sigh. "Can we just move things along, please?" the woman sitting opposite of Zane asked, rolling her eyes. "I want to get home."

Harmony grunted as she got to her feet and cast Shadow a disparaging glare. "You're just lucky they came here first. I supposed them teaming up with Adam was a good thing, after all."

Shadow stiffened behind Scraps. "Wait... Where are the others?"

For the first time that night, genuine concern tugged at Harmony's face, straightening out the crow's feet in the corners of her eyes. "What others?"

Scraps' mind flickered to the team he had watched Flit teleport out of the waste management room. They had not heard anything on comms from them.

"The rest of the Blue Team... They split up for some reason." Acumen tilted his head, his face contorting in confusion.

Scraps winced. If Acumen had plucked that thought from his mind, it meant Fortune's control was slipping. That wouldn't be good, especially with so many max-capped Registereds in the room.

"Joel?" Harmony barked, turning to the group of Oligarchs.

"Not possible. We haven't had any security alerts," a man cowering beneath the console said, sounding confident in his assessment. He slipped out from his hiding spot and tapped on the screen. His eyes widened.

"They've meddled with the security system, haven't they?" Harmony groaned and rubbed her brows.

Scraps couldn't help but smile at her frustration, even with the blade still pressed against his throat. He caught Flit's gaze and could see the tension coiled within her as she glared at Shadow's knife. She wanted to jump over, Scraps could see it, but he bit his lip and shook his head ever so slightly. Not now.

If Shadow wanted to kill him, he would have done it already.

Just as an image of the Blue Team, mid-battle with a contingent of Government Agents, flickered onto the screen, Scraps' earpiece burst to life.

"Uh, guys, I don't know how much longer we can hold out," Swipe panted through the comms. *"They're up here guarding some sort of device. I don't know what it is. We need urgent backup."*

Flit's hands balled into fists as she rounded on Harmony. "Device?"

Acumen's eyes grew wide. "It's on level one hundred and fifty!"

The blade at Scraps' throat disappeared. His back cooled at the sudden absence of his hostage-taker.

Shadow reappeared behind Harmony and slit her throat.

Blood poured out of the gash that stretched across Harmony's skin like a macabre smile. It gushed over the floor and splattered the agents near her. Cries of shock drowned out her gargled moan.

"About time you let us know where it was," Shadow hissed. He pushed Harmony away, and her spasming body collapsed to the ground.

"Agents, drop your weapons." Fortune coughed. She stumbled closer to the Registereds.

Several raised their hands towards Shadow, but nothing happened, and they grunted in surprise. Scraps was relieved Fortune was still capable of negating their abilities.

Scraps and Flit used the opportunity to surge towards their enemies. Shadow joined them, and in a flash of limbs and steel, they made short work of securing the Registereds gathered there. Panting and holding a blade dripping with blood, Shadow turned towards the Oligarchs who were staring at them, agape.

"Get up. Backs to the walls. Hands where we can see them,"

Shadow ordered, pointing the blade at Joel, the man sitting at the console.

Joel met Shadow's eyes and then started to rise, his hands pressed against the screen. Then, his fingers shifted and—

Acumen fired at the Oligarch, hitting him square in the chest and causing him to slump over onto the console as he bled out.

"No!" Adam yelled. He burst forward and shoved Joel's spasming body out of the way as the screens in the room turned black and shut down. "He locked us out!" He slammed his fist against the console.

"I'll fix it." Acumen stepped towards the console.

Flit pointed the tip of her dagger at him. "Don't you dare."

"We don't have time to fuck around. We're on your side. Just let us—" Acumen went to touch the console.

Scraps shook his head. "Don't touch it."

"If they mess it up, we've got no hope of getting back in. We need to call a ceasefire." Adam started tapping at one of the keyboards on the console.

Concerned, Scraps looked at Flit. She just shrugged in response. Scraps considered the choices and decided to let Adam keep working. Right now, he didn't know what Shadow and Acumen wanted.

"Maybe we should get Tweak and Andy on it," Flit suggested, just as the screens flared back to life. "Oh, that was fast."

"You shouldn't underestimate me." Adam grinned then tapped the screen one more time.

"*Uh, guys... can you undo whatever you did?*" Tweak spluttered. "*The device is on a countdown now.*"

Quick as a flash, Shadow teleported over to Adam and put the knife against his throat. "Undo it!"

Adam laughed. "It's impossible. Once it's started, it can't be overridden."

Shadow turned to Acumen as he pressed the blade's edge hard enough against Adam's throat that the man's eyes bulged.

"He's telling the truth," Acumen said, dread lacing his tone as he moved over to Fortune and helped her put pressure on her wound. Her blood was now congealing between her crimson-stained fingers.

The sudden turn of events made Scraps dizzy. He was trying to understand what was happening but could not make sense of any of it.

Shadow cleared his throat. "Scraps, Flit, I need you to listen to me," he said, speaking slowly and far too calmly for the situation. "Acumen and I have been trying to figure out what Harmony has been up to for months. Between the research you gave us and our own network of intelligence, we knew she had a weapon, but we couldn't figure out where it was. The device Swipe mentioned was a bomb." Shadow paused to let that sink in. "That bomb contains an aerosol that binds to cells that have been marked by the VOKZ radiation. If it goes off in this city, every single Derivate that has been exposed to that weapon you were investigating, or the new inhibitors, will die within seconds."

Gooseflesh rose all over Scraps body as ice-cold dread drenched him from head to toe. His body was still aching his mind frazzled, but he remembered that Harmony and Divvy had ordered every single member of the Underground to wear those inhibitors. Flit had been shot by that weapon.

He glanced over at his girlfriend, and his throat was suddenly thick, his collar too tight. His extremities still tingled, and he knew his powers were useless. It had hit him too.

"Go up there. Deal with the bomb," Shadow finished, as if speaking to children.

Flit pointed at the Oligarchs and Adam. "But—"

"Go! Your team has enough skill to deal with it," Acumen barked, his face suddenly contorted with frustration.

"I'll take care of this," Fortune wheezed, leaning heavily against Acumen. Her skin was worryingly pale, and the neckline of her fake Government uniform was wet with a mixture of sweat and blood. "I promise."

Scraps stepped towards Flit. "We need to go," he said.

Suddenly, he didn't care if the Government was in control. He just needed to make sure she and the other Underground Derivates made it out of this alive.

Flit rounded on Shadow. "You fuck this up, I'll fuck you up. Got it?" she snapped.

Then, she teleported to Scraps' side. Even though the only reason she stepped in close and wrapped her arms around him was to translocate with him, it felt good to return the embrace. Her clammy cheek pressed against his chest, and she took a deep breath.

"Let's finish this," she whispered.

Then, they teleported to level one hundred and forty-nine.

70

FLIT

FLIT'S HEAD spun as her feet slammed onto the concrete floor of the emergency stairwell just beside the door that led to level one hundred and forty-nine.

Her vision blurred, fuzzy and black around the edges.

If the early morning, long day, multiple missions, and dozens of multi-person translocations weren't enough, she was also trying to process the twists and turns of what had happened in the basement. She clung to Scraps as he pushed through the door for one hundred and forty-nine and navigated them to a secondary stairwell that led them up to level one hundred and fifty.

Flit's legs shook as she and Scraps burst through the door. They were immediately met with the echoes of frantic shouts and blinding flashes of weapons fire. The voices of her friends were woven into the mix of macabre fleshy thuds and grunts, but her mind was too muddled to figure out whether they sounded like they were winning or losing.

With a collar soaked in cold sweat and vision that made her feel like she was standing on a boat rocking on a stormy ocean, she stepped back from Scraps.

A warm, firm hand on her shoulder held her steady. Scraps' blue eyes found hers as he leaned down. "Flit, you're pale and clammy."

"And you're tall and handsome. So what?" She shrugged his hand away and forced a grin.

"But—"

"Don't fuss over me! You're the one that got hit by that abomination. Are you okay?"

She looked him over. He was definitely looking more haggard than usual, but he seemed otherwise fine. It must have had something to do with the fact he hadn't tried to use his powers.

Reassured that Scraps was okay, Flit leaned to the side to look past him. The fight between the Blue Team members and the agents had migrated towards a set of windows that ran all along the east side of the building. Several panels of the window were smashed to pieces, letting in a high-pitched, howling wind. Even from this distance, the fractured and newly altered skyline of Old City was clear to see. The glow of the electrostatic fence was within the Hub, leaving the vast space between the Hub and Old City dark and void of movement.

Between Flit and the view of the city were the profiles of her closest friends. They were locked in combat with a dozen people dressed in Government uniforms. Judging by the way the fight was going, at least half of them were Derivates.

And between Flit and her friends? A vast, marble and glass boardroom was home to a large, round projector table that had been smashed to smithereens. The whole space was littered with bodies of agents.

In a moment of panic, Flit took stock of the situation. Her mind seemed to process it all in slow motion as she swayed on the spot.

Swipe was standing at the back of the group by the broken windows. She was causing utter chaos with her powers, throwing shards of glass and parts of splintered chairs in the direction of her foes. Layla was near Swipe, a hand on a panel between some of the intact windows. The lights above the melee combat remained on, but those above the ranged combatants flickered off.

Link and Tweak were together on the opposite side of the fray, with Link calling out orders from Swipe as Tweak attacked the tech the agents were wearing. Several of the enemies had cast their visors aside and were frantically tossing misfiring weapons away from themselves.

True to his strengths, Hawkeye was deep in the fray with Sway and Clarity. Between Hawkeye's advanced senses and reactions, Sway's telecoercion, and Clarity's ability to predict the short-term future, they were holding their own against the agents focused on them.

More than a few of her friends had wounds or were moving stiffly in some areas, but they were all alive and fighting.

In the middle of it all, in the base of the broken boardroom table, was the device blinking away with only nine minutes and thirty-five seconds on the clock.

"Flit!" Scraps stepped between Flit and her view of the bomb that could destroy almost everyone she loved.

"What?" Flit blinked, shaking her head. Her processing slammed back into real-time.

"I'm going in." He leaned down and pressed a swift kiss against her forehead. "I know better than to tell you to keep out of it. Just... stay safe. You are looking close to burnout."

"I'm fine."

They both knew it was a lie.

Scraps stepped back, turned around, and ran into the melee. He shoulder-charged one of the agents and knocked him off their feet. Seeing the move, Hawkeye spun away from his own combatant and kicked the one Scraps had knocked prone in the chest. The momentum caused the person to cry out as they fell through one of the broken windows.

That was enough to cause Flit to leap into action.

The appearance of Flit and Scraps seemed to reenergise the Blue Team, and there was extra oomph in their attack. Sensing the change in energy, the remaining Government Agents lost confidence. Their defences became sloppy, their communication non-existent. The chaotic fight was no longer about winning, but to delay death.

Despite the new throbbing in her head and the way her vision split and doubled, Flit teleported around the room with her dagger out. Her slices hit home more often than not, and it was only a matter of a couple of minutes before blood was dripping down the sleeve of her counterfeit uniform. Through it all, she kept Scraps in the corner of her view. His face was set in hard, determined lines, and his movements were swift and precise. Every second of time he spent building his body and in combat training was paying off.

When the last Government Agent fell, the Blue Team stood, panting and on edge, looking around the room to make sure there was no unexpected movement. Flit was tempted to slump back against a nearby wall, but a flicker of red light caught her attention.

"The bomb!"

The next instant, she was there. She leaned over the cracked screen of boardroom table and peered down into the marble base. The bomb itself was half her height and filled the entire space of the round base that had a diameter of close to two meters. She had never seen technology like that before, but there was a definitive purple glow emanating from cracks in the shell-like dome that was almost as wide as the bomb itself. Her stomach churned, and she stumbled back.

"Ouch!" Hawkeye yelped as she trod on his toes. He caught her just before she fell. He righted her and frowned.

"So, it is a bomb." Link jogged over to her side. "Layla, Tweak!"

The rest of the team, the micros included, crowded around the base of the table. They all looked over the edge, their faces glowing purple. The numbers on the timer counted down.

4:39

"Do we stop it or evacuate? What are we looking at here?" Hawkeye glanced at Tweak.

Tweak paled. "Layla, get Cogs on the line." He put his palm over the control panel and closed his eyes.

"It's a new type of bomb," Scraps explained. Compared to the others, he was relatively clean, but he still wiped some dust off his hands and onto his pants. "It has an aerosol agent in it that will bind to the cells of anyone who has been exposed to VOKZ—"

"For the love of—" Swipe dragged her hands down her face. "Speak in a language we can understand!"

"The inhibitors!" Flit snapped, glaring at Swipe. Scraps was trying to answer the damn question. Interrupting him wouldn't help. "If you've been shot by those ability-disabling weapons or worn one of the new inhibitors, this will kill you!"

Seven sets of eyes blinked back at her.

"Well, shit. That's not good." Cog's voice through the comms sounded just as concerned as everyone else appeared. *"Show me what we're working with."*

Reaching into his pocket, Tweak retrieved one of the patches and slapped it onto the screen of the timer just below the numbers.

4:12

"Tweak, help me out. Swipe, Scraps, see if there is a way to move the thing. Layla, look for weak spots in the construction."

Flit was thankful for Cog's quick wit and level-headedness. Having worked in Control for long enough probably helped with that. Not to mention she wasn't directly in the field. That had to take some of the punch out of the fear.

"Guys, move back. Scraps and I will get rid of the marble." Swipe pushed Link and Clarity aside, and those who weren't critical for the mission also stepped back.

The slab must have been insanely heavy, but between Swipe's telekinesis and Scraps' muscle, they managed to crack opposite sides of the circle. They pushed one side away, casting it to the edge of the room, before working on the other.

"That's not good." Hawkeye stepped back towards the bomb and frowned as he started to move around the perimeter of the bomb.

"You're gonna need to give me more than that, Hawk."

"Sorry. Uh, the... the mechanism beneath the bomb is welded to the floor on each side."

"It's got a kill switch," Tweak added.

Layla stepped back and hung her head. *"The dome is integrated into the mechanism. We can't remove without activating it."*

"Cogs? Give us some good news, please," Swipe said, making it sound like an order.

However, no amount of determination could order something into existence if it wasn't already there.

"It looks like it used to be connected to a network, but once it was activated, the circuit burned up. I can't get in. I would have to be

there in person, but even then, tinkering with the program could set it off."

3:20

Flit's stomach sank, and she looked over at Scraps. His eyes were wide, lips parted with horror.

In that moment, she wished they'd had more time together.

"Bust the welding," Flit ordered, gesturing to Swipe. "I'll be back."

Scraps stiffened. "Where are you—"

Flit heard the *"going?"* through her comms. The instant her feet hit the floor of her booth in Nightmix, she started running. Cold sweat poured down her body, and her limbs trembled. She let out a yell of frustration as she forced her fatigued body to move.

When she burst through the door of the bunker, she didn't stop to answer questions. She heard Scraps calling for her through her comms and also from the console where Cogs and Andy were sitting. The bunker itself was relatively empty of personnel but full of action. Every single person at the consoles scattered across the room were commanding some part of the battle between the Free Citizens, Derivates, and the Government.

A battle the rebels appeared to be losing.

"Flit!" Cogs choked out her name as she swivelled in her chair. Her eyes were wide beneath her tousled red hair.

The alarm in Cogs' expression didn't stop Flit. She ran over, barrelling straight into the micro. With all the strength she had left, she dragged her from her chair. "Hold on," she warned.

Half a breath later, Flit and Cogs tumbled onto the glass-littered floor of level one hundred and fifty. They rolled and slammed to a stop against the twitching body of a Government Agent. With several cries of alarm, they were surrounded, the arms of Flit's teammates prying them apart and helping both women to their feet.

Whoever had hold of Flit went to let go, but her body was limp. She stumbled over to the bomb and fell against the side of the casing. "Cogs, please!"

Cogs didn't waste a moment. Despite the shards of glass buried themselves into her legs, she ran to the bomb and sank down beside it. Tweak and Layla joined her. Everyone else watched with horror.

A black haze closed in around the edge of Flit's eyes as Scraps grasped her shoulders and shook her. "Flit, Flit! Hey, Flit!"

Flit ignored Scraps. Her head lolled to the side, and the world shifted on its axis.

1:46

She tried to push Scraps away, but he shoved his face between her and the bomb.

"She's going to go into shock," Link said, suddenly appearing by his side.

A giggle spluttered from Flit's lips.

For some reason, the others weren't as amused by her predicament as she was. Their eyebrows creased.

"Guys, I know we like drama, but if you don't sort this out, I'm gonna shit my fucking pants," Sway called out from behind Flit.

Or was he beside her?

"I can't do it!" Cogs' voice shook. "I need more time."

Flit snorted. "Anyone know where we can buy more time?"

She thought the joke was great, but no one else laughed. Seemed their sense of humour was as off-kilter as her vision.

"We need to get out of here," Cogs warned, a new sense of urgency in her tone as she turned to face Flit.

Flit's skin prickled as she felt the attention of her team members narrow on her.

"She'll burn out before she can get us all out." Scraps stepped in front of Flit, shielding her from what had become a rather uncomfortable sense of being watched. "If we get Shadow to take us out of here, then we leave the Government to claim the city back."

"*What's going on up there?*"

The voice over comms this time was Shadow. Or was it Acumen? It was so hard for Flit to tell. Her mind had started to melt.

"*We can't deactivate it,*" Cogs replied. "*We have to evacuate.*"

"*We don't have time to evacuate. You need to get the bomb out of there.*"

No, that was Shadow. Definitely Shadow.

"*We can throw it!*" Swipe suggested.

"*Tearing it from the foundation will activate it,*" Cogs argued.

"The blast radius will still cover most of the city anyway. We'll lose everyone." And there was Acumen.

Flit slumped against the console and peered past Scraps. "One-ten!" she announced, reading off the numbers that seemed to dance and shimmer in her mind long after they changed to *1:09*.

"What?"

Scraps turned to look back at her. There was such panic in his eyes that her heart broke, but her spinning brain ground to a jarring halt.

They had to get the bomb away from the city.

"The welding," she said, taking Scraps' hand. Her voice now sounded slurred, even to her.

His hand tightened around hers. "What are you—"

"Finish breaking the welds!" Link called out, pulling Clarity, Hawkeye, and Sway back from the device. "Now!"

Flit had never been so grateful for an uninvited intrusion into her mind.

There was an undeniable metallic screech as the everyone worked to free the bomb from its bindings.

Flit grunted as she got to her knees and draped her arms over the side of the bomb. The purple radiation that glowed against her skin as she climbed higher onto the dome was a welcome pain. Even though it made every cell of her body feel like it was burning, it centred her.

"Done!" Tweak stumbled back from the device.

0:26

"Flit, what are you doing?" Scraps leaned over, slipping his arms under her.

She shook her head. "No, leave me." She tried to squirm away.

"Oh, fuck." Clarity's rare expletive made Scraps tense around Flit.

"I'm sorry, but I have to do this. I'm the only one who can keep you all safe." She tugged him down for a kiss.

He pulled away, shaking his head. "There has to be another way. You cannot do this. I love you."

Flit kissed away his protest. She wished the moment could have lasted forever.

But she had a job to do.

0:11

Pushing Scraps away, she looked into his altered blue eyes. "Tell my parents I love them," she whispered. The effort of breathing and talking in quick succession made her lungs seize. "And don't forget I love you too."

0:09

Before Scraps could do anything to stop her, Flit looked over at the view of Old City in the distance and picked a spot right above the heart of it. She let out a sigh of relief, knowing that, with this bomb gone, the Underground would finally be free.

0:08

"Flit, no!"

She blocked out Scraps' protest took a deep breath, and—

Instead of the familiar force of teleportation tugging at her cells, a flash of purple seared through her and she fell to the ground beside the bomb, convulsing. Flit gasped as she looked up to see Shadow standing over her, VOKZ gun in hand.

0:06

"No, what are you—" Flit's words cut off with a wheeze. Dread filled every part of her as she realised she couldn't get the bomb away from the city anymore. "Why would you—" She stopped speaking, unable to force out the words. Her head throbbed. Every part of her sizzled with pain. Her vision blurred black around the edges, and she struggled to string her thoughts together.

0:04

Shadow threw himself over the bomb. His dark eyes met hers. "I'm sorry. This never should have fallen to you."

0:02

Before Flit could protest, Shadow teleported out of the building, taking the bomb with him. Her ears rung as the sound of the distant explosion cracked through the night air and her head fell back against the marble floor with a painful thud.

71

SCRAPS

THE EXPLOSION from over Old City was blinding. Cool, purplish light billowed up high in a catastrophic mushroom cloud that lit the night sky.

Scraps blinked and turned to face Flit. All he could see in that moment was the lifeless sag to her mouth as it hung open. The blood tricking from her nose and ears was black and tar-like as her head lolled to the side.

Panic surged through him as he ran towards Flit and collapsed over her. He grasped her shoulders and shook them desperately. "Flit, wake up. Please wake up!"

"Let me look." Tweak pulled Scraps aside.

Scraps collapsed back against a broken slab of marble as Tweak placed a hand on Flit's forehead. Tweak wasn't a healer, but at this stage, any micro would do.

It felt as though the group, shocked by Shadow's sacrifice, watched Flit with a new sense of horror. It had been one thing to lose her in a sacrifice, but the possibility of losing her to burnout and VOKZ radiation felt *wrong*.

Losing Flit in general just felt wrong.

The Blue Team all waited, breath baited, as Tweak seemed to spend an eternity hovering over Flit.

Then, finally... "She's alive!"

That was all Scraps needed to hear. He leaned back in, sliding his arms under Flit and pulling her body against his. Her clothes were soaked with cold sweat and blood. He settled her onto his lap, shards of glass caught in the fabric scratching his pants.

"I take it, by the lack of kaboom, that the bomb is gone?" Acumen spoke through comms. They didn't need a visual to hear his frown.

"Yes," was all Hawkeye could reply. His voice was thick with emotion and weighed down by fatigue.

"Very well." A pause. *"As much as I hate to rush you, Fortune's lost a lot of blood. If you happen to have a teleporter handy, she could do with an emergency evac."*

Scraps winced.

"I'm afraid that isn't an option." Hawkeye put an arm around Swipe as a sob bubbled from her.

"Then get down here and say your farewells. She won't make it out of this building."

The trip down to the basement was a blur for Scraps. Not only was he exhausted, but every ounce of energy he had went to keeping Flit safe and unjostled in his arms as he watched for signs of improvement. The more he watched, the more he noticed the subtle signs of her weak breath. The relief that flooded through him was so welcome.

He leaned closer, breathing her in and pressing a kiss against her forehead. "Flit, you need to wake. You need to say goodbye to Fortune."

But when they stepped out of the elevator an into the underground bunker, Flit's skin was still pale, her limbs floppy.

Shadow, Acumen, and Fortune appeared to have done a good job of securing all the Government Agents and Oligarchs. They were all sitting, backs against the far wall, with their hands cuffed over their laps. The Derivates were wearing the new inhibitors, and Scraps couldn't help but wonder if they sensed the very real burden of their own decisions as they waited for the Blue Team to deal with the bomb that would have killed them too.

"Do we need to worry about the aerosols from that bomb spreading into the city?" Cogs asked Acumen as she broke from the group and walked over to him.

Acumen, who was kneeling on the ground and holding onto a

pale Fortune, shook his head. He looked at who had emerged from the elevator, seemingly doing a mental count. His shoulders sagged as he clearly came up short. "Shadow didn't seem to think so. It might be best to stay inside and keep the air on internal cycle until we can confirm it, though."

"Oh, Fortune…" Swipe ran over, sinking to her knees beside the older woman.

Scraps held Flit tighter to his chest, knowing that she would wake and hate herself for not being able to help the woman who was like a mother figure to her.

Swipe settled onto the ground and gingerly pulled Fortune onto her own lap.

A weak smile tugged at Fortune's lips as her eyes fluttered open. Her unfocused gazed wavered over Swipe before falling on Flit.

"Just hold tight, Fortune. I'll get you to a medic." Swipe slipped her arm from under Fortune's back, to below her knees, and she started to rise with her.

"No." The word came out with a cough and splutter of blood that matched the crimson stain on Fortune's shoulder. "T-Too late."

"No!" Swipe shook her head, the tears streaming down her cheeks sliding off her face and soaking her shirt as the rest of the team crowded around her. "I'll get you there. I'll—"

"Rook and Vector are w-waiting… for me."

Another sob burst from Swipe, and she rested her forehead against Fortune's.

"H-he'd be so p-proud… of you… all…" The final words were followed by a long, rattling breath that shook Fortune's body for several seconds before she sagged, dead, against Swipe's lap.

Crying echoed around the room. Scraps' eyes burned as he watched Swipe rocking Fortune in her lap. He immediately looked down at Flit, a moment of abject terror freezing the blood in his veins and then…

She breathed in.

It felt wrong to be relieved, but he didn't care.

A throat cleared beside Scraps. "We've used the Government system to call a ceasefire. We need to get this situation under control before we lose our foothold."

Scraps blinked as he turned and saw Adam standing right behind him. He hadn't even noticed the man when he had walked in. Adam's hands were bound in front of him in a set of handcuffs, and he looked like he might have taken a couple of hits. Scraps had no sympathy for him.

Scraps turned to the man who he had been working alongside warily for so many weeks. "You knew about the bomb."

Adam's shrug was so careless, so unaffected, that Scraps' blood boiled.

"You could have killed the people I care about the most!"

Scraps slipped his arm from under Flit's knees and then elbowed Adam in the face. A satisfying crack snapped through the sobs, and his friends watched him, aghast, as Adam fell to the floor beside them.

"I thought he just wanted to bring the Government down. I should have known that he hated Derivates, too. He tried to stop us joining the Free Citizens, but then he realised he could use us," Scraps explained, the true chaotic genius of Adam's machinations finally coming to light. "He knew we were after the same thing, so he tricked us into bringing him here so he could take over himself, and then set off the bomb to get rid of us."

That seemed to be enough for Sway to step away from Link and Clarity. "Adam, you will sleep until I tell you to wake." When Adam's eyes closed, Sway nodded with satisfaction then asked, "So, how do we go about taking out the trash?"

THREE HOURS LATER, Scraps settled Flit on the bed of a hotel a block south of Centre One. It was a swanky place, and the room that he had been assigned was high enough in the building that he knew he wouldn't have been able to afford it on his modest salary.

Not that the salary mattered much. The owners of the hotel themselves had been bowing and scraping when Acumen and Hawkeye requested some rooms for the displaced rebel fighters.

Thankfully, following a thorough medical examination from Tinker, Scraps had been given the okay to bring Flit back to the room he was staying in. Tinker had warned him that she would be weak when she woke, but she *would* wake. He was worried Tinker might have been suspicious of him after everything, but she actually seemed relieved to have someone to watch Flit while she worked on clearing the backlog of medical concerns at the field hospital.

With a heavy sigh, Scraps ran his fingertips over her cheek, pleased to find it much warmer than it had been when he first picked her up in his arms on level one hundred and fifty. Tinker had done a good job of cleaning the congealed blood, glass fragments, and smudges of dirt. He had been out of the small room for the process, but when he had returned, Flit had been changed into the casual tights and tank she preferred. They didn't quite fit right, so Scraps could only assumed they had been loaned from someone else.

Scraps stood back, not wanting to dirty the thick, pure white sheets with the blood and gore over his own body. He watched Flit as he shrugged off a backpack Andy had given him and used his powers to drag a nearby couch to cover the door. Even if the owner seemed genuinely relieved to see that the rebels, not the Government, had won, Scraps did not trust the strange, tense calm that had fallen over the city following the ceasefire.

As Scraps walked to the bathroom and stripped off, his mind played back the blur that was the past few hours. Following Fortune's death, the Blue Team and Acumen had called for backup to deal with Adam and the Oligarchs. They, along with any agents and Registereds who refused to surrender, were taken to the Hub's holding cells in North One by a convoy of vehicles driven by Citizen Derivates and Free Citizens. The building remained under guard of those factions, with a sprinkle of Underground Derivates thrown in for good measure.

Acumen, Hawkeye, and a few members of the Free Citizens who had previously held leadership roles within the Hub had made an official announcement once Andy and Cogs had gotten the network up and running. They had warned that, whilst the fighting was over, the Hub still needed to be on lockdown until a new ruling order could be put into place. Similar orders had been put in place for the other cities. They had made provisions for people who needed to move about to see family or seek medical or practical assistance, but overall, the populace had been asked to remain patient and stay at home for a little longer. From what Acumen had told him, the Underground were planning to use some of the quiet time to go back to their base and see if there was anyone left alive after the latest explosions.

Still, when Scraps stepped into the glass-walled shower and looked down at the city, he noted the roads were busier now than they had been during the initial lockdown. As the sun rose in the distance and the hot water cascaded down his back, he let out a sigh of relief.

The sigh was cut short by a yawn. Something about the steamy shower reminded his body how long it had been awake and active. He put aside his desire to soak in the massaging spray until his legs collapsed beneath him and started to scrub himself clean. Even though he wanted to let the water wash away the stress of the past few weeks, he would much rather be in bed with Flit.

"What a night," Scraps muttered to himself, shaking his head.

He turned the water off, stepped out of the shower, and started to towel himself off. His body ached in places he didn't know existed. When he was dry, he hung the towel and returned to the main suite.

Lips cracking into a smile, he saw that Flit was still peacefully asleep on the bed. Scraps pulled on some boxer shorts and a T-shirt and slipped between the sheets with her. He carefully slid an arm under her and pulled her against his chest. He fell asleep the moment he closed his eyes.

Several hours later, before the sun had reached its zenith, Scraps was woken by the feel of Flit stirring against his chest. He forced his eyes to open, working against the grit and grogginess weighing them down.

Flit's disoriented, hazel gaze found his. "W-What... Where—"

He silenced her worry with the gentlest brush of his lips against hers. "We're safe. We're in a hotel room, resting," he whispered, moving his lips to her forehead. Her temperature now seemed a little high, but Tinker had warned it would fluctuate for a few days at least.

"The war—"

"We won," Scraps said, even though there was little sense of victory in his voice.

Flit blinked. It took her several long moments to process that. "The others?"

"They're safe—" he started to say, but then he paused.

Even in her dazed state, Flit's expression sharpened. Scraps wished he had kept going and just committed to that statement, but he couldn't lie to her.

"Fortune didn't make it."

A strangled cry spluttered from Flit's dry lips.

He pulled her against his chest. "I'm so, so sorry."

He wished he had more words for her as she sobbed against his chest. She cried until her tears soaked his shirt, and her grief taxed her enough to make her fall back asleep.

As much as it hurt to think of Fortune, of Shadow, and of all the people who were lost in the uprising and the destruction of the Underground, Scraps felt an undeniable sense of relief at having Flit safe and alive in his arms. This was the knowledge that allowed him to sink back against his pillow once more and fall into a restful sleep with the feel of her chest rising and falling against his.

A PIERCING, irritating chiming broke rudely through Scraps' slumber.

He rolled over, covering his ears and trying to ignore the sound. He had no idea what time it was, but from the way his body and brain felt, it was too early.

"Stop!" he groaned, hoping to silence the alarm.

It only grew louder.

"Off! Sleep! Stop!" Scraps half shouted, half begged. "Please, stop!"

A muffled groan fluttered against his shoulder blades as a warm body slumped against his back. "Loud voices confound the voice recognition software."

The gritty-voiced comment made him wake. The mocking in the words threw him back to the first time he had told Flit as much.

The last few weeks, right up until him collapsing in the hotel bed, slammed back into Scraps, and he quickly rolled over.

Flit yelped, but he wrapped his arms around her and hugged her tight.

"Ouch. Shit," she spluttered. "Easy there, tiger. I feel like I've been hit by a hover truck."

"Close. It was the VOKZ weapon." Scraps smiled as he watched Flit yawn. He was feeling the impact of his own hit from the weapon, too, but he was nowhere near as burnt out as Flit had been, so he imagined she felt much worse. "Are you okay?" he whispered, raising a hand to push some loose strands of hair off her face.

"Not sure you could call it okay, but I'll get there if that alarm shuts up," she whispered back. Then, she pressed her lips together and glanced at the communication panel on the wall. "Not an alarm."

Her comment drew Scraps' attention, and he sat up carefully to see that what he had initially thought was an alarm was, in fact, a call. He apologised to Flit as he slipped out from under her and half walked, half stumbled to the door. He tapped the screen and bit back a yawn as Acumen's face appeared on it.

"Sorry to wake you, Sleeping Beauty, but we've got work to do," Acumen said. There were bags under his eyes that told Scraps he probably had not slept a wink, but he seemed alert enough. "How's Flit?"

Scraps turned to observe his girlfriend. She laid, tangled in the sheets, yawning and stretching weakly. Even though she was still pale and drawn, she had never looked more beautiful to him.

He smiled. "She is okay for now."

"Good." Acumen nodded firmly. "Bring her along, too, if she's up for it."

"Bring her where?"

"Centre One. Floor one hundred and forty-nine," Acumen said. "We're having an important meeting. We need you both there. We are all tired and need of rest, but this city never sleeps."

The soldier in Scraps snapped to attention. "Copy that. How long do we have?"

"How long will it take to get over here?"

"We'll be there in twenty minutes."

Acumen smiled at him and ended the call.

Flit groaned. "Twenty minutes?"

The enthusiasm Scraps felt at being needed beyond his part in the revolution faltered as he turned around and saw her lying there.

"You heard him," Scraps said with a sheepish shrug. "The city never sleeps."

Flit pointed at the window. The late afternoon sun was streaming through, casting long shadows over the room. "Really? It looks like it may in a couple of hours."

"Yes, but he said he needs us. I can go on my own if you—"

"No!" Flit shook her head. She reached out for him, making grabby hand motions. "I'm never leaving your side again. I just need one more hug."

Scraps walked over, but the second her fingertips made contact with his shirt, she pulled him onto the bed and rolled on top of him.

It was a trap.

He should have known better.

"Your mother said you have to avoid strenuous activity," he warned as her lips found his neck.

Oh, how he hated himself for saying it.

Flit rolled onto her back, the grip she had on his shirt ensuring that he rolled over with her. Her legs parted, and he settled between them. He let out a strangled groan at the warmth of her body against his.

"But she didn't tell *you* to avoid it," she whispered. "Can you help a girl out?"

At that moment, there was nothing else Scraps could do but oblige.

AN HOUR LATER, Flit and Scraps made their way to Centre One. Scraps had used the trip over from the hotel to brief Flit, but any thought of the previous night disappeared as the elevator doors opened onto level one hundred and forty-nine. It was just as white, modern, and pretentious as any other level in the building. As Scraps draped his arm around Flit's waist and took stock of the place, footsteps clicked against the smooth marble to his left.

Hawkeye, looking freshly showered and rested, walked out of a corridor that led away from the main elevator. A few other people milled about. Scraps recognised some as Free Citizens and others as Underground Derivates. Still, they all did their own thing as Hawkeye approached him and Flit.

Before Hawkeye reached them, Flit broke free of Scraps' embrace and threw herself at her best friend.

"Ooof!" Hawkeye grunted, catching her and stumbling back a step. "You were almost dead this morning. Where the fuck did this energy come from?" His smile was so wide Scraps was worried his cheeks might split.

"Oh, shut up for once," Flit muttered, hugging him tight enough that he did just that.

When it was done, Hawkeye gently peeled Flit off himself. He squeezed her shoulders and stepped back. "As much as I want to have this reunion, we need to get to that meeting."

Turning on his heel, Hawkeye led them through a corridor, bypassing several well-furnished seating areas, and into a meeting room that overlooked the Hub and all the way out to Old City.

As much as Scraps' attention threatened to snag on the view and the vast and horrifying changes to the skyline of both the present and ruined metropolises, he was distracted by the people in the room, silhouetted against the pink and purple hues of the approaching sunset. He spotted Acumen and Cogs. Chris and Liana waved at him from their seats at the wide, round table. Swipe and Layla were seated beside Mitch and Iris. Iris' music was thumping in full force through her headphones, obscuring the soft conversation that a couple of the Citizens who had made the announcement with Acumen were having beside her. Even Agent Greene and CC-9832 sat at the table, the latter giving him a nod of greeting. Scraps frowned as he noted TB-219 was not present, and

CC-9832's face darkened in a way that told Scraps he did not make it through the night.

Scraps swallowed as he took in the array of people gathered. A combination of Registered, Underground, and Citizen Derivates, Free Citizens, and even an ex-Government Agent stared back at him. All the groups it the city were represented in a place where most would not have even been welcome twelve hours ago.

"You guys took your sweet arse time," Swipe said, cocking an eyebrow at them both.

Scraps chuckled and scratched the back of his neck. The heat rose in his cheeks. "Sorry. Took a detour through Tunnel Forty-Two."

Flit laughed softly beside him.

"Where's Tunnel Forty-Two?" Mitch asked, frowning. "Weren't you staying across in the hotel too?"

Iris put a hand on their arm and shook her head slowly. Mitch went to argue, but Iris leaned in and whispered something that turned Mitch's cheeks red. They sat back in their seat, taking a sudden interest in a chip on the surface of the table in front of them.

"So," Flit asked, linking her elbow through Scraps' and then crossing her arms over her chest, "what's this all about?"

"We need to figure out what leadership will look like now the Government is gone," Acumen said. As he gestured for Flit and Scraps to take two of the several spare seats at the table, a projection of the Hub rose up off the surface of it, ruined streets and all.

Scraps was impressed. The others must have been busy taking scans while he and Flit slept.

Flit, however, only frowned. "And what do you want us to do about that?"

Acumen frowned, his bushy brows knitting together. "Um... help? You're never short of opinions, and Scraps has unparallelled knowledge of Government policy and procedure."

The expressions of the people sitting at the table morphed from impatience to confusion as they all looked at Flit. Scraps glanced down at her too.

An amused, chaotic half-grin tugged at her lips. She raised an eyebrow. "You... woke us up to talk politics?"

"You needed to be involved in this." Hawkeye skirted around her and took a seat beside Acumen, as if trying to set a good example for Flit to follow.

Scraps beamed, chuffed at the offer. He did not think he had anything nearly valuable enough to contribute to the running of a city, but he would advise on policy and procedure if they asked. He went to step forward but was stopped as Flit held the crook of his arm tight to her chest.

Flit laughed.

The sound was so discordant, so unexpected, that everyone watched her, dumbfounded.

When she stopped, she wiped away tears of amusement. "Thanks, but no thanks." She tugged on Scraps' arm as she turned around to walk out of the conference room.

"Hey, wait!" Acumen's chair scraped against the marble as he stood up and moved around the table. "This is all you've been talking about for decades. Sit down. Help us out."

"No." Flit levelled Acumen with a serious, no-bullshit stare. "I've been talking about the *rebellion* for decades. *Politics?*" She snorted. "Count me out."

Scraps shook his head. He should have known it would come to this. Flit was a woman of passion. Of action. Of impulse and righteousness.

None of those qualities had any business in the drudgery of politics.

"You can't just tear down a government and walk away, Flit," Acumen said, lowering his voice. "The conversations we have in this room over the next few days will determine the trajectory of our society for generations to come."

Flit held up a hand. "Let me stop you there," she said, shaking her head. "I did not sign up for this. You're kidding yourself if you think that I'll be a productive person to have any sort of say in—" she waved her hand dismissively in the direction of the others "—whatever that is. I don't care about economics, or transport systems, or health care. All I ever wanted was equality."

"Which is why we need your voice," Acumen interrupted. "You have a duty to—"

"Don't you dare tell me what my duty is!" Flit pointed her finger at Acumen. "I spent my entire life telling you lot to get your arses into gear and fight back against the Government. You all dismissed me, or ignored me, or called me irresponsible. Scraps and I have been risking our lives for over a year to make this shit happen. *We* are the reason that you have a seat at that table, so now *you* do *your* duty and bloody-well take it."

Acumen winced.

Scraps stepped closer to Flit, putting a hand on her shoulder in silent support. Even though he understood what Acumen was getting at, he agreed with her. He loved his girlfriend dearly, but if she had to sit through all the meetings it would take to get their world up and running again, she would probably lose her mind.

Or start another uprising.

Neither of those were good options.

Acumen bowed his head in resignation and turned to Scraps. "What about you? You love policies and procedures. We could use your skills while we try to sort this mess out."

All it took was one look down at Flit to know that the only place he wanted to be was where she was. "Maybe later," Scraps said, returning his attention to Acumen. "Once you have got some ideas in place, I would be happy to review them. Until then, I need time to reacquaint myself with my girlfriend, without having to worry about the Government, the Underground, the Free Citizens, or whatever else is going on."

"Well, you heard the man." Flit peered past Acumen and offered the others a lackadaisical salute. "Sorry, my friends, but Scraps and I have a sunset to catch. Good luck with the policies and shit. Don't act like arseholes and everything should be fine. You've got this."

Then, she tugged on Scraps' arm. Flit led him to the elevator, his heart warming as they stepped in.

She leaned back against the wall of it and grinned at him. "You wanted to stay in there, didn't you?"

Scraps shrugged and focused on her smile. He loved the way it reached all the way up to her eyes and added just the slightest hint of crow's feet. She was more relaxed than ever before, and he decided it was a good look on her.

As much as Scraps thought it would be interesting to sit in on the meeting and discuss how the cities would be ruled, he knew he would hear about it eventually. He and Flit had worked hard enough recently. They had earned some recreation leave.

"Oh, I fully intend to read about it and give them advice later." He pressed the button to close the elevator door.

"Good. I hope you will tell me all about it in excruciating detail." Flit pushed herself off the wall and kissed him. Her arm snaked past him and she entered the floor number for their destination.

Scraps was about to really invest in the kiss when the car stopped and the doors pinged open. He frowned as he turned around, half expecting to see someone had chased after them and caught them before they could get away. Instead, they were met by the vast, open space that was level one hundred and fifty. The bodies, blood, and debris had been cleaned up, and the shattered windows temporarily boarded over.

Flit took his hand and led him out of the elevator. At this point, the purples and pink in the sky had started to darken as the sun threatened to dip below the horizon. "I've always wondered what it would be like to see the city from up here. Last night was too chaotic and too dark to allow me to take in the view. We've still got some sunlight left for us now, though. "

They walked together until they reached the boarded-up windows. Flit let go of his hand to tear at the panels, grunting and struggling to pull them off. Scraps gently shifted her aside and took them off for her. The concrete and metal scent of the city air streamed in on a cool, refreshing wind. Flit sank down, sitting at the edge of the window, her legs dangling over the city below.

"Is that really a safe place to sit?" Scraps frowned.

Flit rolled her eyes. "Don't worry. If we start to fall, I'll teleport us to safety," she promised.

"You will not be able to. Your powers are drained."

"Then let's live a little dangerously."

Scraps pressed his lips together but still settled down beside her, resigned. He draped his arm around her shoulder and dangled his legs out over the edge too. She leaned against him and let out a contented sigh.

"So, I guess it is finally all over?" Scraps said. The realisation that he didn't have to fight any more finally hitting him as the sun started to dip beyond the horizon.

Flit kissed his cheek. "Are you kidding? The fun has only just begun."

THE END

ACKNOWLEDGMENTS

My goodness. What an adventure.

This story began life over a decade ago as a back-and-forth writing project with my husband. We wrote the entire thing together from Scraps being dragged to the Underground by Flit, right up until the pair helped bring down the Government. When we were finished, we realised there was so much more we could put into the story. My darling husband, probably tired of my constant yapping about it, said that he was happy for me to rewrite and expand to my heart's content. We both agreed the story would lend itself well to a trilogy.

I think it is safe to say that Flit's and Scraps' adventure has grown significantly from its origins. My husband has been involved every step of the way, and I have to thank him profusely for making sure Scraps remained true to character, and the story evolved in a way that was authentic to the original themes. This literally would not be here without his foray into writing the early version with me, his commitment to reading over four-hundred-and-fifty thousand words and providing his insightful comments.

My darling husband, I cannot thank you enough. Not only for what you did to help bring this story to life, but for building a rich life with me outside the pages of these books.

I would also like to thank my family. I don't think this kind of story would have been the same without the fighting spirit I inherited from my father, or the passion and empathy from my mother. Thanks to my mother for buying the *banned* book anyway, and to my brother for being such a supportive shithead the whole damn time. I don't know if you'll ever read the series, but I just want you to know I followed through on my threat to name a character after you and kill them off. You're welcome.

Thank you to my kids who, mostly unknowingly, accept the fact that Mum always has projects on the backburner, and who come along to conventions and share their sass and charm whilst helping me sell books. You guys are the way of the future, and I know it is in safe hands with you two as part of it. This story is, at its heart, about fighting for what you believe in. If nothing else, I hope you two are able to take that forward into life with you. I love you both more than words can express.

No publishing journey happens in isolation, so please sit tight for a short while longer so that I can thank some more people who have been critical in this process.

To my amazing friend K. Isabella Frost. This last book would not be here without our regular sprints. Not only are you the best body double/sprint partner I've ever had, but our chats about life and our stories in general have been so fulfilling. Thank you for cheering Flit and Scraps on throughout this journey, and for having my back when those feelings of being an imposter wanted to drag me down. I am so excited about the other projects we are working on, and can't wait to see them come to life. Also, dear reader, if you get time to check out K. Isabella Frost's work, you will not regret it. Her writing is engrossing and her world-building enthralling.

There are some other wonderful bookish friends who have been so important in this journey. There are so many things to love about the indie publishing world that go far beyond being able to share my stories my way. One of those things is the connections I have made along the way. So, thank you to indie authors Tjalara Draper, Nikki Minty, JP McDonald, Kristen Dovnic, Maxx Victor, Sarah Cole, and all the others who have been there to share the victories and pitfalls of authorship. Thank you to the incredible bookish community, wonderful people like Treece, Lou, Mel, Ashlee, CJ, Kira, Ebony, Grace, Sammy, and Leaha to name a few. I am new to TikTok, but would also love to thank the beautiful people I have found there, especially Tanya. I am sure I have missed someone in the list, but please know that I appreciate everyone who has engaged with my content or read my work.

From a technical perspective, the story would have just languished in a folder on my Onedrive without the expertise of my editors and cover designers. So, thank you to Chelsea Visser for the first edit of The Underground, and then to Nicole Zoltack for taking on the mammoth task of looking over the first book, then doing fantastic editing work with the rest of the series. Thanks must also go to Piere d'Arterie for creating the moody covers for the paperbacks, and the talented artists at MiblArt for creating the hardcover designs. Special thanks also to the immensely talented Cyberaeon who has created gorgeous prints that go along with these books.

Now, I know you're probably sick of all of these acknowledgements, but I can't stop until I have also thanked my beautiful friends Rachel, Alison, and Rhys for all of the support. You guys are nothing short of legendary. Thank you for looking over so many cover designs and blurbs, for reading the books and hyping me up, for helping out at cons, for keeping me somewhat level-headed, and for everything else along the way. I love you guys and don't think I have thanked you nearly enough.

Then last, but certainly not least comes you, dear reader. Even though I tell everyone I have written these stories for myself, there is a special kind of honour that comes with knowing people have decided to spend precious, irreplaceable hours of their lives in a world of my creation. I hope you enjoyed as much of the story as you could, and that you take a little of Scraps' integrity and Flit's passion with you once you close this book.

Read. Resist. Rise.
Xx Liv Evans

IF YOU ENJOYED THIS BOOK...

If you enjoyed Free Citizens (Book Three of the Derivates Rising Trilogy), please consider leaving a review on one of the following sites:
GOODREADS
AMAZON
Reader reviews are crucial for helping indie authors share their stories with the world.

If you would like more news, updates, sneak peeks, and bonus content, you can find it on any of the following sites:
www.livevans.com.au
@LivEvansWrites on Instagram, TikTok, and Facebook.

BONUS CONTENT

THE UNDERGROUND

ART BY CYBERAEON

EXIT

THE HUB
ART BY CYBERAEON

FREE CITIZENS

ART BY CYBERAEON

The Code of Us

"Some things are worth breaking for..."

When Mia and Arden Drew are in a horrific car accident, the dreams they shared for their future balance on a precipice. As a talented neuropsychologist working for one of the world's foremost experimental human research facilities, Mia uses the resources at her fingertips to save her husband's life.

Mia's grief-fuelled decision catapults her into the depths of a messy court case. Her intentions, relationships, and career are put to the ultimate test as the people around her question how far she should have gone to save her husband, and whether he is still the man she fell in love with. Now, she must face the truth of what she's done or risk losing her husband once and for all.

DREW V. SYNTHESIS LABS

"WILL the plaintiff please present evidence item four-c to the court."

A rustle of curiosity ripples throughout the courtroom at the judge's request. The antique mahogany benches groan under the shifting weight as hundreds of people turn to face the door at the side of the room. The air is so thick with tension and humidity that I could swear I'm swimming, but the water stinks of perfume and sweat and anticipation. Protesters, supporters, and reporters alike, wait for their first in-person sighting of the man at the centre of all of this.

And that man?

Well, he is my husband.

The door opens and my heart lurches into my throat as I see him again. It is the first time I've laid eyes on him since the National Security Bureau banged on our door and dragged him from our home. Or, as the official report states, since they "confiscated" him. He looks a little worse for wear. I pulled the crisp black suit he wore to our wedding out of storage and sent it through to the evidence lock-up, but it is all crumpled and hangs on his frame wrong because of the weight he has lost since he wore it last. His chiselled jawline is clean-shaven, his thick brown eyebrows furrowed over bewildered blue eyes.

He hates being the centre of attention.

It is hard to watch him here, looking like a fish plucked out of a river and thrown straight into a frying pan. Still, a warm smile tugs at my lips as the flashes of the reporters' cameras reflect off his bionic leg. The leg of his pants mustn't sit over it properly, as he has the hem rolled up to just above his knee to show off the intricately engraved chrome and glowing green water-cooling channels. His prosthesis is the most modern thing in this relic of a chamber.

When he looks up, he squints his ocean eyes to see past the bursts of light. He scans the courtroom until he locks his gaze onto mine. My hands ball into fists on the table, nails scraping against the polished surface. Our lawyer, Alice McGoward, puts her hand over mine. The small motion is enough of a reminder to take a slow, deep breath, and I let my shoulders fall.

"*I love you.*" I mime the words and, for a moment, it is only my husband and I in that room.

His nod is firm. Resolute. It reinforces his confidence as we face an impossible situation. *"I love you, too."*

His reply is a relief. After spending almost three and a half months apart, I can't help but wonder if he hates me. If he resents me for getting him into this situation. I'm sure I am far from forgiven, but his reply is a start.

"Synthetic freak!"

The hate-filled curse bursts forth from the crowd at my back to a riotous clash of cheers, and boos follow. My husband winces and stumbles over his own feet as he makes his way towards the witness stand. That accidental, clumsy slip silences the chamber. It is such a simple, human mistake to make. *A mistake that most people in the room believe he is incapable of.*

"I am sorry, but you cannot take the stand. *The stand is for witnesses.* Technically, you are *evidence.*" Justice Lorenzi's voice is tinged with genuine apology. The wizened man watches for my husband's reaction from beneath bushy grey eyebrows.

Head bowed, cheeks flaring with a blush, my husband nods. The bailiff gestures towards the table and they make their way over there instead.

My back stiffens with indignation. "They can't make him do that! It ... it ... it's inhumane!"

"Mia, we've talked about this," Alice whispers back, her voice an island of calm in the rolling sea of tension. "It isn't fair, but we need to pick our battles."

The palms of my hands sing with pain as I dig my nails into them. I jam my fists into the pockets of my skirt and sit properly again. I am forced to watch as my husband tries to figure out how to get onto the evidence table with some modicum of dignity. Beside me, Alice's chair screeches as she gets to her feet.

A hush falls upon the court. It is like the room it is holding its breath, waiting to see how Alice will make her case. The only sound is the clacking of her expensive shoes on the polished timber floors. She walks around the plaintiff table, and over to the evidence table until she is so close to my husband that she could reach out and touch him if she wanted to. She doesn't, of course, *but if that was me, I wouldn't be able to resist the temptation.* The two share a short look, the weight of the law suspended between them, before she turns her green eyes to the judge.

"Your Honour, as the legal representative for Doctor Mia Drew in *Drew versus SynThesis Labs,* I would like to present evidence item four-c to the court. Or, as he is better known, Mr. Arden James Drew."

Arden bites his lip, looking back at the judge, then at the crowd, and offers an unsure shrug of his shoulders and a tight-lipped smile in greeting.

Alice graces him with a reassuring smile before she returns her attention to the judge. "Your Honour, I know it is customary for the legal officers to summarise the purpose of the evidence, but in this case, I believe the evidence will speak for himself."

A ripple of surprise goes through the courtroom at Alice's wording. No one knows how to react to it. But ... Arden does. A small, awkward chuckle bubbles from his lips and some of the tension he holds in his shoulders melts away.

"Thank you, Ms. McGoward. After so long being locked up with broken holo drives and forensically cleaned drug canisters, I could do with a chance to speak to an audience that will understand me," Arden says, giving in to his natural inclination to make jokes in stressful situations.

Like the rest of the court, I find myself leaning in towards him. His voice is magnetic. I'd forgotten how much I crave the sound of it. His tone is as deep and warm as always, but a wavering of sheer social anxiety plucks at the vowels.

"You are more than welcome, Mr. Drew. As I said to the judge, this is your chance to speak. So please, be my guest." With a sweep of her arm towards the waiting crowd, Alice steps to the side. Now there is no barrier between Arden and the courtroom.

I can hear my own heart beating in the silence, like the low thunder that rumbles in dark blankets of clouds before a storm. It's a visceral reminder of just how high the stakes are for Arden and I. The whole point of this case is to determine whether Arden should have the same rights and responsibilities as everyone else in this room, or whether his augments make him the property of SynThesis Labs. If he *is* declared their property, I have no idea what they will do to him.

Arden scratches the back of his neck as he looks at the ground. He draws in a long, shaking breath. When he looks back up, his gaze is filled with a hint of apology as it locks onto mine. "When my wife first started working for SynThesis Labs, I didn't know I would become her most controversial experiment."

The Voidstalker Extraction

The galaxy is a dangerous place. Habitable planets are controlled by powerful factions, and the space between them is fair game for pirates and expansionists alike. The best way to get ahead in the Void is by hiring mercenary companies to use their mechs to claim and defend territory.

Most mercenary groups are run by morally gray upstarts who will do anything for the right price. One company is the exception: the Triple C. Led by former mech pilot Henri Durroguerre, it has gained a reputation for honoring contracts and minimizing collateral damage.

Astera Ramos, a runaway turned mech pilot, is new to the Triple C. Eager to prove herself, she volunteers for a supposedly straight-forward reconnaissance job on Baldalan that quickly turns deadly.

After guiding Astera back to safety, Henri realizes that the fatal contract was not as simple as the Kolos Admiralty made it out to be. He recruits Astera to help him uncover what is happening on Baldalan, and the Triple C unwittingly becomes entangled in a sinister plot that threatens to disrupt the balance of power in the Void.

CHAPTER ONE

THE OPS ROOM onboard the Latagarosh was quiet as it orbited a sleepy planet called Baldalan in an unclaimed sector of the Void. The glow of a dozen holographic projectors, dotted around the room, illuminated the faces of three tired and bored Operations staff members as the lights on their headsets blinked their steady, standby rhythms. Until the scouting team on the planet broke radio silence, there was little the Ops staff could do but monitor their own stats.

As Martin Englethorpe, one of the officers, kept an eye on his allocation of the output, he remembered the saying he had heard when first joining the renowned Triple C: "If Operations Specialists have time to get bored, it means more pilots come home alive." He had never worked on a mission with a casualty. They didn't happen often in this company. So, even though he could barely keep his eyes open, Martin was glad for the quiet.

"Okay, Scout Wing. Top three most fuckable ..." began the specialist beside Martin, as he smoothed his sleek blond hair back against his head and grinned.

"Norgard, this isn't the time," chastised Hermedilla, the man to Norgard's right. Martin had only worked with him once before, but clearly, he was the more serious of the two. "Plus, you know Sergeant Johansen will snap your neck if you talk about any of the women in her wing like that."

Norgard snorted. "Come on, it's just us on this deck. Who's gonna know?"

Martin frowned as he looked around the darkened room. "The commander will. I swear he has this area bugged to know what's going on in here."

"He was a mech pilot once. Don't let his present rank fool you, Eggles." Norgard leaned forward and changed his output display as he spoke.

"Don't call me Eggles. I hate it when people use that—"

"But it's so much easier than ... what is it, *Englethorpe?*" Norgard teased.

Martin bristled at the slight as Norgard and Hermedilla laughed. He wasn't sure if Norgard was teasing him because he was the new guy, or because Norgard was generally just a jerk to everyone. He reminded Martin of those kids he grew up with who seemed to enjoy making others uncomfortable. Usually, Martin tried to avoid people like that, but the Ops Team loved Norgard, and if he wanted to ingratiate himself with the crew, he'd have to make some sacrifices.

"Oh, like 'Norgard' and 'Hermedilla' are any easier? Yeah, those two names just roll off the tongue." Martin glanced at the men, figuring that he'd rather go along with the expected banter than let them think they'd bothered him as much as they had.

Hermedilla raised his hands in self-defense. "Why are you bringing me into this? I'm not the one acting like a dick."

"Well, you found my name so funny," Martin snapped.

Hermedilla shrugged. "You sound like some medieval duke or something."

A loud yawn broke through the space, and Norgard leaned back in his seat, kicking his heels up and crossing them over the edge of the console. "Anyway, like I was asking," he said, reclaiming the attention in the room. "Top three most fuckable scouts?"

Martin drummed his fingers against his own console loudly. The base of it was made of the same dull, burnished steel as the floor and wall panels, and carried sound far too well.

"Seriously, can we *not* do this?"

Norgard rolled his eyes. "You don't wanna play, Eggles, you don't have to. I'm sure Hermedilla will."

Hermedilla shook his head, the spikes of his dark hair wobbling slightly, and fixed his teammate with a pointed stare. "Actually, I think it's messed up for you to be asking about them like this."

"Man, fuck both you of you." Letting his feet fall from the edge of the console with a loud bang, Norgard flopped forward dramatically. "You guys are no fun at all. No wonder you're alone during our downtime." With a huff, the disgruntled man turned his attention to his screen, idly scanning the orbital sensor data.

Once again, the Ops room fell quiet, the hum of the coolant system for the electronics filling the space. Tension was never a good thing in the Ops room and the three of them knew it. However, Hermedilla had nothing to lose by pissing off Norgard, but if Martin kept making mistakes when dealing with the other guys in the team, his social awkwardness could cause them to tease him relentlessly.

After taking a deep breath, Martin admitted, "I think I don't want to play because my number one is down there on the mission."

"Ha," Norgard jumped upright in his seat. "I knew it. I knew there was a reason you volunteered for the shift tonight. Only an idiot would swap what you had for a mission like this unless he had some ulterior motive."

Hermedilla tilted his head to the side. "Oh, right. Wasn't Specialist Kernwick supposed to be on this shift? I just figured she was sick or something."

"Nah, I swapped with her," Martin explained, ignoring the fact Norgard called him an idiot. He was content with his decision, knowing that's all that counts. "I let her have my data credits for a week so I could be here."

"You got played. Damn rookie," Norgard tutted, his voice full of pity. "Having someone offer to take a dead shift like this from you *is* the reward. You gave a week's worth of data to sit here and occasionally hear the voice of some hottie? Dude ... you need to get laid." Norgard shook his head slowly, and Martin's cheeks burned. He had never felt quite so stupid before.

The lights on the monitoring deck flickered a split second

before a new voice broke into the room. "Nest? This is Starfall and Sleeves, doing our hourly check in. Do you copy?"

Norgard nudged Martin. "Hey, you take it."

"What? Why?" Martin frowned at him. "You're on the radio. I'm tracking signatures."

"How are you supposed to speak to your number one fuckable if you're on signatures, huh?" Norgard tapped the unit and assigned the mic control over to Martin. "Do you ever want her to know who you are? Or are you just going to keep creeping from the shadows?"

While there was an insult mixed into Norgard's comments, he had a point. This was the sort of opportunity Martin had been hoping for. He smiled, glad that taking the hit to his ego had paid off.

"Please tell me you birds are still awake?" There was a groan through the radio. "Honestly, the frequency with which you Ops guys fall asleep while we're on missions is alarming. You're meant to be watching our ass-"

"Copy that, Starfall," Martin spluttered, realizing that being on mic meant that he had to actually talk, not just daydream about it. He leaned forward, resting his elbows against the console. "We're watching your ass and it's looking fine."

Silence fell on the radio, and in the Ops room. Martin frowned as he tried to figure out why, and then he replayed his comment in his own head. "Ah, Void," Martin groaned.

Norgard and Hermedilla burst into laughter.

"Right, well, hopefully you like what you see," Starfall replied, a hint of amusement in her tone.

"But not so much that you haven't been doing the right scans," Sleeves interjected, sounding a little less appreciative of the blunder.

"No, not at all. I just messed up my words earlier. You're both looking peachy from up here. We haven't had anything worth reporting. Thanks for checking in, we'll keep you updated," Martin promised.

"Peachy?" Norgard mouthed.

Martin winced, cursing himself again. *Why am I like this?*

"And with that juvenile double entendre, we're out," Sleeves announced. "Don't fall asleep, and make sure you're not too trans-fixed by the thought of Starfall's ass to catch any pings," Sleeves said before the lights on the comm unit flicked off.

Exhaling with relief, Martin sank back in his seat and scrubbed at his face with both hands. Norgard reached over, ruffling his dark black hair. Martin batted him away. At least, he tried to, but Norgard was too fast.

"Working with you two is like dealing with a couple of toddlers." Hermedilla suddenly sounded far more tired than before as he switched up his readouts. "I'm gonna kill Kernwick for swapping her shift."

Silence blanketed the room as the specialists conducted the required scans and monitoring to ensure the mech pilots on the planet surface were still in the clear. It was easy work for them, as there was nothing that stood out or raised any red flags. Working in operations meant accepting the monotony. It was part and parcel of their job, but it wasn't why they got paid so well. They earned their money during the real action on a mission. There was a certain level of trauma induced by having to listen to a firefight, but having so few ways to help, beyond providing technical readouts. Banter between specialists was often accepted, as it was a coping mechanism to deal with both the drudgery and the stress. Unless it was Norgard's kind of banter. Hermedilla was right about that. Locker room antics were generally frowned upon, and Johansen had a reputation for obliterating anyone who talked shit about her all-female team.

"So ... Sleeves or Starfall?" Even though he had to know Johansen would tan his hide for it, Norgard did not appear to be dissuaded.

Martin supposed it was his own fault for dangling the "number one" comment in his face like a carrot. Ignoring the bait, Martin brushed some wrinkles out of his gray uniform shirt, his fingers passing over the Triple C logo on his chest. After fourteen months with the company, he still enjoyed the symmetry of the symbol; the concentric Cs were easily read from any angle. The choice to make them look like circuit trace paths around the hexagon background helped them stand out from a distance. Martin snapped out of his trance as he heard Hermedilla's voice.

"Surely not Sleeves," Hermedilla said as he scanned through the readouts of energy signals on the planet.

"Yeah, I don't picture you as a tattoo-loving kind of guy." Norgard smirked victoriously, probably pleased he finally managed to rope Hermedilla into the conversation. "You're more the girl-next-door type. Besides, I don't think Sleeves goes for the lads."

"I'm not uptight." Martin narrowed his eyes at Norgard.

"Whatever." Norgard snorted. "Still, as a rookie, I'll have you know that Starfall's no girl-next-door."

"Seriously?" Hermedilla turned on Norgard. "How in the Void would you know?"

"When you've been around long enough, you get a radar for these kinds of things." Smug cockiness radiated off Norgard as he straightened his shoulders.

Martin realized he'd made a mistake. When he admitted that his number one was on the mission, he was hoping they could move on. He didn't want Norgard, or Hermedilla, to start saying unsavory things about Starfall. She was a skilled pilot, and one of the tamest scouts.

Despite the teasing, Martin smiled to himself as he thought of Starfall. He hadn't spoken to her beyond a casual greeting in the hallway, or when she'd walk through Operations on her way to mission briefings and debriefings. He was always struck by how beautiful she was, with her hot pink hair, and dark brown eyes he could drown in.

Like Martin, Astera was still relatively new to the company. Pilots usually covered their slick black jumpsuits in all sorts of patches and trinkets, but Astera's was always crisp and unadorned. Some people whispered that it was because she wasn't settling in well, but Martin believed she was beyond all that fussiness. She was elegant, classy, and clearly didn't have time to waste on accessorizing her clothing when she should be training. It was probably how she managed to avoid a lot of the social drama too many people in the company got roped into. He liked that about her. She was just the kind of woman he was looking for.

That thought helped Martin get a grip on himself. "I know, we could call Johansen in and see what she thinks?" he suggested sarcastically, suddenly feeling protective of his crush.

Norgard cocked an eyebrow at him. "What crawled up your ass?"

The silent tension returned to the room as Martin decided to ignore Norgard. He'd already embarrassed himself and given far too much away.

As the monotony dragged on, Norgard's foot started tapping against the ground. At first, it was irregular and light, but it got louder and more persistent, and Martin swore the guy would implode with the building energy.

"Okay, if not the scouts, how about the Infantry Wing? Everyone's got a top three for that group."

Hermedilla sighed and Martin's shoulders stiffened.

"Guys, come on—"

"Stop," Martin snapped to attention as an energy signature crossed his screen. Martin held his hand up to forestall any further protest from Norgard. "Nest to Starfall, come in, Starfall." Martin radioed, waiting, and watching the new signal warily. The other two specialists leaned in, whispering to each other as they realized what he had seen.

The comms crackled. "This is Starfall. Go ahead, Nest."

"Starfall, we are reading a new energy signature within the target zone. Can you confirm?" Martin asked as he assigned a designator to the signature.

The pregnant pause that followed was unsettling for the group. Then again, Starfall was probably relaxing in her powered down mech and had to spool it back up and turn on the passive sensor display. It was a relief when Martin heard her voice again. "Um, yup, Nest, I'm picking up an energy signal, too. Looks to be a mech powering on. Do I need to act?" Norgard leaned across Martin to take over the comms from his console. "Negative, Starfall. So long as you've been powered down and running on your passives, they shouldn't have picked you up on sensors yet. They could be cycling out their patrol mech. Hold position until further orders."

"Copy that, Nest. Starfall, out."

Martin frowned as the plume of the energy signature on his readout continued to grow. "Our surveillance didn't see anything bigger than a few infantry mechs for their perimeter patrols, right?"

"Yeah, should be one on active patrol and two more on standby. Why?" Hermedilla asked.

Martin paused the scroll and pointed at the readout. "This energy output is too high for an infantry class mech's power plant." He figured it had to be a spearhead class instead; the mechs containing the heaviest weapons. Weapons that would wipe out Starfall's and Sleeves' petite scout machines as easily as an elephant would crush an ant.

"We are running at a lower orbit than usual. We're probably reading higher flux because of our distance to target," Norgard reasoned as he flipped the channels on his display to check what Martin reported.

"Nah, I compensated for that. I think they are firing up their backup mech," Martin said, looking over at the ranking specialist in the room. The blob of energy grew until it had to be a cluster of mechs. "Or ... mechs."

"Could be." Hermedilla narrowed his eyes, his jaw clenched as he changed the settings, most likely hoping to pull the signatures apart. "Doesn't mean they have picked up our scouts, though. You two keep an eye on the new marks. I'll radio Sleeves."

Martin turned his attention to the energy readings and it became clear the new mechs were nearly warmed up. They would be on the move soon.

His chest tightened, as he thought of Sleeves and Starfall sitting down there, while these new enemies were powering up just miles away from them. He rolled his shoulders and told himself that they still had plenty of time. Starfall would be fine. She knew how to handle herself on a mission.

Meanwhile, Martin heard Hermedilla raising Sleeves on the other channel. "Sleeves, this is Nest. Come in."

"Nest, go ahead."

"Sleeves, we have multiple energy signals detected. It appears the base is waking their mech defenders. No indication of purpose or intent. Stand ready to cover Starfall's escape path to the pickup."

Sleeves was in a Falcon, which was one of the few mechs that could dance between being a scout or infantry class depending on fitout. Sleeves' particular machine had exchanged the heavier armor plating for information gathering systems but had kept the firepower. So, it wasn't quite as light, or smart, as Starfall's Hummingbird, but it was the perfect passive data sweeper, that could sit back and cover the stealthier mech while still sweeping for intel. Martin felt that getting Sleeves to cover Starfall's extraction was a wise decision on Hermedilla's part.

"Understood, Nest. Moving to nav Delta to cover exit lane."

Norgard shook his head as he pulled up the navigation map. "Negative, Sleeves. Remain on station. Stay in position," he advised.

Martin figured Sleeves would have to find a more creative way to get into place to cover Starfall's retreat. He had read the reports as part of his pre-mission prep. The intel from the client on this mission was clear that the base had seismic sensors to pick up mechs in motion. They only work to a certain sensitivity which was another reason why Starfall, in her Hummingbird, had gone to scout base, and Sleeves had stayed farther back.

"Maybe the energy signatures are trying to mask the signal we've been waiting for?" Martin offered, hoping he was right so that the situation would feel less dire.

"That seems like a stretch, rookie," Norgard grumbled, rubbing his chin.

"You got a better explanation?"

The three specialists all looked at each other. It was clear that no one had a better idea.

Hermedilla sat up. "Norgard, contact Command. They'll need to be down here for this. It's above our grade."

Norgard nodded and picked up the phone at his desk. Now that he was on his feet again, Martin got a better look at the yellow framing on his Ops Section patch. Mech pilots would call a pilot wearing that color "Lieutenant", but amongst the Ops Specialists, it was more an indicator of seniority, than rank or achievement. Thankfully, Norgard wasn't the most senior staff member in the room. Hermedilla held that honor. It was also why it was his call to reach out to the command staff. Everyone seemed to hold their breath as Norgard waited for the phone to connect. When it finally did, he cleared his throat and spoke. "Officer of the Watch? This is the Ops Room. We are requesting Command verification of mission critical asset … yes, immediate Executive Class escalation … Roger that." He hung up the phone and looked at the other two. "They're going to wake the top brass. Should be around ten minutes."

"Starfall may be under attack in ten minutes," Martin protested.

"You wanna go up there and wake the XO yourself, loverboy?" Norgard snapped.

Martin started to drum his fingers against the console again as he looked between the door to the Ops room and his control screen. He knew better than to bust rank on a mission like this, but that didn't make it sit any easier, especially when Starfall was down on that planet. Major La Plaz's room was only a few corridors away. As Head of Intelligence and the Triple C's XO, it was important to keep him close to Ops. Martin muttered a curse as he returned his attention to the screen, making sure his breathing was slow and steady as the pulsating energy signal expanded.

"Nest to Starfall." Hermedilla leaned forward as he radioed in, glancing at Martin as the anticipation in the room reached a suffocating level. "Hold position until target determination has been made."

"Copy that," Starfall replied via comms, any hint of earlier teasing, or amusement, in her tone wiped away by the new developments.

Time in the control room slowed to a crawl. As the seconds dragged by, measured by the frantic tapping of Martin's fingers on the console, the three Ops Specialists had no choice but to assume no news was good news. Even if waiting was the hardest game on a mission like this, it was preferable to the alternative.

"Signals are still growing." Norgard stated the obvious as the dots on the holographic projection warbled into a more threatening mass.

Martin turned his head to the side, hoping that looking at it from a new angle would help him take it all in. He figured it was either one big mother of a power signal, or the initialization of a full unit of hulky mechs coming online.

Neither option was good for Starfall.

The radio flared to life again. "Starfall to Nest. Did you guys go out for a cup of tea or something? Even my passives are picking up on this now."

Hermedilla leaned forward, even though it made no difference as his mic was on his headset. "Repeating orders: hold position until a determination has been made."

"Right, shall I tell that to the Harrier and two Eagles that just woke up inside of the compound?" Even through the radio, it sounded to the team like Starfall was speaking through gritted teeth.

Martin grasped Hermedilla's shoulder as he interjected. "Starfall, location scans were negative for hostile mechs."

"Of course. I'll tell them to power down because your sensors didn't pick them up, so they can't exist. Gimme a minute, I'm sure they'll gladly oblige," Starfall retorted.

Martin winced.

Before anyone could respond to Starfall, the door at the rear of the Ops room cycled to reveal Commander Durroguerre, holding a sealed thermos of coffee, and doing up the final clasp on his collar. His navy uniform jacket was wrinkle free, and the purple trim of his rank stood out against the inky fabric. Even though he must have been asleep just moments ago, his dark eyes were alert as he strode over with the kind of confidence and purpose that came with decades of experience.

The specialists glanced at each other. Being as late as it was, Major La Plaz was the one who was supposed to be on call. Seeing the owner, and commander, of the company here in the flesh was a rare occurrence in the Ops room.

"Status report," the commander ordered, looking between them. His chiseled jawline was sprinkled with salt-and-pepper stubble that he rubbed while waiting for their answer.

"Uh, multiple energy signals on the planet in the target area, sir," Martin said as he jumped up from his seat and saluted. "Unclear if the base's mechs are powering up to engage our assets on the ground, or if the mission critical asset is already on site."

"Sit down, Specialist. I need you at your console, not saluting me." The commander waved his hand at Martin, whose cheeks reddened as he sank back into his seat. "Have you performed a spectral analysis on the energy signatures?"

"Negative, sir. Initial energy levels are consistent with a mech's fusion core activating," Hermedilla answered. Being the senior specialist in the room, it was his responsibility if something wasn't done as mission protocol dictated.

"Perform one now," the commander ordered. His mouth opened to say more, when a feminine voice blared through the comms.

"Nest? Please tell me you guys haven't drifted off to dream about peaches again. I've got three hot mechs getting antsy, and I need to fucking move."

Turning to a spare console, Commander Durroguerre pointed to the headset laying on it. "Who's that on the comms?"

"Private Starfall, Scout Wing. She's our forward OP mech, running passive and powered down," Martin explained.

Even as he did, Hermedilla was trying to talk with her on the comms and encouraging her to not break cover.

"Hermedilla, I'll handle this." With a frown, the commander picked up the headset and slipped it on. "Starfall, this is Knuckle Duster," he announced, using the callsign all the pilots would recognize.

Martin bit the inside of his cheek as he waited to hear Starfall's reaction to the commander being on the comms. It was a clear sign that an increasingly bad situation was about to get much, much worse.

Magnolia

"A girl worth fighting for..."

One-hundred and thirty years ago, an alien race known as the Hunduns invaded Earth. The survivors of their brutal attack now live in space, aboard the *Worldship Honour*. Now their resources are nearly depleted, the Emperor has called a conscription draft for a final attack in hopes of retaking Earth.

Determined to save her father from having to fly in the Fenix army, Magnolia steals his flight suit, disguises herself as a man, and joins the armada to fight in the last desperate attempt to save the human race.

Magnolia is the first in the "Reawakened" collection, which is a series of fairytale, legend, and mythological retellings. Stay tuned for the next adventure...

CHAPTER ONE

"MISSILES LOCKED AND LOADED."

Magnolia "Mags" Hua announced as she locked her missile on her target. The simulator console vibrated beneath her as the crosshairs settled right over the slick armoured carapace of the alien Hundun.

"I'm covering your six," Willow chimed in through the comms. *"We have two ships coming in from your seven o'clock. I've got eyes on them. You keep following the others."*

"Gladly." Mags observed the way the naturally armoured plates overlapped, and the stretch of its double pair of membranous leather wings made her stomach churn. It reminded her of a mix between the bats and cockroaches her Earth Studies teacher showed her as a child.

She fired her weapons.

A missile blasted from the launcher on her bird-shaped craft and through the foggy atmosphere, rocketing toward the beast and hitting it in a spectacular display of fire and sparks. The Hun's leather wing started to sizzle away, the creature letting out a low, resonant yowl.

Without hesitation, Mags shot a second missile. It hit the alien beast right in the sweet spot. A shower of gore bloomed across her windscreen, and she grunted as she banked her own plane right to try and avoid the debris.

"Watch out! One of the ships is—"

Mags yelped, pulling to the side hard as her evasive move put her right in the path of an alien Willow was tracking. She tried to avoid it, but she was too slow, and the creature shooting toward her had a death wish.

"Mags!" Willow cried in warning as Mags peered at the alien and prepared to meet her doom—

"Alert! All males aged eighteen and over are required to report to the meeting deck immediately. Alert!"

The simulator whined mechanically as it powered down. The interface helmet Mags wore went black, so she tore it off and slumped back in the seat, placing a hand on her chest as her heart hammered beneath it so hard it hurt.

Red lights pulsed on and off in her living room, and all peripheral electronics around her faded to emergency reserves.

"Alert! All males aged eighteen and over are required to report to the meeting deck immediately. Alert!"

Catching her breath, Mags slid off the seat and staggered from the small, cluttered living room into her bedroom. It had a bunk bed in it and two wardrobes set on either side of a desk. The bottom bunk was stuffed with a pair of threadbare blankets, two pillows, and the pyjamas her siblings had discarded that morning. She ignored the fact that the twins hadn't made their bed, yet again, and climbed the ladder to her bunk, where she shoved her hands under the mattress and pulled out a back-up communicator. She plugged it into the charging socket in her headboard and opened a chat window with Willow.

Hey, you around?

Mags bit her lip and wiped a sheen of sweat off her forehead as the blasted alert hollered through her room. She hoped Willow hadn't left her communicator out in the open again. Last time she had, and her parents had been so scared that she had the contraband tech that they threw it in the trash cycle. Luckily, they'd been too scared to run it outside of their allotted time, so Willow was able to retrieve the device.

"Don't I know it," Mags grumbled under her breath. She sighed and collapsed against her bed.

Mags had recently decided to take advantage of her father's old training simulator while he and her mother were out for work and her siblings were at school. Her grandmother was asleep in a bunk in her parents' room, but lately she had been sleeping deeper than space. Mags had always hated the stupid rule that only men were able to fight.

Rolling over onto her back, Mags blew dishevelled strands of hair off her face. Her hair was another thing she had always hated, envying how the boys and men got to cut theirs short. Not that she wanted it that close-cropped, but something shorter than the regulated minimum of fifteen centimetres below the chin would be cooler and easier to maintain.

A wide grin stretched Mags' lips and she forced herself to sit up. She didn't bother with the ladder, instead jumping straight down to the metal floor, then yanked the communicator from the charge port and ran into the living room. She plugged it into one of the ports beneath the large wall screen her family used to watch the evening news or research different plants or historical stories from Earth.

Her foot bounced impatiently against the deck of its own accord, the rhythmic drumming matching the pace of her still elevated heart rate.

It had been a while since those in charge had called an all-hands meeting. Willow and Mags had snuck into that one, too. Digitally, at least. That had been two days before her sixteenth birthday, which was just over two years ago now.

The wall screen flared to life, showing a little window in the top corner where Mags spotted Willow's smiling face. Her friend's dark brown eyes were bright as she gave Mags a playful salute, her hair also messy from the sim helmet.

"Hey, you," Willow said.

Mags couldn't help but think she looked pretty like that. *"Hey."*

Instead of letting her mind wonder what situations they could get into together that would tousle Willow's hair, she returned the unnecessary salute with a lazy one of her own. Then she tore her eyes away from the excitement on Willow's pretty, heart-shaped face and look at the rest of the screen instead.

The meeting deck was the largest empty space on the Worldship Honour. Ever other level was crammed with a mix of living spaces, community rooms, storage, or critical systems such as air purifiers, water generators, engineering spaces, and the like.

With walls barren except for a screen here or there, the wear and tear of humanity's hundred and thirty odd years in space was clear for everyone to see. The scuffs on the floor, however, were covered by the congregation of hundreds of men crammed in together. There was a range of uniform colours represented, from the pieced together grey of engineering overalls, the bronze-trimmed black of slick pilot suits, to the deep green of medical staff.

Mags leaned forward, taking great interest in looking at the proportions of different uniforms. Given that the Empire wanted every single fit and healthy male on flight duty, they made up at least seventy percent of what she saw. Engineering easily made up another fifteen percent. The rest was a hodgepodge of the rare few who were assigned to things like medical, leadership, education, and maintenance.

It took about twenty minutes for the last stragglers to arrive, and just as Mags wondered why there were so many more engineers than she remembered seeing two years ago, a blast door to the rear of the deck opened. The emperor emerged, dressed in a resplendent suit of red trimmed in gold, with his eight cabinet members in white and two guards in black. He was taller than a lot of other men of his generation, his smooth, flawless skin free of the dark bags and stress lines of the pilots or the scars that were hallmarks of the more dangerous positions in engineering or maintenance.

Silence automatically fell over those gathered as the tall man stepped onto a dais at the front of the space. He raised his hand, and the blaring alert finally stopped.

"I guess it's easy to keep your handsome looks when you don't have to lift a finger in your life."

"You think he's handsome? Seriously? You need your damn eyes checked, girl." Mags shook her head. She could count on one hand the number of times she'd ever looked at a man and thought he was handsome. She had hoped Willow was the same but was too scared to bring it up.

Willow and Mags had been born a few weeks apart. Given their close birthdates, they were in the same year at school. They'd known each other since they were five and had been friends ever since Mags punched one of the boys in their year in the face for trying to steal Willow's lunch ration.

"Why? Jealous, Magnolia?"

Mags pressed her lips together and glanced at Willow. She wanted to wipe away the smirk she wore with a kiss, but...

If anyone caught them, they would both be sanctioned.

Mags' heart ached as she pushed any thoughts of a kiss or possible sanction aside. She would take whatever punishment was dished out if it meant being with Willow, but she would never want to drag her friend through that.

The emperor three generations earlier had decreed that same-sex relationships were to be outlawed, as they would be *fruitless*. Nevermind the fact that fertility or adoption options were available for heterosexual couples who were unable to conceive due to infertility or sex organ variations. Apparently, the rule was good for some and not others. *Utter crap, of course,* Mags thought, but any dissenters were swiftly dealt with.

She was just about to hit Willow with an epic retort when the emperor lowered his arm as he peered around, surveying his minions with a chin tilt that spoke of the superiority complex he had been born with. "Greetings, men of the Worldship Honour. Thank you for assembling swiftly and calmly. It is with a sense of great regret that I gather you all today. But I come to you with dire news."

"Maintaining the remaining population of humanity was never the goal of the Worldship Honour. It was meant to be a temporary host whilst we fought back with the other nations to reclaim our planet." The emperor spoke clearly, slowly, but his tone grew deeper, which made something in Mags' gut twist. "As such, we have now reached a critical point. We are no longer able to manufacture the materials required to replace crucial parts in our oxygen and water systems. And, as you all know, without those two things, this ship cannot survive."

"Oh, crap..."

Mags internally echoed Willow's sentiment. That was terrible news. What were they supposed to do without those parts?

"The current estimates from engineering tell us that we have another two months, at best," the emperor dropped the new information as if it didn't hold the same destructive power as a nuclear missile.

Conversation tore through the room, the men all turning and speaking to those around them, yelling in shock and alarm, demanding more answers.

General Li, the leader of the Fenix armada, stepped forward and raised his hand for silence. "I know that this does not sound promising, but there is hope yet." Then, he gestured to the screens secured on the walls of the space, which flickered to life with a view of Earth. It rotated in space, a green and blue spheroid that looked far more innocuous than it was. Several generations ago, it had been filled with human life. Overfilled, some said. Regardless of the population debates, humanity thrived. Then, a hive of aliens warped into the system and overpowered the humans with a combination of surprise and air superiority. The creatures were like those of nightmares; with armoured bodies and leathery wings, they reminded the people of the destructive, chaotic Hundun from ancient Chinese mythology. The years of the Great War were a brutal, deadly fight between the Hundun, or Huns as they were sometimes known, and the inhabitants of Earth.

Millions had died during the war, but even worse, the Huns

began pumping noxious gas into Earth's atmosphere to make it more liveable for themselves. It created a thick blanket of toxicity on the surface of the planet, quickly making it inhospitable to humanity. Scientists had spent months trying to find the devices they presumed were generating the gas, but none were found, and it was assumed the creatures themselves were the source. Plans had been made to evacuate humankind before they all perished due to the poison.

Humanity had captured fallen Hun to study and understand how they worked together, the nations of Earth combining their efforts to create their own fighter ships to take on the Huns. Ships that could survive in the toxic atmosphere and interface with the human mind and react organically so they could finally catch up with the alien's air superiority. The ships were a mix of stolen alien biology and human technology. To honour the collaboration between the engineers from different nations who created the bird-like fighters, they were named Fenixes. The name paying homage to the Fenghuan, the mythological ruler of all birds, and the phoenix, the avian fire creature that is reborn from its own ashes.

The Fenixes proved to be extremely effective in combat due to the addition of human weaponry; however, the Hun were too great in number and too spread out across the planet to effectively fight. When it was clear the Fenix fleet was not able to protect humanity, the nations panicked. Each continent had created its own World-ship to evacuate the civilians into space. However, launching through the Hundun-controlled atmosphere proved dangerous, and only the Worldship Honour survived.

The image of Earth on the screen zoomed in. It was a dizzying sight as the scope dove into the cloudy atmosphere and the ominous shadows of the aerial beasts shimmered through the toxic fog.

"The Hundun have started amassing in a single location. It is the first time their population has gathered in such a way, and it makes them prime targets for a full-scale ambush," General Li announced.

The cheers of reply were so loud that Mags had to turn down the volume on her device. The men pumped their fists into the air, and the cabinet ministers wore satisfied expressions at their enthusiasm. The emperor retrieved an electronic slate from one of his advisors as the cheers died down.

"As such," he said, continuing as if he hadn't paused, "All ship operations will be dependent on the needs of our pilots, and any ancillary operations will cease. All pilots, whether active or not, will be required to serve. Any retired pilots will be recalled upon the conscription conditions that at least one male of maturity must serve per household."

The emperor continued to rattle off conditions, but they all sounded like gibberish to Mags. Her stomach was somewhere on the floor, and her heart hammered in her throat.

"Mags? Hey, Mags!" Willow's voice sounded a million miles away. *"Magnolia, speak to me!"*

Mags blinked and looked at the corner of the screen. Willow's face was so close to the camera all Mags could see was her eyes and nose. It would have been comical if she hadn't just realised that her father was the only man in her family who fit the requirements of the conscription notice... but he'd left the corps years earlier. At first, the doctors had suspected that he may have suffered neurological damage from a mission injury—the cause of his night terrors, low mood, irritability, and the way he trembled every time he heard reports of a new loss in the armada. However, when all the medical tests were exhausted, the psychological experts on board said it was most likely a condition of the mind. Other people in his old social circle had a hard time understanding the concept that her father had no visible injuries but was unable to fly, and she knew he carried a heavy load of shame and frustration over this.

Mags never understood the shame. For generations, they had given men no chance but to go to war and die, or watch their friends die. It was a brutal life, and she couldn't even imagine some of the horrors he had lived through. As much as he might try to hide it, she knew he was still struggling. The thought of him being forced back into a Fenix...

"Father!" The word slipped from her before she could stop it. Her hands flew to cover her mouth.

"Mags, it's going to be okay. He was deemed unfit to fly. They

won't take him back!" The conviction in Willow's voice didn't register.

Despite Willow's attempt at reassuring her, Mags knew that he wasn't officially deemed unfit. According to regulations, only a physical injury excused a pilot from serving. However, her father's reputation, and his continued emotional difficulties, meant that he had been offered an honourable discharge to save his reputation. During a conscription, though? His excuse would no longer be valid.

It was different for Willow, Mags thought. Her older brother, Onyx, was one of the star pilots in his year. He was fit and healthy, and her father had retired with honour after an injury to his arm made it hard for him to pilot effectively. Nothing would change for her. There would be no added risk to their family.

But Mags?

"I can't lose him," she said, shaking her head. Her eyes burned as the emperor passed over to General Li to explain the training regimen they were setting up to account for the new and returned pilots.

"You won't," Willow promised. *"We'll come up with something, I swear."*

www.ingramcontent.com/pod-product-compliance
Lightning Source LLC
Chambersburg PA
CBHW031946130726
47904CB00012B/7

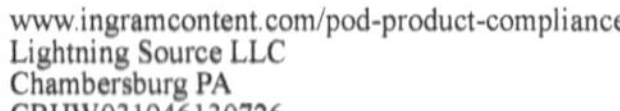